D0713550

WINTER OF THE HEART

ALSO BY LINDA J. LAROSA

The Random Factor, a novel
written with Barry Tanenbaum

WINTER

—OF THE—

HEART

*

LINDA J. LaROSA

G. P. PUTNAM'S SONS / NEW YORK

Copyright © 1984 by Linda J. LaRosa
All rights reserved. This book, or parts thereof,
must not be reproduced in any form without permission.
Published simultaneously in Canada
by General Publishing Co. Limited, Toronto.

LIBRARY OF CONGRESS CATALOGING IN PUBLICATION DATA

LaRosa, Linda J., date.
Winter of the heart.

I. Title.
PS3562.A727W5   1984   813'.54   84-4815
ISBN 0-399-12900-6

PRINTED IN THE UNITED STATES OF AMERICA

IN LOVING MEMORY OF MY FATHER,
PETER,
WHO ALWAYS BELIEVED.

Hate is the winter of the heart.

—VICTOR HUGO

PART ONE

CHAPTER
1

A voice from a madhouse called her name.

It grew louder, piercing and shrill in the dark. The floor began to tilt as she ran to the stairs to be safe. Climb, she told herself, but the banister fell off and spiraled down thousands of feet into an empty, hungry chasm. She pulled herself along the steep angle that grew sharper with each moment, crawling and straining against the gummy surface of the marble.

Faster, she breathed, but she barely moved at all. "Someone help me," she shrieked, but no one heard.

The deafening hiss behind her swallowed up the space between them. "Help me!" she screamed, pulling free from the marble and dragging herself up to the hallway. The floor moved and pitched from side to side like a stormrocked ship as clammy hands with large palms slapped at her skin, swarming all around her. "Stop it, stop it," she screamed and tried to protect herself as she ran forward in the dark. The walls began to crumble, and her bare feet stuck to the floor as the swarming hands tore at the white linen nightgown.

The hiss came closer . . . closer . . .

There. At the hallway's end—the window.

A silhouette appeared in front of it as the lead veins began cracking and the stained glass exploded from the outside in, sending the slivers down the hallway. The tall shadow's blue eyes glistened in the half-dark as it blocked the window. She felt the raw air pushing her backwards toward the tunnel of the clammy hands.

"No, God, stop it, stop it, no more," she screamed, but the laughing hiss drowned the sound. The blue eyes grew, turning slightly from the window. It left a space. She ran toward it, then felt her feet on the ledge, cut from the slivers and numb from the cold.

The hiss laughed.

The lightning blue eyes were hypnotic.

The clammy hands were trying to choke her.

Straining forward, she tried to breathe, then braced herself on the jagged ledge, staring at the dark abyss below. Now, she thought.

JUMP.

Julienne's eyes shot open. Everything was bright and blurred, every part of her shook. She was covered in sweat and the sheets of her bed were damp and sticky. "That . . . that nightmare again," she shivered, trying to massage the palpitations away by tracing small circles on her skin over her heart. Gently, she thought, careful not to touch the bruised ribcage. "It's all over," she whispered to herself, "be calm," then took several deep breaths.

But the bed was suddenly too damp, too cold, and her nerves made gooseflesh on her skin. She flung the sheet back and had to pause at the edge of the bed. She'd moved too quickly and it hurt. She stood up slowly, then paced the bedroom.

Stopping by the windows, she parted the curtains and stared down at the gardens below her. The marble statues of Greek and Roman gods looked sinister, phantom sentries positioned by the manicured hedges. Something moved. Was it a person or just a bush rustled by a breeze? She reached, and felt the ache and the burning throb in her side, then pulled the curtains trying to shut them again. The sudden clatter of the rings made her jump and she backed away from the window and bumped into the carved oak spindle at the corner of the bed. "God help me," she shuddered. Stop it now, she told herself, there is no one in the garden, no one is watching me. And from today, until the end of my life, there will be no more fear, no more, not ever again.

But what if he comes back, Julienne thought instantly, what if he suddenly changes his habit and comes back too soon? He's only been gone two days— he could change his mind, he could . . .

The book, she thought, and moved with an aching slowness to the nightstand next to the bed. She knelt, peeled back the loose panel of silk wallpaper and felt behind it for the small hole in the wall. She touched the slim volume, a guidebook to Italy.

Leave it be, she thought, but it was no use. She had to open it. Page thirty-five was marked by a ribbon. Several passages at the bottom were underlined: the city of Florence and its points of interest. It had been exactly as she had left it the night before. Will he believe it? Will he find it? She put the book back in the hole. One hundred times I have read that passage, she thought, and I have forgotten to seal the hole.

She went to the dressing table, felt in the side drawer and took out the blue sealing wax. She lit the end of the wax stick with a match she took from the nightstand. Thick royal blue bubbled then slid away from the center. Though the wallpaper was white and gold silk, there was just enough of a wax dribble to catch his eyes when he would rampage through the room looking for hidden letters or clues, or something. "God," she prayed, "give us good fortune. A month, please, it isn't a very long amount of time; hide us, please, for at least a month." She moved the nightstand a little to the left, away from the bed to barely show the wrinkle she'd deliberately made.

The light in her room changed. The warm, yellowish tint coming from the oil lamp became a greyish haze from the open windows. Morning. It must be near five, she thought. The servants would be about their duties soon. She heard the mournful cries of doves drifting over the gardens and their velvety calls gave her a momentary peace. There was no point in trying to sleep now, she decided.

Her mind seemed dulled by the lists that kept nagging at her: Kollmer, the photograph-plate album, the basket, the petticoat—is the petticoat secure enough? She shook her head. Pacing will not make the time go faster, she thought, and turned down the wick on the oil lamp, watching a puff of smoke trail up and disappear. Putting on her linen dressing gown and stepping into her slippers, she thought Friedrich, my Friedrich, at the junction near—near what? God, what is the landmark? She panicked, feeling the anxiety prickles break into sweat again. "I, I can't think anymore," she swallowed, and sat down wearily in the chair by the small table in the corner. Her heart was pounding again and she was cold. Leaning into the high-backed chair, she closed her eyes and felt herself drifting; floating in that restless twilight, half-aware of wooden chair arms, half-hearing the muted sounds of birds somewhere outside the closed window to keep out the night vapors. A sound, a soft rustle soothed her. It was the sound of air.

A knock startled her. "Yes?" Julienne said, opening her eyes to a fuller brightness.

"Breakfast, Your Grace." The maid's voice was respectful, quiet.

And now it begins, Julienne thought, then yawned. "Yes, come in." She rubbed her eyes with her hand, then combed her fingers through a long lock of her dark chestnut hair.

The underhousemaid brought in a large silver tray and noticed the open curtains. "Oh, but I'm sure I closed them last night."

"I opened them earlier. Set the tray here, Edda, and I shall serve myself this morning," Julienne said. "You may go." She flicked the linen napkin open and across her lap, then tightly closed her hands under the table.

"Yes, Your Grace," the maid said.

"Send Gelber to me."

"Yes, Your Grace."

Julienne listened. There, the door closed. She was up from the table and peeling off the robe as she walked to the dressing room. I can't eat, I don't want to eat, she thought. I want to be dressed and ready and out of this prison within the hour. God, what if he's on his way back *now* . . .

Quickly, she pulled on her thin handkerchief-linen chemise and drawers, tying them at the knees. Hurry, she thought, as she drew up the white cotton hose. She stood up too quickly and felt dizzy. She steadied herself against the wall, then stepped into the petticoat she had embroidered herself with hidden treasures in every bud of every flower. She buttoned the fitted waist at the back. Will anyone know, she worried, and grabbed a fistful of the petticoat, squeezing the centers of the flowers. Nothing, she thought, relieved. No one will know what is inside them.

Julienne looked at the corset. No, she thought. The pain would be too much to bear. She thrust her arms into the blouse, buttoned the back as best she could, then had her skirt and jacket on when she heard a knock at the door and then, Gelber's voice from the hallway. Julienne called out permission to enter the room.

Marthe Gelber was a pleasant-looking woman in her early thirties. She had blond hair tightly braided in a knot at the nape of her neck and wore a plain dress suitable for her position as a governess.

"Are they ready?" Julienne asked, buttoning the frogging on her jacket. Gelber nodded.

"And the basket?"

"Cook has prepared it with all kinds of cheeses and breads, apples, preserves, cooked meats, jugged meats—all that you have ordered has been done. Cook has been told only that it is a present for the old Aunt. It should last you three days."

Julienne turned too quickly and in the wrong way. She felt the sharp spasm by her bruised ribs and doubled over, gripping her arms as if to steady the pain. Gelber helped her to sit down, then tried to massage the tension from the shoulders.

"Try to breathe," Gelber said. "It is too soon. You try to leave too soon. Perhaps you ought to rest. Lying down may ease the pain."

Julienne breathed deeply, then sighed. "No position is comfortable. It isn't too soon, Gelber. It is years too late." The sharp pain subsided and went back to a dull ache. "I'll . . . I'll manage. I must." She wiped the gloss of perspiration from her forehead.

Gelber let go of the shoulders. She looked at the table near the windows. "You haven't eaten your . . ."

"I'm not hungry."

Gelber sighed. "You must try. You need your strength for the journey."

"Well, if I must," Julienne answered, "but please sit with me, as you have done before." She watched as Gelber hesitated, then sat down in the chair to her left. "I've a gift for you, a gift for my teacher." Julienne squeezed Gelber's hand, then let go and walked to the settee, moved a cushion, and took out the small box and a large book wrapped in cheesecloth that she'd hidden there. "Here," she said, sitting down, "this is for you," and placed the flat box next to Gelber's hands.

Marthe Gelber shook her head. "I think it most unwise to give something of yours away. He might see it and I'm afraid—for you and myself."

Julienne touched the box. "He's never seen this and doesn't even know it exists. It belonged to my mother when she was a child. I want you to have it as a remembrance. If anyone should ask you, just say it belonged to a friend, now dead."

Gelber knew there was no refusing her and opened the cardboard box. It was a child's fan, made of mother-of-pearl with white silk in between the blades. She opened the fan and saw the magnificent embroidery work—swans by reeds in streams, gold fleurs-de-lis in a small pattern outlining these miniature tableaux. Gelber knew the fleurs-de-lis were a family symbol, from the mother's side, the Bourbon dynasty of France.

"My mother loved swans because they meant fidelity," was all Julienne said.

"Thank you," Gelber whispered, then gently folded the fan and put it back into the box. Her eyes drifted to the book wrapped in cheesecloth. It was no larger than an ordinary Bible or prayer book, yet it was a treasure, a connection with the past.

"You know what to do with this," Julienne said, pushing the photograph-plate album closer to Gelber.

Gelber nodded, studying her for a moment, watching the tremors in the hands as she tried to drink a little of her coffee, and then, struggle with the spoon as she tried to break the shell of a soft-boiled egg. She is like her mother, Gelber thought, having a sensitive beautiful face with fine features and large brown eyes. She stands five-feet-six, lean, like her mother had been; and her accent, her voice, lilting, French, like her mother's must have been. Still, Gelber knew, there was evidence of the Weiskerns, the father's side. It was in the coloring—fair skin, dark eyes, dark chestnut hair. And, Gelber thought, it is in the determination now in her eyes, and the willingness to learn, and in the ability to change.

Julienne gave up after she'd eaten half the egg. "No more," she said, "I can't. It will make me ill."

Gelber nodded. "Your shoes," she smiled.

"Oh," Julienne grinned, "I can manage."

"And don't forget your gloves."

"I won't." She took Gelber's hands. "It is time now. Go and bring my children to the carriage and let them wait there with Kollmer. If you linger there, I shall be upset, I know it, and I must not be. You must pretend it is like any other day."

"I know," Gelber answered.

Julienne stood up from the table, and when Gelber did likewise, she reached, and held the governess. "Live well," Julienne whispered, "and be safe. Thank you for all you have done for me."

Gelber swallowed as she nodded, and holding the cheesecloth-wrapped book, left the room.

Alone, Julienne fastened her shoes with the button-hook. Then, she walked to the dressing room, to the large rosewood chest in the corner where she kept her jewelry. She opened the small bottom left drawer, made a space in the back, then took off her wedding ring and tossed it onto the black velvet, hiding it with a long strand of pearls, and closed the drawer. She took one last look at herself in the mirror as she put on her hat, and then adjusted the long veil. Hide me, she thought. She grabbed her gloves and looked at the bedroom for the last time. "I hate you," she whispered to the room. "You were never mine, never. I hate you and this house. And him. God forgive me, I hate him most of all."

She looked neither right nor left as she strode down the hall to the center staircase under the large dome. As if in a dream, she began descending the marble steps, not looking at the stained glass windows, not caring about the Italian fresco in the dome above her. She saw only the large mahogany door. She kept her pace even, but she found it difficult to keep her breathing under control. Walk slower, Julienne thought, and wondered if any servants were near, anyone to report her movements later when he would question them, anyone cleaning, watching, listening . . .

Ten more steps to the door.

She reached for the handle in an ordinary manner, stepped outside, and pulled the door shut behind her. She took a breath. The July sun was inviting, bright, and she felt warm in the blue traveling outfit.

"Momma!"

She heard the little-girl voice from the front seat of the Phaeton carriage. Gisela, hair tumbling down in loose curls under the straw hat. She wore a green visiting dress. Gisela, five years old and growing so quickly. "One moment," Julienne called out and remained where she was, pretending to adjust her gloves. Sweat ran down the center of her back. Was anyone watching, she thought, and wondered if she should turn around, but decided against it. She held a velvet pouch in her right hand and casually went over to the large stone flower urn on the left and placed it there, hiding it under the geranium leaves.

From inside the protective netting of the veil, she watched Kollmer, the butler, give an instruction to the groom, but was unable to hear their words. Hurry, she prayed, hurry . . .

The groom nodded, then held the horse by the bridle and stroked the long black neck of the champion stallion Domino, bred for strength and endurance. Kollmer left the carriage and walked over to her, climbing the seven large stone steps.

"Everything is ready,". he said quietly.

Julienne smiled, then nodded to the flower urn. "For you," she whispered. "It belonged to my father." She heard Kollmer sigh, and saw he was about to object, but she gave one quick shake to her head to stop his words. "There is no time to argue. Take it. He's seen it once or twice, so be careful and hide it very well. I owe you my life, Kollmer. Take it, please, it is only my father's wooden rosary. He preferred it above all others because it is plain and simple. He treasured it, because my Uncle blessed it the day he was ordained."

Kollmer turned his attention back to the horse and carriage, watching them for a moment. "Thank you," he said. "I am most grateful." He paused, then looked at the stone steps, intently staring at a small crack with slender blades of grass beginning to grow through it. "Each time it rains, I shall worry and wonder if you are safe. I have no right to, but I shall."

What did it mean anymore, to be safe, Julienne thought, watching the fifty-year-old butler. "Kollmer," she said, "my father taught us to choose life, always. Anything, even the rain on the open road, is better than this."

He stopped staring at the grass-threads and looked straight at her veiled eyes. "Yes," he answered, peacefully, "you are quite right. Have you the small handkerchief with . . ."

Julienne nodded discreetly.

"You remember the turn-off point, by the wheat field bounded by the stone wall with the . . ."

". . . wild rose bushes, yes."

He paused and smiled. "All your instructions will be carried out. Go then, Your Grace. God bless you and always be with you." He had done so much, taught her so much, and saved her more times than he cared to remember. When she held out her hand to him, he took it, bowed, and kissed her gloved fingers lightly.

Julienne quickly squeezed his hand in appreciation, whispering, "Thank you for my life and the lives of my children," then walked with a regular pace to the carriage.

The groom helped her with the step on the Phaeton's left side. While she adjusted her skirt, he still held the reins to Domino. Julienne glanced at Gisela, who had moved to the back seat and sat next to the large straw basket made into a little bed for her baby brother, Maximilian, thirteen months old. He was sleeping. The picnic basket was tied to the back of the Phaeton behind the seats and below the leather top. The groom gave her the reins with a smile and a respectful bow.

Now, Julienne thought, freedom.

Her nod was polite and distant to the groom, then she slapped Domino's backside with the reins. They moved. She felt a leap in her stomach, a knot going tighter and tighter. Gravel crunched beneath the horse's hooves as the fountain pond drew closer. Roses, shrubbery and hedges brushed by them. The iron gates were open, waiting for her to pass through them and take her away from this hateful house and life in Eisenstadt.

Don't rush, she thought, steady, steady, keep the pace even, smooth, there's time, alarm no one.

"Why are you driving and not him, Momma?"

"Him?" Julienne asked, not turning her eyes from Domino's bobbing head.

"The groom."

"Oh," Julienne smiled. "Because I wish to."

Gisela shrugged. "Fraulein Gelber gave me . . ."

"Gave me," Julienne corrected.

". . . gave me my most special doll, the one I love best, the one Uncle Steffie *gave* me."

"Oh how nice," Julienne said, feeling herself allowing the barest more rein to the horse, letting him move the carriage a little quicker. "You brought Marianne with you?"

"Yes, Momma," Gisela answered. "My favorite, and she has blue eyes and pink lips and blond hair . . ."

"How sweet," Julienne replied, half-listening, watching the road ahead, searching both sides for anyone who might see them and report it later. People were off to the right in the fields, but it was too far for anyone to remember anything except that a carriage had passed. Her throat was tight, so tight it caused a pressure pain in her ears. Her mouth went suddenly dry and she licked her lips, not daring to look back, terrified that someone might be following them.

Silly, she told herself, no one's the wiser, not yet. He isn't here—yet. Keep calm.

The dust was fine and drifted up when a breeze disturbed it. The air was hot and Julienne leaned back slightly, watching the horse move in an even trot.

"Are we there yet?"

"No," Julienne answered.

"When will we be there?"

"In three hours."

"How long is three hours?"

"Three hours," Julienne answered patiently, "is when the sun will be overhead and we shall have a little picnic. That is three hours."

"Oh."

She slowed Domino down for a moment, then pulled him to a stop when the road took a sharp bend to the east. "Gisela," she said, carefully turning around, gently, so she would not cause herself any pain on her sides. "Why don't you try to sleep? It's a very long ride and you'll be much more comfortable. Will you try?"

The little one nodded.

"My good girl," Julienne said, checking once more on Maximilian. He was still sleeping, even though the Phaeton had a fair amount of bounce to it. Perhaps it is like his cradle, she thought absently, then smiled again at Gisela.

Five miles . . . seven miles . . .

Domino walked a bit without strain. Eight years in that house, she thought. Eight years of marriage and six of them hell. It was eight years ago that I first saw that house. 1861. Ahhh, she sighed, painfully, he was alive then. Papa.

———

She saw him from the stairwell, opening a sealed envelope. The greying-brown hair was neatly combed. His face was large and craggy with deep laugh and wrinkle lines. Tall and solid with a barrel chest, he stood like a statue staring at the letter.

"Finally," he said, then noticed his daughter watching him from the landing. "It is a note from your fiancé's family. They recognize me at last," he said sarcastically.

Julienne walked down two steps. "What do they say?"

He grunted. "We are finally to meet them, the phantom parents. They have invited us for a week's stay in their country house in Eisenstadt."

She saw the comment lingering in his eyes. "Is that all?"

Heinrich waved at the air. "You needn't worry. I shall allow this insult to pass."

"Wait," Julienne said, racing down the remaining steps and cornering him by the doors to the drawing room. "There's more, I know there's more."

He sighed. "No. You're quite wrong. That's all they say. But there *should* have been more. Ridiculous, how insulting. You have been engaged to their son Franz for nearly eleven months and they have refused—reasonable excuses or not—every invitation I have issued them. They are traveling; they are away; they are indisposed, they are doing this or that. Really, an effort should have been made, it is only polite. Tradesmen do as much, but, because I love you, I will stop all comments from my mouth."

Julienne shook her head. "It seems you've already made them."

He tapped her chin with affection. "Ah, my wise daughter. The little nuns in Belgium taught you so well, didn't they?" He gave her the note with a sharp click of his heels. "For you, Princess. How *nice* of them to want to meet you—and so close to the wedding."

Julienne followed him for three more steps, trying to soothe his feelings.

15

"A, a week with them, in Eisenstadt, it is, it is almost like a birthday present."

Heinrich frowned again. "Yes, and late for *that* as well." He left his daughter standing in the hallway as he walked into the drawing room on the left, closing the doors behind him.

She heard a whistle of amazement above her.

"He is angry," Stefan said.

Julienne sighed. "He has every right to be. What am I to do?"

Stefan shook his head. "Nothing. You are trapped in the middle." He walked down the steps lightly, with a fencer's grace and easy stride. He was a good-looking man of twenty-five years, with dark hair and eyes and the typical Weiskern pale skin. His smile was warm and comforting. "I, uh, particularly liked the comment about the Belgian nuns," he said, trying to help his sister to smile. "Yes, how clearly it comes to my mind—all the little nuns teaching you languages, the arts, history, geography, politics. All of the little nuns, standing in their classrooms near the famous plains of Waterloo, expounding on the intricacies of political balances—marvelous, absolutely marvelous."

She giggled, remembering the years of complaints sent home because she was taught nothing except petit-point and embroidery, the current court dances, the barest hints of geography and the arts only as a means of conversation. Both of them knew their father had taught her everything.

"There," Stefan said, pleased at her smile. "I knew I could chase the sadness away if I set my mind to it."

Julienne looped her arm about his waist. "He seems so irritable, so . . ."

"Have patience," Stefan quietly interrupted. "Many things have upset him today." He led his sister out the front door to the cobblestoned courtyard that faced Hauptstrasse. He listened to the distant chimes of the bells in St. Karl's steeple, soon to be echoed by the other churchbells in Vienna.

"Something's happened," Julienne said. "Tell me."

Stefan shrugged. "He has collided again with Aunt Sophie. You know how he is, he cannot abide interference in the way he handles himself or his family. In many ways, your wedding is just another game of who controls what." They began to walk around the outer edge of the large courtyard, a slow walk over the smooth ancient cobblestones. "We all know that Sophie controls the goings-on in the Palace and the Imperial marriage. Cousin Frou will side with his mother against his wife, and he has done it again over your wedding."

She stopped walking.

Stefan squeezed her arm. "There has been trouble in that house from the beginning, but SiSi and Frou did that to themselves. You understand that, don't you?"

She nodded. "What happened today?"

"Papa and I went to the Palace to see Frou on business. This particular fight was over who will perform the rite and where the ceremony will take place. Then, dear Aunt Sophie said ever-so-sweetly, 'but the wedding breakfast must take place here. It is only right, Heinrich, surely you must see that?' "

"Uncle Teo is performing the rite," Julienne said.

"Not as of this morning," Stefan replied. "Frou has decided his favorite

16

cousin will be married in St. Stephen's Church as befits a member of his family, and the rite is to be performed by the Archbishop of Vienna."

"No," she said, "they can't . . . I won't let them do this," she said, lips trembling.

Stefan only shrugged.

That night, she stared at the photograph-plate of Franz as she usually did before getting into bed. How lucky we are, she thought, to marry only for love and not for a "proper alliance." But Frou was in love with SiSi, he told me he was, even though his mother did not approve and did not want her to be Empress of Austria. She shrugged. Perhaps Stefan is right. Their trouble is their doing. She smiled at the photograph-plate. Has it been only three years since that Christmas when Stefan brought you here and we met? My brother's best and dearest friend in all the world. You are so charming, so intelligent, so handsome . . . I do love you, Franz.

Heinrich sat quietly, deep in sour thought as they rode on the train to Eisenstadt. Julienne, he thought, will be married in St. Stephen's Church as befits her position. The ceremony will be presided over by the Archbishop of Vienna. It must be so, her wish for my brother, Teo, notwithstanding. If she wants the wedding breakfast to take place at Schönbrunn Palace, I shall agree to it and let Society pay their respects in the Emperor's house. If, however, she wishes it at our own country home, Birngarten, or in our Palace in Vienna, nothing will change my mind. The decision is all hers.

When the train pulled into the station, they were met by the head coachman who took them to an ornate carriage with a team of dappled stallions. The country house of the Duke and Duchess of Eisenstadt was fourteen miles outside the city of that name. The estate had not been given a name, like "Birngarten," Julienne's family home in the countryside of Kahlenberg a little northwest of Vienna along the Danube. This house was simply referred to as "Eisenstadt," as if the estate extended its borders to the town itself. The property overlooked the Neusiedler See, one of Austria's most beautiful lakes.

Through the trees, they saw the beige color of the house, then, the house itself. It had two clock-towers, turrets, a cupola at the center of the massive building, fountains, gardens, mock ruins, all shimmering and casting shadows to the neatly trimmed lawns in the afternoon sun.

They were met at the main entrance by the butler, Kollmer, a pleasant-looking middle-aged man with fair skin and respectful brown eyes. He had the deferential manner of any highly trained servant and instantly took charge without appearing to do so.

Julienne had heard stories of the main hall at Eisenstadt, but they had fallen short of the truth. The cupola dome, she guessed, was perhaps seventy feet high. Marble columns banked the walls to the ceiling. The Doric columns led the eye to the fresco in the dome by an Italian master, depicting the Roman muses.

In the great center hall, and maintaining the beige and black marble floor, was the double-staircase, also in marble. Julienne looked it over very carefully, wondering what it would be like to live here. She met her father's eyes. They both knew the same thing: though all of this was magnificent and artistically perfect, it did not feel like a home. It was cold and impersonal, like a museum, a grave for the artwork of another time.

Kollmer led them to a drawing room off the center hall, and it was, mercifully, more comfortable. It had large windows and carefully arranged furniture. The room was primarily blue, and they waited only a few minutes for Franz and his parents.

Franz gave Julienne a slight kiss, shook hands with Stefan and Heinrich, then introduced his parents, the Duke and Duchess of Eisenstadt, to Prince Heinrich, Archduke of Tulln-Kahlenberg, and his family. They sat down and had coffee with afternoon refreshments.

Julienne watched Franz's mother. She thought the woman distant but pleasant, wondering what it would be like to have a mother again and to know a mother's care.

Heinrich began to get a peculiar feeling up the back of his spine. He watched this little group with practiced eyes, participating in the conversation, yet settling inside himself and becoming an observer.

It was a long time in meeting them, he thought. They always had an excuse and always found a way to reject my invitations. Why? They retreat from Society and keep mostly to themselves. Why? The Duke, Heinrich thought, is slightly taller than Franz's six feet and is of average weight. Father and son have the same blue eyes and blond hair, and although the faces are similar, the Duke's features are sharper. Franz's face is on the round side. Why does the Duke constantly keep watch on his wife? He never looks at his son, Heinrich noticed, but always watches his wife. He seems a hard and brittle man, Heinrich decided.

The Duchess made Heinrich nervous. She was thin, angular, extremely beautiful—but it was a peculiar kind of beauty. Her skin was light and her hair was light and her eyes were a bland blue without life. Hers was the pristine beauty of a statue, exquisite but dead. Kissing her marble hand, he saw no movement, no recognition, no response. She looked past a person and not into their eyes. Her smile was practiced and false. Why?

The Duchess' dress was somewhat out of fashion, which seemed odd to Heinrich in a house so obviously concerned with the perfection of beauty and good taste. Women's day dresses *did* button up the front to some sort of collar, and their shoulders *were* covered, but this day dress seemed out of place for meeting a son's betrothed and her family. The collar was unusually high. The sleeves of the dress, instead of being loose at the wrist, were tightly bound, and had lace which covered half her hands. When he'd kissed her hand, Heinrich noticed a scar, long and thin, tracing along the top of the right hand and cutting down underneath the thumb. It was an old scar, fading. Perhaps she is vain, Heinrich thought, but what kind of accident would make such an unusual scar?

By the evening meal, Heinrich was extremely uncomfortable with these people. Once or twice, the Duke unexpectedly asked a question of his wife and Heinrich saw her flinch when he called her name, Iren. The sound of the husband saying "Iren" made the wife shiver. She quickly recovered and instantly answered his question, immediately agreeing with him, and when she'd finished speaking, she hid once more behind her placid dead smile. Heinrich noticed all of it.

Much later that night, Heinrich filled his pipe and wandered out of his bedroom. He walked down the hallway toward the marble staircase. They sit perfectly, he thought, talk perfectly about the theater, chat perfectly about the government, smile perfectly, laugh mildly but perfectly and always at the right moment—actors. All of them, actors. Except for her—the dead woman. What is the secret in this house? It is obvious they have one. There is no warmth or love here. What is it these people try so very hard to hide from me?

The following afternoon, he made a point of taking a walk with Stefan through the gardens. Heinrich admitted to himself it was partly to remove himself from the house and partly to gain information.

"Hate is the reason," Stefan answered matter-of-factly.

"How do you know?"

"Franz told me, quite some time ago when we were at the Theresianium. Why do you think he spent all those Christmases alone in Vienna whilst they were here at this house?"

Heinrich shook his head, far from convinced. "There is more to it than that," he muttered. "I don't believe hate between a man and his wife looks quite like that. She never looks at him, but he watches her all the time. And the perfection," he said, jutting his head toward the house, "in every little thing. It is so unnatural, so disturbing, like trained animals."

"Fine way to talk," Stefan sighed. "And how should they look, Papa? They meet their son's fiancée and her family, a Royal family. What do you expect them to do, behave less than they would for the Emperor himself?"

Heinrich shook his head. "I am accustomed to that look, Stefan. This," he sighed, "is very different. They are hiding something."

"No, I don't agree," Stefan replied. "Every house has its secrets and dark corners. I am certain one could make a most convincing argument about Schönbrunn. The Emperor's Palace has its secrets, does it not?"

"Yes," Heinrich reluctantly agreed.

"And its husband and wife have their share of troubles?"

Heinrich did not answer.

"Papa," Stefan said, "make no mistake on this. Franz told me himself. They do hate each other, but they try to behave for our sake." Stefan watched his father for a moment. "Not everyone has had my advantages, a father like you. Most of the men I know have varying degrees of Franz's father. And I know I could never speak this openly, this freely to a father like that. You've seen the man, you've spoken with him, and you know yourself the countless stories Franz has told of *never* being able to please his father. Is it any wonder this place is like a grave?"

19

Heinrich did not reply.

"I thought you, more than anyone else, would understand and appreciate how sad and terrible Franz's childhood must have been with parents like that." Stefan looked away and stared at the rose bushes for a moment, then turned and looked sharply at his father. "Do you condemn Franz for the shortcomings of his parents?"

Heinrich shook his head. "And neither do I deny them."

"You must admit that he is not like them."

"Yes," Heinrich said, "but one cannot deny the 'breeding ground,'" he said rather grandly, waving his arm with an annoyed jab toward the house. "He has not told us everything."

"He does not have to," Stefan answered. "Papa, allow Franz the dignity of the 'grand lie,' and let us pretend to believe that they are a 'happy' family."

The breeding ground, Heinrich thought, troubled by his own phrase, and suddenly found himself thinking of a phrase from Ecclesiasticus: "Though his father is dead, it is as if he were not dead, for he hath left one behind that is like himself." He sighed; could it be true with Franz, and if so, Heinrich wondered, what is the father *really* like?

A need from childhood called from deep within her, erasing the austere disposition of the Duchess and filling in the gaps with imagined warmth and love. Julienne felt the need for a mother, and here was a woman who could *be* a mother to her. But the refusals, the coldness and the distance remained over the week's visit.

Julienne walked with the Duchess down a lane called the "Monks' Walk," a narrow, winding dirt path with overhanging branches of trees that arched with natural spires to the heavens. Tomorrow, she and her family would leave and they would not see Franz nor his family until the ceremony at the church in Vienna. But Julienne had the feeling her company was something to be endured, like the walk now. The Duchess' eyes were lowered to the path, or she stared ahead at the low pine branches and streams of dusty diffused sunlight, but she never looked at her companion.

"Have I done something to offend you?" Julienne finally asked.

"You've done nothing of the kind, my dear," Iren answered, as if expecting the question.

"This visit was important to me for many reasons," Julienne went on, watching the woman through glazed eyes. "I, I had hoped so very much that I might call you mother . . ."

"NO," the Duchess instantly glared.

Julienne was so startled she began to say, "I don't understand," but was interrupted a second time by the Duchess, continuing with the sharp rebuff.

"You will *not* call me that. I have suffered enough for . . ." She stopped, the flush left her pale cheeks as the anger subsided from her eyes. It was immediately replaced by another emotion. She smiled, but it was false and prompted by desperation, just as one backed into a corner must retrace hasty, terrible steps. She laughed slightly, but betrayed herself and her fears by the quick tumble of her words. "How silly of me, it was only an, an amusement. I do that, I play little jokes on people when they least expect them. It was silly of me, when the purpose of this walk was to give you this family ring. My husband told me to give it to you as a small token of our love, just as it was given to me for my wedding." She nearly ripped it off her finger, smiling and trying to keep the features on her face under control. Her eyes filled, salty tears began to trickle down her high cheekbones, yet she continued to force a smile on her lips. "You must take the ring. He would be so displeased with me if I . . . please, for the love of God, take the ring . . ."

Julienne nodded and the ring was placed in her palm. It was a very small ring with a pearl in the center and small diamond chips surrounding it, a delicate woman's ring. "Thank you," Julienne managed, not caring about the jewelry but mesmerized by the sight of the ghostly Duchess.

"You must forgive my outburst," Iren went on, quickly. "If, if it pleases you, yes, you may call me mother. I, I shan't object. But you mustn't say anything of my joke. Please, say nothing, not even to Franz." Her blue eyes, the eyes that had looked bland and lifeless, were now wide open. Her thin hands shook uncontrollably and she did not relax even when Julienne agreed to the secret.

Julienne stepped closer, but Iren backed away, clasping her shaking hands to herself. "I am, I am so very tired," Iren whimpered, "this walk has made me tired. You must excuse me. I have much to do, but I should rest before dinner, I should . . ." Iren turned, and was momentarily confused, not knowing where to walk, as if she had lost her sense of direction. When she realized which way she had to go, she moved as if she were being chased.

Julienne watched her, not knowing if the Duchess was an intelligent woman, what were her likes and dislikes, for she had remained as mysterious and distant as the first day of their visit. It no longer mattered. Julienne's own mother had not been like this, and if she needed a mother's care, she would do what she had always done: rely on the fragmented memories of her own mother and try to make them into a guide for herself.

She looked at the little ring. I will not put it on, she thought, and I probably will never wear it. I will never beg to be liked or loved.

∽

The baby gurgled from the straw basket and Gisela made noises back to him. Julienne stared at the road ahead. Papa had been right, she thought, remembering Stefan had told her all about that particular conversation ten months ago, when he'd come to Eisenstadt and learned the truth and she told him of her plan. She swallowed. Papa had been right from the beginning. If Papa had told me, and I had told him of what I saw—but nothing would have changed because I was in love, she thought bitterly, and that makes all the difference, doesn't it?

She saw the turn-off point ahead, the stone wall, the boundary marker with the wild rose bushes, and slowed Domino to a walk, then to a stop. The slight breeze, fresh, clear, jostled the trees and the wheat field to their left. There was no other sound. Where is he, she thought, feeling the tightness in her

21

stomach. Something's gone wrong, they've locked him in a room because they've found out, and the old Aunt has told Franz, and he'll find us on the road and kill us all . . . God in heaven, where is he?

The silence made her nervous and the time dragged as breezes came and went. The moist palms inside her gloves turned cold and she shivered. She undid the netting from the hat and lifted it up to the wide brim in order to see the fields and the lanes clearly. Friedrich, she thought, my Friedrich.

There! From the wheat field . . . the blond hair.

He ran, kicking up dust from the road, faster, faster, arms pumping, sleeves clinging to his skin as he pushed himself harder and harder.

"He did it," she breathed, then jumped down from the Phaeton. She ran to him, and opened her arms to her seven-year-old boy and hugged him tightly. "I was afraid something went wrong."

He shook his head. "Momma, please," he wheezed, then kissed her. He led her back to the carriage and held out his arm to help her with the step. He jumped up beside her with ease, tickled Gisela, then turned back to his mother, studying her for a moment. "We should hide your face," he said quietly, placing his hands on the netting and lowering it to her chin. She flinched, and he knew he'd hurt her feelings. He kissed her cheek gently, saying, "People know you, Momma. We don't want them to see you."

"Of course," Julienne said, then smiled.

"I'll take care of you," he said softly. "I promise."

"I believe you," she said, then gave him Kollmer's linen handkerchief with the ink notations. "You be the map reader," she smiled. "What do we do now?"

"We must go right," he said without the slightest hesitation. "Kollmer told me that. This road leads to the town and Kollmer said stay away from it. Go that way, Momma."

She slapped Domino's backside with the reins, then slapped him again. They moved quickly from the shady lane to the open road bordered by two wide rolling meadows and the horse was finally given his head to do the running he'd pulled for all morning.

"I did everything Kollmer said," Friedrich said loudly, the wind in his face. "I told Tante Hannah I was going exploring, and would pick berries for her, because I loved her and because Father used to do that. She liked that. Kollmer knew she would. I asked for a treat in a basket, and I made sure to leave it by a trail at the other end of the meadow. I've been out since nine o'clock."

"I thought she would make one of the servants go with you," Julienne replied, shouting to be heard above the rattle of the Phaeton.

Friedrich smiled. "I promised I would not go past the meadow." The sound of the wheels drowned out his laughter. Julienne grinned at him.

"Is it three hours yet?" Gisela asked.

"Almost," Julienne answered. "We must find a good spot far far away from here for our picnic."

She drove Domino hard and they went for several miles without speaking. Then, he needed to rest, so at a bend in the road they drove over silken grass to a shaded spot behind lilac bushes now just green, their flowers long gone. They were near a cluster of birch trees, a spot neatly hidden from the road.

It felt good to eat. Maximilian crawled across the blanket and was carefully watched by his older brother. They ate slowly and drank water that had been put into a wine bottle. They rested, watching the trees moving in unison and clouds making pictures in the sky, as Domino grazed. Soon we will discard these clothes, Julienne thought, and change into something more suitable for the journey. They had a long way to go before nightfall.

"Momma," Friedrich said, "I have to . . ."

She nodded toward the trees at the end of this oasis off the road. "There, for privacy's sake."

Friedrich raced to relieve himself.

"Me," Gisela said, "me, too."

"We'll wait for your brother to come back first," she said, watching the surprise on her child's face. "It's something new to learn," she said calmly, thinking it was a fair answer and that it just had to be done.

As they waited for Friedrich, she led Domino back to the carriage and re-harnessed him, as she'd been taught to do. Then she packed up the remaining food that had been allotted for this meal and placed it back in the basket, re-strapping that to the carriage. Friedrich returned and held his brother Maximilian, giving him a bottle of cool water. He sat in the front seat of the carriage, the reins draped across his knees and his brother in his arms.

Julienne led Gisela to the woods, where they would both learn to hold their skirts and be as graceful as possible in a squatting position.

For the rest of the day's travel, they were in a rhythm. Julienne drove Domino and the older children took turns sitting next to her or minding Maximilian. They were heading northwest, skirting the edges of a town named Mannersdorf, struggling to cross the Leitha River before four o'clock. They had an appointment at four, on the other side of the Leitha, at a deserted milk farm three miles down a lane with a broken rail fence.

"You go to the west now, Momma," Friedrich said, studying the linen handkerchief, reading the numbered instructions. "It says, 'go west at the point where there is a blacksmith's shop, burned out.' See," he said, pointing to the charred remains by another crossroad. "We go west now."

Julienne looked at the sun, then tugged on the left rein as Domino trotted on the dusty road going west. Two miles later they came to the Leitha River, the water almost green with its reflected beauty of the overhanging trees and mossy vegetation growing on its banks. A calm little river, it wasn't very wide and the road led directly to the wooden bridge at this particular crossing. On the western bank they stayed with the main road, following it west as the sun bled through the trees and caused them to squint their eyes and shade their faces. West, she knew, always west.

She felt for the lady's pocket watch pinned to her traveling coat, found it, and looked at the time. Fifteen minutes past four; they were late. "He said three miles," she mentioned to Friedrich. "We must have gone three miles by now. Where is it? Where's the farm?"

Friedrich shrugged. "Kollmer wouldn't tell a lie, would he?"

The boy was right and Julienne smiled tautly. Kollmer had prepared all the directions with care. And everything had been where he said it would be. There was no sense in succumbing to panic now.

"There's the fence," Friedrich said, pointing to the split rails barely holding together at the mouth of a shady lane. Julienne felt foolish. Of course it would be there, she thought, as Domino kicked up the loose dirt on his way down the path, and then to the back end of the barn.

Uncle Teo was waiting for them. Seated in the cool shade at the base of an Elm tree, he watched as the little carriage was expertly maneuvered and brought to a stop. "You've done very well, my dear, very well," he said, then stood up and quickly brushed the dust from the bottom of his brown robe.

"I'm sorry we're late," she said.

"I am here," Teo replied. He helped her down then softly kissed her. He tied Domino to a tree a moment later. "Come, children," he called, clapping his hands and then scooping Friedrich and Gisela into his arms with a great hug. "Time to change your clothes. It is time to begin the game."

There is a calm about Teo, Julienne thought. He had a soft voice, much softer than her father's had been, but Teo's physical resemblance to his older brother was astonishing. She watched as Teo gave a bundle to Friedrich. "Go quickly now," he said, "and be sure to bring all your things out with you again." The boy was off like a shot, running to the dilapidated barn.

He gave Julienne a bundle for herself and one for Gisela. "I chose them with care. I think these are the best for your needs." She nodded, then threw her arms around him, bundles pressing against his sides. He held her for a moment, then took the netting off her face to kiss her cheek. He kissed her gently, where the purplish swelling was not too pronounced. "I am so proud of you," he said. "My brother raised you very well indeed. And what you are doing is right—never doubt that. You are right to do this."

"Sometimes, I am so afraid and I wonder if . . ."

Teo firmly shook his head. "Listen," he said quietly, "and remember this all of your life. Remember Lot's wife, Julienne. Never look back, and never, never come back." He lifted her chin with a gentle hand. "If you are to keep to my schedule, you've a long way to go before you lose the light."

She took Gisela's hand and they ran to the barn, meeting Friedrich on his way out. "I think I look rather well," he said, giving a smart brush to his soiled breeches, patched and torn almost beyond repair.

"Help Uncle Teo with the horse," Julienne smiled, then took Gisela into the barn. Teo had picked a stall at the far end for his belongings, and had tied his own horse there. She saw the swish of a roan's tail flick at the sides.

"What game is this?"

"A special game," Julienne answered, as she undressed her child down to the skin and began putting the peasant rags on Gisela. "You remember this

24

game. You remember how *hard* we practiced. This is the game where we pretend we are not Austrian."

"Oh, the pretend game. I know."

"The French game."

"We speak only French," Gisela recited.

"Yes."

"No German . . ."

"Yes," Julienne said, "and anyone who speaks German .

". . . will get no dinner," Gisela replied.

"Who are we?"

"We are nobody, we are peasants," Gisela answered. She watched her mother take off her clothes and exchange everything beautiful for the peasant garments, all loose, ill-fitting, with a pungent smell of perspiration clinging to each faded article. Julienne saved only one thing: the embroidered petticoat. That she would always wear. Then she took her hair down, tossed the pins away and tied a rag about her head.

"This is the running-from-home game," Gisela said, suddenly.

"Yes," Julienne answered.

"And we're never, never going back?"

Julienne left the last button of her blouse undone and held her arms out to Gisela. The child hesitated, then strolled into her mother's arms. "No, my little one, we're not ever going back. It isn't safe, it isn't a home. Would you want me to still live there?" She traced a finger through the curls draped over Gisela's shoulders.

The child's lower lip trembled for a moment. "No," she whispered.

"You have me," Julienne said, rocking her back and forth, "and you have your brothers, and your very favorite doll." She hugged her daughter. "And soon, we shall have a real home, I promise you. One that will be all ours, and no one else's. And we'll not ever be afraid again. We shall live in peace and quiet, and always, always be safe. It will be so easy, but I need your help. Gisela, you must help me. Will you do that?"

Gisela quickly kissed her mother's neck. "Yes." She touched the dark chestnut-colored hair, loose and smooth like silk. Then, she wrinkled her nose. "They smell," she said.

"We'll wash our clothes tomorrow," Julienne said.

They gathered up all their old clothes and wrapped them in a bundle, using Julienne's blue skirt to hold them. They made sure Friedrich had left nothing behind, then left the barn.

Teo had changed the baby's clothes and was now hitching Domino to an old cart. Inside the lightweight two-wheeled cart, a former owner had made a small seat in the front for the driver and a seat along one of the sides. Entry to the cart was from the rear. It had a small step, and a wooden door mounted above it. The cart was open on top so they would be exposed to the elements. Teo took Julienne's hand and walked her away from the cart toward the Elm tree.

"Everything you need is in here," he said, and gave her a flat leather courier's pouch. "You've maps, travel instructions, baptismal certificates—and I have left the names blank for you to write them in later. I have included a letter of introduction to all the Abbots and Mother Superiors. I have also charged each of the Religious to silence."

She took the pouch and held it tightly in her hands.

"Try to send word to me, or ask one of the Abbots or Mother Superiors to write to me saying only that they helped a stranger, a woman and her children, safely on their way."

Julienne nodded. "I make no promise, but I will try." Her eyes suddenly filled. "I, I did as you asked," she said. "I did not write to Stefan. Tell him, tell him . . ."

Teo held her. "We agreed your silence would protect him and his family. He'll be able to look at Franz and say truthfully he does not know where you are."

"But I may never see him again," she cried. "He's all I have, my brother, my friend . . ."

"Sometimes," Teo said, "a journey must be made alone. Remember what my brother taught you: choose life. Do not be afraid. Go and choose life. Take your babies and run and never, never come back to the hell that you leave behind." He kissed her, held her, and whispered, "I shall pray for you, always, as I have always done. My brother would have been so proud of you, Julienne."

She wiped her eyes and composed herself. She was determined not to cry in front of her children and scare them. Three little lives depended on her for everything now. She had to do so much more than was ever asked of her: she had to be a governess, a teacher, she had to cook for them, do their laundry, wipe their eyes, care for their needs, raise them and comfort them—and all without outside help. No one must know where they are. The four of them had to dissolve into obscurity. Their only chance for life was that they must cease to exist.

He smiled, then walked with her back to the cart, blessing them, saying goodbye and watching as they settled into their seats. "Oh, one last thing," he said to Julienne. "This seat, here, along the side." He motioned for Friedrich to stand up. "An added surprise," Teo said, and lifted the top. Inside she saw two lanterns, blankets, a box of matches, a large hunting knife sheathed in a leather scabbard and a small axe. "For your journey," he said, "a few supplies." Teo squeezed her hand. "Go while there's still light." He nodded toward her carriage. "I'll see to all of this."

Teo found this cart, she thought, and it must have been Teo who redesigned it, adding the seats and giving them storage space for supplies—and also, to hide a child. They could pass through larger towns now in this nondescript cart and Friedrich or Gisela could hide in the seat. She could appear to have two children, or three, or just the one baby. She would never look the same in each town along the way.

There was an overpowering need to see him just one more time and, despite his warning, she turned and saw him with his hands on his hips, looped in the white rope belting his brown habit. He shook his head at her, then raised his right hand and wagged a finger in warning. He startled her so much, she quickly turned around, suddenly afraid. She would always remember that— Teo, standing like a guard, barring the way to disaster. This country was no longer hers. And he was right. There was no looking back or going back, ever. Starting now.

"We'll begin the French game," she said lightly to the children, and felt Gisela's small hands on her shoulders.

"How?"

"We start by a song, yes?" Julienne said, and they switched their language, sliding into the melodious tongue of her mother's family as easily as she knew the German of her father's family. She had brought her children up the way she'd been brought up—in a house with two languages.

Teo could hear the faint song carrying in the silence of the countryside. He smiled, then rolled up the sleeves of his monk's robe. He eyed the carriage, the ducal arms of Eisenstadt painted on the sides, proclaiming the owner in a loud voice. Like a beast of burden, he picked up the wooden shafts and hauled the carriage into the broken-down barn. There, he walked to the far end where opposite his tethered roan horse, he'd placed his own belongings in a pile and had covered them with a blanket. He uncovered the pile and reached for the large axe.

With the first swing, the blade bit into the side of the carriage, splintering the polished wood. He dismembered the carriage, swinging the axe like a woodsman. He was a strong man, like his brother had been; a large man, like his brother had been. Seeing him now, reducing the carriage to small planks, no one would ever imagine he had once been a Habsburg Prince.

As darkness came, he took his lantern and walked outside the barn. There, in what would be a shaded, hidden spot, he began to dig a grave.

His rough, woolen monk's habit was soaked through by his effort when he made a layer of kindling and set the pieces of the carriage into a box formation. He doused it with oil from a bottle he'd brought, then lit it, watching as the first parts of the carriage began to burn.

By dawn, his face was lined with sweat and grime. Exhausted, he doused the bundle of their clothing, and tossed it into the dying flames, watching as they burned hot for a moment when the oil caught fire, then died when there was nothing left to burn.

He poured well-water over the charred remains, hearing the sizzle of the hot fragments and smelled the last scent of burnt wood. Quickly, methodically, he began to fill in the grave, packing the earth down with his shovel and his sandaled feet.

By two o'clock in the afternoon, he was finished and washed himself just before leaving. The job was done. And he'd left the grave without a marker.

CHAPTER
2

Franz lay in the afternoon sun using his arms as a pillow behind his head. It was the smell, he decided; the smell made him sleepy. The smell was summer's perfume—warm, moist earth, the vineyards, the cut grassy sweetness of the hillsides and the dank mustiness of the forest behind him.

A breeze rustled the wooden rattles strung along the vineyards and the sudden cacophony screamed the quiet away. "Damn!" he said and sat upright, nerves jangling and edgy. He saw the flock of starlings escape the noise, leaving the tender baby grapes behind. They circled above him for a moment, confused, then flew into the forest. He stood up and stared at the vineyard. "Damn rattles and damn birds," he muttered. "Doesn't do one damn bit of good."

There was no point in staying, he realized; the peace of the afternoon had flown in a panic like the birds to a darker, more secret quarter. He descended the gentle slope of the hillside to the valley below and walked through his vineyards. Eyeing the vines, he shook his head, mumbling, "There must be a better way to save the grapes," and gave an angry, half-hearted swipe to the last rattle in the line.

He made his way down the lanes to the main dirt road which would lead him, some two miles away, to his house on the outskirts of St. Marein in the Styrian Province of Southern Austria.

Why is she so willful, he thought miserably. Why does she make me do these things? Disobedience, always disobedience, and she tries to make me out to be the fool. Why? I try to help her, and I always end up begging for forgiveness. He stopped walking and listened for a moment. A dog barked, birds sang, gnats buzzed and the occasional bee hovered nearby, but there wasn't a voice of a man, woman or child anywhere near him. He kicked at a loose stone in the road, feeling the emptiness and the loneliness around him. What did it matter, he thought, what does this house and property, the vines, the factories, the money . . . what does any of it matter if I sleep alone, and my days are spent alone, and she never speaks to me unless I prompt her. . . .

She lies all the time, he thought. You made me break my promise, Julienne. You made me do it. He felt a sharp pain in his right hand and massaged the palm and wrist to ease it. The swelling had gone down, but the knuckles were still somewhat raw and the center of the palm ached.

The depression took hold, but he was used to it. He continued down the dirt road. When the chalet came into view, he didn't have the strength to go inside, to sit alone in the study, or the library, or the drawing room. He simply could not bear being alone inside another house peopled by servants. The gazebo, he thought, and walked slowly around the back to the latticed summer porch, then settled into the stuffed lounge chair and put his feet up. Sleep, that was the only answer. Sleep it away, and he tried not to think, lulling himself into a calmness by listening with his whole mind to the sounds of the woods.

Footsteps broke his concentration.

"A telegram came for you, Your Grace."

Franz opened his eyes and nodded to Baumann. He sighed, looking at the servant, who was just like any of the other servants in his employ. Baumann held the silver tray out to him, he took the telegram, and then dismissed the servant as he tore open the envelope and read the message.

Five words, he thought, and a world collapses.

He did not remember the eleven-mile carriage ride to Graz. It was a blur, a mystery.

The hours did not seem to pass. He had bought a ticket for the early train, the first one out of Graz in the morning, and this interminable night had to be spent at the Kauenhofen Hotel. Wandering, lost, he lingered in the lobby and thought perhaps he ought to have dinner, not remembering the last time he'd eaten. Was it this morning? Breakfast, perhaps, he thought.

He'd ordered his dinner and sat at his table in the corner, scratching his nail on the embroidered flowers on the linen tablecloth. When his plate arrived, he heard the other patrons, and their whispered chatter, their conversations, their good times and seductive laughter.

"Friedrich missing. Come home. Hannah."

He kept seeing the five words dance in his mind. The dining room smells of meat and gravy, sweet wine, fruity desserts, chocolate, hot bread soured in front of him. He gagged and pushed his plate away, knocking over his wine glass. He sat there, numb, watching the red stain seep into the white linen.

"Oh, let me help you, Sir," a waiter said. "I'll clean this up and then move you to another table." He began to sop up the wine with a cloth.

Franz shook his head. "Clumsy of me." He reached into his breast pocket and took out a gulden. "For the damages," he said, and placed the coin on the table.

"But you needn't . . ."

"Please," Franz insisted, and then, quite suddenly, he stood up and backed away, sensing the place, the atmosphere, the people, the sounds, closing in. "Have . . . have a brandy sent to room five."

"Yes, of course, Sir," the waiter answered, watching the tall blond-haired man walk out of the dining room.

Somehow the dark made the time go faster. At the very least, Franz could lie to himself that it was going faster. Friedrich could be hurt at this very moment. Or dead. There was that possibility, too. He held himself tightly and felt the cold waves of tension hit him in the darkness. He'd drained the brandy glass and felt no better for his trouble. Two days of travel yet, he thought. Two days from Eisenstadt.

Thoughts of coffins and candles and images of Julienne's ashen face tormented him, toying with him like a child afraid to go to bed, knowing that monsters lurk in the halls and wait for the dark.

God, he prayed, God save my child, Let him be safe. Missing, he thought. How could so small a word cause so great a chill in my heart?

"Answer my question. How long did you wait?"

Ahrens felt his body go taut and continued to stare down at the carpet in front of his boots. "He . . . he had a picnic lunch with him, Your Grace. He dismissed me, he sent me away. He promised me he would not wander." The tapping of the Duke's hand on the back of the chair made him nervous.

"You've still not answered my question. How long did you wait?"

"I . . . I had my duties to attend to, Your Grace, and when he'd not returned by five o'clock, I began to worry and then I began to search for him." Ahrens saw the shadow cross in front of his feet, then instantly felt the large hands grab the lapels of his coat and twist the cloth. He felt the blood drain from his cheeks when he saw the Duke's narrow-eyed malevolent stare.

"You let my son wander about, alone, for eight hours?" Franz hissed, tightening his grip and his voice. "He's been missing for four days. *Four days.* My son has a good sense of direction. My son knows this property well. You found the picnic lunch, did you not?"

Ahrens nodded.

"My son is either terribly hurt, or he's dead, do you understand? I hold you responsible. I ought to . . ."

There was a knock at the door.

"Yes," Franz snapped, letting go of the servant's coat.

The door opened and a maid stepped in. "Excuse me, Your Grace, but Madam is waiting for you now, in the drawing room."

Franz nodded, then eyed the footman. "You will remain in your quarters until I decide what's to be done with you. Go."

Ahrens gave a shaky bow and quickly left the room.

Franz tried to calm himself, then walked out of the library in his Aunt's house, down the hall and turned right into the drawing room. Poor old woman, he thought, looking at his Aunt. She was seventy-eight and her skin was as grey as her hair, and her spotted hands shook from age and all this anxiety. He walked over to her, took her hands in his own and kissed her lightly on the cheek. He could smell the brandy. "I'm here now," he said quietly.

"Franzi," she whispered, "I am so sorry . . ." She shook her head and looked very confused. "I simply could not see you when you arrived. I've seen no one, talked to no one except my physician . . . I've taken to bed since . . . since . . ."

"I understand," he said. She was trying, with little success, to pronounce her words with clarity. He knew she'd been given quite a dose of brandy to settle her nerves. He kissed the grey braid on the top of her head. "We will try to talk now, yes?"

She gave an unsteady nod.

"I've sent one of your servants for Julienne, but she hasn't come yet."

Hannah looked up at him and tried to focus her eyes. "But I sent for her."

"Good. We will wait, then, until she comes down."

"No," Hannah managed, shaking her head a bit too vigorously. "I sent for her four, yes, four days ago. When I sent for you. She . . . she never responded."

The pit of his stomach dropped and for a second he stopped breathing. He blinked as if it would clear his mind. "Tante," he said, wrapping his hands around her face, "Tante, listen to me. You must try to think about what I'm saying. You must be mistaken. Of course Julienne is here."

She looked at him with vacant eyes.

"Tante, she is here, is she not?"

Hannah shook her head.

"Then where is she?"

The old woman shrugged, her lower lip trembling.

He couldn't think. He felt as if his skin caught fire, then lost all sensation and stood for a moment, unable to swallow, unable to breathe. What in God's name has happened, he thought. Home. He had to go home. He turned away from his Aunt and stumbled to the bell rope in the corner of the room. He rang, and kept ringing, until his call was answered.

"A horse," he breathed, "saddled and ready. Now."

He'd arrived not half an hour ago, he knew, walking to the front door of his Aunt's house. It was three o'clock; several hours of light left, he thought. Take the short cut through the North meadow, through the fields—save an hour's travel. Be at Eisenstadt in two hours, not three. Plenty of light left, plenty . . .

His hands shook as he tried to pull on his riding gloves. He couldn't remember if he'd eaten. He'd been moving for three days. Exhausted, he thought, exhausted . . . dirty . . . must get home.

He mounted the grey stallion and then had to wait for a minute until his own mind cleared, until he could remember which way he had to go. He cantered the horse to the back of the house, eased the animal down the gentle slope, then dug in his heels and rode hard and long through the fields along the dirt lanes.

Every part of him ached, every muscle felt stretched and in a knot. Familiar sights rushed by him without recognition; the grounds of his childhood were ignored for the sight of the road between the horse's ears. God, he thought, God what's happened . . . She died.

He was a man possessed, oblivious to the pressure on his hands from holding the leather reins too tight, unaware of the dirt clinging to him or the labored breathing and uneven run of the horse beneath him. The animal balked and had to rest. He had to allow a few moments, and slumped forward in the saddle as the horse lowered his head and took an unsteady step. Franz tried to stop his own panicked gasps for air, and wiped the silt from his face. The grey was lathered and had to be walked for quite a distance until he cooled down. Franz could feel the sweat clinging to his own body, the clammy wetness covering him in the dead July air.

He'd walked the horse long enough, mounted up, and dug in his heels for another long stretch of a run, trying to shave minutes from the remaining hour of the trip. This nightmare of physical pain, constant movement and battling time ended when he saw the turrets of his house. He dismounted and his legs felt rubbery, unsure, so he leaned for a moment against the horse. Dizzy from exhaustion, he walked slowly to the front door. It was locked. He pulled on the bell.

Kollmer looked surprised, then concerned. "We had no way of knowing, Your Grace. I received no telegram; I would have met you myself . . ."

Franz waved him off, swallowing, trying to clear the dust from his throat and find his voice.

"Let me help you, are you hurt, are . . ." Kollmer's words trailed off and he watched as Franz steadied himself against the wall and began climbing the stairs. Halfway up, he stopped, listening to the house.

He sensed it. Looking quickly at Kollmer, an unasked question made Franz's eyes widen, and he ran down the hallway, hoping, praying that the hostages were still here. Franz pushed open the nursery door, and the silence told him everything.

He wanted numbness, but couldn't find it. He wanted to be drunk, but couldn't achieve it. The agony was everywhere, and there was no escaping it. For two days, he wandered through the upstairs halls like a dumbstruck animal confused by a sudden fog. Then, he found himself in her room, going through her things, lying on her bed, holding her pillows and smelling the faint traces of her perfume. The scent lingered, not for pleasure, no, but as a tormenting harpie to augment the black mood and unspeakable loss he now knew as the truth. He'd found her wedding ring.

Nothing had happened to Friedrich. She'd stolen the children and they'd run away.

The stillness of the conference room at the Hofburg made Stefan uncomfortable. The curtains were partially drawn, yet now, without the Crown Council or the Council of Ministers gathered around the large table, it was an eerie empty space haunted by their voices.

Stefan remembered. It had been nearly a year since the 1868 revolution in Spain deposed the Bourbon Queen Isabella II. And since that time, this room had echoed with the heated discussions. He remembered giving his opinion on the matter:

"I remind this Council of the discussion that took place two years ago in October, 1866, in Biarritz. Please recall that the Prussian diplomats and Spanish revolutionaries who attended that party played an entertaining after-dinner discussion game of 'who-shall-be-on-the-throne' after Queen Isabella is deposed."

He knew the Council had paid no attention to the reports by the Austrian diplomat who had heard about that "innocent" discussion and reported it at once. The Council decided it was a mere dinner-party amusement. But it was two years *before* the fact. And the revolution *had* taken place. He had reminded the Council of two active players in that game: Baron George Von Werthern, the former secretary of the Prussian Legation to Madrid, and Don Eusebio de Salazar, a Deputy in the Spanish Government. They even had a candidate, Stefan said to the Council, Prince Leopold of Hohenzollern-Sigmaringen—a Prussian.

The door opened at the far end of the room and Stefan's mind returned to the business at hand. The Emperor strode in, taking his usual long measured steps. Stefan bowed to his cousin.

"You look tired," Franz Josef said.

"It has been a long journey, Your Imperial Majesty." He waited, watching the Emperor pull a chair away from the head of the conference table and sit down.

"Well," the Emperor sighed, "the rumors have been with us for quite some time now. Do you still believe them true?"

"Yes, Your Majesty," Stefan answered. "They have been most discreet, but like all hidden activity, there are signs that betray them."

"Give me your report, then."

"My visit to Madrid, unhappily, coincided with new rumors circulating in the newspapers suggesting that a Habsburg Archduke would make a suitable King."

"You denied any interest, of course."

"Instantly, Your Majesty." Stefan then explained the casual social meetings with government members, and their contradictory opinions of the rumor concerning Prince Leopold's supposed candidacy.

"You spoke of hidden activity?" the Emperor asked.

"Yes. Outside the Government House in Madrid, I happened to see two men by a large fountain, speaking in a very excited way. I recognized Don Eusebio de Salazar immediately. The second man I did not know. I learned later, Salazar was speaking to Adolphe Lothar Bucher."

"And who is he?"

"A personal aide of Chancellor Bismarck."

The Emperor thought about that. "It could mean nothing, a private conversation unrelated to government." He looked at Stefan. "But you are determined to believe that nonsense about Leopold, aren't you?" He did not wait for a reply, but continued speaking as he stood up. "Why do you imagine Prussia desires one of her Princes to sit on the throne of Spain? It would gain Bismarck nothing in his quest to unite Germany or to increase Germany's power in the world."

"But . . ."

"No," the Emperor said, "there will be no war *with* Spain or *concerning* Spain."

"Your Majesty, I agree that there will be no war *with* Spain. But I think it *will* concern Spain." He saw the quizzical look, then continued. "I do not believe that Prussia was in any way involved with the revolution. However, I think they are making the best of this 'opportunity.' Bismarck knows Louis

33

Napoleon would *never* allow a Prussian Prince to rule Spain. It would place German sympathies on two of his borders. I think Bismarck is *counting* on that. That man has such confidence, he even told an English journalist some two years back, that Prussia would never begin a war. He said Prussia would not attack France, but that *France* would undoubtedly attack Prussia."

"Does he believe in horoscopes too, like Louis Napoleon?" The Emperor grinned in a strained sort of way.

"He believes in himself and his chosen mission—Prussia, as a major force in Europe. In answer to the journalist's question of what might bring about this war with France, he stated 'an excuse would not be wanting if the French really needed one.' "

"And I am supposed to believe that the Spanish throne is the pivotal point in Bismarck's plans?" the Emperor chuckled.

"He has put his case very bluntly—France would be the aggressor, Prussia would be the innocent party to the world," Stefan pressed. "It is an all-too-familiar story, isn't it?"

The grin left the Emperor's lips. He flushed, clicked his heels together, then strode decisively out of the room.

Stefan closed his eyes. "Damn," he sighed, thinking the Emperor had always done that to end an interview that had turned unpleasant. He will close his mind now, Stefan thought. He will refuse to see history repeating itself: Bismarck manipulating the pride of a nation to engage them in a war, and then, gaining territory and prestige for Prussia. Bismarck doesn't give a damn about Spain, he thought, but he has said, rather slyly, that Alsace and Lorraine are old territories—and he'd like them back. Stefan sighed. I should not have reminded him of our own war with Prussia.

Bismarck is a manipulator, Stefan observed. He gambled with us and drove us to defeat in a mere six weeks' time. This could involve us, he thought. France has been trying for two years to form an alliance with us.

"I will send for you soon."

The sound of the voice jarred Stefan and he whirled around to see the Emperor standing by the open door.

"Perhaps a trip to Berlin will show you the weakness of your position."

"As Your Majesty commands," Stefan managed.

"Yes, I command it. I will send you to Berlin to observe—unofficially."

The door slammed shut.

Franz waited patiently in the drawing room of 35 Hauptstrasse, and saw Stefan's carriage come into the courtyard. Stefan will know, he thought. She loves Stefan, and she would never leave without telling Stefan where she was going, of this I am certain. Stefan has always been more than just a brother to her; he is her dearest friend and advisor, too. And sometimes, he behaves like her father.

He stepped back from the window and walked closer to the small sofas near the fireplace. Stefan is hiding her here, or at the country house, or perhaps even at Schönbrunn with her cousins. If she is not here . . .

The door opened.

"What a nice surprise," Stefan said, and walked to his brother-in-law. They shook hands. "You look exhausted," he said, seeing the pasty color of Franz's skin, the greyish circles under the eyes and the tired lines at the corners of the eyes.

"So do you," Franz said.

"May I offer you a sherry?"

"Please," Franz answered, then followed Stefan to the other end of the room, watching the eyes, the hands, the expressions on the face. He watched as Stefan poured the sherry from the cut-glass decanter with steady hands. "I received a message," Franz said slowly, studying every movement with unblinking eyes. "I was to meet Julienne here."

Stefan replaced the decanter top. "Here?" he said with a shrug, handing Franz a glass. "Are you quite sure you were to meet her here and not at Birngarten? This is news to me."

Franz smiled. "Oh," he breathed casually, "then she's at Birngarten?"

"Not as of this morning," Stefan replied, walking to the sofa. "My family is in the country," he went on as he sat down, noticing the tense shoulders of his friend. "I've been doing some work for my cousin, and I stopped there this morning, on my way here. Busywork, really," he lied, sipping the sherry-wine. He saw Franz's shoulders droop slightly, then saw the posture straighten before Franz turned around. "Are you sure about your message?"

Oh my dear God, he doesn't know, Franz thought, then fixed a smile on his face. "Actually, no." He felt his stomach tighten. "I received a confused telegram at the train station in Graz. I was there, you know."

"No, I didn't know," Stefan replied evenly.

"Yes, well, the message was not all that clear, and I couldn't decide if I was to meet her here or in Eisenstadt. It must have been Eisenstadt, now that I think of it." He gave a hesitant boyish grin, took a sip of the sherry, then placed the glass down on the side table to his left. "Well," he said, "I ought to be going."

"You've only just arrived," Stefan said.

"I know, another time, my friend. I must get back to Eisenstadt, collect my family, and go on to Graz, for something of an extended stay . . . the grapes, the turpentine factory, you understand."

"I understand," Stefan smiled.

"I'll see myself out," Franz smiled as they shook hands.

Stefan nodded, and the smile faded as soon as the door was shut. He walked to the window and saw Franz step wearily into a hired carriage. "You God-damned Judas," he breathed.

Though standing only five feet nine inches, and built on the thin side, Stefan might appear to some as a weak, almost phlegmatic man. But he had been schooled for years in the fine art of controlling nervous and muscular horses at the Spanish Riding Academy; he was a marksman, a fencer, lean and graceful and deceptively strong.

His eyes narrowed. "So," he said, watching the carriage as it turned onto the street, "she's taken the children and left you. She swore to me she'd do it, but only when she was ready." He emptied the glass with a long swallow.

placed it down on the windowsill, then hooked his thumb into the waistband of his uniform and slightly shifted his weight. "Ten months ago, she made me swear on my father that I would say nothing, do nothing, and forget what I had seen. The day she writes me she is safe, I swear before Almighty God I will kill you for what you did to my sister."

CHAPTER

3

Julienne sat down and leaned back to the base of the large Elm tree, squirming and shifting herself to fit in between the roots half-buried in the ground. Six weeks, she thought. Six long weeks. We pass strangers on the road, families moving or others on their way to visit friends; farmers pass by with vegetables on their carts on their way to towns to sell food. Workers come and go, and we smile as our cart passes these people, and we limit our conversation to asking directions or buying food. Her head pounded at the temples and she closed her eyes against the hazy glare of the morning sun. She could smell the fragrant breeze, a warm and heavy August scent around the glade. Perhaps it is true after all, she thought, all the things he screamed at me for all those years. Perhaps I am not a fit mother.

She traced circles in the cool, smooth earth next to her with her finger. It is so different from the few hours spent each day with them at home. Home, she thought, yes, at home they had a governess to care for them and teach them their lessons; maids to clean them; laundry maids to wash their clothes; cooks to prepare their food. And what did I do, she thought. I played with them, and fussed over them, and made decisions that other people carried out, and spent time with them when I wished, and later, when I was allowed to . . . She brushed that thought away. And I read to them, she continued to herself, and of course they loved me. I was special. They put on their best clothes to come and see me.

And now, she thought . . . I saw the look in their eyes. Now I yell at them and frighten them. They looked at me like they looked at Franz.

A twig snapped behind her and her eyes instantly opened wide.

"Momma?"

Friedrich stood next to the tree. He blocked the sun and the yellow-white light in a wreath around him made her smile. She squinted, then had to shade her eyes to see him. "Yes?"

"Are you still angry?" he asked.

"No," Julienne replied. She patted the ground next to her on the left and waited until he sat down cross-legged on the earth. In the tree's uneven sunlight, his knees looked more dirty than they actually were. He seemed nervous and unsure. His breeches had new rips by the seams, and the clothes had a pungent smell that would not come out no matter how many times they'd been washed. It was hard for her to see him in this condition. His skin was darker, tanned by the sun and dirtied by the road. He was thinner, ill-at-ease, and he was dressed in little more than rags. Gisela was no better, she knew, playing with sticks and rocks, and her milky baby skin had turned the color of reddish clay.

"Gisela says she's sorry, and I am, too," Friedrich said.

Julienne smiled briefly, then shook her head. "It's no one's fault. The heat made the milk turn. I try, but I am not doing very well, am I?"

Friedrich hung his head and turned away, concentrating on a squirrel scaling down a tree, not ten feet from him. It raised its head, looked around, then scampered off into the brush in search of food. "We know," he whispered, then half-swallowed the words, "you'd be safe and away if it wasn't for us."

Julienne sat up straight and reached for him, turning him around to face her. "Look at me, Friedrich."

He struggled and pulled his chin, letting his eyes drift from her eyes, paling himself to a shadow.

"Friedrich, look at me. You're wrong. I could not live, knowing I deserted my children."

He crooked his head slightly to watch her.

"What you are thinking is wrong, but you have *done* nothing wrong," she said, and drew him closer, cradling him on her lap.

"Then why . . ."

"Why did I become angry?" she asked, finishing his sentence. She felt him nod against her. Julienne sighed. "Sometimes, it is very difficult for me. I am only one person, and there is so much to do. But, that is no excuse."

He looked up at her.

"This is not the life I was born to," she said gently. "And many times, I must force myself to get up, start the fire, and do everything I did the day before, once again. Some days, Friedrich, I just want to hide in the back of the cart and not open my eyes at all, and then, pretend that there is someone there to take care of me."

"I, I promised I would take care of you," he said. "I can, too."

She kissed his forehead lightly. She'd forgotten, somehow, that little people had feelings, too, and all this movement, all this running might upset and frighten them. We have left a lonely life, she thought, and are lonely now, and we are all feeling unsure.

"Do you ever get, get scared?" Friedrich asked in a small voice.

"Yes," Julienne answered. "Everyone is scared at some point in their lives. Are you scared?"

He looked away.

"You may tell me, Friedrich."

He hesitated, then spoke softly, saying, "Sometimes, those people scare me."

37

"What people?"

"The ones in the town, or the ones we speak to on the road. I, I don't know them, I'm afraid of them, and they stare at us sometimes."

"This bothers you?"

He nodded, thoughtfully.

"Why?"

"Maybe, maybe they know who we are."

Julienne smiled. "Friedrich, *I* wouldn't even know who we are. We are dirty and we wear other people's clothes."

"They still scare me."

"They are just people, as we are just people. We don't frighten them, and they ought not to frighten us. We are all the same, Friedrich."

He thought it over and seemed a bit relieved.

"Come along," she said and stood up. Then she winked at him. "I'll race you to the cart, go!" She laughed as she ran back down the road, but Friedrich won. It had only been about twenty yards, but Julienne felt the pinch in her sides and had to take several deep breaths. She walked around to the back of the cart and saw Gisela sitting in the corner on the floor half-heartedly tapping a stick to a private rhythm as she hummed a toneless child-song. Maximilian sat between her legs and kept trying to grab the stick, but Gisela held it out of his reach.

"I'm sorry," Julienne whispered, and opened her arms.

Gisela looked up, let go of the stick, unwound herself from Maximilian and fell into Julienne's arms, her little body trembling with sighs and cries larger than herself.

Julienne held her, then hugged her. She felt wet kisses on her neck and they tickled. "Better?" she asked and wiped Gisela's face, streaked by tears and the dust of the road.

Gisela nodded.

"Then it is time we were on our way."

In a little less than an hour, each felt the gnawing cramps and growling in their stomachs.

"I'm hungry," Gisela complained.

"I know," Julienne answered, "we'll . . . we'll find something to eat soon, I promise."

Gisela smiled.

Yesterday afternoon, Julienne thought, we ate the last of the bread and cheese I bought two days ago. The milk must have soured during the night, and we haven't had meat since the beginning of the week. What poor planning, she thought, angry at herself for not stopping at the farm they'd passed yesterday morning. Julienne tried to help them forget their hunger by beginning a song about Cadet Rouselle, a French rascal with three of everything—three houses, three coats, three sons and three dogs. It was a funny little song and the children clapped their hands to the bouncy rhythm and melody.

In the early afternoon, Julienne needed to rest her arms and ease the strain on her hands. She walked alongside Domino, feeling tired and hungry. A little to her right, she saw a farmhouse on a hill with a patchwork of fields in front of it, reaching all the way to the road.

The wind changed, and she could smell the barn, that earthy sweetness of manure. "Cows," she said softly, hoping . . . she felt her mouth moisten in anticipation. She pulled on Domino's headcollar and led him on the winding dirt road that gently sloped up the hill. Stopping the cart a short distance on the road before the farmhouse, she motioned for Friedrich to come to her. "Will you help me now?"

"Yes, Momma," he said.

"The woman, there in the yard?"

Friedrich turned around and saw a woman dressed much like his mother coming from the barn. She carried a large basket under one arm and her plain skirt billowed slightly at the ankles as she walked. "Yes," he answered.

"Go and ask if we may buy milk."

His blue eyes opened. "I, I don't know what to say, I don't know her . . ." He took a step back and brushed by Domino's forequarter.

Julienne bent down and tilted her head slightly. "You've seen me do this hundreds of times, haven't you?" she smiled. "Friedrich, think of it, if she has things to sell, we'll have food. There's a chicken coop. I saw it. Look, over there, at the far end, do you see it?"

He had to stand up on his tip-toes, but he did manage to see the top of the coop.

"And, perhaps, they have sausages and bacon. And, we might buy bread here, or at the very least, she might tell us *where* we might buy bread. All you need do is ask, Friedrich. And be polite. Oh, and ask how much things will cost."

He was breathing quickly, from nerves and from hunger. She could see him clench his jaw against the distasteful job, but he did turn around, and walk three steps. He looked back at her for encouragement. Julienne shooed him on, waving her hand and smiling. He was so reluctant, but he walked up the remainder of the hill into the farmyard and approached the woman with the basket.

"She didn't understand French," he said in between breaths, "so I had to speak German, I had to."

"What did she say?"

"They, they have food, but she wants us to come to the house and eat."

That was strange, Julienne thought, what has selling food to do with going into the house to eat? "What did you say to her?"

"I said we were hungry and wished to buy food, please."

"And?"

"And she looked at us, and said, 'but first you come sit at my table.'"

Gerda Schlubach wiped her forehead with her apron. "Poor child," she whispered to herself as she took the flat baking tins off her worktable and moved them to chairs at the other end of her kitchen, away from the hot oven. She gave the table a few quick smacks with her apron to remove any remnants of the flour from her morning's work. She then went to her cupboard and took out three plates and set places for the woman and the two children.

The air was still and warm near the wood-burning stove, and she had to fan herself for a moment. Gerda was a tall woman, solid and sturdy with wide shoulders and strong arms. Her skin was as ruddy and clear as it was smooth. Though middle-aged, she still had mostly brown hair, and her brown eyes reflected her inner contentment. Her face was comely, and anyone could see that in her youth she must have been a handsome girl.

They were hungry, the boy said, and she shook the sight of his haunting eyes from her mind. Gerda collected the boiled potatoes from yesterday's dinner and with a large knife, quickly sliced them in a bowl. Then she shredded the bacon left from this morning's breakfast and sprinkled all of the pieces over the potatoes, along with onions and spices. Now she was ready to crack the half-dozen eggs for the omelet. She whipped them feverishly with her fork as if the act could wipe away the boy's face from her mind. The rags on him, she thought, and worked harder.

She turned around, holding the skillet and the spatula, and saw them standing in the doorway. Oh God, she thought, aching, the woman has a little one, a baby no bigger than my granddaughter. Gerda motioned for the family to come and sit at her table. The two older children had big saucer eyes and licked their lips.

Gerda watched as the young mother sat the baby on her lap and the older children took their places across the table from her. They had washed their hands and faces at the pump outside, Gerda knew, not wishing to come to her table dirty.

She leads them in Grace, Gerda thought, and she's taught them to eat slowly, like well-behaved children and not like animals.

Bread, Gerda thought suddenly, and went to the wooden box her husband had made and took out the pumpernickel loaf. And jam, she thought, they must have jam.

She placed the slices on a plate, then put that on the table. The children waited, watching their mother, and only when she nodded, did they each take a slice of bread.

I'll give a little surprise to the children, Gerda decided as she put fat into her skillet, watching it slowly melt down into liquid. There was time before it would heat up sufficiently, so she walked into her larder and came back with three glasses of milk. She placed them on the table and looked at the young woman feeding the baby bits of cooled egg. "Does the little one drink from a cup?" she asked gently, with a warm smile.

The woman returned the smile. "Sometimes."

Gerda took a small metal cup from its hook on the far wall. "I use this cup for my granddaughter," Gerda said. "Sometimes she drinks for me, and sometimes not."

Julienne poured some milk from her glass into the cup. The baby gripped the cup and tried to tip it faster than he could swallow, but Julienne held it firmly, guiding the angle of the cup as if it were a bottle.

Gerda laughed. "They are all the same, so eager. I am the eldest of nine children, and I have seven children of my own, and I have one granddaughter with three others on the way. Their little hands are always so much in a hurry." Gerda left them for a moment and picked up one of the flat baking tins covered with cheesecloth. She heard the little boy sigh when he saw the uncovered tin as she walked by him. "So," she smiled, "you know what they are."

He grinned. "Krapfen."

"Yes," Gerda answered, and with her fingers took out the cut doughnuts that had gone through two risings and watched the seven Krapfen fry quickly and evenly in the hot oil. When done, she looped them on her fork, let them drain over the skillet, then set them down on a flat platter to cool. "Have you something for the milk you wish to buy—some container or bottle? And have you a basket for the food?" Gerda asked the young woman.

Julienne softly smiled, then looked at Friedrich and said, "Go to the cart and bring what Frau . . . ?"

"Schlubach."

". . . what Frau Schlubach requires."

Gerda left the room and paused briefly by the door. "Send him down this hall to my larder. I have what you need there."

In the larder, she gazed at the full shelves, thinking: we have been blessed with good crops and good stock. We are healthy, happy, and we have been given so much.

They will need bread, she thought, and reached into the cloth-lined basket, taking one pumpernickel and one rye. Jams, she thought. All children love sweet jellies and jams. The preserves had been the best she could remember in years. Twelve eggs she felt would be plenty, and counted them from the straw basket, then cut a large wedge of cheese from the wheel on the corner work table.

She heard a foot scrape, and she turned to her left. The little boy with the piercing eyes stood there. He held a rather worn medium-sized basket. She peered inside and saw two liter-sized ceramic bottles with rubber stoppers. "Good," she said, and took a step closer to the boy.

A look crossed his eyes. His smile paled and he stepped back from her.

Gerda did not understand why he was suddenly afraid of her, but she did not move closer to him. "Little one," she said softly, "I need the bottles for the milk." She bent down and held out her hand to him.

He swallowed, then with an unsteady hand, gave her the basket.

"Go and finish your meal," Gerda said gently.

He quickly left the larder, backing out.

As she filled the bottles with milk, she wondered about that family. Where was the father, was there ever a father living with them . . . then, she scolded herself, thinking, hunger is hunger, with a father or without one. Ah, Gerda, she said to herself, it is not your place to ask or even think about such things.

41

If you were hungry, you would not want to answer a lot of questions about how you got that way.

She packed the basket with food and, as a parting gift from the larder, wrapped one of the nudel-pudding pies in an old cloth napkin. Nudel puddings were solid fare, layers of large flat egg noodles filled with sour cream and cheeses. It would travel well, she knew.

Gerda left the larder and walked back into the kitchen carrying the heavy straw basket under her arm. It moved her when she saw the young woman washing the plates her family had used. Gerda said nothing and continued out the door. Generosity meant more than giving—it meant accepting, too.

She walked across the yard and went into the smokehouse where she placed a few slabs of cured bacon, strips of salted beef and a small cut of smoked ham into the basket. Closing the door behind her, she saw the family standing by the doorway of her house. Gerda walked to the horse cart that had been placed in the shade and slid the heavy basket into it, then loped to her kitchen door again. "Wait," she said, "I have something for you," and disappeared into the kitchen before anyone could say no.

She took the Krapfen and sprinkled powdered vanilla sugar over the dough-nuts and brought the plate out. "These are for you, for the journey." When the boy hesitated, she took a doughnut and brought it to his mouth. "My mother taught me how to make them," she said, "and her Krapfen were the best of all."

He took the doughnut, and she saw the pleasure in his eyes whilst he ate it. The little girl was not hesitant at all and gave a healthy bite into the doughnut.

Gerda was pleased and carried the plate to the cart, where she placed the remaining five doughnuts into the basket. She was about to walk back to the house when the young woman holding the baby blocked her path. With her free hand, the woman held out a fistful of copper pfennigs. Gerda wanted to refuse, but the firm look in the young woman's eyes and the pleading that was silent, yet present, told Gerda to hold out her hand. Gerda closed her fist without ever looking at the pfennigs and dropped them into the pocket of her apron.

"You are kind and generous, Frau Schlubach. Thank you for my children and myself. God bless you always," Julienne said.

Gerda lowered her eyes. "God go with you," she said, and then watched from the fence as they stepped into the cart and then slowly traveled down the hill.

She watched them for some time, and then heard her husband's steps behind her.

"Who was that?" he asked. Karl Schlubach was the counterpart to his wife, a tall, sturdy solid man of fifty years. Sweaty and tired, he took off his cloth cap and wiped his forehead.

Gerda looked across to him and shook her head. "Poor people. Hungry."

He sighed. "They always find you," he said, and nudged her waist with his elbow.

Gerda shrugged. "We have plenty."

He knew this was true. "Did they pay you anything?"

She nodded. "But it is not for us."

"I know, Gerda," he said, "it is always for the poor box in the Church." He pulled at her waist and gave a tired, sweaty kiss to her cheek. "Were they German people?"

She shook her head, recognizing the boy's accent from the first spoken word. "Austrian," she said.

Julienne wondered if it would ever stop raining. She trudged alongside Domino and watched with tired eyes as delicate streams of water made rivulets in the muddy road. That good woman, she thought, remembering the food given had lasted nine days. They had traveled northwest and were well-fed because of Frau Schlubach's generous nature.

Ignoring the clinging feeling of the wet wool, she drew the shawl closer around her shoulders. Two weeks ago they'd passed through the ancient city of Ulm on the river Danube. Uncle Teo's instructions were to continue on through the city, taking the main road out, and when it forked in three directions, to take the left fork bearing slightly northwest. She smiled, thinking of Teo. She let the cart pass by so she could walk behind it and view inside, under the tarpaulin. She lifted it up slightly, rain trailing off down the sides. "Are you warm enough?"

Friedrich opened his eyes, then nodded.

"Good," she smiled, then walked quickly for a few steps to catch up to Domino's pace and keep abreast of him. A little over two months, she thought, and for the most part, the weather had been good.

The unpredictable German summers had kept true to their reputations. Some days were cool and comfortable and the bright sun was tempered by sweet-smelling breezes; others were still and heavy with steam-like heat and a merciless sun that glared all day. And then there were days like this, chilly rains and grey skies and roads that were nearly impassable and treetops obscured by a cover of mist.

What was that, she thought. It was difficult to isolate the sound she thought she heard behind her. It competed with all the rhythms of nature—the rain drizzling into puddles, the sloshing of the cart's wheels, the muffled sound of moving water to her left, as a tributary of the Nekar River fed the sloping land around her.

There it was again. She tilted her head slightly. Was it something plodding in the mud, a horse or some other animal? Reaching up, she pulled on the side of Domino's noseband and he stopped walking. She listened for a moment but heard nothing. Oh this is too idiotic, she told herself, really now, listening for noises in the woods like a child afraid of . . .

She heard the whinny of a horse and felt her jaw tighten. The road wasn't straight. Why couldn't the road lie straight now so I might see who is coming? She strained on her tip-toes as if it might give her a better vantage point, but still saw nothing. She took the small whip down from the holder on the side of the cart and held it a little too tightly, then pulled on Domino's noseband, urging him on There's no one there, she told herself, no one.

43

A horse whinnied, then plodding became a series of rapid thuds and a man on horseback—no, three horses—suddenly blocked her view. One of the men grabbed Domino's headpiece. A second man dismounted. They were all around her. And they looked oddly familiar.

They wore cloth caps, like workmen, and their soaking shirts were of dark colors, blue or black, she could not tell. Their boots all needed repair and each wore patched corduroy breeches.

The Wiesenteig market, she thought, yes . . . in the Wiesenteig market, they were drinking beer at a little table across the courtyard when I bought the cheese and bread. She felt a sudden chill. My God, she thought, they've followed us for half a day. Franz sent them. They're working for Franz and they've come to take us back.

The three men began speaking to each other, glancing at her.

What language is that, she thought quickly, what language are they speaking? They couldn't be working for Franz, they just couldn't . . .

It all happened at once.

The fat one dismounted and took Domino's bridle from the bearded one, and began stroking the horse to keep him calm. He leered at Julienne, speaking to her in a cooing whisper of unintelligible words.

The bearded one stepped closer.

She took a step back, suddenly afraid.

The three men continued to speak to each other, eyeing her, nodding toward her, laughing at private jokes, pointing to themselves and counting.

The rain was instantly very loud, even though it was barely a drizzle. The children, she thought, I mustn't scream, but that thought made her more frightened. There was no one to hear even if she did scream.

The fat one and the bearded one took turns in pretending to step closer to her, sniggering when she didn't know which one to watch.

The bearded one reached and grabbed her thin wrist, then wrenched the little whip away from her and tossed it into the brush to their left. She tried to pull away. He was tall, a little taller than Franz. His hands were rough and strong. She kept trying to pull away, and when he grinned she saw he had rotten, broken teeth. With his free hand, he pulled the soaking kerchief off her head, and seconds later, grabbed a fistful of hair, twisting and tightening.

"No, stop, stop," she wheezed through a clenched jaw, "let go of me . . ."

When he yanked the hair and tried to force her to her knees, she went for his face, scratching him with her short and broken fingernails.

Friedrich dreamt he was home again, hearing the sounds of many Eisenstadt nights. His breath tightened, his heart pounded; the bad dream stayed with him even when he opened his eyes . . . the scuffling, the slap . . . He pushed Gisela, jumped up and tore the tarpaulin off the top of the cart screaming, "Momma!"

Only then did the third man move, the quiet one with the brown cap pulled low over his eyes. He managed to grab the boy by the scruff of the neck as Friedrich jumped out of the cart. The boy strained and pulled, screaming and kicking, calling his mother, trying to get to his mother.

The quiet one struggled with the boy, looked at his companions, and then pulled out a hunting knife from the sheath at his waist.

Julienne screamed.

He held the knife to the boy's neck.

"Friedrich," Julienne cried, begging, "please, please, please don't move, don't . . ." Her voice seized.

He saw the man gripping and pulling his mother's hair. He saw her wide eyes and the way her mouth trembled, as he'd seen her so many times before. He began to cry like Gisela his sister, and Maximilian, his brother. Kneeling in the mud, he was as wet and soaked as they were in the open unprotected cart.

The quiet one held the boy's jaw firmly, and when he spoke the other two men listened. He nodded toward the woods. Then he looked at the woman and motioned with his eyes for her to go. Reluctantly, he tapped the boy's neck with the blade of the hunting knife, and heard her gasp, then saw she no longer resisted.

The bearded one pulled her away from the cart, down the sloping hill, past clusters of Birch trees and clogged underbrush. She tripped. He slapped her, hauled her to her feet and pushed her farther away from the area of the cart, closer to the small river, parallel to the road.

She tasted the salty warmth of her own blood from her cut lip as the icy shudders inside her own body increased. Her mind felt heavy and swam in a murky tension that closed her throat and made her hands clammy and cold. All the sounds around her became dull thuds, echoing and far away.

He pushed her to the ground in a hidden spot where the underbrush and large rocks formed a natural barrier against the road, some fifty meters away. She'd scraped her hands and face on the rocks, and the pain was burning and stinging. She felt the blood drain away from her face in the nauseating whirlpool of distorted blackness that followed.

She woke in the mud. She shook her head and tried to clear her mind, but she couldn't move at all. She was on her side in the mud, and he was behind her with his left leg wrapped around hers. She couldn't pull free—he'd pinned her arms to her sides.

The soaking blouse had pulled down and bunched at the elbows, the chemise with it, and his arms were around hers, all around, everywhere, grabbing at, pulling at her breasts; rough, callused hands pinching and scratching her with his nails in a private frenzy. His gasping was next to her ear, and she had to listen to the groans and cries he made while his scraggly beard scratched her shoulder and the side of her neck.

He suddenly pushed himself inside her, but she swallowed the screams when he scraped her, pumping violently as he kept pulling on her breasts and moaning. The jerks were harder, faster, and he suddenly grabbed her neck with his right hand for better leverage, as he pushed and pulled, pushed and pulled convulsively with his body, slamming her over and over until he climaxed and mercifully stopped.

After a moment, he pushed her shoulder away, pulled himself out of her,

45

then straddled her with his legs. He caressed himself with a breathy laugh, wiped himself and his hand dry with her skirt, then buttoned his breeches. He stood up and she saw his boots as he bent down and gave a hard pinch to her cheek, laughing as he left the site.

She could smell him, a disgusting odor that seemed to cling to her and linger all around her, a common smell of bodies and manure. She started to cry, but was interrupted by the push of the fat man who suddenly sat on top of her. He was panting like a dog, throwing himself over her, trying to force his tongue into her mouth, but she bit him and tasted stale wine for her trouble. She gagged, and he slapped her. He pulled her hair back and slapped her again. She felt as if clumps were coming out of her scalp. He was beefy with fat cheeks and perspiration dripping down a flushed face. He tried to open her knees, but she locked them in defiance and tried to push him away. That made him angry, and he cursed at her and slapped her again with the flat of his sausage fingers, then forced his knee between hers and pried her legs open. He pinned her legs with his own, then took both her wrists in one of his hands and held them up, tightly, as he unbuttoned his breeches. He separated her wrists, taking one in each of his hands, sliding his hands up to her forearms, pinning them to the wet ground, and then plunged himself inside her as if he were a sword piercing the inside of her body, and enjoyed the painful breaths and aborted cries beneath him.

He was heavy and she felt as if her bones would crack and break at any moment. She gritted her teeth and closed her eyes to the grinning ugliness on top of her, feeling him shake and bounce and pounce until he was through.

There was no air, and the trees above her all ran together in her mind. She could not feel herself anywhere, as if her skin had become the dirty, muddy ground and she was being swallowed alive. She bolted upright and sat with arms tightly clenched over her breasts and her chin tucked low into herself. She never heard the third man, the one with the hunting knife.

Feeling a tug at her elbow, she opened her eyes to see hands trying to ease the torn blouse and chemise up to cover her again. He was kneeling next to her, and when she stared at him with dull eyes, he let go of the material and brought a finger to his lips, gesturing for her silence. He nodded back toward the road and, again, made the sign by his mouth, warning her of his companions.

Her hair was matted and hung in muddy clumps around her face and neck. When he moved his hand closer to her face, she flinched. He looked surprised, as if to say he was not like his companions. Slowly, he moved his hand closer again, and then wiped the soil from her cheek. He helped her button the blouse and then, with his cap in his hand, he got up and walked to the river's edge, where he dipped it and used it as a rag to wipe the dirt from her face, to wash her hands and to clean the scrapes on her cheek.

He'd brought her kerchief with him and, with a hesitating hand, gave it to her and helped her by gathering the hair together so she might tie it back without struggle.

Everything hurt and ached, but he helped steady her when she stood up. The skirt was bunched at the waist, but he helped unravel it and smoothed it over the petticoat and let it fall to her ankles, to the boots with the broken hooks at the tops.

The smell from the other two, the rancid sour smell of them, was all over her. She felt the queasy sickness rise and began to gag. The quiet one helped her walk the few steps to the river's edge and held her when the nausea buckled her knees. She vomited what little food she'd eaten several hours ago. He helped her to wash her face and cupped his hands to give her sips of water.

She didn't want him to touch her; she didn't want his help anymore. She just wanted him to go away. When he tried to give his arm to help her stand up, she sat back down and stared with exhausted eyes at the expanding circles made by the rain at the water's edge. She hurt, and every part of her felt like ice.

He touched her arm and she turned to him and stared, seeing him for the first time. He was probably in his late thirties, about average weight and height. His eyes were deep-set, brown or hazel, she didn't know, and his hair was reddish-brown. Great locks of it fell across his forehead. He stared down at the ground in silence, then suddenly wiped his nose on his sleeve and took a deep breath. He shook his head back and forth, slowly, pointed to her gently and motioned for her to wait, to stay where she was. He was going back. He walked a few steps, backing away from her, motioned for her silence, then turned and walked at an even pace as he pushed through bushes and rounded the curving path.

She listened. Quiet, followed by muffled shouts and the sound of horses galloping away.

Bruised and hurt, Julienne stood up with difficulty, smoothed her skirt, and tried to present a picture of calm before she had to face her children. She found the horse tethered to a tree. The cart was still half-draped by the tarpaulin; a blanket lay strewn in the road; the water bottle was uncorked and lying on its side, and two large fistfuls of bread were half-buried in the mud. The children were missing.

Her heart began to beat faster, and there was a stabbing fear inside her. "Friedrich?" she called.

He scrambled out from around the other side of the cart and nearly knocked her over when he wrapped himself around her. He was followed by Gisela. She held them both and felt comforted by them.

"Where's Maximilian? Where is he?"

"On the other side," Gisela said, shuddering, "in the dirt."

They followed her to the opposite side of the cart. She found him lying in the mud. He was cold and dirty; his little dress, soaked with the clay, clung to him and was wrapped around the dimpled baby legs. He shivered and whimpered, and mucus ran from his nose. Julienne picked him up, kissed him, tried to comfort him and then swaddled him in the only dry blanket they had. "Tell me what happened," she said, looking at Friedrich.

He shrugged and stubbornly wiped the rain droplets from his face with the flat of his hand. Then, he settled for staring off down the road, looking at nothing.

There was a sullen look about him, and the anger in his eyes only hinted at his feelings. He stood there in the road, a defeated little soldier, staring at a private target that had disappeared. Julienne knew she would get nothing from him. Bending down to Gisela, she whispered, "Did they touch you?" She tried to smile and keep her face calm. The child looked away and then down at the ground. "Gisela," she said, "did they touch you?"

Gisela finally nodded.

Mother of God, Julienne thought, and wanted to cry with relief when Gisela pointed to her arm.

"They, they touched you on the arm?" Julienne asked.

"Yes," Gisela said with a frightened pout. "The one, the one with the knife, he made us sit here, he made us face the rocks and sit in the mud. He made Friedrich cover his ears and when Friedrich kicked him, he slapped him and pulled him by the hair and made him sit next to me in the mud . . ."

"So he pulled you by the arm?"

"Yes," she whimpered.

Julienne kissed her, then kissed the spot on the arm where she'd been touched, and then motioned toward the cart. "Get in," she said, and placed Maximilian in the corner.

Friedrich heard her walk to him, he saw her hand coming, reaching for him, but he stepped away.

"Friedrich, please . . ."

"I hate them," he said, eyes glaring, shoulders thrown back ready for a fight. "I hate them all."

Julienne lowered her eyes and saw their possessions littered on the wet ground. "I want to leave here," she said quietly.

Friedrich moved to pick up the blanket.

"No," she said, "leave it, leave everything they touched."

He stood up and turned around. His lip curled and his eyes were wet. "That, too?" he said, jerking his chin toward a bush five feet or so behind her.

Julienne looked and saw a piece of blue material. It was Gisela's doll, Marianne. They'd touched the baby's doll. Those animals' hands had touched her children and Gisela's favorite doll.

Numb, she walked to the bush and picked it up. Like everything else, it was soaked. Several fingers had broken off on both hands, and there was a horrible spider-web crack in the face where chips had shattered and left holes. The doll was ruined and Gisela would be terrified if she saw it. It was ugly, like everything else here.

She gripped the soiled material and in a rage, threw the doll deep into the woods and then watched with shaking clenched fists, standing ready just in case something, anything, brought it back to her. "Filthy vipers, you scum, you're all the same," she whispered.

The smell of them was on her, on the cart, on her children and coming from the woods, a lingering reminder. She couldn't breathe and backed away from the spot, then turned and grabbed Friedrich. She pushed him into the cart, then flipped the tarpaulin back over the top and tied it down quickly.

She untethered Domino, then ran to his left and pulled on the noseband. Eyeing the woods behind her, she turned around long enough to spit.

The drizzle let up half-an-hour later, but the light was fading. She kept pace with Domino and would not allow herself to think at all, concentrating completely on the road and their destination, the Dominican Priory outside of Kirchheim. They would not be caught on the road after dark. They would not be defenseless again. The children were filthy and hungry, but she would not stop and ignored their pleas for food.

At some point later, she was able to ride in the cart for several miles, but it began to rain again. She had to get out and walk.

Her legs were stiff and cold and her knees ached, but by evening she saw the outline of the old Priory at the top of a hill. Thunder rumbled behind her, and Julienne held Domino's bridle firmly and pulled him the last half-mile.

Parapets and towers were the silhouettes in the grey-black sky as she approached the fifteenth-century cloister. There was a stone wall and a heavy wooden door. She felt for the bell rope next to the door. She touched the cold wet stone, and inside a hollow was a knotted rope held by a small thin metal hook. She gave a healthy pull, heard the jangle of the bell, and felt the shadows behind her disappear at the sound.

Dizzy and cold, she walked to the back of the cart and had to steady herself by leaning against the side. "Give me the pouch," she said to no one in particular and held her hand out in the darkness. Someone, probably Friedrich, placed the leather pouch in her palm.

The smooth leather was a touch of home and a floodgate of comfort opened as she held it tightly to herself. The door creaked and she was aware of a flurry of robes swirling around her. A hand touched hers, but she pulled back and away from it.

The pouch, she told herself, they need the pouch. It will explain everything. Reluctantly, she gave it to someone. The courtyard seemed large, but she didn't remember crossing it. She blinked and they were inside, standing under large, dark-cream colored arches that swept like wings to the arched ceiling. It was a long hallway with one or two lanterns giving it yellowed light. The arches had marble columns supporting them.

". . . to the warming room," she heard, somewhere behind her. Julienne turned around and saw four Dominican nuns huddled together staring at her. They lowered their eyes and slid their hands up the opposite sleeves of their white tunics, and took on the pose of silent carvings. Julienne shivered and lowered her eyes and saw the puddle of water and dirt underneath her boots. Her skirt clung like gauze, and the thin, ragged blouse was beyond repair. It had rips in it, and the chemise could be seen. She felt naked and tried to cover herself with tightly folded arms.

The nuns are so composed, so dry, so clean, she thought. And the smell of the men was still around her. She gagged, then followed one of the shadowy Dominicans down the hall, where someone opened a wooden door. Inside the large area, without furniture or rugs, was a fireplace. Two nuns had followed

49

her and one of them brought her a blanket. It was placed about her shoulders and she drew it tightly around her shivering body. A metal goblet was brought to her hands, but they shook so violently she could not hold it.

The clean, white hands then brought the goblet to her lips and made her drink the golden Benedictine liqueur. She sputtered and coughed, but the clean hands never moved. When she'd taken two long sips, the hands gently moved the soaking matted hair back from her face and she saw the two perfectly serene brown eyes staring back at her from underneath the black veil.

"I am the Prioress, Mother Veronika. Do you speak German?" She spoke in a soft and soothing whisper.

Julienne found the strength to nod. "My children . . ."

"Your children are being cared for, you needn't worry about them now." The Prioress sighed. "My child," she said, "you're shivering. You might have caught fever. We must put you in warmer clothing, but before that, a hot bath. Then, I think some warm soup might help you. We've some left from our dinner. Sister Agnessa will take you to our bathing room where Sister Paola is waiting for you. Go. I'll join you presently." Her sandals made little padding sounds when she left the room.

Julienne followed the silent Sister Agnessa and walked down another drafty stone corridor that wound around to the back of the Priory. Sister Agnessa stopped at a large door, knocked twice, then opened it for Julienne. The nun kept her head lowered and her eyes watched the trail of dirty droplets on the floor and did not gaze on the woman.

The door was silently shut behind Julienne.

The room was small. It, too, had a fireplace and because of its size was not drafty like the other room. There was a ceramic basin on a small table near the old metal tub that would just about allow someone to sit in it. Wooden buckets with rope handles were lined up near the tub which was, itself, half-filled with hot water. A shadow moved and she saw the habit of Sister Paola.

"I am to help you wash," Sister Paola said. She reached out to lead the young woman closer to the fire, but the woman jumped back a step and avoided her hands. "You mustn't do that," Paola said, "I am here to help you."

"Don't touch me," Julienne hissed, backing away, nearer the fire. All she could see was the nun's staring eyes and a jaw that was firmly set.

Dirt repulsed Paola, and the rags this woman wore would be burned as soon as she could take them away. Paola inwardly prepared herself for the lice she would no doubt find in the woman's hair and on her body. Many peasants had come here for sanctuary or help, and Paola always supervised the cleaning of these unfortunate people. She could not bear the thought of any of God's children covered in dirt or riddled with lice. "Let me help you," Paola said firmly, and grabbed the woman's arms, not listening to the screams.

When the door opened, Paola let go of the woman's arms and watched helplessly as she scurried like an animal to a dark corner.

The Prioress saw the woman clutching the shreds of her clothing about herself. She was a pitiful sight, huddled and shivering with her face turned against the wall. The screaming hysteria was subsiding, but the choking cries were long and hard, almost as if they would never stop. She looked at Paola, who only shook her head, not knowing what to do. "Leave this to me," the Prioress said quietly and knelt down next to the woman, using her soft black veil to wipe away the tears.

Paola watched from the doorway.

"You've done your best," the Prioress said, "now I will try." She said nothing further until the door was shut. "I know of the men on the road," she whispered. "Your daughter has been speaking of how they were made to sit in the mud—and that the men took you away for a long time. I need no further explanation."

"Can you smell it?" Julienne asked, eyes wide and darting about the room in search of other moving shadows.

The Prioress saw the terror and thought of a small child gripped and frightened by an awful fear that rested solely in the imagination. There was no reasoning with children in this state, and the only way to help them find calm again was to convince them—as in a game—that the thing had gone away. "Yes," the Prioress said, "I smell it."

"It won't go away," Julienne whined. "I can't make it go away."

The Prioress held the woman's hands. "I can help you. We will wash the terrible smell away." Wild eyes stared at her as she gently let go of one hand, then reached behind her on the floor and felt for the large, rough square bar of soap. She found it. "See," she said, and held it to her nose, then brought it to the woman's face. "Smell, see . . . see how strong it is?"

The eyes calmed slightly, and Julienne closed them as she cried.

The Prioress gathered the broken woman in her arms. "Let me help you. You'll feel better once you're clean. You are safe now." The Prioress helped her stand up, then discreetly turned whilst the woman disrobed. She busied herself by pouring the hot water from the kettle on the fire into the metal tub, then she faced the fire until she heard the water slosh.

The rags were in a pile on the floor, but the petticoat lay by itself near the tub. The Prioress bent down to pick up the clothes, and with her free hand, reached for the petticoat.

"NO!"

She turned her head and saw the woman grabbing at the petticoat.

"Not that, no, that's mine. Those other things, give them away—no, burn them, burn them all, but the petticoat is mine."

The Prioress threw the offending clothes into a dark corner out of the light of the fire where they could not be seen. She rolled up her sleeves, tied a towel about her waist, and took the petticoat from the woman's hands. "If this is yours, then it, too, must be washed." She picked up the soap, dropped the petticoat into a large bucket of water, and began to scrub the surface until a soapy lather had formed. "Clean, all clean. No smell at all."

The woman looked at her with exhausted eyes, then took the soapy petticoat and held it in her arms against herself.

Picking up one of the buckets next to the tub, the Prioress poured warm

51

water gently over the head and back of the young woman in the tub. From her position behind the tub, the Prioress could see them when the caked dirt melted away. On the fair skin by the shoulders and the spine and the sides of the woman were scars. They were old scars that had healed badly. They were small near the shoulders, but near the base of the spine were the larger ones, and at first the Prioress had to look away. She stopped her mind from imagining the pain suffered during this scourging, and gently washed the area with a soft towel.

Julienne washed off the dirt, scrubbed her long hair, and then, the Prioress rinsed her with bucket after bucket of warm water. Afterwards, she sat shivering near the fire wrapped in a hot blanket that felt itchy and uncomfortable. The Prioress sat next to her and dabbed at the long hair with a towel, helping her to comb it through and then spreading it to dry before the fire.

"Perhaps we should not have washed your hair tonight," the Prioress said. "It will take so long to dry and you're sure to catch a chill."

Julienne sneezed. "Mother, it makes no difference now," she said, her eyes glazing and teeth beginning to chatter. "I've . . . I've been cold and wet all day." She shook her head. "I'm glad we washed it. I . . . I wanted to be clean."

"And so you are. I can't smell it anymore," the Prioress smiled. "Can you?"

Julienne shook her head. "No. It's all gone."

Hours later, hair still damp in the back, she was taken to a cell in the long hallway of cells where the cloistered Dominican nuns had their quarters. The bed was little more than a wooden slab with a blanket tossed on it, but for guests or those seeking sanctuary, a mattress was found. Julienne was dry now and wearing a thick night-shift, yet her skin was icy and her teeth would not stop chattering.

Drawing her knees up under the bed covers, she shook and shivered. More covers were brought to her and piled on top of her. It did no good at all. She felt frightened and small.

The serene brown eyes watched her from the bedside. Julienne timidly brought her fingers to the tip of the covers. The Prioress' warm hand took them and held them as she gradually stopped fighting off sleep.

She couldn't tell if it was day or night, just that a smothering heat burned through her. Sweat beads formed. She felt dizzy lying flat on the bed and struggled under the mountain of blankets to sit up. Waves of nausea beat her down again. She moaned. The room was moving and she was choking in the hot stillness. Material clung to her neck; the shift was wet and hot and she felt as if it was strangling her. She pulled with weak fingers to free her skin to the air.

"No," a voice said, "leave it be."

"I . . . I can't breathe . . . there's no air . . ." Her head lolled back and forth drunkenly on the pillow. There was a sharp smell of alcohol under her nose as a damp cloth wiped the sweat away.

"Lie still," the voice said. "You have fever."

She opened her eyes but everything seemed bathed in a distorted light. No position was comfortable, every part of her ached from deep within the muscles and joints, and the heat, the interminable heat was killing her. Julienne tried to talk but a coughing fit made her forget the words.

Then she gagged. A hand cupped her face gently, eased it to the side of the bed where a cool basin was placed under her chin. The phlegm and the soup churned in her stomach, but the basin was there and a cool rag wiped her mouth clean. A metal cup was brought to her lips. ". . . water," she heard, ". . . rinse your mouth." The voice was soft, kind; she'd heard it before, somewhere. Who was it, she wondered, as the hands helped her to lie back again.

The cold came; reaching through the piles of blankets, it wrapped itself around her, bringing convulsive shivers and delirium. She felt herself being lifted, and watched with glazed eyes as the arched ceiling of the endless hallways moved above her. People were talking, but she saw only fluttering veils, then a doorway, and after that flames behind a grating. Orange fingers reaching high, hypnotic orange fingers . . . the sounds were moving far away.

"Mama?" Julienne breathed, "Mama?"

She smelled of lilacs. Even in frozen winter she smelled sweet and clean like the soft flower scent of her perfume. A woman, delicate and tall with large brown eyes, and a laugh that was beautiful and honest and light. Mama . . . bending down and touching the little girl's chin with slender fingers . . . then, the touch, the special mother-touch across the little forehead to the hairline, a feather's brush to sweep away bad dreams. Only Mama touched like that.

She was in the hallway of dreams, a place that was fogged and blurred, but filled with memories . . .

The kitchen. She was in the kitchen at Hauptstrasse. They sat at a dusty table on tall wooden stools, and hands were molding flour and water. It was sticky and smooth at the same time. Laughter played against the rain. Stefan made a horse. Julienne made a cat. Mama made a swan with little eggs and a nest to hold them all. Mama's lips were moving but there was no sound.

She was running . . . the green dress Mama wore was large and flowing and the crinoline petticoats underneath were like clouds of whipped cream. The columned halls of Schönbrunn Palace looked faded and far away. It was a game of hide-and-seek, and they were running down the halls, past the statues, past the corridor with all the portraits of the Habsburg ancestors. She followed the green dress as it disappeared around a corner, through a door and into the conservatory.

The fever broke. Julienne slept in a peaceful calm, exhausted. Her skin glistened underneath the piles of blankets. She woke and saw Sister Agnessa sitting quietly by the bedside.

"My children . . ." Julienne began, raising herself up slightly on her elbows.

53

"There is no change."

"Change from what?"

"From the illness. Didn't you know?"

Julienne opened her mouth but could say nothing. She shook her head slowly.

"I'm sorry," Sister Agnessa said. "I've only just come to your room. I thought you knew. They are down the hall, but the Doctor is with them."

"Help me," Julienne said, trying to kick the covers back and get out of the small bed.

Sister Agnessa looked undecided. She thought a moment, then shook her head. "No. You can do nothing for them."

"They need me," Julienne said.

"The Doctor is caring for them. You can barely sit up. Let him do what he was trained to do. You rest."

It was meant kindly and Julienne knew from experience it was pointless to argue with the nuns. She decided to wait. Her head suddenly felt heavy and with a sigh she lay back down on the pillows and stared at the ceiling above her. That was not the voice from before, Julienne thought. The nun continued with her prayers and the vigil of caring for the young woman.

Julienne closed her eyes and was content to listen to the whispers. Sister Agnessa left her quite some time later, thinking she was asleep. Julienne continued to listen; she heard the door shut softly, and the sound of the footsteps in the hall faded within seconds.

Propping herself up, she slid her legs to the right and then out from under the many layers of blankets and sat up on the edge of the bed. She felt dizzy, and the stone floor was very cold. She was weak, tired, and standing up took a long time, but she did it.

She walked very slowly to the door and opened it. The hallway was dark. It must be night, she knew, but what time was it? Were they all at dinner?

Sister Agnessa said they were down the hall, Julienne thought, but looking to her right she saw nothing, all darkness. To her left she saw a small shaft of light from a partly open door. Still leaning against the wall, she walked barefooted to the door and eased it open. An elderly man in a dark frock-coat was sitting in a chair. He had grey hair with a few strands of brown, and his face was heavily lined.

Friedrich and Gisela were on beds much like hers and they, too, were under piles of blankets. Maximilian was bundled and in a large basket. "How are they?" she asked in a whisper, leaning against the doorframe.

He looked up. "Madam, go back to bed. There is nothing we can do." He continued to watch the baby.

"What are you saying to me?" she said, walking into the room.

He shook his head, then stood up and held her back by the shoulders. "You and your older children, you all have strength. You were able to withstand the terrible fever. Did you know you've been sick for three days?"

She looked him directly in the eyes. "What are you trying to tell me?" she repeated.

He sighed. "The little one . . . I can do nothing for him. He has pneumonia. The three of you could survive the influenza, but for little children, it sometimes develops into pneumonia. It has settled in his lungs now."

She felt dizzy. God help me, she prayed.

"He will probably die within the hour. I'm sorry."

She heard it now; for the first time she heard it clearly—the labored wet and shallow breathing, baby gasps for air, the last stages of life. She took a step toward Maximilian, her arms open for him.

The Doctor blocked her way again. "You needn't do this to yourself. I'll stay."

"You don't understand," she whispered, her throat tight and dry. "My family has its own way." She stepped around the Doctor and picked up Maximilian, holding the unconscious child against herself, supporting his head with the crook of her arm when it dropped back. She kissed his forehead. She felt weak and numb as she watched him trying to breathe.

"Where are you going?"

"Where is the Chapel?" she asked, looking only at Maximilian.

"I understand he's already been given the Last Rites."

The words made her shake, but she turned to look at the Doctor and asked again, more firmly than before: "Where is the Chapel?"

He saw her wide eyes and the tears spilling from them, and that she was completely unaware she was crying. He sighed and told her which hallway to take until she found the mahogany doors. He watched her walk away from him, then went back inside to stay with the sleeping children.

The Chapel was a large room with a vaulted ceiling and sandstone walls that had gone a yellowish-grey. The altar was set back and above, with two marble steps below it. Behind the altar hung the large crucifix. Prayer stalls lined the two walls leading to the altar, where the nuns prayed and meditated. Votive candles flickered along the sides of the chapel at small altars dedicated to patron saints, and on the side walls were small wooden crosses representing the Stations of the Cross. One large brass ceiling candelabrum was lowered and lit, to give a small amount of light to anyone praying at any hour during the night.

Julienne walked toward the altar. When she reached the marble altar steps she stopped and sat down, laying the rag-doll form across her lap and holding Maximilian's small face close to her breast. She rocked him slightly, giving the remembered mother-touch to his smooth skin, like her own mother had done countless times to her forehead, as if it might make all this pain go away.

She prayed for a long time, holding Maximilian, kissing his forehead, caressing his hands which lay open and did not respond to her touch. The skin was cool. It was a familiar coolness that she'd felt before . . . How, she wondered within a suffocating whirlpool in her mind, how did he do it? How did he sit and hold Mama in his arms and not cry out or scream out in pain? . . . She was aware of a sandal scuffling behind her, then a robe dragging slightly across the floor. From the corner of her eye she saw the rough habit next to her on the right. "I had to come here," she whispered, looking only at Maximilian.

"There is no better place."

It was the voice from the fever and the delirium; and those were the hands that held the cool basin and the damp cloths that wiped her face and mouth and sponged her arms, "Thank you, Mother, for . . ." she turned, expecting the Prioress.

Paola sat next to her on the floor. Her face was calm and sympathetic. Her eyes were a soft and gentle brown.

"You?" Julienne asked, remembering her from the bathing room.

"Yes."

"You helped me, when I was ill?"

Paola reached and caressed the side of the baby's face. "I could not help you when you first came to us. I am grateful I was of some help at a later time. Perhaps, I may help now. Shall I hold him for a time?"

Julienne hesitated, then shook her head. "He . . . he should die in my arms." It was so hard to say the words. They were painful and sharp and she wanted to call them back, wishing that if she could, everything would change and Maximilian would live. Her lips went dry, her eyes hurt, and she could only whisper, "I'm frightened . . . and I . . . how did he do it?"

"Who?" Paola asked as she closed her arm around the shaking and trembling shoulders.

"My father. I, I have been remembering my mother, and the night she died. I was frightened then, too."

"Speak of the fear. Offer it in prayer," Paola said. "Our Lord always listens. He will give you strength."

"She was in labor," Julienne began, speaking in a small whisper like a child, remembering. "I heard the screams . . . there were screams from down the hall. I was only five. I did not understand what they meant when they said it was two months too soon. I remember beating my hands on the door to her room, screaming her name. They hurt . . . my hands hurt. Then, my father was there and he looked frightened and worried, and he scared me because I'd never seen him look like that before. He took me away from her room; he took me away to the Library and made me sit next to my brother, Stefan. Stefan was ten, and he held my hand as we waited. We could feel it, we knew something was very wrong. Then, it was quiet. The screams stopped." Julienne looked over to Paola. "Did you ever feel it was *too* quiet?"

Paola nodded. Her face was placid, her eyes comforting in their non-stare as she gazed at a point at the bottom of the altar steps. She continued to hold the shoulders with her left arm, and with the right hand, placed it on top of the woman's hand and they both touched the child. Paola could feel the cold tremors beneath her warm hand. "It was too quiet," she prompted.

"My father stood by the window," Julienne went on, her vision blurring until she closed her eyes and whispered in the darkness. "He, he gripped the sides of the window so tightly as if something awful were about to hit him. There was a knock at the door and we all jumped. It seemed deafening, but it wasn't loud at all. I didn't know the word then. I was just a child and I didn't know what it meant. We heard it from the other side of the door.

Hemorrhage. I heard him cry out, and then, it was quiet again. Stefan jumped up and ran, pushing past the doctor and my father. He ran all the way down the halls to Mama's room. I followed him."

"What did you see?" Paola asked, her grip a little tighter.

"My mother," Julienne swallowed, "my beautiful mother, lying on her bed. There were lit candles around her, and she was breathing so softly, in shallow little gasps . . . her skin was grey, and she had circles under her eyes and deep pasty hollows in her cheeks. She, she tried to move, and I saw all the pain on her face. Servants were collecting the sheets with blood on them . . . there was so much blood . . ."

Paola let go of the woman for a moment and pulled a linen handkerchief out from inside her right cuff, hidden by the sleeve of the habit. She wiped the woman's eyes. "Was the child born alive?"

Julienne sighed and with a shiver, nodded. "I looked inside the cradle and I saw him. He was smaller than any of my dolls. He had a tiny mouth and tiny eyes that were tightly closed . . . and he was blue. He had blue fingernails and blue skin, and he didn't look real at all. He looked . . . he looked as if he'd been carved out of blue marble." She drew Maximilian closer, kissed him on his forehead, and felt better when Paola's arm was again closed around her shoulders. "The smell was awful—sweet and heavy. It was all around the room, this sickening sweet odor . . . My father was there, and he put his hands around my face and said, 'There's nothing to be afraid of, Julienne, I'll show you.' Then he went to the bed, gathered my mother in his arms and sat behind her. He said to us, 'Come and sit with your mother while there's still time.' We climbed up on the bed. The smell was so very strong near her. Stefan and I curled up next to her, and I could feel the little spasms in her arms. My father was saying that someday we would understand. In his family, he said, they did not believe in standing at the bedside with their arms folded. They did not like to look down on the bed, or watch and pray so far away whilst someone died. He said, he said it was a lonely journey that way." Her body felt numb as she looked down at the baby in her arms. "But how did he do it? How did he hold my mother, speak to my mother, pray with my mother, and not die inside . . . and not scream inside . . . and not want to run away?"

"He must have loved your mother very much," Paola said.

Julienne paused and looked at the baby. "We all spoke to my mother. We all, in turn, told her how much we loved her, what we remembered best about her, and things that we shared with her." Julienne shook her head. "Her eyes were dulling. She touched the gold cross around her neck, held it and moved those tired eyes to me. My father said 'yes.' She touched a ring and motioned to my brother. We kissed her. Then my Uncle Teo came and we had to move back from her. He gave her the Last Rites."

"Your Uncle is a priest?"

"A Capuchin monk."

Paola's eyes sharpened, but she forced her mind to forget what she'd just heard.

"She died," Julienne said, "a few hours before dawn. She was thirty-six years old. She died in our arms." Looking down, she said, "My son, my Maximilian, I named him for my cousin, the one they killed two years ago."

"Who?"

"The Mexicans murdered their Emp . . ." She stopped talking and suddenly looked away. "Nothing. Forget what I've said. It's nothing. He was named for no one."

Paola shut her ears to all the sounds around her and was able to think only of the child, and watched him quietly stop breathing. Gently, she took the edge of the blanket and covered his face and then tried to take the child from his mother's arms.

"No," Julienne cried, "no, not yet."

Paola released her grip on the child and, instead, put her hands around Julienne's face, then stared into the woman's grief-stricken eyes. "You've done well," Paola said. "He was comforted to the last, and rested in your arms. But now, he rests elsewhere. He is in the comfort of God's hands. Let go. His journey is over."

Julienne lowered her eyes, then brought the covered child to her lips and kissed the blanket where she thought his forehead might be. Her fingers caressed the sides of his face as if imprinting his image on them so he might be remembered and the touch of him would be with her forever. "My beautiful son," she whispered, "I loved you." She hugged him for a moment, then gave up the bundle to Paola.

Rosaries and the scent of burning beeswax candles seemed to be everywhere. The coffin was small. She remembered watching it from a doorway, some-where . . . she couldn't look inside, then did, and felt a swimming blackness with a sense of falling. She heard prayers near chipped stone angels in the sunshine. Moist earth was pressed into her palm and faceless people held her up, whispering, "Sprinkle it over the coffin." A shovel cut the earth and dirt thundered on top of the small wooden box.

Wrapped in her blanket, the musty smell of the wool filled her as she watched the dark V-shapes of birds flying south in the sky until, lulled by the quiet, she slipped into a dead sleep with no dreams. God, she prayed every night, I hurt. It is my fault. I know my child died because of me and my foolishness. End my life. I have known nothing but pain for six long and terrible years. Please, God, have mercy, let me die.

At night, the squawking shadows of geese crossed the full moon. She won-dered why they bothered. They fight so hard to survive, and yet, at dawn, they are prey to hunters. Why don't they just give up, she thought.

Give up? It was a hard and alien sentiment to her. A part of her was amazed that she could think that, and unconsciously she brought her hand away from the photograph-plate album and stopped caressing the images there. She closed the album, not to be shamed near the last tie to her family.

She'd been at the Priory three weeks, and one afternoon near the end of the third week, she discovered by accident a walled-in garden behind and to the left of the far wing. It was a separate place, away from the cemetery, away from the priests' quarters and quite a distance from the main building with the nuns' cells, workrooms and chapel. It was a quiet little place where rose bushes still kept their green with a futile stubbornness. All the other flowers had withered and gone dry; only their stalks remained, blanched by the sun and curiously, still beautiful.

There was a small pond in the middle of a semi-circle of evergreens. At the opposite end of the pond were stone benches. A meditation garden, Julienne thought, eyeing the high stone walls with overhanging yellow strands from the willow trees.

She felt tired and went to sit on one of the benches. She watched the autumn-colored leaves fall into the pond and make hypnotic gentle circles as they drifted on the water. One maple leaf, gold and perfect, fell near her feet. Julienne leaned over and, in reaching to pick it up, saw the face in the water: long wild hair that was loose and in knots; skin, paler than grey, a color without life; eyes that were sunken, outwardly showing the inner torment and grief.

A madwoman, she thought, horrified, watching herself with a fixed stare. A madwoman.

She hadn't seen herself since Eisenstadt. None of the Priories or Abbeys had mirrors and the cell windows were small and usually high up on the walls. This would have killed my father, she thought, closing her eyes. What a disgrace. He cherished life, and this madwoman waits only for death. I ran away from Eisenstadt to save my life and the lives of my children. It's all gone wrong. If I wanted to die, I should have stayed at home. Franz would have killed me—or I, him. He'd said it often enough. There was no escape. He would find me no matter where I went. He had spies, everywhere, on the coaches, the trains . . . Julienne got up from the bench. Walking away from the pond's edge, she drew her arms tightly about the woolen habit they'd given her to replace the night-shift. The open sandals they'd given her dragged and scuffed along the ground.

The rose bushes caught her eyes again. All were bare save the one near the end. Stubborn to the last, it had a blossom with two buds growing even at this late time of the year. She watched it for a moment, and felt a strange feeling, as if she'd just walked through a door. I wander about like a ghost, I pick at food, I am afraid to sleep, afraid to see my children, afraid to hold them, just like at home. Papa taught us, as he was taught, as his father was taught—*always* choose life. Smiling at the stubborn rose, she touched the velvet petals.

"Should we gather violets for you and put them in a bouquet wrapped in rosemary?"

Paola. Julienne knew that voice so well. She also knew the reference. Violets, she thought, for the early dead, and rosemary was for remembrance. Lines from a play—Ophelia spoke them, in *Hamlet*. She felt her skin crawl for a second, feeling as if Paola had looked into her mind. "What is the line," she sighed, "about the violets . . . they, they did something."

" 'They withered all when my father died.' "

"Yes, I didn't quite remember." She turned around and saw Paola standing under the archway. "I'm hungry. Is there any food?"

Paola smiled.

After ladling hot broth into a wooden bowl, Paola brought it to the table with a thick slice of bread, placing both in front of Julienne. They were alone in the Priory's kitchen and it was a warm and friendly place. Paola watched her eat just as she had watched her for over three weeks—at a discreet distance. Even if she had not mentioned for whom she named her baby, Paola thought, there is no mistaking it: her table manners, her posture, her poise even in grief—she is an aristocrat. Poor woman, what has brought you to this?

"Are they well?"

It took Paola a second or two to focus her mind. "Oh, yes." She moved closer to the table. "Your son is very bright, but shy. We have been reading to each other for an hour every day."

Julienne smiled. "He's, he's a good boy. And Gisela?"

"Well," Paola smiled. "A lovely child. She's brought us much joy. There is nothing quite like the laughter of little children . . ." Paola bit her lip. "I'm sorry."

"No, you needn't apologize. Gisela has an enchanting laugh."

Paola noticed the bowl was empty. "Let me fill this for you again. It would do you good and help you to build your strength."

Julienne hesitated, then shook her head. "No, thank you. Perhaps tomorrow."

"Well at least you're thinking of tomorrow," Paola said. She took the bowl away, washed it in a bucket, then set it with the others to dry for the evening meal. "Come and rest now. I'll walk you to your room."

When they reached the door to her cell, she turned to Paola and said, "I had a petticoat, the night I arrived . . ."

"Yes," Paola answered. "We've washed it and ironed it for you. It is in your room, in a small basket under your bed." She watched Julienne for a moment and saw the decision being made in her eyes.

"I need your help."

"What must I do?"

Julienne took Paola's hand, relieved. "For a start, I need a pair of scissors. I want to show you something."

Paola returned to Julienne's room a few minutes later, with a pair of embroidery scissors.

Sitting down on the edge of the bed, Julienne unfurled the petticoat across her lap. "I made these flowers," she said, a gentle smile beginning to play at the corners of her mouth. "I was taught by Dominican nuns, in Belgium, where I went to school. They took me such a long time, but I had a great deal of time."

Paola watched, fascinated by the expression on Julienne's face. She couldn't decide if the memories were pleasant or bad—they seemed a combination of both, and both moods were in her eyes.

Julienne calmly looked over the petticoat, chose a daisy, and began snipping at the center of the embroidered flower. She then pressed the colored strands together and it gave up its secret: between her thumb and forefinger, Julienne held a small diamond.

"My husband used to give me presents," she said quietly, eyes beginning to narrow. "He'd try to make amends that way, after he'd hurt me, as if he could buy back my love and trust with little trinkets. He'd run away for a week or two, and when he came home, he would always bring a bracelet or a necklace or a ring or a brooch in a black velvet case. And it was supposed to be proof of how much he loved me," she scoffed, then shook her head. "It never worked. I never wore the jewelry and he never asked me to wear it. I hid them, and later, I found a way to take apart some of the larger pieces. This is from a necklace. I knew the children and I would need money. It was the only way I had of getting money without his knowledge. We had to start a new life on something, and I thought why not let these awful presents do something worthwhile? They could not buy back my love, but they could buy me freedom."

Much of what Julienne said was a mystery to Paola. She had no personal experience of what life was like for a married couple save her parents' marriage. Physical passion was something unknown to her, but her lack of experience did not dull her senses to appreciating the problems of others. Whatever life this woman had, it was obviously traumatic and unpleasant.

Julienne undid the centers of three more flowers. "In desperation, I went to my Uncle in confession so he could never speak of what I had to tell him. I felt so ashamed, and he helped me to understand the shame was not mine. My husband claimed otherwise, and, and I almost believed his lies of everything being my fault." She looked at the four diamonds of varying sizes, then gave them to Paola. "Help me," she said.

Paola sat next to her on the small bed. "What is it you need of me?"

"I want," Julienne said, swallowing and clearing her throat, "I want to go to Paris. My mother was French. I have been to Paris, many many times, and I have always felt that city to be home. We will be able to hide there, as ordinary people, and live quietly without any fear." She paused. "That is what I want. That is what I have been trying to do since July when we left Eisenstadt, a town east of Vienna. But I have failed, you see."

Paola's eyes opened wide. "You've come here, by yourself, all the way from Austria?"

"Yes."

"How can you call that failure?" Paola asked. "Did you come part of the way by coach or train?"

"No. I drove the cart myself," she said, holding out her hands to Paola and showing her the deep calluses and dried cracks in the skin.

Paola touched the hand. "And you think you have failed," she smiled. "Nonsense."

"It had to be that way," Julienne said, feeling a little better. "My husband made threats. He said he would kill my brother and my nephews if I tried to go to my brother for help. I believed him. I knew he would do it. I, I had to

61

find a way to Paris by a route he could not trace. I had to do it alone, but now, I, I don't want to travel that way anymore. I'm afraid. I just want to be in Paris as quickly as possible."

Paola thought a moment. "We'll arrange for you and the children to be taken to Stuttgart. You'll be able to get the train to Paris from there."

Julienne touched the neckline of the woolen habit. "Like this?"

"No, no," Paola shook her head, "we've clothing here for the poor that . . ."

"New," Julienne interrupted softly. "Everything new. I . . . I don't want to wear anyone else's clothing, not ever again."

Paola agreed and said they could be purchased in the town. She looked at the diamonds in her hand. "There are several jewelers in Kirchheim. I am sure they will give you a fair price for these."

Julienne shook her head.

"Why are you afraid?"

"Please. I don't care about a fair price, or the market value or anything else. Please, do as the other Religious have done—arrange for someone to take them to a jeweler, say they have been donated to the Priory and get whatever you can for them. Three of them are for my needs, the fourth I give to the Order to help the poor or for whatever use you see fit. And the horse, too, if you'll have him. He's earned a quiet life now."

"Thank you," Paola said.

Julienne shook her head. "No, it is I who thank you."

Somewhere in the distance, she heard a high-pitched shriek, a small voice, someone pulling, someone grabbing at her arms. "MOMMA!"

"What . . ." It took Julienne a moment to place where she was, the rattling, the bumping . . . The train, a private compartment on the train to Paris. Gisela was crawling into her lap. Friedrich was kneeling next to her on the seat, his face was ashen and his hands were like ice.

"You, you were crying in your sleep," he said, choking on his words. "It was terrible, I didn't know what to do . . ."

She drew him close and hugged them both. "A dream," she said. "I cannot even remember what it was." She gave a little smile, then felt the smile warm to reassure them. She kissed them both. "Sleep now," she whispered. "I will take care of you."

They leaned heavily against her, little arms held tight around her, then gradually eased their grip. They calmed, and drifted into sleep as she ceased touching them and went back to looking out the window at the darkening countryside.

My father suffered as I suffer now, she thought. And he held his children as I hold my children. He survived, and so will we. I have not forgotten. Three days after my mother, my little brother died. And just like my mother, he died in my father's arms.

CHAPTER
4

Franz stared with dull eyes at the canal below, watching the full autumn moon reflecting in the Venetian wet. Slick images were cast on the wharves and gondolas and in the murky canal itself, the rippling moons were mesmerizing, yet, he could only think she had not gone to Florence.

A month, he thought bitterly, feeling the vise-like tension across his forehead tighten a notch. A month of searching and wandering the slate-colored streets, walking in and out of the cream-colored buildings with the orange roofs clustering around the churches of antiquity. Franz felt his jaw set as annoying memories of failure pricked his mind. All those eyes, he thought, black Florentine eyes staring back from the peaceful faces of the priests. He shook his head. "Padre," he recalled, reciting the planned speech, "I am searching for my sister and her three children. We were separated by an accident and I am trying to find her. My name is Stefan Moritz Weiskern." By the end of the first week, he'd known the priests of Florence had not come to her aid.

The second week he sent his card around to the aristocratic families and the visiting Austrian nobility. He called on them in the afternoons and began cautiously asking after Julienne. "It is a surprise, you know. I was to join her here but I am a month early from America. It was a bore, you understand." They understood and would nod in sympathy. They thought him delightful and they vowed to keep his surprise a secret but would send a quiet word if she came to visit them.

During the second week, his mornings were spent suffering the glazed subservient eyes of hotel concierges; men who dutifully searched large registers and always gave the same answer: "No, Signore." He maintained his composure though a frightened voice inside his mind began to scream. "Send word," he remembered saying aloud, "should she arrive, send word to me at the Hotel Porta Rossa."

The third week, he was reduced to asking the maîtres d'hôtels of fine restaurants, and after them he paid waiters for information as he lingered over too many cups of coffee and far too many brandies late into the night. Clerks at the telegraph office gave little hope and the baggage men at the train station could not remember seeing her, but then, he told himself, they saw so many people and she might not have come by train but by private coach.

He stuffed his pockets with coins and in the fourth week began walking the banks of the Arno River. He had seen the gangs of noisy boys near the Bridge of Santa Trinità, and watched them throw rocks into the water competing for distance in a game of Hercules. They were ragged little children, laughing and pushing each other without concern. He saw the lines of dirt caked on their hands and faces, and when they laughed, many of them showed broken, discolored teeth. They gathered around him and he thought they looked old. It was the dirt on their hard, thin features, he reasoned. There was a smell, a sour odor coming from them, but he held his expression and did not step back in disgust. He paid them to look for his children, to roam the city and find an Austrian boy, about their age, playing with his sister, mother and baby brother.

Over the next two days he went to the Piazza Santa Croce, then to the Piazza Santa Maria Novella and finally over to the other side of the Arno River to the Piazza Santo Spirito and paid children to be his eyes. They all looked alike, and when the anxious hands were cupped in front of him holding the large coins, their split fingernails with dirt jammed underneath was all that he remembered.

By Thursday, he was tired. Walking slowly back to the Hotel Porta Rossa, he crossed the Piazza della Signoria feeling the momentary change on his back from the hot afternoon sun to the sliver of shade cast by the gigantic white marble statue of Neptune. Eager young voices called and yelled out to him across the piazza. He turned around to see four boys waving their arms and running after him. He waited, and in the distorting sunshine their crooked smiles and dirty faces melting in sweat made them look like marionettes. They took deep breaths and tried to explain that they had had no luck, then waited with expectant eyes as he nodded, and dug into his waistcoat pocket for the shiny new coins.

Franz saw himself at that moment in a shop window, a glass without the glare of the sun. The scavengers in rags and sandals waited in a half-circle around him, hungry. And he, the tall blond man bending slightly to give them the money, but that strained anxious smile he wore had a petrified look like the dead grins of Egyptian mummies.

So. She had not gone to Florence. It had been a trick, like all the other tricks and lies. The tension went through him, spreading like a fan to all parts of his chest and arms until his hands began to shake. Duped, he thought, feeling his heart pound slightly harder. Duped, made to play the fool because of her lies. Someone's helped her, he thought.

He backed away from the verandah, but did not turn around in the darkened room. "Idiot," he breathed to himself, "stupid, sentimental idiot." After Florence, he thought, to stop here, to come to Venice, of all places, and worse, to stay with the Count Giacomelli, knowing full well he would put me here in this room and I would drown in memories of that bed.

The slow change from child-woman to wife was in that bed, he thought. He closed his eyes but could not stop himself from stretching out on top of the sheets and tracing a finger across the pillow-edges next to him. That night, she'd playfully twisted a finger in his side, and he had been half-asleep and was unsure if it was real or a dream. Turning, he reached for her in the dark and found a bare arm next to him. She moved, taking his hand and then caressed his palm over herself, eager, naked. In six weeks of marriage she had never been naked. His bride had always hidden behind the muslin barrier of her nightdress. She'd been frightened, and he'd said the ease would come with practice. Trust was something, he'd said many times in the dark to her, that could not be rushed.

The barrier was gone, voluntarily.

"Love me," Julienne whispered into his neck. He'd taught her how to move with him, the currents of her body like the currents of the canal below, rolling, even, and then a quickening as he felt her back arch and the soft moaning sigh as a fingernail trailed up his neck and hands closed over him.

Franz suddenly felt clammy and cold as sweat clung to the small of his back. Bolting up from the bed, he slammed into the table near the wall in the dark. "GODDAMN HER," he hissed, kicking the table out of his way. "Some man helped her. She's run off with one of her lovers, and they touch and make love every night while I sleep alone. They laugh at me. They touch and love and laugh at me. Goddamn that woman!"

He felt his hands close and the tight fists vibrated at his sides. The unending scream inside his mind grew louder, and quite suddenly, he couldn't breathe.

He had to get out and away from this suffocating room. Three flights of marble steps were quickly taken and then the candles in the center vestibule blurred as he saw only the large front door and the night beyond it through the side glass panels. He stood for a moment in the small courtyard, trying to clear his mind and decide what to do. Franz could hear the canal water lapping at the steps some fifty paces around the side of the Palazzo. Where to go, what to do, the smothering night fears came with him and did not stay behind in the room.

It was no different than those Vienna nights, wandering and looking for the right person. It was an old problem, to be solved in the old way. He knew exactly what to do.

Walking to the side of the Palazzo, he lit the lantern at the edge of the dock and waited until he saw the lantern from a passing gondola.

"Where do you wish to go?" the gondolier asked, leaning on the long pole.

"Canale di Cannareggio. I'll tell you when to stop."

"Get in," the gondolier sighed.

It was not a very long ride. A good many of the gondolas were moored and they were able to move easily, if at a slow pace. By the time a clock tower clanged for the half-hour, Franz told the gondolier to stop by the Santa Germia Church on the Grand Canal. It faced the mouth of the smaller Canale di Cannareggio. Behind the church was the Lista di Spagna, a fairly good-sized street lined with pensiones and four or five cantinas.

He knew it was the right place to start his search. Cantinas in Venice, or the poorer coffee houses in Vienna, *always* had the same atmosphere and the same clientele. He walked into the first cantina, bought a goblet of wine, threaded his way through the crowd to a corner wooden table and then sat down, leaning his back against the cool stone wall. He sipped his wine and watched, then listened for the right sound. He didn't find it here.

By the third cantina, his eyes were glistening slits as he drank with an attitude of eerie ice-like calm.

Venice, he thought in a haze, so absurd to come here. Sentimental idiot, he thought, but she did this. She sent me to Florence to chase after shadows. She did this *deliberately*, hiding that book, arranging with her lover to send me on a wild chase for no reason whatever except to make a fool of me. She enjoys that, making a fool of me, cavorting with gardeners, strangers, my friends. I am married to a whore, and I have tried to help her, but she is a disobedient, spoiled bitch. He took a long swallow of wine. Hiding that book in the wall, he thought, miserable woman, as if I wouldn't find it. She'll come back to nothing now. It is totally her fault that the room is destroyed.

Trailing along the Lista, he crossed the bridge over the Canal and turned left, walking up the Fondamenta di Cannareggio, also lined with four or five cantinas. I remember, he thought, I remember it all, the grand wedding tour—to the estates in Western Austria, then on to Italy, to this soggy, miserable city that stinks of garbage and open sewers. I remember her family, her miserable cousin and his unbalanced wife intruding on our wedding tour. How could anyone forget or forgive such a thing. And then, having to accept a position in the Foreign Office through a wife's influence instead of by merit . . . how could she *do* that to me? She said no, she said she never spoke a word to him and it was all his own idea, but Julienne lied to me, I know she did. God, I hate this city, and all the people in it.

Mid-way, at an obscure little place called the Cantina di Zorzi, he heard the right sound.

Look at him, Franz thought, leveling a stare at the ruddy-faced Venetian fisherman at the table to his right. He sits like all the others, low in the chair, rounded shoulders, slumped in the spine. He laughs like the others, eats like the others, peasants are like sheep—unquestioning, too sensitive, and easily provoked.

The dark quarter of his mind took hold, he could feel it happening. It was as if he ceased to be, and someone else spoke the ridiculing words. Some other man's finger poked and jabbed the fisherman's shoulder. A voice not his own laughed and mocked the simple patriotism of the Venetian stranger. The verbal assault continued in low threatening mutters. He felt himself moving, edging his way past other people in the cantina.

He began to walk, and though the scream in his mind was piercing, he heard the steps behind him. He felt the fisherman's hand grip his shoulder and pull him around. It was the only time the fisherman's hands touched him.

His fists were so hard they shook with the relentless punishing blows. His eyes saw nothing except the victim. His ears were deaf to all sounds from the scream in his mind. His hands went numb as he kept up the murderous attack in the street.

He only stopped when the scream in his mind was finally silenced, then walked away from the man at his feet, only slightly aware of where he was.

Blessed quiet, blessed relief, no clamminess, no noise, he thought, as he turned left onto Strada Leonardo and walked, vaguely aware of the dark buildings and echoes of his own footsteps on the street. It was late, he knew, but did not care about the actual time of night. It no longer mattered. He relied entirely on his ability to memorize anything at a glance, and followed a street he knew would bring him to the Piazza San Marco.

He crossed the Piazza, then stopped walking, suddenly aware of the stinging pain in his hands and the cracking of dried blood from his skinned knuckles. He shook his hands, flexed them, and finally had to wrap his linen handkerchief around his right hand to stem the flow of blood and ease the ache.

He was alone in the Piazza, and in his mind's fog, turned to get his bearings. He noticed the Basilica behind him.

What was he talking about, Franz wondered, that fisherman. He shook his head. It was all a blur. He felt tired and confused.

The cool stones of the Piazza seemed strange in this shimmering moonlight, but the Basilica itself captivated him. He cocked his head to the left and tried to understand his own sudden fascination with the shapes of the facade. The doorways, he wondered.

He walked a few steps backwards, still studying the Basilica. It *was* the doorways, he knew, three rounded arches; two smaller side arches and one large one in the center leading into St. Mark's Basilica. He stared, but St. Mark's was fading from his mind. The vision of something was hidden in memory, just out of his reach.

He took a step back, heard the click of his boot on the stones and stopped. The portals, he thought, and his eyes opened full. He saw it. As clear as this Renaissance facade in front of him now, he saw the other one, and heard her voice speak. The slender fingers, her beautiful long fingers holding the pen, when she was living at Hauptstrasse, while they were courting—yes, it was in her father's study.

She held the pen and fixed the drawing on the heavy white envelope. "Not rounded portals," she had said, "arched portals. Three of them, and all the same size, and a stained-glass Rose Window. Oh, how I loved it . . ."

"Notre Dame," he breathed, "Paris."

Stefan came out of the Hofburg's main entrance, going slowly toward the right. The meeting with the Emperor had left him drained. To ease his own headache, he dismissed his carriage and decided to walk home in the brisk November air, trying not to think, just to walk. It was the drifting scent of the horses that calmed him.

He looked up and saw the entrance to the Spanish Riding Academy, and a part of his youth returned. He could feel the cold and heavy dampness of the winter arena, the saddle sores and pulled leg muscles, and the sharp scent of the liniment that was applied at night lingered in his mind and senses. He remembered the drills of complicated maneuvers and the magnificent stallions, so difficult for the novice rider to control at first. How many aristocratic young men had been sent here to learn how to ride, he wondered, and all of us became accomplished horsemen . . . Calm days, he thought sadly, staring at the ground, a time for being a student, a time for being young without care, a time when the only responsibility in life was doing well in the arena. What a small world it was then, he mused.

A heaviness settled and he walked quickly away. That time is over, he thought. Papa had said learn from the past, it is life's greatest teacher, but never wish to return to a time already gone. It serves no purpose.

He continued to walk in the late afternoon's quiet, worrying about his sister, his meeting with the Emperor, and the disquieting situation growing within the Council concerning a proposed alliance with France.

No one listens, he glowered. After I reported what I'd seen in Madrid in July, my cousin waited a full two months before he made good his command, sending me to Berlin to ease my suspicions, yes, that was how he put it. Ease my suspicions.

Stefan shook his head. It didn't ease my suspicions. That particular journey *increased* them. I stopped in Munich on my way to Berlin, and I saw them dining together: Baron Von Werthern, who was supposed to be elsewhere, his secretary, and Prince Charles, Leopold's brother.

Stefan crossed the street. I felt a gnawing in my bones, he remembered, the way Werthern's hands were knotted on the tabletop, and the way they unwound and gestured close to the linen with definite strong movements. I'd seen that all my life—a minister explaining and outlining details for a Prince.

I played the spy, he thought, and followed Werthern when this "innocent" dinner party ended. Werthern went to the Hotel Maximilian, on Promenadenplatz. I chased that carriage on foot, and kept telling myself it is nothing, he is meeting someone at this late hour, an assignation, an opera singer, he's in Munich on private business.

Yes, private business, Stefan thought, irritated. Very private business— with the Spaniard Salazar.

I even followed them on the train, he thought. And I saw them met by liveried footmen at an isolated station. We were in a little town in the middle of nowhere, with no surrounding places of importance—except the Hohenzollern family castle. They'd gone to visit Prince Leopold, but did my cousin think that important? No. Did the Council find that the least bit interesting? No. They dismissed me as an alarmist.

He passed the Augustinian Church, passed the Capuchin Church, and finally turned into the Burggarten public park. Leaves fluttered from half-naked trees above him as he sat down on a bench and dug his hands deeply into his frock coat pockets.

People walked and strolled past him, and he watched them, expressionless. Changing his position, he looked across the open park. A man robed in brown caught his eye, a man quite a distance from him. One of the monks, Stefan thought, watching the figure in the habit with the brown pointed hood over his head.

Stefan felt his pulse quicken. The hunched shoulders, the size of the monk, the way in which he walked made Stefan bolt up and run the fifty or so yards across the open ground.

"TEO!" he said, breathing hard, and then grabbed the arm of the monk from behind.

The monk turned around, marking his place in the Breviary. "Nephew,"

68

he smiled warmly, and hugged Stefan, kissing both pale cheeks. "What an unexpected pleasure."

Stefan knit his brows. "Welcome home," he said curtly. "Did you have a nice trip?"

Teo feigned surprise. "Trip? I have been on . . ."

"Retreat, yes I know," Stefan interrupted.

"You seem annoyed. It is an obligation in my life, Stefan."

"Really?" Stefan said sharply. "A four-and-a-half-month retreat?"

Teo's face remained calm. "I made a pilgrimage as well. My Order sent me to Rome. Would you have me disobey my Cardinal?"

"I'd have you give a better explanation than that," Stefan said quickly.

"Lower your voice."

"Did you travel with my sister?"

"What an odd question," Teo answered.

"Did you?"

"No, of course not. My Order sent . . ."

"I am not interested in your maneuverings within your Order. My *only* concern is my sister and her children. Where are they, Teo?"

Teo looked steadily at his nephew. "And how would *I* know such a thing?"

Stefan's eyes turned cold. "Because I think you helped her escape from Franz."

Teo's eyes quickly searched the area near them. "It is a subject I am not able to discuss."

"You *will* discuss it," Stefan snapped.

"I have already told you to lower your voice," Teo said. "If you behave as a child, I will treat you as one—good afternoon," he said, and took long strides away. He expected the hand on his arm, and was not surprised when he felt it. "This is a public place," Teo said softly, "kindly remember that."

Stefan flushed at the quiet reprimand. "I apologize," he whispered. He thought for a moment, then said, "So you did not escort Julienne anywhere?"

"No."

Stefan's throat tightened. She's all alone, then, he thought. All these many months, alone, unprotected. I have deceived myself in thinking she was safe with Teo.

Teo felt sorry for his nephew, seeing the face lined and clouded with worry. "Did Franz come to see you?" he began slowly.

"Yes," Stefan muttered.

"When?"

"In July."

"What was the nature of your meeting?"

Stefan's eyes cleared. Why is he treading so gently with his questions, he thought. Why doesn't he just ask me? "Franz seemed to think Julienne was to meet him at my home or at Eisenstadt. He wasn't sure. He mentioned a garbled telegram sent to him at St. Marien."

"A confused young man," Teo replied cryptically.

"I did, however, receive a letter from him last week. It was dated October 25th."

"Did you? How interesting."

"From Venice," Stefan volunteered.

"A wonderful city."

"Everyone is well, Franz wrote. Everyone except him. He is not well."

"How sad," Teo commented and began walking.

Stefan kept pace with his uncle. "He said, due to his illness, he was taking the family to Egypt to see the opening of the Suez Canal, and, incidentally, he had resigned his position in the government. He would write me again, once they were settled."

Teo smiled.

"It is all rubbish."

Teo said nothing.

"But you already know that, don't you?" Stefan said evenly.

Teo cleared his throat. "When you last saw Franz—in his mild confusion—what did you say to him, concerning Julienne's whereabouts?"

"I answered with the truth: I did not know where she was."

"And that is precisely what she wished." Teo held up his hand to stop Stefan's words. "Do not question me further. I am not permitted to speak of it."

Stefan, stubborn as ever, did not obey. "She came to you, didn't she?"

Teo did not answer and fussed with the rope belt about his waist.

"Did she come to you in confession, Teo?"

Teo lowered his eyes. "I am not allowed to answer you."

"You just did," Stefan whispered. Now it was clear. She'd gone to Teo as a priest. She had invoked the silence of the confessional and in a sense, received sanctuary from the Church. Teo, as a priest, could not reveal their conversation, his advice, or any information about her. Julienne, he thought, how well you planned your escape . . . Stefan tried to smile, but settled for squeezing Teo's arm and left his uncle in the park.

The walk home was not a long one, yet Stefan's mind erased all the intersections, all the streets. It surprised him to find his wife in the hallway by the drawing room when he closed the front door.

"I'm glad you're home," Rosl said.

"Is something wrong?"

"No, but the carriage has been back for quite some time."

"I needed a walk," Stefan sighed, then kissed her. She always smells so sweet, and her skin is always soft and warm, he thought.

Rosl caressed his cheek and had felt the tension in his back the moment he touched her. "We are supposed to go to the Opera tonight. Would you like me to send a note to the Swiss Ambassador and his wife, canceling our engagement?"

"Please," he said, loosening his arms from her waist.

She watched him for a moment, his eyes narrowed and staring at the floor. "Why did the Emperor send for you?"

Stefan nodded toward the drawing room, then closed the doors behind them once they were inside. "He'd just received a letter from Franz and wanted further explanations."

"Was it similar to your letter?"

"Oh yes," Stefan managed. "I spent the better part of an hour lying to my cousin and defending my brother-in-law." His eyes flared and his breathing quickened as he began to pace the room. "I had no choice *but* to lie, damn him. God, God, how I hate that man."

"Did he hint to the Emperor he had tuberculosis, as he suggested to you?"

"The hint to the Emperor was broader than the one to me. My cousin had a splendid idea. My cousin decided he'd send one of his doctors to Franz. I had to talk him out of that but quick. And that made him angry. I had to stand there, and listen politely, to the litany of favors done for Franz, and how could Franz do this to him, and wedged between the Emperor's hurt pride in Franz's sudden disappearance, was his hurt in not hearing from my sister in so long a time. I then had to broaden my own lie, and tell him how I'd last seen her and remind him of how much she cared for him, and how her whole concern at the moment was her husband—and, I did not recommend the Emperor try to see her later this month when the Suez Canal opens because at our last 'meeting,' my sister said they would leave for Egypt in December, not November . . . I sickened myself with the lies, Rosl. All for a man I hate . . ."

"No," Rosl said, "all for the sister you love."

His mouth trembled. "And I have helped her so much, haven't I!" he said in an accusing voice. "I'll be upstairs in the library," he said flatly.

When he reached the top of the stairs, a door opened and light spilled out into the grey hallway. Children's laughter filled the empty space.

"Papa!"

He turned and saw them racing to him. Kneeling down, he opened his arms and held his two sons close to himself, touching them, caressing them, marveling at the two happy, healthy children. Yet, looking closely at his eldest son Karl, dark eyes wide with childhood, a sudden desperate feeling came over Stefan, and he frantically hugged the boy tighter, as if his embrace could protect the boy who now had no worries and suffered no guilt.

Two little arms draped about his neck, and the younger son, Bernard, breathed into his ear. He kissed Bernard's cheek, to let him know he'd not been forgotten.

"Will you play with us now, Papa?" Karl asked.

Stefan shook his head. "I've had a most difficult day, and I'm tired."

"Must we be quiet?"

"Yes," Stefan managed.

Karl took his brother's hand, then leaned quickly to his father and pecked a kiss on the stubbled cheek before leading his brother back to the nursery.

Stefan paused for a moment, watching them, then got up and slowly walked to the library.

It was a room untouched by time. The books, the large desk, the oval paintings of his mother on the wall, everything was the same. Sitting in his father's leather chair, he caressed the metal studs as if it might bring back the touch of his father and bridge the terrible loneliness. His hands shook, and the ghosts of his own broken promises haunted his thoughts.

∾

The stroke had done such terrible things. A man gifted with many languages could now speak none of them. A man whose eyes had seen so much could barely keep them open and the strong hands hardened by life and experience were limp and deadened to the touch. Stefan caressed the grey wrinkled skin on his father's face. It was cool, loose. He tightened his grip and held his father closer, trying not to count the breaths sounding in his ears. "I love you," he said, struggling to keep his voice steady. "You've been more than a father to me, you've been a teacher, a friend. I've shared my life with you, all my dreams and hopes. I . . . I cannot bear to say the word goodbye . . ." His eyes filled when his voice broke in the still and balmy August night.

The good hand, the left hand, touched his own. He looked into his father's eyes and saw the hint of a smile at the corners.

He felt a moment's comfort and smoothed the hair near his father's temples. Stefan sighed, leaning back against the headboard, holding his father in his father's bed, the bed where his mother had died so many years ago. "Your harvest has come, Papa," he said softly, still smoothing the greying hair. "Both your children are happily married. You have a grandson, and Julienne expects her first child in late October . . ." He swallowed hard, realizing his father would never see that grandchild.

Stefan felt the "J" written by the left hand on his palm.

"She's coming," he said. "I sent a telegram to Eisenstadt. She'll be here. Teo is coming. And so is the Emperor. We are here. Your family will all be here."

Heinrich seemed agitated. The "J" was written again, and partly closed frightened eyes pleaded and tried to say what a dumbed mouth could not.

"I will always take care of her," Stefan promised. "You know this is the truth. She will always have me and she will never be alone. I shall be her brother, father, and friend until I die. I swear this to you, Papa. No harm shall ever come to her, I swear it."

Lips tried to kiss him, and the attempt shattered what little composure Stefan still possessed. He wept, then hugged his father tightly. He felt a large, shivering palm close gently on the back of his neck, just as it had done for the whole of his life.

∾

Stefan looked at the photograph-plate, framed in silver on the corner of his desk. She was in time, he thought, and was able to hold Papa, and kiss him, before exhaustion claimed him to sleep, a quiet sleep, a calm end. I'm sorry, he thought, looking at the face of his father. I betrayed you. And her.

Later that night, lying next to Stefan in bed, Rosl listened to him breathe. He'd barely spoken at dinner, and had wandered from room to room upstairs until they'd gone to bed. He has always been like this, she thought. He was like this for months after the war with Prussia in '66. It takes him time to sort out within himself all that troubles him. She felt herself easing gently into sleep, and had the fleeting thought that he would speak soon.

・　・　・

At three A.M., Stefan tied his robe about him and walked downstairs to the
drawing room in the dark. Shivering, he poured himself a brandy and sipped
it. He took it with him to the window. He parted the curtains and stared out
at the courtyard for the remaining hours of the Vienna night.

All the lies, he thought. I believed every lie he told me that horrible night
fourteen months ago. September, 1868 . . . He'd come to the door with Friedrich and Gisela. And he lied to me as easily as he spoke to me.

∽

"I need a small favor," Franz said, sipping his sherry.

"Anything."

Franz motioned for Stefan to leave the drawing room and go out to the
hallway, away from his children. "Will you keep them here with you for a
week or. so?"

Stefan looked surprised. "Of course, but . . ."

"I know, I know," Franz sighed. "It is a long story, an involved one. I am
to go to Hungary tomorrow. It is very sensitive and I am not permitted to
discuss it. You understand, I know you do."

"Yes," Stefan replied.

"Before I continue, I tell you there is no reason for you to worry."

"What's happened?" Stefan asked quickly.

"Julienne is fine, but . . ."

"What's happened," he repeated, feeling his stomach tighten.

"We . . . we had a slight accident with the carriage." He saw the look on
Stefan's face, then swallowed. "Nothing's broken, but she is somewhat bruised.
The doctor's been to see her and he's prescribed rest—and quiet."

"Oh," Stefan breathed, closing his eyes for a moment.

"That is why I need you to care for my children. My Aunt has gone to
stay with Julienne, and Maximilian, well, how much disturbance may a three-
month-old infant cause," Franz said, then added, "he is in the care of his
nurse. But you know from your own family, older children make noise, need
attention, like to play loudly, and Julienne cannot bear the sounds of their
voices just now."

"Of course they may stay," Stefan nodded. "My home is your home, and
you did not even have to ask, Franz." He noticed Franz's hands, the discolored
bruises across the knuckles. "Did you have the doctor see to your hands?"
Stefan asked.

Franz quickly shook his head. "It's nothing."

Stefan thought a moment, then said, "Would you like me to go to Eisenstadt
in your place, or perhaps Rosl should go to be with her."

"No," Franz said, "thank you, but no. As I've said, my Aunt is already
there. And a doctor visits her daily. She has told me she wants no one to see
her just now, and I must respect her wish." He studied his brother-in-law for
a moment, then brightened to a dazzling smile. "I know. When I return from
Hungary, and after she has recovered, I'll bring her to you. I think the change
will do her good. Do you agree?"

He is such an actor, Stefan thought, a charming, polished, refined, lying actor. I agreed, oh yes, I agreed. And it would have worked, too, except the children were not as good at maintaining the lie as their father. They hadn't the practice, Stefan thought.

They were so nervous, but we found excuses for it, didn't we? Rosl said it was the journey. A long journey upsets children. Children need their own surroundings, their own rooms and of course it was difficult for them to sleep comfortably in someone else's home.

They were off their food, too, but we excused that as well. Their parents' accident, being bundled off one day with their father, and travel will upset delicate little stomachs . . .

But on the third day, and from this window, I saw them. Karl and Friedrich in the courtyard—Karl had been playing with his tin soldiers, Friedrich watched him. Friedrich suddenly decided he wanted the soldiers. They argued, and I saw Friedrich punch my son's face.

I ran outside, pulled them apart, and then he lied to me. Yes, Stefan remembered, he lied and said Karl had started it. And he looked up at me with the most sullen expression I would not have imagined possible in a six-year-old child.

We even tried to excuse that, Stefan thought. Rosl said perhaps he learned that from friends, or from the children of estate workers. Children learn from other children, he thought quietly, but Gisela learned a different lesson, didn't she?

Stefan shook his head at the window. I will remember that day, always. I passed by the library, and the door was partially open. I saw her. And heard her.

". . . I told you to be good."

A sound.

". . . I told you not to lie to me, but you *always* lie, don't you, yes you do, bad girl, what a bad girl you are . . ."

The sound again.

"You make me do these things, you make me do it, it's all your fault, it's always *your* fault . . ."

Stefan looked inside the library. Good God, he thought. Gisela was sitting on the floor and slapping the doll's face. "Gisela?"

She gasped, jumped up and turned around with astonishing speed.

"Why do you hit the little doll?"

She glanced at the floor, then grabbed the doll, held it tightly, and stepped back. "I love her," she answered.

Stefan walked into the library, then knelt down on one knee. He reached for Gisela, but she stepped back from him again. "Don't do that," he said firmly, seeing the four-year-old child begin to shake. "Gisela," he said quietly, "come stand here, next to me."

She did not move.

74

"Gisela, come here."

When her Uncle reached for her, she dropped the doll and ran from the room.

∾

She hid herself somewhere, Stefan thought, and Rosl tried to find a reason for that as well, but it was becoming harder and harder to excuse the bizarre behavior.

The following day tore it all apart, he remembered. I'd had a bad day, arguing with the Council over something . . . Rosl and I argued that night over something totally unimportant and now forgotten. I only remember that I was unusually loud.

Then, we heard her scream.

∾

Stefan stopped yelling and looked quickly at Rosl, then ran to the door of their bedroom.

The screaming continued and he saw Gisela in her nightdress running down the stairs, followed moments later by Friedrich.

She ran, confused, Friedrich tried to grab her but she pulled and kicked her way free, then ran around the back of the hallway heading for the music room.

Stefan raced down the stairs. He was barefoot and half-undressed. Rosl followed in her robe.

"Light the lamp," Stefan said to Rosl. "I can't see them."

Rosl turned on the gas-lamp, lit it, and they looked around the large gilt and mirrored music room for the children. The whimpers came from under the piano.

Stefan knelt down.

Gisela was shivering, sucking her thumb, eyes clamped shut. Her face leaned against her brother's chest and he was holding her, rocking her back and forth.

"Come out of there at once," Stefan said.

Friedrich ignored him.

Unsettled and unnerved, Stefan roughly grabbed the boy and hauled them both out. Gisela began screaming again.

"Don't hit me!" Friedrich shrieked.

"Stop it!"

"Don't hit me, don't hit me," the boy wailed hysterically.

It was all so horrible. Gisela's screaming finally stopped when Rosl imitated Friedrich's pose, smothering any sound to the child's ears.

"Don't hit me," Friedrich begged, trying to pull free from his Uncle's hands.

"Stop saying that," Stefan said, jerking the arm.

"We . . . we had . . . we didn't do anything, we had to find a . . . a safe place . . ." the boy shivered, tears spilling from open terrified eyes.

Stefan shuddered, then turned around, looking helplessly at Rosl, hoping she could explain this. She had no answer and stared at Friedrich. Stefan faced the chalky-skinned boy again and pulled him closer. "Why do you have to find a safe place?"

The boy's hands covered his own mouth.

Stefan pulled the small fists down. "Answer me."

"He'll . . . he'll lock me in, in the wardrobe . . . in the dark . . . I, I can't, I can't . . . I'm not allowed to tell . . ."

"Answer me," Stefan repeated firmly, his own eyes widening.

"Momma, Momma told us to, to hide, always . . ." The words were tumbling out as fast as the tears.

"Why?"

Friedrich shook his head violently from side to side.

"Why?" Stefan repeated.

"Because, because he'll kill us too . . ."

Stefan's hands went suddenly clammy. He loosened his grip on the boy and watched as Friedrich sank to his knees. "Friedrich," Stefan whispered, trying to control his voice as he sat back on his heels, "don't lie to me. Look at me and tell me the truth."

The boy did not move.

Stefan's hands shot out and grabbed the boy's face, forcing it up. "Look at me," he said to the closed eyes, and when they did not open, he shouted, "I SAID LOOK AT ME!"

Friedrich's eyes opened wide.

He stroked the boy's jawline to ease the sudden fear. "Did your mother have an accident in a carriage?"

The boy shook his head.

Stefan swallowed. "Is your Aunt at the house, with your mother?"

The boy shook his head.

"Is your mother hurt?"

The boy's eyes welled up again when he nodded.

Jesus, Jesus, Stefan thought as he looked at Rosl, then at Friedrich and asked the last question. "Is your mother alive?"

"I . . . I . . . I don't know," the boy wailed.

∾

Stefan felt an arm touch him as he cried at the window.

"Come and sit down," Rosl whispered.

He shook his head, then slammed his open palm against the wall. "I begged her," he cried, "I begged her not to make me swear . . . God forgive me, I should have killed that animal the day I found her . . ."

Finally, Rosl thought. She eased him to the sofa, made him sit down, and just let him talk.

"I should not have listened, I should have hidden her away myself, I should not have given in to that promise she wanted, because in agreeing, I betrayed her and my father . . ."

"You're much too hard on yourself," Rosl said quietly, brushing back a long strand of her blond hair that had slipped over her eyes. "Julienne said she would not trade one prison for another. And she fully believed he would find them one day and kill them all."

"I would not have given him that chance," Stefan snapped.

"Easy," Rosl soothed, rubbing the shivering shoulders.

Stefan shook his head and wiped his eyes with the flat of his hand. "For the second time in my life I don't know if she's alive or . . ."

"For so long now, you've believed she was safe."

He nodded. "I believed Teo was with her. He wasn't. I saw him today. Rosl," he whispered, "she's all alone. A woman traveling with three babies, alone, unprotected . . . " He closed his eyes.

"Stefan," Rosl said, sitting next to him, "you mustn't do this. You mustn't play morbid games and imagine the worst of all possibilities. It does nothing but harm."

"Then why hasn't she written me? Why hasn't she sent me word, unless, unless she can't."

"She might be afraid to write you. She always said he had . . ."

"Yes, he had *so* many friends."

"It *is* a possibility."

He looked at her. "Maybe."

She touched his wet cheek. "You know her better than anyone else. Anonymous and ordinary, she said, correct?"

"Yes."

"Where might she go?"

"Paris."

"Then you go."

He weakly smiled. "You know me so well, don't you?"

"When will you leave?"

"As soon as the Emperor allows."

"Resign."

"I tried to do that today. He won't permit it. And he reminded me, rather tersely, that members of the Imperial family do not resign their posts. It is maddening. He only humors me, pretending to listen, but rarely listens to advice—from anyone. He keeps me at a safe distance, yet, never too far from his sights. I suppose I ought to feel honored that he hasn't set his spies on me, noting down my every movement—as he's done with others in the family."

When he sighed, Rosl climbed into his lap and sat comfortably with his arms around her and stared now into his tired brown eyes. "It is an awful trap, isn't it, duty and loyalty to family pulling in opposite directions."

He nodded. "It will only get worse. I am imprisoned here, trying to work for the good of my country, and she is God knows where, perhaps in Paris, perhaps not." Exhausted, he leaned his head back against the sofa. "What time is it?"

Rosl looked at the clock in the corner. "Nearly half-past six."

Stefan sighed. "Duty calls, and soon. I've a conference later this morning with the French Ambassador, the Duc de Gramont, and I know he will try to pressure me again about that alliance with France. I have been told to delay an answer. I have been told that Gramont has an unhealthy preoccupation and hate for anything Prussian and I have been told he is not to be trusted." He cleared his throat. "If my cousin has a brain in his head, he will send me, or someone else, to Paris. He cannot ignore this situation for much longer."

77

Stefan sighed again. "I hope he sends me, I really do. You know the old saying . . ."

"All the world eventually meets on the streets of Paris?"

He smiled. "I pray to God it is true."

CHAPTER
5

It was a glorious French confusion: porters, stocky old-looking men running and calling, pushing carts without a clear direction, each and every one of them gesturing wildly and speaking rapidly; mobs of people milling about and having conversations wherever they pleased; stacks of luggage and trunks sitting on carts placed at strategic points to deliberately clog the passageways while people stood and decided what they ought to do. Typical, Julienne thought happily, and felt a confidence in the sameness. Holding the hands of her children, she guided them toward the large open doors of the railway station.

They walked from one confusion into another, and she felt her own eyes widen slightly as her smile faded when she saw the crowded boulevard and realized it wasn't as she had remembered it. The names of the streets had changed. The buildings looked different. Her memory began to play tricks on her. Things she remembered looked new; new things looked familiar. Every three blocks she had to stop and ask directions and it frightened her to think she had studied a map of a city that no longer existed.

But Notre Dame was unchanged. Even in the drizzling rain, and not having any idea where they would spend the night, the fear eased as she led the children through the center door. They stood for a moment, looking down the Central Nave at the high columns and arched stone ceiling. An immense chandelier was still and imposing over the Sanctuary so far away from them.

Julienne felt small, dwarfed by the statues and the carvings, and the windows that gave so little light to the cathedral. Their steps echoed on the stone floor and the chill inside was worse than the rain outside.

Still, a spot of warmth glowed from the beeswax candles at the altars around the sides. She led the children toward the right, and knelt with them in front of the statue of the Blessed Mother holding the Christ Child; she, chiseled from a grey stone, older than the cathedral itself, smaller than any other statue there, having a delicate foot worn smooth and now shining from the kisses and gentle touches of the faithful throughout the centuries. Julienne dropped a coin into the box, picked a beeswax candle, kissed the shaft and lit the wick from another person's burning prayer. She placed the candle at the far end of the line, in the corner, away from the glowing crowd directly beneath the statue's feet. Help me be brave for my children, she prayed. I have no parents, no family, no friends, and the city I knew and loved has gone as well. Help us, please, to live a peaceful life here, and to call this place our home.

They walked out of Notre Dame Cathedral. The sky had darkened, and the drizzle had increased to a driving rain. Julienne decided to just walk to the Left Bank, as she had planned, and find any place at all for shelter.

What began as a night's stay in a noisy, miserable little hotel, turned into a week's lodging because she could not find a suitable flat in any of the apartment houses she'd seen so far. Drawing the newly purchased woolen cloak around her neck, she shrugged to herself and side-stepped a puddle on the Boulevard St. Michel. Perhaps I expected too much, she thought. Perhaps because I was so desperate, it was immature of me to think we would find a place quickly, and live a quiet life instantly. She sighed. It never once occurred to me that places, like people, change.

She stopped walking, and still felt slightly awed by all the new buildings and the wide grand boulevards on the Left Bank in the Latin Quarter of Paris. Franz told me he fell in love with the photograph-plate of me he'd seen on Stefan's bureau in his quarters. But a tin photograph isn't a person. It doesn't breathe or laugh, grow or change, she thought, then smiled to herself. Like a map of a city, she thought. Well I've a new map now. And if Paris has grown into a new city, we will become new with her. I am twenty-nine years old, and I am still trapped in that limbo between the old life and the new one that has not yet begun. She smiled. We begin, tonight, she decided.

After a cold supper in their small hotel room, Julienne sat with the children on the bed the three of them shared. "Let's play a game," she said.

Gisela, bored and listless, opened her eyes. "What sort of game?"

"We have to make up a story about who we are, what our names are, where we used to live and what our house looked like. Do you want to play?"

"I'll play," Friedrich said, suddenly interested.

"My good boy," she said. "New names for a new life, in a new city." She looked at her daughter. "Gisela isn't a French name," Julienne began, "but the French have a similar name to yours."

"What is it?" the child asked.

"Gisèle," Julienne smiled. "It is a sweet name, soft and lilting like a song."

She wrinkled her nose and whispered it several times to herself.

"And in French," she said to Friedrich, "your name would be Frédéric."

"I like it," he said.

"Now we need a last name, and for the game, I want you to try to remember any names you might have heard on the streets or in the cafés."

"I heard a man," Friedrich said, "talking with his friend, and he called his friend 'Jamelin.' Then I heard a butcher talking to someone on the street, and that man's name was 'Lobinet.' "

Julienne shook her head. "No, think again."

"I . . . I heard a name once," Gisela said, looking shyly at them both. "In the café, before today?"

"You mean yesterday," Julienne corrected.

"When we had hot chocolate?"

"Yes," Julienne said to the not-quite-a-whole-question.

"Barbier," Gisela said. "I think that was it. Barbier."

"Oh I like that," Julienne smiled and then turned to Friedrich. "Do you?"

"Frédéric Barbier," he said rather grandly. "I like it."

She gathered Gisela in her arms and gave a big kiss to the child's forehead. "My good little Gisèle. From this very second on, that is your name. Gisèle Barbier. And we are the family Barbier."

"You need a name, Mama," Frédéric said. "But Julienne is a French name, isn't it? Couldn't you keep your name?"

Her smile softened. "No," she said quietly. "There must be a new name for me, also. I, I like the name 'Jeanne.' It is an ordinary name, for an ordinary woman. Jeanne. Jeanne Barbier. Do you like it?"

"Yes," Frédéric said.

"People have noticed our accents are not Paris French accents. And we must have a story, a reason why we sound the way we do." Julienne pretended to think. "Ah, we are from Alsace."

"Alsace?" Gisèle said.

"It is a region of France, in the northeast. Near the Vosges mountains. And," Julienne said with a broad smile, "there are farms and vineyards, too."

"I know what they look like," Gisèle brightened.

"Yes, you remember, don't you?"

Gisèle nodded.

"Did we live on a farm?" Frédéric asked.

"Why not," Julienne agreed. "We lived on a farm, not a very big farm, just an ordinary farm in the countryside many many miles outside of a town named—Belfort. Can you remember that?"

"Belfort," Frédéric repeated.

"Did I have toys?" Gisèle asked.

"Yes of course," Julienne answered, pained by the question. "You had the same toys you had in Austria."

Gisèle smiled, closing her eyes and seeing the dolls with their dresses, and the tops that spun, and the puppets and puzzles and the carved wooden set of Noah's great ark with all the animals that stretched in a line across the nursery's floor. "I remember," she sighed. "In Alsace."

Walking up and down the Boulevard St. Michel, Julienne continued her search and investigated some of the side streets that fed into this main boulevard, watching for small hand-lettered signs in windows advertising rooms to be let. The children had been most cooperative, either waiting at the hotel or walking for many hours without complaint, each hoping as much as their mother for a place to finally call home. They visited the magnificent Jardin du Luxembourg and they played along the pathways and had seen the restful fountain ponds and ate little bon-bons bought from a vendor's cart in the park, just like other French children.

The second Thursday of November, Julienne walked again up the Boulevard

St. Michel, this time without the children. She turned left onto Rue Gay Lussac, searching the windows for signs, then turned onto another street, Rue Royer Collard. It was smaller than the Rue Gay Lussac, with a slight incline and narrow pavements. Midway, in the window of Number Seven, she saw a sign: Rooms to Let. It was a beautiful building, sand-colored, iron-grated balconies with tall double-windows that opened into the rooms. It seemed a fairly quiet street, yet not all that far from the Rue Gay Lussac which fed directly into the Boulevard St. Michel and all the new shops. Such an ordinary street, she thought, no one would ever think to look for us here. No one, she thought, and shook her head at the euphemism. *Franz* would never think to find us here, and certainly not on the Left Bank. Over the large double wooden doors was an arched stone transom. A carved decoration, something like a vase, was at the center.

She walked into the building, stepping inside to the cool center hall. The floor was made of large black and white octagonal tiles. The white stone stairway leading to the upper floors was wider than most stairways she'd seen. But it was the banister that caught her eyes. Spindles of mahogany carved with rounded lines, a curve to the end of it, concave furrows on both sides, it was elegant and beautiful and had been made by a talented craftsman, perhaps the same person who'd made the beautiful front doors.

"Bonjour."

She jumped slightly at the sound of the male voice and felt a blush burn her cheeks. She'd never heard the front door open behind her. "I, I am interested in the rooms to be let," Julienne sputtered, then took a breath. "You startled me."

"I did not mean to, Madame." He was a tall man, on the thin side, with a heavily lined face. He smiled a broad toothy grin, much like a child's. "You like my banister?" he suddenly asked.

It took her by surprise. "Oh, yes, very much. I was admiring it when you . . ."

"Yes, when I startled you." He seemed to puff out his chest. "My son and I made it ourselves. And the doors, too. Did you see my doors?"

"Yes. You are a very talented man, Monsieur."

"I used to be a carpenter," he shrugged, "now, I am a landlord."

"So this is your building?"

"Yes, all mine. And my wife's of course." He looked around the hall with a smile. "We have a small piece of France to call our own." He seemed lost in private thought for a moment, then turned back to her. "I am Armand Mabilleau. And you, Madame?" he asked, waiting for a response.

The game begins, she thought and smiled. "I am Madame Barbier."

He nodded respectfully. "There are questions I must ask, Madame Barbier, and please excuse me for it, but my wife and I are very proud of our home and we wish it always to be so. Are the rooms for yourself?"

She nodded. "I am a widow, Monsieur Mabilleau, with two children." She waited for a reaction and did not expect the kindness to remain in his expression. "They're not babies, Monsieur, and will make no noise, I promise you."

"But I did not ask, Madame."

Julienne liked him. His smile reminded her of her father's, all lines and teeth and big brown eyes that crinkled with a dancing delight. He had thick brown hair with silver-grey strands making it seem lighter. His attitude and expressions seemed to be of a very large child yet having the responsibilities and body of a man.

"What can you tell me of the rooms, please?"

"There are two sets of rooms to be let, Madame. The ones on the third floor and the ones on the fifth floor. Both are furnished, but the fifth floor is less expensive."

"Why?"

"Well, you will have to come down each day when the water cart passes, and haul up your own water supply." Mabilleau shrugged. "The other, well, slightly more expensive, but there you will have a water pump in the kitchen. Would you like to see it?"

"Yes please." Julienne watched him as they walked up the flights of stairs, the way he held the banister, the secret glances toward it and the affectionate pats he gave tò it at the end of every flight. She thought that each spindle and each curve held its own memory for him, a history of a time spent with his son.

Mabilleau said he and his wife lived on the second floor. An older couple, Monsieur and Madame Dardé had the apartment across from them. Probably eight or nine families in all lived in this building, Julienne thought, not too many people, yet enough for us to blend in with them.

The salon was a good-sized room, comfortable-looking with a sofa, two upholstered chairs and an eating area off to the left. The fireplace was on the left wall.

"It is because of the chimney, Madame," Mabilleau explained, indicating the fireplace. "Your stove in the kitchen is on the far wall, and it has its own little chimney." He strode across the room and opened the middle set of double-windows, letting in the full afternoon light. "Two bedrooms, Madame," he said, and pointed to the opposite side of the salon. "The one opens onto Rue Royer Collard, and the other, to the courtyard." He saw the surprise. "Ahh, you did not know, yes, we have a courtyard, so your children might like to play there. It is a cheerful little place with a small flower and herb garden, and roses, beautiful roses, and an old Birch tree. The 'convenience' is in the hall. Each floor has its own. I am honest with you, Madame," he said pleasantly, "the rooms are not as large as I would like, but I was not the architect or the builder." He sighed. "Ooh-lah, I am only the owner."

She walked to the two bedrooms. They were L-shaped, somewhat small, but had plenty of light and were very clean. She felt a warmth in the apartment, as if she belonged here. It was a quiet street, a quiet building, cozy rooms, and a coal-heater in each bedroom with metal flues built into the walls. There was a permanence here, a home. She walked across the salon and looked at the kitchen. It, too, had a small window looking out to Rue Royer Collard. The iron stove was large and black and had some white porcelain on it. There was a wooden work table, the water pump and sink, a small larder, and shelves to hold the dishes and pots. But there were just a few dishes and glasses, and only two pots.

"Yes, my former lodgers," he said with obvious annoyance. "Clumsy or careless people, I have not decided which." He shook his head. "My apologies, Madame. You will have to supply most of this yourself. There is a Triangle Bazaar not far from here where you may buy whatever household items you may need."

They walked back into the salon. "How much does it cost, Monsieur Mabilleau?"

"This one," he said, "two hundred Francs per year, which comes to seventeen francs a month."

More expensive than the others, Julienne thought. It was difficult, having never made a decision quite like this before. "All right," she said, feeling a little strange, the sudden responsibility of it beginning to settle on her shoulders. "I like this one. I'll take it."

He seemed pleased, yet surprised. "You don't want to see the other one?"

She shook her head.

"You're quite sure, Madame Barbier?"

"Quite."

"Then we are agreed," he smiled. "When would you like to move here?"

She grinned shyly and sighed. "Had I known, Monsieur Mabilleau, I would have moved here one week ago. My children and I have suffered in a terrible hotel. Is this evening too soon?"

He chuckled. "Not at all, Madame. It is as you see it. There is no wood but I will bring you some from my own rooms to allow you to cook for your children tonight. Tomorrow, we will talk and I will give you all the information you need—when the coal carts make deliveries, when you can buy your wood, where you might buy oil for the lamps, all that you need to know. Will you require a cart or some help to move your belongings?"

Julienne shook her head. "We came to Paris with, with very little, Monsieur."

His smile turned sad for a moment. "As I did, so many years ago."

From their salon window, they watched her jaunty walk down Ruy Royer Collard. "She does not look like a widow," Cécile Mabilleau said.

"And what does that look like? Tell me, my love, do they have a special look?" Armand asked, shaking his head.

Cécile arched an eyebrow. "Look at her clothes, she's not in mourning. They're so simple, and they're not even black."

"Well, maybe she no longer mourns."

"Maybe she was never married," Cécile said, facing him.

Armand frowned. "You are wrong, you know, just wrong. And much too suspicious."

"You are much too trusting," Cécile replied, stepping back from the balcony and placing her hands on her waist. "I think I shall meet this 'widow' and her two children when they return . . ."

. . .

"Is it a good place?" Gisèle asked, holding Julienne's hand as they walked the Boulevard St. Germain.

"Very nice. And clean, too." They'd left the hotel with a great deal of pleasure, and she'd stopped on the street to buy another small woven basket to hold the groceries. On the way to the apartment house, she bought meat and vegetables for a soup, cheese and bread, wine, a gâteau and nuts for dessert.

Turning back to the Boulevard St. Michel, they saw a man by a cart filled with dolls, trying to sell them to people as they passed. It had been so long since Gisèle had a toy and the child's grip tightened as they stopped in front of the cart.

Julienne bent down. "They're very sweet, aren't they?"

Gisèle could not speak and stared at all the beautiful porcelain bisque faces—dolls looking like little babies in white bedgowns; dolls with faces of small children; dolls looking like ladies with fine wide dresses and hair piled up in curls and hands covered with gloves and glass jewelry around their necks.

"Madame, they are all made for children to love and all of them have horsehair," the cartman said. He wore a cloth cap and a woolen coat and seemed tired at the end of his day.

"Which one would you like, Gisèle?"

Her eyes went from face to face, as if searching for a friend. "That one," she said.

The cartman reached up to the second level and held a small doll that looked like a three-year-old child. She had rich brown braided hair, a bonnet, a dress of bright royal blue, and her face had pink lips painted on the creamy bisque. Gisèle gently touched the lace collar and the buttons on the bodice.

"Her name, Little Gisèle, is Marie," the cartman smiled.

Gisèle closed her eyes and hugged the soft body filled with straw and rags. Julienne did not argue the price of forty centimes. Gisèle's contented face meant more than the price of a doll.

They walked away from the cartman and she squeezed Frédéric's hand. "Tomorrow, it is your turn."

"Not a doll," he quipped.

"No," Julienne smiled, "perhaps lead soldiers, or something else that interests you. We have a home now, and our home ought to have our things in it. Do you understand?"

He shook his head.

"It doesn't matter, someday you shall understand," she replied and led them up Rue Royer Collard to Number Seven. Frédéric opened the door and they walked up to the second floor. She put the baskets down and knocked at the door.

Impassive eyes stared at them from the opened door. "You are Madame Barbier?"

Julienne nodded and tried to smile as Cécile Mabilleau introduced herself. The eyes, Julienne noticed, were hard and small, and the woman's mouth seemed to be set in a pursed-lip frown of disdain. It took a moment for Julienne to see that the tips of the mouth naturally drooped down. The woman had a strong chin, high cheekbones, and in a few years, Julienne thought, she'll have jowls. The hair, however, was a beautiful brown, with a soft roll back and high off the forehead. Madame Mabilleau seemed to inspect them, and Julienne thought that she must have seen much joy and sadness in her years to cause such deep wrinkles on the face.

Frédéric took a step back when the stocky woman moved toward him.

But her eyes softened for a brief moment, when she saw Gisèle clutching the doll. "And what is your name?" Cécile asked the child.

"Gisèle."

"And your brother," she asked sweetly, "what is his name?"

"Frédéric," Gisèle answered, "and my baby's name is Marie."

"Well, she's very pretty," Cécile answered, "almost as pretty as you." She turned her eyes on Madame Barbier. "My husband is upstairs. He's brought you some wood and I believe he's started your fire."

"That was most kind of him."

"Yes, it was," Cécile replied coolly. "Follow me," she said, walking at an even pace, and making no move to help with the baskets.

It was the sudden scent of the perfume that made Julienne's eyes fill. She tried to calm her expression, but it released a flood of memories in her mind, watching the older woman climb the stairs, seeing the brown hair pinned up in a roll, the handkerchief held in the woman's left hand scented with that perfume . . .

"I have your key," Cécile repeated firmly.

"Oh, yes," Julienne said, and quickly brushed a tear from her cheek.

"Is something wrong?"

"No, no. Your perfume reminded me of someone."

Cécile watched her with unblinking eyes. "I hope the memory is not a bad one."

Julienne managed a smile. "My mother wore a perfume similar to yours. One remembers so many things by their scent."

"How true," Cécile said, forcing a smile.

"We have a chair!" Gisèle squeaked, and raced into the room, flinging herself onto the green upholstered chair with soft arms and a pillow behind her.

"Two, you have two chairs, and a sofa," Armand Mabilleau corrected, walking out from the kitchen, brushing coal dust from his hands. "Madame, your stove is heating, and I have shut your windows to prevent a draft. The night air is not good for anyone. One must seal it out," he said, and smacked his hands together.

"You are very kind, Monsieur," Julienne said, taking off her gloves, and then introduced her children. She was pleased when he shook Frédéric's hand, making the boy feel like the strong grown-up man of the house.

"Here, let me take your food basket into your kitchen," Armand said, and picked it up before Madame Barbier could refuse.

"We will speak tomorrow about any questions you might have," Cécile said coolly.

"Thank you, Madame."

"Good evening to you, Madame Barbier," Armand said, ushering his wife toward the door. "And welcome to all of you."

Cécile stared at him in the hallway. "Widow, uhn?" she said.

"Why do you frown so much?"

"Why doesn't she have a wedding ring?"

Julienne quickly prepared the soup, and while it cooked for several hours, they explored their new home, making lists and deciding what had to be bought, and where the furniture might be moved to change the arrangements in the bedrooms, what clothing they had to buy, and talked about living in this place.

After dinner, they played the Armada game, walnut half-shells with wooden matchsticks held inside by a drop of candle-wax as the mainmast, floating in a shallow pan of water. Whichever boat remained sailing after the "rainstorm" was the victor.

She kissed the children, hugged them, and put them to bed—Frédéric in one room, and Gisèle would sleep with her until she bought a bed for the child and would put it with Frédéric's bed, making that room the children's bedroom.

Placing the oil lamp on the small wooden table next to her, she sat wearily in the upholstered green chair. She drew her knees up and stared for a long time at the far wall, watching a moth's frantic shadow flutter in the dim light. I still have fifteen diamonds, and the money from the four that were sold in Kirchheim, she thought.

We have a new home, and new names. Frédéric must go to school, and Gisèle must be taught, also, somewhere, somehow. Ordinary lives, she nodded.

She looked around the room. And what do *I* do with my ordinary life, for the rest of my life?

Franz wearily crossed the street, his mind's eye lost in a memory of that first Christmas. Eleven years ago, he thought, and I still remember the snow. It fell in confused patterns because of the wind—clinging and clogging the evergreens, the bushes, and collecting in the joints of bare tree branches. Stefan and I were bundled against the cold. We were twenty-one years of age. In the vestibule, the butler assisted us, and the maids appeared, taking our packages and luggage away to the rooms upstairs.

Then, I saw her. This vision, this exquisite beauty ran to her brother, kissed him and hugged him, saying, "Welcome home, I've missed you so very much!"

Stefan returned the hug, then tapped her back with the flat of his hand. "Mustn't be rude now," he said softly, "we've a guest." He eased her arms from his shoulders and took her by the hand. "Julienne," he said, "this is my dearest friend, Franz Victor Berend-Schreier."

Franz sighed, feeling old. I remember, he thought sadly.

∽

He stood six feet tall. His hair was blond, the blond of sand, not yellow-blond. She saw that his face was a curious blend of imperfections—his eyes were very blue and turned down slightly, sensuously at the outer corners; his upper lip was thin, but the bottom one was full. He could be called handsome, but it was the handsomeness of a puppy, that vulnerable blend of innocence and warmth. He smiled as she held out her hand in greeting. He had a beautiful smile; honest, gracious, charming, inviting.

"It is a pleasure to meet you," she said.

Her hand rested so easily on his fingers. It took him a moment to speak, he was so captivated by her. He bowed, then kissed her hand lightly. When he spoke, he saw the smile play at her lips and knew she'd been surprised by his voice. He knew his voice was a powerful friend, even and smooth as if he were speaking a song. He used it often to his best advantage, and he saw the success of it in her eyes.

He met her father, and they spoke in the drawing room for a time. Later, Franz settled into his room. His suitcase had been unpacked by servants, and he began to undo his uniform and change into dinner evening clothes.

That photograph-plate of her on Stefan's bureau does her no justice at all, he thought. Her skin, like porcelain, how could a grey photograph-plate compare with that? And her eyes, she has such beautiful eyes, large and brown. And there is the barest trace of a pout around her lips, so lovely, so very French.

For eighteen months, he thought, I have loved a photograph. And it has held a dossier in my mind of all the questions I have asked about her—what she likes, reads, enjoys, her friends, her studies, everything—and yet—only fragments, seen through someone else's eyes.

Franz checked himself in the mirror before leaving the room and quickly brushed his hair. Not too anxious, he warned himself, and with a whimsical grin, gave a second brushing to his hair. He hesitated at the door, then sighed. Practiced calm. Franz knew all about practiced calm and set the imaginary mask on his face—he knew what they expected and watched the anxiety leave his expression. There is the face, he thought, the clever, comfortable young man, the able aristocrat-soldier with a hint of shyness about him.

At the dinner table, Franz was pleasantly surprised to learn that not every family was like his own and not every man was like his father. Prince Heinrich was so unusual, he credited both his children with having opinions and encouraged them to express their thoughts at will. At times, Franz noticed, he encouraged his daughter more than his son in participating in conversations.

Franz had a difficult time concentrating on his food. She sat near to him, and having loved a photograph-plate for so long a time, the sight of her in a chaste blue satin evening dress allowed his mind to picture her with the evening dress of a woman—her shoulders bare, her neck exposed—not as now, covered. She will be exquisite then, he thought, then corrected himself. She is exquisite now.

I want to belong here, he thought, with my best friend, the young woman I love, and with him, the father who gives me the dual pleasure of learning from his years of experience and crediting me with intelligence by listening when I speak. God, he prayed quietly, don't take this from me . . .

After dinner, Julienne and Stefan excused themselves and went to the drawing room. Franz thoroughly enjoyed the private conversation with Prince Heinrich. About an hour later when they rejoined the other two, he heard the last words of a story Stefan was telling Julienne:

". . . he sat there, and took care of me all night . . ."

He's told her what happened two months ago, Franz thought, that drunken party when we continued drinking long past the others, in workmen's establishments all over the poor sections of Vienna, after I received my father's letter . . . He looked at Julienne and tried to understand her expression. He wondered if she disapproved of the common behavior that had lasted all night; if she was appalled at the story of the fist-fight against three men on the street, one of whom had a knife. What did she think about Stefan being much too drunk to do any fighting at all, leaving it all to Franz? He protected Stefan, and stilled the screaming voices in his mind at the same time. He had severely punished the three men for their offensive attitude. Stefan had been stabbed in the side, but it wasn't very deep, more of a large scrape rather than a gash. It bled a great deal in the beginning, but had healed nicely. Franz thought he saw worry in those beautiful eyes when she looked at her brother, but it disappeared when she looked at him. The smile was discreet, small, and it was one of gratitude for helping Stefan.

∾

Franz took off his gloves, then sighed. Years later, he thought sadly, she never smiled anymore. She never spoke to me unless I asked her direct questions, and no matter what I said, she always agreed with me. Just like my mother, he thought.

Seeing Julienne's face in his mind, he thought: She took it all away from me. All that happiness, gone. I loved her more than my own life, I loved her family more than my own, and despite all she has done, I still love her.

He slowly climbed the stairs to his right, and continued his search down the long corridors of the Louvre.

CHAPTER
6

Julienne watched Frédéric leave for school in the rain. He turned at the corner, looked back and waved to her before leaving the street. Her eyes drifted to the other people below her window on Rue Royer Collard. They all have things to do, people to visit, friends . . . She left the window, listening to the rain splashing in puddles on the balcony. It was a cold, early December's rain, and brought with it the promised chill of winter.

To keep Gisèle busy, Julienne gave her one of the grammar books she'd bought from the bookstalls on the Quai and had the child copy out passages to learn to make her letters correctly.

Even Gisèle has something to do, she thought, just as the other families in this lodging house have things to do. And I? All I manage to do is say a simple "hello" to the others in this building—they seem so distant. They smile when we meet on the stairs or in the lobby, then continue on to their destination, somewhere outside or back to their flats. The two gentlemen on the top floor tip their hats, the family across the hall says "hello," the people above me I have never seen, and the old couple across from the Mabilleaus rarely come out. I have never lived like this before, she thought. I had no idea living as "one of many" could be just as lonely as living in a large house owned by one man. The only difference is that we are safe—and I am grateful for that, yes, thank the good Lord. Then, she smiled in a sad way. What is the old proverb— be careful what you wish for, for you may get your wish? Ah well, she sighed to herself, I have gotten my wish—anonymity.

To keep herself busy, she went back to work on making a winter dress, but when she tried it on, something was wrong with it. She looked at the material and tried to find her mistake, but dressmaking had never been one of her talents.

Frustrated, she took it off and put on her brown day dress, one that had been made by someone else. I could see it so clearly in my mind, she thought. The pattern was a simple one. Gelber taught me to sew seams and to cut material with straight and even lines . . . Gelber. The memory made her sad. Gelber taught me so much . . . and Kollmer, bless him, he taught me even more: to care for the horse, harness him, feed him, how to drive the carriage, how to build a campfire . . .

And, at the small farmhouse, Gelber's sister taught me to cook. Julienne kept all her notes in a small book and remembered the sister's patience in teaching her how to hold the pans, how to cut the vegetables for soup, how to buy the food, and still had limitless patience with something as basic as how to make and light the stove fire. I did not even know how to feed Maximilian at that time, she thought, but that memory hurt and she brushed it aside. Looking at the dress, she wondered: What have I done wrong?

The sudden bittersweet whistle coming from the stairwell made her look at the door. Armand Mabilleau kept himself company by whistling or singing old French songs from his childhood. Julienne knew he was polishing his beloved banister. Every Friday, he oiled the wood and kept it a living monument to a summer's pleasure with his son.

The whistle nagged at her and she listened to it for nearly half an hour. When it finally stopped, she thought of asking his wife if she knew of anyone who could sew.

The thought frightened her for a moment. But, she decided, I must do it. Otherwise, I really *have* brought the prison with me, and only the guard was left behind in Eisenstadt.

Julienne walked to the door, and then down the flight of stairs. The hall was thick with the scent of furniture oil. It was warm and inviting, a pleasant smell. She knocked at the Mabilleau door.

There was a sound, and it opened.

"Yes?" Cécile Mabilleau said, "did you want something?"

Julienne smiled. "I, I am sorry to bother you, Madame, but I was hoping, perhaps, you might know of someone who sews?"

"Yes," Cécile replied, staring with cold eyes at her, the quiet one, the mystery lodger, the fake widow, the woman made of contradictions. She kept to herself and Cécile liked that, yet, Armand insisted she was kind and sweet. And he adored her children, even the strange little boy who sulked in hallways and gingerly stepped away from people and always had a guilty look about him in the afternoons. But, Cécile thought, Armand adores all little children. Still, his accusations had stung her deeply. She was too suspicious, he'd said, too cautious, too cold and indifferent to strangers. Everyone is a stranger someplace, he'd said. And perhaps she buried her ring with her husband. But he was from the country, and openness was his way, not hers.

"I am trying to make a dress," Julienne went on, "and I've done something wrong."

There was a look in the large brown eyes, a vulnerable look, or perhaps it was need, Cécile wasn't sure. "I sew," she answered. "Would you like me to see the dress?"

"Thank you," Julienne smiled, surprised at the answer.

Cécile shut the apartment door behind her. The Widow Barbier was kind, Armand had said, the Widow Barbier was well-spoken, the Widow Barbier was this or that, she thought. Well, we shall see. We shall see who is right about the Widow Barbier.

The apartment has been kept clean, Cécile thought, and she saw Gisèle at the table working on her letters. Cécile noticed all the personal touches to the room, especially the books arranged on the corner table. "Ahh," she said, "you have been to the stalls, near the Quai."

"Yes," Julienne said. "I love to read, and they're company, you know."

Cécile tried to ignore that understanding, vainly pushing aside the knowledge of her own life—books had been read for more than amusement, they were necessary friends to a young girl ill-at-ease with people.

"For some reason," Julienne said, holding the dress, "it just does not fit correctly and I cannot understand what I have done wrong."

Cécile saw it immediately. "But you have reversed the material."

"I don't understand," Julienne said.

"Come see what you've done," Cécile said, and walked over to the window for better light. "You have not cut the bodice piece with the same grain of the fabric as you have cut the sleeves and the separate skirt piece. It will never be right now."

"I've ruined it," Julienne sighed.

"Maybe not," Cécile clucked. "Show me how much material you have left."

Julienne opened the large remnant square and watched as Madame Mabilleau measured it with her eyes.

90

"I think it will fit," Cécile said.

"It was to have been my winter dress." Julienne said, "but my ambition had more talent than my hands."

"You abandon the dress too quickly," Cécile smiled, then sat down on the sofa.

The task was a pleasant one. As they worked, they spoke of books and Cécile found Madame Barbier to be well-read, and well-spoken, as Armand had described. They spoke of children, and she learned that the boy was attending the La Salle School, taught by the Jesuits. She began to speak of her own children, her son Denis, a grown man now and in the Army. "We had another son, but he died many years ago." She saw a sudden clouding in Madame Barbier's eyes, a memory given fresh pain.

"I understand," Julienne said quietly, her eyes returning to the new seam she was basting.

"Do you?" Cécile asked, more surprised at herself than the question.

Julienne nodded. "I had another son," she said, then added softly, "pneumonia."

Cécile studied the Widow Barbier for a moment. Perhaps Armand was right about the ring, too. So young, she thought, and to have buried a husband and a child. To be so young and so alone . . . Hesitantly, she said, "Claude . . . my Claude was an apprentice. He was to be a mason. He liked working with his hands. He could have been a carpenter, like his father, but he wanted something else. It was a good job, and Paris was in need of workmen then, many workmen, much more than now . . ."

Julienne looked up and saw the softer expression in Cécile Mabilleau's weary eyes.

"He was a good boy," she said, staring down at the material. "He was sweet in his voice and so kind with everyone." She sighed, and said matter-of-factly, "It was a wagon, you see, making deliveries of wine barrels. They told me the horses bolted and it ran him over."

Julienne reached and touched Cécile's wrist, but there was no response and she withdrew her hand. "Would, would you like some tea, Madame? And perhaps a little cake, to refresh you?"

"Yes," Cécile said calmly, working intently on joining a sleeve to the bodice. She heard the footsteps leave the salon and go into the kitchen. She stopped sewing and slowly touched the spot on her wrist. It had been a warm and gentle touch; comfort from a stranger. And she is a stranger, Cécile told herself, feeling suddenly unprotected. Why did I speak of him, she thought, why did I speak of my Claude to a stranger . . .

"Sugar?" Julienne asked.

"Please, two." Cécile watched her pouring the tea, scooping out the sugar, stirring it and then handing the cup and saucer over. What beautiful hands she has, Cécile thought; long fingers with a delicate shape to them. And why not, she is a beautiful young woman. Cécile looked at the dress. "It will do," she said aloud, "but it will be rather plain."

"I thought to embroider the skirt and do . . ." her hand fluttered by her neckline, "do something here. Would you like to see my samples?"

"Yes," Cécile said.

The two dozen little squares were magnificent. The Widow Barbier had fashioned all sorts of flowers, stems, leaves in the centers of the squares. Some had borders, others did not. The stitches were tight and even, and she had obviously been taught to do this by an expert who knew all the different kinds of embroidery stitches for all the different effects they would produce. Cécile looked at her. "You do beautiful work," she smiled. "They are good enough to sell."

Julienne was surprised and opened her eyes slightly. "Do you really think so?"

"I am sure of it," Cécile said. "There are many shops that would pay you for such fine work. I do not know your circumstances, Madame, but with two small children— Ahh, I apologize. It is too personal a subject."

"No apology is necessary, Madame," Julienne smiled. It seemed almost indecent to consider it, yet, it might be a chance to blend in with Paris life one step further, to speak with people, and be near people every day, and perhaps, find a friend. And, Madame Mabilleau, as others, might wonder about her "circumstances." "Where would I go?" Julienne asked slowly, watching Madame Mabilleau.

Cécile sipped her tea. "I do not speak from experience, you understand, just from little things I have heard. There are many shops near the Quai des Grands Augustins, and the woman who makes my dresses sometimes has the material embroidered by them. I do not know for certain, but they must do piece-work as well as the full bolts of materials."

Well, Julienne thought, I have broken so much from the past, why not this, too? "What might I say to these people?"

Cécile shrugged. "Bring your samples. That will say it all."

"Would I have to work in the shop or might I work here?"

"I don't know," Cécile said, surprised at the question. "Why do you ask?"

Julienne looked at Gisèle. "My daughter is too young to spend her days alone."

Cécile watched the expression on Madame Barbier's face change from a pleasant possibility, to what looked like longing for something out of reach. The little girl is too young, Cécile thought. The boy is in school and does not come home until four or half-past in the afternoons. But she is such a well-behaved child, Cécile thouht, so quiet, so sweet, sitting there at the table doing her letters. She'd heard the child playing in the courtyard on sunny mornings, and the sound of her voice singing songs was a delight. It was a sound she'd not heard for many years.

Images of Claude and Denis came back to her, precious sights locked in her heart and hidden in dreams: young boys playing soldiers with wooden horses carved by Armand; rainy afternoons spent in her salon holding pieces of white paper over the oil lamp, waiting for the sooty smudge to appear and letting them scratch out pictures with the dulled points of old pens or hatpins. Did the Barbier children scratch pictures, she wondered. The wooden horses were in boxes in the cellar, part of that private shrine to Claude's memory and Denis's childhood—their toys, their shoes, some of their clothes that she had made, schoolbooks, and now letters from Denis. Armand had gathered them all and locked them away. But he was like that, she knew.

"Perhaps," Cécile said slowly, looking at the finished seam on the sleeve, "perhaps I might help you." She glanced up to see Madame Barbier's expression. There was no look of rejection, no hint of annoyance or intrusion, so she continued. "I am home, most days," she said, pacing her words, "I might help you for a time, until you could make other arrangements for Gisèle." She forced herself to sit back into the chair and to look at Madame Barbier's face.

Julienne reached for the hand. "Thank you," she said softly, feeling the fingers underneath her own relax. "This is most generous of you. I don't even know how to repay such kindness, to speak of what it means to me."

Cécile patted the hand, then pulled hers away. "Tut," she said, "come now and try the dress and we shall see what has to be done."

Julienne returned from her bedroom some five minutes later, wearing the blue dress, her left hand clutching at the as-yet-unfinished front to keep it closed.

"It will do," Cécile said with a broad smile, "yes I think it will do." She stood, left hand on her waist, the right forefinger tapping at her closed mouth as she carefully observed the lines of the dress. "Yes, almost," Cécile said, then walked the few steps to Madame Barbier. She tugged the back of the bodice piece, then sighed. "Ahh, no, I've pulled it too high here, in the center of the back. The seam is not even. Pull your arm out and I will fix it now, a little snip of the thread to loosen this one spot and adjust it here, and . . ."

Julienne felt the tugging and pulling stop when she heard the sharp intake of breath behind her. "What is it, what's wrong?" she said, then felt the chill of the air on her upper back, just above the chemise. The scars, she thought.

Cécile turned her face away and tried to look just at the bodice piece. All that dead white skin, she thought.

"It, it happened such a long time ago," Julienne said, trying to smile, and pulling at the bodice to hide her back. "An accident," she continued, thinking quickly and liking the sound of it. "An accident, when I was much younger, and they did not heal well."

Cécile met her eyes for a brief moment, then smiled, graciously accepting the lie.

"So," Armand said, draining his wine glass then pulling off a piece of bread from the baguette. "Why do you make something more of it?"

"An accident?" Cécile said smartly. "You did not see them, Armand, scars, criss-crossing all over her back."

"What I cannot understand is why you insist on making a story to go with it. Anything could have happened to her," he said, and went back to cutting the veal on his plate. "Anything."

"Of course," Cécile said, hardening her stare. "You always accept what people tell you, don't you?" She shook her head and then concentrated on her food.

"And you always look for little secrets and lies."

Cécile looked up at him. "Then you explain it."

He grunted at her. "I have no explanation."

"Because there is *only* . . ."

He slammed his fork down on the table. "Leave the woman in peace," he said firmly. "She hurts no one, always has a kind word to say, is always pleasant—at least to *me* she is always pleasant—she is alone, she has no friends, leave her in peace."

Cécile bit her lower lip. "I have always done so," she said.

"No," he said, "you are sitting here, inventing stories about her past, trying to find the little hidden lies to explain what she has plainly told you was an accident."

"I could see the lie in her eyes, Armand."

"I will hear no more of this," he said, and left the table, roughly shutting the door out of the room and leading to his salon.

"Obstinate, pig-headed man," Cécile mumbled to herself, staring at his half-eaten dinner. She shook her head at him. "She had no accident," Cécile whispered to herself, "she was whipped like a dog."

After the children said their prayers, Julienne tucked them in their beds, kissed both their foreheads, and whispered goodnight before closing the door to their room.

"You promised I could see," Gisèle whispered.

"I'm not so sure now," Frédéric answered, staring at the bumps of his feet under the covers.

"But you promised."

"Ohh," he sighed, "all right," and kicked off his covers. He felt his way in the dark to the other end of the room. Opening the middle drawer, he touched inside for the box. "Come by the window," he said, moving to the area between their beds, and then opened the curtains to let in the light from the gas-lamps in the street. He looked at his sister. "Do you really promise?"

"I promise," she said, tossing back the long braid of her hair behind her shoulder.

"And if you tell," he said in a threat.

"I will *never* tell," Gisèle insisted.

"Well, all right then," he said, and placed the box down on the window sill. "Jeannot and I found these things," he said easily.

"Jeannot?"

"My friend," Frédéric said, "my most best friend in all the world."

"Does he go to school with you?"

Frédéric shook his head. "Jeannot doesn't go to school. He says it's silly."

"Then how . . ."

"I met him in the park. He lives near the cemetery, he told me once, near Montparnasse. Sometimes . . ." he looked at Gisèle again. "You really promise?"

She gave several vigorous nods.

"Sometimes," he said, lowering his whisper even further, "I don't go to school. And I meet him by the pond in the Jardin du Luxembourg, and we play all day."

"Mama will be angry with you."

"But you promised you'd never tell, so how is she to know?"

Gisèle frowned, then touched the side of the box. "Show me," she said.

He opened the lid and took his treasures out, one by one. He held a man's leather glove, the left one, with two buttons of pearls at the wrist. He touched the soft leather, then gave it to Gisèle. She tried it on, her tiny hand lost in the large palm. It came back to him, the first day . . . that first time. He could remember crawling up behind the bench, snaking his hand through the slats and quietly reaching for the glove. The fear had been terrible, and it gave him stomach cramps so powerful he was nauseated . . . but he'd done it. Jeannot had shown him exactly what to do. Only later did Jeannot yell at him. One glove, he'd said. Of what use is *one* glove? *Two* gloves, and then we could sell them at the Mont Pieté pawnshop. But one glove, how stupid . . .

He felt sick all the way home. He felt as if everyone on the street was looking at him, knowing he had stolen the glove.

He took out the small wooden whistle from the box, one that could be bought for a centime or two. But he hadn't bought it. He'd stolen that from a young boy playing with stones near a path in the Jardin des Plantes. Careless boy, Frédéric thought, to leave it all alone behind him. That had been easy, but still, he'd felt sick afterwards.

"Smell," he said to Gisèle, holding the lady's handkerchief.

She sniffed, then smiled.

"You can still smell her perfume, can't you?"

"Yes," Gisèle whispered.

He placed the handkerchief down on the bureau; that, he'd found. It had been blown by the wind into bushes and he'd picked it up because it was interesting. He took out several feathers, all of different lengths and textures and colors. "From the birds," he said, "aren't they beautiful?"

Gisèle nodded.

He smiled, knowing still hidden in his drawer was the small pouch of money from the real things they'd stolen and then brought to Mont Pieté: scarves, walking sticks, gentlemen's hats. Once they'd stolen a watch from a fat man who'd fallen asleep in the sun. Jeannot had done that. Jeannot had unhooked the fob from the waistcoat and drawn the watch out ever-so-delicately. They would've taken his hat, too, but they heard footsteps on the path and darted into the bushes.

And the apples—how many apples had they stolen from the carts in the market? Or chestnuts? Or pears, even. They took their lunch from the vendors on the street, sneaking and grabbing and running.

"Take the handkerchief," he said, rather grandly.

Gisèle held the linen to her nose again and sniffed it deeply. "Thank you. Where did you get all these things?"

"We found them," he said. "Maybe . . . maybe we'll find something for you someday. Would you like that? Would you like me to find something for you?"

"Yes," she said. "I hope someone loses something nice."

"They might," he smiled.

Shopkeepers, Julienne thought, gritting her teeth and walking quickly along the Quai des Grands Augustins. Those shopkeepers, those tradesmen, those miserable, offensive, rude excuses for people. Pawing over my squares like that, she thought, giving those mean haughty looks to me. The work is so-so, they said; no positions available, they said, sniggering little laughs and leering at me . . . Well, I don't need the position, and if Madame Mabilleau or anyone else asks questions, I'll explain it, somehow, I'll think of something else to do . . .

Passing a boulangerie, she paused and looked at herself in the window. I am the same as everyone else, she thought, touching the ribbon of her bonnet. Or am I, she wondered, leaving the window and stopping by the passageway at the side, watching a young woman walk out of the boulangerie carrying a large basket of trash. Her hair, though pinned up and back, was falling down at the sides and hung limply over her ears. Unkempt wisps fluttered on her forehead. Her hands were bare. Her head and eyes were downcast. Perhaps it was her posture that made Julienne recall all the people that had walked through her life asking for positions in her household. She had interviewed enough young women recommended by the housekeeper to remember how they stood before her, how their hands were clasped, how they slightly lowered their heads and had answered, "Yes Sir," and "No Sir," to the butler.

She walked from the passageway and pulled wisps from her own hair. Then she took off her gloves and hid them in the basket. Oh this is too silly, she told herself, as a bright red pony cart caught her attention as it clattered down a side street. She watched it stop a little farther down the block and a man jumped off and went inside a door. It is too late in the day for deliveries, Julienne thought, and decided to watch and see what would happen.

A few moments later, the man came out and carried an armful of material bolts. She looked at the street sign: Rue de la Bucherie. It is near enough to the Quai, and to the bridge at the end of Rue St. Jacques to go to the Right Bank and all the great dressmakers. When the cart turned around and passed her on its way, she saw it turned right. So he is going across the river, she thought, then walked closer to see this place of business.

There were several business establishments along Rue de la Bucherie: a laundry, a shoemaker, a triangle bazaar for copper pots, two other businesses that gave no indication of what they were, and this one, where the man had gone. The name of the establishment was painted in white on a blue board above the door. It said CHAVASTELON.

The door, also, was painted blue, and the business had a single window on either side showing the wares of the shop: bolts of material arranged in a display with embroidered flowers. Needles had been stuck into the material with embroidery thread dangling to give the impression of a work-in-progress.

Oh, why not, Julienne thought, and tried to relax the smile on her face. She opened the door and a little bell jangled above her.

Displays, all neatly arranged, of both embroidered and plain material were on tables in the small area to her right. A desk and chair were toward her left and a doorway, leading somewhere else, was ten feet in front of her. It opened and a man walked in, a man of ordinary height, slightly overweight, of perhaps fifty years with the much-used fashion of mustache and beard emulating the Emperor Napoleon III. He wore pince-nez glasses on his nose, which was a shade too pointed.

"Yes," he said.

"Excuse me, Monsieur," Julienne said, keeping her head and eyes low. "I am looking for someone who might speak for me to the owner about employment."

"I am the owner," he said stiffly. "I am Monsieur Chavastelon." He waited. "Well, speak up, speak up."

"I, I am looking for a position," she said, and timidly gave him the samples of her work. She watched him walk toward the window. How humiliating, Julienne thought, and stole another look at this man Chavestelon. He examined her work by the window's light, flipping the squares like a card dealer, adjusting his pince-nez glasses and wrinkling that too-long nose. Shopkeeper, Julienne thought, and quickly went back to staring at the floor the moment he began to turn around.

"So-so," he said, walking back to her. "What is your name?"

"Madame Jeanne Barbier."

He grunted. "So you are married, uhn?"

"Widow, Monsieur."

"Oh," he said. "I am willing, Barbier, to give you a chance. I pay the usual rate: one franc, seventy-five centimes for each day's work."

"Yes, Sir," she smiled.

"You will start here tomorrow." He gave her the squares and then placed his hands on his waist. "We begin at seven, and we close our doors at six. And, Barbier, you do not enter from the front. You and the others come in through the passageway two doors down and enter from the small common courtyard in the back."

Julienne suddenly thought of the servants' entrance in the homes of the rich. "Yes, Monsieur Chavastelon," she said, looking at the floor and controlling her voice.

After supper that night, Julienne had drawn the water from the pump in the kitchen, filled many pots and boiled them on the stove, and then poured the hot water into the metal tub brought into the kitchen for their twice-weekly baths. Gisèle had already been bathed and was now in bed. It was Frédéric's turn.

He frowned as he washed. "But why do you have to do something?"

Julienne shook her head as she leaned against the doorway to the kitchen. "Why shouldn't I? You do something. You go to school, you go out, you meet people and have made friends. Why should it be different for me?"

He said nothing.

"It . . . it might not last for very long," she sighed, nervously picking and tugging at the cuffs of her dress. "Perhaps I will not enjoy it, or I will not like talking to the women in the shop, but there is no way of knowing this until I try. Can you understand that?"

"No," he sulked.

"Well I mean to try," Julienne said firmly. "I won't be afraid anymore."

She heard a slosh, then the sound of feet on the floor. Stepping into the kitchen, she saw him shivering with a towel wrapped tightly about him. "Come by the fire, quickly now, or you'll catch cold." She shooed him out of the kitchen and ran behind him as he stood close by the fire. Taking the edge of the towel, she dried his face. "Did you wash your hair?"

"Yes, Mama."

"And your neck?"

"Yes, Mama," he sighed. "I am a man now. I washed everything, just as you said."

Julienne pursed her lips and tried not to smile. An eight-year-old man, she thought, then knelt down and kissed his cheek. "Frédéric, it isn't the money, or the work itself. Being ordinary is more than just taking a new name and living in a new place. It is trying to belong." She rubbed his hair with the towel. "You will come home directly from school and collect your sister from Madame Mabilleau. Then the two of you will come here and wait for me. If it is a cold day, you will ask Monsieur Mabilleau to start the fire. Do not start it yourself. You will wait here for me, you will not go out, and you will not allow anyone to come in here whilst I am gone. You say you are a man. A man has many responsibilities, Frédéric. Caring for your sister is one of those responsibilities."

He thought about it, then nodded.

"My good boy," she said, and hugged him, then began to rub his back dry with the edges of the towel. "We have Sundays," she said. "After Mass on Sundays, we will go out to the parks, or the zoo, and then, to a café for a tart or little bon-bons. I will see to it that Sundays are very special days for all of us, I promise." Julienne stood up, and took his nightshirt, now warm from hanging by the fire, and gave it to him. He slipped it over his head, gave her a quick kiss goodnight, and raced to his bed.

Julienne spent the better part of half an hour emptying the tub's dirty water by potfuls into the sink. Then, with the work all done, she sat down at the table and began to draft a letter to Stefan, missing him terribly and trying to put down the information without appearing to do so. It was difficult, and she still worried that the letter would be intercepted by one of Franz's spies in the Post Office. She used a different name. Stefan will know my handwriting, she thought, and still struggled with the rough draft for a little time more.

After breakfast the following morning, she wrapped a piece of cheese, a large slice of bread and a small tart into a linen napkin and put her lunch into the small basket. She left the apartment a little after half-past six, still trying to focus her eyes in the grey light just before dawn.

Julienne marveled at the activity on the Boulevard St. Michel. Passing the many boulangeries, she could smell the bread already in the ovens, its warm scent filtered out to the street and making her hungry again. The hidden people, she thought, the separate society that made so simple an act as buying a loaf of bread, or a pair of shoes—or embroidered cloth—possible.

She had to stop herself at the main blue door of Chavastelon's. Yes, the back door, she remembered with annoyance, and continued on to the passageway and common courtyard shared by several businesses. There was a stern, plain-looking woman at Chavastelon's back door with a small notebook in her hands. She had placed a mark next to someone's name and was about to close the door.

"Chavastelon's?" Julienne asked.

The woman looked at her. "You are . . .?"

"Barbier."

The woman nodded. "You are late, Barbier."

"But Monsieur Chavastelon said seven o'clock."

"It is now five past," the woman scolded, "but we will forgive you this time, as it is your first day." She held the door open. "Inside."

It was the stench Julienne first noticed the moment she stepped into the room, the sour smell of perspiration from twenty women and countless women before them. She swallowed hard at her first real sight of poverty.

The work place was only slightly larger than the salon at her apartment. Gas-jets flickered on the walls, a fire burned in the open fireplace at the far end, and these women, these hunched-over, round-shouldered, sweaty women, were already working at their assigned benches and tables.

The older ones had candles next to them and large goblets of water in front of the candles. The young ones, twelve or thirteen years old, clustered together in a corner. Women of twenty-five or thirty years of age had bone-thin hands with pieces of wool wrapped around their palms. The sound of needles clicking against the thimbles made a strange rhythm, like chattering teeth.

Julienne felt faint from the smell. The closed windows and the stale, hot air made beads of perspiration break out on her forehead, while others trickled down her neck to her back.

"Barbier," the woman said, "this is your place." She pointed to a bench near the window.

Thank God, Julienne thought, and saw she could pull out the rag that had been stuffed into a hole in the broken pane of glass.

"Dubord," the woman called out. "Show Barbier what to do," and then she left the backroom, shutting the door to the shop behind her.

"Little Marquise Dubord . . ." someone sniggered.

"Show her what to do," someone said rather grandly.

"Hags," Dubord said, and pulled her bench to the woman Barbier. "My name is Isabelle," she said softly. "Pay no mind to the hags. Bent-over, dried-up hags," she said for their benefit. "that's what they are. That's all they've ever been."

"Jeanne," Julienne said. "My name is Jeanne." She was somewhat unnerved by the word "Marquise," and asked quietly, "Why do they call you that?"

Isabelle shrugged. "Jealous."

Julienne didn't understand, but let it pass and noticed that Isabelle was a striking woman, with brown hair, light brown eyes, clear skin and high cheek-bones. She was attractive, in a brittle sort of way, with her unflinching eyes and their direct, hard stare.

"You are doing a border piece, Barbier. You have a hoop, a needle, there is your thread, and your pattern—you can follow a pattern, can't you?"

"Yes," Julienne answered, seeing the intricate design of stylized rosebuds with half-circles on both the top and the bottom. The rosebuds had three shades of red, and the circles had two shades of gold. The border piece itself was black satin.

"It's from one of the shops on the Rue de Rivoli," Isabelle said, then added wistfully, "for some rich woman's cape." She touched the satin, saying almost in a whisper, "maybe for the theater, or to wear over a grand dress when she goes to a ball . . ." Isabelle let go of the satin and said quickly, "It has to be done by Saturday."

Three days, Julienne thought, shaking her head and looking at the length of the satin in the basket at the end of her bench. "I don't know . . ." she said quietly.

"You'd better know, Barbier. Chavastelon's promised it for Saturday, and he accepts no excuses. And you'd better get started. The Egyptian is very fussy."

"Who?"

Isabelle shrugged. "Her, the one we call the Egyptian, the matron. She keeps us working. Chavastelon himself has little to do with us—except on a few occasions." She smiled to herself. "Yes, except on special occasions when we become important."

"Why do you call her that?" Julienne asked as she stretched a portion of the black satin across the embroidery hoop and secured it tightly. Then, she reached up and unplugged the hole in the window glass.

"I should leave it be if I were you. The draft is very bad," Isabelle said, embroidering her own border piece of green leaves.

"But I need the air," Julienne said, wiping her forehead with the back of her hand. "It is so hot in here."

She should know better, Isabelle thought, then shrugged. It is none of my business, she decided.

Julienne began with the rosebud, bending over slightly, counting the stitches on the pattern and working from the softer shades of the inner bud to the darker colors outside. "Why do you call her that?" she whispered to Isabelle.

"Oh," Isabelle said, "I did not give her that name. Some woman, three or four years back, before my time, gave her the name. The hags told me that this woman heard a Bible story once, from some priest, and the name just seemed to fit that one. The Egyptian—the one who drives the slaves at their work."

It is such a different and terrible world, Julienne thought, remembering the charitable work done by her father, and soup kitchens organized by aristocratic women to feed the hungry poor during the winters.

She shook the thoughts from her mind and concentrated only on her work and the cool breeze at her side. They worked steadily, the needles forever clicking, the fire spitting and giving its heat. The flickering uneven light from the gas-jets all around the room occasionally cast shadows on their work and by mid-morning, she found herself wet from her own perspiration and squinting at the black satin.

"Barbier," Isabelle said, barely looking up from her own work. "Faster . . . you have to go faster, or you'll never finish it on time."

She tried to work faster, but her fingers felt stiff and she was unused to the smothering concentration, and having to stay in one position for such a long period of time. By two o'clock, she'd done five rosebuds and their half-circles—a mere ten inches of work. She placed her hoop and needle down, and when she tried to straighten her back to stretch, she moaned from the sudden cramp in her side and at the back of her neck. Her right hand shook from all the work it had done during the half-day.

A shadow came behind her, and Isabelle reached down for the rag and plugged up the hole in the window again. "Where does it hurt?" she sighed.

"Everywhere," Julienne replied.

"Barbier, from the draft, where does it hurt from the window draft?"

Julienne looked at her sharply. "Dubord, my name is Jeanne."

Isabelle grinned. "You're not like the others, are you?"

"What does that mean?"

Isabelle shrugged. "Only that you're different." She smiled. "Rub the spot with your hand, where the draft made a cramp. You'll feel better in a few minutes."

Julienne rubbed her side. It hurt, but then began to ease.

"You've never done this work before, have you?"

She looked at Isabelle. "Why do you say that?"

Isabelle chuckled slightly. "Anyone who does this work knows about the drafts. And your hands, they tell me you haven't worked like this before. Look at them."

Julienne looked. They were just her hands. There was nothing special about them. "So?"

Isabelle held out her own hands and Julienne saw the difference. The skin, on the balls of the fingers, was cracked, split, blackened and dead from years of needles stabbing them; the skin on the top of her hands was thin and tight, stretched white over bony ridges; thick blue veins moved and pulsed like small worms on the top of her hands to the wrists; her knuckles were red and large. The hands looked cramped and arthritic. They were the hands of an old woman, the hands of a servant.

"I never had to do this kind of work before," Julienne said quietly.

"I thought so. We ought to eat. There isn't much time left. Get your cloak and wrap it tightly around you. We'll go outside and get some air."

As soon as the door opened, Julienne felt the shivering cold from the world outside.

"You see, Jeanne," Isabelle said, "you feel the difference now?"

Julienne shuddered a nod.

"We live in the heat, and the slightest chill is so much more to us. It gets worse you know, never better." She took Jeanne's arm and led her to the far

101

end of the courtyard where they could set their food down on a barrel-top and lean against the wall. Isabelle closed her eyes to the sun.

Julienne undid the linen napkin and placed the cheese on top of the bread. She was about to bite it when she noticed that all Isabelle had to eat was a piece of meat with a black spot at the edge, and a small bottle of wine, partly filled.

"You shouldn't eat that," Julienne said, nodding toward the meat.

"Why not?"

"The black spot," Julienne answered. "It's gone bad."

"So?" Isabelle said, and picked the small black spot out of the meat with broken fingernails. "It's this, or go hungry." She turned away from the stranger and bit into the meat, chewing and staring at the opposite wall to their left side.

Julienne watched her for a moment, the defiant stance, the effort to straighten her posture, the deliberate way she bit into the meat and chewed it thoughtfully, the desperation in her eyes. Julienne ate half of the bread and cheese and took a small piece of the tart for herself, then said, "I'm too tired to eat. I'm so exhausted, I can barely swallow."

Isabelle turned her head left. "You have nothing to wet your throat, that is why you can't swallow. Have some wine," she said, and held out the bottle.

Julienne brought the bottle to her lips and told herself to drink, just like the other women were doing. She swallowed a mouthful of the cheap, slightly sour wine. "Thank you," she said, clearing her throat, "it is better, thank you. But it seems such a shame, a sin, really, to waste the food. Whatever you wish, Isabelle, is yours." Looking around the courtyard, Julienne asked, "Where is the convenience? I think I'll use it now."

"Around the back," Isabelle answered, watching her walk away. What a strange one she is, Isabelle thought, eyeing the food on the linen napkin. The hags would take it out of her mouth as soon as look at her, if they could. And she gives it to me as if it were nothing. She touched the cheese, then slowly picked it up and ate it, savoring every bite. She took a swallow of wine, and then looked at the pastry. Breaking off a corner of the tart, she dissolved it in her mouth, letting the sugared apple flavor linger for a long moment.

I have not tasted something like this, she thought, since Philippe . . . two months since Philippe came here, in his fine carriage, and picked me . . . and he took me to the rooms with the waiters bringing in the dinner on their silver platters. It was duck, with that sugary glaze made of something, I don't know what, and champagne to drink, and later, brandy, wonderful brandy . . . and tarts, as many as I wanted, tarts of all different kinds with cream and fruit. I made him laugh, and he had them bring me more.

Eating the last of the tart, she thought: You promised me a better life, Philippe. You promised you'd come back for me, and give me a set of rooms all my own . . .

"I'm glad it was not wasted," Julienne said, then folded the napkin and put it into the small basket.

Isabelle managed a grin. "You don't belong here. What brought you to this? Ahh . . ." she waved it off. "It's none of my business. I was just curious."

"I am a widow," Julienne said.

"Ooh-lah," Isabelle sighed, "so he left you unprovided, uhn?"

Julienne did not answer.

"So typical of them," Isabelle said, "to think only of themselves. But you won't be back tomorrow, little widow You're not the kind that spends her life here."

The door to Chavastelon's opened and the women began filing in.

"So, you think I'm not strong enough for this, uhn?" Julienne said, copying the tone of Isabelle's expression.

She smiled. "I think you were made for better things in life."

There was a kindness in the desperate eyes of Isabelle. "We do what we must do," Julienne answered.

"Until the day, when we are free to live as we have wished," Isabelle said softly.

Julienne smiled in agreement, thinking someone finally understood.

It was half-past six that evening when her turn came, at the table where the Egyptian sat with the notebook. "Barbier," she said, peering at her book, then counted out the money.

Julienne took the coins and counted them herself. "No, Madame, this is not correct."

The Egyptian's eyes burned. "It is most certainly correct, Barbier."

"Monsieur Chavastelon promised one franc seventy-five centimes for each day's work." Julienne gripped the coins in her hand. "You have only given me eighty centimes."

"Yes," the Egyptian replied coolly. "One franc and seventy-five centimes, *less* the cost of the thread you used today—two spools at forty centimes each, and *less* the cost of the needle you broke, the needle that belongs to Monsieur Chavastelon. It must be replaced, and it costs fifteen centimes. Can you add that Barbier? Can you add that quickly enough in your selfish head—eighty centimes is what you earned, and eighty centimes is what you hold in your hand." She shut her book with a snap and stood up. "Good day, Barbier."

Julienne closed her hands around the coins, numbly staring at the table.

"I said, good day, Barbier."

Julienne walked out of the shop. The thieves, she thought, the miserable shopkeeper thieves. She pulled her cloak around her neck a bit tighter, and walked in a fury up to the corner and turned left.

They stole from me what was mine, she thought. The coins felt cold and tainted in her hand. I've a mind not to return tomorrow, she thought, then decided: No. A shopkeeper will not cheat me of learning to belong, she thought. Other people manage. Isabelle has, I'm not sure how, but she has. I will learn to belong. Besides, she thought, I've survived worse lessons than this in my life.

"There he is," Frédéric said and waved his arm wildly.

Julienne watched as the skinny, scruffy young boy waved back and walked toward them. He had a cap on his head, with strands of dark hair falling over his eyes and ears. He seemed to be all legs and arms, and was several inches taller than Frédéric. "How old is he?" she asked Frédéric.

"Twelve," Frédéric answered with a sigh. "That really makes him a man, doesn't it?"

Julienne raised her eyes slightly toward the sky. A man, she thought; first an eight-year-old man, now a twelve-year-old man, then smiled as Frédéric introduced her to Jeannot Dessard, the rough little boy with the pouty lower lip. "I like to meet Frédéric's friends," she said, watching the boy blush and then kick at the dirt on the path with his shoe. "I am sure Frédéric has told you how special Sundays are for us," she continued. "I hope your parents will allow you to join us later, when we go for a little refreshment." She waited, watching his surprised open eyes.

"Thank you, Madame," he said softly, "my parents will not mind."

The Jardin du Luxembourg was crowded with people on this rare and warm mid-December sunny afternoon. Julienne took a deep, relaxing breath of crisp air and looked lazily at the couples and the children. "I shall be at the gazebo, listening to the military band. You know it, yes, Jeannot?"

He quickly nodded.

"I know you children want to play. Try very hard not to distrub other people, Frédéric. And mind your sister now. Don't lose her in all the excitement."

Frédéric gave a toss to his head. "I won't," he said, stealing a look at Jeannot.

"Just an hour, and then we'll go to a café. And mind your clothes, they've just been laundered."

"Oh Mama," Frédéric said, then loped to catch up with Jeannot.

"Your mother's very beautiful," Jeannot said, "and very kind, too."

Frédéric shrugged. "I suppose."

Jeannot pinched his arm.

"Ow," Frédéric complained.

"At least you have a mother."

"Don't you?"

Jeannot shook his head. "I don't need one," he answered.

It is a day for leisure, Julienne thought, a day for enjoying the fresh air. She listened to the sounds of life in the park: trickling water from the fountains; words and phrases from different conversations; graveled paths crunching quietly as people took unhurried strolls. As she walked, she looked up to the nearly bare tree branches forming a lattice-work of grey against the blue sky. And she heard laughter. Children's laughter. There was so much beauty in this park, and it fed a starving portion of her mind.

Confined in the small workroom all week, she had no opportunity to see anything of life, of nature, but on Sundays—true to her word—they went out all day. Last week, they took an omnibus and went to the Right Bank. She brought the children to the Tuileries Gardens, but Frédéric seemed nervous and, for some reason, he didn't like that park at all. They didn't stay very long. His only reason had been he liked Jardin du Luxembourg better. And why not, Julienne thought, it is more lush, has more winding paths, more greenery, and is more beautiful than the Tuileries.

She followed the paths around the still-green lawns and, as was her habit, went to the kiosk selling hard candy. She bought a small paper cone of the many-colored sugared balls, putting one in her mouth and letting the sweet taste melt. She would eat a few and then save the rest for the children. Children love sweets, she thought, then smiled. I must be part child, too.

She continued to walk, and heard the band before seeing the cast-iron gazebo. They were playing Handel's *Water Music,* and it sounded as peaceful as the sounds of the park. She walked past the gazebo, seeing the gleaming instruments of the band, the spotless uniforms of the musicians, and found her bench— her particular wooden bench facing the gazebo on the other side of the path. It was empty. She sat down and ate another candy, smelling the air and the warm scent of coffee coming from the café behind her and to the left, some twenty feet away.

The music was soothing, and later, she knew, they will play the old French songs, as they do every Sunday, and some people will sing, and others will smile, and everyone will be lost in their own private memories.

"I don't like it," Frédéric whispered to Jeannot as they walked slightly ahead of Gisèle.

"Why not?" Jeannot whispered back. "There's lots of good things here today, lots of fancy people with fancy money. Look at all the hats on the benches, all the gloves, and my God, look at all the walking sticks with the silver tops, and some—did you see, did you see the ones made of gold?"

"Not here," Frédéric insisted.

"Idiot," Jeannot said, "everything goes to the Mont Pieté pawnshop."

"But not here."

"Why?"

Frédéric shook his head. "We live near here. We come here all the time. And so do they," he said, jerking his head toward the people in general. "They might remember me. No. If you want to, then you do it. I won't. Tomorrow, maybe, at the Tuileries. Not here."

"How can I do it if you don't help me?"

"How did you manage before?"

"I had a different partner," Jeannot replied, eyeing all the potential money now out of his reach.

"And?"

Jeannot shrugged. "And nothing. One day he just never came back."

Frédéric thought about that. "Did he get caught?"

"I don't know," Jeannot answered. "I went to look for him, but I never found him. He just disappeared. People do that sometimes; one day they're there, the next, they're not . . . Gone."

"Who's gone?" Gisèle asked.

"No one," Frédéric answered quickly. "It's nothing. You wouldn't understand."

"You always say that," Gisèle whined.

They walked past the Medici Fountain, past the long stretches of green. They watched men reading newspapers and other groups of workmen bowling on flat, dusty ground. Still others sat comfortably while old women fed the pigeons.

They heard the people singing as they saw the top of the cast-iron gazebo. "I know that song," Jeannot sighed as they walked closer. "If the King only knew you, Isabelle," he sang, "then the King would love you, Isabelle . . ."

Frédéric looked at the people. He saw him. He saw the blond-haired man sipping his coffee at the last table in the café, near the path.

The music became unbearably loud. Frédéric instinctively took two steps back and collided with Gisèle. He grabbed his sister and pushed her backwards toward a hedge marking the end of the corner path.

"SHUSH!" he said to Gisèle. "Be quiet! Don't move—don't move at all!" He was breathing harder and felt himself shaking. He felt sick as tears spilled from his eyes.

"What's wrong with you, you're very strange today," Jeannot said, crouching behind the bush with them.

"Over there," Frédéric sputtered, "over there . . . that man, the blond one, near my mother . . ."

Jeannot snaked himself partway around the hedges. "Yes, I see him," he whispered.

"That's, that's my father, he's, he's followed us, he'll kill us if he finds us . . . we, we ran away." He gripped Gisèle's mouth tighter when he heard muffled screams from her mouth. "Help me!" he cried to Jeannot. "Please, please, I don't know what to do . . . if he sees us, if he sees my mother . . . tell me what to do, Jeannot . . ."

Jeannot saw the terror on their faces. He looked around the bush again, first watching the blond man, then Frédéric's mother, barely twenty-five feet apart, separated by a few low hedges and several other benches with eight— no, nine—people singing with the band.

"He can't see you," Jeannot said. "Go home." He looked at Frédéric, who had not moved. He grabbed Frédéric's shoulders and violently shook him. "Stop it, it's all right, he can't see you here. Do what I've always told you to do— _Don't run._ If you run, people will look at you. Do what we do at the Tuileries, Frédéric."

"But my mother . . ."

"I'll see to your mother," Jeannot said. He crawled around the bush and watched until the blond man signaled to the waiter. "Go now," he said, "the waiter is talking to him. Hurry, and don't run until you pass the bowling courts."

They scampered out from behind the hedge and walked quickly away from the gazebo. Jeannot watched them until they had rounded the turn and were out of his view. He knew it was safe for him, the blond man didn't know him. He strolled out, shoved his hands into the pockets of his jacket and walked to Frédéric's mother.

He sat down next to her, on the left, so she would turn away from the café and face the opposite direction.

"Where are . . ."

"Frédéric says his father is behind you," Jeannot interrupted. "No, don't turn, please face me, Madame."

Julienne shuddered so hard the paper cone of candy slipped from her hands and spilled on the path. "Oh, God," she whispered, "oh God, God, somebody help me . . . he's found us . . ."

"He hasn't," Jeannot said, looking past her and watching the blond man sip his coffee. "He is like everyone else in a café; they look, but they don't see." Jeannot heard her begin to cry. "Madame," he said, tugging on her cloak, "please, stop. I know what to do. I know how to escape when people are looking for me or chasing me. If you cry, you make people look at you."

Julienne forced herself to stop and then wiped her eyes. "Frédéric and Gisèle, where are . . ."

"Safe. I sent them home."

"Tell me what I must do," Julienne whispered.

"When he turns away, " Jeannot began, still watching the blond man, "you stand up and walk down the path next to the gazebo. You stay a little longer in his view, but it is the fastest way out of the park and he will only see you from the back."

Julienne nodded.

"But you must not run. I know you want to, but you will make people look at you if you do."

She took several deep breaths and tried to calm the pounding in her chest. Her heart was beating so fast and so hard it hurt. "Tell me when."

"He does what everyone does," Jeannot said. "He lets his eyes just look, but he does not really see. He looks at me, he looks at your hat, now he looks at the old man walking in front of the gazebo, and now he reaches into his pocket and takes out a cigar case. He opens it, he picks a cigar . . . wait until he strikes the match . . . he clips the end, he puts it in his mouth . . . NOW."

They stood up and began walking alongside the gazebo. Julienne fixed her eyes on the path, trying to see where she was going, but was, instead, counting her steps. Fifteen . . . sixteen . . .

"Slower," Jeannot said, "walk slower."

She slowed down and kept pace with him. Her body was cold, shivering. "He said he would find us, he said so, and he has . . ."

"But he hasn't," Jeannot said. "He would be following us and he's not."

"You don't know him," Julienne whispered. "He won't leave Paris until he finds us, and brings us back, and then . . . then . . ." She began to cry again.

"I'll watch him for you."

She wiped her eyes and glanced at Jeannot.

"It's a game, a spy game," the boy smiled. "I play it all the time. I pick someone from a crowd and I follow them. It's so easy," he said with bravado. "I know how to do that. I learned things."

"From whom?" she whispered as they rounded the hedges that led to the bowling courts.

"I learned . . . from people," he said quickly. Jeannot turned himself around and stole a look. "No one," he said proudly. "Safe again. I'll watch him and I'll tell you when he leaves Paris."

Julienne touched his arm and he smiled.

"You can run now," he said, watching for a moment until she disappeared.

They were safe inside the little apartment with the windows shut and the curtains drawn and the door bolted.

Julienne started the fire and then sat close to it on the floor with the children. "We're . . . we're safe," she said, trying to believe her own words. She touched Frédéric's hair. "My good boy," she said, kissing his forehead. "You saw him first."

"What . . . what do we do now?" he asked quietly, looking nervously about the room.

"We'll stay here until we know it is safe to go outside again."

A little later, the children had calmed down and went to their room. Then, Julienne took the letter she'd been writing to Stefan and burned it in the fireplace. I love you too much to place you in danger, she thought sadly, watching it burn. He swore he would kill you and your children. Stefan, I'd rather die of loneliness than jeopardize your safety.

The sheets of thoughts and hopes, so carefully worded, disappeared, and though she told herself it was only paper, she felt as if that last avenue had been permanently blocked. Teo's image came back to her mind, barring the way.

So it must be, she thought. Live well, my brother. I love you.

Franz stared at his cup of coffee, then looked again at the people near him. They all look the same, he thought. That happened in Florence, too. None of them have her face, that exquisite face . . . He swallowed. Nineteen, she was. I kissed her first, and felt a lover's welcome, and proposed to her after the first kiss . . . she'd never kissed a man before. I kissed her first, loved her first . . . I could have died of happiness that first year we were married. Perhaps, I should have. How much better, to have died when filled with happiness, than to face this slow, bitter death of life without her.

I am here seven weeks, Franz thought miserably, and there is no trace of her at all. It is as if she never even existed. What to do, he wondered. Vienna is not possible. Too many questions, and I've resigned my post. Travel? He sighed. Where, he thought, and to what purpose? Home? He shook his head. I . . . I can't. Christmas is two weeks away. I cannot be alone in that house, that grave. I have endured five months without her. If those five months have been a hell, what in God's name will the next five bring?

When the blond man stood up and decided on a path, Jeannot followed at a distance.

He still looked at people, but in a disinterested way. He left the Jardin du Luxembourg and waved at a cab.

Jeannot stood close enough to hear:

"Hotel Bristol," the man said, "Place Vendôme."

Jeannot made a skinny but efficient little shadow. The tall, strong-looking blond man had a melancholy air about him. And Jeannot noticed, whenever the man stopped for a cognac—which he was doing more frequently with each passing day—he seemed to stare into his drink for a long time, lost.

It is so easy, Jeannot thought, watching his quarry walk so slowly back to the Hotel Bristol.

It was easy because Jeannot knew the streets of Paris. He'd been called a guttersnipe, a rag-boy, and his teachers had been the friends of his uncle— thieves and pickpockets, prostitutes and ruffians. He knew how to find food from the streets, how to find shelter from the rain or snow, where to steal and what to steal, and like any thief in Paris, he knew where to bring the items—the Mont Pieté pawnshop, where the clothing of the poor was often pawned so they would have money to buy food. A gentleman's hat, or cane, or gloves or watch could be brought and sold with no questions asked.

Jeannot could not read words, but he could read situations and the faces of people. And this one, he thought, studying the face of the blond man, the despondent one, his walks grow shorter, he drinks more often, he lingers longer over his cognacs, and now he barely looks at the faces of people passing him by in the streets. He seems weary, Jeannot thought, and hopeless.

The game ended all too soon. Three days after he had become the spying shadow, Jeannot saw the blond man watch quietly as his bags were loaded onto a carriage. The blond man gave the doorman a coin before stepping inside the cab.

Jeannot waited, and when the four-wheeled closed carriage turned around, he scampered across the street and wormed himself into the shallow outside back of the cab, his feet dangling in between the two large wheels.

They moved slowly to the north of Paris, on Rue St. Denis, and Jeannot had the idea they were going to the Gare du Nord, that railway station with the iron and glass arched roof.

Two or three blocks before, Jeannot waited until the cab slowed down because of traffic, then jumped off and went the rest of the way on foot. He'd often stolen rides that way. It was a game of danger and he loved the thrill of never knowing if he would jump off safely or be caught by the cab driver.

He watched as the blond man's luggage was unloaded from the carriage, then followed the porter's wagon inside the train station. The blond man gave his ticket to a trainman, then stepped inside and disappeared into a private car.

Jeannot smiled, very satisfied with himself. He looked around the platform and saw the boys with the lucky jobs of selling newspapers. They are here every day, he thought, they must know where the train goes. He walked up to a boy younger than himself and asked, "Where does this train go?"

"It is the daily train to the East," the boy replied. "First to Germany, then people change if they wish to go further, to Austria."

Jeannot nodded and began strolling to the end of the platform. He waited, not bothering anyone, just watching as the great black engine began to move. Jeannot was fascinated by the steam and the sight of the massive iron hulk pulling the cars out of the station. It must be so wonderful, he thought, to go someplace, to go on a train.

"You, boy, get away from here," a trainman yelled, and made a grab for Jeannot.

Jeannot ducked out of his reach, and scampered out to the confusion of the Paris streets.

CHAPTER
7

It was probably the way in which the snow edged the stone buildings that made her think of Austria. Three weeks had passed since Christmas, and they had welcomed the New Year, 1870, with presents bought from stalls that lined the Boulevard St. Michel and the Boulevard St. Germain. They had done as every other French family had done: she'd purchased little French toys for the children; they'd gone to Mass, and wished people and tradesmen a good New Year . . . still, a lifetime's habit of her own holiday had been with her, in her mind, like a faint voice in a lonely and placid valley.

The morning was a numb stretch of hours, but at least they were warm. Sweat clung to them all like a blanket, yet by their lunchtime, they did not dare go outside for fear of the sharp cold and the illness it would bring.

"It's too terrible, uhn?" Isabelle said, passing the bottle of wine to Jeanne Barbier. "How I hate the winter, but not in the daytime. Here, at least, I am warm."

"Too warm," Julienne answered, wiping her forehead and pushing back a long strand of hair that had fallen in front of her eyes.

Isabelle laughed. "Little Jeanne," she said. "You are still not like the others."

Julienne grinned at the remark, then waved it off with a toss of her hand. She took a swallow of the wine, then shared her bread with Isabelle.

"Your children, are they well?"

Julienne nodded. "My Gisèle enjoys the time with Madame Mabilleau."

Isabelle bit the edge of the bread.

"She's never known a grandmother," Julienne went on. "My own mother died when I was very young, about Gisèle's age."

"Pity," Isabelle said. "My mother works in a shop like this. But for how much longer, who may say . . . I hate the machines." She saw the confusion on Jeanne's face. "Ah, I forget, you are a stranger to this world. She makes lace, and there are so few women left in Paris who make the lace by their hands . . . Now, it is mostly machines—looms, and men who run the looms.

Looms," she said with a sigh, "they steal the sous out of the lacemaker's crippled hands, after a lifetime of knots and strands and eyes that go blind . . . I hate them, and the men who make them work."

Julienne's eyes drifted around the room, to the women and the work being done for Chavastelon's rich customers. The rich, she thought, and its companion phrase—the deserving poor. My father hated that term, she thought, and he criticized anyone who used it or made a show of charity. He believed true charity was anonymous. The looms are not the only thieves, Julienne thought, glancing at the door to the main room of the shop, and there is something very wrong with this kind of world.

They went back to work.

It was half-past four when Isabelle heard them from the shop's main entrance. The laughter and the loud voices were slightly slurred from too much wine. Isabelle stopped working, as did the young ones in the corner. They wiped their sweaty faces with the hems of their skirts, combed their hair with their fingers, pinched their cheeks and bit their lips to make themselves look rosy.

What are they doing, Julienne wondered, as the young women sat up straight, almost posing.

The door opened slightly, and there were hushed whispers behind Chavastelon. He stood at the entrance and turned his head to the side to speak to the unseen visitors. After several nods, Chavastelon shut the door.

A few moments later, the Egyptian appeared. "Patenaude," she said, and one of the young ones stood up with a smile. "And Barbier."

Isabelle's shoulders sagged and, after a sigh, she picked up her embroidery hoop again.

"There's a good dinner for you tonight, Barbier," an old one cackled, the others joining her.

"What are they talking about?" Julienne whispered to Isabelle.

"Go," she said, staring at her embroidery. "Go, you've been chosen—and bring your cloak."

Julienne followed Patenaude through the door. She saw two men in their early thirties dressed in fine clothes, one in maroon, the other in blue, speaking with Chavastelon. The maroon one had light brown hair and was not very tall. He was stocky, with an odd, almost primitive unrefined face.

The other one, the blue one, was his opposite. He was tall, on the thin side, with a very handsome face. He had a dimpled chin, high cheekbones, pale skin and eyes of a deep blue color which he struggled to keep open. He had thick, dark brown hair and traces of a stubble on his face. Neither man had shaved, and they both smelled of wine.

"Come, come, I will not haggle with you," the maroon one said.

Chavastelon licked his lips like a snake. "My dear Marquis de Roquetanière, have I ever disappointed you?"

Marquis, Julienne thought, he looks like a farmhand.

The Marquis considered the question. "No," he said finally, then laughed.

"Ahh, here they are," Chavastelon said, behaving in a strange grandiose manner.

When Chavastelon approached her, Julienne did not move, and when he

111

placed his arm through hers, she pulled away from him. "What do you think you are doing?" she said.

"I, I wish to introduce you to the Marquis de Roquetanière."

"No, no," the Marquis slurred, "not for me, she is for my friend, Lord Harlaxton."

"Ah, my mistake," Chavastelon groveled.

Two noblemen, Julienne thought angrily, two disgusting drunken noblemen. Chavestelon took her arm again. "Let go of me," she said firmly as her cloak dropped to the floor.

He laughed nervously. "Barbier, don't be difficult, behave yourself now."

"You should listen to your own advice," Julienne snapped, wrenching her arm free again and glaring at him. He's put us on display, for their pleasure and amusement, she thought.

"Leave her be," Lord Harlaxton said, and stepped closer.

She could smell the stale wine on him, a smell that lingered, like the smell of the men on the road in Germany.

He inspected her face, then went to touch her cheek but she stepped away from him. "Beautiful," he said, "absolutely beautiful."

"Chavastelon, is this reluctance a new maneuver to raise your prices?" the Marquis asked.

Julienne's eyes opened wide.

"No, no," Chavastelon shook his head. He turned to Jeanne Barbier. "This is nothing unusual, Barbier."

"Really?" she said sarcastically, "and who decided that?" Julienne turned to go back to the workroom.

Lord Harlaxton blocked her way. "Now, now," he said, "nothing to be afraid of, you know, Chavastelon's right." He grabbed her arms.

"Let go of me!" she yelled. She pulled her arms free and when he tried to grab her again, she backhanded a smack across his face as hard as she could. "You filthy, worthless drunk, you disgusting animal, you are a disgrace to your family! How dare you touch me . . ."

"Barbier!" Chavastelon shouted, "enough."

"Yes," she sputtered, "quite enough. Who do you think you are, you bug, you pig, to try to sell me as if you own me? To the devil with *you*, and your disgusting shop, and your disgusting side business."

"You are dismissed, Barbier," Chavastelon said, red in the face.

Julienne narrowed her eyes. "Not until you pay me," she breathed. "And this time, you pig, you will pay me what you *promised* me—one franc seventy-five centimes for a full day's work, and by God, you'd better not deduct *anything* from it."

"Leave my shop at once," Chavastelon ordered.

"You'd like that, wouldn't you," Julienne smiled meanly, her eyes wild as she stepped closer to him. She poked him in the chest with her finger. "No, shopkeeper, slaveowner, pig. Pay me what you promised me that first day six weeks ago. Pay me. NOW."

He backed away from the wild-woman and went to his desk. "Here," he said, fumbling with the coins. "Now get out."

She looked at them, and tossed the extra coin down to his feet. "I said one franc seventy-five centimes and I meant it." She picked up her cloak from the floor and walked out the front door.

"I will call the police after you," Chavastelon yelled, "you have robbed me, you have disgraced me . . ."

"No, you won't," Lord Harlaxton said and tossed a gold Louis to the shopkeeper. "Leave her alone." He smiled, hazy from the wine and feeling the cold draft from the open door. He turned to the Marquis. "She's quite right, you know."

"About what?" his friend asked, crooking an arm around Patenaude's waist.

"Everything."

The Marquis shrugged. "Ah, but you have no one for tonight."

"Doesn't matter, Philippe," Lord Harlaxton said, and walked unsteadily to the door jamb, leaning against it. "Which way did she walk? I didn't notice, did you?"

Philippe sighed. "Is it important?"

"Yes," he said and took a deep breath of air. "What was her name? Barbier?" he asked, looking at Chavastelon.

"Jeanne Barbier, yes."

"Where does she live?"

Chavastelon took off the pince-nez glasses from his nose and made a great show of cleaning them as he shrugged.

"How can you not know?"

Chavastelon kept cleaning his glasses. "Who is concerned about such matters with such girls . . . they work for me, that is all."

"Does anyone know? Has she a friend?" Lord Harlaxton pressed.

"She used to speak with Isabelle Dubord," the pretty little Patenaude offered.

"Yes," Chavastelon said with a weighty sigh, "I have heard that to be true."

At the door, the Marquis de Roquetanière suddenly remembered. He turned to his friend. "Ahh, Isabelle, yes. Sometimes, they all become confused in my mind. I cannot remember if she is the one who loves cakes, or something, ah, no matter. All the little embroidery girls are such sweet flowers."

Patenaude smiled as he squeezed her waist.

"Shall I see you later this evening, Edward?" the Marquis asked.

The English Lord nodded, then turned to Chavastelon. "You know nothing more of Jeanne Barbier?"

"Madame Barbier is no longer in my employ," he said stiffly. "If you wish further discussion, question Dubord. I will speak that one's name no more."

Madame, Edward thought. Married. He shook his head and left the shop.

The door to the apartment house slammed shut so hard it startled Armand as he carried a bucket of coal up from the cellar. "Are you all right, Madame?" he asked, seeing her flushed cheeks.

"No, I mean, yes, fine, just upset."

"Is there anything I might do for you?"

"No," Julienne said, then calmed down. "No, thank you."

113

"Well, if you need anything, just let me know."

"I will, thank you," she said, and walked up the stairs.

Armand took out his pocket watch and looked at the time. Twenty past five, he thought, she is home early today. Something must have happened at her shop, he thought, closing the door to his own apartment.

Kneeling by the stove in the corner of his parlor, he shoveled scoopfuls of coal into its belly.

"I heard you speaking to someone in the hall," Cécile said from the kitchen.

"Yes," he said, shaking his head at her too-sharp senses.

"Well?" she said, coming into the parlor.

There was no escaping the questions. "Madame Barbier is home early today. She seemed . . . a bit upset."

"Is she unwell?"

"No, just upset," he said casually, closing the stove's door. He heard Cécile walk back into the kitchen. She will find a reason, he thought. I know her and her habits, she will find a reason to go upstairs and learn what has happened. As much as she pretends to be busy with the dinner, she will find a way. He stood up, warmed his hands for a moment, then walked to his chair and sat down. Curious as a cat, he thought, she cannot resist this little string trailing on the floor; she has to pounce on it.

He lit his pipe, listening to the absence of activity in the kitchen. Come along, he thought with a smile, you kill me with the suspense of waiting. Find your reason and have done with it.

Cécile walked out of the kitchen carrying a covered ceramic bowl. "She must be ill," she said matter-of-factly, "and is probably sick with a cold. She cannot possibly find the strength to cook tonight. I am taking her some soup— for the children, too. The little ones cannot suffer because their mother is ill."

Ah, he thought, stood up and kissed her on the forehead, saying, "My little kitten."

Cécile managed a small smile. "Somehow, I have this feeling you meant that differently."

Armand only grinned and drew on his pipe as she walked out the door.

It had taken him nearly two hours to walk to the Roquetanière Palais on Avenue de la Reine Hortense, which backed the Parc Monceau, but Edward needed the walk to clear his mind from the day's drinking. Numb, cold and tired, he told the servant who had drawn his bath that he did not wish to be disturbed this evening, that he would retire early, and to tell the Marquis he would join him for breakfast the following morning.

He sat in the porcelain tub for a long time, at first with his eyes closed, unable to sense where the water began and his own body ceased in this warm, steamy womb. When the water cooled, he opened his eyes and washed himself quickly, feeling more relaxed and clean. He stepped out of the tub and dried himself with a towel by the coal stove in the corner.

In his nightshirt, dressing gown and slippers, he walked unsteadily down the drafty hallway to his own room at the far end. He yawned, then rubbed his eyes and face, feeling the scratchy stubble. I ought to shave, he thought, one is not completely clean unless clean-shaven. At the washstand in the corner, he felt the weight of the pitcher when he picked it up and poured the water into the bowl. He nearly dropped the pitcher when the man in the mirror startled him, then shamed him by the common ugliness of bloodshot eyes, puffy lids and skin drawn and pale. His hair was dripping and unkempt, and the stubble on his face seemed darker. Edward backed away from the mirror, not looking at himself again.

He shivered and sat down on the floor, close to the heat of the fireplace. Filthy worthless drunk, she'd said, disgrace to my family, she'd said. True, he thought, hugging his knees. All true.

In Paris since November, he thought, all a haze. How many embroidery shops and dressmaking shops, and other excesses . . . It was a foggy dream and even the faces melted together. He shook his head and closed his eyes to hide himself from his building shame. Philippe had said it was the thing to do, and everyone did it. It was a public service. The girls were paid next to nothing. They led miserable deprived lives and were eager—nay, hopeful—to please aristocratic "gentlemen." It is normal, Philippe said, it is the way of their lives and what they expect from their lot in life, and quite different, almost charming, from the ways of professional prostitutes.

But she stood there, proud, defiant, and was appalled by the actions of "gentlemen," Edward thought. Chavastelon dismissed her, and she demanded what rightfully belonged to her, then shamed him further by returning the silly little coin that did not belong to her. How magnificent, Edward thought.

His eyes gazed on the corner table to the crystal bottle of brandy glistening and reflecting the fire's light. He hesitated, then told himself "no." She'd called me a filthy worthless drunk. No drinking to bring on the black comfortable oblivion, to spend the night without thinking or dreaming or to silence the nightmares. No, no brandy tonight; he yawned, and thought instead of Jeanne Barbier's lost job.

All because of me and my arrogance, Edward thought. And still . . . such courage. She must have known she would be dismissed, he thought, but I suppose it didn't matter to her. Right is always right, he thought, just as the truth is always the truth.

He stood up and walked slowly to the bed. It took him a long time before he closed the oil lamp down. He kept reminding himself, it is just a room, like any other room in any other house. He crawled under the covers and told himself tonight there are no ghosts, no dreams, no memories, just sleep.

He jabbed the pillow with his elbow and settled down, closing his eyes. If she has so much courage, he thought, she won't mind if I borrow some of it—just for tonight. Tomorrow will take care of itself, but for tonight, I'll borrow courage from Jeanne Barbier.

Two days later, Julienne felt the sudden grief, almost as if she'd turned a corner and collided with a wall unexpectedly there. Pulling at the bed-linen in the children's room, the heaviness settled as she jumbled the sheets into a ball and tried to forget she'd dreamed of Maximilian.

Just gather the laundry, she told herself, keep busy. But the laundry in the straw basket had a soft, rounded form, like a child's form swaddled in blankets. She watched the form, expecting it to move, to see it breathe, to hear it cry out.

"Mama?"

Julienne gasped and, with the spell broken, turned to the sound of the little voice at the door.

"Marie and I are ready," Gisèle said, hugging the doll.

Julienne stepped closer to the laundry basket and picked it up with unsteady hands. She put on her cloak and led Gisèle down the stairs. She was glad now she had arranged with Madame Mabilleau to watch the child for the morning. Better to be alone, she thought, to walk outside and not have to talk or answer questions or amuse Gisèle. And to repay Madame Mabilleau's kindness, she would help her by doing the Mabilleau marketing.

She watched her feet on the slippery pavement, crunching snow beneath her shoes, and walked with a deliberate pace to the Blanchisserie. "Good morning, Madame Bédard," Julienne managed, shutting the door quickly behind her, feeling the heat from the back room warming her face.

"Ah, Madame Barbier," the old woman said. "I have your order, all pressed and ready."

"Thank you," Julienne whispered, and quietly wiped her cheeks.

Madame Bédard was a stocky, short, white-haired old woman with an ill-fitting blue dress with the sleeves rolled up, exposing wrinkled elbows. Her nieces were busy at work, one of them washing in the back room, the other ironing at the rear of the front room.

"Here," Madame Bédard said, "six sheets, four shirts, two little dresses, two trousers, one large dress, three chemises, two petticoats, five drawers, thirty centimes, Madame."

Julienne paid the laundress her money.

Madame Bédard noticed the pale complexion, the shivering hand, and said, "Are you unwell, Madame Barbier?"

Julienne smiled. "It is the cold. It makes my eyes tear."

Madame Bédard nodded. "It is so awful today, but, that is natural for January, is it not?"

Julienne swallowed, then tapped the edge of the basket. "For next Thursday?"

Madame Bédard reached in and grabbed the bundle, roughly pulling apart the sheets and counting them. "Only the six? Oh, yes, they will be ready for Thursday, Madame."

Silly of me, Julienne thought, doesn't look like a baby at all.

And yet, on the boulevards in the cold and damp morning, she was now acutely aware of mothers and their children. Julienne tried to close her ears to the sound of them and tried to think only of her errands, but there, inside Jevelot's butcher shop, she came face to face with one of them.

The little eyes opened and closed and dripped fat tears onto his mother's shoulder. The mother held the baby and tried to soothe the hysterics, swaying back and forth, caressing the child's back.

116

That cry, Julienne thought, that helpless baby cry when they are so young. She was unable to stop herself from reaching to touch the perfect little hand wound around the mother's cloak. The skin was soft and smooth, the velvet of baby's skin on the dimpled hand.

All her errands were a blur, and even having tea with Madame Mabilleau was a haze with answers given in echo by some part of her that did not ache.

I should have protected him from the rain, she thought, viciously pulling the freshly laundered linen tight on the beds. I should have done something for him when he was ill, nursed him back to health, then he would be alive today. I should have loved him more . . .

She smoothed the blankets, then walked to the corner chair and picked up Frédéric's trousers and shirts. She wiped her eyes as she opened the second drawer of the bureau.

Look at this, she thought, all his shirts, jumbled and messy, I've told him a thousand times to care for his things, but he never folds them and never puts them away.

She moved the disorganized pile of shirts from the center of the drawer and saw a box.

Julienne only went cold when she saw the strings of a pouch hidden under the shirts, and in lifting the pouch, felt the money. Her hand shook when she emptied the pouch into her palm, coins rattled, then lumped together as she clenched her fist around the centimes and francs and gold Louis.

"Marie is going to a party," Gisèle said, wandering into the room, "and I must change her dress."

Julienne watched her daughter fuss with the small basket of doll's clothing. Then, she took out the box from the drawer and placed it on the bed. "Gisèle, what do you know of this?"

"Oh, that's Frédéric's secret and his treasure box," she said, then her eyes widened. She dropped the doll. "I, I don't know, I'm . . ." She looked around the room.

Julienne stepped closer and let the coins rain down on the bed. "Tell me," she said.

"I . . . I . . . he made me promise . . ."

"Tell me," she said firmly.

Gisèle tried so hard to keep the words inside her, but they tumbled out. "He and Jeannot found them when they, I can't say, he made me promise, and I did, but he found them when, he said, they'd . . . he said he'd find something for me, and he did, so . . ."

"Gisèle," Julienne said, eyes narrowing.

"Sometimes, he, he doesn't go to school, and they find things, but he made me promise, so I can't tell you," the child trembled.

"And the money?"

"I, I don't know about that."

Julienne turned away from her daughter. "Go inside and leave me to think about this."

The child backed out of the room, grabbed the doll, then ran to the salon and hid in a corner.

117

He doesn't go to school sometimes, he finds things, *they* find things, Julienne thought. She sat down heavily on the bed and stared at the box. How many little presents has he brought home, she thought, a few bon-bons, then a bag of hard candy, and how many times did he say "a man selling flowers just gave me these for you, Mama," she remembered. And, "I won a race in school and the prize was a paper Harlequin puppet, and I give it to you, Gisèle."

Lies, Julienne thought, all lies. She opened the box. No one *finds* a gold watch and chain. And no one finds this amount of money.

She wiped her eyes and felt the weight of the disappointment in him. God, I thought all the horrible little surprises in life would just end if we left, but it doesn't happen that way, does it?

Her jaw tightened and her hands still shook. Wait, she thought, looking at Frédéric's bed, just wait until you come home . . .

He was late by half an hour. His cheeks and nose were beet-red from the cold and he slapped his hands together to warm them. "Hello," he said, dropping his schoolbooks on the chair nearest his mother. He pecked a kiss on her cheek, then ran to the fireplace to warm himself. "Jeannot says hello and hopes you are well."

Jeannot, she thought, the very sound of his name an annoyance now. Yes, he helped us once, she thought, pricked by a moment's guilt, but he has obliterated that good by leading Frédéric to do wrong. Stealing is wrong, it is a sin, and it was obvious the lanky street urchin lived by his wits. And I was so blind, Julienne thought. "Did you have a nice day in school today?" she finally asked, her eyes glaring, her hands gripping the skirt of her dress much too tightly as she sat rigidly in the chair.

"Yes," he answered, staring at the fire.

Julienne stood up and moved closer to him. "Did you go to school today, or did you meet Jeannot somewhere and spend the day playing?"

Frédéric's mouth opened. He looked quickly at Gisèle and saw her hide herself from his eyes. "I . . . I went to school . . ."

Julienne closed the distance between them, then reached into the pocket of her apron and drew out the gold watch and chain, gently placing it onto the table. "What do you suppose this is?"

He stared. His heart began to pound. "I, I don't know . . ."

"And this," she said, dropping the pouch of money with a thud alongside it. "Tell me, Frédéric, where did they come from?"

"I, I don't know," he said, blinking rapidly several times.

"You know where I found them, don't you?"

"No, no," he sputtered.

"Don't lie to me, Frédéric, they were inside your treasure box in your drawer."

"I haven't a box in my drawer."

"Stop lying to me," she snapped.

"I'm not lying," he said, raising his voice.

"Gisèle told me all about your treasure box."

"I don't know how they got there," he said, backing away from the table and his mother's narrowed eyes. "I, I don't know about them . . . somebody put them there. Somebody came into the house and put them there to get me into trouble. I, I didn't do it."

"No one came into the house," Julienne said sharply.

"Gisèle," he said, "Gisèle did it, to get me in trouble."

"She did no such thing," Julienne said, her voice getting louder. "Stop blaming your sister when we both know the truth."

He began to shake and stepped back from her again to get away from her, and the peering eyes, and the way her hands were on her waist, and the angry face.

"You have not been going to school every day, have you?"

"Yes I have," he said quickly, his heart pounding faster and faster as if it would jump out of his chest at any moment.

"I *know* you've been seeing Jeannot, and I *know* the two of you have been doing bad things . . ."

How, how could she know, he screamed inside, Jeannot, help me, I'm scared, Jeannot, help me . . .

"You've been stealing, you've been running wild, you're lying to me and you're lying to protect Jeannot. I won't have it," she yelled at Frédéric. "I will not have you lie to me, not ever! I shall punish you, and you must not *ever* see Jeannot again . . ."

He could not stop the frantic tears when he heard the words.

". . . you will not ever leave this house again until you tell me the truth!"

"Yes," he shrieked, his entire body shivering. "I did it, they're mine." The sobs were hysterical; caught and confused, he shook his head from side to side, his hands clenched tighter and tighter into white-knuckled fists as he backed away from his mother. "I hate you, I hate you," he screamed.

He felt the door behind him, opened it, and ran down the stairs, still screaming, "I hate you, too! I'm never coming back, never!"

"FRIEDRICH!" Julienne called from habit, then ran out after him, calling him by the French name, "Frédéric, come back . . ."

He was too fast and all she could do was hang limply over the banister in the stairwell, hearing the front door slam, three floors below her.

She felt dizzy, and the tears she'd been fighting all day finally came. She wept, not hearing the other doors to the apartments opening and closing. She continued to cry, for Frédéric, for not teaching or helping him enough; she cried because she lost her temper and yelled at him; she wept for Maximilian, because she should have been a better mother and protected him from the rain . . . there was no escaping the avalanche inside her, and she did not even try.

She did not know how long she was there, but felt an arm close around her shoulders.

"I was across the hall at the Ribière apartment," Armand Mabilleau said, "fixing a window. Come inside," he said, and when she did not move, he repeated, "come inside. No need to let the others see you this way." He led her to her own rooms, then shut the apartment door to the hallway. He sat her down in the chair near the fireplace and gave her his handkerchief.

The hysteria began to subside, lasting, like most others, only a few minutes. Her eyes and nose hurt, and she wiped her face with his handkerchief. It smelled vaguely of tobacco, a warm, fatherly smell, and it reminded her of how alone she really was. She cried again . . . softer, less frantically, from an old pain deep within her that had never really gone away.

A glass of wine appeared in front of her eyes.

"Drink," Armand said.

She did, but swallowing hurt her throat.

"He will be fine," Armand said, quietly, when she had calmed down. He held her shaking hand and tried to warm the icy fingers. He sat down next to her on the footstool. "Sometimes, I thought to myself, it must be very hard for you, to raise a young boy alone."

She could not answer with words, but gave him a small nod.

"Cécile and I have raised two boys, and that was hard sometimes, for two people. And," he said lightly, trying to make her smile, "I was a boy once, a very long time ago."

"He . . . he . . ." Julienne tried, nodding toward the door.

"Yes, but he will be fine. It is the nature of little boys to run away. My Claude ran away from home, once. He broke a vase, fighting with his brother, and he could not face his mother. So, he ran away. And, when it was dark, he came home. No matter how much a little boy says he is not afraid of the dark, don't believe him. Outside, they are *all* afraid of the dark. He will come back, Madame Barbier, and very soon, too."

Julienne wondered about Frédéric. He knows stealing is wrong, she thought, but he ought to be punished in some way, so he will not do that again. "Did you punish Claude?" she asked Armand.

"But of course," he said with an easy smile. "I punished both of them, because they were both wrong."

"How?"

"I punished them with kindness—and, a little extra work." He saw the warm, appreciative smile on her face. "Ah, you understand, don't you?"

"When Claude came home, you did not send him to bed without his supper, did you?"

Armand shook his head. "He punished and frightened himself more than I could, or more than was necessary. It was only a vase. Yes, we had his supper waiting for him. My poor little Claude was shivering and crying when he came home. First we comforted him, then he was punished. I made him work with his brother. They both carried coal up from the cellar, they both washed the walls in the hallway . . ." He chuckled. "They were so small, the two of them, how high could they reach, Madame? I made them work together, and speak together, and be together, and by the end of the week, all was as it should be."

"You are a very wise man," Julienne said.

He shook his head. "Just a father."

"My Frédéric," she smiled, "does his chores willingly. He enjoys helping me, and has said so, many times. Would it be too much to ask you, if . . ."

"If he could wash a few walls, big, strong, tall little boy that he is?"

Julienne nodded.

"Of course," he said. "And he is so tall, I will not have to do the walls over myself . . ." The grin was toothy and boyish. "You seem better now."

"Yes," Julienne answered. She stood up and led him to the door, saying, "You have been kind to me from the very first day, Monsieur Mabilleau. You understand a great deal and my life has not been without its troubles."

He kissed her hand. "Madame, I will tell you one last thing. I am from the country, from the Graves region near Bordeaux. The soil in Graves is full of rocks, all rough and horrible. But, it is the kind of soil that makes the grapes sweet and worthwhile. A mystery, yes? The people of Graves have a saying to explain that—and themselves. They say: 'The vines are like people; the more they must fight for life, the better and sweeter they become.' Madame, if you will please forgive me, you would make the people of Graves very proud."

She watched him walk down the stairs, holding onto his banister. Then Julienne went inside to wait for Frédéric.

Faster, he thought, darting around the crowded streets, pushing past old women with kerchiefs tied around their heads. He bumped into legs and walking sticks and did not hear the swear words of the tall men call out after him as he continued to run. He shivered in the grey twilight. His feet were soaked from the dirty sluh that made splattering marshes at the curbsides too wide for him to jump and stay dry, and he thought only of Jeannot.

He knows how to escape from trouble, Frédéric thought, remembering Jeannot said he lived somewhere near Montparnasse Cemetery. But on which street, Frédéric thought, and which house on which street? No matter, he decided, I will find him, I will . . .

He was confused by the streets, but felt better when he saw the name Boulevard du Montparnasse. He found the courage to ask a couple which way was the cemetery, and lied that he was to meet his mother there.

The gentleman had smiled, and gave him directions, and even offered to walk him there, but Frédéric said no, thanked him, and ran away.

But the dark came. He blinked and it was dark, with gas-lamps on the streets casting monster-like shadows on fences and the sides of houses. Lights came from the windows, and in the dark they looked like eyes staring down at him.

He found it very hard to stop looking at all the eyes and bumped into a small wall made of bricks with iron rods embedded into it. He turned around and saw the white tombstones, with tree limbs looking like bony fingers pointing at the graves.

Dead people live here, he thought with a shallow breath, and was frightened by the stone angels and the way their wings seemed to flutter every time the trees above them moved with the wind.

When his teeth began to chatter, he told himself he was cold. He did not dare turn his back on the cemetery, lest one of the dead people walk out and surprise him.

He began to retrace his steps toward the main boulevard and the bigger lights on Boulevard du Montparnasse. I am never going home, he thought. I shall become a pirate, or an adventurer, and I don't need anybody at all . . . but he felt relieved when he saw Jardin du Luxembourg to his left. The shadows were not so ugly there, and he knew the fences and the houses on the boulevard, and the streets and all the shops. He hid himself in a doorway for a long time, trying to warm himself and keep the sharp wind from his face. A dog barked, somewhere, and startled him. He began to walk again. I will never go home, he told himself, but turned right onto Rue Royer Collard anyway.

Two hours and some, Julienne thought nervously, where is he? She tried to stop the thoughts of disaster—that he was hurt, that like Claude Mabilleau, a wagon had run him over . . .

She tried to be calm, but her stomach was knotted and tight, and she could not eat her dinner. Gisèle had eaten, and Julienne had put the child to bed soon after, then returned to her vigil by the window.

Footsteps in the stairwell made her breath quicken, but when they continued up the stairs or stopped at floors below, the heaviness returned and she would pull the shawl tighter around herself.

At half-past seven, she heard footsteps again on the stairs, but they sounded lighter, smaller than all the others. The relief was wonderful when the door opened. "I'm glad you're home," Julienne said, not knowing how to begin. "I've kept your supper warm."

Frédéric stared at his wet shoes. "I'm not hungry . . . I, I want to go to my room."

"Take your shoes off first," she sighed.

He did as he was told, then strode past her into his room, roughly shutting the door. Then, it was quiet.

Julienne listened at the closed door for a moment. "When you are hungry, your supper will be waiting for you." There was no answer. She walked away from the children's room, bolted the hallway door, then took her seat by the fire and tried to understand what he'd done. At least he is home, she told herself, but the sound of his little voice plagued her, and the way he avoided her eyes hurt her deeply. He is a little boy shamed, she thought.

She thought she heard a sound behind her and looked, only to see the closed door of the children's room.

When the mantel clock chimed nine, Julienne decided to put an end to the silent dead hours and went to the closed door. "Frédéric," she said, knocking softly, "I want you to come inside now. We will talk about this later, but for now, I wish you to sit by the fire and warm yourself, and have your supper. You must be very cold and hungry. I know I would be . . ."

He did not answer.

She opened the door and saw the boy hidden under the covers. The memory of a boy disciplined by his father, with his face turned away, shivering and frightened as he was now, unsettled her. She bent close to the mound she took for his head. "I am not going to hurt you," she whispered, then deliberately left the door open on her way out of the room.

The sudden light made him squint, but he slowly came out from his hiding place, thinking: She knows everything, I don't know how, but she does . . . He sat up on the edge of his bed and finally took off his coat and scarf.

Julienne watched him inch his way over to the table, eyes down, lips in a tight line, head bent low. He picked up his fork, but at first, only moved the vegetables from one side of his plate to the other. He struggled with the chicken, nibbling, trying to swallow, but not tasting anything at all. He heard the scrape of a chair next to him and saw the movement of her skirt, and then her hands folded on the table.

"We will speak now," Julienne said.

Frédéric put his fork down and played with his thumbs under the table.

"I wish to know about the watch."

"I found it," he said quietly, watching his own hands on his lap.

"Where?"

"On, on the Pont St. Michel. It was just lying there, and I thought, I had better not tell anyone because, because they might be mad at me. I found it. It's mine."

"So a man lost his watch?"

"Yes. I don't know how, but he lost it and I found it."

"Did you find it on one of the days you did not go to school?"

She does know everything, he thought. "Yes," he said.

"Why did you not go to school?"

He did not answer.

Julienne saw the little lips trembling and his head seemed to bend lower. "Don't you like school?"

He shook his head, slowly.

"Why not?" she asked gently.

"They . . . they don't like me . . . all the, the boys, they don't like me. They make fun of me, of the way I speak . . ." He saw her hand come closer to touch him, but he moved away.

"Why haven't you told me of this . . ."

A hot tear dripped from his eyes, then another, until a stream fell steadily down his pale cheeks. "Brother Laurence, he doesn't like me. Nobody likes me. I hate school. I hate it there."

Julienne tried to touch him, to wipe his eyes, but he would not let her do it. Looking at the watch, she decided to address one problem at a time. "Frédéric, someone must be very upset about the watch. We must go to the police, and we have to say, 'someone lost this.' "

His eyes opened wider.

"And, as Jeannot was with you, he must come with us to the police and tell them what he knows of this."

"NO," Frederic blurted, "no, leave Jeannot alone. He can't come with us, he can't . . . you, you can't tell Jeannot about this."

"Why, what will he do?"

"He told me not to tell anybody because I would get into trouble, and you'd be angry at me, and you are. I, I don't want Jeannot to hate me."

"Frédéric," Julienne said, "I know Jeannot steals. I want the truth now, do you understand?"

She knows everything, he cried inside as his face turned red and the tears continued spilling. "It . . . it wasn't my fault," he wept. "It wasn't. Jeannot, Jeannot made me do it, he made me take it from the man. Don't tell him, please . . ."

She took his hands down from his mouth and wiped his eyes. "Shhh," she whispered, trying hard not to cry in front of him. It was awful and horrible to see him so upset, but he had done something very wrong, and it had to be stopped. "No more now," she said, and wiped his nose with her handkerchief. She steadied herself, then said quietly, "You know it is wrong to steal and to lie, don't you?"

"Yes, I'm sorry, I'm very very sorry . . ."

"You will have to be more than sorry, Frédéric. I see I must take you to school in the morning and meet you there in the . . ."

"NO!" he shrieked, "no, don't come to school, don't." He jumped off the chair. "I'll go every day, I promise, I promise, please don't come to school, they'll laugh at me, they will . . ."

She grabbed him and held him, whispering, "I shan't come to school. I will trust you."

It took him a moment, but he calmed down, sighed, and stepped away from his mother.

"But . . . you cannot keep the things in your treasure box."

He nodded.

"Nor the money, Frédéric. As we do not know who their rightful owners are, we will do the next best thing: Tomorrow we will put *everything* in the Church's poor box."

"You . . . you won't come to school with me?"

"I've already said I wouldn't."

He wiped his nose with his wrist.

Julienne held the handkerchief in front of his eyes. He took it and wiped his nose again. "As a punishment, you shall help Monsieur Mabilleau for a week after school and do whatever job he gives you."

Frédéric nodded, staring at her shoes.

"And, I'm sorry, but I cannot allow you to see Jeannot again." Julienne watched him look at her, first with surprise, then with a terrible sadness when he fully believed her words.

"He . . . he's my friend," Frédéric said, and when she tried to touch his chin, he jerked it away as he began to cry softly.

"A friend would not let you do wrong to yourself or to anyone else," Julienne said.

He missed Jeannot already and knew Jeannot would wait for him tomorrow. Jeannot would wait, all by himself at their meeting spot, and maybe not ever go home.

Without a word, Frédéric walked back to his bed and hid himself in the dark again.

Philippe slouched in the chair by the fireplace and sipped his brandy, watching Edward comb his hair. "I've not seen you—really seen you—for many days now."

Edward looked at him and smiled. "I have things to do."

"What things?" Philippe snickered.

Edward finished combing his hair. "Nothing special," he replied. "I suppose I just want to go out, take a walk, something like that. I need time to think."

"You seem to be doing that a lot lately," Philippe commented.

"So?"

"So I miss you. Is that so strange?" Philippe took another sip of his brandy and tugged at his dressing gown, trying to cover the bare legs stretched out in front of him and dangling over the armrest. "And, Edward, tell me, please, why do I drink alone? Lately, that is all I do. I drink alone. You don't go to the theater with me, you don't laugh with me over late-night suppers, you don't go out with me to find lovely ladies. I am always alone."

"Philippe, you are never alone," Edward chuckled.

He wrinkled his nose at the answer and went back to sulking and staring at the fire. "That is not true. Even in a crowd, I am alone."

Edward straightened his cravat, tugged at his sleeves and strode over to the chair. "*You*," he said, taking the glass from Philippe's hand, "are melancholy because of *this*." He placed it down with a thud on the table next to the chair. "I'll be back in a few hours."

"Ooh-lah," Philippe sighed, "you condemn me yet again."

"You have a friend in your bedroom," Edward said at the door.

"No. I have a woman in my bedroom. My friend stands here, deserting me in my hour of need."

Edward shook his head. "You ought to shave. It will make you feel better."

"You . . . you . . ." Philippe coughed at the closing door. "you English! You have to walk, uhn? Walk all the way to the devil and see if I care . . ."

Edward ignored the ramblings from the bedroom and hummed a song on his way out of the house. It had taken him three days to clear his mind, thinking about himself and his amusements with Philippe, and decide on a different way. In the twilight dream of that remarkable afternoon when so many things were swallowed in a liquored fog, her face remained clear in his mind. It was no struggle at all to remember the beautiful features, the lovely hair, the sound of the anger in her voice. And that magnificent courage. Her husband is a fortunate man, Edward thought.

He was shamed by his foolishness, and all the silly games he had played with Philippe, and on his own. This would not be one of them, he decided. I wronged her. I must say I am sorry and try to right the wrong.

He glanced at the windows of Chavastelon's for a moment, then crossed the street and entered the shop. He remembered the name spoken by that girl, Patenaude, who'd been with Philippe. When he tossed Chavastelon the money, he asked quite simply, "Isabelle Dubord, is she still in your employ?"

"But of course," Chavastelon answered, then snapped his fingers to the starched, dry-looking woman seated at the desk, sending her to find the worker Dubord.

When this Isabelle Dubord appeared from the back room, Edward saw that she looked like all the others, with the same desperate hungry look in her eyes. She seemed disappointed at first, having the fading smile of a child expecting a particular present, only to discover something else in its place. He led her out of the shop, watching as she draped a woolen scarf over her head.

"You have no carriage, Monsieur?"

"No," he said quietly. "I do not wish you to misunderstand me."

"There is no need to explain."

"I only wish to speak with you."

She stared at him, trying to understand.

"I am seeking information about a friend of yours."

She stopped walking. "You are from the police?"

"No," he said. "Perhaps you'd like a hot chocolate or something else to drink on this cold day, and then, we may talk."

"Which friend?" Isabelle asked, suspicious of this Englishman.

"Madame Jeanne Barbier."

Isabelle looked the English Lord over for a moment, thought about it, then shrugged. "I'll have a hot chocolate with you, Monsieur."

She told him there was a café not very far away on the Île St. Louis. And only after several warming sips of the chocolate did she feel like answering any questions. "What would you like to know?"

"Is Madame Barbier well?"

Isabelle shrugged. "I have no way of knowing. I have not seen her since she left, and do not expect to."

"I thought she was your friend," Edward said, nervously tapping the wooden top of the table.

Isabelle grinned slightly. "Friend . . . a good word. We shared some food. Well, that is not exactly true. She shared her food with me, and I shared my wine with her. We spoke a little, but in shops like Chavastelon's," she shook her head at the Englishman's foolishness, "there is not much speaking done during the day."

"Do you know where she lives?"

"No, Monsieur, I am sorry, I do not." Isabelle saw the sudden disappointment come to his eyes. "Someone," she said, much softer, "someone has misled you, Monsieur. I do not know very much about her. Just little things."

He sat there, uncomfortable in the silence. I tried to undo the wrong, he thought. "What things?" he said, more out of ending the silence than out of curiosity.

"She has two children," Isabelle said, watching the Englishman, whose face seemed to cloud with every word.

"Two children," he repeated. "And her husband, what does he do?"

She frowned. "Do? He's dead, what can he do?"

"Oh, I see," Edward said, then opened his eyes. "What?"

"Her husband is dead. What he did before, I don't know, but . . ."

126

"Dead?" Edward sat straight up in his chair.

"You seem pleased at her tragedy," Isabelle said, annoyed.

"Pleased?" Edward said, trying to control the smile on his face. "How can you suggest such an awful thing? A widow, with two children, alone, and now without work? I am certainly *not* pleased. Are you quite sure you don't know where she lives?"

"Somewhere in that area," she said, jerking her chin toward the Left Bank. "She mentioned to me her landlady cared for her daughter during the day while she worked in the shop."

"A little daughter," he smiled.

"Yes, Gisèle," Isabelle said, wondering about this strange man. "And a son, in school. Frédéric."

"A son . . ." He smiled again. "What else?"

"Nothing else," Isabelle said. "She shops, she works, she takes her children to the park on Sundays, what else do you expect from the kind of life we live?"

"Which park?" he asked quickly.

"How should I know?" Isabelle said, then drained her hot chocolate, suddenly feeling her wrist in the tight grip of the Englishman's hand.

"This is very important to me," he said, his eyes pleading to her eyes. "I must know. Try to remember."

Isabelle had to look away from him and stared for a long time at the grains of wood on the tabletop. "She liked the music . . . and she liked to play with her children, and buy them little candies . . . I remember now. Jardin du Luxembourg. Every Sunday."

Edward loosened his grip, then let his fingers lightly travel from her wrist to the swollen aching fingers of her hand. He kissed her fingers and said, "Thank you." He reached into his waistcoat pocket, then pressed three gold Louis into Isabelle Dubord's palm before he stood up.

"I cannot, Monsieur. I've done nothing for . . ."

"It is a gift," he said, leaning his palms on the table. "You've no idea how much this means to me."

Isabelle smiled. "Oh, I've some idea, Monsieur."

The air in the room was stale and dry as Frédéric sat with rounded shoulders. He stared down at the blank paper in front of him on the desk he shared with two other boys. The recitations by the class were in a perfect rhythm, a numbing monotonous sound, but he only mouthed the answers and did not speak, barely moving his lips.

He did not hear his name, but was jolted out of his thoughts of Jeannot when Brother Laurence smacked his desk with the wooden pointer. Frédéric jumped and sat up straight.

"Barbier," Brother Laurence repeated, the long dark cassock in front of the boy's eyes. "Did they not teach you your numbers in your other school?"

Frédéric heard muffled snickers. He looked up. "Yes, Brother Laurence."

"What is the answer, then?"

Frédéric hung his head. "I, I don't know."

"You are stupid, then, is that the reason?"

"I, I did not hear the question, Brother Laurence."

"So you are deaf as well, uhn? Stupid boy," Brother Laurence said and smacked the desk a second time. "Stupid boy. What are three twelves?"

Frédéric shook his head.

"Answer me," Brother Laurence ordered.

"Twenty-four," Frédéric sputtered.

"No," he said, then turned to the class. "You see what they teach little boys in Alsace? You must be grateful you live in Paris, my children. Bretillot," he called out, not having to turn around. "Tell Barbier what are three twelves."

"Thirty-six, Brother Laurence."

He nodded to the shivering Barbier. "You see, it can be done. But you must work to know the answers, and you, Barbier, do not work. You are a lazy, stupid boy, but I will teach you. You will write the tables over and over until you learn them, until you are able to say them perfectly. Begin writing, Barbier. You do not deserve to be in my class, but I will make you learn. You are not in Alsace now, you are in Paris, and in Paris little boys learn their tables. Write, Barbier, and write clearly, one mistake and I rip it up."

Frédéric dipped his pen in the inkwell and, with a shaking hand, worked as he had been ordered to do for the rest of the afternoon. When Brother Laurence dismissed the class, the cold air in the halls chilled Frédéric terribly, and he sneezed.

He walked alone, separate from the boys who chided him and said his name just loud enough for him to hear. "The Alsatian," they called him, and others said, "Stupid Alsatian peasant boy . . ."

He came to the gate and was about to turn left when he heard his name again, but it was a different voice, a friend's voice. He whirled around to find Jeannot, leaning against the wall and biting his right thumbnail. "Where were you?" Jeannot said, spitting out the nail sliver.

Frédéric could not find the words and stepped closer to Jeannot.

"Well?" Jeannot said. "I waited for you. What happened to you yesterday?"

Frédéric shook his head. "I, I couldn't," he finally said, ashamed to look into the eyes of his friend.

"Why did you make me wait all afternoon for you?"

Horrible visions of Jeannot waiting and waiting in the cold came to Frédéric's mind. "I couldn't," he repeated. "I had to promise my mother . . . She, she found the watch."

"WHAT?" Jeannot shrieked, then quickly looked around to make sure no one else had heard, that there were no spies from the police there, that no one would take him to prison. He stepped closer to Frédéric and grabbed the shoulders of the boy's coat. "Idiot," Jeannot snarled and shook him. "Idiot, idiot, I told you not to keep it, I told you it would be trouble, why didn't you listen to me . . ." Jeannot kept shaking Frédéric back and forth. The panic grew, the panic made his eyes wild, the panic made him afraid of the prisons and what would happen to him there. "I should never have trusted you, never, never," Jeannot said, suddenly hating Frédéric. "I'll kill you for this, I'll kill you, you stupid idiot!"

Frédéric pulled free, shaking and backing away from the anger, the yelling, the wild eyes, and the terrible names. "She's not going to tell," he screamed, as he started to run away from Jeannot. "She said she wouldn't tell, she won't tell . . ." he wailed before he rounded the corner.

Jeannot only shook his head. "Idiot," he breathed, "of course she will. They all do." He walked away from the school, deciding it wasn't safe for him there anymore. Frédéric was not a good partner because he did not obey instructions. He cannot be trusted, Jeannot thought. He looked back one more time at the corner. Go home to your Mama, Frédéric. I don't need you. I don't need anyone. I can find another friend just like that, he thought, with a snap of his fingers, then walked quickly to the Boulevard St. Jacques and disappeared.

"Why must I play with them?" Gisèle complained, turning her eyes up toward her mother.

Julienne re-tied the woolen hat under the child's chin. "You make it sound like a terrible punishment," she smiled. "I thought you wished to play with them. They see you here every Sunday, and I think they want to be friends with you. Wouldn't it be nice to have a friend or two?'

Gisèle shook her head, then turned her eyes to the ground.

It is always the same, Julienne thought, she is so frightened of anything new. Julienne shaded her eyes and looked back down the bright snowy path in the Jardin du Luxembourg, watching the group of three little girls, standing and waiting for Gisèle. "I think they want to make snowballs and throw them at tree trunks, just like you used to do."

"And will it be all right to make snowballs today?"

"Yes," Julienne sighed, "but try not to get too wet. Your brother caught cold from getting his feet too wet the other day."

"But . . ." Gisèle pouted, "but what if I cannot throw the snowballs as far as they can?"

"Do your best."

"Maybe, maybe I will play with them," Gisèle said.

"Good," Julienne smiled. "I shall be here, walking the large square path," she said, indicating the path that banked the frozen pond and, after it, the snow-covered lawn and flower beds directly behind the Palais Luxembourg. "You stay here, Gisèle, and go nowhere else."

Gisèle smiled.

"And later, we shall go to the café and drink some hot chocolate."

The child nodded, then half-walked, half-skidded to the girls building a wall.

It was a cold day, and when Julienne finally neared the massive grey shadow of the Palais Luxembourg, she felt much colder in the shade of the building and drew the woolen cloak tighter around her.

I suppose it was silly of me, she thought, a job, to work at something, and in such a terrible place. I shall not do that again, she decided. I must accept my life as it is. It is what I chose, and what I wished for.

"Madame Barbier?"

The voice of the man was familiar. She stopped walking and turned around to see the tall gentleman removing his hat.

"I, I hope I am not intruding on your afternoon walk," he said.

"Not at all, Monsieur," she replied. "The Park, as you see, is open to everyone." The face was clean-shaven, and his eyes were no longer bloodshot and half-closed by wine. It surprised her that the haunting deep blue color of his eyes had managed to stay in her mind.

"You do not remember me," he said, a blush of relief coming to the pale cheeks.

"On the contrary," Julienne replied, "I remember you very well, Lord Harlaxton."

His eyes drifted to his hat and he touched the brim of it with gloved hands. He cleared his throat, then said, "I was hoping you would not remember."

"You made a rather strong impression, Monsieur."

"Yes," he said, glancing from the hat in his hands to her eyes, "and I am embarrassed for it, and more sorry than I am able to express." He tried to smile, a boy's smile, making two sharp dimples on the handsome face, adding to the constant dimple in his chin. "I am truly very sorry, Madame."

His smile was warm, but the sound of his voice and the look in his eyes made her uneasy. He means what he is saying, she thought, not like the false and empty apologies given by Franz—this one acknowledges his own wrong-doing. And his eyes, she thought, they have a sadness to them, a subtle tenderness and pain. "Thank you," she finally said, yet taking a step away from him. "And I hope you have a most pleasant afternoon walk."

"May I walk with you?"

"Why?"

The question surprised him. "To speak with you, to tell you how sorry I am."

"But you've already done that, Monsieur," Julienne said. Suddenly feeling the terrible chill of the winter shade, she began walking out of the shadow toward the warmer sunlight.

"Not nearly enough, Madame," Edward said, keeping pace with her. "After all, it was I who cost you your position at Chavastelon's."

"Only in part," she said. "Chavastelon himself must share the blame."

"Yes," Edward pressed, "but surely there must be something I might do, to make amends for my own share of the blame."

"You've said you were sorry and that is more than enough for me," Julienne answered, keeping her eyes straight ahead, yet very aware of his strides next to her.

Edward sighed. "I think, Madame, your forgiveness is held only in words."

She stared at him. "What can you mean by that, Monsieur?" she said with an edge to her voice.

"They are only words," he answered. "But you do not really mean to forgive me, or allow me a way of showing you how sorry I am for costing you your position. That is simple enough to understand."

"Simple enough for a shop-girl, you mean," Julienne said with narrowed eyes.

"I never said that," Edward replied, turning to her.

"But you meant it, didn't you?"

"No, not at all," he said quietly. "You see," he added with an engaging smile, "you *are* angry with me."

She was forced to smile. "No, I am not. I am rather glad to be rid of Chavastelon, in a strange sort of way."

"Why?"

Julienne shook her head. "It . . . it is much too complicated to explain."

"Too complicated for a drunkard to understand?" Edward said quickly.

"I never said that," Julienne answered, turning to him again.

"But you meant it, didn't you?" he grinned.

"Uh . . . no, I, I meant it is too private a matter."

"Fair enough," he nodded, then looked away from her. They walked silently for a time, down a path with deserted grey benches covered with snow.

He is a curious man, Julienne thought, feeling very confused. The quality of his voice is sweet and encourages conversation; his smile is quick and open and enchanting; he has an expressive, handsome face, a pleasing manner, and is so totally different from our last meeting. But which man is the true man, she wondered. "You speak French very well," Julienne said, finding it necessary to fill the silence as they neared the end of the walk.

"The result of a 'gentleman's education,' " he said. "I learnt it as a child, soon after Philippe's first visit to England." He sighed. "That seems more than a lifetime ago."

"Philippe?"

"Yes," Edward said, "my childhood friend, You've met him," he said, then paused and blushed with embarrassment. "At uh, at . . ."

"Ahhh," Julienne grinned smartly. "The other one."

Edward laughed slightly. "Yes, the other one. The Marquis de Roquetanière."

"A fine citizen," she quipped.

"And a bored one."

She saw the expression change in his eyes. "And is Lord Harlaxton a bored English citizen?"

"No," he said, then added softly, "please, never call me that." He looked away for a moment. "My name is Edward. Edward Atherton-Moore. I don't use that title."

"But it is yours, isn't it?"

"Well, it is, but it isn't. At least, I've never felt it to be mine. It . . . it belonged to someone else."

She saw Gisèle waving to her and waved back as they stood in the cold. "All titles belonged to someone else, unless they are created," she said casually.

He looked at her again, very puzzled by her knowledge. "You're quite right," he said. "My brother's title was Harlaxton."

"And you must be the second son, to inherit from him," she said.

Edward blinked. "How . . . how did you know that?"

Julienne was flustered by her mistake. "A guess. You said his title *was* Harlaxton. There could be no other way, Monsieur. After all, I read books and newspapers, like anyone else in our world. It it is not unusual knowledge."

131

His stare was an unbroken one. It was a logical answer, he thought, but the casualness, that certainty of knowledge, had been so unexpected. It was as if she'd known such things all her life.

"I must be going now," Julienne said. "Thank you for your apology."

The little girl strolled closer. She had the same coloring, the same eyes, the same hair as her mother. "That must be Gisèle," he said, looking at the child walking on the path.

"Yes," Julienne answered, then widened her eyes at him. "How did you know my daughter's name?"

A fear surfaced in her eyes and he watched as she stepped back from him, as if to protect herself. "It is nothing, Madame," Edward said calmly, trying to put her at her ease again. "I've been trying to find you for a week's time now. I was told you are a widow with two children, Frédéric and Gisèle, and that you often come here on Sundays. Isabelle Dubord told me. You needn't be afraid of me, Madame Barbier, I know nothing more of you."

"I'm sorry," she stammered. She tried to smile. "I realize it must have been Isabelle. I cannot imagine what I must have been thinking." Julienne felt her cheeks redden again. Gisèle tugged at her skirt and she placed her hand on the child's shoulder. "I really must be going."

She seemed to be drifting back from him, a shadowy woman disappearing further into an unknown place with every step she took. In desperation, Edward looked to the child and suddenly had an idea. "Hello, Gisèle," he said, and bent down to take her tiny hand in his own. "My name is Edward, and your mother and I have had a most pleasant conversation."

Gisèle wrinkled her nose at him, liking the way he bent down to talk to her, but still partly hid herself behind her mother's cloak. "Where are you from?" she asked, hearing something strange and different in his voice.

"England," Edward said. "Do you know where that is?"

She slowly shook her head, fascinated by the look of him.

"I shall send you a map, then, and you shall see for yourself where my country is. It is, I must say, quite a distance from here." He squeezed the wet mitten in his hand. "You've been playing with the snow, haven't you?"

"Yes," she said, watching the funny crinkles at the corners of his very blue eyes.

"And what game did you play?"

"Castles," she said, amazed at his questions. "And I threw snowballs at the army."

"Did you, now," he said. "Good for you. And did the army run away, or break into the castle?"

"They ran away," Gisèle said, smiling, taking a step out from behind the skirt. "Do you know that game?"

"Oh, very well," he said. "I used to play that game when I was a child. You must be cold," he smiled. "You ought to have something warm to drink."

"Mama promised me a hot chocolate."

"What a splendid idea," Edward said quickly. He stood up and smiled broadly at a very surprised Madame Barbier. "And I invite you both to join me at the most wonderful place directly across the street. I do think, Madame

Barbier, we ought to go there now, as the child is so cold. A hot chocolate would be just the thing to warm her."

"Please, Mama," Gisèle asked, tugging on the cloak. "Please, may we go?"

"And of course, a little sweet," Edward said, not waiting for Jeanne Barbier's reply. "After all, defending a castle in the snow from an attacking army is exhausting work. My apologies for hurrying you, Madame," he said, taking Gisèle's hand and beginning to walk, "but it is turning colder and the child does need her hot chocolate."

Julienne took Gisèle's other hand and managed a tight smile. "Clever," she whispered, "very clever."

The boyish grin warmed and he winked.

After several long strides, Gisèle complained, "You walk too fast, I can't, I'm tired."

Edward stopped walking and peered down at the little girl looking up at him. "I'm sorry," he said. "I forgot I am so much taller than you," he said softly, bending down. "Are you very cold and tired?"

She shivered a nod.

"I am a very strong fellow," he smiled, "and I promise you we shall arrive at Pons ever-so-much faster, little Mademoiselle Barbier, if you will allow me to carry you."

"Really," Julienne began, "I don't think that is . . ."

"Yes," Gisèle said, opening her arms.

Julienne stared at the child. This is impossible, she thought. Gisèle? Gisèle allowing a stranger to be near her? Gisèle actually speaking about her games to a stranger? Is this the same Gisèle that one hour ago had to be prodded to play in the snow with other little girls? What kind of magic is this? What kind of man is this who bends down to talk to a child, face to face, and apologizes to a five-year-old for walking too fast and speaks so sweetly to a shy little girl? What kind of terrible man is this?

He picked Gisèle up with ease.

"You are so tall," she squeaked.

He hugged her slightly, properly. "Six-feet-two. I suppose that is very tall, isn't it?"

"Yes," she said.

Edward smiled at Madame Barbier and had the good sense not to look too pleased with himself. "Shall we go then, to Pons? 'Tisn't far, as I've said. And I did rather promise the child . . ."

It wasn't a long walk. And inside the parlor, the green and white marble circular stairway led to the second floor of Pons, a most respectable establishment where good families brought their children on Sundays or young women met their friends in the afternoons during the week. The small, octagonal wooden tables had glass insets and were just the right size for intimate conversations. They sat near the windows which gave a marvelous view of the Jardin du Luxembourg's ornate black iron gates, looking very cold in the fading sunlight. And beyond the gates, the bare trees with snow clustered on the near-purple bare branches looked darker when the sun had gone and snow flurries began to fall.

He is a strange man, Julienne thought, stirring her hot chocolate in her cup. He nearly disowns his title, doesn't he? I've disowned mine, she thought, but for reasons. I wonder what *his* reasons could be? And look at him, she thought, speaking to Gisèle the way he does. It isn't false. He tells her stories and chats with her and entertains her with a genuine kindness. Children know when they are being lied to—and when someone is being kind. How does such a man come to be—no, better not to know, she decided.

"Have you ever been to India, Madame Barbier?" Edward repeated, waiting patiently as her eyes lost their glazed private look and her expression sharpened.

"I'm sorry," she said, putting the cup down on the saucer. "I did not mean to be rude."

He let it pass and said simply, "I was speaking of India. And I was telling Gisèle I'd spent some time there, in the Army. I wondered if you had ever traveled to such a faraway place."

"No," she answered.

"It has all sorts of strange and wonderful animals," he continued, looking at them both. "Elephants and tigers, snakes and monkeys, and beautiful, beautiful birds."

"Snakes," Julienne shivered.

"Yes," he intoned.

"I saw two elephants in the Zoo," Gisèle said.

"Did you, now?" Edward smiled.

"They're very big," she said.

"Quite." He turned to face Madame Barbier. "When we arrived in Madras, the place at which I was stationed, we had to leave the steamship by rowboat, and be rowed onto the beach."

"How dangerous," Julienne said.

"Yes, it was. Not as bad as rounding the Cape, though. That was simply awful."

"How long a time did you spend in India?"

Edward's expression changed slightly, as if he'd suddenly remembered something. He drank the last of his hot chocolate, then looked steadily at the beautiful Madame Barbier. "We used to say: 'not a very long time, and yet, too long a time.' " He dabbed the linen napkin at his mouth and watched as Gisèle finished the pastry on her dish. "Eight years," he said, noticing the child seemed to fight back a yawn. "She's tired. If you're ready, I'll see you home."

"You needn't . . ." Julienne began, then saw the surprised hurt look come back to his eyes. "Yes, thank you," she said, reconsidering. "We live nearby."

He paid the bill and held the warm hand of the little girl as they walked down the winding stairs. Outside, she held her arms up to him. He picked her up again as they walked toward the Boulevard St. Michel.

"Why did you leave India?" Julienne asked.

He sighed, the cold air streaming from his mouth and that sad look returning to his eyes. "I resigned my commission along with a friend," he said quietly.

"But . . ."

He shook his head and pleaded silently. "Not today," he said finally. "This has been the most wonderful afternoon I've ever had in Paris. It, it isn't the time for unpleasantness."

She felt shamed by her questions. "I did not mean to pry. I apologize," Julienne said, and looked away from him, leaving his secrets to himself.

They walked quietly in the snowfall and turned onto Rue Royer Collard. When she stopped in front of a building, he put Gisèle down and took Madame Barbier's arm, but she gently withdrew it.

"I shan't forget my promise about the map," he began. "And, for the other matter, we'll speak again," he said, his voice making it nearly a question. "On another day, perhaps, I shall speak of it." He looked first at the ground, and then back at her. "Perhaps, a quiet talk during an afternoon tea at Pons? I assure you, it is most respectable and no one would disapprove of your meeting me there, you would not be embarrassed or . . ."

"I have been to Pons before," Julienne said, "and I know of its reputation."

"Will you consider it?"

"Perhaps," she said, opening the door to the apartment house. He reached for her hand and kissed the top of her gloved fingers lightly.

"When?" he said.

Julienne looked away. "I thank you for your kindness to my daughter. But this is quite improper and I shall not make such a decision whilst standing in a doorway on the street. Goodnight, Monsieur."

CHAPTER
8

Why did I speak of India, Edward thought, rattled and walking quickly through the snowfall as if the speed would leave the gathering furies behind him. The past belongs to the past, he told himself, let it rest; let it stay buried; never look back, never, never. The child, he thought, quickening his strides. I did it to delight the child with stories.

A gust of wind blew his hat off by the Rue de Rivoli, but he did not stop to retrieve it, trying to outrun his own memories. He saw an empty cab coming toward him on the opposite side of the boulevard and frantically waved both arms.

"Yes, Monsieur?"

"Number Five, Avenue de la Reine Hortense," he said after a breath, and jumped inside the cab, shivering and then leaning against the side.

Philippe, he thought, feeling the wound inside him opening, I need Philippe.

Philippe will want to laugh and drink and that will drive the specters from my mind. He had done this before. Four months earlier, he'd come to Philippe. He'd disobeyed his father's explicit instructions and ran away to Philippe to finally end the pain in his mind.

He paid the driver, then walked in front of the large Palais where he was staying, as Philippe's houseguest.

It looked odd in the snow, like an ornament for a cake, he thought. In daylight, the stone had a creamy look to it with its carved balconies and arches, and highly decorated windows and gargoyles laughing down with frozen eyes at the courtyard. But in the snow it looked almost artificial, an ancestral town palace carved out of buttercream and ice on the Parc Monceau. He held onto the wrought-iron rails and peered through the gold-colored spearheads that lined the top of the fence and stared at the courtyard, seeing grey slate, wet and paled by the snow. His tired eyes drifted up the three stories and then looked at the much plainer fourth story, the servants' quarters.

The relief dissipated and the panic came back when he thought that Philippe might be out visiting people or carousing or meeting girls of the Corps de Ballet. He pulled the gate open and ran the length of the courtyard, then climbed the fourteen small steps to the main entrance.

"I was hoping you'd be home tonight," Edward said from the doorway to the study, feeling the warmth beginning to thaw his skin.

Philippe opened his sleepy eyes and turned in his chair. "You look terrible," he said and tried to stand up, but staggered. "And I cannot see why," he slurred, "come closer."

Edward shut the door behind him and stepped closer to Philippe.

"My God," Philippe breathed, "what has happened to you? You're soaked. Come sit by the fire before you die from the cold."

"Doesn't matter," Edward shrugged, and let Philippe fumble with his coat.

"Take some brandy to warm you," Philippe said, offering his own glass.

A shiver helped his decision. Sitting on the floor by the fire, Edward pulled off his boots and warmed his cold feet. Philippe tossed him a cushion from the chair and kept refilling his glass.

After a time, the room slowly began to look brighter, and Edward felt so warm by the fire that sweat began to drip from his forehead. Philippe looked strange and silly, slumped in the chair, chatting about the new girls in the Corps de Ballet. The calm is wonderful, Edward thought, easy and familiar and wonderful. He tried to focus his eyes and saw that his glass was empty. He squinted and saw that Philippe had the decanter. Edward struggled to sit up from the floor, his elbow slipped. He tried again. Another drink, he thought, then said quite naturally, "Trāgutaku emina immu."

Philippe convulsed in laughter. "What did you say?"

"I said, give me something to drink."

"No," Philippe said, "no, you didn't. You spoke something else. What talk is that? Are you so drunk you invent a new language?"

"What did I say?" Edward asked, feeling his smile paling.

"Trāgu—something," Philippe managed.

The tears welled up in Edward's eyes. It's coming back, I'm not drunk enough to stop it or make them go away . . .

Philippe watched Edward cover his ears and eyes to shut out the sounds and sights of the room. He stumbled out of the chair and crawled over to Edward. "What is it, Edward, Edward," he said, trying to pull his friend's arms down, "tell me what's wrong?"

"Jesus, Jesus, help me, they've come back," he cried, "the faces, all their faces, the ghosts . . ."

"Who? What ghosts? Edward, my dear friend, the brandy has made you morbid."

Edward shook his head. "I can't bear it, I can't, do something, make it stop, make them go away . . ."

Philippe tried to think, and then remembered the other bottle. "Yes, yes, I know what to do," he said and staggered over to the cabinet.

Edward felt the hands a moment later.

"Come," Philippe said, "sit up. I've an old friend here. A good friend who will make it go far away. It has worked for you before. Open your eyes, Edward."

Edward opened them and saw the cut-glass decanter in Philippe's hand. The ruby-red color seemed alive and moving inside the large, slender decanter bottle.

"Do you remember this friend?"

Edward took a deep breath and stopped crying.

"You remember, don't you? When you first came to stay with me, and you could not sleep, we took this many, many times."

Edward was mesmerized by the red liquid.

"I don't have a teaspoon," Philippe sighed. "We'll . . . we'll have to approximate, then. Give me your glass."

Edward reached behind him and gave Philippe the brandy glass.

"Yes," Philippe said, pulling the glass stopper out of the decanter, "the genii from the bottle to chase all the phantoms away." He poured with an unsteady hand, first a trickle, then a steady stream until the glass had roughly two ounces in it. Philippe stared at the glass with blurry eyes, trying to measure, then gave it up and poured a little more. "Beautiful color," he murmured. "Look at it. It is just beautiful. Poppy wine, special wine, dearest friend, Laudanum."

"I remember," Edward mumbled.

"This supply is very good," Philippe said, pouring himself a portion of the Laudanum. "It isn't as diluted as the other one was. It is much stronger. Drink, Edward. Let the genii make you calm."

Edward brought the glass to his lips, drank, then took a long second swallow. "I . . . I can't taste anything."

"It has a strong taste, what do you mean you can't taste anything?" Philippe demanded.

"My mouth is numb and I cannot taste anything."

Philippe sighed. "Small wonder. You're *already* drunk. That is the brandy's doing, you idiot."

"I suppose," Edward said.

"Let us make a toast," Philippe said, bringing his glass to Edward's. "To de Quincey," he smiled, "our spiritual father."

Edward clicked his glass against Philippe's, then drank again. De Quincey, he thought, the opium-eater. He stared dully at the empty glass. Opium. Tincture of opium. Laudanum was just another name for it, he knew. He leaned heavily against Philippe for a moment, then took his pillow and stretched out in front of the fireplace, watching the flames.

They grew larger. At some point later they grew brighter and larger still, sharp and clear and as rich as drawing room curtains, they grew up and out of the fireplace. Yet nothing burned. The colors of the flames began to melt together, forming parting curtains with large endless stretches of blackness opening between them. Rich blackness, empty blackness that suddenly sharpened into tall trees and cobblestoned pathways; a building grew from nothing, a fountain appeared. He knew. He recognized it immediately. Oxford.

No, he thought, I shan't think of it, I shan't remember it . . . but his voice was without panic and, though he tried, he could not control the people in the mist taking real shape as the paintings came to life.

He saw himself turn a corner and there, sitting under a tree was John Sherringham, his brown hair tousled and a bit too long, like Byron; sparkling devilish eyes that took on a life of their own; a large square jaw; a nose a shade too large for his face; a wide, crooked grin and that laugh, hearty and full.

Edward saw him speaking but no sound came from his lips. The trees darkened and changed into wooden columns. Beams grew from them, a white-washed ceilng appeared and then, a wooden table.

"My father's Viscount Sherringham, of Worcester," he said. He seemed to grow out of the darkness from the candle flame flickering on the table.

"Mine's a peer also," Edward said.

Sherringham laughed. "Aren't you modest, as if we didn't know. Harlaxton, that's you. I've heard of you. Marquess Harlaxton, and your father's Duke of Middlesex. Mine's a peer also," Sherringham mimicked and laughed again. "But you don't fancy the title Harlaxton, do you, so you've said."

Edward's face appeared from the blackness. "Quite right."

"I shall call you 'Ted.' "

"I shan't answer to it," Edward replied.

"Why not? It's a perfectly respectable name for Edward, as you don't care much for Harlaxton."

"My brother called me Ted," Edward replied as his face began to disappear.

"Ahh, and he's dead now, isn't he?"

"For quite some time."

"All right then," Sherringham said, gazing deep into the face. "I shouldn't want to upset you. I like you. You're not like them, the toady boys who come here and have no imagination. Neddy. Yes, I rather like that. Neddy."

Edward did not answer.

"Will you respond to it? I mean, shall I look a fool, shall I be a toady boy, calling out to you on these decrepit paths, 'Neddy, Neddy,' and not have you answer me?"

He felt the blackness smile.

"Good. I'm glad I shan't look a fool, then," Sherringham smiled. "You like it, don't you? I'll call you something else if you'd rather . . ."

"I like it."

"Then Neddy it is."

Time seemed to bend and press itself into more curtains as silhouetted people sat in lectures and laughed around a table at dinner. Sherringham sat in the center, telling funny stories about Italy and amusing his friends. Edward tried to listen, but the sound was far away and muted as he felt himself drifting through the red Laudanum veils.

At ten o'clock, Sherringham left, excusing himself with wide exaggerated grins and secret winks, letting the toady boys believe what they wished about his plans for the evening.

He did it all the time. They'd gather, laugh and drink and tell stories, and at precisely ten o'clock, John Sherringham would leave.

The friends grew quiet, and the vista changed to the paths of Oxford town late at night; trees rustling, the air cold and black. Edward knew it was later, months later, and he was following to see what John Sherringham was up to. Winding paths became cropped and shaped hedges as a church bell chimed and John Sherringham whistled "Rule Britannia" as he strode toward a building in the distance.

Edward hid himself and saw John Sherringham push up a window and climb in, leaving it partly open. Edward felt the blackness follow as he, himself, climbed in moments later. It was a hallway, with an open door at the far end. A building, in one of the colleges. He felt his way along the walls and pushed the door slightly. Stairs. Small, spiraling, wooden stairs leading to the basement. Edward tried to be quiet and crept down the stairs, holding onto the railing.

A door opened at the bottom, then a light was struck.

There were sounds from inside the deserted storeroom and, as he sat on the bottom step, he could see Sherringham in profile, lit by a single candle at the far end of the room.

There was a glow to his face, a soft and loving expression Edward had never seen before. Sherringham took off his coat, and stripped to the waist, then ran his hand over his smooth, muscular, hairless chest.

Edward could see his eyes, wide-open, burning with a passion Sherringham had never before shown to anyone. He was speaking softly, in a caressing, sensual tone of voice.

A woman, Edward thought. He's hidden a woman, his lover, in the storeroom. But the dream remembered the truth.

Sounds came from the storeroom, warming-up sounds. Rapid scales.

Edward felt the blackness leave the landing and move closer to the door, it changed his view of the storeroom.

Sounds . . . beautiful, gifted sounds came from the room as Sherringham

139

performed one complicated piece after another. Mozart, Chopin, Beethoven, Bach, Handel . . . hours of the Laudanum-vision stretched to infinity as Sherringham made his own private love to the piano.

Edward watched the receding vision, an exhausted man standing up, sweaty and tired, a chest breathing hard and glistening, yet, he was the vision of peace. A hand, Sherringham's hand, strong, finely shaped, touched the piano. It was gentle, a lover's parting, with words spoken later, quietly in the stairwell.

"I knew it was you. I would play for you, Neddy."

"Why?"

"Because you understand what it is to have a life's dream. You had one yourself, from childhood." Sherringham's kind face began to disappear from him and Edward desperately tried to control the Laudanum and make it come back, but the narcotic had a mind of its own.

"You are my truest friend," Sherringham was saying from some dark tunnel leading to another place. "I needn't hide anything from you. You are the most honest, most genuine understanding man I ever met. You know my fears, my pleasures, my thoughts. I joke with the others, but with you, I may really talk. With you, I may open my mind, and share all of myself."

"You wrote the last few compositions, didn't you?"

"Yes, I did." In the fading grey, he smiled. "You know almost everything now."

"Has no one ever told you how truly gifted you are? And that it is sinful to hide your talent?"

He saw Sherringham's brown eyes clouding in the darkening vision. "I knew you would understand. I . . . I want so much to . . . I knew you wouldn't ridicule me, like my father." The eyes were half-shrouded in pain.

"John, you have such talent, how sad that . . . "

"That I am not able to use it, yes," Sherringham managed. "It is a torment, a haunting, help me, Neddy . . ."

The shift was sudden, abrupt and brutal in the change. A downhill sleigh ride from a dizzy height and a sharp, hot fall. Brown faces appeared, and men stood at attention; sweaty horses with their riders were in a perfect precision as the drill fields opened up and the shadow of the encampment rose up behind them from the deadened dusty earth. Tall trees were in the distance, and the calls of wild birds mixed with a language not his own.

"Tupākulanu bhujamulapai pattandi."

Edward watched as the separate Madras Native Army shouldered their arms, ready for the daily drill.

All their faces came clear: the Sergeant Major "Belfast Jack," the Captains, the Lieutenants, and Sherringham . . . consorting with Indians, fascinated by their music and instruments, always asking questions and seeking to learn a new musical expression in this hot and strange land.

The pressure in Edward's mind increased, his heart began to pound harder and harder until the accelerating beat was the only sound the Laudanum would allow.

The faces changed rapidly in time with the heartbeats.

Hollow-faced children, the dead of Orissa, Sherringham standing at attention before the Colonel trying to explain, the Indian moneylender shaking his head in his kampong in the village as he held out a brown hand, crooked and bent with arthritic knuckles.

The scandal destroyed a childhood dream, and in his mind, the whirlpool of images continued—Sherringham's father would not make good the debt. Edward resigned his commission along with Sherringham, honor was satisfied, and they returned to London. Sherringham would live only three years more, virtually disowned by his father.

They sat in the Solicitor's office. Sherringham could taste his freedom, to do as he wished, to pursue his music, all would be well now that his wretched father had died.

But the Solicitor's fat and sweaty face promised no hope.

"No," Edward called out, "no, don't read it . . . don't read the will . . . " The Laudanum turned vicious and its sudden cruelty colored the already horrible words:

" . . . as John is irresponsible, a drunkard, a disappointment to me from the day of his birth, my revenues and the contents of my several houses are not required by law to pass to him. But I give them to him, provided no new additions are made: He is *not*, under any circumstances, to add any musical instruments to his possessions. Should he do so, all allowances will be permanently severed. He is not to travel to the Continent. Should he do so, all allowances will be permanently severed. He will have his ancestral lands— which he will not be permitted to sell, as I am not permitted to sell. They are in trust for his son, should he surprise us all and marry, providing the family with legitimate issue.

"His obsession with music has led him to consort with unsavory persons, and has been my cross in life. Even now, there is no rest or peace, and my responsibilities to my son do not end with my death. He must learn to behave. He must learn this lesson, or forfeit all."

Sherringham was a man without hope, trapped by comfort and money as the grand furnished houses became silk and satin cages. He detested his own weakness, hated himself and died a little more inside with each passing day.

Edward watched that night come back. Standing in the shadows of the Laudanum dream, he watched the four people, drunk and disorderly, steal a rowboat from a dock in the slums of East London.

"It will be fun," Sherringham said cryptically. "An adventure."

"No," Edward said.

"You're too drunk to see the fun," Sherringham insisted with a peculiar smile. "The Thames is perfectly calm. Pretend we're at Oxford."

The rowboat rocked and with oars in hand, Sherringham began to guide them out to the center of the river as he whistled "Rule Britannia."

A winding river, a deceitful river, the Laudanum made it more alive than ever . . . it slithered and breathed and began to buffet the small boat.

"We should not be doing this," Edward said.

Sherringham laughed. "All right then, do you wish me to turn back? Well, do you? My God, Neddy, I have never met anyone such as you. You haven't a smile in you. Shall I turn back, tell me, and tell the ladies, shall we all turn back and settle in for another boring evening and grow another day older by the doing?"

"Yes," Edward managed, hearing the giggles of the barmaids they'd bought for the evening. "Well . . . "

"Ahh, you're not sure, are you, Neddy?" He stood up.

"Don't do that!" Edward shouted.

"Christ, you sound just like my father. Don't do this, don't do that. I shan't suffer that from you. I'll do whatever I damn well please to do, at least here, at least here and now I'll do what I please . . ."

"John, sit down, for God's sake, sit down!"

"NO!"

The girls, as drunk as he, stood up with him, laughing and doing a silly dance as they tried to step closer to the bow. The boat pitched and swayed with them.

"I just don't care anymore," Sherringham laughed.

The small boat, in one long horrifying moment, overturned as the black water swallowed them all. The cold surrounded him, and as Edward surfaced, he heard the scream that haunted his every waking moment:

"NEDDY! HELP . . ."

He couldn't see, he could barely keep himself afloat. The dock piles were so far away and the Laudanum made them alive, pushing him back, as the water, like grabbing hands, pulled and tried to drown him. An arm crooked around his neck. A woman's arm. He kicked and fought the tangled skirt, swallowing much water, the black water from the black night as he tried to turn her around, then swam for the piles that seemed to be forever out of his reach. Stroke after stroke, he fought the water's deadly enticing pull.

He grabbed for the thick piles and held on, hauling the woman out of the water with him. She sputtered, coughed, and only then began a drawn-out moaning cry.

The night was quiet . . . too quiet. He heard only the woman and the ripples of the hungry water lapping at their bodies against the dockpiles. "JOHN!"

But there was no answer.

They called it "The Grace of Wapping," where the body washed up with the morning tide, on the stairs next to the old execution dock, a place reserved for pirates and smugglers hung in chains until three tides had cleansed and drowned their sins along with their bodies.

The Grace of Wapping. A grace that the body should be found at all, they said. The Thames has a way of hiding her victims for eternity.

The colorless face stared up at him from the flames. Sherringham's sad brown eyes, swollen and open, looked at him with a stunned amazement.

And in the Laudanum state they called "dog sleep," he heard himself screaming.

❧

Julienne passed by the window and casually watched the few solitary figures walk to some unknown destination. She lingered, expecting a taller, thinner man to be there amongst the shadows. What am I doing, she thought, and quickly closed the curtains. Sometimes, my silliness surprises even me. How absurd, she scolded herself, what can it possibly matter, a map promised to a five-year-old.

Still, she thought a moment later, he'd meant well. She picked up her book and then sat down in the chair by the fire. And, he'd been kind when there was no cause or encouragement to be so.

Like Franz—once, she thought. But it was all a pose. The Englishman's kindness must be a pose, too, and what does it matter anyway, a brief polite conversation, a promise to a child not kept in three days, a kiss to the hand. They're all the same, she thought, as indistinguishable as poplar leaves from any poplar tree. Men are all the same.

The following morning was an ordinary Thursday, overcast and grey, and with only the laundry left to do, Julienne bundled the clothes in the large sheet and put them into the basket. Just this last little errand, she thought, walking out the front door, and then home to a warm fire, hot soup for luncheon, and a quiet afternoon on such a miserable day.

"Good afternoon."

She turned around and saw the tall, thin Edward Atherton-Moore. Thinner than usual. "Good afternoon," she replied.

He smiled.

It must be the light, she thought, studying his face. He looks nearly as grey as the sky.

"I, I did not forget my promise," he said, and tapped the circular tube under his arm. "The map, for Gisèle." He noticed the basket under her arm, then said, "You seem in a great hurry. I shan't keep you, then. Please tell her it is a gift from me. And I hope she enjoys it. It is a map of the world, and I thought it might be of greater interest than a map of England only."

He sounded withdrawn and dispirited and the question escaped her before she could stop it. "Have you been ill?"

He bit his lip. "Yes," he said, "for nearly three days." He tried to smile, but it was a lost effort. He held out the tube to her and said "I shan't keep you from your errands and . . ." he paused, "unless, if you prefer, after your errands, you might consider going to a café with me, for luncheon?"

She looked away from him, wondering what to do. Why not just say no, she thought, almost angry with herself at her hesitation. It is an easy word, no. But her thoughts softened when she saw his face. His eyes had such sadness in them, and his shoulders drooped with the weight of some hidden burden. His voice was so dramatically different from last Sunday's lightness and kindness.

Julienne thought a moment, then said, "Yes. There is a café on the Boulevard St. Germain. It is comfortable, a very respectable place."

Relief eased into his smile.

"But not with this," she said, and tapped the basket. "The blanchisserie isn't far."

He offered to carry the laundry, but Julienne shook her head and refused with a smile, saying, "I manage it each week."

For ten minutes or so, he said nothing further, and just walked alongside her to the blanchisserie, then waited outside.

Julienne chatted with the laundress for a few moments, heard the latest news and gave congratulations on learning that the older niece was now engaged to be married. Her fiancé had two years left to serve in the Army. Julienne wished them luck. "In about an hour, then," she said, leaving her basket with Madame Bédard, then took Edward's arm when she joined him outside.

The café was small, like its menu. When they were seated at their table inside, Edward's expression had changed again when he gave their order to the waiter. In his silence, it was still evident he was troubled, but his eyes had softened and his posture seemed more relaxed, and he was—as he was obviously trained to be—calm and elegant.

Trying to fill the silence, Julienne said, "This is very kind of you, Lord Harlaxton."

"Edward," he quietly corrected.

"Edward," she repeated.

"It's not so very kind, it's really a bit selfish. You spoke an unpleasant truth to me, once, and I was hoping you'd speak it again."

"I'm not sure I understand you."

"Well," he sighed, "that first time we met, you held a rather large mirror up to me and made me see something I preferred to ignore. But, see it I did, and I'm grateful to you for your honesty. So grateful, in fact, I'd like to see that mirror once more. I'm . . . I'm feeling a bit lost, at the moment."

The waiter brought them their orders of leek soup. When he left the table, Julienne took her spoon, then said to Edward, "Could not your friend, the Marquis, help you more than I?"

"No. He's avoided that mirror as long as I have."

Julienne had seen the quick sad look in his eyes, eyes bare of warmth and trapped by a restless mind. "I realize we are strangers, but if it is your wish, I will listen, and tell you what I think."

"Thank you," he said. "I suppose I ought to be surprised, but somehow, I'm not. I know of no other woman who would speak to me like this. Have you always been so outspoken, Madame Barbier?"

She smiled. "I've had two very fine teachers, my father and my brother. My brother and I were raised to speak our thoughts, and later in life, he was more than a brother to me, he was a friend, too." She stared at the bowl in front of her. Remembering Stefan in spoken words brought the ache of his absence back to her.

"Was? You've lost him, then?"

"Yes."

"Have you no other brothers or sisters?"

"No." She looked at him. "Do you?"

"I've a sister, much younger than I, but the difference in our ages and my own 'confused' state did much to discourage any real friendship."

"Pity. But you had a brother, didn't you?"

He winced, then said, "An older brother, yes. He died when I was ten years old." Edward put his spoon down, completely disinterested in the soup.

144

"I'm thirty-three years old," he said, looking straight at her, "and almost everything in my life has been someone else's idea."

"Do you mean the responsibilities to your family?"

He felt his eyes narrow. "My brother was more suited to that than I. My brother wanted to join my father in his work, not I."

"What sort of work, Edward?"

"Government. He's a member of the House of Lords. Takes it quite seriously, too; laws and debates and the gentle application of pressure to encourage people to do the right thing."

"You sound angry."

"Do I?" he said, then looked away. "Sorry. It's . . . it's a sensitive subject with me. And quite a separate matter." He went back to his soup, and waited until she spoke first.

"Why is your father's work so distasteful to you?"

"It isn't," he said. "My single objection is that he has consistently denied me my own life and my own hopes because . . ." He stopped speaking and chose his words carefully. "He . . . he has his reasons."

"Punishment?"

Edward met her stare. "Very good," he said. "Very observant, Madame Barbier."

Julienne sipped her wine without comment.

"And there is some truth in that," he continued, then picked up his wine glass and drained the remaining Beaujolais. "It is so peculiar. I hadn't meant to speak of those things at all, but of something else." He shrugged. "Doesn't matter anymore."

"Sometimes, we speak the most important words of all when we least expect it."

"True," he nodded. Though the waiter brought them their order of veal, Edward no longer had an appetite. He looked at the plate, then poured himself a little more wine. He sipped his wine and glanced at the other patrons in the small café. Clerks, probably, he thought, from banking houses or business firms and shops. Then he looked at Jeanne Barbier. There was something oddly familiar about her, about the way she spoke, the way she sat straight in her chair, the poise . . . She is so unlike the other embroidery girls, he thought. It is familiar and peculiar—at the same time. Her manners seem so proper, so schooled.

When they left the café, he walked with her first to the laundry, and then to Rue Royer Collard. Edward had the tube under one arm, and the soft gentle arm of this curious woman on the other. Two and a half days of a drugged nightmare, he thought, and a third day of hopelessness . . . until seeing her.

She took her arm from his when they reached the doors to the apartment house.

"Here," he said, handing her the tube. "And thank you for a lovely afternoon."

Julienne gave the tube back to him.

"You do not accept it?" Edward asked.

She smiled. "I was taught that a gift should be given by the giver. You've gone to a great deal of trouble to please my daughter. Come inside and speak to her yourself. She is with my neighbor."

He followed her into the lobby and then up the flight to the first landing and the door on the left. She knocked, and they heard a woman's voice from inside the salon, followed by Gisèle's laughter.

Cécile opened the door, laughing and wiping her hands on her apron, wet flour stuck to her fingers and dry dustings of it were on her nose and chin. "You have missed all the fun. We have been making dough, and with the scrapings, little animals for a zoo." She looked to her right and saw the tall, smiling man.

"Madame Mabilleau, may I present Lord Harlaxton," Julienne said.

Cécile was flustered, blushed, put out her hand to him and saw the wet dough clinging to her fingers, then hid the hand behind her skirt. Not knowing what else to do, she curtsied.

Edward extended his hand and waited patiently until she placed her hand in his. He kissed her hand, paying no mind whatever to the dough caked on her skin.

"Lord Harlaxton has a present for Gisèle."

"I, I forget my manners," Cécile said, stepping back from the door. "Do come in, please."

They went inside and he saw the child kneeling on a chair, squeezing dough between her fingers. "Hello, Gisèle," he said.

She looked up and smiled. "Hello!" she said, and bounded off the chair.

"I didn't forget my promise. I've brought the map," he said, bending down as she threw her arms around his neck.

"I knew you'd come back, I knew you'd bring it!" She kissed his smooth cheek. "Thank you."

"Gisèle, your hands," Julienne said. "You've soiled Lord Harlaxton's coat."

Edward returned the hug, then stood up. "Doesn't matter. It's only a coat."

"Please, sir, let me see the map and the place where you were, I don't remember the name," Gisèle said.

"India," Edward said calmly. He looked over to Madame Mabilleau and caught her fixing her hair and wiping her face. "I do not wish to impose, Madame, is it all right?"

"Oh, yes, certainly," Cécile said. "Some coffee, perhaps?"

"Thank you," Edward said, and unbuttoned his coat, then gave it to Madame Mabilleau's waiting arms.

"Here, this way, at the table," Gisèle said, and pulled on his hand, walking him to the dining room.

When they reached the table, he looked at the white cloth that had been spread for doughmaking, and then at the animals. "You've done quite well," he said, inspecting the dogs, birds and snakes that were hardening on a platter.

"I made the snakes," Gisèle said.

"They're very real," he smiled.

"Madame made the other animals. Sometimes . . ." She looked up at him. "You won't tell Mama?"

146

He shook his head. "I shall keep your secret."

She sighed a smile. "Sometimes," she whispered, "I may call Madame 'Grandmama.' It is our secret and only when we are alone. And she calls me . . ."

"Granddaughter?"

Gisèle shook her head. "My little granddaughter," she corrected, then tapped the tube. "Please, sir, may I see it now?"

Edward rolled up the tablecloth with the fine dusting of flour and exposed the wood top of the table. He took off the leather tube top, tilted it down, and a heavy-grade paper tube dropped out. He spread the map before her and was delighted by the gasp and the wide dancing eyes when she saw the gaily colored map of the world. The map-ends curled and he looked up to find Madame Barbier holding two books, which she placed on either end.

"Thank you," Edward said.

"Where is it, where is India?"

"Here," he said, standing behind the child as she knelt on the chair and leaned over the map.

"And where were you?"

"I was here," he said, and pointed with his index finger to Madras, in the southern quarter of the country. "But not all the time. We moved about several times."

"Where do you live?"

"Here," he said, and tapped England.

"And how did you get there, to India?"

"By boat. We left Southampton," he said, tapping the port, "traveled all the way down the continent of Europe, and then all the way down the continent of Africa, rounded the Cape, and sailed this way to India."

Gisèle shook her head. "Did it take a long time?"

"Six months," he said, "but now people travel differently. There is a canal open."

"A what?" Gisèle asked, wrinkling her nose at him.

"A canal, it is a kind of passageway, where a boat may travel. It is called the Suez Canal, and it is here," he said, pointing to Egypt. "Now boats may go from India, through the Suez Canal, and then out to the Mediterranean Sea. It is a much shorter journey, Gisèle, now it takes only three months, instead of six."

"Is six months a long time?"

"Yes," he smiled, knowing how difficult it was for a child to understand time.

Julienne watched him as he talked to Gisèle. He is so patient, she thought, and he explains things to her in a simple language so she will understand. Perhaps the kindness was not a pose, she thought, moving closer to them, letting her eyes explore the expensive and very beautiful map.

"And where is Vienna?" Gisèle asked.

Edward was about to answer when he heard the child gasp. He looked up to see Madame Barbier's hand on the child's shoulder, squeezing it ever-so-slightly. Gisèle's eyes had widened, but she said nothing more. "Here," he said, pointing, "and France is here," he said, watching the child examine the country intently. He was far more interested in Madame Barbier's lips, drawn tight in an even line.

A short time later, Madame Mabilleau had prepared the coffee and brought it to the salon along with tarts she'd made herself. Edward could see that she had tried very hard to please him, and she still felt nervous to be sitting at table with him. They spoke of the usual things—some travel, living in Paris, food.

Not one to overstay a welcome, he left about an hour after he'd arrived with Madame Barbier. He thanked Madame Mabilleau for her hospitality, and delighted in her second series of blushes and flusterings.

As Madame Barbier saw him to the door downstairs, Cécile went over to Gisèle. "What a nice gentleman," she said, looking over the child's shoulder as she stared at the map. "And such a nice gift he brought you. Your Mama would do very well to see more of him."

Gisèle looked up. "Do you like him? I like him," she said, caressing the map. "He smells nice, too. He smells like cinnamon biscuits."

Cécile laughed and pinched the child's chin. "All young men do," she sighed. "It is the macassar oil they use on their hair."

Gisèle shrugged, not understanding what that meant. "I still like him."

Edward kissed Madame Barbier's hand. "May I call on you again?" he asked softly.

"Yes," Julienne answered. "Gisèle and I would enjoy your company very much."

"And perhaps, on the next occasion, might I meet your son?"

"Yes, of course, how kind of you to ask." Julienne smiled and slowly, gently, withdrew her hand from his.

"Frédéric, isn't it?" he asked, crinkling his eyes, searching his mind for the name.

"You have quite a memory."

"Only for things that are important." He smiled and walked out the door.

As he walked away from the apartment house he thought: It is so odd, how much one's life may change in a matter of days, or hours. Last night, a scant twelve hours ago, to sit alone in Philippe's study, despondent, after having lived two and a half days, drugged by Laudanum, in a living nightmare. To think that I held a loaded dueling pistol and debated with myself for hours trying to decide if I should just pull the trigger and end my misery. He stopped for a moment at the corner. That is why I came to Paris, he thought. I came here to die, not to live. I also knew it would not take very long, knowing myself, and what I wanted, and a willing companion in Philippe, though I never spoke the words aloud.

He sighed, feeling the cold air on his face and watching the grey steam from his mouth. I was, he thought, so very close to the abyss, and how strange that a lovely little girl and a map would stop me, and hold out to me a slender thread of hope. I shall love Gisèle for that, always.

He turned around and looked up at the apartment building. He saw a shadow by the window where he thought the Mabilleau salon might be. The shadow waved, and he waved back. Then, the curtains were drawn.

There is an extraordinary treasure in that woman, in Jeanne, he thought, and to think I almost threw this day away . . .

Tired, marooned in his own worries, Stefan dressed himself at four o'clock in the morning and quietly left the house. It is an old trick, he thought, an exhausted mind needs an exhausted body, and he walked the length of the stables to the far end. Placing the bitless Hacamore bridle over the stallion's head, he led his horse to the center of the stable near the lamp on the post, fixed the bridle to the post rope, and then undid the jute night-rug from the animal's back.

Stripped to the waist, he looped the body-brush on his right hand and the square curry-comb on the left and began to groom the horse.

I knew they were idiots, he thought, but Bismarck knew *that* long before I did. He called Gramont "the stupidest man in Europe" years ago, and Jesus, he was right . . . all that petty schoolboy gossip, Stefan bristled, I'm sick to death of Embassy parties and idiots minimizing the danger . . . bringing up our war with Prussia, chuckling about the rumors of a goat and Bismarck's supposed pact with the devil, and then, to ask me if I thought them true, for God's sake, and didn't Gramont look disappointed when I told him it was only a mascot, frightened by the gunfire. The idiot. He didn't understand the entire battle had turned 'round in less than two hours, our forces were split, we had three armies to fight, and *they* had modern rifles and cannons, Krupp Cannons, and *their* soldiers could afford a five-minute footrace to catch a goat. Our war was over in six weeks. Six weeks.

Although he was sweating, he shuddered, seeing in his mind the aftermath of Königgrätz, the rain, the smoke and the smells of the battlefield in July.

The screams of the wounded, waiting, dying. And the other tent, men lying upon the ground sprawled on rough blankets, men with amputated arms, legs, everywhere he looked he saw bloodied cotton batting and the stunned calm brought on by morphia to deaden the pain. When the morphia ran out, he saw the doctors measuring a red liquid, and then filling the remainder of the glasses with brandy, forcing this combination down the throats of struggling and screaming men. Laudanum, they said; it would have to do, they said. Most of them died, Stefan knew. A hopelessness descended on them, their eyes with large black pupils staring at nothing, their bodies, weakened by the surgery and by the loss of so much blood, allowed the men to simply give up and die.

When he'd finished grooming the horse, he sat down for a moment on the stool, wiped his forehead and then brushed his hands clean on his trouser legs. After saddling the horse, he dressed himself, doused the light and led the stallion to the courtyard. He mounted, and with a slight kick to the ribs, let the horse walk slowly at first up Hauptstrasse, heading vaguely in the direction of the Burggarten.

It was a bitter cold morning and Stefan felt it acutely in his hands. Though he wore gloves, the slight wind seemed to go right through them. The ride on the frozen ground was a slow one. He couldn't jeopardize the horse or himself and, after an hour, he headed for home amidst the merchants' carts and sounds of the city waking from the night.

Roughly one block from the Capuchin Church, he felt a sudden need to go there and be near his father. Dismounting, he led the horse to the rear of the Church and tied the reins to a post. It was early and he knew it, but it did not stop him from pulling on the bell rope and saying to the monk who answered the door a few moments later, "I wish to pray by my father." He thought he'd seen an odd look in the monk's eyes, but he didn't particularly care. They could not refuse him, and he knew that, too.

It was a dank, cold and lonely place. His eyes drifted sadly to the effigies and monuments and statues of glorious Habsburgs gone and turned to dust. He knelt by the effigy of his father, and after he'd taken the gloves off his hands, touched the closed carved marble eyelids. You taught me too well, Stefan thought, and now, I am being slowly crushed by stupidity. There is a war brewing which may or may not affect us. We are unprepared for war. We are bankrupt—in our purses, in our men, in our pride. And those who wish to remain neutral, do so for the wrong reasons. But it is a twin grief without end that I suffer. Work—and my sister. With each day that passes, each day I am imprisoned here in Vienna and shackled to my desk, my worry for her grows, my helplessness grows and I have no one to turn to for advice or comfort.

He felt a hand touch his shoulder.

"I do not wish to be disturbed," Stefan said crisply.

"Yes, Brother Anthony told me you looked distraught."

"Leave me, Teo," he warned.

"You do not dismiss your uncle as if he were a stable boy."

Stefan looked up. "I'm tired. I apologize."

"Have you been to bed?" Teo asked, noticing the pale skin, the sunken eyes and the stubble on the cheeks.

Stefan wearily shook his head. "It's not important."

"What troubles you, nephew?"

"You would not understand," Stefan answered and stood up from the kneeler.

Teo's eyes burned. "Do you believe me stupid? Do you believe I know nothing of the world, just because I have renounced my position in my family to serve in another kind of life?"

"What can you know!" Stefan snapped. "You live *here*, protected by the Church. You are . . ."

"Your father would be shamed by your stupidity and the way you speak to me."

"Don't you say that to me—ever!" Stefan shouted. "He taught me far too well to . . ."

"And you have learned nothing," Teo interrupted. He stepped closer to his nephew. "Your father held your position long before you, my boy. Your father suffered, as you do now, before you even *knew* what the word suffering meant in *your* little protected life, in your nursery, playing with your toys.

And when doubt raged in *his* mind, to whom did he turn for help? To the dead, here in this Chapel? No, he turned to *me*. ME. Your sister knew that truth. But you, you have learned nothing."

Stefan felt a small boy's shame at the chastising truth-filled words. When Teo's brown-robed arm cradled his shoulder, he leaned slightly against his uncle, yet still touched the clasped stone hands of his father's effigy. "Help me, then," he said, and spoke to Teo about the political intrigue he suspected, but did not mention Julienne, knowing Teo could not speak of it.

Teo listened patiently, then thought for a moment, and when he spoke, he spoke in a soft tone of voice. "You are right to distrust Gramont," he said. "But he is harmless where he is. Let him enjoy his anger—he can do nothing with it. He has some influence, as Ambassadors do, but he does not write policy within the government."

"And Napoleon?"

"Ah," Teo sighed, "that is another matter. What is in your favor is the fact that Napoleon strives for peace. He is, I believe, a man of peace and would be reluctant to go to war . . ."

"But . . ." Stefan prompted, meeting his Uncle's eyes. "I hear the word in your voice."

"But," Teo nodded, "those around him may have other ideas."

Stefan sighed. "Peace," he said tonelessly, "but a peace with honor."

Teo shook his head. "Don't fool yourself," he said quietly. "There is no such thing as peace with honor. This is just a kind way of saying the other side must make all the compromises. Never believe it to be true."

"Bismarck is playing the same game. Only the faces have changed."

"Yes," Teo agreed, "but it is not a fait accompli just yet. No one has joined in battle on the fields—yet. There may still be time to apply the right kind of pressure and to urge people into doing the correct thing, honorably."

"How?"

"You cannot attempt this on your own. You haven't the influence or the years in service that would command that measure of respect. But there is one man who has those qualifications. Your father knew him. All of Europe respects this man. Lord Clarendon, of England."

Stefan thought it over and saw the logic in Teo's answer.

"Remember something, Stefan. The intrigue is there, it is real and does not rest only in your imagination. If you have seen this, others may have seen this as well. Clarendon is a student of history, a man whose opinion is respected throughout the world. You travel a road he most likely has already traveled, and if you see disaster, it might comfort you to know he sees it as well."

"But I am not free to visit him," Stefan sighed.

"Write to him, then, unofficially. You must not, under any circumstances, embarrass your government. You do not have the Emperor's blessing in this venture—not yet—and if you are not believed in your own house, why should anyone else believe you?"

"True," Stefan said. "I thought of writing to Metternich. He is a special close friend of . . ."

"The Empress Eugénie, yes, I know. A splendid idea. Our French Ambassador has exceptionally large ears," Teo smiled. "He should be able to advise you and relay court whispers. Write to him, but privately."

Stefan smiled, somewhat relieved. "Thank you."

Teo gave a rough, bear-like hug to the thin shoulder. "Come upstairs with me and have breakfast."

Stefan shook his head. "No, I think I will be able to sleep now. I want to go home."

Teo kissed his nephew's forehead. "Go, then."

Stefan walked toward the door and turned around before opening it. "You see," he said, "I did learn. I shan't make this mistake again," he smiled, then left.

Alone amongst the effigies and monuments, Teo stood for a moment near his brother and gazed down on the calm stone face. "I know you rest easy," he said. "I have always known that, and though I miss you, I know your prayers for me help me each and every day. I have kept my promise, Heinrich. When our beloved Nathalie died, you made me promise to care for your babies when you died." He caressed the cold cheek of the marble. "My dearest brother, you did not think you would live so long without her. But I did not forget. I am still caring for your babies, Heinrich."

CHAPTER
9

He hated the map. And he hated the way his mother smiled every time she looked at the map. Buttoning his trousers, Frédéric stared meanly at Gisèle's empty bed. Oh, he mimicked her silently and with a curl to his lip, he's so nice, and so very tall . . . He kicked the side of her bed. All grown-up men are tall, he shuddered. He sat with a sigh on the end of his bed. Stupid, ugly map, he thought, as he pulled on his boots, wondering why his mother was doing this to him.

"Are you nearly ready?" Julienne asked from the doorway.

Frédéric's face calmed to a pout. He turned around to face his mother and shook his head. "I can't do this," he said quietly, letting the button-hook drop on the bed. "Help me, please," he said, looking up at her.

Julienne walked into the room, closer to him. "This is awfully silly," she said. "You do this every day for school."

He looked at the boot. "I can't do it," he said.

She sat down next to him on the bed. "I'm very surprised at you," she said, and began hooking the buttons.

"My collar is too tight," he complained, pulling at his shirt. "It pinches me."

"It didn't pinch you yesterday," she said, "and I'm quite sure it hasn't changed overnight sitting in your top drawer."

"But it doesn't fit right today," Frédéric insisted.

She looked at him but did not reply and finished hooking his left boot.

"Do the other one," he said, watching her.

"I will not. You're a big boy and you know very well how to hook the buttons."

He shook his head. "Please, Mama, help me, you do it, please?"

Julienne heard the knock at the door. "Come along now. We shouldn't keep Lord Harlaxton waiting."

"But my boot," he sniffed, sitting helplessly and staring at the right boot. "Please?" he asked, looking up at her with moist pitiful eyes.

She sighed, then called out, "Gisèle, be a good girl and answer the door, please?" Rather than argue, Julienne took the hook and quickly did the other boot.

A moment later, Frédéric heard his sister squeal a delighted hello. He felt the hairs stand on the back of his neck when the man's voice said it back to her. He's tall, he sounds tall and big, Frédéric thought, and he has yellow hair, I know it . . .

He didn't move and stared at the floor. "I, I don't feel well."

"This is too much, Frédéric," Julienne said.

"My stomach hurts," he whispered, shaking his head.

She lifted his chin with her hand. "You've eaten your breakfast, and enjoyed it, too. Your forehead," she said, touching him, "is as it should be. Why are you behaving like this? Don't you wish to see the puppets, and have a nice dinner in a restaurant and ride in a beautiful carriage?"

He shook his head. "I want to go back to bed."

She thought a moment, then said quietly, "I know that sometimes it is hard to meet new people." She caressed the side of his face. "You have no reason to be shy with Lord Harlaxton. Come and say hello to a very nice man, and try to be pleasant."

He shook his head. "I don't want to go. May I stay home? I'll be good. I'll stay in bed and I won't leave it until you come back. May I stay here, please?"

"No," Julienne answered quietly. "You're not at all ill, and I will not let you spoil this day for everyone. Lord Harlaxton has gone to a great deal of trouble to find interesting things to do today and he's done this with you in mind. I will not let you disappoint him or anyone else." Julienne held out her hand to him and waited until he'd thought it over. Frédéric placed his left hand in her right one and shuffled alongside his mother as they walked into the salon.

Even in a plain and simple blue day dress, Edward thought, she is fantastically beautiful.

Then he saw the boy.

He does not resemble her much, Edward thought, but he's quite a handsome little boy, very fair, like her skin, and a touch of ruddiness in the cheeks, probably from playing outside. But the hair is so very blond. Much more so than my brother's was . . . and blue eyes, I think they're blue, can't tell, he's staring at the floor.

Frédéric managed to look up for a second when introduced.

Yes, blue eyes, Edward thought.

Brown hair, Frédéric thought, not yellow. The man's hand was held out to him nearly under his nose. His eyes widened, and instinctively he moved his head slightly back to keep the hand away from his face. He felt a tap on his shoulder and shuddered.

"Take Lord Harlaxton's hand and say hello, Frédéric."

When he bent down, Edward saw the boy's hand shivering at his side and the unbroken, wild-eyed stare at the floor.

"Frédéric," Julienne repeated.

"No," Edward said quietly, and withdrew his hand. Standing straight again, he said, "Don't force the boy."

Julienne frowned and was somewhat embarrassed. "He's been taught his manners, Edward," she said softly, "and it isn't right for him to be discourteous."

Edward looked at the boy and had the peculiar feeling Frédéric was little more than a shadow. "Perhaps, Madame," he said gently, "on another day Frédéric might wish to shake my hand in friendship. I shall look forward to that. One may not force friendship upon another." He brushed the rim of his hat, then said, "We ought to go."

Julienne agreed, and allowed him to help her with her cloak, and then, to help Gisèle put on her small frock coat.

"Mama?" Frédéric said, looking up and waiting for help.

Julienne sighed and did his buttons for him, then followed Edward out of the salon and into the hallway. She locked her door and walked down the stairs.

Edward took Gisèle's hand. I should not be surprised, he thought, a little voice from a little boy. He shook his head. Yet, it had sounded so small, so helpless and distant.

The sight of the large closed carriage with the emblazoned arms on the door, the elegantly matched grey horses and the two liveried coachmen startled Julienne.

"I, I realize it's grand," Edward smiled. "Philippe has given me the use of it—and one other—during my stay with him."

Stepping onto the metal footrail and then into the carriage, Julienne said, "Your friend is very generous."

Edward poked his head inside the cabin. "He can afford to be," he quipped, and then helped Gisèle up. He held out his hands to Frédéric, but the boy stepped in quickly by himself and took the seat next to his mother. Edward was the last inside the cabin and he sat down next to Gisèle on the opposite seat, as the footman closed the door.

Gisèle quite enjoyed looking out of the small window, and kept up a constant chatter about the sights of the city and all the other lovely carriages out on this day, and especially how fast they were moving on the streets. Edward half-listened, but found himself watching Frédéric more and more. At first, the boy did not look out at the passing streets, and stared instead at his hands, as he played with his thumbnail.

I used to do that, Edward thought, when I first went away to school. "Do you like carriage rides, Frédéric?" Edward asked.

The boy shook his head and leaned farther back into the leather seat slightly closer to his mother.

Edward tried again to put the boy at ease. "I much prefer walking, myself," he said lightly. "Habit, I suppose. My family has a country house and there are long meadows, and acres and acres of farmlands, and soft rolling hills, with many brooks running through them. I used to ride my pony out to the meadows, and then walk for hours when I was about your age, Frédéric." The sleeping memory suddenly came clear in his mind. He could see his brother, Michael, racing ahead of him in the south meadow, toward a field of green corn. And NanaMac, he thought, walking behind us . . . He brushed the thought from his mind. "My brother and I would walk and play in those meadows," he said quietly. "Did you ever run and play in meadows like that?"

Frédéric's eyes opened, but he shook his head.

"There are lovely fields outside of Paris. We must do that sometime, we must find a special . . ."

Frédéric turned his head sharply to look out the window and pressed himself very close to the side of the carriage, staring with a total concentration at the passing pedestrians and buildings.

What has upset him, Julienne thought. She sighed, then met Edward's eyes. She shook her head and shrugged.

Edward smiled warmly. "Don't be concerned," he said softly, wondering what the boy was thinking.

The frustration Edward felt in the carriage built steadily throughout the day. Though the dinner conversation was pleasant, it hurt Edward that Frédéric continued in his silence. The boy had enjoyed himself, Edward thought, I saw him smile when the puppets and marionettes performed. However, as soon as we'd gone back to the carriage, and I asked him "did you like the puppets?" he'd said "no," and then quick as you please, corrected himself with a pointed "no, Sir." It was a stinging answer, and why had he done that, Edward wondered. He watched Frédéric sullenly move the food on his plate rather than eat it. I gave him no cause, no reason to fear me. But it is there, in his voice, in the way he stands, and for one moment, the true Frédéric appeared in the way he stole a look at me. Why this fear? And why to me?

But it was the way in which the darkening cabin of the carriage altered the boy's appearance that made Edward go cold inside. The boy's face was more shadowy than ever, and for one moment, Edward saw a different boy, a dark-haired boy with sad blue eyes looking into a mirror and combing his hair after Michael's death; a frightened, dark-haired boy, so terribly alone. It was a memory he'd tried so hard to forget.

He walked them upstairs and bent down to receive a thank-you hug and kiss from Gisèle.

"Good night, Frédéric," Edward said, and held out his hand.

"Thank you," the boy managed with a whisper, and walked quickly into the salon, stepping away from Edward's hand.

"I, I don't know what to say about him," Julienne sighed. "You've been very patient and kind. And I had a wonderful day." She was about to walk into the salon when she felt his hand take her arm. A firm touch, yet gentle in its caress.

"A moment," he said, nodding to the area just before the stairs. "Please?"

"Yes, of course," she said, and told the children she'd be in directly.

Edward closed the door to the apartment and then walked the few steps closer to Madame Barbier.

"He's never done this before," Julienne said. "It's something of a mystery to me."

Edward took her hand, held it warmly and kissed it, then stared for a long moment at the long delicate gloved fingers. He continued to hold her hand in his own. "The boy and his father," he began, "did they go riding together? Did they play with toy soldiers, or tell stories, and did the boy try to please his father with new things he'd learned?"

The questions were a complete surprise and she had to look away from the gently searching eyes in order to compose herself. She slowly withdrew her hand from his.

"I am sorry to ask, and I apologize if I have stirred any memories, but it is important for me to know these things."

"Why?" Julienne asked, thinking: He is a stranger, and a stranger has no right to know.

Edward sighed. "How long . . ." he began, then started again, "how long have you been widowed, Madame . . . Jeanne?"

What do I answer, she thought quickly. I haven't felt like a wife for years . . . the time we left? No, she thought, longer. "Almost . . . almost eighteen months," she lied and looked away from him.

"Then he must miss his father very much."

She saw his point and the assumption he was making, but it isn't the truth, she thought. "No," Julienne answered cautiously, "no I don't believe he does."

"I don't understand," Edward said.

"The things you've described," she continued, choosing her words carefully, "it, it wasn't like that. His father," she thought quickly, "was a busy man. And, sadly, did not have a great deal of time to spend with Frédéric."

"Yes, I know that feeling myself," Edward said.

"Well, then, you must know one cannot miss what one never had."

"No," he said, "I don't agree. Jeanne," he said, using her Christian name for the second time, and when she did not object, went on, saying, "I cannot speak for your son. I speak only for myself, and I missed them all the more because I wanted those things and never had them."

She thought about that and saw the possible truth in his words. Frédéric probably misses Stefan more than anyone else, she thought. "Perhaps you may be right."

"Does he have friends?"

156

She shook her head. "I have tried to encourage him to make friends at school. But, I think it is difficult for him."

"It is, for a great many people," he said softly.

"He had one friend, but that boy was a bad influence."

Edward sensed what was coming, and waited patiently for her to continue.

"There . . . there was a bit of trouble." Julienne saw the expectant look in his eyes. "The boy," she hesitated, then decided to speak of it, to trust him. "The boy lived by his wits, a child of the streets."

"He was a thief," Edward said calmly.

"Yes," she said, feeling awkward.

"And your son adored him."

"Yes," she answered. "I have forbidden him to see that boy ever again. Frédéric was punished for his wrong-doing."

"And rightly so. It must have been very difficult for you."

Julienne wondered why he understood so much.

"Has he spoken of anyone else at school, any new friend?"

She shook her head. "At one time, he did speak of the other boys, but no longer."

Edward sighed.

"You seem to understand a great deal," she said, a bit crisply.

He smiled. "Unhappily, yes." He looked steadily at her large brown eyes. "I know what it is to have a friend out-of-step with 'Society.' It isn't difficult at all for me to put myself in the boy's place." He shook his head. "People say: time is a gentleman. It isn't true, you know. Time has been no gentleman to me because it has neither erased nor healed. I often wish I could forget, and, God help me, how hard I've tried, too. It would be lovely to lock the past away and leave it all behind me. That is a blessing I've not been given."

She felt a sadness at his words, and reached for his hand. "But the past is a teacher, not an enemy."

He kissed her hand. "Dearest Jeanne, we have had different pasts." He looked away from her and glanced back at the closed door to her flat. "I ask a small favor," he said, moving from her and starting down the stairs. "Don't reproach the boy for his behavior today. I know most people believe that children have no feelings. That was believed of me when I was a boy and I know it was not the truth then, nor is it now. Given time, he may grow to like me." He looked back up at her and smiled. "Who can tell about the future? Perhaps, one day, his mother might grow in that direction, too." He saw her smile before she stepped back from the banister, and heard the door open to her flat.

In the carriage, he sat in the right corner and let his eyes stare where Frédéric had been sitting. In the cold darkness, he remembered again that warm Spring, that fleeting thought: Michael running toward the green corn-fields, and NanaMac following them.

"NanaMac," he sighed, and realized he hadn't thought of her for years. It saddened him to think that once, she had been his whole world. He knew her disapproving eyes and tight knot of hair; he could smell her starched dress and soap-perfumed hands, and before all this, was her voice, and the comforting phrase he remembered from earliest childhood: "Um-ma-num." She'd used the phrase whenever he refused new food and was afraid of the strange colors and strained mush on the plate in his childhood nursery. It was a toddler's game, and, when older, he'd turn away from food just to hear her say it . . . "um-ma-num."

A distant memory, a pleasing memory, and Edward smiled in the dark, remembering her.

❧

"No," NanaMac said, grabbing Edward's hand away from the plate of buns. "You'll kindly remember, that you must eat the slice of bread *before* the cake."

"Let Ted have the bun now, he's been a good man today," Michael giggled.

NanaMac pinched his ear with unexpected speed. "That's for encouraging him to be naughty. Did you learn such rudeness from 'that' tutor?"

Michael's lips tightened. "No, and you oughtn't to call Master Chester 'that' tutor," he sulked.

"I'll thank you not to stare at me so," NanaMac said, arching an eyebrow. "And if you keep that face, God shall punish you and it shall be your *only* face and you'll grow up to be the ugliest man in England."

As much as he resisted, Michael had to smile.

"That's better," NanaMac said. She turned to Edward. "You've had plenty of time. Well?"

"I'll eat the bread, if it pleases you so much."

"Doesn't please me in the least," she said, watching Edward nibble at the corner where the strawberry jam had been spread thickly over the buttered bread. "You shouldn't play at table, it's not seemly," she went on. "Society would toss you out without so much as a wink if you played like that at your meals."

"Oh Nanny," Michael sighed, "we know."

"You think you know," she said. "And you shouldn't make me cross, should you, of course not." She reached elegantly for the pot of tea and refilled their cups. Michael used the moment to stuff the last bits of his bread into his mouth, barely chewing and swallowing at the same time. His hand reached for the bun, but her hand was there before his.

Michael swallowed with a gulp and a cough. "Be fair," he wheezed, "I've finished the bread."

"So I've noticed," she said. "Eaten like a common little boy. I'm surprised you could swallow at all."

He coughed and wheezed again.

"I've told you, haven't I, a thousand times, a gentleman eats *slowly*. I suppose 'that' tutor taught you to eat like a chimney-sweep."

"He hasn't," Michael managed, coughing.

"So it's your doing, is it?" she glared.

"Please may I have a bun now, NanaMac?" Michael said, watching her think it over, and then gave a pained shout of "the *small* one! That's not the one I wanted."

"You'll say thank you or you'll go without."

Michael muttered a thank-you, and picked at the bun in front of him, wishing he'd been given the large one with the mountains of icing that dripped over the sides. Resigned, he took a large bite and felt a quick pinch to his arm.

"Slowly," NanaMac intoned.

He chewed carefully, deliberately, then swallowed politely.

"Spiteful child," NanaMac said with a trace of a smile.

∞

The carriage wheel hit a small ditch in the road and the sudden jolt broke Edward's concentration. That was such a long time ago, he thought. She left us soon after that, he thought, a few weeks after I'd turned five. My father took me aside and told me it was of her own choosing because she only wanted to care for very small children, and I wasn't small anymore.

He closed his eyes by the Place Vendôme. I begged her, screamed for her, chased after her, but she left. I couldn't eat or sleep, didn't get dressed, and sat in a corner of my room in mirthless play with my miniature lead Napoleon.

∞

Someone walked across the nursery room floor and he saw large shoes and grey trousers in front of him. "Come sit with me, Edward."

He looked up to his giant-like father and obeyed.

He was led to the table, where he sat down. His father sat next to him in the other chair and placed the linen napkin across the boy's lap, saying quietly, "You must eat something. You haven't eaten anything since yesterday."

Edward shook his head and stared at the table, then began to cry.

"Richard," his mother said, "do something, please."

Michael walked to their father and whispered something in his ear. The Duke nodded, then took a slice of buttered toast and liberally spread strawberry jam all over it, then placed it in front of his son. "Now I know you like this," he smiled. "Everyone likes this. Come along now, um-ma-num?"

Edward's eyes went quickly from the table's corner to his father's worried face.

The Duke said it again. "Um-ma-num?" and this time, the smile was warmer.

Edward picked up the toast from his plate and took a small bite. Rolling the sweetness inside his mouth made him suddenly hungry. He finished and asked for another.

His father prepared a second slice of toast exactly as he'd done the first, then stood up, tousled the boy's hair and walked toward the nursery door and his wife. "He's on the mend, Beth. No need to worry any longer."

She smiled and looked quickly at her son. "He'll soon forget all about Missus MacPhee. They don't really remember much, do they, children I mean. They haven't the feelings yet. He'll soon forget all about this day and this unpleasantness."

∞

Edward shook his head in the dark as the carriage clattered through the iron gate of Philippe's courtyard. I never forgot, he thought, and despite what my mother and her social set believe, children *do* have the capacity to feel

159

things—love, pain, fear, loss, especially loss. I knew it then, just as Frédéric knows it now.

"And the children Barbier," Philippe said, "are they as ravishing as the mother?"

Edward nodded across the dining room table. "They're very handsome."

Philippe grinned, then shrugged. "How tedious, though, to care for wet-nosed children all of the time."

"It's not quite like that," Edward replied, sipping his wine.

The servants cleared the soup bowls while others brought in the second course. They served Philippe first, he absently nodded, then said to Edward, "What are your plans, then, for this beautiful creature?"

"My plans, for the beautiful woman, are the usual sort of things—the theater, the ballet . . ."

Philippe laughed and shook his head. "Edward, really, I am surprised at you."

"Why?"

"Oh come now, little embroidery girls do not like that normal sort of evening. You should know that by now. They are, shall we say, 'socially embarrassed' at such places."

"She's not like that," Edward said, paying no attention to the servants at his elbow.

"And how do you know such a thing? Tell me, please. A cup of hot chocolate in the afternoon, a little lunch at a workmen's café? How do you know she will not embarrass you at the theater, in full view of Society? Or that she will even consent to go to such a place?"

"Her manners are exquisite."

"Beauty has made you blind."

"How can you judge someone you've never met? You haven't seen her at table, or listened to her conversation, and I have. I . . ." He glanced down at his plate and saw the filleted fish, slit lengthwise. The fork and knife dropped from his hands as he stared at the white, moist fish and felt the blood draining from his face.

"Edward? Edward, are you ill?"

"Take it away," he said, quickly pushing the plate and toppling his wine glass. "Take it away," he said, breathing harder.

Philippe suddenly noticed what they had been served. He left his chair instantly, strode to Edward, and tossed the plate and the fish to the floor as he reprimanded the frightened servants. "I have given explicit instructions that fish was not to be served at any meal during my guest's stay."

The manservant backed away from the Marquis and began to stammer. "I . . . I . . ."

"Be quiet!" Philippe snapped. "You," he glared at his butler, "inform my Chef he is no longer employed."

Edward turned his back on the table and took Philippe's arm. "There is no need for that."

Philippe bent down slightly and placed his hands on Edward's shoulders.

"They have offended you, my friend. They have upset you and disregarded my explicit instructions. I will not employ such people."

Edward left the table and led Philippe away from the flustered servants. "It was an oversight," he said quietly, "nothing more. No harm has been done. But if you do this, a lasting harm will be done to your servants. I ask you, please, let it pass."

Philippe searched the eyes of his friend, then saw the color begin to return to the pasty cheeks. "As you wish," he said, then said to his servants, "You may tell that man, that he may remain here at the specific request of my friend." He smiled at Edward, tapped his arm and said, "Come, let us sit down again. The offense has been removed."

Edward managed a small grin. "Don't be angry, but . . ."

"You have no appetite," Philippe said, newly annoyed.

"I . . . I am quite all right, but please, for me, give it no notice."

Philippe pursed his lips, then nodded. "Rest, then. And I shall see you in the morning."

Edward left the dining room and went upstairs.

Several hours had gone by, and Edward made a conscious effort not to let his mind wander. He'd changed into his nightshirt, wrapped himself in his robe, and forced himself to read a book and think only about the book.

There was a knock at his door.

"Yes," he said, marking his place and then looking up to see Philippe's butler, waiting patiently just inside the room.

"I am sorry to disturb you, My Lord, but Chef has prepared a small tray for you and begs a moment of your time."

"Of course."

A middle-aged man entered, a man with a worried face and mousy-brown hair and a touch of grey in his mustache. He carried a silver tray, and bowed slightly. "I am most grievously sorry to have upset you in any way, My Lord. I have no excuse. It was unthinkable to forget the Marquis' order."

Edward shook his head and said gently, "This is unnecessary. All is well."

"You are most kind, My Lord. And I hope you will accept what I have made for you. I was trained not only as a cook, but to bake, as well. I know you have a fondness for special English cakes. And, and I have made you some hot chocolate, and the little cakes you like so much. I thought, perhaps, something sweet before you retire, might dispel the sour taste of my mistake."

"That is thoughtful," Edward said, "and I accept, with pleasure."

The Chef brought the tray to him and set it down on the small wooden table to his left. Edward saw the plate of buns, rich with snow-white icing that dripped down heavily on the sides. He smiled.

"Thank you, My Lord, and good evening to you." The Chef bowed, and left the room quietly as the butler poured a cup of the hot chocolate from the silver pot.

"If you require anything else, My Lord," the butler said, "you have only to ring for me."

Edward nodded as the butler left the room and quietly shut the door. Do your magic then, he thought as he ran his finger over the icing. Hide from me the fact that it has been nearly twenty-four years since I have eaten fish. Um-ma-num, he thought sadly, and let the sweet icing linger in his mouth.

CHAPTER
10

Two days later, Julienne read and re-read the letter Edward had sent her and tried to keep the unusual request in perspective. Polite greetings, she thought, then Tuesday next is his thirty-fourth birthday, an invitation to accompany him to an early dinner, and then the theater, plain enough, normal enough, and then she looked at the disturbing paragraph again:

". . . One may suppose, dearest Jeanne, that an evening such as this might, in a broad sense, be viewed by Society as a 'fancy dress ball.' Society is on parade for the express purpose of being admired by others. It is a harmless pastime—the obtaining of a 'costume' and the wearing of it, all according to Society's codes of such matters. In this light, then, I hope you will permit me the honor of furnishing you with several 'costumes . . .' "

It is so delicately worded, she thought, putting the letter down. She had to smile, in spite of herself. Delicate, and ironic. A costume, she thought, I am living in a "costume" now, and he thinks of me as an ordinary woman, with a meager income, and offers me a costume, which will return me to what I was.

She heard a knock and walked across the salon to answer the door.

"Hello," Cécile said lightly, and then, "Oh, but you're not ready."

Julienne saw the buttoned coat and realized they were to go out and shop for children's clothes at the Bon Marché store. "I'm sorry, come in, Madame." She stepped aside and let Cécile Mabilleau into the salon and closed the door after her.

"Gisèle is settled downstairs with Armand and he has her quite fascinated with stories of all the animals near his family's home. I think he is quite enjoying himself and . . ." As she was loosening her scarf, she saw the worried expression. "Is something wrong?"

Julienne decided to speak of it. "I am in need of advice . . . to know what is the right and proper thing to do in . . . in a strange situation."

"You say that as if age has some magical property," Cécile smiled, then sat down in the chair nearest her. "What is the problem?"

Julienne took the letter and handed it to Cécile. "Read for yourself," she said, and watched Cécile calmly reading, then the surprise, then her face returned to a calm expression.

"Well . . ." Cécile said, the word half in question, "it is . . . it is a generous offer."

"Doesn't it presume too much?"

Cécile saw the hard expression in the young woman's eyes. She stood up and returned the letter. "No. He has gone to great lengths to see that you are not embarrassed. He is only saying that if you agree to accompany him, he considers it his responsibility to provide you with proper clothes, as he must provide the carriage. That, at least to me, appears to be his reasoning."

Julienne said nothing.

"Please forgive me for saying so," Cécile went on, "but you are too young to be forever a widow. He seems a kind and considerate man."

Julienne looked at her.

"If you were my own daughter, I would encourage you. It is not often a man such as this, a titled man, walks through our lives. If he displeases you, then you send him away. But for the right reasons. This," she said, indicating the letter, "is not the right reason. It is a generous letter, and worded with care because you haven't the means for a proper 'costume.' " She led Madame Barbier to the chair with the cloak draped across it. "My Armand is a thoughtful and caring man. People who do not know him, see only the bluster and the noise and the arguments he has with all the world—and with me. They do not always see him in quiet moments, when he sings his cheery little songs, when he is thoughtful and considerate, when he is with children, and plays with them like a child. It is rare to find such a man."

They went outside and Julienne took a deep breath of the cold air. Cécile had said all she wished to, and spoke of it no more. Julienne appreciated the silence and when they took their seats on the omnibus going to the Right Bank and eventually to Rue de Sèvres, she tried to make sense out of her thoughts.

What should I believe, she thought, staring out the window. Kind words, considerate words, yet at one time, Franz spoke like that to me. But my brother is not like Franz, and neither was my father. And Armand is different, too. Edward might be different, and he might not. It could all be a disguise, another Franz waiting underneath the pose of a gentleman.

She shook her head. But it doesn't solve the other problem, she thought. Society. How can I sit with him in the theater, or go to a fine restaurant with him when titled Society people who look and inspect and gossip like mad will be there. It is impossible.

Still, it bothered her. His face, his smile, his eyes, his wit, his conversation, his patience and kindness with the children came to one point she had to admit to herself. She liked him.

But it is an awesome risk, she thought. Oh, why did I ever say yes to that cup of hot chocolate at Pons, she sighed.

"You needn't ask again, because I shan't tell you," Edward grinned.

"I've never been fond of surprises," Julienne countered, watching that smile on his face as they sat in the carriage.

"I think you'll like this one."

"You are so sure of that, are you?"

He laughed. "Well, I'm sure of one thing. If it displeases you, I know you will tell me precisely what you think."

The carriage passed by the Place Vendôme and went straight through to Rue de la Paix. It was only when the carriage slowed and stopped in front of Number Seven, Rue de la Paix that the little smile left her face. This is a terrible surprise, Julienne thought, staring at the stately town-house establishment. Worth—the House of Worth, couturier to the noble, the rich, the wives of statesmen, he's even dressed my cousin SiSi . . .

"Everything has already been settled," Edward was saying as she stepped out of the carriage, "so choose precisely what pleases you, Jeanne. Any color, anything you desire. The carriage is at your disposal. It will be waiting for you and will take you wherever you wish."

"But . . ."

"And don't let them bully you. They are there to serve you, remember that." He kissed her hand, winked, then said, "Go on. Appointments are very difficult these days, but Philippe used his influence."

I suppose I could run away, Julienne thought, watching him walk down the street. No, she sighed. Impossible. I think I would miss him—and his smile. Ah well, it isn't a firing squad, so better to have done with it. She straightened her shoulders and walked through the door held by the doorman.

The reception area was beautiful. Many couches and sofas and stuffed chairs were bathed in a bright yellow light from the crystal chandeliers. It was filled with women, talking and chattering away.

"Good morning, Madame," a smartly-attired young man said. "Your name, please, Madame?"

"Barbier," Julienne whispered.

He looked at a list in his cloth-bound book. "Ah, yes, Madame Barbier. Please follow me, Madame." He led her up the long winding staircase on the left, up and above the reception area.

On the first landing, she heard a loud shrill voice from the room to her left:

"He is monstrously expensive!"

The door opened in a flurry and Julienne saw the distinctive profile instantly: the yellowish skin, the large eyes that seemed to pop out of her face, the thick lips, and that memorable, familiar complaining voice—Metternich, Princess Pauline Metternich, wife of the Austrian Ambassador to France.

Julienne lowered her head and hid part of her face with her hand as she quickened her steps behind the page. How could I be so stupid, she thought. They're all here, the court ladies, the noblewomen . . . stay calm, she ordered herself, and felt strange remembering Jeannot's words of don't run . . . And I thought he would bring me to a dressmaker, a small shop somewhere on the Right Bank . . . I never expected this . . . Pauline . . . Pauline is here . . .

Once she was safe inside the private room reserved for her, and the door was closed, she took an easy breath. I must have been mad, she thought, and listened at the door to the main hall. Pauline had not noticed her. Had anyone?

She opened the door and peeked out. Everyone below was going about their own business.

And who am I in the scheme of their lives? To Pauline I am someone, she thought, and to other Austrians I would be someone, but here, with these Society women? Now she felt silly. What vanity, she decided, and quietly closed the door, looking for the first time at the room. It was of a good size, with rich wooden floors, a large triple mirror, gas-lights on the walls and a high-backed sofa next to a brown upholstered chair. There was a second door at the far end of the room, and when it opened, she saw an attractive woman walk across the floor. She wore a plain brown day dress unmistakably designed by her employer.

"Good morning, Madame Barbier," she said. "I am Madame Sophie." She courteously nodded her head.

After taking off her hat and cloak, Julienne sat with her on the small sofa.

"It is our understanding," Sophie began, opening a small book, "that you are ordering three day dresses, two evening gowns, two dinner gowns, two ballgowns, one opera gown and an evening cape. We were also informed that it is of the greatest importance that one of the evening dresses and the cape be ready by Tuesday next. Is this correct, Madame Barbier?"

I am not mad, Julienne thought, he is mad, quite mad, but she smiled at Edward's generosity and nodded to the waiting Madame Sophie.

"It will be difficult," Sophie went on, "but as we informed the Marquis de Roquetanière, we will, of course, accommodate you. Unfortunately, the final fitting will be Tuesday morning. I apologize for the inconvenience this will cause you, but it is the only time we could find. Eleven o'clock, Tuesday morning, and again, we apologize to you. If I may make one suggestion, Madame?"

"Yes," Julienne said.

"If you were to choose that particular gown first, my assistant will begin the preparations for it immediately. We shall measure you after you choose the dress."

"Yes," Julienne said, feeling very much at ease. It had been such a long time since she had dealt with dressmakers of this kind, and watched as Madame Sophie rang a small silver bell.

The assistant entered the room from the rear door and quietly approached her superior.

"We shall begin with the evening gowns," Sophie said.

The assistant nodded, and disappeared as quietly as she had come in.

"Madame, you may either choose the actual gown the mannequin wears, or the general style and then choose other colors more to your liking. My assistant will bring in our samples of colors later."

Julienne was amazed by the magnificent Worth designs. Some had embroidered skirts; others had intricate lace over the plain skirt material; some were made of satin; still others, of velvet; and one had the bodice and skirt edged with brocaded satin.

It was only then that she noticed the lines of the low bodices, and when the mannequins turned around, she saw the lines repeated on all seven dresses—the sloping front, just above the bosom, to the bare shoulders, and nearly half-exposed back.

The scars, Julienne winced. In Vienna, on those rare occasions when Franz allowed friends to visit, she had draped herself in shawls, and feigned a cold. She had seen in the mirror, not herself, but her mother-in-law, Iren, a living corpse of gauze and lace.

"And now," Madame Sophie was saying, "come in one at a time for a closer inspection.

As the mannequins glided from the room, Julienne turned to Madame Sophie. "They are exquisite," she said quietly, "but there is one problem."

Madame Sophie's eyes had remained cool and passive.

"Several years ago," Julienne began, "I suffered a terrible accident. It left scars and I am reluctant to have them seen."

The assistant poked her head through the door.

"No, not yet," Sophie said, and waited for the assistant to disappear.

"The scars are on my back, and . . ."

"We are able to raise the back, Madame Barbier. If you would accompany me to the mirror, I will measure the distance now."

The tension in Julienne's shoulders lessened as she walked across the room to the triple mirror.

"Turn sideways, Madame, please," Sophie said as she produced her small measuring tape. "The gowns, as they are now, come to here," she said and gently touched the point mid-way between the shoulder blades.

Julienne studied the line and knew it was too low. She shook her head.

"We might raise it to here," Sophie said and brought her finger up three inches. "In this way, we preserve the line of the bodice and it will still remain off your shoulders, as is the style."

She knew her back and the scars on it. Most of them were in the middle and lower. Only a few were near the very upper back and shoulders. "Yes, that will do," Julienne said.

Madame Sophie dutifully noted the distance from the waist to the new top of the back, measured Madame Barbier now, and then led her back to the sofa to choose her dress.

". . . and?" Cécile said, leaning closer across the table.

"And I inquired about a shoemaker, because as you know, I have nothing suitable."

"Yes, yes," Cécile prompted.

"And she told me that orders had been placed with a shoemaker, a M. Massez, Number Nine on Rue de la Paix—Worth recommends him highly—but not only that, she also told me orders had been placed at a glovemaker and at a store for undergarments. I need only go and pick what I want, and everything will be waiting for me with the gown on Tuesday. And after the fitting they will, of course, deliver everything to my door."

Cécile sighed. "Oh, he must love you, he must adore you," she said. "Such thoughtfulness, such . . . such generosity."

Julienne smiled. "Thoughtfulness, yes." She opened a small box and took out a handful of velvet ribbons. "This is the color of the flowers, on the gauze."

Cécile sighed again, holding the rich-looking apricot-colored ribbons. "Exquisite," she breathed, "exquisite . . . Did you see *him* at all?"

"Worth?"

"Yes."

"No," she said.

Cécile took a sip of her tea. "I've read in the newspapers that he tells the woman how *she* should look."

Julienne shook her head with a smile. "I thought I would use some of the ribbons for my hair. You don't think I'm too old for that, do you?"

Cécile shook her head. "Do you have combs, and beads, perhaps, to fasten to the end of the ribbons?"

She shook her head.

"I do," Cécile smiled, "leave it to me."

"I thought I would put the large ribbon around my neck, women still do that. I've seen them wear velvet ribbons instead of jewelry."

"You will be the jewel," Cécile said.

"I'll have to, won't I?"

Cécile laughed. "I will help you all you need on Tuesday."

"I was hoping you would."

"Oh it is too exciting," Cécile breathed.

Five sets of hands touched her. Five strangers pulled and tugged and adjusted and pinned in an organized confusion as her feet ached in the new shoes.

The corset pinched, the padded crinoline underneath the layers of the skirt was heavy and Julienne could barely breathe.

"So," Madame Sophie said with a weighty sigh, "only an inch then."

Julienne craned her neck. It was the hem again, this time at the rear of the large dress forming a hint of a train. The style had changed slightly, because Worth decided to change it. The dress was not as wide at the sides, but was now fuller in the back.

"And now, Madame Barbier," Sophie said, "if you will please accompany me, we will go downstairs to the Salon de Lumière. It is our examination of what the dress will look like in proper surroundings."

Julienne nodded and with the help of the assistants, all very careful not to dislodge any pins, she followed Madame Sophie down the steps to the Salon de Lumière for the inspection of the gown in a ballroom setting. She gathered the dress slightly at her sides and moved across the floor. She turned, watching her reflection and the line at the upper back.

I wonder who she is, Sophie thought, watching the woman glide across the floor. I have seen them all, and I have assisted "himself" on the special calls to the houses of aristocrats . . . once, even, to the Tuileries for the Empress. This one, she thought, is not the usual class of woman the Marquis has sent to us. The others, she smiled to herself, those other women were first all wide-eyed, and then came the airs. Not her, she thought. This quiet one knows

167

how to stand, how to move, how to speak and it is all so natural. She must have been taught when she was a young child.

Julienne turned and smiled at Madame Sophie. "It is lovely," she said. "I am very pleased."

Sophie gave a courteous nod of her head. She is delighted, Sophie thought as they left the room. But Sophie knew it was spoken with the restraint of an aristocrat to a dressmaker.

It happened at some point after Julienne had bathed, then washed her hair and dried it before the fire, then partially dressed and covered herself with a robe. As she sat in the kitchen and listened to Cécile hum a little song as she began braiding a portion of the thick hair, Julienne could feel other hands touching the hair, smaller hands with long fingers lifting and combing and separating a little girl's hair. She saw in her mind the edge of her bed and the reflection of her mother in the mirror sitting behind her. She closed her eyes for a moment and felt that mother's touch, the special gentle smoothing of the hair near the brow. It was a moment's warmth, a fragile mist that disappeared when Frédéric returned from school and mumbled a hello before going to his room and quietly shutting the door behind him.

"Doesn't he want to watch?" Gisèle asked as Cécile wound a strand of hair around the hot iron, and she heard the sizzle and saw the steam.

"Tut," Cécile smacked her lips. "Little boys have no interest in this sort of thing."

Julienne smiled at Gisèle. "Madame Mabilleau is right."

By six o'clock, they had finished her hair. Long thick braids had been looped and drawn back up to the crown where Cécile would later fasten the combs with the ribbon strands and beads. Underneath this rich cascade, the crimped ringlets and curls drifted beautifully down the center of the back.

"I am surprised," Cécile sighed, "we did not even need the padding for fullness. But then, you have such beautiful hair. Come along, now, we haven't much time."

Julienne and Gisèle followed Cécile to the bedroom and shut the door. There, she slipped out of the robe, then stepped into the crinolines which Cécile drew up from the floor and tied securely at the waist in the back.

Over that, Julienne put on the new cambric petticoat which buttoned at the waist. Then, the large skirt of the dress was drawn up and buttoned at the back.

The bodice piece of the dress was next, and as Julienne slipped her arms through the tiny sleeves just below the shoulders, Cécile adjusted it and made sure it was properly aligned with the skirt. Then she hooked and tied the small lacings which had been ingeniously designed and were hidden by a flap that fastened and was made to look like a design in the dress. "It is too beautiful," Cécile said. "And I am too old for this," she sighed, feeling an ache in her lower back.

As Julienne lifted the back curls, Cécile tied the embroidered velvet ribbon around her neck. Then the combs and the ribbons for the hair were gently put in place. Julienne turned slowly and looked at the exhausted Cécile. "Well?" she asked.

Cécile arched an eyebrow. "Almost," she said, and then with a secret smile, went to the box she had brought with her. From it, she took out a white and gold fan. "My Armand gave this to me for our wedding. I thought, I thought you might like to borrow it."

Julienne smiled. "How kind you are, yes, thank you. You *and* I shall go to the theater now."

Cécile grinned, then turned away for a moment. "There is one other," she said. "You admired it once. And I thought, perhaps wearing it would please you." From the box she took out a small bottle of perfume.

Julienne undid the stopper and the fragrant scent of lilacs filled her heart and mind with soft images of pastel-colored dresses and warm, loving eyes.

"You mustn't cry," Cécile said, stepping closer. "Ooh-lah, if I thought it would make you cry I would not have brought it. You mustn't, it will spoil everything." She hesitated, then placed her arms around the small back. She drew the younger woman closer and gave a comforting pat between the shoulders. "You loved her very much, didn't you?"

Julienne returned the hug. "Yes," she answered. "My mother was a kind, thoughtful woman. Like you." She kissed Cécile's cheek.

"Oh, your eyes," Cécile said, turning away. "They're red. Let me get some water and we'll make a compress to take the red away." She walked to the door and then quickly walked to the kitchen. After she'd pumped the water into a glass, she stopped and quietly, privately, touched the spot on her cheek. Such a soft kiss, she thought, a little daughter's kiss . . . She shook her head, took a breath, and went back to the bedroom with the water and a towel.

She was a woman he'd seen only in the twilight dreams of restless nights, when the mind conjured visions of imagined happiness forever out of reach. He'd sought a life's companion, yet never found one in all the women he'd ever known. The others had been so incomplete, never caring enough, never bright enough, never kind enough, never honest enough. But not her. Edward vaguely remembered speaking to Madame Mabilleau, and giving her the bonbons he'd bought for her and the children; and Gisèle, giving him a quick hug and a kiss; and from the doorway to the children's room, he'd seen the distant eyes of Frédéric before the boy had stepped back inside and closed the door.

But mostly, he saw Jeanne Barbier, the soft and elegant Jeanne Barbier, a woman with sensuous shoulders, large brown eyes, and that warm, inviting smile. As he helped her with her cape, her scent was as fragile as the lilac blossoms themselves, and from that moment, the two for him would be a single memory.

There was something remarkably new yet oddly familiar about her. He could not place it and did not trouble himself with it until they reached the restaurant, the Maison Dorée on the Boulevard des Italiens.

"I ought to explain," he began, "to save time, I took the liberty of ordering dinner when I reserved the table."

"But of course," Julienne replied.

He stood where he was for a moment.

Julienne smiled, then waited for him to follow the Maître d'Hôtel into the dining room.

Her answer startled him. And it was that disturbing voice from the corner of his mind asking again, how would she know such a thing? The embroidery girls are always so impatient in fine restaurants and, yet, she walks with such ease and seems so at home with the white damask walls and all this red plush.

He watched her with a critical eye, noticing that nothing surprised her, nothing awed her, and her calm and elegance at the table as she maneuvered the dress, and settled into the chair, were flawless.

She's living a lie, he thought. There was never a Monsieur Barbier. She has been someone's mistress, which is why she has no wedding ring. He was someone highborn, who taught her manners and bought her dresses, someone before me. Perhaps he died . . . But then he shook his head. No, if he had died, Edward thought, he would have left her something, he would have provided for her. No, he thought, they must have quarreled and he left her. Despicable man, Edward thought, to leave her with nothing, and with two children, perhaps his children . . . He sighed, wondering how she came to be at Chavastelon's, not wishing to think of the poverty or the hunger that led her there.

They spoke of literature, and her knowledge was considerable—Shakespeare, Voltaire, Dickens, Victor Hugo. After they finished their Consommé, he noticed she was listening to the music from the small orchestra at the far end of the large dining room.

She is so unlike the others, he thought, sipping his wine. Some of them were beautiful, but cold, as impersonal and as distant as works of art in a museum. But she, he thought, radiates a warmth from within. "You seem pleased with the music," Edward said.

She smiled. "They used to call him Chubby."

"Who?"

"Schubert. The orchestra is playing several of his most famous songs. That was his nickname. Chubby."

Edward felt his eyebrow arch slightly. "Oh," he said, "and was he?"

She laughed. "So I'm told."

"By whom?"

"My father."

Three waiters arrived at the table and his questions ceased as they were served the filet de boeuf Chatelaine. He meant to return to the conversation about her father, but before he could ask, she had mentioned Frédéric.

"He seemed a bit shy, earlier," Edward said.

Julienne smiled sadly. "I wish I knew what to say about that."

"Was he always shy?"

She thought, and recalled his hesitancy of meeting new people en route to Paris, and his growing silence even before they left. Finally, she nodded.

"Gisèle is so different," Edward said, "but I suppose that is often the case."

170

"Are you so very different from your brother?"

"Yes," he said, after a moment's surprise at the question. "We . . . wanted different things. We had . . . different points of view."

Julienne watched him concentrate on his food. His face changes every time his family is mentioned, she thought. His eyes cloud, and he looks bewildered. What a large wound it must be, she thought, and one that has not healed with time.

Throughout the rest of the meal, they spoke of impersonal things . . . safe in discussion of George Sand, Racine, Diderot and, most surprising of all, the Greek Classics, which led them to art and music, painters and the theater. By the time the dessert came, an elegant timbale d'Aremberg filled with layers of pears and apricot jam, the orchestra played Handel's *Water Music*. It reminded Edward of England, and with memories of England, he thought of the Queen.

"She was quite attractive when she was young. One wouldn't think so, to see her now. Widowhood and the increasing demands of the world have made her old. It has changed her face forever."

"Sad," Julienne said.

He thought for a moment. "I wonder if it will happen to the Empress."

"Well, we must all grow old," Julienne said.

"Oh I realize that," Edward replied, "but the world is changing, and she seems so burdened by her position."

Julienne shook her head slightly. "She has never become used to it. She was such a free child and now, she is a prisoner without a voice," Julienne sighed with more than a touch of sadness.

Edward eyed her. "She was never like that," he said. "She enjoys her power and it is considerable."

"No," Julienne said, "she is powerless. SiSi's only true power is her freedom to run away from the court whenever she wishes."

"I was speaking of the French Empress, Eugénie," he said evenly.

Her spoon clattered slightly against the rim of the dessert bowl. A blush spread slowly up her neck and to her cheeks. A moment later, Edward saw a peculiar smile crease her lips.

"Ah well," she said quickly, "they are all the same to me. We, we shall be late, if we stay much longer. What time does the play begin?"

"Nine o'clock," Edward said, with a hard stare. "We'll leave now, if you wish."

"Please," Julienne said, and for the first time did not meet his eyes.

Frédéric listened to the rhythmic breathing from Gisèle's bed. She was finally asleep. He gave a vicious kick to his covers and got out of bed, listening for a moment at the door of their room. He opened it a crack and saw that Madame Mabilleau had fallen asleep in the chair. She had been sewing and the dress now lay on the floor next to her feet.

He crept across the room to Gisèle's bureau, reaching in the dark for the top, and felt for the leather tube. He touched it and quietly pulled it toward him.

The covers will hide the noise, he thought, and buried himself beneath the woolen blankets. In the dark of his little tent, he opened the tube, drew out the map, and began quietly to rip it to shreds.

When he'd finished, he gathered up all the pieces and, on his toes like a thief, walked past the sleeping landlady toward the fireplace. He showered the pieces on the flowing embers, smiling with delight as the gaily colored countries went up in flames.

SiSi, Edward thought, uncomfortably, as he followed Jeanne Barbier up the stairs to her apartment. She had called the Austrian Empress SiSi. It had bothered him all evening, and during the play he had ignored the voices of the actors and listened only to the uneasy voice in his mind. He had tried to piece together the confusing elements that formed this woman, Jeanne Barbier. Had she been someone's mistress? Was he French? And why would a French-woman, hearing only the word Empress, assume it was the Austrian Empress, Elisabeth? That, in itself, was incomprehensible, but she had done it—and so calmly, too. She *must* be Austrian, he thought, despite her claims of living in Alsace.

And was she merely assuming airs, that gossipy chat reported so often in the newspapers? That irritating pose favored by so many mistresses to titled men, or was she speaking from personal knowledge, as she had done all evening?

And how did she get those curious little scars, he wondered. He had first seen them when he helped her with her cape, and had noticed them again in the restaurant. They were old, and some were nearly faded, but he had seen the handful of whitened streaks almost hidden by her hair.

He shrugged to himself. She could be from Alsace, and it could be newspaper nonsense and the pose of a mistress. Or she could be Austrian. And if Austrian, was she the mistress of an Austrian noble, which would explain very nicely her manners and education and poise . . . unless, of course, she was his wife.

And if she was his wife, how in God's name did she come to be here?

She turned and smiled at him and his doubts eased slightly. In time, he thought, she may speak of it, she may trust me with her secrets. And if she doesn't, he thought, it doesn't matter at all. We all have our dark secrets, and, God knows, I have so many of my own. She has just as much right to hers as I have to mine.

He took her hand and gave her gloved palm a lingering, affectionate kiss, then brought the hand to his cheek. "You have made this day a memorable one for me," he said softly. "This is a birthday I shall never forget. And you've promised not to forget Friday, haven't you?"

"Yes," she smiled. "I shan't forget."

"And Saturday, my afternoon with Frédéric? You will not forget to mention it to him, will you?"

She shook her head. "My memory is a good one."

"I've known that from the first."

She laughed. "That seems so long ago. And how different you are now, from that day."

He grinned, slightly embarrassed. "Too much wine makes one much too bold."

She withdrew her hand slowly from his.

He walked to the steps and tapped the edge of the banister. "That first day, yes, I was rude and numbed by wine. But the second time we met, that was my true self. You see me now as I really am. You believe me, don't you?"

"I cannot say," she answered, "because I don't really know you, do I?"

He laughed slightly. "What a cautious woman you are."

I've had a lot of practice, Julienne thought.

He took a step down and reached for her hand, and when he did, she squeezed his palm. "I suppose caution is not so terrible a thing," Edward commented. "No one may force trust in another." He watched, surprised, as that friendly, delicate hand slowly pulled away. He wanted to reach for her again, to tell her silently with his eyes and his touch that she need not do that, but he could see that his words, somehow, had disturbed her. God knows what she is thinking, he thought, and what sort of memory has unexpectedly hurt or frightened her. Edward felt the sudden chilling distance and when she finally looked at him again, he hoped to bridge that distance with a tender smile. "It's late," he said. "You must be tired."

She nodded.

"Goodnight, then." He watched as she backed away from him and could only see this phantom woman disappearing within herself, and then into the darkness right in front of his eyes. When the door had closed and she had gone, all the warmth in the stairwell had gone with her.

CHAPTER
11

It had been a dismal afternoon, a grey day echoed by a grey little boy. And though Frédéric had answered politely the questions put to him, he had not given himself to the world of the marionettes; the sad, faraway look stayed with him all through the performance and lingered still as Edward led him out to the overcast street and then to the waiting carriage. It was all an uncomfortable reminder of the last outing Edward had spent with the children.

When the carriage stopped at the Boulevard St. Michel entrance to the Jardin du Luxembourg, for the briefest of moments Frédéric looked surprised.

"I thought," Edward smiled, "we might walk for a short time, and then go to Pons for a treat. Would you like that?"

The sad look returned and the boy did not answer.

"Come along, then," Edward said quietly, stepping out of the carriage and holding his hand toward Frédéric. This time, as the last, the boy jumped out of the carriage without assistance, and then shoved both his hands deeply into his pockets, tight little fists making tight little balls inside the cloth. Edward sighed, wondering what to do.

It was a silent walk along the path and then down the steps by the small pond, where he had seen Jeanne Barbier walking some seven weeks ago. It hasn't been so very long a time, Edward thought, and yet, it was enough time to change my attitude toward life. He smiled to himself. One of life's little ironies, he thought, when, at the strangest of moments, one individual alters forever the course of another's life. He looked down at Frédéric and saw the boy watching a group of boys chasing each other in front of the imposing Gothic Palais Luxembourg.

"They seem to be having a good time," he said to Frédéric, and when the boy made no response, added, "Do you have friends—in school, I mean?"

"Yes, I have many many friends, Sir."

But it was said without pleasure or confidence. I sounded just like that, Edward thought, telling my father how much I liked Eton, and how well I was getting along, and how many friends I had. I lied, as he does now. I had never belonged and was an isolated boy in the midst of other people's friends. As they walked on the path leading to the gazebo, Edward thought Frédéric an eerie reminder of himself. They sat down on a wooden-slat bench facing a small stark green, an area that in the spring would be alive with color and flowers, but now had only the cold emptiness of winter. Edward shifted slightly and turned his head left to look at Frédéric. The boy slouched, his eyes staring at the methodical private rhythm of his swinging left leg.

"Do you like school?" Edward asked.

"Yes."

"So you find pleasure in your lessons?"

"Yes."

"And do you visit your friends?"

"Oh yes."

"Do they come to visit you?"

Frédéric shook his head.

"Why not?"

Frédéric shrugged and looked farther away.

Though the boy sat next to him, Edward felt as if he were struggling to see clearly through a window nearly frosted by snow—a fragmented boy's shadow distant and remote hinted at the form, but the small words and phrases were muted to silence by an impenetrable layer of ice.

Frédéric's hands came out of the pockets, and he played with his thumbnail.

Edward quickly looked away as a chill tickled his spine. Good God, he thought, just like the train ride. He tried to stop thinking of it, but his mind kept connecting Frédéric's hands, the swinging leg, the posture, to that particular June day in 1846.

I was ten years old, Edward thought. And Michael, Michael had just died in London. And we were bringing the coffin to Chadwell for burial.

～

It was a confused dream of ghostly images, and a pungent smell of Lavender salts in a small vial held under his mother's nose. She would jerk her head back and away, then cry from beneath the thick black veil, but the smell would linger in the closed and stifling train car. His father's skin was grey, the deep-set blue eyes had dark circles underneath, and there seemed to be more wrinkles on the skin overnight.

Hours passed. Hours of the same quiet, the same dull thudding in the ears as the train continued on its journey. Edward, not knowing what to do, where to look, if to speak at all, played with his thumbnail.

When they came to Melton Mowbray, the coffin was lifted out by pall-bearers and brought to a waiting hearse, drawn by black horses. It led the procession the remaining four and a half miles to Chadwell.

He saw the church, St. Mary's, on the slight hill in the distance. It had been built by the Duke's ancestors in the sixteenth century. Rising above the trees, the tall sandstone belfry tower had aged badly and it now was a dullish yellow against an extremely blue and cloudless sky.

Edward stepped out of the carriage and tugged at his collar. It itched and felt tight. Master Chester, his tutor, shook his head once, and Edward stopped fidgeting. He then followed silently behind his parents.

They were met at the Lych-gate by the Reverend Mr. Dowd. He had a kindly look about him, and though his hair was thinning, his face was full and round with clear brown eyes and a gentle smile. Mr. Dowd waited until the pall-bearers and the family were all in order, then he turned around leading them through the churchyard, holding his open book and reciting in a clear voice, "I am the Resurrection and the Life, saith the Lord: he that believeth in me, though he were dead, yet shall he live: and whosoever liveth and believeth in me shall never die . . ."

Walking through the South Porch and along the south transept, it felt cool inside as Mr. Dowd intoned: "We brought nothing into this world and it is certain we can carry nothing out. The Lord gave and the Lord hath taken away; blessed be the Name of the Lord . . ."

The four large perpendicular windows on both sides of the church allowed a soft and generous light. As they walked down the center aisle, Edward saw the tenant farmers from his father's lands sitting alongside the townspeople from Chadwell. Some of the servants from the house were there. Even Gerald and the boys who worked the stables were there.

They took their seats in the family pew with the carved wooden pulpit in front of them. Then, Mr. Dowd began the Psalm readings. Edward's mind began to drift. The words were large and complicated and his mother kept sighing. He found himself counting the sighs and not listening to the words.

When it was time for them to return to the churchyard, Edward followed behind his parents. Half-way down the aisle, he was startled by the sight of his father suddenly helping his mother to keep her balance, and then, to continue walking.

175

The sun was bright, the Yew trees in the churchyard smelt clean, and Edward counted the tombstones all the way to the corner of the yard where people stood quietly near a small building. Birds called loudly from the trees and Edward shaded his eyes to try and see them, but Mr. Dowd was speaking again and his mother had moaned.

"Thou knowest, Lord, the secrets of our hearts; shut not Thy merciful ears to our prayer, but spare us, Lord most Holy, O God most mighty, O Holy and Merciful Savior . . ."

Edward looked inside this little building and saw strange names. Lady Caroline Atherton-Moore, beloved daughter, he read. But there was only one year under the name, 1834. Why was that, he wondered, and who was she? And who was Lord Charles Atherton-Moore, beloved son, who died at birth in 1838?

They shut the door.

No, don't, Edward thought, he doesn't like small rooms, don't lock him inside that small room.

His mother was crying, and Master Chester's hand was on his shoulder. He turned around to go back to the small building, but Master Chester led him away.

That night, when Edward should have been in bed, he lay awake by the window watching the sky's gradual darkness and then, the quarter moon and the stars.

I never told him, Edward shivered. I have to and I didn't . . . and, and they put him in a small room. He doesn't like small rooms, he's afraid of small rooms . . .

He pulled on his breeches. Carrying his shoes, he crept down the long hallway and saw the light from his father's study at the other end. Hugging the wall, Edward looked inside and saw his father. The heavily lined face was greyer than ever, the lips were trembling, and he was sitting at the desk with all the prize medals Michael had won at Eton spread before him.

Edward shifted his weight, the floorboard creaked, and he almost stepped into the room, but stopped when he heard his father's voice:

"Michael?"

Edward stepped back deeper into the darkened hallway, hearing only the sound of tears from the study.

The little hands holding the shoes and touching the wall felt their way downstairs. He couldn't move the big door in the front, and when the clock chimed ten he was so surprised he dropped the shoes. The white drawing room, he thought, and went there. He put on his shoes, parted the curtains, opened the doors to the stone portico and let himself out.

He began to run in the cold night air down the main drive toward the road. He kept remembering all the stories Michael had told him of bloodthirsty wolves and ghosts that came out at night and ate bad little boys whilst they were still alive, and screaming, too. He was frightened, and thought of turning back, but he thought of Michael, trapped inside the small room, and kept going.

He walked, then ran, then walked and ran the two and a half miles to St. Mary's. He saw the belfry tower, a dark structure with shadows playing at its base. He stood for a long time at the Lych-gate, unable to move, touching the wood. The hoot of an owl scared him inside.

He tried very hard not to notice the strange white crosses and tombstones, and just ran to the small building in the far corner. Exhausted, every part of him ached and he was terribly cold.

All the flowers and wreaths people had left behind looked strangely black in the quarter-moon's light. He pushed the wreaths away from the door.

"Michael?" He knocked softly on the door. "Michael, come out of there. Michael, you don't like small rooms, come out, answer me, please Michael?" He hit the door with his fist and pulled on the handle. It was locked.

"MICHAEL!" he shrieked. "Come out, I'm sorry, I'm sorry, come out of there, it's my fault, I didn't mean it, I didn't mean to make you laugh . . ."

∾

Edward watched a fragment of a leaf, brown and dry, dead as all the others, flutter by his feet on the path in the Jardin du Luxembourg. He took a breath and noticed Frédéric's leg had stopped swinging. "I'm cold," he said to the boy and stood up. "It is time we were going."

In the warmth of Pons, he watched Frédéric only nibble at the pastry, then take a sip of hot chocolate. When he took a second sip, a lock of the blond hair fell onto his forehead.

Edward reached across the table to brush it from the boy's eyes.

Frédéric jerked his head away in a wide-eyed flinch. He stared for a moment, then nervously looked at his plate.

Why had he done that, Edward thought. What did he think I was going to do to him?

Stefan must be safe and well, Julienne thought, standing near the fireplace. I've read nothing strange in the newspapers. And, God forbid, if anything had happened, I know it would have been in the papers.

The door opened and she jumped.

"Oh, sorry," Edward said, holding the door for Frédéric. "Didn't mean to startle you."

Julienne tried to smile. "Did you have fun today?" she asked Frédéric.

He looked at her, nodded, then asked to be excused. When he was given permission, he barely glanced at Edward, then backed into his room, closing the door after him.

"Was he any better this afternoon?" Julienne asked.

Edward shook his head. "He seems frightened of me."

"Habit," she sighed, preoccupied with thoughts of Stefan, then realized what she'd said. "It's nothing," Julienne amended quickly, "nothing at all. You needn't concern yourself."

Frustrated, Edward tossed his hat, gloves and walking stick down on the chair by the fireplace and stepped closer to her. "For pity's sake," he said, taking her hands in his own, "don't make the same mistake my mother made about me. I know you have more kindness than that, and a child's fear or awkwardness or . . ."

A loud yelp followed by a shriek came from the children's room. Edward

177

reached the door first and flung it open. He saw Gisèle sitting on the edge of her bed, holding the side of her face, crying.

The instant Edward entered the room, Frédéric jumped back from Gisèle and flattened himself against the far wall. And when Edward walked closer to him, the boy's eyes widened dramatically, his body visibly shook, and now he stared only at the floor.

"Gisèle," Julienne soothed, holding the little girl, "tell me what happened."

"He, he pulled my hair," she stammered, "and, and he hit me, he hit me in the face, and he, he pulled my hair," she cried, leaning into her mother.

Frédéric was breathing very hard and very fast, and his fingertips turned white from pressing them against the wall. All he could see were the large black shoes and the man's shadow.

"Why did he do all that?" Julienne asked, watching Frédéric.

"Because, I said, I said he took my map, and it's gone, and then he pulled my hair and he hit me."

Frédéric's mouth opened a fraction, but no sound came out. He knew what was coming from the tall man towering over him.

Edward knelt down on one knee. Good Lord, he thought, he has the eyes of a cornered animal. "Did you take the map?" he asked softly, moving his hand slowly to smooth the rumpled shoulder of the boy's jacket. He stopped when he saw Frédéric watching his hand, and then take a step to the right to avoid the hand. "Did you?" he repeated.

Frédéric shook his head.

"I believe you," Edward said, noticing the large tear that suddenly appeared and slid down the pale cheeks. Edward moved his hand slowly, gently, and though the boy turned his head away and braced himself for some unseen avalanche, Edward managed to wipe the tear with his thumb. "Brothers do not fight with their sisters. You must tell Gisèle you're sorry you hit her," he said, then stood up and left the room.

As he finished pulling the glove onto his left hand, he heard the door to the children's room close, and then a moment later, a floorboard creaked with her step. He saw the confusion in Jeanne Barbier's eyes. "I apologize," Edward said. "It wasn't my place to speak to the boy in that manner. I'm sorry for intruding."

Julienne brushed aside his apology. "You know he took the map," she said quietly.

"Of course."

"Then why did you say you believed him?"

"Because he seems troubled and frightened and he has lied to me all afternoon," Edward replied in a soft voice. "Before the puppet show, I asked him about his father. He told me how much his father loved him, all that they did together—playing soldiers, riding together, playing chess, his father taught him this or that and spent so much time with him and his father was so wonderful and never never hurt him." He glanced up when he heard the sharp intake of breath. "Yes, and more. In the park, he told me he has many many friends, and he visits them, but strangely, they never visit him here. He's not a very good liar, Jeanne." He tossed the hat back onto the chair and tugged a little too hard on his right-hand glove.

Julienne stared at the fire, arms crossed tightly in front of her. She felt the gloved finger lift her chin and then saw his clear, friendly blue eyes.

"When one is lost, it is a terrible unique fear. Even a small boy may feel that. And for him, the world is that much more an awesome and ugly place. It is a bitter business when one's dreams are shattered, one's hopes destroyed, and one's trust misplaced. I know those feelings only too well." Edward bent down slightly, and gave a brief but tender kiss to her lips. "I have run away from far too many things in my life," he whispered, "but I shan't ignore him, this . . . or you." He left quietly and shut the door behind him.

Outside, taking a deep breath of cold air, Edward felt suddenly tired. He stepped closer to the carriage and looked up toward her apartment as he usually did. From the salon's window he saw her, as always, and courteously tipped his hat to her.

But something moved at the other window, the window to the children's room, the window between their beds. He looked and saw a small form, now partly hidden by the wall. A moment's glimpse was all he needed—the hair was blond.

A confident smile began to play at Edward's lips. So, he thought, curious after all, and perhaps confused as well? I shall never give you up for lost, Frédéric. I may know it now, but you shall know it, too, and very soon.

Philippe saw less of him than ever. Though it would have pleased Edward to think of his actions as some sort of military campaign, he knew that was not the truth. He had told Jeanne that no one may force trust, or that which accompanied trust—affection. And what was the truth for her, was also the truth for the boy.

It surprised him to discover, some three weeks later, that he was content to spend his afternoons with the children. Gisèle always sat close to him, and participated completely in the story-telling, laughing and listening, but when Frédéric came home from school, he lingered in the salon, taking a chair as far as possible from Edward, and never joined in the conversation, yet, he was there.

Frédéric, Edward thought, hasn't changed—or has he? Sipping a brandy in his room by the fireplace, Edward remembered the Zoo, and how delighted the boy had been. He laughed and stared at the animals, but that stubborn little beggar wouldn't admit it, would he? Edward chuckled and then shook his head. No, he would not admit it. He insisted he did not have a good time, and wanted to go home. The little liar, Edward smiled. And at Jardin des Tuileries, last Sunday . . . I sent him out to the boulevard to buy bon-bons from a vendor. He clutched the centimes in his hand, then scampered away, happy as you please, skipping and kicking loose stones with his feet just like an ordinary boy. I saw the smile on his face when he came back. And I saw how quickly that expression changed when *he* noticed that *I* noticed the smile. Crafty little boy, Edward thought and placed the brandy glass down.

He is still squabbling with Gisèle, though, Edward thought. Jeanne said they had another fight last night and he made her cry again. Pinched her, or something.

He lit his pipe and stared into the fire. I fought with Michael, he thought; many times, sometimes brutally. All he had to do was mention things he'd done before I was born—places our father had taken him, a ride on a horse, anything before I was born or when I was very, very young. He could push me into a black and ugly rage.

Jealous, he thought.

The following Saturday was a mild day, and Edward stood in the salon with a mysterious smile on his face, hands placed at his waist as he looked down at Frédéric.

"I've a surprise for you," he said, grinning so broadly the dimples in his cheeks seemed deep as dark chasms. "Just you and I are going out."

Frédéric looked up at him and turned away. "I, I don't feel well," he mumbled and took a step behind his mother's skirt.

Julienne shook her head, exasperated.

"Pity," Edward went on, not in the least dismayed. "It's a fine surprise. And you know my surprises are quite good." He watched the boy think it over. "What a pity," he said, playing the actor and emphasizing all the right words. "I thought long and hard and decided on a special surprise every boy in the world would enjoy. Ahh, well, I suppose I'll have to enjoy it all by myself, then."

"What is it?" Frédéric managed.

Edward shook his head. "It wouldn't be a surprise, then."

"May I go?" Gisèle asked.

Frédéric glared at her, then his defeated eyes stared once more at the floor.

"No, sorry," Edward said pleasantly, noticing it all. "This is a surprise for a boy. Shame, really, that Frédéric doesn't wish to have it. I suppose I'll have to find some other boy . . ." He watched the slow movement, the quiet movement, the boy stepping out from behind his mother's skirt. "Come along," he said easily, watching as Frédéric shoved those hands deeply into his pockets.

They sat opposite each other in the carriage, Frédéric looking out the window and occasionally stealing glances toward Edward. "Is it the Zoo?" he asked.

Edward shook his head "no."

"But the Zoo is this way?"

He shook his head. "It lies in the opposite direction."

"Won't you tell me, please?"

"No. I'd spoil it then," Edward smiled.

The boy looked very confused when they'd passed the Arc de Triomphe and kept traveling on the Avenue de la Grande Armée. When they passed Porte de Neuilly, and after a time turned left onto Avenue de Longchamp, he simply accepted it would be a surprise, and no amount of asking was going to change it. Avenue de Longchamp went through the Bois de Boulogne. Frédéric saw huge trees, cool paths, large open greens and people riding horses or promenading in their carriages.

Ten minutes or so later, the carriage stopped.

"We're here," Edward announced, and opened the door of the carriage, knowing full well the boy would follow unassisted. He waited and saw the quizzical look on Frédéric's face. "A friend has lent me your surprise for the day. It doesn't belong to me, but for today, it is all yours." He led the boy down the path to one of Philippe's stablehands holding the bridles of a large saddled bay, and alongside it, a small grey pony.

The boy's smile warmed and brightened. He ran to the pony, touched it, caressed the velvet nose with his hands and then rubbed his cheeks back and forth on that smooth and lovely muzzle, giggling when the pony breathed.

"Do you know how to ride?" Edward asked.

Frédéric closed his eyes as he leaned against the pony's neck. He nodded.

"I would have taught you, had you not known how." He paused, then said, "What are you waiting for? Mount up."

The wide eyes were filled with delight and Frédéric could not put his foot in the stirrup fast enough.

Edward gave his walking stick to the groom, mounted the bay, then watched as the boy followed him on his pony. He led Frédéric out to the main bridle path.

"I had a pony, once," he said to Frédéric, "when I was a boy. Taffy-Anne, that was her name. She was cream-colored, and I learnt how to ride on her. I think she was my favorite."

They rode along the cool path, underneath trees that had the first hints of buds. They heard the calls of birds, and could feel the sudden warmth of the sun when they walked out of the patches of shadows.

"Taffy-Anne," he went on with a smile. "She and I had many favorite places on my father's lands. A special stream, a special meadow, a special hill. I discovered them all when I went riding alone. Wonderful," he breathed, "it was wonderful. Have you ever been here before?"

"No," Frédéric said, keeping pace.

"Then we shall find a favorite place today, a special place."

Frédéric smiled.

Edward gently kicked the sides of the bay, spurring him on a little faster, always making sure the boy could keep up and not lose control of the pony. He'd asked for a gentle little pony, and Philippe had sworn the grey was as sweet as they come. He heard a giggle next to him, a pleased and excited giggle of a little boy having fun.

"Faster?" Edward asked.

"Yes, yes," Frédéric answered.

They went faster for a stretch, leaving the path and heading through an open green with centuries-old trees forming a huge circle around them. There, they slowed to a walk and allowed the horses to cool down.

"Did you always have Taffy-Anne?" Frédéric asked.

"For most of my life, yes."

"What happened?"

Edward looked at Frédéric. "Like anything that lives, she grew old. Before I went to Woolwich . . ."

181

"The military school?" he asked.

"Yes," Edward answered, now knowing the boy had heard every word of the stories told in the afternoons to both children. "Before I went to Woolwich, I gave her to one of the tenant farmers. He had small children, and she always liked to be near children. They loved to groom her and comb her mane."

"Did you see her?"

"Yes," he said. "I would visit her. You would have liked her very much. She was sweet and gentle. She had lost some teeth by then, so I would make a mash for her to eat. Carrots and apples, some grains mixed in. Looked very nasty, but smelled good. And she did love it so."

"She . . . she isn't there anymore?" Frédéric asked.

"No," Edward answered calmly. "She died, some years back. But she lived a good life, a long life. A happy one, too. Isn't it odd, I may say that about a pony's life, and many people could not say the same about their own lives . . ."

"Did . . . did those children miss her, Sir?"

"Yes," Edward said. "I miss her. Do you know what I used to do?" he asked, looking down at Frédéric alongside him on the right.

The boy shook his head.

Edward smiled warmly. "When I was small, and the world seemed too big a place for me, I would ride Taffy-Anne as fast as I could, then I'd walk her a bit so she might cool down, and when she was, and I was near my most favorite place of all, I'd leave her and run and run and run as fast as I was able, until I could run no more. And then, I'd sit beneath my favorite tree in all the world, and rest for a bit in the shade, listening to the birds, watching them fly, or trying to see shapes in the clouds . . ."

"I play that game, with the clouds."

"Do you? Well, I used to play it, too. And if I was very quiet and had a bit of luck, I saw deer. They're very beautiful, you know, and very fast. And easily frightened. Like people."

"Did they run away when they saw you?"

"I'd try to be quiet," Edward laughed, "but I suppose I wasn't. Yes, they ran away when they knew I was there. But I'd seen them, and that was good enough for me."

"Do you think there are any deer here, Sir?" Frédéric asked.

"Possibly. Shall we try it—riding and running and resting and then waiting for the deer and see if they pass by?"

Frédéric nodded vigorously.

"Then I'll race you," Edward said and kicked the bay with his heels.

They galloped across a field, then up a slight incline and saw it, far ahead, a gathering of bare trees surrounded by bushes. Edward kept turning around to watch Frédéric, but the boy was riding splendidly. After a few minutes, he tugged on the reins and slowed the bay down.

"Good," Edward breathed, "good. Now we'll let them cool a bit. There, do you see it, far ahead, those trees?"

Frédéric was completely out of breath and could only nod.

"That's a good place, isn't it?"

Again, the boy nodded.

"We've discovered it, then, a special place, the most special place in all the Bois."

They walked a bit more, then Edward suddenly dismounted. Frédéric followed his example. Edward took the reins of both horses, tied them to a bush, then tossed his hat to the ground some distance away from the horses.

"Now," Edward said, "that way. You run until you can run no more." He ran as he had run as a child, wild and hard, a game he hadn't played for years. His long legs and speed put quite a distance between himself and Frédéric, but when he heard the muffled cry behind him, he stopped quickly, whirled around and nearly slid off his balance. He saw the boy on the ground, and ran back as fast as he could to Frédéric. The boy was holding his right knee and trying not to cry.

Edward knelt on the ground in front of the boy. "Let me see your knee."

Frédéric looked up with those all-too-familiar terrified eyes. "I'm—I'm sorry, Sir," he stammered. "I, I didn't mean to spoil everthing. I'm clumsy, I know I'm clumsy, everybody, everybody says so."

"What rubbish. Let me see your knee," Edward repeated.

"It, it doesn't hurt. It doesn't."

"It should. That's quite a cut you've got there," Edward said, spreading the hole in the trouser leg. He looked up at Frédéric too quickly and the boy flinched back from him. He paused, then said firmly, "You are not clumsy. It could have happened to anyone. I've fallen, everybody does at one time or another. You are *not* clumsy, and don't you believe those lies other people tell you. You haven't spoiled a thing, do you hear?"

The boy managed a nod, but still fought back his tears.

"I'm glad we understand each other," Edward said, and looked at the wound again. "You're bleeding." He loosened the silk cravat from around his neck and pulled it free. "It's not a proper bandage, but it will have to do," he said, and tore the trouser leg from the rip made by the rocks. He wrapped the cravat around the boy's knee and then said with a smile, "You'll survive." Sitting back on his heels, he took a deep breath and looked around the deserted area. "I think we've pretty well finished running for the day. A race wouldn't be fair now, would it?"

Frédéric shook his head.

"I agree. We'll go back, then. And we'll come back here when your knee is better—for a proper race and deer-watching." He stood up and waited, watching the boy struggle to his feet. When they began to walk, he could see Frédéric was limping. He stopped and waited for the boy to come alongside him. "It hurts, doesn't it?"

Frédéric looked up at him, then away. "Yes, Sir," he said, and discreetly wiped his eyes.

"Let me carry you, then," Edward said, and bent down. He waved the boy toward his back and, when he felt the small hands on his shoulders, hooked his arms beneath the boy's legs and stood up.

He took long and even strides and could feel the boy's chest leaning into him. "Better this way, isn't it?" he asked, not turning his head. He could feel a nod against his shoulder.

When he'd reached the horses, Edward bent down to let Frédéric off, then turned and lifted him up to the saddle. "I think it's best for the horses to walk back," he smiled, giving the boy the pony's reins. Then, he mounted the bay.

They spoke very little, but he watched Frédéric most of the way and when they reached the carriage, he dismounted quickly and then helped the boy down.

They walked silently to the carriage and Frédéric paused for a moment, eyeing the metal step. Edward scooped the boy up under the arms and lifted him into the carriage. "There you go," he said. Frédéric paused, then sat down on the right. Edward had seen what he had done, and sat where he usually did, on the right.

They traveled quietly for a time, and Edward saw that the boy was rubbing the palms of his hands.

"What've you got there," Edward said easily, and turned the boy's hands over. "Oh that's right, you didn't have gloves, did you?"

Frédéric looked up at him. "No, Sir."

"I should have known better," Edward replied. "I'm sorry." He cupped his hands over the boy's and rubbed them gently. "They've just been roughened up a bit by the reins. We'll ask your mother to put some salve on your hands. That will make them feel better. And next time, when we ride, I shall see to it that you wear gloves." He smiled and let go of the boy's hands.

When they reached Rue Royer Collard, Frédéric said he could manage the stairs. Edward was behind him, ready to pick him up or break a fall. The boy slowly climbed the three flights.

Edward knocked at the apartment door before opening it, and as the boy limped across the room to a chair, he explained what had happened.

"He can barely walk," Julienne said.

Edward grinned. "It's just sore, but he'll be fine, I promise."

Julienne went to look at the wound, and began to untie the cravat. "I'll have this washed for you."

"As you wish," Edward said, "but if Frédéric would like to keep it, he may, and if not, don't bother with it. Throw it away. We needed a bandage and that's all I had."

She touched the knee. "How is that?" she asked.

"It . . . it doesn't hurt so much now," Frédéric said, and as Edward walked to the chair, he looked up and smiled at the tall man.

Edward bent down and placed his hand on the boy's shoulder, giving it a warm squeeze. "I must go," he said, "so do precisely what your mother says and get that knee well as fast as you can."

"Yes, Sir," Frédéric said, "and thank you, Sir," he added as Edward walked toward the door.

In the hallway, Julienne caught up with him and took his arm. "He was better today, wasn't he?" she asked softly with a smile. "He had fun, didn't he?"

"Yes," Edward answered lightly, "he was absolutely wonderful." He smiled, then kissed her quickly. "He was pleasant," he said, and gave her another kiss, "and asked questions," he said, punctuated with a longer kiss, "and he actually laughed and smiled," he said, drawing her closer for a warm and lingering kiss that was as effortless as it was gentle. "I do love you, Madame Barbier," he said, stepping backwards and then around the banister onto the first step.

"You, you can't possibly," Julienne sputtered, leaning over the railing. "You hardly know me."

"You'd like to believe that, wouldn't you?" he grinned.

"What a wicked . . . wicked thing to say," she said and shied a step away.

"Absolutely," he quipped, thinking her like a startled deer when one steps too close and too quickly.

"And, and awful, too."

"Unquestionably awful," he said, taking another step down.

"You're a wicked, and cruel, and presumptuous man," she said.

"I am heartless," he laughed as he rounded the first landing. "Ask Frédéric. He will tell you exactly how cruel and wicked and heartless I am," Edward said, then took the steps two at a time.

He must be mad, Julienne thought, leaning against the closed apartment door, but then shook her head and smiled. She noticed Frédéric had left the chair. She saw him now across the room waiting by the window.

Julienne stood next to him and placed her hand on his shoulder. A moment later, they saw him in the street below and she saw what Edward could not see: Frédéric's hand moved slightly against the window. He waved.

CHAPTER
12

"But you must come," Edward insisted as they walked the main path in the Jardin des Tuileries, feeling a March breeze against their faces. "It will be Carnival Night, and it is the last party until Lent has passed. You must. And I've a better reason, too. Philippe is anxious to meet you."

Julienne stared at him.

"Well," Edward grinned like a boy, "meet you *again* is what I meant to say."

She laughed and continued walking with him, seeing both children far ahead of them watching a paper-boat race in the small fountain pond at the end of the path.

"It's . . . it's not a 'formal' sort of gathering," Edward said delicately, "if that is the reason for your hesitation. I can assure you, it will be just a pleasant evening with some of Philippe's friends—actors, artists, a few theater managers, people from the Opera, a few of his friends who have been traveling. It will be quite informal, so informal, in fact, you won't even have a dance programme. Philippe can be very perverse about those things. In his home, people do as they wish."

"Oh," she said, feeling herself relax. It might be safe then, Julienne thought. After all, I've been in Society's view at the Opera, the ballet, the theater, art galleries, the Louvre, and the earth hasn't swallowed me yet. If Franz had known, he would have been here by now. She waved to both children when they turned around, and watched as they walked to them.

Edward took Frédéric's and Gisèle's hands in his own as they walked out of the park toward the carriage.

They do cling to him, Julienne thought, walking alongside Frédéric. They hold his hands and stretch their necks up to see him, to speak to him, to laugh when he laughs.

When they sat in the carriage, Julienne thought how near they are to him. And how patient he is with children. His voice is always filled with the same honest kindness.

"I nearly forgot," Edward said, and let go of Frédéric's hand. "I saw this yesterday, and I thought you might like it for your treasure box." His long fingers dipped inside his waistcoat pocket and drew out a smooth, oddly colored stone, nearly violet in shade.

"Is it a fossil?" Frédéric asked, inspecting it.

"I don't think so," Edward said, "but you know what everyone says about Paris—even the grass is old."

"Where did you find it?"

"In my friend's courtyard. I've never seen one quite like it."

"Thank you," the boy beamed.

Gisèle sulked on his right.

"What a long face," Edward said, pinching her nose. "Could I possibly forget you—ever?"

"I don't like pebbles," Gisèle frowned.

"Gisèle," Julienne scolded.

The child pouted.

"I know you don't like pebbles," Edward said. "What about this?" he asked, and took out a small object wrapped in thin white paper. It was a miniature doll, fit for a small doll's house, made with wooden arms and legs, and had a tiny dress and a painted face.

"Does she have a name?" Gisèle asked.

"You name her," Edward said, and gave Gisèle the doll.

"Marie?"

"Your other doll is named Marie. Wouldn't do to have two dolls with the same name. They might get confused," Edward smiled.

"Oh." She thought, pursing her lips tighter and tighter. "Patricia?"

"Perfect."

She suddenly climbed into his lap and kissed his cheek. "Thank you," Gisèle said, then sat down next to him again.

Edward never forgets, Julienne thought, studying the calm, angular face. A pebble for the treasure box, a treasure box now filled with new things they have found together on their rides or walks; a beautiful new doll for Gisèle's sixth birthday; he replaced the map, too, and then explained that birthdays were so special, all children ought to celebrate and have presents. He gave Frédéric riding gloves, new breeches, a riding jacket and a new silk cravat for a fine young man, though Frédéric loves the one used as a bandage best of all.

When he visits, she thought, they don't want *me* to tell them stories. They want to hear *his* stories, they want to show *him* the things they have done, they want *him* to read to them and to tuck them in their beds at night, and the very last kiss goodnight *must* come from Edward.

Back in the apartment, Julienne put the tea-kettle to boil and only partially listened as Edward sat with the children in the salon, reading them a story. She'd laid the table for their afternoon tea and now set the sweets and cakes out on small platters.

Some time later, she heard his voice at the doorway.

"You've not given me your answer," he said softly.

"For what?" Julienne asked, as she arranged the apple tarts in a circle on the platter.

"The party," Edward replied, coming into the kitchen. "Shall you come?"

She looked up at him, leaning against the cupboard. "Yes."

The blue eyes brightened. "Splendid," he smiled. "And, as long as I am Father Christmas today, I'll not have you think I had forgotten you. Never you," he said, and took his left hand from behind him and placed a flat, square black case on the work table near the small window.

Julienne did not move and eyed the box with an unbroken stare. "That was not in your pocket," she said quietly.

"No. I left it in the carriage with the driver. Won't you open it?"

She shook her head.

"Why?" he asked with a small boy's innocence.

Too many bribes, she thought, I have seen too many like it . . . "It, it is generous of you," she said, "but I cannot possibly accept it."

"You don't even know what it is," Edward said.

"It makes no difference," Julienne said too quickly and too harshly, then softened her voice. "Did you think it would?"

"No, you misunderstood my words," Edward answered, then thought for a moment. "If you will not accept it as yours, then allow me to loan it to you—for Philippe's party. Is that more acceptable to you?"

She stared at the case again. "Why is it so important to you?"

Edward watched her eyes, and the disturbing way she kept her distance from the case, yet kept watching it as if it contained something awful instead of beautiful. "If it is more pleasing to you not to have it, I shall take it back."

"Yes," she said.

"Then it is done," he said easily and took the case from the table, noticing she had closed her eyes and seemed relieved. He stopped by the door and leaned in toward her, half in the kitchen and half out. "But, how am I to know if we are still friends? You're frowning, Madame Barbier," he quipped.

She felt her shoulders relax when she smiled. "We are still friends."

"That is more important to me than anything else, Jeanne," he whispered from the doorway.

She dreamt of Franz that night. A fragment of a moment, from that life so long ago. He stood quite clearly at the side of her bed and looked down at her with sad, contrite eyes.

"Why do you make me do this? You kill me a little more each and every day, Julienne. I've begged you, and begged you until the words strangle me, and you just ignore me, don't you?"

She heard him weeping, then felt the mattress sag next to her as he sat down on the bed.

"You . . . you must stop lying to me, you must . . . We cannot continue our lives like this, in this hell . . ."

She closed her eyes underneath the cold compress and wished him far away.

"My mother lied to my father, and you've made me just like him and our lives duplicate their lives. It's all your doing. How could you *do* this to me when I love you more than my own life?" he asked, placing the black case next to her hand on the sheets.

She woke in the dark and fumbled with the match on her night table and lit the oil lamp. Only then did she realize where she was. I am not afraid of the dark, Julienne told herself. There are no ghosts, and he's far away, but she still watched the corners of the room and slept with the light on.

"Oh *there's* Philippe," Edward said, indicating the entrance to the music room.

Philippe stopped speaking when he saw them begin to climb the stairs. "Do excuse me," he said to his guests and moved away from the small circle near the music room's entrance. What a creature, he thought, seeing her in the burgundy-colored Worth gown. Such magnificent skin, and shoulders. Philippe shook his head. And Edward found her in the back room of Chavastelon's—how incredible life is at times. But what nerve she had—to reject the present *I* gave to Edward so he could give it to her! What splendid nerve . . .

"Philippe," Edward said, "it is my pleasure to present Madame Jeanne Barbier."

Julienne extended her hand.

"Madame," Edward continued, "the Marquis de Roquetanière."

Philippe bowed slightly and kissed her gloved hand. "A pleasure, Madame, to meet you under better circumstances."

"For me as well."

Philippe grinned and saw the sparkling strength in her beautiful warm eyes. "I hope you will allow me some time, later this evening, to speak with you and perhaps to dance with you?"

"I have no programme," she said, looking at Edward.

Philippe chuckled. "Madame, in my home, no woman has a programme. I am a revolutionary at heart. If I had the power, we would turn back the clock to another age—and, another fashion of dress for women. The style of the great Napoleon's time was so much more 'pleasing' to the eye."

She grinned. "But if you did that, my dear Marquis, you might not have this house to enjoy. As an Aristocrat you might have forfeited your head, for a more 'revealing' women's fashion."

Philippe laughed. "You are very clever, Madame. I look forward to our conversation later. You must make yourselves comfortable. The champagne is excellent, due completely to my father's exquisite cellar, and regrettably, you must excuse me now."

Julienne smiled as Philippe returned to his circle of friends. He has a beguiling face, she thought, remembering their first meeting at Chavastelon's. He is not an attractive man, but there is an unspoiled boyish sweetness that shines in those deep-set green eyes.

Edward kissed her hand.

"He considers himself a revolutionary, does he?" she smiled.

"A decadent radical," Edward chuckled. "He strikes back at Society by detesting dance programmes, and thoroughly delights in any confusion that results."

"How very wicked," she said.

He shook his head. "It's harmless. A child's game, nothing more. Some champagne, Madame—or would you prefer to dance?"

Julienne listened to the music and met Edward's eyes. "I would like to dance."

Edward was about to lead her into the Music Room when Philippe caught his arm.

"She doesn't need to wear my mother's pearls, you know," Philippe whispered in Edward's ear.

"Yes, I know," Edward grinned, then led Jeanne Barbier to the dance floor.

Like the rest of the house, the Music Room was magnificent. It had cream-colored walls, gold cornices, gold moldings, gold bas-relief panels on the doors, and mirrors. It captured light in every direction.

"And at first you did not want to come," Edward said to her.

"I was wrong," Julienne laughed, enjoying the pleasure of the waltz.

She met many of Philippe's friends that night, including his special guests, the Comte and Comtesse de Bouvard. They had been traveling all over the Eastern world, and she had always loved listening to travel stories.

The Comte asked her to dance, and she happily accepted, feeling as if she had to make up for lost years and recapture a youth denied her. Edward turned to the Comtesse, but she declined, feeling fatigued.

"I think our host is in need of you, though," she said, giving a discreet nod toward the open double-doors.

Edward saw Philippe leaning against the wall. He held a champagne glass in his right hand, and when their eyes met, he beckoned toward himself.

Edward excused himself and walked over to Philippe.

"Look at her," Philippe said quietly.

"Who?"

"Your Jeanne Barbier, who else?'

She was dancing and speaking and laughing with the Comte de Bouvard. "Yes, so?" Edward asked.

"She dances quite well, don't you think?" Philippe asked, staring at the lovely woman.

"Yes, I know, I've been dancing with her all evening. Does this conversation lead somewhere?" he asked and took Philippe's champagne glass for a sip.

"Wait for me here," Philippe said.

Edward watched for a good ten minutes as Philippe first led Jeanne in a courtly gavotte, and then a waltz. Afterwards, he stood with her for quite some time, speaking and asking questions, laughing and teasing, all with a comfortable easy air. Edward, still waiting by the doors, watched again, as Philippe led Jeanne back to the Comte and Comtesse de Bouvard.

What little game is this, Edward wondered, studying Philippe, and then the rest of that small circle at the far end of the Music Room. What is he trying to prove?

It came to him as quietly as the strains of the music. The Music Room, like the restaurants, the theater, the ballet, the opera, was not a foreign place to her. He had not forgotten how at ease she always seemed to be in those places. Now, seeing her next to the Comtesse and seeing no difference in their posture, their expressions, their poise, a thin veil lifted from his mind.

The Comte de Bouvard again asked Jeanne to dance, and the Comtesse, still fatigued, had refused Philippe.

At that point, Edward saw Philippe excuse himself and walk decisively toward the doors.

"Well?" Edward said, "did you enjoy your dances and conversation?"

Philippe looked about them to make sure no one could hear them. "That is no embroidery girl," Philippe said softly.

"Yes, I know."

"Do you also know she is very well versed in the arts, in literature, in history, and . . ."

"Yes," Edward nodded, "I know that as well."

"Do you imagine she learned all of this at Chavastelon's knee?"

Edward shook his head, still watching Jeanne Barbier dance.

"That woman is a fraud, you know."

Edward gave a single nod.

"That woman is not from Alsace, either. I believe she has never even *been* to Alsace. Look at her, at the way she stands, the way she carries herself, the way she speaks." Philippe stared at Jeanne Barbier. "She is an aristocrat."

Edward smiled and sipped his champagne. "Yes, I know."

"Yes you know," Philippe said quickly, mimicking the tone of Edward's voice. "What do you know? Who is she? Where is she from? Not Paris, no, that is most obvious. Her accent is all wrong. Yet, it is French, but there is something else in her voice. I cannot place it. She must have lived for many years in another country, but which one, I . . ."

"Austria," Edward said calmly.

Philippe eyed him. "Well?"

"Well what?"

"Well have you looked through the *Almanach de Gotha* to see the family pedigree—oh, but you need to know her maiden name. Do you?"

Edward shook his head.

"Did you ask her?"

"No."

"Love has made you stupid, Edward," Philippe scoffed, "and I think you have gone quite mad as well. Have you no curiosity at all?"

"Of course I am curious," Edward replied, looking at Philippe. "But whoever she is and whatever she was simply does not matter. She will speak whatever truth she wishes me to know, at the time she wishes me to know it."

"And the children?" Philippe asked, pointedly. "What are they?"

"Just children," Edward answered kindly, "and legitimate or not, they are lovely and sweet, like their mother."

"I am speaking to a lunatic," Philippe said.

Edward laughed.

Philippe shook his head slowly. "And I must be more of a lunatic than you, for I am envious of a lunatic. What luck you have," he sighed, "to find a jewel in the dungheap of Chavastelon's."

Much later that evening, Edward led her to the main hallway and said, "The hallway to the right at the far end is a private gallery. Philippe's father was quite a collector in his youth, and there are several fine paintings there: some from the Flemish school, two from the Renaissance, many French, and four or five Italian masters. If you are interested, I will be pleased to show them to you."

"Yes," Julienne said, "I think I would enjoy that."

They walked down the hall, and as they passed a small sitting room, they saw Philippe standing with the Comte and Comtesse de Bouvard. He beckoned them inside.

"Edward will know," Philippe was saying as they stepped into the small room.

Julienne had never seen anything quite like this small room. The rosewood walls were painted with scenes of country life and gardens, roosters and cats, and trellises of wisteria in full bloom. The golden light from the chandelier seemed to enhance the golden colors of the paintings and the wooden floors and the carved wooden moldings under the paintings. It made a soft glow, for an intimate room.

"What do I know?" Edward asked.

"The Comte was just speaking of his travels," Philippe began.

"And of my liver, dear Marquess," the Comte de Bouvard laughed, saying it to Edward.

"Well of course, what may one expect from a long sea voyage and protracted overland travels," Philippe said.

"Yes, but the food was by far the worst in the Eastern countries. Still, the Suez Canal was worth the agony of my liver."

Edward's eyes opened a fraction.

191

"A true wonder of the earth," the Comte went on, then looked at Edward. "You were in India, were you not?"

Julienne had seen the subtle change in Edward's eyes. It was as if he had suddenly taken two steps back behind them, hiding within himself.

"Our guide, Laxman Bhargavi, was greatly moved by a statue he showed us in the Elephanta Caves . . ."

"Near Bombay, yes, the representation of Shiva," Edward said in a small voice.

"But what does it mean?" the Comte asked.

Edward swallowed. "It . . . it represents the absolute power of Shiva. Shiva, in the center, the impersonal judge; and on either side, Shiva as male and Shiva as female, showing all the universe divided, yet contained, within the one statue."

"But who is Brahma, then, and why do they pray to him? Laxman Bhargavi always whispered his prayers to Brahma."

"They have a trinity—Brahma, is creator of the universe; Vishnu, sustains life in the universe, and Shiva, is the great destroyer."

"A strange, ambiguous land," the Comte said.

"Yes," Edward said, uncomfortable.

"You should have been with us," the Comtesse said. "Your knowledge would have meant a great deal to us."

Edward shook his head. "My knowledge is marginal, Comtesse. Mine . . . mine was a wasted journey there. Please excuse me. I was just about to show Madame Barbier the gallery." He gripped her arm tightly and led her quickly down the hall, but his enthusiasm for the paintings had gone and he stared blindly at them, offering no commentary or opinions.

Seeing the shadow of agony in his eyes, Julienne said, "I would prefer not to see the paintings after all."

"As you wish," he said in a clipped tone of voice, the evening's champagne beginning to cloud his mind and free the buried memories and faces. "Would you prefer to go back to the ballroom?"

"No. I'd much prefer to sit quietly and talk with you."

He turned his head and smiled sarcastically. "Talk?" he said, annoyed. "Talk of what—travels?"

"I'd rather you speak to me of important things, things that trouble you."

"No," he said sharply, "absolutely not. It is an old wound, and a private wound, and I make no apology for it or myself."

"I did not ask you for an apology," Julienne countered, "but all the world knows that a wound—be it an old one or a new one—needs to be opened, drained, cleansed in order that it might heal and thus be forgotten."

His smile was mean. "Common knowledge, is it? Open it, drain it, clean it, forget it, huhn? It doesn't signify, Madame," he said, drawing the word out in a nasty tone. "It isn't that way in life, only in the theater."

"You are quite wrong, you know."

"You haven't lived my life," he snapped.

"And you haven't lived mine," she answered sharply, seeing the surprise in his eyes from the tone of her voice. "So, Monsieur," she said, drawing out the word in an annoyed fashion, "I'll leave you with something that *does* signify: the sort of people who only share the calm moments in life, are people one must not trust, for they disappear when one needs them most, when one is in trouble or pain. You know nothing of me, *nothing*, and yet you have the rudeness to suggest I am incapable of understanding. When my child died in my arms of pneumonia because I could not protect him from the rain, I wanted to die. I trusted and depended upon others at that moment, people who were true friends because they did not desert me and did not run away from sadness. You lied when you said we were friends. You don't even know what the word means. Keep your wound to yourself, then," she said, and ran toward the main hall, but felt a hand catch her upper arm. She saw him standing beside her.

A burst of laughter came from around the corner, and there was suddenly too much noise, too much light, the music seemed wrong and out of place. Edward hesitated, then led her back down the hallway, and when they'd reached the end of it, they climbed a flight of stairs to the upper floor. Midway in this darkened hall, he opened the door to a room on the right.

It was a cold, dark room, and when she'd shivered and said she was cold, she felt his jacket about her shoulders, still warm from his body. He lit a taper, then the candles in the double candelabra on the mantlepiece.

A library, Julienne thought, feeling calmer by the sight of the bookcases lined with beautifully bound volumes.

She saw Edward had taken off his gloves and tossed them carelessly to the floor as he made up the fire. Only when he stoked the fire with an iron poker did she sit down on the small sofa facing the fireplace. Edward sat down on the floor. Julienne thought he had the look of a pouting boy about him, the way his thick dark hair tousled and fell upon his forehead, the way he ran his fingers through the hair to push it back from his eyes, and then, that faraway stare in his troubled eyes.

She was about to speak, when he suddenly pulled his stiff collar so violently he nearly ripped it from his shirt.

"India was the hottest place I'd ever known," Edward said, staring at the orange flames. "A sweltering, awful heat. Our day began at first light, and by noon we were finished with our 'work.' It was too hot by then, and by necessity, everything had to stop. People moved slowly, and slept anywhere they could in any sort of scrappy shade they could find. That was Madras."

He looked away from the flames and saw her listening, as if the unbroken stare might help in the understanding of his words. "You cannot appreciate how terrible it was, but India was the end of the nightmare. No one knows the whole of it, not even Philippe or my family. So I did not lie to you. I have never lied to you, and it was unkind of you to think that I did."

"I'm sorry," she said.

He nodded, then said, "The only one who lived through it with me is dead. It is difficult for me to speak of it, because India has become in my memory not just a place, but a Pandora's box of what went before, and the wreckage that came after it. Can you understand that?"

"Yes," she said, and thought of Eisenstadt.

He didn't know why, but he believed her. He looked away from her again, and began to describe a childhood obsession, a goal just out of his reach. Ever since he was a child, he'd dreamed of only one thing—a career in the Army. He devoured memoir after memoir of professional soldiers, relived battles with his set of tin soldiers, and ignored the cautions given by his father about the reality of war and the destruction it always brought. After his brother died, the conversations with his father changed.

"He spoke more and more of his work," Edward said, "but I had no interest in going with him on fact-finding tours. He was always doing that, going on his missions all over the country and reporting directly to Prince Albert. They were friends, you see. Besides, I'd heard all those stories of children misused in the labor force—bald, coughing children sweeping chimneys; illiterate children working the farms; thin, hungry children imprisoned for all their lives in the mines. I knew all of that, and all of the bills he'd worked on with his dearest friend, Lord Shaftesbury."

"You sound angry with him," Julienne said, wondering why such splendid work from a caring man would so enrage Edward, who was himself a caring man.

"Do I?" he shrugged, then a moment later, shook his head. "He tried to speak to me as he'd spoken to my brother. I'm not angry with him. Not anymore. It doesn't matter anymore."

From the expression in his eyes, Julienne knew he was lying to himself.

"He wanted me to go to University, to 'broaden and discipline my mind,'" Edward grunted. "Indeed. I wanted the Army. We argued, he said I was too young, I didn't agree, and the subject was closed—for a time. Well, at seventeen, I decided I would not be cheated of what I wanted for myself. I did not want a direct commission that he could purchase for me. Anyone could do that. Anyone with money could be an officer. So, Philippe and I arranged a conspiracy. He wrote to my father and asked if I might accompany him and his uncle on a 'grand tour' of the continent for seven months. My father gave his consent and wished he could go with me, to see the world new in my eyes, he said. What rubbish," Edward breathed.

Julienne watched that chilling smile return.

"He even wanted to see me off at Dover, but I talked him out of that because I didn't go to Dover. I went straight off to a small village southwest of London—Wimbledon—and a Crammer's School under the direction of Captain William S. Grimshaw."

Julienne shrugged, not understanding.

"It is a period of study of about six months' duration in preparation for the entrance examinations to the Royal Military Academy at Woolwich. Cadets at Woolwich trained for the Royal Engineer or Artillery Corps. I wanted the Engineers because it was the most difficult of all. Money couldn't buy a commission in the Engineers—one had to earn it by intelligence. Do you understand now?"

She sighed, then nodded.

"I swore I would show him what I could do with my own idea for my *own* life."

Why does his voice change whenever he speaks of his father, Julienne wondered. Why does the bitterness come so sharp in his words when his father's actions do not warrant it?

"That first day in Wimbledon, I'd felt as if I'd spent all my days in a deadly shadow and was only now touching the sun's warmth. I never worked so hard in my life."

His obsession flowered at the Crammer's, this single-minded purpose to overcome unbelievable obstacles and succeed at all costs. For six months he worked so diligently his colleagues nicknamed him "The Mad Monk."

But it was a naive young man's respite from the world, hiding in a town, his nose in his books, thinking all was well. When it came to the entrance examination itself, his father discovered the lie.

"I had to submit my name to the Duke of Cambridge, the General Commander-in-Chief of the British Army." He saw her confusion. "For Woolwich," he said, "I could not sit the exam unless he approved my name. And he was my father's friend."

"Your father must have been . . ."

"He most certainly was," Edward interrupted. "Livid is the word that comes closest, but it falls short of the mark, I think. I lied to him, and he cannot abide deception of any kind. He'd written to me on the Continent and heard no word for months. He said he worried, sent telegrams, and was about to pack his bags and go looking for me when he met Cambridge who gave him the 'happy' news of my activities. He sent me to my room, like a child, to think about what I'd done. I thought only about the medals my brother had won for Latin and Greek translations. My father cherished dead medals for dead languages. It made little difference to me. The house was nothing but a crypt anyway. Michael *still* lived there. Edward was the son who died and then I realized, Edward never existed at all."

"What did your father do?"

"He came to me and said he'd been trying to understand why I'd lied to him. I apologized for *that*, but not for what I'd done. He asked me what I wanted, and I told him I wished to sit the exam. He didn't understand why I'd chosen this particular way, and it seemed to me, he didn't even *try* to understand how important it was for me to earn my place." Edward stared at the fire. "My mother, his friends, all held the same opinion: Woolwich? For a Marquess? Unseemly. Purchase a commission, if he wants it so deeply."

"What did he do?"

"He said I could sit the exam."

"But how wonderful," Julienne smiled.

Edward set his jaw. "It took four days to complete the tests. A candidate needed a minimum of 3,000 points to even be considered, point values being ascribed to each exam."

"And?"

He turned his head, but did not smile. "I was placed third, in a field of thirty-one successful candidates. I earned 4,750 marks."

"Edward," she glowed, "how simply wonderful for you."

"I knew he hoped I would fail."

Julienne stared at him, amazed. "You lied to him, and he forgave you. He disregarded the opinions of others because your happiness meant more to him than . . ."

"My happiness?" Edward said, sarcastically. "Oh no, no, Madame, not at all. The happiness of his little chimney-sweeps meant more to him than the happiness of his own son. He is a patient man, though, I'll give him that. It took him the whole of my first year at Woolwich, but by God, he had *his* revenge."

"You never thanked him, did you?"

Edward looked away.

She continued to stare coldly at him. "You never did, did you? You never kissed him and said, 'Thank you, Papa, for giving me what I've always wished for.'"

"I haven't kissed him since I was ten years old."

"I am sorry for you."

"Save your pity, Madame," he glared in the dark.

"Oh, I shall," Julienne replied firmly and then stood up.

"Where are you going?"

"Home. It's late and I really don't wish to hear any more."

He was up from the floor and took her arms before she reached the door. "Don't," he said, "not just yet."

"Edward," she sighed, "I loved my father very much, and to hear you speak with such bitterness of your father, who still lives . . ."

"And didn't you speak such fine grand words not long ago, in the hall, about friends not deserting one another . . ." He let go of her arms and stepped back.

"I meant every word."

"But you've already judged, haven't you? You stand there, having had a loving father, and cannot imagine a parent who does not love—nor even *like*—his own son, so therefore, it cannot be possible."

I do know, she thought, getting angry at him. Franz had one. And you do not.

"So, Madame, 'friend,' there's the door. I won't stop you. Run away from the unpleasantness." He stepped toward the window and roughly parted the curtains, then looked out to the darkened park below him.

The sharpness to his voice had returned in full, and he formed an eerie silhouette against the window. Julienne knew she could not leave him in so despairing a state. She walked over to the window and placed her hand on his arm, and gave a reassuring squeeze. "What happened?" she said quietly.

He shook his head. "I had so much to prove . . ." He smiled in a sad way. "Let me give you some good advice: never challenge a ghost to a joust—you will never win."

"What ghost?" she whispered.

"What ghost indeed," he said. "My brother's medals haunted me. I wanted my father to see that I, too, could do something well." He closed his eyes for a moment and turned his head away.

"Was the Academy so very difficult?"

He nodded. "More than the Army itself. I loved mathematics, but at Woolwich, mathematics became arithmetic, algebra, logarithms, geometry, trigonometry, heights and distances, analytical and descriptive geometry, mechanics, hydrodynamics, and so on. I was 'The Mad Monk' again, and I loved it. My God, the challenge was magnificent."

He explained he had worked continuously from the Crammer's six months to the examination, then in the two months before he started the Academy, he continued to study. He studied late into the night the whole of his first term—from February through June—and continued his studies throughout the summer during the six weeks' vacation. He never stopped, never desired a rest, and wanted only to be the best. He continued this awesome pace when he returned for the Autumn term, August through December, and the award ceremonies, the giving of prizes by the Duke of Cambridge.

"What sort of prizes?"

He stared out the window. "Books, memoirs of professional soldiers, mathematical instruments. And for superior work, he gave medals." Edward's voice cracked and he turned away.

"You won, didn't you?"

"I won the medal for mathematics. Everyone applauded and said 'well done . . .' and he wasn't there."

Julienne touched his shoulder and felt the shiver. "There must have been a reason."

"Reason?" he spit out. "No *reason* would have served at that moment, Madame. All I could think of was that in the six years Michael had been at Eton, he did not miss one award ceremony."

"But Edward . . ."

"Something happened to me. Something inside of me died at that moment. I ran from the enclosure, kept running until I dropped. Then I tore the medal from its case and hurled it as hard as I could into the Thames."

Julienne placed her arms about his waist and held him, feeling the dampness that clung to the back of his shirt. "I don't understand why you threw away the reward for such an achievement."

He held her and gently rubbed the small of her back. "The soldiering part, that was what I wanted. But the medal was for him. I wanted to show him, in the only way I could, that I loved him, too. And I wanted him to love me. Stupid, isn't it, silly of me, it could never be that way and I should have known it."

"But he does . . ."

"No. He knows what I've done. He's always known. It's a fog after that. I only really remember looking in the mirror and seeing a stranger look back at me."

Woolwich became a cage for him, and he was trapped inside an evil game—doing just enough work to pass the weekly tests, and stepping out of bounds just enough to annoy them. He was twice expelled by the Lieutenant Governor, but the Duke of Cambridge overturned both those decisions after a quiet talk with a highly-disturbed young man who kept promising to reform. The third time, Cambridge could not alter the decision: Edward was expelled because he'd failed his examinations. He never graduated and never received his position in the Royal Engineer Corps. All of his work and efforts were wasted.

"And where was your father during this time?" Julienne asked.

"Making weekly trips to Woolwich, mostly, looking all grey and stern and trying to understand why I was in solitary confinement. He asked all the usual questions—why had I made a disaster out of such a splendid start, why did I keep my silence with him, why wouldn't I explain what was troubling me, what was wrong, was I ill? Why wouldn't I speak to anyone, even the Chaplain. . . . Rubbish. He didn't really give a damn. I was just an embarrassment he had to rectify."

Julienne felt an exasperated scream building and simply added these facts to the growing list of inconsistencies. He didn't even realize what he was saying, and it painted a disturbing picture in her mind: no matter what Edward's father did, he was wrong in Edward's eyes. Any show of concern on the father's part was viewed by Edward as false, and yet, a dedicated, caring man, whose life had been devoted to the poor and unfortunate, left his work every week to visit his troubled son. And Edward calls that 'rubbish,' she thought. "Did he never mention that day, the ceremony?"

"I think he did, I don't remember exactly. He arrived late. He was at Windsor, or something . . . I don't know anymore."

She shook her head. How unreasonable of you, Edward, she thought. He tried, and in all probability was delayed by the Prince Consort. And because he wasn't there at the exact moment you wanted him there, you punished not only him but yourself as well. What a contradiction you are, she thought. You are reasonable, patient, understanding and kind with everyone—except your father, and, I think, yourself. "But you said you were in the Army."

He nodded. "Later."

"How?"

He shrugged. "The distance between us was . . ." He sighed. "I tried to please him, one last time. I went to Oxford, for him. It didn't work. I was sent down after a year. Then he offered to buy me a commission. He held it in front of me, like one might wave a carrot in front of an ass. I accepted— on my terms. Because of the Mutiny, a regiment was being raised to help relieve the garrison at Madras. They would accept *anyone* in this emergency— even a Marquess. It was the only time a commission could be purchased for service in India. Every other officer came out of Sandhurst or Woolwich. At any rate, that's what I wanted—the 120th Fusiliers. The Infantry. My mother was appalled. What did it matter anymore? By the time we got there, it was just about over, the Mutiny was nearly suppressed. We'd missed it. No combat. No medals. No glory. In the evenings, in the officers' mess, I listened to tales told by others who'd lived through the battles I never saw." He noticed the troubled expression in her eyes and said quietly, "Let it pass. You're much too beautiful to be bothered by such nonsense."

Franz had said something similar, she thought, pricked by the eerie reminder of those words. That photograph-plate, the vision of an untroubled woman. Franz had said it must always be so, perfect . . . serene . . .

It began to rain and Edward saw her jump slightly at the sound of drops beating against the window. He wondered why. A moment ago she had been a true and sympathetic friend who had not deserted him in a time of need. "Jeanne?" he said, softly.

She looked at him with wary eyes.

"Why are you afraid?" he asked, watching as her eyes changed expression, becoming the eyes of a child with a guilty secret.

"What . . . what an extraordinary thing to say . . . I'm . . . it's late, Edward. I really must . . ."

"Why do you step back from me?" Edward asked, stepping closer to her. "There, you've done it again."

She was breathing harder, and stepped back a third time.

Edward grabbed her by the waist with both his hands and felt the surprised shudder. "You've no reason to do that," he said.

"Let go of me," she cried.

He released his hands and watched as she stepped back from him and closer to the window. For one moment, she had looked like Frédéric, when the boy had cowered against the wall, but being near the window seemed to upset her. The sound of the rain, the clap of thunder made her shiver. She stepped back from the window, into the darkness of the room.

"Where are you going?"

"Home," she answered by the door. "I, I may do as I like. I'm not anyone's prisoner."

"Shut the door," Edward said, seeing the shaft of light crease the floor.

She froze.

"Shut the door," he repeated firmly, and when she did not move, he said, "Can't you trust me even *that* much?"

Julienne hesitated, then shut the door, her hand still on the knob, ready to turn it quickly.

As he walked closer to her, he said, "I never once suggested so distasteful a thing as you were my prisoner. I've made too many mistakes in not-too-long a life, Madame, and . . ." he paused, then said coldly, "if you take one more step away from me, I will walk out of that door before you, and I swear to Almighty God, you will never see me again." He stood directly in front of her and could hear the shallow breathing. "If, somehow, I have upset you, or frightened you, tell me what I have done. I have always accepted responsibility for all my mistakes. But I do not deserve this, and you know that is the truth."

"You . . . you don't understand."

"Tell me, then."

"No."

Edward held her.

"Let go of me."

"No."

199

"Let go of me, don't touch me."

"I love you," he said, and felt her arms between them, tight gloved fists pushing against his chest. He took the right arm and placed it about his waist, then the left, feeling the fists at his back near the buckle of his waistcoat. "Tell me," he said, then said nothing more, feeling her fists calming long enough to hold him firmly, with a measure of trust. She started to cry, turning her face deeper into his chest, and told of the last time a man's hands had touched her, the men on the road, the rain, the mud, and that they had raped her.

God help us, he thought, listening to the rain and closing his eyes for a moment. He tried to lift her chin, but she jerked her head away from his hand.

"Don't look at me."

"Open your eyes," Edward said.

"No."

He grabbed her face and shook her slightly. "Open your eyes, goddammit," and when she did, he said more quietly, "How can you look at me with such, such shame?"

"Because it is shaming and ugly and so very dirty . . ."

"Yes," he said sharply, "but the shame and the ugliness and the dirt is all *theirs* and not *yours.*"

She shook and cried when the thunder clapped, and held him fast like a clinging child lost in the dark. "Edward, help me. I'm frightened."

Her skin was so cold, it was like touching marble. He thought for a moment, then said, "Wait here. Let me look in the hallway."

When he saw that the party had ended and all was quiet, he came back to the room and led her out of the library to the other wing of the house, to the room at the far end, his room.

She flinched when he lit the oil lamp. "No, don't," she whispered.

He blew it out. The only light in the room was the light from the fireplace. His bed had been turned down. He walked to it and picked up his thin satin robe. "Here," he said quietly, "put this on. You'll be more comfortable. I'll . . . I'll get you a brandy."

He took his time walking slowly down the hall and back to the library. He collected his coat and his gloves, the brandy decanter and two glasses. The servants will see to the candles and the fire, he thought absently, then walked slowly back to his own room. He knocked, and when he heard no answer, opened the door and looked in. Some of her clothing lay in a pile on the floor. Then he saw her, with the robe pulled tightly about herself. She was sitting, curled in the chair with her knees tucked under her chin and her face buried away from the light.

He shut the door. "Drink this," he said, and gave her the glass. "Jeanne, I didn't say sip it, I said drink it, all of it."

She shook her head, and when he took the glass back, her hands were trembling.

Perhaps if I spoke of something else, he thought, and noticed she had taken some of the pins out of her hair. He bent over the back of the chair and took out the remaining pins, beads and combs. "Why do women put these things in their hair," he said, and tossed the handful of them down on the small table next to her. "There," he said, running his fingers through the long, silky, chestnut-brown hair. "It has to be more comfortable than before." He offered the brandy to her again, but she shook her head. He knelt closer to her, and whispered, "When I was a child, I had a Nanny who was more a drill-sergeant than the ones I'd met in the Army. And when I refused food, she'd whisper in my little ear, 'Um-ma-num?'" He saw the flicker of a teary smile and watched her drink the brandy.

Thunder clapped again, she jumped, then coughed.

"Well," Edward said lightly, taking out his handkerchief and wiping her mouth, "you drank most of it. It'll do. It should warm you soon enough."

"This is too silly," Julienne said, taking his handkerchief and wiping her eyes. "I'm ashamed of myself. I'm not a child. I feel such a fool, a storm, it's . . . it's too silly. A night like this, a long time ago, I'm not afraid of storms, or the dark, or . . . or ghosts from the, the past, I'm not," but the voice was weak and she was still shivering and hid her eyes against her knees again.

"You're a fine one to talk," he said, walking nearer his bed. "I suppose opening wounds and draining them so they may heal only applies to other people and not to you." He took off his waistcoat, tie, undid his collar and removed it with the cuffs of his shirt, then took off his shoes. When he padded back to her, she seemed to be listening to the rain, not even realizing she was crying.

He took her in his arms and brought her to the floor, closer to the fire. He sat behind her with his back against the chair, cradling her against himself, warming her with himself and his arms. "Silly," he whispered, "letting me prattle on about nothing whilst you kept all this poison inside of you . . . I am still here. I have not deserted you. I love you, and I am your truest friend. If you believe nothing else, believe that."

Tears spilled from closed eyes. She nodded.

He let her cry until there was nothing left inside, then he swallowed to ease the pull in his own throat. "I'll see you home soon, so the children will find you there when they wake up. You're safe now. Let the past stay where it belongs. Rest," he whispered, holding her shoulders with his left arm, and with his right hand gently rubbed her back and sides. He felt the little ridges underneath the thin material of the dressing gown, the mates of the scars he'd seen on her upper shoulders. These were larger, more defined.

Watching her eyes slowly close, he thought to himself: And what else have you not told me?

CHAPTER
13

The Hotel Bristol overlooking the Place Vendôme still had the same luxurious and comfortable rooms Stefan remembered from his last visit, some five years earlier: brocaded chairs, a large Cheval mirror, highly polished wooden floors, a large poster bed and a beautiful fireplace.

Stefan had arrived in the morning, and had spent the better part of the day resting from the journey, bathing, and settling himself into his rooms for what he hoped would be not too long an official stay. He wanted and needed time to himself to look for Julienne, but he knew the situation in Paris had grown steadily worse. My cousin should have sent me here months ago, he thought, or at the very least, last month, when the French Foreign Minister resigned and the Duc de Gramont was appointed in his place.

Teo, he thought, your advice gives me no comfort now: "Gramont is harmless where he is. As French Ambassador to Austria, he cannot write government policy."

But he will write it now, Stefan thought, with a blind suspicious hate for anything Prussian, with words unchecked by reason, and a mind that is inexperienced for that most sensitive position within a government. Even Metternich is worried.

Stefan realized the only hope for continuing peace rested on the shoulders of the seventy-year-old Lord Clarendon of England. A man of his years, Stefan thought, traveling back and forth between Paris and Berlin. He smiled, thinking of Clarendon, and the correspondence between them. Though Clarendon could not say what the specific nature of his mission was, he did say Louis Napoleon had requested his help, and Stefan guessed it could only be some sort of disarmament treaty. Clarendon had been on this mission since January, 1870.

At half-past six, Stefan began to dress for the Embassy party, and as he was in Paris without official posting, he could not wear an ambassadorial sash, or even his army uniform. He was, as was his Emperor's intention, a private citizen visiting Paris, and as such, wore only his evening clothes.

It will be good to meet Clarendon, Stefan sighed to himself as he stepped into his carriage. A man like my father, a man trained in the old school. That first letter he wrote me was so warm and kind and filled with memories of my father. And he continued to write with as much frankness as he was able to give, considering the secrecy of his work. Perhaps Clarendon will put the specters to rest—or if not that, show a way to keep the peace in Europe. No one else has his experience or his influence.

It was not a very long ride to Rue de Grenelle and the Austrian Embassy on the Left Bank. Inside the Embassy, he presented his card to an aide and then climbed the stairs to the second floor. He was about to enter the reception room, when he heard a familiar voice shriek behind him:

"Good God, don't go in there, it stinks of Excellencies!"

He laughed and turned to Princess Pauline Metternich, seeing her large smile and even larger eyes. He kissed her right hand, then both her cheeks and said softly, "Good evening, Princess, you're looking very well."

"Well enough for Sodom and Gomorrah," she grinned and waved a gloved arm toward the open door of the reception room.

Stefan laughed again. "Oh come now, it isn't as bad as all that."

"I only know what I read in the newspapers. See for yourself," she said, and took his arm, dragging him closer to the doorway. "Look at them," she whispered, "see what a decadent lot they are . . ."

It was an ordinary Embassy party, with the visiting dignitaries absorbed in polite conversations. All was proper, and all was very dull for Pauline Metternich's taste and sense of adventure.

"And do you believe everything you read in the newspapers?" Stefan asked as she led him back to the stairs.

Pauline winked slyly. "It depends upon which paper one reads."

"You haven't changed," Stefan grinned.

"Ahh, but you have. Vienna has made you grim."

Stefan's smile paled. "Not Vienna—the times in which we live."

"Richard is waiting for you upstairs in his study. He is most anxious to speak with you privately. We will speak later."

Stefan nodded, then walked up one more flight and turned left at the head of the stairs. A door was open mid-way down the hall, and when he looked inside, he saw Prince Richard Von Metternich seated at his desk with a single oil-lamp burning.

Metternich looked up at the sound of the knock. "I am glad to see you, Stefan," he said, and walked over to the door.

Metternich was six feet tall, had wide shoulders and was ruggedly handsome, having a fine mustache and neatly groomed whiskers of fair hair beginning to show a little grey. He was about forty years old, and with his good looks and superb manners, was the absolute opposite of his wife. She was not attractive, and enjoyed being notorious for her uncensored opinions and daring behavior. She spoke as she liked, when she liked, no matter what the company. Stefan had heard she'd even dressed as a man and ridden an omnibus at night. Pauline smoked cigars with a flair, and let her bawdy behavior be her beauty. Richard adored her, and she, him. And Society's rules about beauty didn't concern them.

Stefan shook Metternich's hand and watched him shut the study door. "You wished to see me privately, Richard?"

"I have news, and I am afraid it isn't good," Metternich said. "Lord Clarendon is ill. He has returned to London."

"Is it serious?"

203

"I don't know," Metternich replied. "I only know he left Paris quite suddenly yesterday and has returned home. He sent his apologies to you."

"Was his endeavor successful?"

"I do not have that information," Metternich said. "I only know the Empress Eugénie was highly disturbed over this news."

Stefan felt if the mission had been successful, some word or clue would have been left for him.

Metternich paused, then asked quietly, "Does the Emperor still maintain he will need six weeks to raise an army?"

"As of two days ago, he raised that figure to eight weeks," Stefan replied, weary of the ongoing attempts for an Austrian-French alliance to counter Bismarck.

"Minister Gramont was, shall we say, mildly curious."

"And I can imagine how 'mildly' he phrased his questions," Stefan commented.

Metternich sighed. "We ought to rejoin my guests."

"How nervous is Gramont?"

"Very."

That will make him careless, Stefan thought. "Is he here?"

"No," Metternich said, opening the door. "You know several people here, but there is one man I know you will enjoy meeting. He was given his post last summer, and I find him a gracious and honorable man, the Ambassador from the United States, Mr. Washburne. He is most interesting, and has, I believe, the most astounding ability to remember names and faces that I have ever encountered. It has become quite a parlor game in Paris, the testing of Mr. Washburne's memory. No one has caught him out yet. I met him last summer at Fontainebleau. The Emperor had invited some one hundred guests, and Mr. Washburne remembered all of them."

"That is interesting," Stefan commented as they stepped into the hall.

"I had dearly hoped for better news," Metternich sighed, facing Stefan.

"So had I."

Somehow, Stefan would not have guessed that the man of average height, greying hair and bushy grey eyebrows was the Ambassador from the United States. He was a soft-spoken man with a pudgy face and had a pleasant smile. He was clean-shaven, and his shoulders were slightly rounded. Though he wore his ambassadorial sash, he had the look of a university professor, and Stefan inquired if he might, at one time, have been a teacher.

"No," Washburne smiled, "I have, Prince Stefan, been in law and government for all of my life. This, however, is my first post abroad."

"You speak French very very well, Your Excellency."

"Thank you," Washburne said, "but I find I am learning more each and every day. It is a most pleasing lesson."

Stefan liked Washburne. His conversation was interesting, his experience with people was very deep, and the self-effacing man was warm, friendly, and a respite from the usual maneuverings done at Embassy parties.

In the following two weeks, Stefan had been invited to many other parties and met what he expected: the Duc de Gramont, or agents of Gramont, or friends speaking for Gramont.

Gramont was more anti-Prussian than ever. He seemed overly sure of himself and spoke now with the full power of his position. Though the conversations were always exceedingly polite, the question of the alliance was never far from anyone's thoughts. It made Stefan nervous to hear the sort of conversation about Bismarck and Prussia he had heard in Vienna—they were still playing schoolboy games and telling ridiculous stories about an extremely dangerous man, poking fun at character quirks to make the tellers of the story seem more elegant, more schooled, more adult than their Prussian counterpart.

". . . I suppose the easiest way to view all this," he wrote to his wife, Rosl, "is that it is now abundantly clear to both Metternich and myself, that the wrong people are in the wrong government positions at the wrong time. Gramont is impetuous and . . ." The sound of several loud knocks at the door jarred the quiet of the room.

He set the pen aside, rubbed his eyes and walked in his stocking feet to the door. "Yes," he said, seeing a hotel messenger boy holding a silver tray with an envelope on it.

"A message came for you, Monsieur," the boy said.

Stefan reached inside his waistcoat pocket for a coin, and exchanged the coin for the envelope.

Alone in his room, he turned the envelope over and saw the seal of the Austrian Embassy. He ran his fingers through his hair and then, standing by the window, tore the envelope open.

The message was simple, as simple as the north-easterly breeze that fluttered the curtains:

"Clarendon died yesterday, June 27, in London." It was signed, "Metternich."

Stefan leaned heavily against the wall. The valiant old man, God rest him, he thought. And God help us. Now there is no one to stop Bismarck . . .

Julienne leaned against the cool grey stone wall of the Château's eastern front and watched Frédéric throwing bread into the moat, feeding the carp that swam near the surface. She closed her eyes and felt completely at peace, listening to the birdsong and the gentle spray of the fountain raining down on the pond some distance away. The Château's vistas—French sculpted gardens, trimmed lawns and the forest that surrounded them on all sides—were restful and beautiful.

She was glad she had accepted Edward and Philippe's invitation to spend the final week of June and the first week of July here at Château de Vaublanc. Philippe loved to entertain friends and he had invited some fifty people to spend a holiday in his countryside between the towns of Melun and Cesson. He'd planned picnics, evening parties, and a large fancy-dress ball for the final

week-end, the food and costumes to be of the late sixteenth century, an an-
niversary party to commemorate the age of the Château.

An arm closed around her waist. "I've been looking for you," Edward
whispered.

"And so you've found me," she smiled.

"Happy?"

"Very."

"And do you like your birthday present?"

"Soon-to-be-birthday present, you mean."

He smiled.

"Yes, I love being here."

"As you wouldn't allow anything else," Edward commented.

She laughed slightly. "No, this is wonderful. I am content."

"Good," he said. "I finished that book, by the way."

"*Man, Woman and Child* by . . ."

"By Gustave Droz, yes," Edward said. "His ideas are quite radical, and yet,
they are so true, so sensible."

"I felt that way, too," Julienne said.

"I was particularly struck by Droz' distinction between 'father' and 'papa.'
The father in Society is that reserved sort of man, untouched and not touching,
unruffled and uninterested in the lives of children. They are something to be
endured—sparingly—until they reach their maturity. Only then are they
interesting people, as if they had magically climbed out of a cocoon and," he
snapped his fingers, "there you have him, a staunch, solid member of Society,
the very image of his father."

She nodded. "He claims that is not normal."

"Not quite," Edward said. "Droz claims it is absolutely wrong. The 'papa'
is the true parent. The papa, who frolics with his children, caresses them,
laughs with them, teaches them with kindness and understanding—*he* is the
true parent. Droz has nothing but contempt for the man who claims to be a
'father.' " He paused, then said, "You had a 'papa,' didn't you?"

"Yes," she said softly.

"But your children did not."

"No," she sighed, then looked at him steadily. "And you?"

"Need you ask," he said with a smile. "Mine was unquestionably a father."

She shook her head. "Then explain to me, please, how you came to know
just how to talk to children, and play with them?"

He shrugged slightly. "Mine was the experience of want and need, rather
than example. Blame my excellent memory."

She had to smile. "Edward, it is too lovely an afternoon to argue this point,
so I won't—for the moment."

He grinned. "You are determined to see what was not there," he cautioned
pleasantly.

And you, she thought, are equally determined to deny what *was* there. You
lie to yourself and see a "father" instead of a "papa," a man who, by your
own words, has given you everything, worried for you, stood by you when all

were against you. Perhaps your actions have grown from *some* want and need, but his example is there as well, if only you might recognize it.

He was puzzled by her thoughtful expression, then gave a long, lingering kiss to her slightly parted lips.

"Where is everyone?" Julienne asked, leaning against him.

"Resting, sleeping, making love," he answered. "What else would one do on such a warm afternoon . . ." He sighed and held her close to himself. "Come with me, inside."

"But Frédéric . . ."

"I'll send him up to the nursery. Gisèle's there. Go on. I'll join you in a few moments," he said, lightly kissing her forehead.

In his room, the room that adjoined hers with a door on the connecting wall, Edward undressed, then drew his robe about him. He thought of the two previous times they had tried to make love, when she had suddenly and abruptly pulled away from him. And though he'd held her in his arms, she had seemed to vanish, leaving only a stricken far-away look in her wake. He'd touched the scars through the muslin shift she never removed, and had tried to ignore their ugliness. She'd only said they resulted from an accident and did not explain what it had been, nor did he ask.

She was so wounded and ashamed on both those previous occasions and he knew it was the past, the men on the road that haunted her still. Such violence, he thought sadly, to suffer that and then the death of an innocent child who became ill because they were so unprotected on the open road. *I cannot blame her.* He looked out the windows of his room to the peaceful gardens below him and an idea raised by Droz came to mind. *The problem in life,* Droz had said—though his meaning was directed toward children—*was to be loved in return by the person one loves—freely.*

Edward leaned against the window frame. *She's never said it,* he thought. *I tell her I love her, and she does not reply.* Yet, he thought, *she is filled with tenderness and love for her children, in everything she does for them and with them, in the way she caresses them and sometimes, in the way she caresses me, but she has never actually said it.*

He sighed, wondering about the paradox, of a woman so intelligent, so kind, so alive and strong in every respect save this one. *No,* he thought, *in this she is a stranger, not a friend.*

But Droz had said that, hadn't he, Edward thought. He championed the radical idea that husbands and wives ought to be true friends, and then passionate lovers.

Friends, he thought. *And what are friends*—patient, kind, generous, honest, placing no restrictions of time on each other. He nodded to himself. *So it must be,* he thought. *Time to grow, and time to trust, for only from this may a true lover come*—a lover and a wife. Not a mistress.

He looked at the door and more or less knew how he would find her. He was not surprised when he entered the room and saw her huddled on the bed under the coverlet, curtains drawn and her hands cold as they might be in winter. Just as before, he thought, but unlike the last time, he did not crawl beneath the covers with her. Instead, he fluffed two pillows behind him, and sat next to her on top of the covers. He leaned back, sighed, and half-closed his eyes in the dim room.

After a moment, he heard the small voice to his left.

"What are you doing?" she asked.

Edward shook his head. "Just thinking."

The mattress moved as she inched a bit closer. "What about?"

"The future, my future, something which hasn't concerned me for years."

"Really?" Julienne asked.

"Yes, really," he smiled. "You find that surprising, don't you?"

"Yes," she answered, and leaned her head on his chest.

He unwound his left arm from beneath her and gently draped it around her back to her waist, then closed his right arm over her as well and caressed her shoulders. "Why are you surprised?" he asked.

"I don't know," Julienne answered, "it just seems natural for one to think of the future. The future is part of life. And my father had always said, choose life, in spite of the obstacles."

"Where did he learn that?"

"It is in the Bible. A small quote, I don't remember it exactly, only the way my father used to say it. It says that each of us is presented with a choice, life or death, and we will be given what we choose. It was never the obvious choice of living or dying, but the kind of life one may live, the quality of life."

He thought a moment, then said, "Isn't it odd, to arrive at the same point from two so very different paths."

She slowly raised her head from his chest. "What do you mean?"

He sighed, watching shadows on the walls. "I had no particular loyalty to life, to anything really, not even myself. In fact, I sought to end my life. In January when we first met, I was nearing the end. It seems almost like another lifetime. I suppose I did choose life, then, that day. I have a happiness now I've never known before, a patience with people, things and situations that I'd never had before." He chuckled slightly. "Perhaps I am just growing old."

Julienne sat up, and then leaned across him, moving her hands slowly up his chest and then placing them on his shoulders. "Silly man," she said to him, staring straight into his beautiful blue eyes. She smiled, then brushed the dark hair at his temples. "No man who plays with children as you do will every really grow old." He seemed pleased by the comment and impulsively, she kissed him.

"Of course I'll grow old," Edward said, "we all will," and then quietly, returned the kiss.

"But not your heart," she whispered, tracing a finger along his jaw. "That remains young, if it has always been kind, and so very generous."

He caressed her soft arms beneath the loose muslin shift, then kissed her hands. "I love you," he said.

"Then hold me," Julienne whispered.

Edward gently eased her to her back as he pushed the pillows behind her away. He slipped his arms out of the robe, then slid under the coverlet and drew close to the muslin shift. He kissed her parted lips long and lovingly, trailing his fingers through the silk-like hair, fine and thick like a child's. He could feel the tremor in the lips, and when he opened his eyes, he saw her watching him, with widened eyes, as she had done twice before. "It is only me," he said quietly, gently, then took her left hand from his arm. "It is," he said with a small smile, "only me." He brought her icy hand to his face and warmed it with a kiss. Then, he traced it down his neck, to his shoulders, to the taut and smooth muscles in his chest, to his ribs and then to the muscle making the right half of the V-shape to his waist. He brought her hand around to his back and let go. "It isn't any good, if I am the only one doing the holding. You must hold me, too," he said, and nuzzled into her neck.

Julienne slowly drew her left hand up his back, smooth, like the back of a marble statue of a Greek or Roman athlete. It was his scent, the scent of the cinnamon hair-dressing he used, drifting in the lazy heat of the closed room that made her smile and lean closer to him. Edward's scent, she thought, Edward, and let her right hand glide up his arm, down his chest around to his back, just as the left had done with his guidance. Edward, she thought comfortably, it is only Edward. She felt safe from the outside world, so far away now it seemed, that there was no world other than the protecting boundary of his body.

Her touch is different, he thought with several teasing kisses into her mouth, and pulled her slightly closer. She hasn't turned away, as before. He felt her leg move against him, a faint caress he made tighter with his hand squeezing her knee. When she did not object, he slid his hand under the muslin shift, pressing his palm on her moist skin, firm abdomen, and then to the lower ribs, slender ribs fanning slightly up and open, then in and down as her breathing quickened gently while he made small circles with the tips of his fingers. Edward felt content in these long moments of peace, caressing her, kissing her, holding her cradled in his arms with a depth he'd never believed possible.

After a time, Julienne slowly moved his hand to the breast, and sighed in his mouth when he touched her, as he pressed just right on the nipple, over the nipple, it was all so effortless and right as time began to disappear under the palm of his hand. Only then did she feel the damp muslin shift clinging to her, acting as a terrible barrier to this fine and caring man. She pulled her arms in from the billowy sleeves and felt him help her draw it up and over her head. Warm and freed, she kissed him hard, touching and squeezing him, feeling as if her skin had been starving for him for the whole of her life.

His kisses moved from willing mouth to neck's hollow, to the slight depression between her breasts, then lingered on the dewy skin of each breast while his hand drifted down her legs, in between, touching and stretching as whispered sighs encouraged him first in his ear and then suddenly vibrated in his mouth during a long, passionate embrace.

The air was hot and still and silent, and Julienne pulled him closer, closer, with quick welcoming kisses, feeling his hand briefly under her hips lifting and then easing himself into her. She gasped, then smiled a sigh feeling the very pinnacle of life within, and closed her eyes as their skin began to lose definition, each equally as warm, each moistened with a shimmering sweat as their bodies moved toward a single end.

"I love you," Edward whispered as he drew his arms tightly around her.

I love you, she mouthed inaudibly against his wet shoulder, feeling herself beginning to drown in the steady, effortless movement of his body, as natural and soothing as inland canal water bobbing and lapping against endless docks on its journey to the sea.

Edward held back and did not allow himself to be lost in the warm, moist baby-soft skin pressing and rippling all round him. He half-heard the creaking of the bed's music, and tried to listen only to her as she wrapped herself tighter than ever to him. Only later, when he'd quickened his movements, and then felt the waving smack of her against him, the sudden arch of her back as her arms trembled and shook at his sides and heard the moaning sigh, only then did he let go of himself to the white-heated dream.

The sliver of his heart that was virgin still began to burn with a new fear. It was the part of him that no one had ever found, that he had hidden behind the abuses of too much drinking, and the excesses of Laudanum and had remained untouched by the faceless women in an endless procession of empty pleasures. In the dark hours before dawn, he had the recurring dream of a loving woman, but whenever he opened his eyes it would vanish and leave him with unspeakable loneliness.

He was suddenly terrified and closed his eyes quickly because she had made the desperate dream travel across the barrier of his mind and live in another person. Yet in the fear, in the newness of finally loving another with all of his neglected heart, he found peace.

Julienne felt the powerful shudders and heard a sighing cry somewhere above her ear.

Edward lay there, breathing shallowly at first, then deeply, eyes closed as he anchored himself for as long as he could to the dream within his arms. Moments passed, he didn't know how many and didn't care, and clung tightly, terrified of losing what he held so tightly in his arms. He felt her hands draw slowly up his sides, and tentatively opened his eyes, seeing her long dark hair loose and tangled with the white sheet. He moved slightly, and slowly caressed his cheek against hers and saw the foggy calm in her large brown eyes. "I love you," he whispered, "marry . . ."

She stopped his words with her thumb. Unable to bear the sudden shock in his eyes, Julienne turned away from him.

A moment later, she began to cry; short exhausted sobs came from a closed throat as tears fell against his trembling shoulder.

Edward's eyes had filled and he weakly closed them against the world. The emptiness came back and though he held her firmly, he felt as if he were holding only the shell, not the woman. Damn you, he thought, damn you. When will you stop running away from me . . .

Julienne held him tightly as she cried. Where were you ten years ago, she thought, none of it would have happened had it been you . . . Why weren't *you* Stefan's best friend . . . Why did I have to meet you *now* . . . Dear God, it is so hopeless . . .

CHAPTER
14

On the morning of July 4th, Stefan returned to Paris after paying his respects to the family of Lord Clarendon in London.

The Prussians wasted no time, he thought sourly. Clarendon has been dead only one week and the newspapers reported the throne of Spain was offered to Prince Leopold and he had accepted. I was right, and my cousin and the Council now know I was right. I have been right for two solid years and it gives me no joy whatever. He looked warily around the hotel room. Idiots. They will involve Europe in a war.

He glanced at the newspaper on the table and felt his jaw lock. Gramont, he thought, blustering and filled with righteous indignation. He is *still* playing the schoolboy game and he has not realized Bismarck is, without question, the upper-classman.

Stefan walked to the window and stared out to the Place Vendôme. Metternich has my message by now, he thought, and with a little luck, he will arrange for me to meet with Louis Napoleon tomorrow. I have my cousin's instructions, but . . . He shook his head. I haven't the influence or experience Clarendon had, still, I must do my best. There is a way to solve this, but the greatest obstacle is Gramont.

The epithets were beginning to circulate in the press and on the boulevards, all the disparaging comments made to minimize an enemy and thereby prove one's superiority—hopsmasters, peasants, uncivilized farmers . . . A patriotic parade, Stefan thought, and Gramont is at its head. He sighed. Yes, he is the obstacle. How in God's name do I convince the Emperor to disregard the prejudice of his own Foreign Minister? And, he wondered, is it my place to do so?

In the private study of Château St. Cloud, Stefan bowed to Emperor Louis Napoleon III. He looks so much older than his sixty-two years, Stefan thought. The hair was thin and lusterless, and he had a fair amount of grey in his mustache and small pointed beard. The Emperor's eyes had many wrinkles and the lids seemed heavy, almost half-closed. The skin on his face was drawn and looked pasty. He was not very tall, standing about five feet eight inches, and looked thinner than all the past official portraits.

When he walked back to his chair, Stefan noticed that the Emperor walked with difficulty, as if in great pain.

"I met with Ambassador Metternich yesterday," the Emperor said quietly. "I seem to have met with everyone in the past few days. I feel as if I am sitting on the top of Vesuvius . . ." He sighed, then sat heavily in his chair.

He is more ill than the press has given out, Stefan thought, watching as the Emperor took a cigarette from the box on his desk, fixed it to the holder, lit it and inhaled deeply.

"I expected my brother Austria to send someone," Louis Napoleon said. "Have you a message for me?"

"Yes, Your Majesty. My Emperor's words, exactly, are: Austria may not promise, what Austria may not do."

"He still insists he needs six weeks to call up an army?"

"At *least* six weeks, Sir."

The Emperor shook his head. "He speaks of one promise, I think of another, of our promise of a peace with honor . . ." He noticed the expression on the Austrian Prince's face. "You seem disturbed. Why?"

"It is not for me to say, Sir," Stefan replied. "I am an outsider and my words would only be an intrusion."

The Emperor smiled sadly. "Sometimes, someone not directly involved with all the partisan sentiments, gives a breath of fresh air. Like Lord Clarendon. He gave good honest counsel."

"I am sure of it," Stefan said.

"Did you know him?"

"Not personally, Your Majesty. I wrote to him last January because of certain fears I had. He wrote to me when he could, saying only that Your Majesty had enlisted his aid as an intermediary to the Prussian Court. Indeed, I came to Paris to meet him, but . . ."

"Yes, his death was unexpected and a most terrible blow to us." The Emperor sighed. "I am curious, Prince Stefan, if your fears parallel my own."

Stefan considered the request, then said, "I wrote to him because of the intrigue in Spain, and the possibility of it being used to begin a war between France and Prussia. Though Lord Clarendon never said, I imagined his efforts might be some sort of disarmament treaty to ease the growing tensions."

"It was, indeed," the Emperor smiled. "I see now Ambassador Metternich did not exaggerate his claims about you. Clarendon failed, you know."

"His failure is now painfully obvious, Your Majesty."

"They led him a merry chase," Napoleon continued, quietly. "He kept returning to the Prussian court only to find that they had re-worded the agreement, or changed their mind on a minor point, or had disagreed and would wait to see what I would do. Chancellor Bismarck kept him hoping, and when a hope is skillfully nursed, it is easy later to see who was in control

212

of the game." The Emperor looked up and saw the clouded expression on the young Prince's face. "I have described a familiar tactic, have I not?"

"Yes," Stefan answered, knowing the Emperor had referred to the power struggle between Austria and Prussia in the early months of 1866—it had been masterfully played, with Austria placed in the position of declaring war on Prussia, only to lose that war six weeks later. The French should have assisted Austria, but Louis Napoleon waited too long a time.

"It was a very black year," Napoleon answered. "It was then my Star began to fall . . ." He smiled gently at the Austrian Prince. "You do not believe in such things, do you?"

"No, Your Majesty. Men interpret the stars, and men can and *do* make mistakes."

"Ahh, but that is part of the destiny. The mistakes by men are woven into the prophecy." He paused, then said, "Do you believe I desire war?"

"No, Your Majesty."

"Why not?"

"Because Clarendon's strenuous efforts began at your request."

The Emperor smiled easily and leaned back into his chair. "Why do you have no official post? You are wasted without one, you know."

Stefan accepted the compliment with a nod.

"I like you," the Emperor said. "Tell me, do you believe France has been wronged in this business with Spain?"

Stefan paused before answering, collecting his thoughts for the solution he had worked out two days earlier. "I believe that Europe has been wronged."

The Emperor noticed he'd smoked his cigarette down to the last shred, and reached again into the box to replace it with another. "And how might Europe right this wrong?"

Stefan stepped closer, picked up the match and lit the Emperor's cigarette. "I believe the only course open to Your Majesty is to convene an International Conference. Because a reigning house is placing one of its princes on a foreign throne and European peace is being threatened as a result of this, International Law has been violated. Prince Leopold's name should be voluntarily withdrawn for the sake of peace. Above all else, we should save the Prince from any embarrassment."

"Exactly so," the Emperor smiled.

"If Your Majesty were to write to all The Powers asking that they write to King William and urge this same course, the King, being a peaceful man, would absolutely agree with you."

"You are suggesting, very quietly, that we avoid Bismarck as long as possible, aren't you?"

"Yes," Stefan chuckled slightly, "I would certainly recommend that, Your Majesty." He sighed. "The individual Ambassadors will help you in this. They would contact their governments and offer the same suggestions."

"And are you free to speak to them as well?"

"I am," Stefan replied.

"And will you?"

"If it is your wish, I will, Your Majesty."

The Emperor nodded, then smiled. "I say this with kindness and without insult, your Emperor wastes your talents in giving you no official post."

Stefan smiled and bowed at the gracious compliment.

Where has the time gone, Julienne thought sadly, slowly opening her eyes on Saturday morning to a hot July sunshine. She listened to Edward's deep and steady breathing next to her. She smiled at the sight of them, tangled, as always. Only one week, she thought, this second week of loving him, waking with him, talking and laughing and sleeping so safe and comfortably. The second week, and it is over tomorrow night . . . and we return to Paris on Monday morning. A week's happiness, and it is nearly gone. It isn't fair, she thought, and closed her eyes as she leaned against his cool skin.

She felt him stir when in the courtyard below, loud voices yelled instructions to the servants hired for the day. She watched Edward wake up, opening an eye, shutting it again, yawning, and then giving a long stretch to his arms and back.

"What time is it?" he managed.

"Early. But they've already begun working outside and in the kitchen. Can you smell the food?"

He grunted. "Blast Philippe and his silly party," he yawned. "Dressing up in Elizabethan costume and lolling about with three hundred people all looking like paintings is the last thing in the world I want to do today. God, I hate these things."

"Last week you said it would be great fun, feasting like they used to, dancing, music, fireworks . . ."

"Last week was last week," he smiled. He turned his head toward her on the pillow. "I've a better idea. Let's run away, the four of us, as a family . . ."

Her smile faded. "You promised you wouldn't speak of that."

"I was only jesting."

She shook her head.

He stared silently and hard for a moment, then leaned up on his elbow. "You're quite right. I am serious."

"You made a promise to me, and I shall hold you to it," Julienne said, pulling on her dressing gown and leaving the bed.

He sighed, then leaned back against the headboard.

She noticed the sour expression on his face and walked to his side of the bed, sitting down next to him. "Edward, be reasonable. Today is a special day for Philippe," she said in a soft voice. "We really ought to try to . . ."

"Damn this party," Edward interrupted, "damn it, and Philippe, and everyone attending this charade. I don't care about it or them, only about you. Why won't you believe me?"

"But I do," Julienne said quickly, "it just isn't the time or the place to discuss it. Let it pass for today."

"Madame," he said, twisting the word as he usually did when he was annoyed with her, "I have let it pass all week, as you made me promise— unfairly, I might add. This cannot continue. Don't you understand? I love you."

She nodded, then looked away.

When she said nothing more, he swallowed hard and stared at the sheet. "Do enjoy yourself today," he said with an edge to his voice. "I shan't attend this charade. Living one is quite enough, thank you." He rolled onto his side away from her.

Julienne leaned across the empty space and gently hugged his back. "Edward, please, the children have looked forward to this all week. If you remain angry like this you leave me no choice—I shall leave and return to Paris today."

He turned over and took her firmly by the shoulders. "Then *you* promise *me* something," he said.

She felt suddenly wary.

"Promise me we shall have our talk—and soon."

"That is so unfair of you," Julienne said.

"No more than you were to me."

She looked away. He is going to take this shred of happiness from me, she thought, just as everything else has been taken from me.

"*Promise*," he repeated.

Julienne slowly nodded.

"That isn't good enough, Madame," Edward said. "Say it. Say you promise."

She pleaded silently with her eyes, but he would not give it up. It is all your doing, then, she thought. "I promise."

"When?"

"Oh Edward," she sighed.

"When?"

"Why must you have a specific time? You've made me promise, isn't that good enough for you? Don't you trust me?"

He felt foolish and his impatient words had upset her. He pulled her closer to himself. "Of course I trust you," he said in a softer, kinder voice, then sighed. "I love you. I need you. What kind of life do you condemn me to live without you?"

Julienne closed her eyes and felt the sting of a tear.

"Don't," he said, wiping her eyes. "I cannot bear to see you cry. I'm sorry I've upset you, but you've hurt me as well."

"Not deliberately," Julienne said, leaning against him.

He curled a strand of her hair through his fingers. "Jeanne," he whispered, "sometimes the unsaid words hurt far more than the spoken ones." Edward kissed her, then kissed her again after she'd said she was sorry, but they were not the words he wanted to hear.

Philippe had spared no expense, but then, he never did when it came to this feast. Acrobats, jugglers and puppeteers would roam about the gardens and entertain his guests at will, as was the custom for feasts. As usual, he had engaged twenty additional cooks, ten pastry masters for the dessert banquet to follow the feast, some fifty additional servants, and the children of his servants would act as pages. All were dressed in sixteenth-century costumes.

The musicians arrived from Paris at roughly ten o'clock in the morning. They would be housed with the servants. These musicians would play on replicas of sixteenth-century instruments during the day. At the feast itself, however, only a contemporary quartet would play because Philippe preferred the softer quality of violins, cellos, violas and flutes whilst he ate.

The guest list had grown over the years and was now numbering some three hundred people—friends, his family, cousins, neighbors and their friends staying at their Châteaux in the countryside. His neighbors always graciously allowed their servants to work at his feast. It was, they all felt, a delightful adventure into the past, and something different and exciting for the servants—as well as extra pay.

The fireworks display in the evening was always a spectacular end to the day's games. Philippe was a great admirer of Handel, and always insisted his orchestra play the *Fireworks Suite* while rockets were shot into the sky and rained down their fountains of white and red and yellow.

My guests should arrive by noon, Philippe thought, and it will be the sixteenth century for a day. We shall begin eating around two, and rest, and dance, and play in my gardens. He gazed at himself in the large mirror in his dressing room, then nodded to his valet. "It looks like his portrait, does it not?"

"Yes, My Lord," the valet smiled.

"Tut," Philippe grunted, "where is your respect? Today I am a King."

"Yes, Your Majesty," the valet grinned and bowed.

Philippe laughed like a boy. "Go, you must dress yourself now. I will not allow anyone to be late."

It is so strange to look like a painting, Julienne thought as the maid left the room. The gown was beautiful. It was made of white silk with blue velvet flowers in a pattern up the sides and the back. The décolleté was extreme, and the corset had drawn in and pushed up both breasts. She wore a small starched ruff, and her hair had been pinned up, curled and frizzed by a hot iron. Philippe had provided a headpiece made of pearls. She heard a loud burst of laughter coming from Edward's room. It continued in spurts for quite some time until she heard him knock on the door.

"Yes," she said, and then had to laugh when he came into the room.

"Do you like Philippe's surprise?" he laughed, nodding toward her gown.

"Very much," Julienne answered. "And now I understand why he would not answer any questions about this dress. He is delightful," she smiled, "and you look . . ."

"Naked," Edward blushed. He shook his head and played with the velvet hat in his hands. "It's very silly," he said.

"Not at all," Julienne answered, admiring his costume, a peascod and belly doublet of royal blue and white, the same colors of her costume. The stocking hose was white and clearly showed the fine lines of his long, lean and muscular legs. He wore a single ruff, and the buttons of his costume were made of silver. He had a short Spanish cape slung easily over his left shoulder. It was made of the most beautiful blue velvet she'd ever seen.

"I ought to have a small mustache and beard, but I don't much care for them."

216

"You look wonderful," she smiled.

"Not I," he said, "but you do." He admired her for a moment.

"Who are we?" Julienne asked. "Are we ordinary people or famous people at court?"

"You are Lady Raleigh," Edward grinned. "And I, I am Sir Walter Raleigh, adventurer, explorer, a mannered and elegant man in service to Her Majesty, Queen Elizabeth—before my execution, of course," he said with a wave of his hat, then bowed from the waist.

She laughed.

"Well he was later executed—by King James the First. I am the younger Raleigh, before his decline and his disgrace."

"How thoughtful of you to be alive and not in decline."

"And not beheaded," Edward added with a grin. He led her to the door, saying, "Come, it is time to go a-feasting," then mumbled softly so she would not hear, "My Lady-Wife."

They found Philippe waiting on the stone porch by the main entrance to the Château. He was splendidly dressed, and his all black costume had silver buttons, and rubies and pearls in a sunburst pattern down the front. It was the costume of the French King, Henri IV.

"Your Majesty," Julienne said, then curtsied.

Philippe beamed, delighted at his game. "I am so pleased with myself for having kept my secret of your costume. And I? Do you think I look like him?"

"Very much," Julienne said.

"Be thankful I do not smell like him, though. I have read he was as rancid as a goat."

Julienne and Edward laughed.

"It is true, he rarely bathed." Philippe shuddered. "That I refused to do, how insulting to one's guests. However, my choice brings back my old worry— how many Marie de Medicis will arrive today . . ."

They laughed again.

"No, it is very embarrassing," Philippe went on. "All the mothers dress their daughters so, and I foresee tall Marie de Medicis, short ones, fat ones, old ones, young ones, parading about as the Queen, or others dressed like Gabrielle d'Estrees, the King's mistress, or others as his annulled wife, Margot." He shook his head. "It is a grand conspiracy to see me wed . . ."

Edward looked away.

They heard the music beginning from the Pavillon d'Entrée as carriages drove up the long drive to the Château.

"I must welcome my guests to my feast," he said, and after kissing Jeanne Barbier's hand, strode to the steps of his Château.

"The children are waiting for us outside," Julienne said, "on the Southern Terrace."

Edward managed a smile and followed her toward the back of the house. It is all disappearing, he thought miserably, tonight, and one last day tomorrow, then Paris on Monday. Thus have I had thee, as a dream doth flatter, in sleep a King, but waking no such matter. Paris, he thought, with our lives unchanged and living in two houses, with two beds.

He watched her caress and kiss her children, laugh with them and smooth their hair and give little tickles to their ribs. He stood apart, and continued to watch her, imprinting the vision on his mind as she took their little hands and walked with the children toward the fountain. A spray of water made delicate rainbows in the air above them, and disappeared each time a breeze disturbed the air.

A fitting end, he thought, a woman in the mist, a charade, a game to crown the game of pretend we have lived all this week.

Still, he had promised, and he tried to keep his promise and buried the questions and the words behind a mask of smiles and laughter. He occupied himself by teaching her the dance steps to an old Pavan.

They walked in the gardens in a stately fashion, enjoying the spots of cool shade and did not hear the conversations from groups of people seated on benches or standing near the edges of the flower gardens.

"Well," a man's voice said, "I heard Minister Gramont address the Corps Législatif three days ago and he was magnificent. Such power, such presence when he declared to all of France 'A German Prince on the throne of Spain will place the interests and honor of France in peril. To prevent this, we shall rely on the wisdom of the German people and the friendship of Spain, but should it be otherwise, we should know how to do our duty without hesitation and without any sign of weakness.' He is right, my friends," the man said. "France will never show any weakness. He is right to warn them."

Politics, Julienne thought, taking Edward's arm as they walked toward the Château, hearing the servants announce the beginning of the feast itself.

"But I don't want to eat in the nursery," Frédéric complained.

"Well you will," Julienne replied easily. "It wouldn't do to have your stomach upset by all the food. You will eat what you normally eat, at a normal hour, and rest afterwards, as well you should."

Frédéric scowled and nearly stomped his foot but saw Edward's wink instead. He slowed his pace to take a few steps behind his mother and listen to Edward.

Edward bent down and whispered to him, "I've had a few little tastes of the food we shall be eating sent up to the nursery. Later, I've a small surprise from the desserts, so we'll have no scowls today, will we?" He pinched Frédéric's nose and was given a kiss on the cheek for his kindness.

Edward touched the spot on his cheek and stood up, watching as the boy raced ahead of them, running and weaving around the guests and then disappearing into the Château.

At the main stairs, Edward took Gisèle in his arms, gave her a kiss, held her whilst she kissed her mother, then placed her on the step and watched as she went up to the landing and out of his sight.

Julienne and Edward walked slowly with the other guests through the main hall of the Château toward the Grand Salon. Like the others, they dipped their hands into bowls of scented water, and dried them on linen towels held by servants.

The room was like a ballroom, but more magnificent, with an enormous cupola roof rising sixty feet above the ground. All around the room, the twelve sets of double window-doors were open, letting in the fresh cool breeze from the gardens. Long banquet tables were covered by platters of food. At the southernmost point of the room, a small platform had been built for the master of the house and his dearest friends.

All along the sides of the room were narrow tables holding the leather jugs of wine and waxed-leather goblets that were in use in that century, but for the master and his special guests, silver chalices were waiting at the narrow table behind the platform.

Edward led Julienne to the main table, and she was surprised to learn she sat on Philippe's right, with Edward on her right.

Philippe grinned when she sat down. "I have counted seven Marie de Medicis . . ."

Julienne heard Edward laugh, but she shook her head. "I think there are nine."

Philippe's eyes widened, then he looked at his guests and quietly began to count all the women dressed as the Queen. A moment later, he whispered to her, "Nine. The two in the corner on the left, I missed them. But, dear Jeanne, you see they have not missed me, yes," he smiled to the women, then gave an imitative regal wave. "Hello, hello, I see you . . ." He sighed. "I think it is time to begin." He stood up from his throne-like chair and waited until the murmurings in the Grand Salon had quieted. A few people began to rise, but he shook his head, saying loudly, "No, I give you permission to sit in the presence of your King," and graciously accepted their enthusiastic applause. "I am pleased you have joined me in my celebration, I wish you a good feast, and you," he nodded toward a servant at the rear of the room, "go tell my musicians to start my music!"

He sat, and a moment later, the soft sounds of the string quartet delighted his guests.

Edward had given his cape to a servant and like all the other men in the room, placed his napkin across his left shoulder, letting it dangle mid-way down his chest.

Julienne placed her napkin across her lap, and stared at the fifteen platters of food in front of them: roast boar, salmon, roast pigeons, carp, quails, oysters in white wine, caviar, sliced lemons, olives and radishes, mussels, stewed mushrooms, a gruel made of many grains that they ate with their spoons, cheeses and stewed pears—the variety accommodating the many tastes of the guests. They used their fingers for most of the dishes, and though forks were in common use in Italy, they were not, at that time, used in France.

Edward had been unusually quiet for most of the afternoon. He commented, occasionally, on the food and made an observation or two about the music, but for the most part, he was silent, lost somewhere in his own thoughts, Julienne assumed. He no longer seemed angry about the promise she'd made him give, nor was he unduly pleased by the promise he'd extracted from her. He just seemed quiet and preoccupied.

Several hours later, they had finished their long and most filling meal and would now rest quietly for a few hours before an evening of dancing, desserts, and the fireworks. The men, if they so desired, could play billiards, or card games with the women, or backgammon, but it was a time for rest or a quiet walk, necessary after so large a meal.

Julienne thought a walk would be pleasant, and was surprised when Edward declined. He kissed her hand and walked to another part of the house. She took her hour-long walk alone, wondering if he were playing at billiards or cards.

Feeling more rested and comfortable after sitting in the cool shade of a group of feathery willow trees, she walked slowly back to the house to find Edward.

He was not in the billiard room, where men discussed France's honor being challenged by Prussia; nor was he playing cards in one of the many salons set for the pleasure of the guests. He was not in his room, nor hers, and Julienne was about to climb the stairs to look for him in the nursery when she noticed the doors to the balcony overlooking the gardens, were wide open.

She found him sitting on a chair, his feet up on the balcony's railing. He was smoking a cigar and sipping a glass of wine.

"You look comfortable," she said.

Edward turned his head to the left, slowly exhaling the cigar smoke. "Not really. I am miscast, today, and most uncomfortable in this costume. I'm not Walter Raleigh."

"Who then?"

He smiled in a cold way, stood up and took a step closer to her. "Well, my dear, I cannot tell you his name, but I do know his function. In earlier times, for any King at any court, one man always played the Fool." He pecked a kiss on her forehead, then said, "Until later, for the dance," and left her on the balcony.

Julienne had little appetite for the desserts, and only picked at one or two cakes presented. Edward, she noticed, ate nothing at all.

Twilight chilled the air. The sky softened with coral clouds and the red sun's color shone through the strands of trees. They danced with the other guests outside on the Southern Terrace as the music played day into night.

The last goblet of wine made her light-headed and giddy and as the fireworks began, Edward walked with her and kissed her as she leaned against the trunk of a poplar tree.

"This will continue for hours," Edward said, watching the fireworks and the brilliant colors in the night sky.

She giggled.

"Someone's had too much wine," he smirked.

"Oh but I love wine, and I love you," she laughed and instantly felt his hands lift her face with a touch that made her stop laughing.

"Don't say it like that," he whispered, "not if you truly mean it. You've never said that to me before, and I've waited a long time to hear those words from you."

She placed her hands on top of his. "I love you, Edward," she whispered. "I love you."

He held her tightly in his arms and gave an urgent searching kiss. "Then marry me," he said, feeling her suddenly try to pull away.

"Let go of me," Julienne said firmly, turning her face away from him.

"I don't understand you," he said, the annoyance and frustration edging his voice. "I love you, I love your children, I want to be their . . ."

"Stop it," Julienne said, pulling free of him. She stared at him for a moment, then walked away. She grabbed the sides of the cumbersome skirt, lifting it slightly to allow her to run back to the Château.

The sound of the music, and the people laughing, and the now irritating sound of the fireworks made Edward feel so apart from the world and her. He left the grove and walked slowly to the Château, unable to stand the night any longer.

When he'd reached the second landing, he could not bring himself to go to his room and instead, went up to the third landing, deciding to look in on the nursery, just to be near them for a moment.

The room was empty, and at first, he was worried, but then he heard the giggles and the sighs from a room across the hall that overlooked the Southern Terrace and the fireworks. Naturally, he thought, what child in all the world would not seize this opportunity to stay up late and watch fireworks? He swallowed hard, unable to smile, and walked into the room where Frédéric and Gisèle, in their nightdresses, were leaning on the window ledge and watching the display in the sky.

They jumped slightly when he shut the door.

"You, you won't tell Mama, will you?" Frédéric asked.

Edward shook his head, brought a chair to the window and sat down with them. A moment later, Gisèle was in his arms and seated on his lap, huddled and cuddled and marveling at the colors raining down.

Frédéric moved closer as well, and made a place for himself on Edward's right.

"The treats," Frédéric said, "they were very good. See, I saved some," he said, holding a fragment of the almond marchpane pastry with the sugared candied violets on the top. "Here," he said, and brought it to Edward's mouth.

Edward bit off a small piece, but tasted nothing, deadened to the sweetness of the confection, the softness of the music or the brilliance in the sky. He held the children, feeling himself overcome by the dark thought of losing them. He held Gisèle closer and heavily leaned his head on her back, sensing that no matter how tightly he held to Jeanne, or the children, it was all slipping away. Jeanne shows me a new family life with children I love as my own, he thought, and then denies me that full and complete happiness. His stare settled on the blackened bowling green spread beneath them.

"Are you sad because we're leaving soon?" Gisèle asked, leaning back against his chest.

He felt himself nodding.

"I am, too," she said. "I wish we could stay here, all the time, forever. I don't want to go back."

Still, when the child touched his face, she made him smile. He hugged her and felt a little better. "Was . . ." he began slowly, "was your mother very happy with your father?" This question was never far from his thoughts as he'd tried to put together all the things she had said to him to fill the gaping stretches of her life before he'd met her. He'd wanted to ask for some time, and the deadly quiet in the small room made him ask the question again, directing it to Frédéric.

"No," the boy answered, then looked away, staring much too hard at the fireworks.

Edward had often wondered about the nameless, faceless man she'd married, but the boy's answer was strangely unexpected. "Were you happy, living with your father?"

Frédéric played with the edge of the marchpane. He slowly shook his head and Edward saw the pained expression on the small face bathed in the lights that lit the night sky.

"Are you happy, when I am with you?" Edward asked.

"Yes," the boy replied, his features easing into a comfortable smile.

"And you?" he asked Gisèle, "are you?"

"Yes," she smiled, "I love you."

"I love you too, both of you," he said, aching, thinking about this strange and confusing conversation, reminding himself that children see the world differently and their view of their parents' marriage might very well be distorted. He thought for a long time, and was a little afraid of his last question but decided to test the waters and ask it anyway. "How did your father die?"

The boy stared doubly hard at the fireworks.

"Frédéric, do you understand what 'die' means?"

"Yes," the boy nodded.

"Well?"

Frédéric's jaw clenched, and he played for a moment more with the marchpane. "I, I don't know," he finally answered.

"How can you not know?" Edward asked quietly.

The boy did not answer.

Edward saw the slight tremble in the shoulders and knew that his question had upset the child. "It, it is not important," he said gently, giving a reassuring squeeze to the boy's arm and feeling the taut muscles relax. "Never mind."

They were quiet for a time, and Edward was more confused than when he'd entered the room.

"Why . . ." Frédéric began with a large breath, "why don't wishes come true?"

Edward sensed the meaning behind the question and looked away for a moment. "Sometimes," he sighed, "they do." He caressed the boy's arm and said, "Is it bad luck to ask what it is you are wishing for?"

"I wish . . ." Frédéric said, beginning to sputter, "I, I wish . . ." he repeated, then suddenly leaned with all his weight into the buttons of Edward's costume and hugged his arms around the large chest.

"I wish I could be your Papa too," Edward answered and held the boy tightly. He kissed the top of Frédéric's head, then leaned his cheek on the soft blond hair. "You keep wishing," he said, "promise me you will keep wishing,

222

every day . . ." He felt the boy nod. "And I, I shall wish, too," he said, and held them both for a short time more before bringing them back to the nursery, putting them both to bed, and saddened all the more by their innocent eyes and the honest loving kisses only children may give, each kiss unraveling his life's new plan.

He went to his room, undressed and was finally out of the ridiculous costume, ending the hateful charade. Through the closed door separating their rooms, he heard a soft and agonized sigh, the last remnant of an evening of spent tears.

When she heard him in his room, the sound of movement there brought the last few straggling tears to her swollen eyes. Julienne wiped them away with the wet handkerchief and tried to blow her nose, but it hurt, and she wiped the slightly raw skin instead. What does it matter, she thought, it is a living death either way—we cannot pretend for much longer, and he wants from me what I am not free to give.

The door handle moved, and a moment later she heard him walk into the room and felt his hand on her shoulder.

Such a soothing, gentle hand, she thought, letting go of his pillow and turning over to look up at him in the dark. This is the worst of all, to see the life we might have had and to know it will never be, she thought.

Edward sighed and sat down on the edge of the bed. He ran his thumb under her eyes and wiped the tears. "God," he said, "I hate to see you cry . . ." He touched her cheek, hesitated, then said, "Answer truthfully, do you wish me to stay?"

"Yes," Julienne said.

"Move over," he replied, and crawled into bed alongside her.

Julienne wiped her eyes with her hand, then leaned as closely as she could to him, holding him tightly. "I love you," she whispered.

Then why, he thought, and would not allow the tears to come to his eyes.

The train ride to Paris was a melancholy one and Edward spent most of it holding her hand and watching the towns and country lanes pass by. A few hours ago, he thought, saying goodbye in bed, loving each other for the last hour of undisturbed time without fear of neighbors or children noticing or disturbing us, now gone—for a time, anyway. He looked at her for a moment and felt his mouth set in a line. I shall hold you to your promise, very soon, he thought.

When they arrived in the early afternoon at the Embarcadere de Lyon Station, Philippe's servants saw to their trunks and brought them to the waiting carriage.

From the peace and quiet of the countryside, the noise of Paris seemed more confused and dissonant than ever as people gathered in groups, gesturing madly to each other, and the cries of street vendors and newspaper sellers annoyed him. He welcomed the quiet of her street and managed to force a smile for Madame Mabilleau.

Julienne and Cécile chatted and laughed about the costumes and the feast, as the servants brought their trunks upstairs. They left, and then Edward and Julienne left Cécile.

He said goodbye to the children in the hall, promising to visit the following day, then watched her as she moved to follow them inside the apartment. Impulsively, he took her in his arms, drew her close, but he heard a door open upstairs and conversation spill out into the landing. I love you, he mouthed silently to her.

I love you, she said in a like manner.

He gave a hard kiss, a fast kiss as the footsteps on the landing above them moved to the stairs. He let go of her and stepped back toward the banister, then turned around and began to descend at a reasonable pace, Society's pace, beginning the agony he had known would come as soon as they left the Château.

CHAPTER
15

Stefan had spent six days in constant movement. He talked with Ambassadors and Envoys for hours in long hallways, in conference rooms, at their individual Embassies, at The Tuileries, and even at Château St. Cloud. He'd sent his telegrams and waited, like everyone else, for the replies from the European Powers. He slept very little, and worked with all his mind to keep the fraying tempers calm.

They had heard that on the 20th of July the Spanish Cortes would vote and declare Leopold their king. Metternich worried. "If it happens," he said to Stefan, "and Leopold is proclaimed King, France will be put in the position of declaring war on Spain."

Stefan told him not to confuse the issue and continued to urge the individual Ambassadors on the course of the conference, staying with the point of International Law. He had avoided Gramont as much as possible, and it appeared the success of his efforts was within reach. The Powers were beginning to reply: Queen Victoria had written to Louis Napoleon stating she, herself, had written to King William urging the renunciation; the Tsar had done likewise; his cousin felt the same; the King of Belgium had agreed with the others.

In going from Embassy to Embassy, Stefan was vaguely aware of activity in the Spanish Embassy. He'd seen the lights burning late in Ambassador Olózaga's office, and twice collided with the dark-haired man in the halls of The Tuileries, as the Spanish Ambassador was leaving the Emperor's office and Stefan was about to go inside.

He wondered what Olózaga was up to, and mentioned this to Metternich late in the night on Monday, July 11th.

But Metternich shrugged it off, deeply concerned about another matter. He tried to soften the blow as best he could, speaking slowly and evenly about his meeting with the Emperor only two hours earlier. "I have been told," he finally said, "that if a reply does not come from King William within forty-eight hours, Napoleon will mobilize the army."

"Goddammit," Stefan snapped, jumping out of his chair. "It is too insulting for words. . . . Who spoke to him about this? Who urged this course?"

"Stefan . . ."

"It was Gramont, wasn't it?" Stefan glared.

"They're fighting amongst themselves now. The Senate, the Corps are impatient for an answer, July 20th is looming in front of their eyes . . ."

"The powers are replying *now*. We are outplaying Bismarck *now*, and that idiot is asking for a time limit? Jesus, doesn't he realize Bismarck's options have run their course!"

Metternich sighed. "Perhaps we might explain that to Gramont."

Stefan arched an eyebrow. "We *might*," he said sarcastically, "but Gramont *might* not want to listen."

Metternich cleared his throat. "Will you speak calmly?"

"You know my temper is a private one, Richard."

"Usually," Metternich quipped, but with a smile.

The following two days were days of total confusion. They spent hours waiting in the main reception hall at The Tuileries speaking with other Envoys and airing the worry about the time limit. Stefan learned that King William was at Ems, taking a cure, and receiving telegrams from the other European powers. Stefan and Metternich still had not seen Gramont. Rumors began to circulate, and on the night of the 13th, the *Gazette de France* made them true.

"The name is withdrawn," Metternich sighed, "the Prince's reputation is undamaged, and all is well. I think we'll sleep easy in our beds tonight." He saw the look of annoyance in Stefan's eyes. "I thought you'd be pleased. You've worked so hard, we all have. What's wrong?"

Stefan smacked the newspaper. "This. It doesn't make sense."

"What does it matter how or by what means, it is done. Enjoy the victory and stop worrying."

"Whose victory?" Stefan asked pointedly, then stepped closer to Metternich's desk. He tossed the newspaper down, then leaned the flat of his palms on the desk. "Richard, think about this for one moment, think clearly, and do not think of any victory. That is a bit premature just now. Explain to me why Prince Leopold's father withdraws his son's name, and notifies only the Spanish Ambassador to France and *not* the government in Madrid. Think about that. Why does the official word come from a French newspaper, and there is nothing but silence from the Spanish capital?"

Metternich paused, then felt foolish. "Oh," he managed.

"Thank you," Stefan said. "I'm going out for a walk. I intend to walk as far as the Spanish Embassy. Care to join me?"

Ambassador Olózaga was a slightly-built man with dark hair and dark eyes. "I see you, too, have a copy of that," he said, indicating the *Gazette de France* held by Metternich. "My efforts are totally embarrassed . . . my efforts *and* my government . . ."

Stefan didn't like the sound of this. "What efforts, Your Excellency?"

Olózaga paused, then said in perfect French with his distinct Castillian accent, "I will only tell you that I felt honor-bound to assist a continuing peace in Europe. Through a person, whom I shall not name, we secured the renunciation. It is absolutely genuine and comes directly from Prince Leopold's father to me. My government was informed at the same time, and only now, and only now, *tonight*, do they tell me *officially* that Spain accepts the renunciation. Yet, here it is, in this newspaper, and I am told, in German newspapers, all having my 'official statement.' "

"Who knew of this?" Metternich asked.

"First, the Emperor, as I was bound to tell him. Then, Minister Ollivier, and later, I saw Minister Gramont." Olózaga sighed. "He already knew, at least that was my impression."

"Why?" Stefan asked.

"He . . ." Olózaga took a breath. "Everything has changed. It is a catastrophe. I . . . I don't even know how . . ."

"What happened?" Stefan asked quietly, trying to calm the Spanish Ambassador.

"Gramont was with Ambassador Von Werther and . . ." He saw the astonished look in the Austrian Prince's eyes. "No, you misunderstand. He asked Von Werther to wait in an adjoining room. We spoke in private."

Stefan nodded. "The Prussian Ambassador left," he prompted.

"Yes, and I told Gramont the news," Olózaga continued. "I read him the dispatch. He was cold, annoyed, complained that I complicated the issue: France was not mentioned, Prussia was not mentioned, everyone would be offended by this because it made France seem as if she were trying to control the voice of the Spanish people . . ."

"What . . ." Stefan breathed.

Olózaga nodded. "Yes, he said those things to me." He watched as the Austrian Prince glanced at Metternich. "There is more," he continued. "Today, when I saw this," he said, indicating the newspaper, "I went to Von Werther myself. He denied this most emphatically and showed me the dispatch he sent to Berlin. He had reported the events accurately, that I had been given a private message and the official word would come from Madrid. It is the idiots in the transcription room," Olózaga snapped. "How could they misconstrue so simple a message . . . how can they employ such people in Berlin, people who cause trouble like . . ."

"It wasn't them," Stefan interrupted. "Your words were changed. Otherwise, the newspaper would have stated clearly, 'transmission incomplete.' The information was deliberately altered—and just enough to cause a stir." He looked at Metternich. "And you thought it was over . . ."

"But who . . ." Metternich began.

"Bismarck," Stefan said coldly. "Who *else* would Von Werther send his report to? He sent it to his superior."

"It no longer matters wnat this newspaper says," Olózaga managed. "As I said, everything has changed. The Tuileries, it is like a lunatic asylum now. They, they have become crazy-people. They believe no one, Gramont even accused me of lying about the renunciation, he sees treachery everywhere, in everyone. He says France has been humiliated. King William himself must apologize to France and give a guarantee for the future this will never happen again."

"Good God," Stefan said. He turned away from Olózaga. "It absolutely defies belief. . . . Prince Leopold's father withdraws the name, Spain agrees to the renunciation, European peace is secured, and even so, Gramont is not satisfied. He's won, and he's throwing it away . . ."

"They feel they have won nothing," Olózaga whispered.

Stefan was no longer listening. Bismarck was right, he thought, Gramont *is* the stupidest man in Europe.

He heard a voice, but it sounded far-away, as if muffled by thick clouds. He heard it again, sharper, then in the dream, he felt a hand grab him and begin to shake him.

"Stefan . . . Stefan, wake up . . ."

He opened his eyes and then closed them quickly in a squint. The light near his face was too bright. "What is it?" he asked, half-sitting, half-leaning up on his elbow while he tried to focus his eyes. Only then did he realize he was in Paris, not in Vienna, and he had stayed the night in Metternich's home. It was Metternich, dressed in a robe, who was shaking his shoulder. "What time is it?" Stefan yawned.

"Eight o'clock."

"Morning or night?"

"Morning, wake up, it's morning, July 14th."

"I *am* awake, Richard, stop, you're making me dizzy."

Metternich let go of the shoulder. "This was brought to me ten minutes ago."

Stefan slowly pushed himself to a complete sitting position, leaning his back against the cold headboard of the bed. "What was?"

"A telegram from our Embassy in Berlin."

Stefan's mind instantly cleared. He opened the folded telegram and began to read what had been published the night before in the *North German Gazette*. He read with a building anxiety, the snide and rude story involving the Prussian King's meeting with the French Ambassador Benedetti. He read that Benedetti pestered and annoyed the King on his morning walk, demanding the guarantee for the future. Finally, Stefan read the tersely worded text of the telegram from Ems, published for all to see:

". . . that His Majesty the King would obligate himself for all future time never again to give his approval to the candidacy of the Hohenzollerns should it be renewed. His Majesty the King thereupon *refused* to receive the French Envoy again and informed him through an adjutant that His Majesty had nothing further to say to the Ambassador."

Underneath the text of the article, was a post-script added by the Austrian Ambassador. He said he had sent a duplicate of this information to Vienna, adding the following: riots had broken out in Berlin, people were massing and chanting for war, and the Austrian Ambassador had been informed by Bismarck himself that Prussia would not sanction any effort made by Austria to mediate in this crisis and would, in point of fact, consider it an offense. The Ambassador added his hope that perhaps the only effort left might come from the Embassy in Paris.

Stefan stared at Metternich.

"I've already sent a telegram back to Berlin requesting more information and a current judgment of the people's mood, but it will be half a day before we learn anything more. If we have this information, so does everyone else— including The Tuileries."

Stefan flung the coverlet back and sat on the edge of the bed. "The train from Berlin arrives at ten o'clock. We'll meet it and read the newspapers there. Assuming this is true, we must remind Ollivier not to let a newspaper article dictate policy. *If* Prussia is severing relations with France, it must come *only* from the Embassy."

By quarter to eleven, the mood of the crowds on the boulevards had turned mean, and Stefan thought it must have been like this in Berlin last night. There were spontaneous angry demonstrations and all along the streets, the people were singing the forbidden "Marseillaise," calling Paris to arms.

The crowd at The Tuileries made it impossible for the carriage to get anywhere near the entrance. Reporters from all the Paris newspapers and the Foreign Press, together with ordinary citizens, called out and yelled to the shaded windows of the Palace to answer this Prussian insult and save France's honor. From the back of the crowd, a chant arose and was like a growing, tumbling wave until the mob spoke with one voice: "TO BERLIN, TO BERLIN, TO BERLIN . . ."

Balanced on the step and leaning on the open door of the carriage, Stefan looked at the crowd. He suddenly bolted back inside the carriage after shouting to the driver, "Move further down and go to the center of the boulevard."

Metternich looked at him and then out the window. "Why?"

"Olózaga's trying to push his way out of the crowd."

Metternich looked again, and for a few minutes, saw nothing. Then he saw the Spanish Ambassador trying to pull away from the journalists. Metternich shook his head. "You have the eyes of an eagle, not a man. How do you see such things," but did not wait for an answer. He opened the door to the carriage, called out to Olózaga and waved him inside.

The Spanish Ambassador broke into a run, then hopped inside the carriage. He was shaking and sweating and completely out of breath. "There . . ." he wheezed, "there is no stopping this now . . ." He took several breaths and tried to calm down. "I, I have offered my services to Minister Ollivier. . . . I am to . . . to speak to Von Werther."

"We'll take you to the Embassy," Metternich said, then called up to the driver from the window not facing the Palace, "Rue de Lille, the Prussian Embassy."

"It is so hard to believe," Olózaga sighed, wiping his brow with a white-gloved hand. "The King, so brusque . . . there is no news from Benedetti yet . . . I wonder what his explanation is of this."

Stefan looked at Metternich, and then at the Spanish Ambassador. "The King and Benedetti were at Ems. But the dispatch and the newspaper article came from . . ." He knew. "Bismarck did this."

"No," Metternich said quickly. "It must be the truth. Bismarck would not *dare* falsify a—"

"He's already *done* that," Stefan interrupted. "He altered Von Werther's report of—"

"Of *my* meeting, yes, he did," Olózaga said.

Metternich was firm. "This is too much, even for Bismarck. Altering correspondence from his King? Never. I cannot believe it."

When the carriage slowed and then stopped in front of the Prussian Embassy, Stefan leveled a stare at Metternich. "Do you suppose anyone is at home?" With Olózaga and Metternich behind him, he strode to the door and repeatedly pulled the bell. When no answer came, he began pounding on the door. Only a minor aide answered.

"Prince Stefan Weiskern, Ambassador Metternich and Ambassador Olózaga to see His Excellency," Stefan said in a sharp, official tone of voice.

The aide looked nervous. "His Excellency has gone to the Foreign Office, to see Minister Gramont."

"We'll wait," Stefan said.

"I . . . I have been instructed to admit no one," the aide continued. "I am to say, His Excellency will be leaving for an extended holiday of indeterminate length. His Excellency will not be returning here. I . . . I shall leave word that you have called. Good day, Your Highness, Your Excellencies," the aide said with a courteous nod as he shut the door.

Stefan felt an amazed smile crease his lips. "My God, what a clever man," he breathed as he stepped away from the door. "It is almost a thing of beauty. He's done it. They've recalled Von Werther—but not officially. Everything will now rest on the shoulders of France. Prussia is the innocent party, and France is the aggressor. Bismarck swore it would be so—Jesus, why would no one take him at his word . . ." Stefan noticed Metternich's strange expression. "What are you thinking, Richard?"

Metternich shrugged. "It is so . . . I suddenly remembered a dispatch from a French official at their Embassy in Berlin. He said, 'Prussia is not a country with an army. Prussia is an army with a country.' "

"*That* man should have been made Foreign Minister," Stefan snapped.

Julienne sighed as Cécile refilled her cup of coffee. "Have you received any word from your son?"

229

"My Denis," Cécile smiled, "he was to have come home to visit us, but he wrote me whilst you were in the country. All home visits were canceled, so." She shrugged. "I hope he will come home when he is able. I have not seen him for a very long time."

"Do you have a photograph-plate of him?"

"Not a recent one, no. He kept promising to send us one, but, the army moves here, the army moves there. I miss him, very much."

"You must be proud of him."

Cécile sipped her coffee and nodded. "My little boy," she said, then shrugged. "Not so little anymore. He is a Sergeant in the Zouaves. I would have preferred a different life for him, but," she said with a slight toss of her head, "he has his own mind, like his father. Still, it would have been very good if he lived not far from us, or with us, with a wife and children. I am selfish that way. I love little children."

"I know," Julienne beamed.

Cécile looked at her for a moment, then said, "But I think you will leave me too, and soon."

Julienne shook her head. "And where would I go, Cécile? This is my home now."

"But he loves you, yes?"

Julienne felt her smile fading. "Now. I don't know about the future. No one does."

Cécile reached across the table and gently squeezed the hand that drummed fingers on the linen tablecloth. "You worry for nothing, Jeanne."

"I have reasons," Julienne said, then smiled too quickly. "But that is part of being a mother, isn't it?"

"Yes," Cécile replied, "to worry for your children, for the future, yes. My Denis is twenty-five years old and still I worry for him that perhaps, someday, he might be alone. But Edward loves your children. I see it in his eyes."

Julienne looked away. "It isn't that," she said, pausing for a long moment, then looked again at Cécile. "When I was a child, I had my room, and all my things were given freely by a loving father, and so they were mine. But when I was married, Cécile, nothing belonged to me—not my clothes, the things in the house, not even the house, and worst of all, not even my children. I didn't live in a home, I shared a place with a man, my husband. He took everything from me, and he made me feel that I did not even belong to myself. Everything was his, and everything could be taken away whenever he so wished it."

Cécile said nothing, but her eyes spoke the sadness for her.

"Now," Julienne continued, "I have a home, my home, my children, myself. 'Tisn't very much, but it is all I have in the world, and everything is truly mine."

"Do you love this man?"

"Yes," Julienne said, then shrugged. "I think so."

"Why do you think it would be like that with him, as it was with your husband?"

"Because when I married my husband, I loved him, too."

"Everyone is different, Jeanne," Cécile said slowly.

Julienne stared at her coffee. "It isn't the same anymore. There is so much—unsaid."

"That is no way to live," Cécile breathed. "We have a saying—when it is finished, it is finished," she said, and smacked her hands together, wiping them clean. "Say what you must say, and see what happens. This unhappiness, this confusion is bad for everyone. You may find it is different from what you imagine."

"I don't think so."

"Ah, you are like me," Cécile clucked. "You have the argument in your mind and you imagine you know what he will say. But, as I have found with my Armand, he still surprises me. Will you see him soon?"

"Tomorrow."

"And are you so very certain of his feelings?"

"Not of his," Julienne said slowly, "of mine."

Walking down the main hallway of Château St. Cloud, Stefan felt exhausted and wondered why the Emperor had sent for him. The Corps Législatif was in session, the newspapers had stirred the people, it was all over save the doing. Still, Stefan knew, he would try one more time, for only the Emperor himself could declare war.

He marveled that the Emperor looked older still. Stefan graciously bowed to Louis Napoleon.

"I would very much appreciate a few last words of advice from the 'Ambassador without a post,' " Napoleon said with a melancholy smile.

"Of course, Your Majesty."

"I have been told you fought against my army in '59, and against the Prussian Army in '66. Is this true?"

"Yes, Your Majesty."

"It has been suggested," Louis Napoleon said, walking slowly to his chair, "that perhaps the South German States may use this opportunity to separate themselves from the supremacy of the North, and in particular, from Bismarck. Many favor a return to Austria. Do you believe this may happen?"

Stefan thought for a moment, then shook his head.

"Why not?"

"With all due respect, Your Majesty, I have no gift for seeing into the future, but in my opinion, they will not, because Bismarck's policy has been one of *uniting* all German-speaking people. Whatever the differences between the North and the South are at present, they will be put aside now, because the issue is one of nationalism, and that will take precedence over everything else."

Louis Napoleon sat down heavily. "Has my brother Austria changed his mind?"

"No, Your Majesty. I received word this morning. Nothing has changed. I am returning home tomorrow."

231

"You will present my respects and greetings to His Majesty at Court, and let me know immediately if anything should change?"

"I will, Your Majesty."

Napoleon studied the expression on the face of the Austrian Prince. "You have done your best and worked long and hard for us and for peace. We are grateful, Prince Stefan, but it seems to me, something troubles you."

Stefan smiled, then nodded.

"You may speak freely."

"Sir, the final voice is yours. Can you not go against the old proverb— answer a blow with a dagger—and answer it with reason?"

The Emperor smiled, then slowly shook his head. "There is another proverb, and I have learned that lesson well: when it is finished, it is finished."

It was a long ride back from Château St. Cloud. Stefan looked at the countryside, but did not really see it. All the hours, all the days, all the talk, the telegrams, the running back and forth from embassy to embassy, the relentless tension, the sleepless nights, and to see it come to this because one man did not realize he had won the game, and as a result, threw the victory away. Stefan closed his eyes, numb, exhausted, and totally disheartened.

"They expect him to lead the Army in person," Metternich said. "They look at him and see his uncle, the great Napoleon, not a sixty-two-year-old man who is ill. If I were a woman, I think I would weep."

"Save your tears, Richard," Stefan sighed, "you'll need them later. Save them for the Army, and all the young men who *are* the Army. They have no idea what waits for them on the battlefield . . ."

From the moment they entered Paris, the mobs jarred Stefan's listlessness, and his eyes focused sharply on the faces of the people as the carriage passed them by. Anger and delight were unnervingly mixed in their eyes and he heard shouts of "vive l'Empereur," melting and joining with the passionate cries of "to Berlin!" Both, somehow, added to the ominous contrapuntal rhythm of the strains of the "Marseillaise."

They crossed La Seine at the Pont de la Concorde and then moved sharply to the right crossing the Place de la Concorde. Various groups of people were all singing different stanzas of the "Marseillaise" and the cacophony was alarming. He looked at the people buying flags and pears and bon-bons and flowers, all jammed and congested by the entrance to Jardins des Tuileries. All those people, Stefan thought, so . . . unconcerned.

He saw the blond hair of the boy racing by him, a boy clutching a bag of bon-bons.

"Stop the carriage! STOP!" Stefan yelled and opened the door of the still-moving carriage, and half-tripping on the cobblestones as he pushed his way past the people, pushing and shoving his way to the entrance of Jardin des Tuileries, near the stairs that led to the long walk by the trees and the small fountain pond.

"FRIEDRICH!" Stefan screamed, but there was no sign of him. There was too much noise, too many people, and the boy had disappeared into the crowds.

Stefan's hands on the cold stone barricade were shaking. His stomach had constricted into a knot and he felt the blood draining from his face as the "Marseillaise" began to sound in echo, and Metternich spoke words to him, but he did not hear what they were.

Friedrich, he thought.

She's here.

CHAPTER

16

Though Edward had slept late, he knew breakfast would still be waiting for him in the dining room. He dressed, then left his room. As he walked the side corridor toward the main hall, he heard gales of laughter from Philippe's room. A woman, probably, he thought with a smile.

"No, no, the shoulder, it doesn't fit on the shoulder—and do not stick me with that pin again, you terrible man, or I shall dismiss you and go elsewhere."

Curious, Edward walked to Philippe's door, knocked, and called his name.

"Yes, come in, come in," Philippe answered.

Edward opened the door and stood for a long moment, watching Philippe's tailor and the assistants chalking and marking a uniform.

"Isn't it splendid?" Philippe beamed. "Isn't it the most splendid costume you have ever seen? Don't I look wonderful—ouch!" He frowned and smacked the tailor's hand. "I warned you—but I give you a second chance. Do not pinch me again."

"What is all this?" Edward asked.

"I have enlisted," Philippe smiled. "But not in the Infantry. I," he said grandly, "I do not walk. I am a Cuirassier of the Guard. I shall ride my horse to war."

"Philippe," Edward said, then stopped speaking, nodding toward the tailors.

"It is too wonderful," Philippe continued, unaware of the signal. "Look at my costume, it is too fantastic. Scarlet epaulets and trousers, such a brave color, and the helmet has a horsehair plume, the blackest plume I have ever seen. It's long, like a woman's hair tumbling down free and careless after you have made love to her. Magnificent," he sighed. "And I have a sword and breastplate and . . ."

"I must speak with you now," Edward said firmly.

Philippe nodded. "You, assassin, go," he sneered and waved the tailor and the assistants out of the room. When they were alone, Philippe clapped his hands together like a child. "I have never been so happy! Who would have thought it would be so grand to go to war!"

"Philippe . . ."

"My God, it is wonderful, exciting, and dressed in this!"

"*Philippe*," Edward shouted, then made an effort to control his voice. "You cannot do this, it's madness, it's . . ."

"Don't be offensive," Philippe flushed and turned away. "How can you suggest . . ."

Edward grabbed Philippe's shoulders and shook him. "Listen to me, for once in your life, listen to me, goddammit! This is not a game you may play and stop whenever you wish."

Philippe's stare turned cold. "You insult me. My country is at war. I shall defend France. I love her, like a woman, only more so. I shall defend her honor against the hopsmasters. We shall fight those barbarians, those peasants, and after the day's battle, we shall drink champagne at night and tell stories of brave men at the front."

Edward let go of the shoulders. "I've never heard such rubbish in all my life . . ."

"You hypocrite," Philippe said. "You always believed it was a man's duty, a man's honor, and you *always* wanted to fight in a battle. Well we speak of my country, of France's honor, and I am a loyal son of France! You, you are an outsider and I do not expect you to understand. Even in England, you were an outsider without an ounce of loyalty."

Edward drew his head up and back. "That's a damned cruel thing to say."

"But it is true, isn't it?"

"*Once* it was true, and then, only in part," Edward answered meanly. He looked at the uniform. "You called that a costume, and you haven't the vaguest idea of . . ."

"And you do, do you?" Philippe said sarcastically. "When your father gave you your wish, and purchased you a commission in that emergency, you went to Madras—the ordinary, nothing army, with men sitting around and talking only of the past. And it was not even with a horse, Edward. You went to the Infantry, to a place so stagnant it took you *eight years* to reach the rank of Captain. *Yours* was a completely inactive, sedentary service."

"I'm aware of that," Edward said, narrowing his eyes. "But I learned a great deal from those men and their stories of the past . . ."

"Chats around a fireside, Edward. It does not compare with one's experience."

"You pampered puppy," Edward said sharply. "Glory, is it? That's what you want, is it? Where is the glory in watching homes burned to ashes, people burned, or people being hacked to death with very pretty swords, or seeing them shot through the head without mercy, or watching them slowly starve to death? War is base and savage, Philippe, and it isn't a game and it does not stop simply because you grow tired of it."

Philippe stood a little straighter. "But England suppressed the rebellion. England won. And we shall win, too."

"You haven't heard a word I've said," Edward said, the anger building inside of him.

"Yes, I heard you," Philippe said in a superior voice, "I heard you only too well. But *I* was not brought up to be afraid of little nobodies and peasants."

"Peasants, huhn? Was it the little Prussian peasant that overtook the Austrian Army in *six weeks*? Not peasants, Philippe. Seasoned, *professional* soldiers."

Philippe chuckled and drew his chin higher in the air. "And do you think I should flinch at their challenge? Well, not I, and not France. I know *my* loyalty, and I shall defend *my* country. If you are so afraid of little . . ."

"Is that what you think of me?"

"You are behaving like . . ."

"I'm damned if I'll listen to this," Edward raged and pulled the door open so hard and so fast that it swung back and shut behind his heels.

The white-heated anger fed upon itself the further Edward walked from the house. He was jostled by uniformed men clogging the streets and gathering at corners singing military songs: Infantrymen with red epaulets and blue frock-coats; Zouaves in the same colors but with shorter coats; Grenadiers with white frogging on their blue jackets; the Garde Mobile with their kerchiefs tied about their necks and wearing blue uniforms with a red stripe on their trousers.

Everywhere he looked the French Tri-Color was displayed and waving.

The bells of Notre Dame clanged, and their noise startled flocks of pigeons. They flew in patterns to the cloudless sky, dipping elegantly against the sun.

Edward stopped and wiped the sweat from his forehead. He'd left the house without his hat, without his gloves, without money—no, he thought, feeling inside the waistcoat pocket, not completely without money. A few francs, he thought with a shrug.

Then he looked at all the people in front of the Cathedral. Their eyes were shining and opened wide with a vision of glory and an eagerness for war.

What a colossal waste, he brooded, and over a damned stupid telegram and a newspaper account of an Ambassador's meeting with a King. For *that* they go to war. Not because of an invasion, not because of a slaughter of innocents, not to preserve their government, but because of a telegram. How utterly appalling . . .

Julienne dabbed the soft cloth with lemon oil and wiped with a strong stroke across her dining table. It was the oil Armand used on his banister, on all his furniture and on everything he'd made, and she was pleased he had given her a small bottle of it.

She heard the rapid knocks and, leaving the cloth on top of the table, answered the door, startled at first to see Edward, sweaty and flushed and with an odd look in his eyes.

"Are you alone?" he asked, walking into the apartment.

"You haven't even said hello," she answered, closing the door. "I didn't expect . . ."

"Where are the children?"

"Playing in the courtyard. Why?"

"We must talk."

"Would you like some coffee or . . ."

"I want nothing," he said too quickly, then continued a touch softer, "nothing except answers."

Julienne felt her back stiffen slightly.

"I'm tired of this," Edward sighed. "I'm tired of stealing an hour or two with you in my bed or yours. It sickens me to leave you at night and to always listen for the sound of your neighbors in the hall, or for the sound of your children in this apartment. I can't live like this anymore, Jeanne. It isn't living, it isn't even existing."

"I'd rather not talk about this just now, if you don't mind."

"I do mind," Edward said, "and you no longer have that choice." He stared at her. "It's some sort of game, isn't it? I am surrounded by people playing horrible parlor games—Philippe's playing the soldier, you're playing . . ."

"What has Philippe to do with this?"

"He's enlisted. He's going off to war. He thinks it's a grand costume ball, and if it wasn't so tragic it would almost be funny. And this game," he said, staring at her, "what should we call this? What am I, your sometime lover? Do we spend the rest of our lives playing at tenderness and pretending to love each other for a few hours every so often? It isn't enough," he said. "I don't want a mistress. I want a wife."

Julienne closed her eyes and heard him step closer.

"You cannot accuse me of being impatient," he continued. "Whatever you wished of me, I've given you. You wanted time, and then more time to let this subject rest, and I gave it to you. But we must settle this now. I cannot . . ."

"I don't have to listen to . . ."

"Stop it," Edward said.

"You will not order answers from me in my own . . ."

"I am not being unreasonable," Edward countered.

"You act as if you own me. You stand there and tell me how generous you've been and shouldn't I be grateful for . . ."

"I've never done that," Edward argued.

"I don't have to answer to you, to anybody—not anymore. I want you to leave my home."

"Have you no love at all for me? Say it, then, tell me you don't love me."

The words died somewhere in her throat.

"If you love me then marry me."

"No," Julienne whispered.

"Marry me," he repeated, raising his voice.

She shook her head and clamped her lips shut.

"Why not," he demanded, "tell me why not?"

She stepped back from him again.

236

The third step made him furious and he grabbed her arms to stop her scurrying away. She'd closed her eyes as tightly as her mouth, refusing like an obstinate child to say anything. He shook her, and kept shaking her until her eyes fluttered open. "Answer me," he shouted, "answer me, damn you, answer me . . . Why won't you marry me?"

"Because I *am* married," she sputtered.

"I thought as much." He let go of her arms and took a step back.

Julienne felt her eyes narrowing. "What is *that* supposed to mean?"

"It means, Madame, I thought it peculiar that your son did not know how his father died."

She stared at him and his arrogant pose, as if he'd won a point in a private game. "And you decided you had the right to question my children about me, my life and their father, didn't you?"

"Yes," he snapped.

"I never gave you that right," she glared, "and I will *not* be spied upon anymore by anyone."

"You have a very strange view of love if you believe that," he answered, opening the door to the hallway.

"And so do you," she answered smartly, "following me, asking questions to verify your own suspicions, trying to catch me out in lies, forcing me to do what you wish me to do instead of . . ."

"You're not describing *me*," Edward said loudly, turning quickly around from the half-open door. "That's *him*, isn't it? He was like that, wasn't he? If you're going to blame me for something, then blame me for what *I've* done— yes, *I* asked Frédéric, yes, I wanted to know about the man you married. I fully believed you would tell me all I wished to know in your own time because you trusted me and loved me. But you don't, do you? You don't trust *anyone*, do you?"

"NO," she yelled, "and neither would you if . . ." She stopped speaking.

". . . if someone had whipped me and left my back scarred," he said.

Armand ceased polishing the banister. He had tried not to listen, and even considered walking to the door to close it and give them the privacy that had been interrupted by the argument and the open door. Cécile, he thought. Cécile had been right. Madame Barbier lied.

"You think you know," Julienne went on in a cold voice. "It's so easy to say, isn't it, I don't trust you, someone scarred my back," she said and sat down wearily on the sofa. "You know nothing about real hate."

"Of course I know," he said. "Don't you believe I hate the men on the road for what they did to you?" Edward stepped closer to the sofa, then pulled the chair near to her and sat down.

Julienne thought for a long time, trying to decide if she believed his words. "Jeanne?"

She looked at him sitting close-by. "That isn't my name."

Edward held out his hand to her, palm open, waiting. A moment later he closed his hand over hers.

"There is no Jeanne Barbier."

"Yes, I know."

She looked at him, steadily. "What else do you think you know?"

"Only that you're Austrian."

Her smile was a small one. "I'm not a very good liar, am I?" she sighed. "My name is Julienne Marie Christine Therese Sophie Weiskern Berend-Schreier."

"And how did . . ."

"The scars?" Julienne asked, then scoffed, "Which ones?" She looked away from him. "The ones on my back, the ones on my heart, the ones on my children, which scars?" She shook her head. "It doesn't matter. They are all the same, given by the same man. I . . . I was so young, and my innocence was in believing that all families were like my own. My father suspected that family from the first. But I was in love with a charming, intelligent, sweet and handsome man, my brother's best friend, and I had none of my father's suspicions."

"Regarding what?"

"My mother-in-law. I should have seen what I would become."

"No one knows the future, how could you have known? What sort of woman was . . ."

"She was a ghost-woman," Julienne interrupted. "Shrouded and caged in that house, frightened of everyone and everything. Her husband was always right, always, no matter what he said or did, he was right and she always agreed with him, and pacified him to protect herself. The day they buried him, she packed a few trunks and that very afternoon escaped to her family in Hungary. I never saw her again. She looked at me, when she said goodbye, almost as if she knew what was to come." Julienne took a quick breath. "And why not? She had lived it before me. She had scars, too." She looked at Edward. "You don't understand, do you?"

He shook his head.

"How can I explain this," she said aloud, then thought a moment. "Have you ever seen an avalanche?"

"No, but I know what it is."

"It starts with just a little bit of falling snow. A handful of snow, tumbling, gathering strength, and building, building, causes an avalanche, destroying everything in its path."

He nodded.

"The little bit of snow began on my honeymoon tour. It was so—unexpected. He had been drinking, and I said something, I don't remember what, and all of a sudden, he smacked me, just like that. His ring caught my lip, and I bled. No one, no one had ever hit me before."

Edward closed his eyes for a moment.

"Franz, my husband, stood there, stunned, and began to cry. He begged me to forgive him, swore it was the wine, held me, and wept like a frightened child. God help me, I believed him. After that, he was the charming, lovely considerate man I'd just married. Attentive, affectionate, he was always buying me presents, jewels in black cases, and the moment was forgotten. A drunken stranger had hit me. Not the man I loved, not my husband."

Edward caressed her hand with his thumb, understanding now her horrified reaction to the present.

"For a few years, I was very happy. He was a decorated soldier, had a fine position in the government, an important position, one of great responsibility, we were happy. Even when his mother left, we were still happy. Then, my father died."

"Meaning?"

"I don't understand it, and I can't explain why or how, just that he loved my father, relied on him, needed his approval, and behaved differently around my father. When my father died, something inside Franz was set free. That's when it really started, a marriage in a perpetual avalanche. We would be happy for a while, then, slowly, as it built, an edge would creep into his voice. He became annoyed for the most trivial of things. As the months went on, his criticisms became sharper, more angry, more cruel. Why do you wear that dress, you know I don't like that dress, and you do it deliberately to displease me, why? Who are you seeing today? You know I don't approve of that friend, that friend is no good, you can no longer see that friend. All the time, he grew meaner and more cruel in his words, until he became obsessed by the fantasy that I had a lover. I had no one, Edward. Do you believe me?"

"Yes," Edward said quietly.

"He . . . he kept watch on me, came home at unexpected hours as if he would find me with someone. He inspected all the mail, all invitations, and if, by some rare chance, we went to a party, he would watch me with these glaring eyes. I . . . I learned not to dance with anyone, and not to speak with anyone unless he was involved in the conversation. Otherwise, he would imagine all sorts of terrible things, invent in his mind the basest of liaisons, and later, yell at me about liaisons I never had. There was no end to it. We went to the summer house, the country house, and everywhere I looked, or turned, or walked, he was there, following me, watching me, I . . . I couldn't even talk to the gardener or the stable-boys. Maids had to deliver instructions because if I did, if I met them and spoke to them . . ." She shook her head. "He made me cry, all the time. I was always wrong, he began calling me filthy names, criticizing every breath I took, I felt as if he were smothering me with filth, day and night. I couldn't talk to him, I didn't know *how* to talk to him anymore. Then, he started to drink, heavily, and one night, the avalanche, the rage."

Edward felt slightly sick, and watched her stare at the opposite wall. He saw her remembering, and though the sun shone through the large windows and bathed her in a pool of warm yellow light, she was a woman half in shadow.

"It was a sound from hell itself," she said in a dead voice. "I heard him, closer, the door to my room slammed open and he stood there, leaning against the wall. He was going to teach me to behave, he said. I could smell the brandy, and his eyes were different, glistening, ugly. He suddenly grabbed my hair.

He pulled it, twisted it, yelled at me, called me those filthy names, claimed Friedrich was not his baby, then he let go and started to beat me. He punched me, over and over, my face, my neck, my chest, I fell to the floor and tried to hide from him, and he kicked me. Mother of God, the pain, waves of it pounding all over me. I was screaming, I knew I was screaming . . . he pulled me up and shook me so hard I thought my neck would snap, and, and I was so terrified I scratched him on the face and he let go. I ran away from him, screaming down the hall, begging and screaming for help, for the servants, for anyone. No one came. I was so confused, so dizzy, I heard him behind me and tried to run, and then, his hands, his hands were all around me, smacking, punching me, over and over . . . I didn't even know where I was. I grabbed something, threw it at him, and he was more enraged than ever. I saw a light, and I ran to it. I . . . I didn't even know it was my room. I had run back to my own room. I tried to shut the door, but he was so strong. He pushed it open and I fell backwards." She took a breath, then another. "I . . . I saw blood, everywhere. My blood, dripping from my face, my mouth, my nose, it . . . it was all over me. He pulled me up, and then, I felt the most horrible pain, and I knew he'd broken a rib . . . I collapsed. There was no air and I fell to my knees on the floor, but I didn't feel anything. A heavy fog just seemed to come and I couldn't feel anything, I couldn't hear him anymore. He was still yelling and screaming, but I couldn't hear one word of it. All I saw were his teeth, bared, like a chained rabid animal. I fell backwards, and he stood over me. A voice inside me kept saying, he is going to kill me . . . and when he took off the belt from his uniform, I remember, I remember turning over . . ."

As if from the middle of a dark tunnel, she heard the sound of weeping. She turned and saw the tears spilling from Edward's eyes and moved slightly, tentatively, to wipe them from his cheek.

He leaned his face into her palm and held it there. "How can you speak of this, this outrage, in so quiet a voice? Why aren't you screaming?"

"I screamed for six years and no one heard me."

Edward moved closer, drawing her to himself. His hands remembered the touch of the scars on her back. He dismissed the ugliness and tried to erase them by tender caresses.

Julienne closed her eyes against his hair and smelled the warm scent of the cinnamon macassar oil, a scent that circled around her like an insulating blanket and reminded her that here was that friend, that trusting man who wanted the truth.

She opened like a flower and spilled the remaining poisoned drops still held inside.

The butler, Kollmer, was well-schooled in this sort of thing. He had been a loyal servant to Franz's mother and had years of practice. Franz disappeared for two weeks, leaving her to live, or die, and without Kollmer, she would have died. He cleaned her, fed her, dressed the wounds, changed the bandages, sat with her through a four-day delirium because they were not allowed to send for a doctor. It was scandalous, and therefore, had to be secret.

When Franz returned, he was penitent, made promises, shed real tears, begged and pleaded and stopped drinking.

"I didn't speak to him for months," Julienne said. "He never forced me to converse with him, and, strangely, it was as if he were courting me all over again. He was loving and gentle, quiet and calm, spoke pleasantly, quietly, tried to make me smile, and didn't smother me with his eyes and his watching. You have no idea how long five months can be without a single word spoken to a husband. And I hadn't forgiven him. He managed to convince me that what had happened that night was an aberration, a strangeness brought on by liquor. I . . . I forgave him. I was taught to forgive. We had Gisela. And then, it started again."

It was a shifting, confusing inferno. Franz kept saying he loved her, and laced the words of love with criticisms, ever-so-slightly at first, and he didn't understand why she wasn't being a perfect wife, as perfect and as flawless as that photograph-plate he'd seen so long ago on Stefan's bureau. He was trying to help her, he said, because he loved her.

There was nowhere to turn. Friends had been methodically severed from her life. She was allowed fewer and fewer visits to her brother, her cousins, and she discovered, as her mother-in-law had discovered, that she was alone and living in a cage.

He could not bear disagreement, so she never disagreed. But he could not bear the lack of conversation either, and her attitude was too reminiscent of his mother. She'd reached a point where she could not even decide for herself what to wear on any given day for fear of upsetting him and being hit for her "disobedience." If, that is, she got out of bed at all.

"Why didn't you run away?"

"Not without my children, and I was never alone with all of them at the same time."

"What about your family? You said he was your brother's friend. Was your brother alive then?" Edward asked, remembering she had said she'd lost her brother.

"Yes, and still is. I . . . I misled you. I'm sorry."

"Why didn't you go to him for help?"

"Franz said he'd kill my brother, my nephews and my sister-in-law." Julienne sighed. "I stopped believing his teary promises of never hurting me again, but *that* threat I totally believed. I knew he would kill them, and I couldn't live with that."

To fix a trap like that, Edward thought, no friends, no family to turn to, only the servants to gather the pieces of her together and try to keep her alive. That jackal stripped an intelligent, loving, beautiful woman to a faceless, submissive, frightened shadow.

Toward the end, the calm periods grew shorter and shorter. But Franz was a clever man, and whenever he ran away to escape the sight of what he'd done to her, he'd take a child hostage to be sure she would still be there, dead, alive, it didn't matter, but she would never run away from him. And little Maximilian, the son who'd died on the road, was born out of marital rape.

She was a shell that lived in dreams, and they, too, turned against her and frightened her beyond any boundary of understanding or rational thought. At first, she'd dreamed of death, and thought of death as a friend, a liberator from a living death. But when she began to dream of killing him, of repeatedly stabbing him with a knife whilst he slept to end the hell of all their lives, it frightened her more than he ever could.

Frédéric, too, she had sighed in Edward's ear, knew the experience of suffering. Slapped and shaken senseless, he had to be perfect, too, and if he wasn't, he had to be disciplined, that was the polite word for it, the word Franz used. Franz was always a proper and polite man to all the world except his own family.

After the second time he nearly killed her, she began to think of a plan. She would not exchange one prison for another, nor would she place anyone else in danger. Franz had infinite patience and would wait for that one day of carelessness, that one day of an unescorted walk, or carriage ride, and he would kill them, one by one.

Anonymity, a common life, a quiet life as ordinary people, unimportant people, was the only answer.

Though she had no money, she did have those despicable jewels and thought it a fine irony that his presents would buy his children and his wife freedom from the prison.

And, though she did not know how to care for her children, much less herself, she would learn the most basic lessons of life secretly, and then, they would escape.

But it was not without cost. He had to be driven from the house, and there was only one way to do that. When she was ready, and all the plans were made, for the first and *only* time of her life she baited him into giving her a beating.

"I gambled he would not kill me," she said to Edward. "Perhaps I was being selfish in taking such a chance, and possibly leaving my children unprotected if I should die, but . . ."

"Don't say such things," Edward said. "It was a most self-*less* act, an act of supreme courage, an act of love."

"I should like to believe that." Julienne leaned back from him and into the sofa. "It was just a question of time, you see, whether he killed me, or I killed him. I was more frightened of staying than I was of leaving. Besides, what could the world do to me that my husband had not done first?" She heard him sigh and looked at him. "The rest, you know. Chavastelon's was not for the money, or the work. It was just a way of being with people, talking with someone, anyone, hoping and praying for a friend. I was," she said, "so very lonely."

He raised his hand to caress her face, but stopped when he saw her watching his hand. "I . . . I am not Franz," Edward said, wounded. "You do believe that, don't you?"

"I'm . . . trying."

"Then there is hope," he gently replied.

She shrugged. "I thought I'd left all that behind me, all that fear, all that confusion. But I haven't, have I? It's followed me here, with you."

"Nothing has changed."

"I, I don't know if I agree."

"It isn't fair to decide that now. Decide tomorrow, or the day after that, or next week, or next month."

She looked at him.

"Or next year," he smiled. "But not now, when all the mind's dust is swirling about in a terrible storm. It isn't fair to you—or to me."

She nodded.

"Do you wish me to stay?"

She shook her head.

He kissed her hands. "Until tomorrow, then," he said, and stood up. In the hallway, he closed the door to the apartment, and only then noticed the landlord standing by the banister.

Armand looked away, then shook his head at himself and stood taller, prouder. He looked straight into the Englishman's eyes. "I apologize," he said.

Edward stepped closer.

Armand gazed at the closed door for a moment. "You needn't worry," he said softly. "I have always liked and helped Madame Barbier. No one will ever know this secret."

"No," Edward said, "too many people have kept that secret."

Armand was startled by the tone of the voice and the words themselves.

"Continue to like and help Madame Barbier."

"Did you think I would not?" Armand asked.

"I don't know you well enough to make that sort of . . ."

"Then I will tell you outright," Armand interrupted. "I am not so stupid a man to change my feelings for someone because of their past, especially *that* sort of past."

Edward nodded.

"Madame Barbier is *safe* in my home."

"Tell your wife."

Armand thought a moment. "If Madame Barbier had wished us to know, she would have told us herself."

Edward nodded toward the closed door. "She has been trapped and friendless for too many years. Friends do not desert each other in times of trouble or pain or grief."

"You are right," Armand said.

"Then you know what to do," Edward answered, and slowly walked down the stairs.

Though he walked at a sluggish pace in the sunshine, he felt an awesome shadow all around him. He was hungry, and then not hungry; grateful for the noise of people and children all around him, yet numbed by their sounds of happiness.

When he reached Philippe's house, he was relieved to learn Philippe was out and the large Palais was empty of noise. Restless and overwrought, he suddenly felt dirty, and though the bathwater was cool and refreshing, it did not seem to cleanse him. His mind became a taunting enemy, tormenting him by fabricating a shadowy image of a faceless man swinging a belt.

He tried to still the image and calm himself with a brandy, then took a second. He was about to reach for a third, when he stopped, seeing not his hand, but another's hand, drinking to release what would become an unchecked rage.

He replaced the crystal stopper in the decanter, and saw the drinking folly for what it was, a false escape, a liquored calm that solved nothing, changed nothing, and always made a deeper wreckage than the one he sought to leave.

Idiot, he told himself. Jeanne, Julienne, she is *still* the same woman. I love her, whatever she is, whatever she was, I love her. Nothing has changed, and trust has not been lost, because I know I am not *Franz*.

He felt a calm settling, a peaceful calm that comes with a certainty when facing the truth. With the calm, came a burning curiosity, and though he tried to avoid the library, later that night he found himself fanning the pages of the *Almanach de Gotha*. He stared for a long time at the section beginning with W.

Holding the red-leather volume, he finally gave in and began to read the Weiskern family lineage: a brother named Stefan; the father, Heinrich, deceased; the mother, Nathalie, deceased; an uncle Teodore; and then, the cousins.

Weiskern, Edward thought, staring at the page. Weiskern. Blood relations through the father to the larger family.

Habsburg.

"And so," Armand said in a tense whisper, "you were right after all. She is not a widow."

Cécile touched his hand and smiled. "No. I was wrong. He made her a widow the first time he hit her."

Armand had to nod in agreement. Then, he sighed. "Come. The time for grief is over. It is the past and it should be forgotten. It was another life in another place, and we must tell her so."

In awkward moments, Armand Mabilleau had a gift that never failed him. His smile was quick and easy and shone brightly, and when they were invited into the Barbier salon, he strode with long steps and set up the chessboard on the table. He called the children over and his gift of humor and story-telling made them laugh. And in the laughter of children, he found his own peace.

Gisèle and Frédéric were to play against him, but more often than not, Armand joined them against himself. He gave the chess pieces personalities, and if the children attempted a silly move, he pretended to scold them, calling the children "my little fleas," and telling them, "Ahh, but the castle grows and grows and moves in a line and protects King Frédéric with its tall grey walls . . ."

He left the quiet talk and the explanations to Cécile, and defused his own anger by playing with the children.

Julienne sat in the kitchen with Cécile, and sipped the calming herbal infusion the older woman had made. "It was good of you to do this," she said.

"Tut," Cécile clucked and waved her hand. "Family and friends always help each other. You would do the same for me, Jeanne."

"Julienne," she corrected with a soft smile.

Cécile nodded, then, in a self-revealing gesture, reached and brushed back a wisp of the dark silky hair, saying, "Julienne. What a lovely name your mother gave you."

I wander in a maze of darkness, Franz thought, and all these harried little people have the license to continue with their miserable little lives.

He felt cold in the Vienna rain, an aging summer's rain from a leaden sky and he knew it had been a little over a year since he'd last seen her.

He walked into St. Stephen's Church and kept his promise. At the altar to the Virgin, he lit a candle for his Aunt. The burial service in Eisenstadt had been brief, and he had been the only mourner. Tante, he thought, staring at the flickering flame of the votive candle, even you have left me.

He walked out of the Church and opened his umbrella against the early evening's rain. A thin and fleeting whim crossed his mind, an avenue grown out of despair to end the mockery of his life. He was one of many people on the streets, an ordinary man with his black umbrella, but he walked slower than the rest, lost in a hollow mood, in a world all his own.

Looking at the lights glowing from inside Stefan's house, he wondered if he ought to go inside. What would I say to him, Franz thought—talk to me, I need you, help me, you're my friend, and by the way your sister stole the children and ran away one year ago?

He shook his head. And how could I tell him the rest of it—that she was unfaithful to me with any man she could find, anyone, even the boys in the stable. He walked away from the house and went back toward the Ringestrasse.

When she stole the children, he thought, she stole my life as well. He knew he could not return to the government, and had the absent thought that he ought to shutter the Vienna house and sell it. No point in staying, he observed. I take a risk by being here at all. All the probing questions that would come, he thought, from Stefan, from her miserable cousin, how would I answer them? How much more could I lie to protect her?

Eisenstadt is a grave, my aunt is gone, my mother disappeared and never writes—well, he thought, she never cared anyway.

He stared for a long time at the main entrance to the Hofburg. I had a purpose once. And I proved myself many times, proved to them my full worth. I helped them with the Hungarian agitators. I helped with the treaty and aided her cousin in forming the "illustrious" Austro-Hungarian Empire. And I distinguished myself in battle, too. But I was young, then, and had hope. And that virgin hope had not been subjected to any trial or scrutiny. I was a boy, with a boy's dream of life-long happiness. And she stole it from me, when I gave her, willingly, everything I had to give in this life.

He saw Stefan step out of the Hofburg, open his umbrella, and begin to walk toward the right. Franz felt one moment of relief in seeing the face of a friend in a strange, lonely city he'd once called "home." He took a step, then stopped and made no other move toward Stefan. His eyes welled up as the ache inside him magnified.

Go, he thought, leave me as all the others have done. You are no different. You've not written to me, you've not come to visit me, you desert me in my most agonizing hour in this life. Go home to your children, your wife, yes, your wife, and the comforting sound of her voice and the warm pleasure of her love. I hate you. I wish to God I'd never met you, he thought, beginning to cry. I wish to God in heaven I'd never seen that damned photograph . . .

It was not a long walk from the Hofburg to the Capuchin Church, and in the summer's rain, Stefan felt curiously relieved at this quiet end of the day. He'd asked for—and had been granted—six months' absence from the Court and his duties. He had lied, and said he might travel to the United States for a well-deserved rest. His cousin believed the lie, and that was all that mattered to Stefan.

When he stepped inside the vestibule of the Church, he brushed the rain from his cheeks and then shook his umbrella before leaning it against the wall. He waited patiently until the monk had unlocked the door to the Habsburg Crypt, and then told him he wished to speak with his Uncle.

He felt cold, but it was different this time. It was a physical cold from the dampness of the underground chamber that made the stone monuments raw to the touch. It wasn't the cold of his soul's desperation, as it had been the last time.

Standing before his father's effigy, he placed a warm steady hand firmly on the stone hands, then felt himself smile. He heard a door open, sandals scrape along the floor, and then saw Teo calmly watching him.

"You wished to see me?"

"I need your help, once more."

"How?" Teo asked, pleased at the resolve in his nephew's voice.

From under his arm, Stefan took a leather pouch stained by the rain and dripping slightly. He placed it gently by the hands of the effigy. "In that," he said, "you will find all my personal papers: my bequests, instructions for my various properties, instructions and lists of payments for my servants, and most important of all, instructions for the education of my sons, and letters for both of them, letters of my love for them. Take care of my family, Teo. See to them, see to Rosl. Be her friend and advisor. Treat her as you would Julienne."

Teo's eyes opened slightly.

Stefan lifted his chin. "I saw Friedrich in Paris."

PART TWO

CHAPTER
17

For two days, Edward and Philippe carefully avoided each other. Philippe always seemed to be out at unnamed places with other friends and Edward made no attempt to find him. Edward spent most of his time at Julienne's, a name he found hard to remember to say, at first, but as the hours with her grew less strained, and their walks less uncomfortable, the name, like the woman, grew more familiar to him.

He enjoyed eating the midday meal with her and the children at home. She took such pleasure in preparing it and it seemed to him so very strange that a woman of her class and background could find pleasure in doing that. But he realized she had learned to do this, as she had to learn everything else, in order to survive. That other life for her was dead and her new responsibilities gave her a purpose. This purpose, outside of Society's suffocating dictums, gave birth to a freedom she had never known before.

He knew that pleasure from his own life, when he'd secretly done as he'd wished in attending the crammer's course. To understand her, he merely magnified the exhilarating feeling of being at the helm of one's life and in not abusing that privilege.

Her father, he thought, had taught her well.

But there was still Philippe, and on the third night of silence, that anger had settled like a cold vapor within the house. Edward decided to speak with Philippe this evening.

When he was called to dinner, he realized Philippe had made his own quiet attempt at a reconciliation by having all of Edward's most favorite foods prepared. But the table was still set only for one. When Edward had finished dinner, the butler came to him and asked quietly, "The Marquis desires to know if Your Lordship was pleased and well served?"

"Yes," Edward said, rising from the chair. "The meal was splendid, but his company was missed. I shall be in the library."

Edward poured two brandies and a moment later, heard the door open. He held out the brandy to Philippe.

Philippe studied it for a moment, then took the glass. "You know I only drink with friends," he said.

"I know," Edward replied. "I apologize for my angry words."

Philippe grinned. "I, too, apologize. We have never fought before. It was most distasteful. We must not do so again. To the future . . ." he said, clinking his glass against Edward's. "And . . . and I have missed your company, too. Ahh, but that is done now, and we must look to other things."

Edward smiled, then sat down in the chair by the empty fireplace.

"You consulted the *Almanach de Gotha* the other night," Philippe said, taking the chair opposite Edward and offering him a cigar.

"How did you know?" Edward asked, striking a match for Philippe's cigar.

"It was on the table and not on the shelf. Did you find her there?"

"No," Edward answered, knowing it made little difference to Philippe, but would make a great deal of difference to Julienne, and his first loyalty was to her now. He lit his own cigar.

Philippe nodded, becoming thoughtful and quiet. "Though we are the same age," he sighed, "sometimes I feel like a sentimental old man." He sipped his brandy and then placed it on the table next to him. "You know how I am. I save all sorts of silly things, and every so often, I take them out and look at them, and memories grow. It pleases me, but curiously, makes me feel old."

Edward drew on his cigar. "My friend, I have never met anyone who embraces the past as much as you do. What did you find?"

Philippe chuckled. "You remember that first summer, we were, oh, six or seven, and though we could not speak to each other, we found a way to play."

Edward leaned his head back against the chair and grinned. "I remember. I had a set of soldiers, a grand set, with horses and cannons, and so many infantrymen."

"And that summer, as a parting gift to your new friend, you gave me the Napoleon, mounted on his white charger."

"Wellington seemed inappropriate," Edward smiled. "I remember."

"I still have it."

"After all these years?"

"Yes." Philippe's eyes warmed for a moment, then he sighed as he looked sadly around the room. "Many of my servants have asked my permission to leave and enlist in the army. Do you wish to stay in this house? If so, I shall keep it staffed for you."

"No," Edward said, "there is no need. They have served you well and to keep them here for me would be wrong."

He looked at Edward. "I shall close this house, then, and send the maids to the Château." He sighed. "You have been in my thoughts, all the time, and I have wondered how to care for you in my absence."

"Philippe, you needn't . . ."

"Edward," Philippe interrupted, "let us be practical. You are my dearest friend again, so do not insult me. When you first came to me, you had very little to sustain you. You left England . . ."

"In something of a hurry, yes," Edward said, finishing Philippe's thought. "But you have already been most generous and I shall repay . . ."

"There is no question of debt," Philippe said. "Had I come to you without funds, without a home, without the necessities of life, you would have given me all, so do not speak to me of a debt."

249

Edward nodded, silently agreeing.

"I shall make an arrangement with an hotel. And I imagine you wish it to be near the 'family Barbier . . .' "

Edward grinned a nod.

"I thought as much," Philippe smiled. "I shall leave you the use of a team of horses, a carriage for the family, a little carriage for your personal use as well, a servant to be your manservant and driver, oh, and the pony, for the boy."

"He'll be very pleased, as I am."

"I have not finished," Philippe said. "I shall leave you a sum of money for whatever you need to sustain you—separate, of course, from the stable fees, the servant's pay and the hotel. Also, I shall leave you one little gift for her. She has refused it once, but will you do what you can for me, and ask her to accept it now?"

"Yes. When are you leaving?"

"In three days."

Edward sighed. "So soon?"

Philippe nodded. "Isn't life strange," he said, leaning back into the chair. "My accounts at Worth may have dressed her, but the pleasure in her eyes, in her voice, and the pleasure of her love was all yours. How lucky for you I even remembered that dungheap of Chavastelon's . . ." Philippe sighed. "Give her my mother's pearls, as a remembrance from me."

Stefan sipped his coffee at a café near the railway station in Lyons. Though they'd had a fair amount of time for dinner, he felt his stomach turning. Was it the journey, he wondered, or the other matter? Probably both, he decided, and thought of Rosl, of making love with her before he'd left, morning love in a warm and still bedroom. She and the children are safe, he thought, and Teo will take good care of them.

But the darkness in his mind came from another quarter. He had suspected that Teo had given Julienne false papers, French papers, and he'd said to his uncle they would be of no use to her now. He asked Teo to obtain other papers, for Julienne, the children, and himself. Swiss papers, he'd said.

Stefan stared at the ring left by the strong black coffee within the cup. I told Teo that after the war Julienne will decide what she wishes to do, but she must be safe now.

Thinking of Teo, he smiled at just how powerful and persuasive Teo could be. It is no wonder Julienne turned to him for help, Stefan thought, and it is because of his help, and those forged papers, and her own mind that she has been able to hide as long as she has. I will lose a great deal of time trying to find her, he thought, and he remembered he had sighed to Teo, "She is so stubborn."

"It runs in the family," Teo had grinned to his nephew.

In the early morning of July 28th, Philippe's carriage was brought round to the courtyard and packed with his trunks and provisions and plate. Large straw baskets were filled with jams and cakes made by his chef; champagne bottles, brandy and wine filled a second basket; a third contained linen, silver, china and crystal for his table. Philippe's comfort would be maintained, even on the battlefield.

Edward watched it all without comment as his own carriage was being packed. He stood in the courtyard in the cool morning air and gazed at the grand house being shuttered and locked for Philippe's "month-long" absence. He still believed that fantasy of being home within the month of August, to enjoy another early autumn in Paris and then go, as usual, to his Château for the hunting season.

Philippe stepped from the house and gave it a last look. He took a breath, straightened his shoulders and strode with long elegant steps toward his carriage. His uniforms had been finished and he wore one now, delighted by the shining black boots, dusting imaginary lint from his epaulets, and then, as he held his helmet, ran his fingers through the long black horsehair plume. Reluctantly, he gave the helmet to one of the three servants accompanying him and walked toward Edward. "Do you wish me well," he asked quietly, staring at the sad blue eyesof his friend.

Edward placed his arms about Philippe and gave him a strong hug. "I wish you a long and happy life. Come home, safe, my friend."

"I shall," Philippe answered. "Have no fear of that." He gave Edward a parting handshake, then grinned like a boy. "Did she like the pearls?"

"Judge for yourself," Edward said and nodded toward the iron gate of the courtyard.

Philippe turned and saw the three of them. He walked over to them, imprinting on his mind the sight of this lovely woman holding the small hands of her children. He sighed, then smiled. "It suits you," he said, seeing the pearls around her neck. "More than it would any of my cousins." He winked, then kissed her hand. "Goodbye, Madame. Be well. We shall meet again, soon, and you shall come to my Château for the autumn, perhaps forever, and I shall tell you stories of Prussian cowardice, and we shall laugh and be content once more."

Gisèle gave him a small bouquet of violets and baby-roses, and Frédéric firmly shook his hand, like a man.

Julienne leaned to Philippe, thanked him, wished him Godspeed, and kissed him lightly on both cheeks.

"You send me to war a happy man," Philippe said, and after an elegant bow, took his leave. He stepped into his carriage and waved his hand, giving the single spoken command to his driver, "Go."

They waved to him, and watched as the carriage clattered out of the courtyard and turned toward the direction of the Boulevard de Courcelles.

It was a strange and familiar feeling, Julienne knew, watching the carriage until it disappeared. She'd done this for Stefan when he had gone to war. Watching the carriage, and then still watching even after it had disappeared, as if the mind might imprison the phantom image in the empty space of the boulevard and keep him safe.

She felt Edward's hand on her waist and it broke the spell.

"Thank you," Edward said. "It meant a great deal to him to see you, all of you, and for you to wear the pearls."

Julienne shook her head. "It is such a small way to thank him after all he has done."

"Still," Edward said softly, "I know how you feel about these things," and lightly touched the longest strand of the pearls.

She smiled at him. "But it isn't the same," she said quietly, and then turned her head to watch the children climb into Edward's carriage. "It was a gift of love and friendship, not one to buy my silence or to make a guilty apology. There is a difference."

He smiled, thinking: Thank God you are now able to see that difference.

On August 2nd, Stefan opened the small, brown, book-like folder with the bold lettering "Paris, New Municipal Divisions, a Guide for the Visitor," printed by Garnier Brothers, Booksellers and Editors, and having cost him three francs. He spread the map open on the table in his salon at the Bristol and eyed the five colors that were used throughout, helping to delineate the twenty divisions comprising the arrondissements which formed the wheel of Paris.

He sipped his coffee, then put the cup down and took out his pen. He began to eliminate the areas he believed to be unsuitable for Julienne's purposes.

The first, he crossed out without hesitation. Although Jardin des Tuileries was located there, he knew she would never live that close to the Emperor's residence and risk, every day, seeing people who might visit the Emperor. The second arrondissement he crossed out as well—the wealthy Rue de Rivoli ran through it. The third, he thought, hesitating—some good areas, some very poor like Chatelet, with long, narrow winding streets and overcrowded . . . perhaps, he thought, and did not cross it out.

The fourth comprised the second half of the Rue de Rivoli to the Bastille, and took in the Île de la Cité and the Île St. Louis—all unacceptable, either too wealthy or too crowded.

The fifth had real possibilities, he thought—the Sorbonne was there, and this part of the Left Bank was far enough away from the wealthy, yet not too far to be really poor. The newly finished Boulevard St. Germain was a main boulevard, and much work, much construction had been done on the Left Bank: new buildings, apartment houses . . . there were parks for the children to play in, yes, he thought, a strong possibility there.

He moved to the sixth arrondissement and gave himself the identical reasons—Jardin du Luxembourg was there, and the Boulevard St. Michel was a main boulevard, with plenty of shops, yes, he thought.

The seventh, he eliminated immediately. The Austrian Embassy was there, and though it was a large area, she might perhaps be taking too great a risk of seeing Metternich's carriage on the streets, or meeting Richard and Pauline accidentally on the Champs du Mars, or by walking toward the Tuileries directly across the Seine, a walk Metternich himself was fond of taking.

The eighth was too wealthy, on the Right Bank again, with the Parc Monceau and many aristocratic houses with the magnificent boulevards and hotels and amusements . . .

He eliminated the ninth, tenth, eleventh and twelfth arrondissements on the Right Bank because they seemed too isolated, and did the same for the thirteenth, fourteenth and fifteenth on the Left Bank.

The sixteenth was too far west, bordering on the Bois de Boulogne and therefore too far away to be practical; the seventeenth, Montmartre, was too poor, as was the eighteenth; the nineteenth was too far to the east, practically nothing there; and the twentieth—having the large Père Lachaise cemetery—held even less promise.

He put his pen down and sipped his coffee again. So, he thought, three of them. He stared at the map. Three possibilities—the third, the fifth and the sixth arrondissements, and how many hundreds of streets, and buildings, and shops, and restaurants, and how many thousands of people crowd those streets each and every day . . .

He shook his head with a sigh, wondering how in God's name to begin.

The following morning, August 3rd, Stefan had heard the beginning of the war rumors, a disease that plagued those left at home in any country at war. In the time it took him to cross the lobby of his hotel, he heard three different versions of the first battle at Saarbrücken. The ending was the same—a resounding French victory—but it had graduated in the telling from a minor skirmish to a major battle. In the dining room, he let it pass from his mind without judgment, reminding himself it was no longer his concern, and gave his full attention to his coffee and to the croissant on his plate.

He thought only of the question that had haunted him for most of the night—where to begin. But after breakfast, it somehow seemed easier to address.

In front of the hotel, he took a hansom cab to the crossing of the Boulevard de Sebastopol and the Rue de Rambulau, in the third arrondissement.

He did not fool himself at all, and told himself, over and over, she may not even be here now, and she may have left Paris for a place of safety for the duration of the war. It will not be easy, he scolded himself, feeling his heart quicken at the sight of a blond boy, only to discover it was not Friedrich. It will take time, a great deal of time, and there is no one who could give information, or aid in the search. His only clue was her own plan of being ordinary and doing ordinary things.

Then the search must begin in ordinary places, he said to himself, with people doing the ordinary things of life. And that, he knew, meant food.

Methodically, he began to search the windows of boucheries, boulangeries, patisseries, the people gathered around vegetable carts on the streets, then laundries, and triangle bazaars where she might buy pots and pans and household items. His sharp eyes glanced at women approximating her height, and ignored those who did not conform to the remembered image of his sister.

CHAPTER
18

Edward hated hotels. Although the Hotel du Louvre on the Rue de Rivoli was a comfortable old establishment, with a fine view of the museum directly across the street, it was an impersonal place. His rooms were passable, with the luxury of another age in the heavy oak canopied bed, a large carved armoire, and an even larger wardrobe. The adjoining salon had a faded tapestry rug on the polished wooden floor, a writing desk, several brocaded chairs, a small table and a rather large marble fireplace. Though the owners had made a faint attempt at modernizing the hotel, they had not installed any gas-lights. In the hallways, there was a permanent stench from the oil-lamps being used at strategic points to give a small amount of light. When he'd described all of this to Julienne, she had had a much kinder view of the hotel. She had called it charming.

"Yes, charming," Edward had said rather sarcastically, "because you live here and not there. The noise from the street is hideous."

"Philippe has spoiled you," she laughed.

It is good to hear her laugh, he thought.

"Oh and I live in such luxury, do I?" she smirked.

"Ah, but you might, if you desired it," he'd said, hoping.

She had not replied and had simply refilled his cup of coffee.

He felt an ache, remembering that conversation, now a week old. She had deftly, and quietly, stepped aside from the first gentle suggestion that they might leave Paris and begin a new life elsewhere, as a family.

Still, he consoled himself, she is only now beginning to be affectionate again.

He looked at her, seated next to him in the carriage as they left the Bois de Boulogne. It had been a lovely Saturday, warm and sunny, and they had spent the day as a family. I ought not to be impatient, he told himself. She has had to learn many things in her life, things outside of what she had been taught as a child. But I think learning to trust and love may be the most difficult of all.

As they passed near the area of the Place Vendôme, a crowd of thousands screamed with one voice, "OLLIVIER! OLLIVIER!" over and over, demanding his presence at a window of the Ministry of Justice.

"I wonder what's happened," Julienne said to Edward.

He shook his head and searched the crowd for anyone selling newspapers, but found no one.

When they arrived back at Rue Royer Collard, Edward took the picnic basket from the carriage, then spoke with the driver for a moment while Julienne and the children went inside.

He found them in the lobby, listening as Armand Mabilleau spoke with several lodgers and friends.

Edward met Julienne's eyes and she stepped away from the small circle.

"It seems there was a battle," she beamed yet spoke in a soft voice. "A tremendous battle, and we won!"

Edward thought a moment. "Is it confirmed?"

"I don't understand," she said.

"When was the battle?" he asked.

"Today."

"Where?"

She shrugged. "No one seems to know."

"Have the newspapers, the evening newspapers, given any report at all, or is this excitement based on rumor?"

"I don't know," she said, knitting her eyebrows. "Why are you asking all these questions?"

"Don't you see? If it were true, the newspapers would have printed a special edition. People on every street corner would be reading the newspaper accounts, yet, I could not find one man selling any papers. And that crowd in the Place Vendôme didn't seem joyous to me. Something is very wrong here. I wouldn't place too much faith in this rumor. Until it is confirmed or denied, I would not believe one word of it."

"How can you say such a terrible thing? What kind of person would lie about something so important?"

"I have no idea," he said, "but we should not be arguing over this. It doesn't concern us."

She felt her lip tightening into a straight line, then gathered the children and went upstairs, followed by Edward.

Inside the salon, he put the picnic basket down on the table and sat on the chair.

"Sometimes," Julienne said, "you really surprise me."

He looked at her, not liking the sound of her voice.

"You said it so easily, didn't you, it does not concern us. How can you think such a thing, of course it does. Well, at least it concerns me. I suppose because you're English it wouldn't . . ."

"Don't ever say that to me again," he interrupted with a reprimanding tone and a glare. "My friend is at the front, and *that* concerns me, not some silly rumor people are all-too-willing to believe. When it is confirmed, I shall be as happy as you, but not until then." He paused, then continued, "You've a mind, use it. Think, with your mind, and not with emotion or blind patriotism."

"You've never said that to me before," she said, watching him.

"What?"

"To think."

"I never had to," he remarked in a softer tone. "I shouldn't have raised my voice. I apologize."

"It isn't necessary," she smiled and sat down in her chair at the table.

He covered her hand with his own. "All I am saying," he said calmly, "is to be patient. Rumors are a dangerous thing. In London, whilst the Mutiny raged in India, people just seemed to lose all restraint over the slightest hint of what might be happening. And the same is true here."

She thought a moment, then nodded. "You're quite right. In Vienna, too. My brother went to war in Italy. We never knew either. I'd quite forgotten that." She squeezed his hand. "Will you stay to supper?"

"Thank you, yes, and as I've already dismissed my carriage," he smiled, watching her eyes, "I shall stay—until you dismiss me."

"Wicked man," she said with a grin.

"I've been called worse—and by you, I might add," he quipped, as she laughed her way to the kitchen.

It was a calm evening, and Julienne enjoyed watching Edward play with the children, help Frédéric with his bath, and then roughly dry him with a towel. When it was time for the children to go to bed, he listened patiently as they argued over which bed he would sit on whilst he read them a story. She heard him gently remind Frédéric it had been his turn the night before, and it was now Gisèle's turn. A small grumble was heard, and then, after their prayers, the story, a long story of fairy Queens and little people that lulled small imaginations to sleep on a warm and still August night.

He found her trying to read a book in the salon, but preoccupied, he thought, by a question or a feeling she was not yet ready to share. He left her to her own thoughts and picked a book for himself and quietly began to read. Once or twice, he caught her looking at him, then quickly away as if it might reveal a too-private thought, and then hide herself again in the pages of her book.

At a quarter-past eleven, he stood up and walked behind her chair, placing both hands lightly on her shoulders. "It is late," he said, "and both of us are tired."

She stood with him and held him for a long time.

"Tell me the truth," he whispered after kissing her, "do you want me to stay?"

She nodded yes, but then glanced quickly at the closed door of the children's room.

He smiled, agreeing to the necessary silence, then turned down the wick of the oil-lamp and led her to bed.

Though he walked the cool grey streets at half-past five in the morning as the sunlight began to burn off the night's mist, Edward felt a boyishly giddy euphoria he hadn't felt in weeks. Hearing only the sound of his own footsteps echoing against the calls of birds, he felt a curious yet delicious sense of freedom. The faceless man that had come between them had crawled back into the blackened past.

It was a moment savored in the silent streets of a sleeping city, the vanquishing of a phantom, and he stood full in the sun unencumbered by someone else's shadow. She had loved him quietly, completely, and with that tender trust he'd once known and that had now returned.

He didn't even mind the room now, and thought of it only as a partial lodging, a place to change his clothes, shave, and rest for a time in the mornings. The mattress sagged under him and he jabbed the pillow twice with his elbow, then closed his eyes. He'd won his battle, and if the faceless phantom had any sense at all it would stay faceless. *He's as good as dead should we ever meet,* Edward thought with a yawn, then pushed the dark thought from his mind and dropped off to a morning's rest after a loving night, knowing nothing else mattered to him but her happiness.

But it was the mid-day quiet that woke him and seemed so strange. Even on a Sunday, there should have been noise, and the quiet was awesome. Edward heard no sound at all in the hallways of the hotel, but in the lobby, he saw the Commissionaire, Monsieur Robinet, half-leaning, half-slumping over the main desk. "Monsieur?" he asked, walking closer. "Monsieur, are you un-well?"

Robinet looked up with tear-filled eyes and shook his head.

"Is there something I might do to help you?"

"Thank you, no, My Lord," Robinet managed. "Read it for yourself. All of Paris mourns."

Edward drew the newspaper closer. It was the early edition of the *Journal Officiel.* He read where Robinet's finger tapped the page:

"METZ—11 P.M., Saturday, August 6th: The Corps of General Frossard is in retreat. There are no details."

Edward read it again to make sure he hadn't misunderstood, then said quietly, "Monsieur Robinet, it doesn't seem to say very much."

"It says enough," Robinet replied sharply. "They have retreated. With all due respect, My Lord, a victorious army does not retreat," and pushed himself away from the desk. He stood tall, and tugged at his cuffs, a habit he had to compose himself.

Edward held the newspaper. "Might I borrow . . ."

"You may keep the hateful . . ." Robinet looked away and took a breath. "I apologize, My Lord. You may keep it for as long as you desire. Shall I have a carriage brought round for you?"

Edward shook his head. "I would prefer to walk."

"As you wish, My Lord," Robinet answered and busied himself behind the desk.

Outside, as Edward walked the same streets where he'd felt so comfortable only hours before, he knew Robinet had not exaggerated. He saw only five people, wandering like himself, but their faces were unlike his—they had stunned sad eyes while his eyes were narrowed and sharp.

He gripped the newspaper as he climbed the stairs to her flat, then rapped on the door. The look in her eyes told him she already knew.

"Armand," she explained. "He went out early for the newspaper."

She poured Edward a cup of coffee, then sat wearily in the chair nearest him. "You were right," Julienne said quietly.

257

"It gives me no joy," Edward replied. "Perhaps the later edition will have more news."

"They're very worried," Julienne said, staring at the door to the hallway. "Their only son is in the Army."

"Who is his commander, do you know?"

"Marshal MacMahon."

"There's been nothing said of him yet," Edward sighed. "This is the worst of it, the waiting, the not knowing."

Around three that afternoon, Edward went out for a walk and to look for the later edition of the *Journal Officiel*. Everyone had the same idea and there were people gathered around every newspaper kiosk.

He bought a copy, then stood away from the moaning, sighing confusion, reading the short cryptic reports of telegrams that had come. There had been another battle, and according to the first report, Marshal MacMahon had lost and was, like General Frossard, in full retreat, but in an organized fashion. Yet the last comment, brief as it was, was the most powerful of all, and its importance was not lost on the crowds. The enemy was now on French soil.

They began to mark time by the newspapers, how many hours to the afternoon editions, how many hours to the late-evening papers, how much longer to the morning papers as the days began to drown in the blackened ink of the censored press.

They read *Le Figaro's* fiery editorials demanding that the 30,000 German nationals in Paris be deported immediately from French soil. They read that the United States Ambassador, Mr. Washburne, had accepted the request of the Prussian Government to see to the safety of those stranded German nationals. And lastly, they read that the Empress had recalled the Corps Législatif for a special session on Thursday, August 11th.

This was enough to draw the people of Paris to the Place Vendôme in the pouring rain, demanding an explanation and shouting for Emile Ollivier's resignation.

It was a hostile mob, but the driving rain sent the people home to wait again for the newspapers.

The wait was not a long one. The evening editions carried the chilling words to a city of millions:

"The Corps are in session. It is declared that Paris is now in a state of defense. To aid military preparations, we declare Paris to be in a State of Siege."

Stefan had moved from the Bristol. And then had moved again from a rooming house in the third arrondissement to one in the fifth. He'd crossed the third from his map and was now devoting his time to searching for her on the Left Bank. He took all his meals in public restaurants and cafés, and spoke as little as possible to people on the street. Though his French was perfect, having spoken it all of his life, his accent could be heard through the French words and now, he decided, he had to be more careful.

People's nerves were being drawn taut, and a nervous mob is a dangerous mob. Sides were silently, methodically, being taken within the city. Strangers, any strangers, provoked an uneasy feeling. To melt further still into the anonymous crowds on the street, Stefan had bought common workman's clothes from a shop in the third arrondissement, but they had been suspicious of him there. He'd seen the look in the shopkeeper's eyes, and the way in which the man turned slightly away from him, speaking behind his hand to his friend. Stefan left quickly and changed directions after crossing a few boulevards before returning to his rooming house.

Frustrated, angry people were now beginning to stand together and focus their eyes on the cause of their betrayal, the cloud of their dishonor. Strangers were the enemy, Prussian strangers and spies living amongst us . . .

There had been a few isolated incidents, a few window smashings of shops owned by Prussian nationals, a few attacks and beatings in the streets. He heard of them. And then read of the thousands of Prussians and German nationals alike, waiting outside the United States Embassy hoping by Ambassador Washburne's efforts to secure a safe transit out of France.

The balance was shifting within the city, and nervous people believed every rumor and distorted story. Emile Ollivier had been dismissed and a new government formed, but the small riots persisted.

In a perverse way, the cold and silent voice of the Tuileries fueled a voice being stirred from a long sleep. It began to gather strength on the boulevards and in the cafés. It was the low rumbling chant for a Republic.

CHAPTER
19

The small bell jangled as Julienne opened the door to the laundry shop. She heard the quick thudding of the hot irons on the long table, too quick, too hard, and the girl's shoulders were shaking.

The old laundress wiped her brow with her forearm and took the laundry from Julienne's basket.

"These are black days, Madame," Madame Bédard said softly, then shook her head and took a long, sorrowful breath.

It was only then that Julienne noticed the small piece of black crepe pinned to the laundress' dress, and then heard the other sound in the shop, the sound of the niece crying as she smacked the iron on the table. The eyes of the old laundress were reddened, and looked so very tired.

"Her fiancé?" Julienne whispered.

Madame Bédard gave a stiff proud nod. "The list was posted this morning."

Her lips trembled, and in a cracked voice, she said firmly to her niece, "He died for France, for us, you remember that, remember there is no better way to die . . ."

The girl made no reply and kept on working, even when she felt the hands on her shoulders.

"I am so very sorry for you," Julienne said. "Have courage."

The girl nodded, and numbly continued to iron.

Julienne left the laundry and walked quietly outside toward the crowd gathering at the Boulevard St. Germain in front of bills posted upon a board. Wails blended with sighs of relief as people staggered away and made room for others to sigh or scream as their turns came.

The lists were long, five long sheets pasted on the board . . . so many names . . . wounded . . . dead . . . missing . . .

Philippe, she thought, but did not find his name.

Yet, the sudden cold came when she saw the other name—Mabilleau, Denis, Sergeant, Zouaves . . . at Wörth . . .

Mother of God, she thought, Cécile.

She edged back through the crowd of men and women, turning her shoulders to push out against the tide of people anxious to read the first lists of tragedy.

The crowds thinned as she walked up the Boulevard St. Michel. When she turned onto Rue Gay Lussac, it was nearly deserted, but ahead of her, almost at the cross-street for Rue Royer Collard, she saw a woman staggering and leaning for support against the buildings, then walking slowly, with uncertain, uneven steps. Julienne dropped her empty laundry basket and ran to Cécile.

Her eyes were wide and glazed, and she kept shaking her head from side to side, unable to speak.

Julienne pulled her close, held her up and steadied her as they walked toward the apartment, listening to the constricted sound from Cécile's throat, until the sound finally became a mumble. "Two weeks . . . he is dead two weeks and we didn't know . . ."

They met Armand inside, and there, Cécile collapsed into his arms, moaning, "Denis . . . Denis . . ."

Armand carried her into their apartment, vaguely hearing Julienne's words, "I'll be back in an hour."

She walked slowly up the stairs, wanting to stay and help Cécile, but knowing it was best to leave them both alone for a short time, to face that first grieving together. Thereafter, it would be easier to grieve with friends.

Julienne felt her eyes filling with tears and wondered what he looked like, what he sounded like, what sort of young man he was. It made her cry to think he had been buried so far from home.

She kept herself busy by making soup, and about two hours later, wrapped her apron around the handles of the pot and had Frédéric open the door to the hallway. She carried it out and met Edward on the stairs. After a quick kiss, she told him what had happened.

"I'll stay with the children," Edward said.

"There isn't any food . . ."

"I'll take them to a café," he added. "Do you want me to carry that for you?"

She shook her head. "I can manage." She sighed and steadied herself on the stairs. "It's awful, horrible . . . I wish I knew what to say to her."

"What did people say to you?" he asked.

Julienne bit her lip. "Words, just words. Nothing really helped."

"When will I see you?"

She shrugged. "I don't know. It all depends on Cécile."

"We must talk, there are decisions that have to be made."

"Not now, Edward. I can think of nothing except her."

"But . . ."

"Not now," she repeated, "later, tomorrow, in a few days," she said and walked by him on the stairs.

Armand let her into the salon, gestured toward the bedroom, then walked within a self-made fog and left the apartment heading towards the cellar.

Julienne put the pot on the stove, then after a deep breath, walked into the bedroom. All the curtains had been drawn to shut out every shred of light. Cécile had undressed and, wearing only her night-shift, lay exhausted and sprawled underneath the thin sheet. She had made an attempt to pull her hair down, and the thick braid of brownish-grey hair, half-undone on the pillow, still had hair pins in it. Her eyes were swollen, and her fingers gripped the top of the sheet, twisting it into a knot.

Julienne brought a chair closer to the bed, then gently took the remaining hair pins out of Cécile's hair, watching as Cécile stared at the opposite wall, blinking every so often. She touched Cécile's hand and felt the gooseflesh, skin that grief had turned to ice in the hot closed room.

I know this well, Julienne thought, holding her warm hand around Cécile's fingers, feeling her slowly let go of the twisted sheet and clasp Julienne's hand.

"I am here," Julienne said quietly, knowing there was absolutely nothing else to say, watching as Cécile's eyes filled and she fell into yet another two-minute hysteria. It comes and goes, Julienne thought, wiping Cécile's eyes. We cry, then stop, we cry, then stop again, like waves at the shore, it comes and goes. Even when we are numb it is like that, for we could not bear it otherwise. It comes and goes until there is nothing left, and we go on.

She sat with Cécile for several hours, holding her hand, wiping her eyes, feeding her soup, listening, always listening to the sound of a mother's agony over her son, her boy, the boy she had not seen for over a year nor even kissed goodbye.

Armand, she had been told, was in the cellar, and Julienne wondered what he was doing.

Cécile had made these, Armand thought, and fondled the clean baby clothes, the few that he had saved, and then knickers and a shirt. He touched a school book filled with times-tables written in a child's hand. He held to himself the wooden toys he had made and had given to Claude and Denis for their birth-days, or for Christmas, or for any special day he chose just to see them smile and laugh and play with a new object . . . a menagerie of animals, then boats, carts, soldiers and a wagon. He set two aside.

Lastly, he came to the letters tied with blue ribbons. He hesitated, then opened them one by one, reading them, laughing sadly as the words made him smile in reading of a young man's ambitions and his travels and adventures in the Army. Each one began in the same way, and each time he saw the faded ink words at the top, his eyes filled anew as he read "My beloved Papa and Mama . . ."

He kissed the letters.

About half-past ten, Julienne left Cécile and walked into the salon. She was surprised to see Armand sitting there and had not heard him come into the apartment. He picked up two small wooden animals from the seat of the chair.

"Here, Julienne, for the children," he managed in a soft but steady voice. "I made them myself. Take them," he said, putting them into her hands. "Take them, please, a gift from my son to your children."

She nodded, pained at the thought of what he must have been doing for all these hours down in the cellar, alone with memories and a killing emptiness, going through the baskets that held the past in the things that he had saved. "I will see you in the morning," she said.

"Yes," Armand answered, and held the door open for her.

Edward saw very little of Julienne for several days. She was either cooking, or downstairs with Cécile as friends of the family made condolence calls. She and the other lodgers all helped in those terrible days, and she had no time for conversation. Whenever she went out, it was for very quick trips to do the marketing. She had not even read a newspaper. He saw quite clearly how much she loved Cécile, and this tragedy had brought them even closer to each other. It was a grief that both women had experienced, a loss unique to a parent.

But Edward's worry and concern for her and the children grew with each day, and at the end of the week, he cornered Julienne on the stairs as she was slowly climbing them back to her apartment.

"We must speak now," Edward said, watching her lean wearily against the wall.

"I'm too tired," she sighed.

"It cannot wait," Edward insisted. "You've been locked away for too long a time and you haven't the slightest idea of what is happening outside of this building."

"I don't really care."

"Madame, you'd better care."

She hated the way he used that word when annoyed, and scolded him with her eyes, but controlled her voice as best she could. "How can you be so unfeeling, when she has lost both her sons?"

Edward nervously tapped the banister. "I grieve for them, I do, but my only concern now is for us—and the children."

They heard a door open, and then quietly close below them. A moment later, they saw Armand slowly begin to climb the stairs carrying his chess board and the wooden box of the pieces. He looked up and suddenly noticed them.

"Oh," he said. "I intrude. I'm sorry."

"No, no Armand," Julienne said, "you do nothing of the kind."

"I cannot stay in that room one moment longer," he said quietly. "I . . . I had thought, if you don't mind, I would spend a little time with the children, and perhaps play a game of chess. Maybe they will help me to feel better."

"They're quite bored," Edward said, "and I've told them all the stories I know. It's a splendid idea."

"You are sure I do not intrude?"

"Not at all," Edward said. "In fact, it would help a great deal." He glanced at Julienne.

"Edward . . ." she began.

"I was rather hoping to take Julienne for a carriage ride, for a little air."

"No, I can't," she said firmly.

"Yes, you should," Armand said. "You have been inside too much. Stale air makes one morose. Go, I'll stay with them. It helps us both."

She watched Armand climb the stairs, then glared at Edward. "You are very selfish."

"When it concerns you and the children, I am very selfish indeed," he said. He took her hand and pulled her downstairs, outside to the two-wheel curricle carriage, and saw the servant Bitran toss the stub of a cigar down to the pavement and crush it with the heel of his boot.

Bitran coughed, then stood straight. "Good afternoon, My Lord," he said, clearing his throat.

Edward took a coin from his waistcoat pocket and gave it to Bitran. "Buy yourself dinner," he said, "I no longer need you today. You may do as you like for the afternoon, but I shall expect you at the hotel this evening."

"Yes, My Lord," Bitran said, delighted, "and thank you, My Lord."

Edward waited until the young servant had turned the corner. "Climb up," he said to Julienne, then sat next to her on the seat and took the double-set of reins in his hands. He smacked the horse's rump and guided the stallion toward the Boulevard St. Michel.

"Why are you doing this?" Julienne said. "I am much too . . ."

"We shall see some lovely things," he said sarcastically.

She felt her mouth purse at his irritating tone of voice. "Why do you speak to me like that?"

"You'll have that answer later, after we spend an afternoon 'sight-seeing.' " He said nothing further until they approached the Jardin du Luxembourg and began to drive alongside its outer boundary.

Julienne wrinkled her nose at the sudden pungent smell and heard the loud confused bleatings. She turned to Edward. "Sheep?"

"Yes, my dear, sheep," he answered snidely. "Thousands and thousands of them, and cattle, herds of cattle grazing on the lawns of Jardin du Luxembourg, and in Jardin des Plantes, and on any tiny stretch of green they can find in this city."

Julienne felt her jaw slacken, and turned away from him. Sheep and cattle, she thought, then began to notice the thousands of soldiers all around them on the boulevards.

The traffic on the streets leading to the Right Bank was nearly at a standstill. The troop wagons and bullock teams hauling armaments mixed in a dusty confusion with people in their carriages loaded with trunks trying to head toward the railway stations.

Edward took her to the Rue de Rivoli and passed by the Louvre, where she saw hundreds of workmen quickly and carefully carrying out the unframed rolled canvases and stacking them unceremoniously in wagons under military guard. Titians, Rembrandts, Da Vincis, stripped from the famous walls and placed in a cart like young saplings of no value, while the museum director stood by, watching as the fully laden cart took a nation's treasure from its home.

"It must be done," she said quietly, "they must be protected, but how . . . how awful . . ."

"I would have chosen a different word," he snapped, then smacked the reins hard on the horse. The two-wheel carriage gave a sudden jerk as it moved quickly to the center of the street.

Julienne watched the people on the boulevards and saw all their faces, proud and fierce, the determined eyes clear, and all the French voices steady and strong. They were magnificent.

Edward suddenly stopped the carriage at Jardin des Tuileries by the Place de la Concorde and nearly pulled her out, dragging her by the hand over to the small stone wall that overlooked the main walk. "Look at it," he said loudly, "take a very good look at the madness."

It was littered with straw, and horses were tethered in long lines as military grooms inspected them and fed them. Small tents to house the troops were pitched to the sides of the main walk. The Jardin des Tuileries, like everything else in Paris, had been commandeered as a military encampment.

"I would have taken you to the Bois de Boulogne," Edward huffed, "to the spot where we had our picnic or to the meadow where Frédéric and I race our horses, but they've closed the Bois. The entrance has been blockaded and every tree is being felled."

She was more upset by his anger and blazing eyes than by the idea of felled trees in the Bois. "Why?" she asked.

"WHY?" He looked at her and felt his breath shorten. "To fortify the old walls of Paris, that's why. For God's sake open your eyes—they've brought in sheep and cattle for *food*, the Army is in retreat, and there is nothing to prevent the Prussians from advancing all the way to Paris."

"Never," she said, feeling her back stiffen. Her patience was wearing thin and she was over-tired from cooking and Cécile's weeping, and his blazing eyes began to grate on her nerves.

"Is that so?" he said sharply. "You're like everyone *else* in this city. Lunatics, every single one of you, lunatics. The City of Light," he laughed meanly, and shook his head. "The village idiots are razing houses near the old walls to make way for the guns, powder magazines, fuel storage, and barracks for the troops while the rest of the fools wave their silly little flags and sing that Goddamned song."

"I will not listen to this raving any longer," she snapped.

He grabbed her shoulders and gave her a violent shake. "Yes you will, we *must* leave, open your eyes to . . ."

She pushed his arms away and yelled back at him, "*You* open your eyes. Look at the soldiers, look at the people on the streets. How dare you call them idiots? They're not afraid, not any one of them. *You're* the only one afraid because you have no loyalty, not to your home, your family, or your country."

"That's not true," he hissed.

"It is true," she said, raising her voice. "If things do not go as you wish, your answer to everything is to leave, to run away. You've done that for the whole of your miserable life." She saw the color leave his cheeks and his eyes shrink to slits but he'd pushed her too far for her to stop now. "I am not like that," she continued. "This is my home, my country, my friends, and the only people running away are those who do not belong here and I belong here!"

"No you don't," he countered, "you belong with me."

"I am not your property and you cannot order me to do anything I do not wish to do," she answered sharply, stepping away from him. "I paid for my freedom. I have already given up one family and one country and I will *not* run away a second time. I do not desert the people I love when they need me the most. You," she breathed, "you do as you wish," and walked quickly away from him.

"Then stay and be damned for it," he yelled back at her, seeing her disappear into the crowd on the Rue de Rivoli. "Yes, stay and be damned," he repeated quietly, aware of the people watching him as they walked by.

He climbed into the carriage and left the sounds of the horses and the military songs drifting from the main walk of the Jardin des Tuileries behind him.

That evening, Edward informed Monsieur Robinet he would be leaving in the morning. Robinet was surprised and reminded him that the Marquis had paid in advance for a full month, and there was still another week left.

It annoyed Edward all the more. Philippe, he thought, Philippe and his month-long war . . . "It doesn't matter," he said to Robinet.

"As you wish," was the reply, "the balance shall be refunded."

"Do you have a schedule of trains leaving Paris?"

Robinet shrugged. "Some are still running, My Lord, but not on any reliable schedule. The stations are, sadly, being used for other purposes. I have heard that Gare de Lyon is now a cannon foundry, and the Gare du Nord is now a flour and corn mill." He shrugged again. "There is talk that the Louvre itself will be turned into an armament factory. It is all . . . very strange."

"Of that I am certain," Edward said in a clipped tone of voice.

"I would suggest," Robinet went on, "that you do not try the trains, but leave, perhaps, through one of the Porte entrances by the ancient walls. You may have to wait a long time, though, because people from the outer provinces coming into Paris have preference over those wishing to leave. The Army, I am told, is supervising the traffic. Though how far one may go in one's carriage, who can say?"

Edward grunted.

"I wish you good luck, My Lord," Robinet said, "and it was a pleasure for us to have served you."

Julienne leaned against the open glass door of the small balcony in her salon. Idiot, selfish man, she bristled . . . to say such things to me, go where you wish, deserter, she thought, though the harshness of the word made her uncomfortable. She stepped away from the balcony. Leave, she thought, and go where? She shook her head. There is no place *left* to go, she thought. I am safe from Franz here. I have friends—no, family—here, now, in this building and the city I call home. I chose to come here and we live without fear of Franz ever finding us or hurting us again. And Edward would have me give up the only place I have ever been able to call mine, and spend my life once again looking over my shoulder for Franz's shadow; wandering from place to place, in some aimless search for a peaceful sleep. She shook her head. Edward thinks he is free, but he is more trapped than I. He is his own jailer, whilst I have escaped mine.

Her words stung him deeply, and even in the darkness of the warm hotel room, he cringed at the memory of them. No loyalty, she had said, to anyone or anything. And only those who do not belong are leaving . . . When, in all my life, he thought, have I ever really belonged? The truth of the words hurt him, and he tried to occupy his mind by thinking of where he would go and what he would do, trying to hide his wounded pride even from himself.

Nevertheless, he spent an angry, sleepless night.

In the early morning light of September the first, Bitran drove the carriage down the winding boulevards of the fourteenth arrondissement to the Ponte de Vanves near the barricaded and fortified walls circling the city. The tree trunks from the Bois de Boulogne were here, the ancient trees with their many ringed patterns were being lined up to block off part of the open gateway leading out of Paris. Wooden soldiers, Edward thought wryly, then shook his head at the madness.

Outside the city on the other end of the wall, the volunteer workmen were fortifying Paris to protect her from the Prussian invaders. He heard them singing old country songs as they mortared the walls, dug trenches for wooden barricades, lifted sandbags to the top of the stone walls to make them higher and give protection to the sentries and riflemen. He eyed the carriages waiting in front of him in the queue and noticed the occupants, mostly well-to-do foreign people. He saw English fops, dandified and annoyed that they were made to wait whilst peasants were allowed to enter the city, carrying or dragging whatever pitifully few possessions they had in the world.

Madness, Edward thought, slumping back into the seat of the carriage. Then, the remnant of his sleepless night began to plague his mind. Where am I going in so great a hurry, he thought. What life am I trying to find when all that I love is here? He looked at his trunks strapped to the carriage and wondered what angry madness had taken hold of *him* to make him leave the only happiness he'd ever found and the only woman he'd ever loved.

He thought a moment, then said in a steady voice to Bitran, "Turn the carriage around."

Damn him, Julienne thought, rubbing the wet plate and watching it slip through her fingers and shatter on the floor of the kitchen. She closed her eyes, annoyed, then took a breath and picked up the pieces, tossing them into the garbage bin. She looked at the wet rag and flung it into the sink by the water pump. Let them dry by themselves, she thought and scowled her way back to the salon.

She heard a knock at the door and looked quickly at the mantel clock. It is only two o'clock, she thought, why are they back so early?

She opened the door, saying, "Why are . . . Oh, it's you," she said to Edward, seeing him lean against the outer wall.

He nodded.

"I don't want to argue with you anymore, I'm . . ."

"Then don't," he said, pushing himself away from the wall. "Talk with me instead." He strode inside the apartment and shut the door. He heard the quiet and knew the children were gone. "They've gone out?" he asked, glancing toward their room.

"Yes," Julienne answered. "Armand took them to see the sheep in Jardin du Luxembourg. He needed company and a walk while Cécile is resting."

"Oh," Edward said. There was an uncomfortable silence for several moments. He realized he'd just have to brazen it out and speak his mind. "You were wrong, you know," he began. "And it was very wrong of you to use my words, words I'd spoken in a loving confidence, in private, and turn them against me."

"I was not wrong," Julienne answered.

"I *have* loyalty," he said firmly, "and God help me if it's been misplaced. My *only* loyalty is to you and to them," he said, pointing his hand toward the door of the children's room. "And if you believe otherwise, then tell me now and save us both further heartache."

She closed her eyes to the sight of him standing there, waiting as if by any spoken word he'd suddenly find himself in an unfamiliar place.

"You know that is the truth, don't you?" he said.

It was, she knew, for he'd not done anything in all this time to show otherwise. She nodded and then heard a soft, relieved sigh, from him, from her, she wasn't sure.

"And is your mind unchanged about leaving?"

"Yes," she said and opened her eyes, staring at the floor, hearing him walk closer. "You ask too much of me," Julienne said, shaking her head. "Can't you understand why . . ."

"I am no longer asking you to leave," he said, cupping his hands around her face and gently lifting her chin. "Truly, I am not."

"Then why . . ."

"We both spoke cruel and wounding words," he said quietly. "But the most cruel was the suggestion that you were my property. No," he said. "Never that. This . . ." he sighed, searching for words, "this . . . liaison, or whatever we might call it, must change. Either we are together, sharing the burdens and joys of life, or we are nothing. It can be no other way."

She felt her lip beginning to tremble. "Why do you hurt me so?" She tilted her head downwards and away from him. "Do you not believe I would change my life if I could? But I have no choice, Edward."

"Yes you do," he said calmly, giving a gentle caress to her soft cheeks. "If I stay, I stay as your husband, here, with you and the children. And we would treat each other as husband and wife, trust each other in that special way and raise the children as our children."

"You make it sound so simple," Julienne said, "but it would not be the truth."

"Yes it would," he answered. "It would be our truth, our pledge." He pulled her closer and held her tightly, whispering, "I love you. I cannot live a life without you, and if this be our only course, then I shall take it, gladly, and pledge myself to you. The man you married gave you up to a living death. He broke the vow he made to you before God. His soul deserted your soul and he left you foundering in the wasteland he called a home. But I have never deserted you, Julienne. And I never will. You once wished and hoped for a friend. You have in me, husband *and* friend. I shall never break my promise to love you, stand by you all of my life, through good and bad alike, and your children will be my children. I shall care for you, honor you, and protect you for as long as I have breath. I give you all that I have to give and all that is mine to give—myself." He paused, then said, "What is your answer?"

She looked into his eyes and saw the truest friend she'd ever had, the kindest eyes that were only the surface of his loving healing self. "I love you," she said, "and I promise to love you in good times and in bad, and stand by you for all of my life, and I give my children to you as your children. I shall care for you, honor you and protect you for as long as I have breath. And like you, I give you all that is mine to give in this life—myself."

"Then it is done," he whispered with a kiss. A moment later, he patted his waistcoat pocket and withdrew a gold ring. "Here," he said, "this will seal our promise, and put to rest any questions from outside that door. It will satisfy the children, and Society. It is our secret, one we will keep all our lives, one we will take to our graves." He put the ring on her finger, asking, "Does it fit? I had to guess and choose rather quickly from the jeweler's."

"Just," she said, caressing it with her left thumb, the smoothness of the small band of gold, a ring that had not been worn on that finger for a long time. It felt strange and wonderful. Julienne looked up at him. "It isn't only our secret, though. Armand and Cécile know the truth."

He pursed his lips and thought for a moment. "And if they cannot accept what we have done?"

Julienne's eyes drifted to the windows of this safe familiar place, home. She swallowed. "Then," she said slowly, "then we must move to another place, together."

Edward hugged her and smiled. "I have been yours ever since that day in January, but this is the first time you are really mine."

Julienne watched him from Cécile's bedroom window as he directed the servant Bitran in unloading his trunks from the carriage. She kept touching the small band on her finger and was afraid to turn around, to see a mother's disapproval, to see condemning eyes that might hurt the happy gift of him and bind her still to that other married life of humiliating agony. "Is it wrong?" she asked softly, waiting for the words that would send them away to a friend-less world.

"I am delighted," Cécile said.

Julienne turned quickly around and walked to the bed. "Really? Are you really happy for me?"

Cécile patted the side of the mattress and moved over. "But of course," she said, beaming a smile. When Julienne sat down next to her, she reached and caressed a motherly hand on the smooth forehead. "How could you think I would not be happy for you? How silly, how ridiculous. He is a wonderful man, I said so from the first. You silly creature . . ." she said, and gently shook Julienne's face. "For shame."

It was too confusing, too wonderful. "But . . . but people, what will people say?" Julienne stammered.

"What people?" Cécile fumed. "I am not people, Armand is not people, what do you care what strangers would say? Armand and I will swear we saw you wed in Church, so there is an end to 'people.' Where were the 'people' when you were hurt? Where were the 'people' when you screamed and cried at his hands? To the devil with the 'people.' "

"That, that is the past," Julienne said, amazed.

"Yes," Cécile agreed firmly, "and it is dead. So let it stay that way and now, live. As we all must do. We live. We continue, we go on as best we can. I love you like my child," she said, "and your happiness is my happiness, as your secret is my secret," she said, kissing Julienne's cheeks.

As he spoke, their little eyes were open and confused, and at times, Edward thought, a shadow crossed their eyes. It must be the word "father," he thought, and the memories of that other life. Edward calmly took their small hands in his large hands, caressing their fingers as he tried to explain what their lives would be like now, reminding them of the summer's visit to the Château and how good it was to be like a family there.

Gisèle, then, accepted his words with a ready delight and climbed into his lap, throwing her small arms around his neck. But he knew her memories were different from her brother's and he watched Frédéric struggling with a summer's wish come true.

He put Gisèle down and gave a kiss to her forehead, sending her to Julienne in the other chair. Then, he turned to Frédéric. He opened his hands to the boy and watched as Frédéric hesitated, then stepped closer and allowed Edward to place his hands on his waist, drawing him in even closer. "I am not a stranger to you," Edward said quietly. "I am the same man who watched the fireworks with you at the Château. Do you remember our promise, our wish?" He saw the boy's eyes relax for a moment, then grow concerned, almost frightened.

"Will I . . . must I . . . call you 'father'?" Frédéric asked slowly, barely whispering the new word for Edward.

"No," Edward said easily, "not father," he continued, lifting the boy to his lap. "Papa." He smiled warmly, watching Frédéric's eyes open. "It is a good name, Papa," Edward continued, "and you will say to me, 'good morning, Papa,' " as Edward kissed the boy's cheek, "and 'will you walk me to school, Papa,' " as Edward kissed the other cheek," "and, 'Papa, will you help me with my tables, please,' " as he kissed the boy's forehead.

"And will you still read me stories and arrange my covers at night and will we still go riding?"

"Yes, of course."

Satisfied that nothing had changed, Frédéric leaned heavily into the shoulder and whispered, "I love you, Papa."

Four little words, Edward thought, spoken by a little boy, and they have such awesome power as to melt my heart with their innocence. How like his mother he is, Edward thought, and in all the hell this boy has lived, he, like her, freely gives all his hard-won trust to me. He watched Frédéric as he moved his hand closer to the boy's face and saw that the boy had not flinched, nor indeed even noticed. Edward caressed the boy's blond hair with his cheek as he whispered, "Sometimes, my son, wishes do come true."

September the third was a warm Saturday evening. In a small crowded restaurant on the Boulevard de Port Royal, Stefan listened to the battle rumors of victory or defeat. No one knew what to believe anymore.

Suddenly, he could see from the window across the small room, a crowd running by the restaurant. Shouts and screams, at first confused, began to clear as people in the restaurant slowly stopped talking and began to listen to the cries from the street.

"DOWN WITH HIM! DOWN WITH HIM! LONG LIVE THE REPUBLIC!"

The waiters looked around nervously, hoping someone would tell them what to do now.

Men began rising quickly from their chairs and went to the doors of the restaurant as people began to leave their homes and spill into the streets.

Stefan looked around the restaurant, dabbed his napkin at his mouth, dropped several coins on the table and left quietly, moving with the crowds as they rushed toward the Boulevard St. Michel.

Over and over he heard "Long Live the Republic," as it mixed with the alarming news of the Emperor's capture and the defeat of Marshal MacMahon's Army.

A massacre, he heard, as the rampaging mob gathered more and more countrymen, calling them to arms with the forgotten screams of the Republic and the strains of the "Marseillaise."

They moved in anger down the Boulevard St. Michel, yelling all the way to the Seine. Stefan slowly, carefully, began to edge his way out of the crowd as Frenchmen began to buffet his shoulders in an effort to keep pace with the tide of humanity.

Stefan watched with horrified eyes as the faceless mob with one voice cheered a workman with a sledgehammer, cracking the Napoleonic N from a stone pillar on the bridge over the Seine. In the hypnotic twilight, he repeatedly pounded the letter until it shattered to dust.

All night, all over Paris, people woke their friends and relations and joined with new brothers in the Infantry, the Marines, the Gardes Mobiles and the Gardes Nationals, armed and ready.

By the morning of September the fourth, they massed outside the government buildings, where no minister dared to show his face. But the mob knew where they had to go, and in the grey overcast light, they marched to the Place de la Grève, in front of the Hôtel de Ville, reliving the past, becoming like their ancestors as they stood alongside the phantoms of another time who'd spilled their blood nearly a century before, who'd marched, as they marched now, to the Hôtel de Ville, the beacon of liberty, the midwife of Revolution.

And by four that grey Sunday afternoon, it was born.

The Gardes Mobiles had invaded the Hôtel de Ville without resistance, followed by the mobs. Leaflets and papers began to fly out from the ancient windows. The Republic was cheered and wept for in its first moments of life.

They waved their arms, tossed their hats in the air and moved with deafening steps down the Rue de Rivoli, down to the black-iron gates of the Tuileries, and by their united force, opened the home of the Emperor.

They smashed the N's off the pillars of the Palace. They tore down the golden eagles from the tops of pillars and cheered as the symbols shattered upon the pavements.

As Stefan leaned against a building across the street, he saw a workman write in chalk "Under the Protection of the Citizens" on the black marble surrounding the doors of the Palace itself and, aided by the Army, the people invaded the Tuileries.

Their shadows and muffled cries passed through the halls of the Tuileries and he saw curtains being torn from their rings, windows were opened and cups and plates and small objects were tossed to the brethren outside in the courtyard. Bricklayers brought gold candelabra out and took them home; carpenters, café owners, kiosk managers and old women linked their arms and carried souvenirs from the Palace as the soldiers tore shreds of green from the bushes and stuck the leaves into the barrels of their guns.

Stefan watched them, chilled on this grey September Sunday afternoon as they carried their personal talismans from the Palace, all of them lost in a frenzied dream of victory, and all of them forgetting that the stolen objects would not protect them from the real enemy.

Paris, he knew, was a walled and barricaded city. And outside the walls surrounding the "City of Light," in a larger ring, were a moat and sixteen forts manned by the French Army and their guns.

And outside that, were the Prussians, drawing closer and closer with each passing hour in an ever-tightening stranglehold as they hauled their Krupp cannons and armaments and supplies.

Stefan felt a pull in his throat. In a battle, he thought, and on the open battlefield, chance and heroism may make the difference in the opposing armies. But they are meaningless now.

He shook his head. The Prussians, he thought, with all their guns, and all their horses, and all their cannons, know that when a city of many millions is trapped within its own walls and has no access to fresh food supplies, there is only one element necessary for victory—patience.

CHAPTER
20

Names. All the lists in all the weeks had only been names of faceless people that had nothing to do with him. But one of them had a face now. One of them, proud of his uniform, brushing his epaulets, running his fingers through the horsehair plume and mounted on a charger, had a face that smiled easily, and laughed quickly, and often scowled like a child.

Edward barely heard the four rows of people at the front of the kiosk asking for their newspapers, as he had only a moment ago, wanting to read the accounts of the fall of Sedan. They would read, as he had read, that on the hilly slopes of Sedan, a place he'd never heard of, that young man's face melted with the legions of shadowy riders and had charged the enemy uselessly.

Surrounded as they were, under heavy shelling with explosions of earth raining down on them and man-made gunpowder clouds filling the air, they had charged headlong into the enemy artillery fire; their swords were held high in the air, and their voices had screamed, "Revenge, Revenge," for the wounding of their general.

They had charged, riding at a full gallop down the slopes, across the fields, riding through the blurry Prussian infantry line only to meet the cannons and the heavy fire aimed at their shiny breastplates.

The survivors had returned to the slopes of Sedan. The survivors of the first assault had regrouped, and they rode again into the cannons, horses and men shattering to pieces and tumbling to the torn earth, mixing with the dead and dying of the first assault.

The second assault gave way to a third, then a fourth.

All they had left was their pride, and the handful of men and horses, wounded and dirty from the clouds of dust and earth and blood, charged again at the Prussian Infantry as if millions of soldiers were behind them and following their lead.

Moved by their courage, the Prussian Infantry did not fire and let this handful of men and horses ride through their ranks, and safely return to their countrymen.

They fought in vain for the rest of the day, trapped in a city being bombarded by Prussian cannons until the Emperor put an end to the bloodshed by surrendering to the Prussians.

Philippe was dead.

The constant jangle of coins in a box became a slow dull hum. People's voices sounded far away, obscured and muted. Edward just seemed to be moving. He crossed one street, then another. He felt suddenly panicked, trying in some morbid frenzy to remember exactly how many days it had been. Did he leave on the twenty-ninth of July? No, Edward thought, the twenty-seventh. He tried to concentrate, to count the days and the weeks. He stopped walking and leaned against the cool metal lamp-post and stared for a moment at the black puddle between the uneven cobblestones in the street next to the pavement. Six weeks, he thought. Only six short weeks.

A grey cat caught his eyes as it trotted across the street, tail high in the air, padded feet barely touching the ground. It disappeared into an alley passageway. His eyes went from the alleyway to the building and then to the blue-and-white sign above the door.

Chavastelon.

He closed his eyes and though his throat pulled taut, he could not cry. He'd come to Paris to die, yet on this street, just nine months ago, a new life had been resurrected from the wreckage in an unplanned moment. A last-minute decision to ride down this street and go to that shop and buy company for that evening changed everything.

He stared dumbly at the ground, seeing the black puddles dance with raindrops. He felt cold and began to shiver.

They are all dead, Edward thought, stunned by his own words as he began to walk again. The traffic and the people on the Right Bank jumbled into a disorganized haze of movement and rain. Philippe, John and Michael. All dead.

John died, one year ago next month . . . and I arrived in Paris in early November. He shook his head and stared at the streets. I don't remember an autumn. It's all just a blur, summer to winter, London to Paris, all one drunken blur . . .

When one has nothing to lose, Edward thought, fear simply disappears. What an uncomfortably curious feeling it was, to be dead inside and to no longer care about anything, anyone, any trouble or amusement. I had no family, no country, no home, no money, nothing.

Except Philippe.

He was in bed, Edward thought sadly, with a girl from the Corps de Ballet.

And when he saw me at the door to his room, he pulled on his robe, jumped out of bed and threw his arms around me like a brother. I was so numb and cold, and he told the girl to care for me. He left me there and went to take a bath.

Edward closed his eyes. I . . . I can't even remember her name or what she looked like, he thought nervously. Just another set of hands touching me without feeling, lips kissing me without love. Practiced hands to give a moment's pleasure and all the time, he thought, I was trying to fill an aching emptiness inside myself by using her and others like her, only to find that emptiness had never left me at all.

He continued walking. Laudanum, he thought, absinthe, brandy, women, gambling dens, virgin prostitutes in private dining rooms at the best restaurants where meals became orgies, and I was always too drunk to know or to care, or to even see my life draining away with every drink, and with every woman we bought for an evening. He helped me forget. I never told him why I'd come to Paris, not the real reason, not about John. Just that I'd had a terrible fight with my family. Philippe decided laughing and carousing was the very medicine for me. He made me forget the cancer-like memories that were killing me. And he's dead.

He felt his stomach tighten as he walked through a dancing puddle. They're all dead, he shivered. I should have stopped Philippe. I should have done something, said something, stopped his foolishness . . . and John . . . dear God, John . . .

A carriage passed by, the sleek black horses dripping with rain. We were in a carriage that night, in October, Edward thought, sinking deeper and faster into that buried memory. We'd already had several drinks at my flat, and I had to go back to the Berkeley Square house for . . . for what? He tried to reach back into his mind for the detail, but it was lost. He sighed and continued walking. John had been strange for nearly two months by then, since the will. And grew worse ever since the Solicitors engaged people to watch him. If I hadn't been so drunk myself, I should have seen what he'd become, and known how much of him had already died. He was in a particularly odd mood that night, with a mean look in his eyes. And in the carriage he said to me . . .

∽

"I don't rightly know what I'd do without that piano in your rooms, Neddy. Still, if the watchdogs found out, I'd lose everything. They'd strip the house bare, they would, rugs and all, and leave me just the shell of it. That's a father's love for you . . ."

"They're all the same," Edward grunted.

"Are they now?" Sherringham said, turning sharply to the right. "And how would you know that?"

"I've one myself, laddie."

"You'd like to believe that, wouldn't you?" Sherringham smiled maliciously. "I used to laugh inside, every time we'd get to drinking at Oxford, and all the boys would trade stories about their dear old dads' love. Sometimes, I thought it was because you were older than the rest of us, but I see now, I was wrong. My father punished me for the whole of my life because I ran away to Italy to study music. He never forgot it and he never forgave it. The only time my father was pleased with me was when I joined the Army with you. Otherwise, he spoke to me through his footman."

"Mine never speaks to me, either."

"No, *you* never speak to *him*, and there's the difference, laddie."

∾

Laddie, Edward thought, watching people walk quickly through the sheeting rain. We heard an argument in the drawing room. My mother was upset over not having musicians for her dinner party. How absurd . . . prior engagement they'd forgotten or something. They apologized to my father, and he agreed they ought to keep their first commitment, it was only right, *that* was the cause of my mother's anxiety and tears—musicians, engaged for an evening's entertainment.

Why did he volunteer? Why did he say he would play for them? It was so great a risk and I told him so.

But his expression had changed. I remember that, Edward thought. He said he was going to put an end to the evil game . . . Yet, whatever hateful reasons were in his mind or glaring in his eyes, when he practiced at the piano before dinner, the music was untainted. He always looked as if he were putting music into the piano and taking it out of the instrument at the same time. It was untainted, Edward thought, but he wasn't. He'd become the will's whore, and he knew it. I told him to leave. I told him to steal the silver and sell it if he had to, or leave with nothing and I'd give him everything I had, but leave and go back to Italy, to the place he had loved and where he had been recognized as a talented man. Brandied nods, teary promises, yes, he would do just that, and do nothing except die a little more every day.

And after dinner, drunk as he was, he gave the performance of a lifetime, liberally mixing his favorite composers with his original compositions. He played fluidly, lovingly, as he had played in the cellar storeroom at Oxford.

He gracefully accepted the comments he'd never wanted to hear from those Society people—such a surprise, they'd said, to be so talented an amateur pianist . . . a hobby . . . gentlemen don't really . . . and how charming to compose as well . . .

But he looked cornered, and pleaded with his eyes for me to save him, Edward thought, and outside the house in the damp and chill October air, he shivered.

∾

"Did you hear, did you hear what they said to me—hobby, amateur . . . useless, utterly utterly useless . . . I thought I could stiffen my back and face them down, but . . . it will never change. I'll . . . I'll never belong. The hypocrites, they're all the same. But I, yes, *I* am the embarrassment, aren't I? My actions and needs occasion comment, don't they? It is *useless!*"

When Sherringham's knees gave way, Edward grabbed him. "You've had too much to drink, that's all," he said, helping his friend to stand up.

"No," Sherringham snapped and pushed free. "I haven't had *enough* to drink, that's the problem." He stepped away and looked with startled eyes at the houses showing through the fog in Berkeley Square. "Look at them," he shrieked to Edward and waved his arm in the fog toward the houses. "Look at them as they *really* are. The hypocrites have their revenues from their lands, and their tenant farmers, and their lands in Ireland, and their rents from the slums, and then, they have their wives open charity soup kitchens to feed the poor people who pay them their rents, and that's all right, isn't it, but *they* would hang *me* in public for what *I* am!" He tripped and fell.

Edward walked unsteadily and slowly knelt down on one knee. "We'll go to my rooms in Knightsbridge now. You'll stay with me."

Sherringham looked with hollow eyes at Edward and shook his head. "I'm not drunk enough to sleep, Neddy. What a good friend you are . . ." He was beginning to slur his words. "And . . . and I love you, more than anyone in all my life. But you know that, don't you?"

"Yes."

"And you love me, but differently, don't you?"

"Yes."

"You've never judged me, or hurt me, not once, not ever. You, you just accept people, don't you? How? Even at University, you stood apart from everyone else. There was something in your eyes that told them all to leave you alone."

They heard a noise, muffled voices from behind the front door of the house.

"They'll be coming out soon," Sherringham said, then looked kindly at Edward. "Help me up."

Edward gave his arm and let Sherringham lean on him as he tried to stand.

"A . . . a gentleman does not fall down dead drunk in the street," Sherringham said with a nasal voice. He tugged elegantly at his cuffs. "It's common."

"We'll find your carriage now."

"No," Sherringham said. "I don't want to go home."

"You'll come to my home and sleep it off."

"No. I've a better idea. Come with me to the Union."

Edward sighed. "It's an awful place, John, and you know I hate it."

"Tonight, it shall be great fun. We'll be watchers tonight. Yes, we'll watch the hypocrites watching the performance. What fun, all those titled people applauding all sorts of depravity. And everyone singing those lewd and bawdy songs."

"How very vulgar," Edward laughed and shook his head.

"I'll play the proper gentleman tonight. I know it well. It's a wonderful pose. Come with me, just once more, so I may say goodbye to the place."

"What do you mean 'goodbye'?"

Sherringham had a dazzling, mysterious smile. "I . . . I shall never go there again. Sometimes, it's even too ugly for me." He looked at Edward. "Just this last time, please, Neddy, my Neddy?"

❧

I should not have agreed, Edward thought, walking up the Rue de Rivoli, splattered and muddied by the rain. I should have brought him home and let him sleep.

He had an amazing capacity for brandy, Edward thought. My eyes had blurred and he, he was still drinking, laughing, whispering dirty limericks to me about the Lords and Judges watching the tableaux on the small stage in that basement.

John left me for a time, I remember that. There was smoke from the cigars and cigarettes clamped in the holders which men held in their teeth. And . . . and one man laughed loudly, and I turned to see who it was, and I saw John by the door. No one else noticed. They were too busy watching the nymphs-and-satyrs tableau. He looked so unbelievably sad as he spoke to that young, dark-haired boy of sixteen or seventeen. He caressed the boy's face, and kissed the boy's mouth so desperately, and then, he wept and held the boy in his arms. He needed from me what I could not give, still, we loved each other like brothers, anyway.

I should have stopped him, Edward thought, crossing the Place Vendôme. I should have told the barmaids to go home, and I should not have agreed to that mad search for a rowboat, and I should have listened to his words—you'll take care of me, Neddy. I know you will, I trust you, you always do take care of me.

I didn't take care of him, Edward thought as he watched the rivers of rain slide down the grey column. I could swim, and he could not, and Goddamn my faithless heart for not remembering in time.

"I've been so worried, oh you're soaked," Julienne said, and pulled Frédéric closer to the fire, taking off the sopping-wet coat and wiping his face with her apron. "Where is your Papa?"

The boy shook his head. "I waited for him, for a long time, in the place where he told me to wait. But, but he never came." He looked down at his schoolbooks. "They're all wet. Brother Thomas will be angry with me."

"He will not," Julienne said and took the books, laying them open by the fire. "They'll be dry by tomorrow." She touched Frédéric's forehead. "You're shivering," she said. "Come along now and we'll get you out of those wet things and into some dry clothes."

"I waited, Mama, I did. He . . . he forgot."

"No," she shook her head and stood up straight. "That's not like him. Something's delayed him, that's all. He's been gone for several hours now. Come, quickly now, before you catch cold."

I stayed drunk for weeks after the drowning, Edward thought, walking the via dolorosa of his dreams. My father visited me, said he was sorry to learn about my friend, how tragic. I don't think I answered him, no, I can't recall if I said anything to him. Until our own fight, some three weeks later. Yes, in the afternoon, to meet my sister's fiancé. Strangers. A family of strangers and I, a stranger to myself.

I know I was drunk, he thought, and my blood was beginning to burn with every word my mother said and every smile she gave me. When would I think of marrying? I had a responsibility, to my family. Suitable young women, suitable to my damned position. It was expected of me.

He stopped walking and saw the locked iron-rod gate. The courtyard was

277

empty. The windows were shuttered. A sign posted on the fence caught his eyes: Thieves will be shot. Respect Property.

He felt his lips beginning to tremble. Philippe's home was deserted. It was cold and dead here. He leaned against the fence and gripped the wet and icy rods.

I bared my teeth at my family and they thought I smiled. And the venom poured out of me, all the hate, all the anger bottled up and trapped for so many sorry years just exploded in the most vile arrogant rage . . . it felt as if the words were cracking pieces of myself apart in a madness to be screamed out loud.

My mother collapsed. My sister burst into tears, but I could not stop myself and I didn't want to. Edward shook his head and gripped the iron rods tighter.

My father came towards me, but I kept screaming at him.

He struck me. I felt his hand for the first and only time of my life. He knocked me off my feet. I was so stunned, I could not stand up, but he'd hauled me up off the floor by my coat.

I wanted to die. I wanted him to kill me right then and there and just stop all the pain. But he didn't. He yelled, said I was offensive and shaming and my arrogance would not be tolerated any longer. He'd suffered my debts, my offensive behavior long enough and if I could not or would not learn manners at home, he would have me learn them elsewhere. And if I would not behave as a grown man, he would treat me like the miserable boy I was. I would do as I was told or I would find myself without a shilling to my name for as long as I lived.

He let go of the iron rods and walked slowly to a wooden bench near the rear of the house in the Parc Monceau. He slumped onto the wet bench and rested his elbows on his knees. Send me to Lisbon, would he? Not a chance. To friends of his? Never. Pack your trunks and be ready in the morning, he said. I went to my rooms in Knightsbridge and actually began to obey that command.

Goddamn him, Edward thought. Goddamn him and all like him. But I showed him. And with no word at all to anyone, I left that very night for Dover . . . For Philippe.

Philippe . . . and did you take that little tin Napoleon to war with you, he thought, beginning to cry.

"I'm going out," Julienne said to the children and took her cloak from the rack near the door. "I'll be back in a short time. Be good. If you need anything, you are to ask Madame Mabilleau for help, do you understand?"

"Yes, Mama," they said, and watched as she took her umbrella and walked out the door.

Perhaps he's been arrested, Julienne worried. The police arrested people yesterday, foreign people they thought might be spies for Bismarck . . . what madness, she thought.

She stopped walking when she saw a newspaper kiosk down the Boulevard St. Michel. What did he read, she thought, and ran to the kiosk. "Have you any newspapers, Monsieur?"

"Oh no, Madame, they are all gone, hours ago. You must wait for the evening editions now."

"Monsieur," she said slowly, "was there a list posted in the afternoon edition?"

"Yes, Madame," he sighed. "The dead from Sedan. You might try the notice board on . . ."

"Thank you, Monsieur," she said quickly and left the kiosk. She walked, then waved at a passing hansom cab. She knew he must have read Philippe's name on the list.

I should have died years ago, Edward thought miserably. My friends, my brother, it should have been me, the fault is mine, all mine . . . Dear God in heaven, there is no justice in this world, no mercy, no forgiveness, nothing but despair.

A warm hand touched his icy wrist. "Edward?"

He looked up from the muddy puddle and saw her sitting beside him on the bench. "Philippe," he whispered, then looked away.

"Come home," Julienne said softly. "You're soaked to the skin and shivering with cold."

He shook his head.

Julienne brushed the wet hair from his forehead. "Where's your hat? Have you lost your hat?"

Absently, he touched his head, then looked at the ground and then at the bench. "I suppose so."

Julienne tried to comfort him by holding his wet, cold, trembling hand. "Frédéric waited for you," she said quietly, and watched him remember he was to meet the boy after school. "Come home with me now," she said, and hooked her arm through his, forcing him to stand, then led him to the waiting carriage.

At roughly two in the morning, the cold shivers left his body when the heavy sweat appeared with the fever. He dreamed he saw them, Michael, John, Philippe, their three faces melting into one and suddenly, he couldn't breathe and kicked the covers off to try to cool himself.

Julienne woke up when he stirred and heard the moaning. She touched his face in the dark and felt the burning wet skin. "No, Edward, keep the covers on. It's better for you . . ."

"I can't," he gasped, "I can't breathe . . . everything's moving, the covers are, are too heavy . . . too hot."

She got out of bed and ran to the kitchen, pumped water into a shallow pan and grabbed a rag before going back to the bedroom. She lit the oil lamp near his side of the bed and saw the flushed skin, dripping wet. Even his hair was wet.

"My eyes hurt," he whispered.

"It's the fever," Julienne answered, seeing how glazed they were. He began to sneeze and cough and she pulled the covers loosely over him.

"Everything hurts," he said after a coughing fit. "I'm dying . . ."

"You're not dying," she said, "it's only a fever." She spent the rest of the night wiping his face, pulling the covers over him and holding the basin for him when he became violently ill nearly every hour on the hour.

When the fever broke in the early morning, he was so chilled his teeth began to chatter.

From the other room, she heard Frédéric coughing, sneezing, and calling for her in pitiful small moans. She closed her eyes and prayed, God give me strength . . .

By the end of the second day, both of them were a little better. Edward had a bad cold, but the fever, thankfully, had disappeared.

He slept a great deal, lost somewhere within himself, trying not to think of the dreams that had come back to him and the faces that had been so clear in his mind.

Perhaps it is still the shock of Philippe's death, Julienne mused, wondering about his silence. Still, he seems troubled, as if he were running away, avoiding something once more. He ought to have learned by now, running away from a problem within oneself does not solve it. But the sight of him, seated on the bench in the Parc Monceau, made an uneasy reminder of how she had looked at the convent in Germany, staring at herself in a pool filled with leaves after Maximilian had died. I felt burdened, she thought, and guilt-ridden.

She heard his voice from the salon and went to the door to see what he was doing. He was dressed and seated in the chair nearest the fire and reading a story to Gisèle. Every few minutes, he cleared his throat and swallowed, and breathed only through his mouth.

At least he is dressed, Julienne thought, though his voice is thin and sad. Gisèle has missed his company, but only a part of him reads the story to her now. He keeps far too much to himself, she thought, and went back to preparing dinner.

Friday, Edward thought nervously. It must be Friday. She always serves fish on Fridays. He stared at the veal on his own plate.

"Edward?"

He looked up at her.

"Is something wrong?"

His smile was tight and small as he shook his head. "Why do you ask?"

"You suddenly looked very pale."

"It's nothing," he said quickly.

Julienne did not question him further. She watched him for a moment. He said months ago he did not eat fish because it does not agree with him, she thought, but why is he staring at the platter? He's never done that before.

It looked like that, he thought, no, stop, don't remember.

Why are his hands trembling, Julienne wondered.

A warm, still June evening, Edward thought, a small dinner party for his fifteenth birthday. He sat next to me. We'd finished our soup. The servants brought us the fish.

The Duchess of Sutherland, he thought, across from me at the table. She wore a gown with puffed sleeves and a low front and a diamond necklace. Diamonds. Reflecting the candelabra's light. Rainbows on her skin, and a few between the soft white mounds of her breasts.

I grinned, and leaned over to Michael, and whispered about the rainbows whilst I still looked straight at her.

He laughed. I heard him laugh, then wheeze, then no sound at all from him when he dropped his fork.

My father bolted up and out of his chair, grabbed Michael, hauled him from the table. They loosened his collar, hit him between his shoulder blades, tried to put their fingers into his mouth . . .

He stared at his own plate for a moment, then took a sip of wine. From the corner of his eyes, he saw the blond hair. He saw the smile, heard the laugh, saw the boy chewing and then heard the awful sound of a cough.

Edward felt the color instantly drain from his cheeks, as the wine glass dropped to the table. He was out of his chair, sweating and his skin had turned a pasty white.

Frédéric flushed and continued to cough.

Michael, he thought, he can't breathe, just like Michael . . . "MICHAEL!" he shrieked, and found himself back at the table, his hands suddenly and violently on the boy's shoulders. He shook the small boy, pounded on his back, ripped the collar open and stared with terrified eyes as the blond hair flew wildly about.

"Let go of him," Julienne yelled, "EDWARD! Let go of him, he only coughed, let go of him," and she pulled his hands from Frédéric.

He stared at his hands, and then at the boy. Frédéric, he thought, it's Frédéric. Timidly, he touched the boy's face, then grabbed him and held him tightly, kissing Frédéric many times. A moment later, he let go of the boy and staggered from the room.

Julienne smoothed Frédéric's hair. "He . . . he thought you were ill, you understand that, don't you?"

Frédéric didn't know what to say.

"He wasn't hurting you, you know that, don't you?"

The boy looked up at his mother, then nodded. "Who's Michael?" Frédéric asked softly, wiping his eyes.

"I'll explain later. Finish your dinner," she said and went to the bedroom.

Edward was sitting on the edge of the bed. She shut the door and sat next to him. "What is it?" she said, holding him tightly, rubbing the back of his damp neck. "Tell me, tell me what's wrong."

He shook his head. "I . . . I never cried for him. I was so young, I didn't understand the ache or the lonely separation death leaves behind. I knew none of that. And when I *did* know, it was too late." He began to cry. "It . . . it was just . . . too late . . ."

"You cry for him now," Julienne said. "It's never too late for that." She held him firmly, saying nothing until he calmed down. "Tell me," she whispered

The words tumbled out and filled the silence, but it was the voice of a vulnerable child, speaking of an older brother who was friend, protector and hero—all in one person. Then, he spoke of that night.

"He was fifteen years old and he choked to death. It happened within minutes. My father held him. The skin . . . his, his face was purple . . . they tried to take him from my father's arms, but he wouldn't let them. He stayed where he was, on the floor, crying, holding Michael, kissing my brother's forehead. I was hiding in a corner. No one noticed. Just as well."

"Why?"

"My father adored him. He was everything I'm not—clever, talented, handsome, affectionate . . ."

"But . . ."

"I loved him, more than anyone in the world. And I . . . and I made him laugh. I did. It was my fault that he died . . ."

"It was only an accident, you didn't plan to hurt him."

"You weren't there," he said, tears spilling from his eyes, "you didn't see . . ."

"Edward . . ."

"No," he shook his head. "I know what I did. Don't . . . don't say anything."

Julienne sighed and gave it up for the moment, knowing there was no reasoning with him now. He was too upset to think clearly, and she knew all he really needed was a quiet comforting.

You blame yourself as I blamed myself, she thought as she held him, and it has haunted you and poisoned you since you were a child. I remember what you said to me months ago—you said you had not kissed your father since you were ten years old. God help me, she prayed, help me, now that this deep and ugly wound is open, what do I say, how do I help him as he helped me . . . God of Mercy and Forgiveness, help him to forgive himself . . .

Stefan pulled his workman's cap lower on his forehead. He drank his bowl of coffee and feigned interest in his newspaper while a troop of Gardes Mobiles marched by on Rue Mouffetard. He breathed a little easier when they turned a corner.

Glancing at the newspaper, he saw the small notice on the bottom of the page: "As a result of the interruption of railway communications, only ordinary letters for the local departments and abroad may be accepted . . ."

He had to smile. So, the Prussians now have the railway lines, and the French call it an interruption of the mail service . . . incredible. He wondered how his letter to Rosl in Vienna should be posted, and thought a telegram would be better. Idiot, he scolded himself, if they have the railways, they have the telegraph lines, too. He sighed, then turned the page of the newspaper.

"He looked so listless this morning," Cécile said to Julienne as they walked down Rue St. Jacques.

"He's been like that for days. I suppose men are different, and he will mourn his loss in his own way."

"Yes," Cécile said. "Grief is a personal thing."

As they turned the corner onto Rue Soufflot, Julienne saw the line. "What's that?" she said, jutting her chin slightly.

"I don't know," Cécile answered, and as they moved closer, they saw the queue of ten women at the butcher's spilling out into the street. Cécile walked to the end of the line and asked the woman in front of her, "Madame, is something wrong inside?"

The old woman with the kerchief tied about her head shrugged her shoulders. "We wait our turn, Madame, that is all I know."

Cécile turned and shrugged to Julienne. "We will have to wait, I suppose. It's very strange."

The line moved quickly and the wait was not a long one. When they finally went inside, Cécile smiled at the butcher. "Good morning, Monsieur Jevelot."

The thin butcher motioned for her to leave the queue and come closer as he wiped his hands on his soiled apron. "Madame Mabilleau," he said, and waited until she stood next to him.

"Is something wrong?" Cécile asked.

He shook his head, but kept his voice very low. "Let me give you some advice," he said, "as you are a good customer of mine, for, ooh-lah, too many years."

Cécile smiled.

"Come earlier tomorrow."

Cécile looked at him and frowned. "But why?"

"You will have more of a choice then, Madame. There is very little left at this hour."

Cécile stared at him and felt her jaw relax slightly. "But, but it is only half-past ten, Monsieur Jevelot."

"Yes, yes," the butcher sighed, "I know. But do as I suggest, otherwise, you will only find the last little bits of meat."

"How can this be?"

"The new government now controls the slaughterhouses and, Madame, I have been informed there will be less for me to buy, and so to sell to my customers. And please tell your friend there," he nodded toward the queue in the shop, "the widow Barbier."

Cécile smiled. "She is Madame Atherton-Moore now. She has remarried."

"How very nice," the butcher said. "But you will tell her, won't you?"

"Yes, of course, and thank you, Monsieur Jevelot."

He stood a little straighter as Madame Mabilleau rejoined the queue. "How may I serve you today, Madame?" he asked in normal tone of voice.

"How long will you be gone?" Julienne asked, smoothing the shoulders of Edward's frock-coat.

"Oh, just a couple of hours," he said in a colorless tone of voice.

"Are you sure you don't wish me to . . ."

"No," he said quietly. "The walk will do me good, and I'd like to find something special for him. From me."

"As you wish," she smiled, then looked up at him. "Edward," she began, "the other night you . . ."

He put his thumb gently on her lips, then shook his head. "Let it alone," he said quietly. "Please. Do this for me."

She saw the hurt in his eyes, then nodded, giving in.

"I'll be home for lunch," he said.

She shook her head. "Lunch," she sighed, "I shall have to look through my little book and find a way to cook the lamb."

"I thought you were going to buy chicken?"

"There wasn't any left. I'll ask Cécile. She'll know what to do."

He stared at her for a moment. "I do wish you'd let me hire someone to help you, this is becoming silly."

"No," she smiled. "I will do it myself," and gave a strong defiant nod to her head.

"Yes, I am quite sure you will," he said, and pecked a kiss on her lips before he left.

He thought about her for a time, as he walked toward the Right Bank. He'd thought, once, she was very much like John Sherringham, for some odd reason. He'd changed his mind, though. She wasn't. She was able to do the one thing John Sherringham could not—she was able to turn her back on the trap, and walk away from it, without caring one moment for "reduced circumstances." Peace of mind and freedom meant more to her than title, country house, and a position in Society.

When he crossed the Seine, he stopped musing on the past and thought only of now, and of Frédéric's birthday present. Edward went to the Rue de Rivoli and began to search the shops for a kaleidoscope. He spent the better part of the morning looking, asking questions, examining the different varieties of kaleidoscopes, and finally saw one he liked in a shop on the corner by the Rue Bordonnais.

The shopkeeper seemed a nervous man, short, stocky, balding, wearing pince-nez spectacles and a brown frock-coat and striped trousers. He left Edward peering through a brass kaleidoscope, and went to the rear of his shop. He whispered to his assistant, nodding towards Edward, and nervously knit his fingers in a frightened, prayerful way.

The assistant, a man in his forties, left the shop by the rear entrance.

The shopkeeper forced a weak smile and returned to his customer.

"Yes, all right, this one," Edward said.

"Fifteen francs, Monsieur," the man replied.

Edward looked at him. "What?"

"Fifteen francs, Monsieur."

"That's a bit high, don't you think?"

The shopkeeper shrugged.

"Your colleagues on the avenue are offering it for less."

The shopkeeper was unmoved.

Edward sighed and paid him the fifteen francs, watching as the shopkeeper wrapped the leather case in paper and tied it with string.

"Thank you, Monsieur," the shopkeeper said and quickly looked away.

Edward left the shop.

He did not notice the assistant speaking with three Gardes Mobiles, and pointing to his back but felt their hands soon enough on his arms, restraining him. He whirled around and saw the assistant step back like a thief and then slink away to the safety of the shop.

"You seem in a great hurry, Monsieur," the middle soldier said, a cocky sort of fellow with a large, pouting lower lip, dark eyes and a sooty smudge on his chin.

"I am, if it is any concern of yours," Edward replied.

"You will come with us, please."

"I will not," Edward said. "What is the meaning of this, you miserable little man, and take your hands off me."

"You are under arrest, Monsieur, you will come with us. Now."

Edward stared back with arrogant eyes. "What is the charge?" he demanded, aware now of a small crowd of curious, nervous people beginning to gather around him.

"Spying."

"Don't be absurd," he hooted, and pulled his arm free from the soldier. A moment later, he felt the cold metal of the gun barrel under his chin.

"You will come with us now, and without argument, Monsieur. Or we shall shoot you where you stand."

"I am an Englishman," Edward said, "and you have no right to detain me in this way."

"We have the right. Tell your story to the Prefect." When the tall Englishman did not move one inch, the soldier smiled in a menacing way. "Do we shoot you here and spoil your very nice frock-coat, or do you walk peacefully, Monsieur? It makes little difference to me."

"I'll walk, thank you very much, and take your hands from me this instant," Edward glared.

"But of course," the soldier answered sarcastically.

They led him to a covered cart and shoved him inside. It was crowded with foreign people, several women, and two deaf-mutes. Edward gritted his teeth and slammed his hat down on the package, muttering in English, "Damned fools."

"I quite agree," a voice said, in perfect Oxford tones.

Edward turned quickly and looked at the young man, three people away from him in the straw-filled cart. He was very smartly dressed, had sharp, clear eyes and a roguish smile. "Are they purging the city of foreigners?" Edward asked in English.

"Yes, I do believe they are," the man replied with a quick bright grin. "Tommy Bowles," he said, "correspondent for the *Morning Post.*"

Edward reached and shook the hand, then lied easily. "Ned Moore, private citizen," he said with a smile.

"You have been denounced," Bowles said.

"Apparently, and by a shopkeeper's assistant, can you imagine . . ."

"What's in the package, they will want to know."

Edward looked at the medium-sized package on his lap. "A birthday present, for a nine-year-old boy. A kaleidoscope."

Bowles chuckled. "The equipment of a spy."

"This is too ridiculous," Edward said, "and it shall not go unanswered. I shall complain to the Embassy."

"I shouldn't bother if I were you," Bowles said. "There's no one there."

The smile faded from Edward's lips. "What?"

"Quite true," Bowles went on. "They packed up five days ago. Closed it, without so much as a goodbye and God bless . . ." Bowles breathed, then added, "Imagine, sneaking off in the middle of the night like that, shameful, absolutely shameful." He looked at the stunned Englishman at the rear of the cart. "We're in quite a fix, Moore old man, you, me, and three thousand other English. Lord Lyons left only a clerk at the Embassy and we're a stranded lot now." Bowles looked around the cart and then peered out through the wooden slats as they moved slowly down the Rue de Rivoli. "Yes, quite a fix. This is my second arrest. I fear I shall have to advertise, as other English are doing, that we are not spies, only English citizens."

Edward found his voice. "Was he officially recalled? I mean, the man could not just leave, how could he, it isn't possible unless he was officially recalled."

Bowles shrugged. "Don't know. One day they were there, the next morning, they were gone. Most of the embassies have closed up shop, you know. Or do you?" He looked at his countryman. "There's only a handful of them open now—the Papal Nunciature, the Swiss, the Dutch, the Belgian and the United States Embassy. Everyone else—gone," he said, then peered through the slats. "Still, wouldn't have missed it for the world. It's a journalist's dream."

Edward felt his back slump slightly against the cart. "They've all gone quite mad."

"No, Moore, they're scared," Bowles corrected. "And looking under everyone's bed. That's the sign of a frightened people. *Le Figaro* prints a story—true or not—about French uniforms 'stolen' by the Prussian Army, and they purge their own ranks. Even the Gardes Mobiles is combing itself for Prussian spies . . ."

Some time later, the cart stopped in front of a solid, greystone building, and they were led out and into the Police Depot of the first arrondissement. They filed silently into the cold and imposing building. All packages were confiscated, they were searched for any "hidden" weapons, and then led to basement cells, small dank rooms with pitifully few wooden stools and straw on the floor, and were locked, like cattle, inside.

About an hour later, they heard the sound of keys turning in locks down the corridor, footsteps scraping along the stone floor, muffled conversation, and then their door was unlocked and opened. A soldier stepped inside and nodded toward Tommy Bowles.

"Well," he said and stood up, "good luck to you, Moore. We'll most likely meet here again until they issue some sort of identification to all honest visitors . . ." He tipped his hat and strode proudly with unflinching style out of the small crowded cell.

Typical, Edward thought with a smile.

"But where could he be?" Julienne whispered in the hall to Cécile. "He should have been home hours ago."

"Calm yourself," Cécile said in a hushed voice.

"Something's happened to him, I know it," Julienne said.

"We have no way of knowing that," Cécile said. "Perhaps, perhaps he's met someone he knows and has just forgotten about the time."

Julienne shook her head. "That's not like him. He said he'd be home for lunch, he said that."

"Well, suppose he stopped by his friend's house, as he did the last time."

"He went to buy a present for Frédéric," Julienne said. "His mood wasn't sad. He seemed more tired than anything else."

"What can I say to you," Cécile said with a shrug. "We must wait and see what happens. If he does not come home tonight, well, I don't know, Armand will help you look for him, but," she said, nodding and trying to calm Julienne, "we must wait and see. It does no good to upset yourself now. Wait and see."

What a sorry lot we are, Edward thought, watching his fellow prisoners. The deaf-mutes were particularly nervous; the two women had been crying and sighing for most of the afternoon. He'd given the older one his handkerchief hours ago and she'd accepted it with a teary silent appreciation. The others, he thought, workmen, foreign workmen who'd come to Paris to begin a new life. He brushed the rim of his hat. All afternoon, he thought, and all evening, and not a scrap of food for anyone. Despicable, he thought.

They expect us to be terrified, Edward thought, looking again at the frightened people in the cell. They expect us to be intimidated, cowed. He felt his jaw set. Well, not me, he decided, feeling a strange, angry feeling churning slowly within him. They will not get the better of me, he thought.

At roughly half-past nine, he heard the footsteps again, the keys, the voices, and finally the door to their cell was opened.

"You will all follow us now," a soldier said, watching the tired, frightened people stand up.

Edward took his time. He stood casually and brushed the bits of straw from his trousers with a deliberately slow hand.

"They are waiting upstairs, Monsieur," the soldier commented.

"Then let them wait," Edward answered and adjusted the sleeves of his coat.

He followed the line of people upstairs, to the second floor, where they were made to wait, standing or leaning against the wall under armed guard, each being led in turn into a room for interrogation.

A soldier approached him and nodded for him to follow.

We shall see who is made of what, Edward thought, and when he entered the room, two other soldiers grabbed him by the arms.

"Take your hands off me at once, you sniveling toads," Edward snapped, and pulled his arms free. Using their moment's surprise, he strode unescorted and with great arrogance to the table at the far end of the room where five men were seated. In front of the center man, the man with the hard features and the clipped mustache, he elegantly tossed his hat down upon the table.

The game's afoot, he thought, and drew himself up to his full height of six-feet-two, hooked his thumb in his waistcoat pocket and let his left arm dangle free at his side. He lifted his chin, put his nose in the air, and stared with hot eyes at the men.

"Your name?" the First Assistant Prefect asked, folding his hands under his square chin, staring with malevolent eyes at the tall man.

"Edward Atherton-Moore," he answered.

"Monsieur . . ."

"*You* do not address *me* as Monsieur," Edward snidely interrupted. "I am Marquess Harlaxton. You address me as My Lord."

"You are not in London," the Assistant Prefect sarcastically replied.

"Yes," Edward answered in kind, "of *that* I am sure."

The Assistant Prefect's eyes narrowed. "Do you have your papers?" he asked, arching an eyebrow.

"I do," Edward said and pulled a small folded parchment from his breast pocket. He tossed it to the table, deliberately out of reach of the Assistant Prefect's hands. He smirked as the man had to stretch for it and watched as the Assistant Prefect examined the sheet of paper with the official seal of Great Britain at the top and listing his physical description below it.

He watched as the Assistant Prefect read the description and compared it with the man before him, examining the height, the approximate weight, the color of his hair and his eyes.

"Your address in London?" the Assistant Prefect asked.

"Number twenty-seven, Knightsbridge."

"Your date of birth?"

"Your date of birth, 'My Lord,' " Edward corrected.

The Assistant Prefect glared above the edge of the paper. "Give me the date, Monsieur."

"Nineteen, February, 1836."

"Your father's name?"

"Richard Atherton-Moore, Duke of Middlesex." He smiled again when the Assistant Prefect momentarily reacted with surprise.

"And when did you arrive in Paris?"

"November, of last year."

"Why?"

"Vacation."

"Just a vacation, and for so long a time?"

"And to visit a dear friend, if that is any of your affair."

"It is, most definitely, Monsieur." The Assistant Prefect smiled when he deliberately ignored the title. "Whom did you visit?"

"The Marquis de Roquetanière."

"We shall ask him to corroborate your claim, of that you may be sure."

"You will have some difficulty," Edward replied evenly.

"I do not think so," the Assistant Prefect answered.

"Do let me know if he answers you. I should like to ask him a few questions myself."

"You shall have that chance, Monsieur. His address?"

"He is buried at Sedan."

The Assistant Prefect flushed briefly, looked away, then cleared his throat while he thought for a moment. He looked back at the tall man with the curious smile. "I . . ." he began haltingly in the English language, "I . . . speak some English."

"That is your opinion," Edward answered in perfect, if exaggerated, tones.

The Assistant Prefect glared at him, then smiled in a superior way. "Englishmen," he said in Edward's language, "are fond . . . yes, that is the word, fond, of reciting. Recite something for me, if . . . if you are able," he said in a chilling voice despite the hesitation in his search for the right words.

Edward arched an eyebrow. You insect, he thought, try to play *me* like a puppet, will you? Better men than you have tried, he thought, baring his teeth in a smile. He stood poised, like an elegant actor upon the stage, and stared directly into the Assistant Prefect's narrowed eyes. Recite, is it? You will get what you deserve and no more, he thought, then, in measured Shakespearean tones, he said, "There was a young man of Peru, who had nothing whatever to do; so he whipped out his carrot and buggered his parrot, and sent the results to the Zoo."

The Assistant Prefect's eyes opened wide and when he laughed, Edward knew he'd won this little game.

The aides asked in French what was so funny, and the Assistant told them the limerick.

"It loses in the translation," Edward remarked in flawless French.

"Yes, I agree," the Assistant Prefect chuckled. "Oh let him go. He is unquestionably English. Only an Englishman would not be afraid at a time like this. Let him go."

Edward took his papers from the Assistant Prefect, then took his hat and reached for the package.

The man's hand closed on top of the string. "Ah, ah," he said, clucking his tongue. "I think not, Monsieur."

"My Lord," Edward corrected.

"As you wish, My Lord. It is confiscated."

"It is a toy for a nine-year-old child."

The Assistant Prefect opened the package. "A spyglass?" he said.

"A kaleidoscope," Edward sighed.

The Assistant Prefect shook his head.

Edward stood tall again. "I shall tell the little French boy his birthday gift was stolen by France."

"No, no." The Assistant Prefect clucked his tongue again as he sat back in his chair. "Not by France, My Lord, by me—*for* France. You may redeem it after the war," he said, then looked to the aide at his right. "Give him a voucher." He faced the Englishman once more. "But for now, My Lord, buy the little boy something less seditious."

Edward leaned the flat of his palms on the table. "Do be sure to read the instructions," he said sarcastically, "it is a complicated toy." With that, he grabbed the voucher and strode from the room.

289

• • •

Julienne inched closer to him, their knees touching under the table. She'd done her best to be calm in front of the children at dinner, and only after they'd gone to bed did the real fear begin to surface. The hours had been long and she'd watched the street from the salon's window, then paced the room. The tears came when she'd undressed for bed. Yet, seeing him now, watching him finish his dinner, listening to him explain what had happened eased some of the fear, but it was the reassuring touch of him that began to soothe her.

"You're still shivering," he said quietly.

She shrugged. "It's been a terrible day."

"For both of us," Edward answered, then covered her hand with his. Her face was drawn. Though wrapped in her robe, her hair tumbling loose over her shoulders, she seemed cold. He picked up his wine glass and brought it to her lips. "Drink," he said, watching as she took a delicate sip.

"You don't seem very disturbed about all this," Julienne said.

He chuckled. "Oh, I was, believe me I was, but strangely, no longer."

He leaned back in his chair and stared at the dark doorway to the kitchen. He thought a moment, and saw in his mind the stern and powerful faces of the Assistant Prefect and his aides and felt that renewed confidence again.

"Why are you smiling?"

He looked at her. "I, I couldn't repeat it, honestly, it's too bawdy a limerick and I should embarrass us both." He stood up, then gave a tired long stretch to his back and his arms.

"Well," Julienne said, "it is good to see you smile, whatever the cause." She began to gather the dishes on the table. "And at least now, it is over."

He took her hands from the plates and kissed them. "No, leave them," he said, nodding toward the table. "Come to bed with me." He drew her closer and trailed his fingers through her hair. "Come and hold me and love me," he said, guiding her toward the bedroom and closing the door behind them.

"You're wrong, you know," Edward said as he slipped his arms from the waistcoat. "It is far from over."

Julienne pulled the covers back and sat down. "What is?"

He grinned as he undid his shirt and drew it over his head. "This. That shopkeeper will not get the better of me," he said.

"Oh Edward," she sighed, "why look for trouble."

He undid his trousers. "No. I'll not be denounced as a spy and say nothing to my accuser in my own defense." He tossed his trousers on top of his shirt on the chair next to the bureau and a moment later was under the covers of the bed. "He will remember me, Julienne. And he will know he's made a most grievous mistake." He blew out the oil-lamp next to the bed and held his bare arms around her.

She hugged him tightly. "What are you going to do?"

"Nothing vindictive, if that is what worries you."

She shook her head. "What worries me is that he might denounce you a second time," she said in the dark. "And I was so frightened here, alone, not knowing what had happened to you."

He kissed the hollow between her collar bones. "What did you think, my dearest love, that I'd gone off my head and just disappeared?"

"Worse."

He turned her on her side and hugged her to himself. "No," he said, "you mustn't think those things."

"But if he denounces you, and you're arrested again . . ."

"I know a lot of limericks," he teased, then muffled her soft laughter with his mouth.

CHAPTER
21

Thursday morning, October sixth, brought the first signs of the winter to come. It was crisp and their breath steamed from their mouths when they spoke. Still dark and foggy, there was a cold mist lingering in the air at six o'clock in the morning as Julienne stood behind Cécile on the queue for Jevelot's. In the distance, the familiar sound thundered through the muting fog, cannon shells, rumbling in their steady explosions.

"They're fighting again," Cécile yawned, "I wonder where," she added, then looked at the head of the line to the women waiting by the locked door. Even at this hour, twenty-five women were ahead of them. "What time do you think they arrive?" she asked Julienne.

Julienne shrugged.

Cécile was irritated. It is bad enough, she thought, that Jevelot, like the other butchers, is now open only one day in three, and he, like the others, has raised his prices. "But what time do you think they arrive?" she asked again.

"Perhaps four o'clock, or earlier."

Cécile grunted. "We must come earlier then," she whispered. "Much earlier."

Julienne looked at Cécile, then sighed. "Is it safe at that hour?"

"What choice do we have?" Cécile asked as an answer to the question.

"We don't have a choice," Julienne replied.

"Shopkeepers," Cécile said in a curse. "How do they expect us to live, raising their prices, closing their doors . . . Madame Laumonier, in the flat above yours? She told me she knows people who are buying tinned meat, at the Nevoret Grocer's on Rue d'Uln . . . Terrible," Cécile shook her head.

Julienne shifted her weight to the other foot. "Did you notice something strange about the meat we bought yesterday from the butcher on Rue St. Jacques?"

Cécile looked at her and nodded. "They swore it was beef, but it did not look like beef, or smell or taste anything like beef."

"I thought I hadn't cooked it properly," Julienne said.

"You do very well in the kitchen."

"I manage, but there was something odd about it."

"Whatever they sold us," Cécile complained, "it was *not* beef."

"I . . . I don't want to think about that," Julienne shuddered.

"Armand was most displeased last evening."

"Gisèle barely touched it," Julienne sighed. "She went to bed hungry. I had no vegetables, there was no fruit, no butter. She ate a little cheese and some bread, but would not touch the meat. Not even for Edward, Cécile, and he tried very hard to coax her to eat. You know she would do anything to please him, and he can be most persuasive."

"And Frédéric?"

"He ate some, but not all."

"We cannot go on like this, Julienne. We run from place to place, and everyone has been there before us," Cécile said, watching the first signs of the sun turn the night sky to a light grey. "We must find a new way of doing our marketing."

"Oh where is he," Julienne shivered. "Why doesn't he open his doors?"

By half-past nine that morning, they took their small portion of meat and vegetables in their straw baskets and walked back to the apartment house. There, they saw Armand unloading sandbags from a cart manned by two Gardes Mobiles while their sergeant wrote in a small book.

"Very good, Monsieur," the tall sergeant said. "And the water, have you buckets of water on each landing?"

"Yes, yes," Armand replied, "four large cans on each landing."

The sergeant noted it in his book.

"What do you know of the coal deliveries, uhn?" Armand asked. "It is three days now and I have received nothing."

The sergeant shrugged. "That is not my province, Monsieur. You must take that up with the coalmen."

Armand tossed his head back in annoyance. "Yes, wherever they may be . . ."

"Patience, Monsieur," the sergeant soothed. "It is difficult for all of us. Please try to remember that."

"I remember," Armand breathed, "believe me, citizen, I remember."

"Good day to you then," the sergeant smiled.

Armand sighed and watched them lead the cart to the next apartment house on Rue Royer Collard. He saw Cécile and Julienne watching him. "I have a message for you, Julienne," he said. "I am to tell you that Edward and Gisèle have gone to Place St. Pierre, Montmartre, to see the balloons leave."

"Ah," she said, remembering the newspaper notice that Minister of the Interior Leon Gambetta was moving the government outside of Paris for the remainder of the war and was leaving by balloon this morning. "Thank you."

"Did you buy meat?" he snorted to Cécile.

"Yes," she replied.

"What sort of meat?"

She shrugged.

He narrowed his eyes. "Woman, do not shrug your shoulders at me."

"I shrug them at the butcher. Go yell at him," she said and walked into the lobby of the apartment house.

Julienne listened to Cécile's suggestions when she prepared the meat for dinner. She used several of the onions she'd bought that morning, and poured wine into the skillet. The onions, Cécile had said, would hide the taste and might be the only taste if she used enough of them.

Edward stood behind her watching the meat go brown. "Gisèle ate well in the restaurant," he said quietly, then wrinkled his nose. "What is that?"

"They told me it was beef," Julienne sighed. "It isn't, of course."

"It looks just like the meat we had last night."

"Whatever that was," Julienne commented, then added a little more wine to the skillet. "This is going to be horrible," she said. "Gisèle will never eat it."

"Maybe if we distract her," Edward said. "She might eat it if she's talking about something else."

"Would you?" Julienne asked, looking at him.

"You have a point," he sighed. "Still, it's worth a try."

"And then what happened?" Edward said, prompting Gisèle.

Her eyes were wide like saucers. "Then, Papa picked me up, and I could see them, climbing into a big, big basket."

"That piece there," he said quickly, "and people sang didn't they?" he said, watching her as she ate the meat. "And didn't we sing, too?"

"Yes," she squeaked.

"You've missed that one there, that piece, and what did the men do?"

She ate another piece, then said, "They took the long ropes, and they walked with them, and . . ."

"Don't forget that other piece, and they looked like . . ." he prompted.

"Like, like men leading a horse," she giggled after she'd swallowed.

"You mustn't leave that piece, and what balloon did Monsieur Gambetta use?"

"The yellow one."

"Oh what a clever little girl you are, and you forgot that one there, and how high did the balloon go?"

"Higher than the birds," she sighed.

"Would you like to travel by balloon someday—that last piece, Gisèle, would you like to see the world from a balloon?"

She swallowed and nodded at the same time. "They went so high, and they had a big flag from the basket, and then, they were gone."

293

"Yes, gone," Edward winked to Julienne. Gisèle had eaten all the meat.

"I wish I'd gone with you," Frédéric sulked, playing with the last piece of meat on his plate.

"And how did you do on your division examination today?" Edward asked, waiting for the right moment.

"It was hard," Frédéric answered.

"Why was it hard—and do finish that last piece there—you know your sums."

"Because," Frédéric swallowed, then had to swallow again, "because the numbers didn't have zeros after them."

"I think it's time for another examination," Edward said.

"But I was given one today."

"By *them*," Edward replied, "not by me."

Frédéric smiled. "Yes, Papa," he said, then took another drink of the watered-down wine in his glass.

Edward stared down at his own plate and quietly picked up his knife and fork, prepared to eat whatever it was without notice or comment.

Julienne cleared the table after dinner, listening as Edward read a story to Gisèle, then gave his time to Frédéric and the division examination, before sending the boy to bed.

As she washed the last plate, she felt arms circle her waist. She dried her hands, then turned around, stood on her toes, placed her hands on his cheeks and kissed him.

"Mmm," he sighed, as he hugged her. "Was there any special reason for that?"

"Yes," she smiled. "You are the most wonderful man in all the world and my father would have adored you."

He lifted her chin and gave her a warm smile. "That is the second nicest thing you have ever said to me."

She grinned. "I'll wager I know the first," she said rather confidently.

"Oh," he laughed softly, "and you know me so well, do you? What was it then?"

"I love you," she answered, and received a long, leisurely fervent kiss for her reply.

"I have never loved anyone as I love you," he said.

"You have kept every promise you made to me," she smiled.

"As you have," he said.

"And you really are the truest friend I have ever had, and so much more, Edward."

"This is how it should be, this is really a marriage."

She nodded, thought a moment, then said casually, "What would your mother think of me?"

He sighed. "Well, I doubt she'd understand this," he said, looking at the kitchen.

"Was your parents' marriage an arranged one?"

Edward nodded. "My mother was titled in her own right, the daughter of

294

a duke. We have a tendency to inter-marry. She was the right sort of woman for my father to marry."

"Did he love her?"

"Yes, and still does." He paused, then smiled. "I just remembered something. How strange . . . they were sitting in the white drawing room at Chadwell. I was very very young, and standing at the doorway, watching. He was explaining something to her, pointing to a newspaper, and he made her laugh. Then, she caressed his cheek. And he kissed her. I'd never seen him do that before." He suddenly looked straight into her eyes. "Oh clever," he said calmly, "very clever of you."

She smiled. "It was just a question, Edward, and the earth didn't swallow you up, did it?"

"Not this time."

"And not the next time you speak of your family," she said lightly, then heard a knock at the hallway door. "They're here," she said, giving a pat to the small of his back.

Edward answered the door, bidding a good evening to Armand and Cécile. After Julienne had brought in their coffee, they sat at the table as the women explained the problems of doing their marketing.

"So we must go earlier," Julienne said, "but we're afraid."

Armand grunted. "It isn't safe. There are too many soldiers who drink and loiter around the streets, and the streetwalkers . . ."

"And the people from the provinces," Edward said. "Thousands of the homeless day *and* night wandering all over Paris. I agree. You cannot go out alone. One of us will go with you."

"No, no," Armand said. "If you and Julienne are both on the queue for meat, who will stay with the children? No, Edward, you and I will take turns. You and Cécile will go one morning, Julienne and I will go the next, and so on."

Edward nodded. "Splendid idea."

"And those not on the queue for meat, will be able to buy the vegetables. Those queues are not as long," Julienne said.

"Have you had any trouble buying bread?" Armand asked.

"No," Cécile answered. "The baskets in the boulangeries are always filled."

"I'll help with that," Edward volunteered, "but you'll have to show me what to buy," he smiled at Julienne.

She nodded.

"And wine?" Armand asked.

"They seem to have plenty," Cécile said.

"I will buy the wine for all of us," Armand said.

"We ought to make up a schedule, so we shall know who rests and who waits on the queue," Edward said, leaving the table, and went to find a piece of paper.

In a twilight sleep he reached for Rosl and touched the empty space in his bed. Stefan's eyes opened in the grey dark of the room and he remembered where he was. He closed them again with a heavy sigh and caressed the pillow next to him, imagining the soft blond hair, the sound of her voice, the scent of her perfume. It was the old agony he remembered whilst he was in the army, the long separation from a loving wife and friend. He missed her more and more each day, and the uncertainty of the post, now being carried by pigeons and balloons, made him worry for her.

What if none of his brief messages got through to her? What if she worried if he were still alive? What if the children fell ill? What if Rosl herself was ill . . .

He shook his head on the pillow and chased the thoughts from his mind. Rosl, at the very least, had Teo and her family and friends to go to for help and the sheer pleasure of speaking to people. He looked around the sparse and worn room of the old hotel. I, he thought, cannot remember the last real conversation with another . . . months, he thought, the end of July. And now it is the middle of October. He sighed heavily. It must be like this in prison, he thought, locked away in a small cell. And I have listened to my own voice in my mind for so long.

It must have been like this for Julienne, he thought, feeling his throat pull. Exiled to a new place, not knowing anyone, hardly speaking to anyone except when buying food or to ask directions. What unspeakable loneliness she must have felt.

He hugged the pillow and tried to go back to sleep. Rosl, he thought, my Rosl, and my children. God keep you safe for me.

He slept a light sleep for another hour, then roused himself again, dressed and tied the small leather pouch about his waist inside his trousers. In the pouch he kept some of the money he'd brought with the forged Swiss identity papers for all of them. He slipped his arms through the worn and soiled frock-coat, then checked the map spread on the bureau for the area he would now go to, then he left the room. He would continue his search, inspecting the long queues of women in front of the boucheries at ungodly hours of the morning.

"It's him again," the Concierge said, watching from his window as the man walked down the street. "Every day now, he goes out when it is dark and does not return until it is twilight."

"He's a workman," his wife yawned from the bed.

The Concierge drew the curtains closed and went back to bed. "I don't like it," he said. "Even the sewermen keep better hours than this one." He grunted in the dark. "He never speaks, he receives no friends, he comes and goes like a phantom. There is something very queer about him, Marie."

"He pays his bill," she sighed, closing her eyes.

"Yes, doesn't he? No excuses, no hesitation, always on time and always the full amount."

"Why do you complain?"

He poked her with his elbow. "And why is he not in the Army?"

She opened her eyes in the darkened room, thought a moment, then sat up next to him. "Why *isn't* he in the Army? Or the Ambulance Corps? Most young men not in the Army have volunteered for that, and some old ones, too."

"They will want to know who he meets at such terrible hours. Yes, they will want to know *all* about him . . ."

It had been a typical exhausting day. Stefan had searched the queues for meat in the early hours of the morning, and as the day went on, he'd broadened his search to the vegetable markets, boulangeries, and lastly, he'd walked the boulevards and lingered near newspaper kiosks. The faces began to look the same to him and he wondered if it was all futile search.

He finished his dinner in the restaurant, some odd-tasting meat the waiter insisted was beef, but he suspected was horsemeat.

He paid his bill and left the restaurant, walking along the Boulevard St. Germain, passing huddled groups of streetwalkers. He turned onto Rue de Poissy and yawned as he drew closer to the hotel.

He saw the closed cart in front of the hotel but paid little attention to it. He had almost closed his hand on the cold knob of the door, but saw through the small window three Gardes Mobiles speaking with the Concierge and his wife.

Strange, he thought, then, he saw it. He was suddenly awake and stood very still, slowly withdrawing his hand from the knob.

Spread on the desk at the far end of the small lobby, he saw his map, his suitcase, and the guards nodding, and the Concierge explaining and pointing and shrugging.

Stefan flattened himself against the brick wall next to the door. He felt his heart pounding and he swallowed air in short gasps. He looked quickly at the cart and saw one other Garde Mobile nodding asleep as he held the reins of the horse-team. Stefan's eyes darted back to the window. They hadn't seen him, and he began to inch away from the door, then quietly walked alongside the team, and quickened his pace to long strides up the street. When he rounded the corner, he broke into a run for two blocks, then slowed down so as not to attract any attention.

He silently thanked God for this escape, then paused under a gas-light to steady his breath. Now what, he thought. They've got more than half the money, but not the papers, he thought, touching the pouch on his waist. He looked around the street, then shoved his hands deeply into the pockets of his coat. He sauntered down the street at an even, unhurried pace. Safety in numbers, be one of many tonight, he thought.

He knew the very poor and homeless were sleeping along the Quais. It was dangerous, he knew, and the poor and hungry had resorted to robbery now, but still found himself drifting toward the embankment. There is no other choice, he thought. I've no suitcase and that would invite suspicion at a new hotel.

He decided on the Quai de la Tournelle, knowing he would not sleep this night, but only rest with his back against the concrete wall. He sat stiffly on the cold and damp concrete, smelling the Seine and glancing at the foggy Île

St. Louis in front of him, then at the older man sleeping near him on the pavement. The man had thin features, hollowed cheeks, a prominent nose and his mouth was open. He looked like a statue, and even in sleep, his features illustrated the agony of poverty.

After four days, they'd settled comfortably in the schedule they'd drawn up, and grew accustomed to one partner from each family rising at an early hour, and standing in the now longer queues for meat. Julienne enjoyed Armand's company. He told her stories of his youth, of living near Bordeaux and growing up near the vineyards. He drew word sketches of his playmates and made her laugh softly in the cold morning air whilst they waited for hours in the dark.

She touched the meat ration card and wondered how they would manage on what they were now permitted to buy. They had waited for half a day to get the card at the local Gardes Nationals Municipality. They had argued with the local Prefect about the amounts of meat they were permitted to purchase for their families, but he had heard it all before and was unmoved. They got their card with the daily coupons dated for today to November fourteenth. One month, Julienne thought, and then we shall have to do it all over again. She sighed, closed her eyes and tried to stay warm by drawing the cloak tighter about her neck.

Stefan saw the light beginning to change. The black velvet clear night had turned a shade lighter at half-past four. He yawned and walked slowly, holding the small broken straw basket he'd found and picked up in the street and now used to enable him to blend in with the poor of Paris. He felt dirty, was unshaven, and had slept in the most miserable of hotels for the past few nights.

His eyes were tired as he walked down Rue St. Jacques. There it is again, he thought, listening to the footsteps behind him. Just far enough away, he thought, and measured with my own steps.

He did not dare turn around, but kept walking at an even pace. He'd already seen five queues at butcher shops, hundreds of people waiting quietly in the dark to purchase their rations of meat.

Another queue, he thought, turning the corner onto Rue Souffelot, and casually walked closer.

In the faint grey mist, he dropped the small straw basket and felt the tears spring to his eyes seeing a lifetime in one person, the child, the young woman, the grown woman, there. He restrained himself and forced himself to walk slowly toward her, and when she turned and saw him, he threw his arms around her, held as tightly as he could, touching her face, her hair, as if to prove she were really in his arms.

"I knew I'd find you," he whispered, then covered her mouth with his hand before she could speak. "Shhh," he whispered again in the smallest voice, wiping her tears with his fingers. With his arms closed around her, Stefan felt a calm for the first time in fifteen months, since she had disappeared. "Listen to me," he whispered, "shhh, you must stop crying, listen to me . . ."

The tall man behind her bent down slightly. "Someone is watching you from the corner. A soldier."

"Armand," Julienne whispered, "this is my brother."

"He is a friend?" Stefan asked quietly.

She nodded quickly.

Stefan thought a moment, then drew her arms down from his neck and kissed her gloved fingers. "Where do you live?" he whispered, bending his head down and listening to the whispered address and directions. "I'll be there in a few hours," he said, "once I rid myself of my shadow."

"I'll watch for you," Julienne said softly, caressing his cheek, then held his hand as long as she could. "Be careful."

Stefan looked at the man Armand, then gave a slight nod toward Julienne.

Armand's eyes darted to the corner and the waiting soldier. "Be well, my friend," he said in a normal voice. "It was so very good to see you again, and please give my regards to your lovely family . . ." He waved at the young man and saw the soldier observing it all.

Julienne held her breath when Stefan picked up the straw basket and deliberately walked by the soldier, going back the way he came. A moment later, the soldier left, following in the same direction. She sighed and felt Armand's hands on her shoulders, but they gave little reassurance.

The hours passed slowly. Pacing in front of the salon window, she had no one to tell the happiness to—Edward had gone out to buy bread and left a note for her; Frédéric was in school; Gisèle had gone out with Cécile. It was an awful wait, watching every person walking the street, searching the corner, examining shadows and wondering all the time about that soldier who had followed him.

Stefan, she thought, my Stefan, here . . .

When she did see him, she didn't wait in the apartment, but leaving the door open, raced down the three flights of stairs and threw her arms around him in the lobby.

"I lost him," Stefan said, then hugged her as they walked up the stairs together.

He took off his cap and looked at the apartment, and then at her as she closed the door behind them.

"I cannot tell you what this means to me, to see you again," Julienne bubbled, holding him.

He sighed. "And to me." He kissed her forehead. "I've been in Paris since August," he said quietly. "Searching for you."

She swallowed. "How did you know I'd be here?"

"Did you think you could fool me, as you fooled him?"

She smiled. "He was here, you know. We saw him first, but he was here, Stefan."

Stefan's eyes narrowed. "I am so angry with you, I cannot even find the words to . . ." he began. "How could you *do* this to me? How could you just leave and send me no word at all?"

"I began a letter," Julienne answered, then shook her head. "I had no choice."

"Yes you did," he snapped, as the frustration of two and a half months of searching boiled to the surface. "Just who do you think we are, nobodies? Do you believe your family have no power whatever in this life? One word, *one*, to your cousin and he would have been imprisoned or exiled under guard."

Julienne shook her head. "He would not have obeyed."

"He would have had no choice."

"You have never understood about Franz," she said. "You have never understood what he . . ."

"Don't say that to me," Stefan commanded, flinging his cap down on the chair. "There is nothing to understand. He is an animal, and that is that."

"If he knew where we were, he would have infinite patience and wait, he would wait for years, Stefan, for that one day of carelessness. And it would come, too. Would you have exiled *me* to a prison, living *my* life under guard, walking with an escort every day of *my* life?"

"You should have come to me," Stefan scolded, his voice getting louder. "I have had to lie about your absence, I have had to lie for your miserable husband, I have wept for you, worried for you, and made myself sick day and night wondering if you were even alive. You were *wrong* not to come to me. I could have sent you *anywhere*—and without a trace, too."

"I was afraid," she said, feeling the tears sting her eyes. "Can't you understand that, I was terrified . . ."

"Of what?"

"Of him," she said, her hands shaking a little. "He . . . he swore to me he would kill you and your children . . ." She felt his arms around her and cried into his shoulder. "He . . . he would have," she sputtered, "I know him, he would have done it, why won't you believe me?"

"Because I would have killed him first," Stefan said tersely. "And I should have done it the day I found you. You and your damned promise, I should have gone after him that very day and put a gun to his head."

She shook her head.

"How can you say 'no' to me?"

She looked up at her brother. "Whatever he did to me is his sin and not mine. To kill him is wrong. That would have damned us both, Stefan. If I plotted his murder with you, how could I look at my children—his and mine— knowing I'd killed their father?" She took a breath and stepped back from him. "No, Stefan. I . . . I could not live with that. This was better. This was the only choice I had to live a life without fear of him ever finding us. I . . . I spoke to Teo, about the bad dreams I had, about wanting to kill him—that frightened me so much. Teo said I was right to leave and he would help me do it."

Teo, Stefan thought meanly, then shook his head. "Teo is just a man," he said after a breath, "and he makes mistakes, too."

"But not this one," she said firmly. "Do you imagine this was easy for me? Do you know how long I cried knowing I might never see you again?"

He closed the distance between them and again placed his arms around her.

"Did Franz come to you?"

Stefan grudged a "Yes."

"And what did you tell him?"

"I knew nothing, what could I tell him?"

She straightened her back. "I knew he would," she said. "And you told him the truth, didn't you?"

"But at a terrible cost," he commented.

"The truth, nevertheless," she said, eyes flaring. "And he believed you, didn't he?"

"Yes," Stefan finally answered.

"Yes, and he left you alone, didn't he?"

He grabbed her arms and made her look straight into his eyes. "I am not afraid of your husband," he said.

"I never said you were," Julienne answered, "but he didn't follow you. He didn't keep watch on your children. He didn't linger about your home, did he?"

"No," Stefan answered.

"He would have, had he suspected anything. And then what, Stefan? Where would I find a peaceful night's rest knowing he would torment you and your children the way he tormented me?" She lifted her chin. "I was not wrong," she said. "I did the right thing—for all of us."

"I shall never agree to that," Stefan answered.

"No, you wouldn't," she said easily and kissed his cheek. "You look older," she said quietly.

"I've aged considerably over the last year," he said wryly, seeing her smile. "But you," he grinned, "you look wonderful."

"Very different from the last time you saw me," she said.

The grin left his mouth, which set in a hard line. "Yes," he said curtly, remembering the bruised and beaten face. He sighed and looked around the apartment again. "How can you live like this?"

"But this is home," she smiled. "And I love it. It's mine. Really mine."

"This? It's so . . ."

"Ordinary?"

He looked at her. "Poor," he said. "Not ordinary, poor."

"It isn't, you know. We're not poor at all."

He shook his head. "You deserve better. You are entitled to better."

"I have all I want, Stefan."

He eyed the worn furniture and the small size of the room. "It isn't right," he said. "Papa would . . ."

"Papa would be proud of me," she said. "I'm safe, alive, happy, I sleep well at nights, I don't live in fear, what more may one ask of life?"

"Safe, uhn?" he said, raising his eyebrows. "My dear sister, you are not safe in Paris."

"It is home," she said firmly.

He let it pass, knowing there would be time to bring the subject up again. He told her he'd seen Friedrich in mid-July. "He's grown," Stefan said. "And the others, where are they?"

She took his hands and led him to the small sofa, and once they were seated, told him of Maximilian's death and the men on the road. She watched his eyes filling, his lips trembling, and felt safe in the compassionate arms that circled her as she quietly spoke.

Stefan did not interrupt her, but simply let her talk and kept the rage inside of him quietly trapped there. He wanted to scream, hearing that she had escaped one hell, only to find another on the road, which had become for her a half-world between death and life. Yet, after she'd found this apartment, and they'd all settled into the routine of daily living, he found a quiet fleeting peace in her ability to survive and in her strength in implementing the lessons of childhood and the remembered words of a loving father.

A key turned in the door and it opened rather suddenly.

"Hello, they were all out of baguettes, but I . . ." Edward stopped speaking and stared at the two of them on the sofa in each other's arms. He felt his mouth set in a line, but closed the door softly, looking first at her, then at the stranger, and waited for an explanation. He put the basket down on the chair and took off his hat.

Stefan looked quickly at Julienne and stood up. He clenched his jaw and took her hand. He felt the ring. He hadn't really noticed it before. It was a different ring, it wasn't the ring Franz had given her. He knew that ring. He'd been with Franz when he'd bought it.

Julienne felt cheated of not being able to tell Stefan everything in her own way, quietly. Feeling a bit awkward, she said, "Edward, this is my brother."

Stefan glared at her. "I'm very tired," he said evenly, "perhaps too tired for this. I may look like a workman, Julienne, but do not treat me as . . ."

"It is a pleasure to meet you, Prince Stefan," Edward said, stepping closer and offering his hand.

Julienne's eyes widened.

"I've known for quite some time," Edward smiled at her.

Stefan placed his hands, knotted in tight fists, on his waist, as he stared at the tall, dark-haired, blue-eyed man. "Edward," he said.

"Marquess Harlaxton," Edward corrected.

"Edward is from England," Julienne offered.

"I understood that," Stefan replied in a castigating tone of voice.

When the Prince made no move toward his hand, Edward quietly withdrew it.

"How did you know?" she asked Edward.

"Uh," he cleared his throat, "when you told me about . . ."

"Franz, yes," she said.

"You mentioned your full name." He shrugged like a boy. "Blame it on curiosity," he said simply. "I'd always had a feeling about you, from the first, and . . . and I looked you up," he grinned. "And there you were, under Weiskern. I told you I had a good memory."

She sighed. "It never occurred to me that you would . . ."

"Well I did," he said easily. "Ever since that day, I've known about your brother, and . . . and your cousins."

"It is nice that *someone* has remembered that," Stefan said acidly, leveling a stare at his sister.

Edward saw her flush, then noticed that her eyes were red and realized she'd been crying. Perhaps the excitement of seeing her brother, he thought.

"Gisèle should be home soon," Julienne said, then saw the quizzical look on Stefan's brooding face. "I . . . I call her Gisèle now."

"And Friedrich? Who is he—now?"

She swallowed. "Frédéric."

"And you? What is your name?"

"Stefan, please," Julienne said. "It . . . it isn't what you think."

"Really?" he breathed. "What could I possibly be thinking?" He shook his head. "What have you done?"

She looked away from him.

"Answer me," Stefan snapped.

Julienne stepped back from him.

Stefan took a step but Edward stopped him, quietly, firmly, and planted his hand on the left shoulder. "Why don't you put some water on for tea, or something," he said to Julienne without taking his eyes from her brother.

"Do not speak to my sister like that," Stefan glared.

Edward's eyes narrowed. "Julienne, please, give me a moment with your brother." He heard her go into the kitchen.

Stefan smacked Edward's hand away from him and was startled by how quickly both hands suddenly grabbed the front of his coat and nearly lifted him to his toes.

"This is *my* home," Edward whispered, leveling a stare. "You will not bully her or make her cry. She will not live like that ever again," he breathed, holding the coat firmly and tightly in his fists. "Do not judge her. You haven't that right," he said, letting go of the coat.

"She is *my* sister," Stefan harshly reminded him, "and I have every right."

"You haven't lived her life," Edward said. "I expected more understanding from you, knowing what little I have been told of your father." He stared at the shorter man and saw the eyes soften. "You ought to take a very good look at your sister now. She is no longer afraid. She laughs, smiles, is happy and quite safe. When, in the last seven years, have you ever seen her like that and known it to be genuine and not a pose for self-protection?"

He is right about that, Stefan thought.

"Her happiness means everything to me, even if it means so little to you."

Stefan met the Englishman's eyes. "That is not true," he said quietly. "And it is very wrong of you to think so." He walked three steps away to the cold fireplace. "You . . . you have not seen what I have seen."

"I saw the result," Edward countered. He studied the Austrian Prince for a moment, then said, "In time, I would hope for your friendship, but I shall settle for less—a quiet tolerance because you will know your sister has finally found happiness in this life."

"You ask a great deal," Stefan said.

"I realize that," Edward replied. "I've a younger sister, and I can easily put myself in your position. But if you are determined to hate me, then by God, find a good reason first. And one that *I* give you, not one that you attribute to me or have carried over from someone else."

Stefan reluctantly nodded to the Marquess. He owed him that much.

They had a few hours to themselves. It was awkward and uneasy, but Stefan spoke of his own family and told them what he had been doing over the past year. At one point, he looked at this "Edward," and said suddenly, "Marquess? Your father is a Duke?"

"Yes," Edward replied. "The Duke of Middlesex."

"I have heard of him, and read about him in English newspapers," Stefan said, then went back to his explanations of his own government work. He noticed the way they looked at each other, the way they spoke to each other, and the invisible binding ties that seemed to be there between them, the same sort of ties he felt with his own wife, Rosl.

When Gisèle bounded into the room rushing instantly to "Papa," he saw what he had never seen with his brother-in-law. The tenderness in the way Edward held her, the delight in her eyes, the lovely childish squeak in her voice and when she saw him, and ran to "Uncle Steffie," she kissed him many times, as she had never done before.

This is not the phantom he remembered, the solemn little girl hiding in his study and disciplining her dolls for lying or being bad. Her voice did not have the high-pitched screams born of abject terror when she hid under the piano. It chilled him to remember that. She was different. She played differently with her dolls now, she spoke differently, and it was awesome to him in its calm and quiet and lovingly ordinary way.

Friedrich had changed, too. Coming home from school, he'd kissed "Papa" first, then noticed his uncle. Stefan saw this affection again, and it was more pronounced in the boy than with Gisèle, a name he had difficulty remembering.

He watched his nephew proudly showing a mathematics examination to "Papa," telling every little detail about his day at school and how all the tutoring "Papa" had done had helped him with his lessons. Stefan remembered a shadowy child, who would barely speak at all about anything. Friedrich was a boy who deliberately lied and provoked fistfights with his cousins. Friedrich was *not* this loving generous boy willing to share a piece of chocolate with his sister, or willingly reading a story to her or playing with her, or the boy spontaneously hugging and kissing his "Papa" or his uncle. Friedrich wasn't this boy, or was he?

They crawl over him like puppies, Stefan thought, stunned at the sight that evening after dinner as they clambered into Edward's lap and argued over whose turn it was to have him sit on their bed and read them their bedtime story. They are no different from my own children, he thought, and looked away, grappling with what he knew was wrong, yet at odds with what his own eyes were clearly showing him.

They kissed him goodnight, and he watched them, each taking a hand and dragging "Papa" into their room, then heard the door quietly close. Stefan wondered what to do. He kisses them like a father, he thought. He smiles and laughs with them, plays with them, teaches them like a father, a true father. And they look at him as they never once looked at Franz. He felt the sofa sag next to him.

"Do you hate me?" Julienne asked softly.

He looked at her and shook his head.

"Do you hate Edward?"

He shook his head, then said, "My hate lies elsewhere."

"Don't," she said. "It will only eat away at you. Let it pass. Think of him as dead."

Stefan only smiled. He will be, he thought, then gave the nod she expected from him.

"You aren't going back to your hotel, are you? Not after this morning, Stefan. I'm afraid for you. They're arresting so many people for no reason at all."

"Well, they nearly got me five days ago," he sighed, then saw the surprised look in her eyes. "Oh," he grinned, "I didn't tell you that, did I?"

"No," she said.

"I shouldn't have mentioned it. Don't concern yourself. I'm here, and that's all that matters."

"Stay."

"Where?"

"Here."

He looked at her. "Bit crowded, isn't it?" He turned away from his sister. "I, I'm not sure I can."

"Stefan," she whispered, "please don't punish me."

He shifted himself on the sofa to face her. "The pair of you . . ." he sighed, "it's beyond words. I find you, living this charade, and you somehow expect me to instantly accept it, when it is against everything I have ever been taught, *we* have been taught. Other people do these things, Julienne. Other people."

"I love him."

Stefan shook his head. "And what do you expect me to say after that?"

"I don't know what to say to you," she countered, "or what you expected of me. Should I have died, Stefan?"

"What a terrible thing to say," he answered quickly, then sighed. "I never thought of you living like this," he said finally. "I never thought of you with . . . with another man," he said, choosing his words very carefully.

"It was a surprise to me, also," Julienne said. "I certainly did not come to Paris to find someone else. But I love him, as I never loved Franz, even when we were first married. Edward is wonderful. A truer husband than Franz ever was, a greater friend, also. And a father, a real father to the children, as Papa was to us."

"That is an offensive comparison," he said.

"Why?"

"Because you aren't married to him, that's why."

"But we are," she said quietly, "here," and touched her heart. "Haven't you noticed a change in the children?"

He stared at her, then reluctantly agreed.

"Edward made all the difference," she said. "I wish you might understand that."

"I do," he said. "It's . . . difficult just now."

"Should I have stayed with Franz?"

"Never," he replied.

"Well at least we agree on that," she said.

"I can't help it, Julienne," he commented. "I can't help being what I am or feeling the way I do. I'm sorry."

They heard the door to the children's room open, and then quietly close.

Stefan took her hand, and shook his head at her to end the conversation.

"Please stay," she said.

He thought for a long time, stared into her eyes, saw the worry and knew that he could not refuse her. With pursed lips, he said he would stay, as distasteful as it was to him, and knew it was right by the relaxed smile he saw on her face.

"What about your things, at the hotel?" Julienne asked.

He shook his head. "There's nothing there. Most of my belongings were confiscated at . . ." He stopped speaking, then smiled easily. "It isn't important," he said, adding, "but I would like to bathe," he said, scratching the stubble on his cheek.

"I'll draw a bath for you," she smiled and instantly felt his hand on her shoulder.

"You're not my servant," he said without rancor. "I'll do it myself."

"All right," she nodded.

"I'm glad we understand that," he arched an eyebrow. "I'll have to buy a razor tomorrow."

"Use mine," Edward said.

Stefan's eyes drifted to the tall Englishman. "Thank you," he said, after a pause.

"You'll need a change of clothes, too. I've another robe and nightshirt. They're clean and you're welcome to them."

Stefan forced a tight little smile. "Thank you, Harlaxton."

"Edward," he said evenly.

"Edward," Stefan repeated.

"You're most welcome, Prince Stefan," Edward said.

Stefan stood up. "Stefan will do," he said, "as we're all in hiding at the moment."

Edward felt a grin beginning and watched as the Habsburg Prince walked to the kitchen to draw his own bath.

Julienne leaned against Edward. "He's very upset," she whispered.

"Well, naturally," Edward replied. "What did you expect?" he asked softly. "I imagine he hadn't counted on someone being here."

She shook her head.

"Wishing me away doesn't mean I shall go away," he chuckled quietly. "He must reconcile himself to that, and this," he said giving a look to the salon. "And I imagine it will take some time. We are living quite outside the rules, you know. Oh, court liaisons and lovers of married women are a way of life in Society, he knows that as you and I know that. But this is quite different."

"Because I am his sister?"

"That, yes, certainly, and we are different. This is not a liaison. He must see that."

"I think he does."

"Well this does present a problem to him. He will always be your older brother, he will always be protective of you and he will always be head of the family Weiskern. He thinks differently and acts according to his position. Let him do what he must. But nothing he says will ever change this family."

"I know that," she smiled.

"Then give him time. It is so little to ask."

"What would you have done, if you found your sister in this situation?"

Edward grinned. "Assuming I hadn't shot the blackguard, I'd probably do what he's doing now—sulk in a bath. And bide my time to convince my sister to leave her 'husband.' "

"Do you really believe he'll try to do that?"

He laughed softly. "An older brother is an older brother . . ."

Stefan lay on the couch in the dark unable to sleep, mulling over the day's conversations, weighing in his mind what he saw and what he felt, and tried to sort out the confusion. The door to their bedroom opened and he heard footsteps. He sat up and saw Edward reaching for his greatcoat. "Leaving?" Stefan asked pointedly, and then heard the soft chuckle.

"Only for a few hours," Edward replied, shaking his head in the dark. "It's my turn tonight to wait on the butcher queue with Cécile. You met her husband. Armand."

"Oh," Stefan said, and placed his head again on the pillow. He fell asleep soon after Edward had left.

Stefan spent the following morning playing with Gisèle while Julienne went out to do the marketing, and he silently cursed all the work she was doing in this situation. They must leave this place, he thought, reading a story to Gisèle. They must. She must.

Later, he watched his sister in the kitchen slicing vegetables, stoking the stove, drawing water, and ached at the sight of her hands, rough and worn like a servant's. "Why?" he said, drawing the word out and watching as she stirred the soup.

"Because I enjoy it," she said, "and I am able to do it."

"And you said you were not poor."

She tilted her head at him. "I learned to do it. I learned to care for my children. It isn't horrible. It must be done."

"But . . ."

"No. I did not want strangers in my home, cleaning and touching my things." She knit her eyebrows. "You sound like Edward. He resents this sort of life, also."

Stefan looked away, disliking the comment.

After luncheon, Stefan watched Edward read a newspaper and smoke his pipe, and bristled while Julienne cleaned the last of the dishes.

She walked to the bedroom, opened a drawer, closed it, and returned to the salon, standing before Edward. "I want to show you something," she smiled and motioned for him to join her at the table. "This," she said, holding something close to her, "is the only thing that was ever really mine, and the one treasure Franz never destroyed."

Stefan recognized it instantly.

Edward drew on his pipe and looked at the back of a sort of book. "Destroyed?"

"Stefan knows," she said, "don't you?"

"Every present our father gave her, every little souvenir of home, even her hairbrush for God's sake . . ." Stefan said and cursed his brother-in-law under his breath.

"Stefan?" Julienne called.

He looked up.

"Come sit with us."

He left the chair and took a seat at the small table.

Julienne sat down next to Edward. "All my things," she said calmly, "slowly, one by one, were broken or destroyed by him. But not this. I hid this. It made me feel like a thief, but I hid it from him and he never knew it existed."

She opened the photograph-plate album. "That was my father," she said, slightly caressing the image on the tin photograph-plate. "He had such a lovely smile, didn't he, Stefan?"

Edward glanced at the Austrian Prince and he saw the man's hard expression noticeably soften as he nodded. "He was a General?" Edward asked, studying the greyed tin face.

"Yes," Stefan said. "A Hussar General. And a Prince. And lastly, an. Archduke." He watched the Englishman.

"You have his eyes," Edward said without blinking, returning the stare.

"And more," Stefan replied and turned the page.

There was a photograph of a portrait of a beautiful woman. "My mother," Julienne said.

"Nathalie?" Edward asked.

"Yes," she smiled. "But you remembered that, didn't you, from the *Almanach de Gotha?*"

"And your father's name was Heinrich, wasn't it?" Edward smiled.

"Yes," she said, pleased that he remembered the names of those she loved.

Edward looked at the photograph-plate and saw the resemblance to Julienne. "Did Winterhalter paint the portrait?"

"Yes," Stefan answered. "How did you know?"

"He painted my mother," Edward replied. "And his style is quite unmistakable. Nice man. I saw him once. He's the favorite of all the courts," he went on and looked again at Prince Stefan, "even the English one." He felt very pleased with himself when the stone-like expression cracked a grin. When Stefan turned the page, Edward nearly lost his breath. There he was, high forehead, large whiskers, and that recognizable stance—the Austrian Emperor. "Your cousin," Edward said calmly.

"Frou," Julienne smiled.

Edward swallowed. "Frou," he repeated, "but only in private."

"Otherwise, Your Majesty," Stefan said, grinning in a superior way and arching that eyebrow again. "Unquestionably, Your Majesty. Blood notwithstanding."

Edward managed a smile.

Stefan turned the page and kept up his advantage. "And his wife, our other cousin," he said smartly. "SiSi," he smiled, "but only in private . . ."

"Of course," Edward said, thinking: Go ahead, twist the knife, as if it makes one little bit of difference. He saw plates of a man and learned it was their Uncle Teo, their father's younger brother before he'd entered the monastery; plates of their Aunt Sophie, the Emperor's mother; other informal plates of the Royal Family with Julienne, then many plates of Stefan—with his sons, with his wife, in riding habit, and then, in an Army uniform. "Colonel?" Edward asked.

Stefan silently nodded.

"I was only a Captain, myself."

"Really? What regiment?"

"The 120th Fusiliers, in Madras."

Stefan tilted his head slightly. "How long were you in India?"

"Eight years."

"Impressive," Stefan commented.

"Not really," Edward replied.

"But the uprising . . ."

"My regiment arrived in Madras in January, 1858," Edward said and turned the page. "The Mutiny was virtually over by then. We relieved the combat troops at the garrison. And there we stayed."

"Oh," Stefan said, noticing the sudden subdued look in the Englishman's eyes and the chill to his voice. "It, uh, must have been difficult then."

"Yes, it was."

Julienne looked at her brother and then at Edward. "Why? Why was it difficult?"

Stefan noticed Edward leaning back into his chair, ignoring the question. "There is a numbing sameness," Stefan said to Julienne. "In a war, an Army has but one purpose—to fight and to win. Without that purpose, it is just routine: drilling, marching, drilling, and the enormous free time given to the troops usually results in a variety of discipline problems."

"And more," Edward said, and though his voice was quiet, it startled Julienne. "The climate was awful, and the mistrust and prejudice to all Indians, even the loyal ones, was . . ." He shook his head. "Doesn't matter," he said quickly, and made a half-attempt at a grin. "It was a long time ago."

The last few plates were pictures of her father with his baby grandson, Stefan's eldest son, Karl.

"It is a lovely treasure," Edward said. "It was good that you saved it."

"Now you know everything," Julienne said.

He shook his head. "Even at the end of my life, I will know and not know everything about you. And that is the joy of it—the discovery." He took her hand and kissed it lightly and though he did not see it with his eyes, he felt the scowl from her brother.

They ought to spend some time together, Julienne thought, for good or bad, they ought to try to speak to each other without me reminding them of a different life. She thought a moment, then said pleasantly, "It is such a lovely afternoon. Why don't you both go for a walk? Gisèle is still sleeping and Frédéric will be home soon and I ought to start our dinner soup now."

Soup, Stefan thought, to bolster what little food they have.

"All right," Edward said, standing up and waiting for Stefan.

Reluctantly, Stefan stood also and followed Edward out of the apartment.

They walked silently for several blocks. Heading down the slight incline of the Boulevard St. Michel, they saw many National Guardsmen loitering in the streets with silly grins on their faces as they spoke to anyone who would listen. Idle soldiers, Stefan thought warily, this is not good. But they're not real soldiers, are they, he thought, just the townspeople banding together into some form of home-front militia. They're armed and they're drunk and that makes them dangerous. He quickened his pace.

It was a beautiful afternoon, with a bright sun and the air cool and crisp. The leaves had nearly all turned to their magnificent autumn colors, and against the blue sky, it was a refreshing cleansing sight.

"You were in a war, weren't you?" Edward suddenly asked, trying to fill the silence.

"Two," Stefan replied. "One as a young man, the other," he sighed, "it is best not to speak of it. It is too appalling a memory."

"Against Prussia," Edward said flatly, hearing a grunt from the Austrian Prince.

Stefan looked at him. "It is madness to stay here," he said. "You must know that."

"I do," Edward answered and leaned his arms on the small stone wall overlooking the Seine.

"Then why are you still here?" Stefan pressed, annoyed.

"Because she would not leave," Edward answered and met the hot stare full. "I tried," he went on, "believe me, I tried. But she would not leave and I would not go without her." He sighed. "To keep her safe, I would have gone back to England, if I thought she wanted that, much as I detest the place." He felt his jaw set for a moment. "I am prepared to do that still," he said, looking at Stefan. "But she is very stubborn."

Stefan smiled. "It runs in the family."

"I've noticed," Edward grinned, then turned away and looked at the Seine, with beautiful brightly colored leaves floating on the green water, lapping at the edge.

Stefan studied the profile of the handsome man, wishing things had been different. Those we call friends, he thought, give such hideous betrayals, and those we should dislike present such a different picture—intelligence and calm, patience and kindness and a quiet strength and persistence that are awesome in their combined depth. "I . . ." he began, "I have not been searching for her, for so long a time, to let her stay here."

"Yes, I am aware of that."

Stefan thought for a moment, then realized it just ought to be said out loud. "I admit to you, I am concerned about, about the situation."

Edward turned his head to the left. "You mean me," he said plainly. "I am the problem you hadn't counted on, isn't that right?"

"Yes."

Edward smiled, grateful for the honesty. "You needn't worry," he said. "I shall help you all I can in that regard, but give it a little time."

Stefan sighed, relieved. "I am pleased to hear that," he said, feeling a burden lift from his shoulders. "I had thought you might go against me in this."

Edward shook his head. "I am not Franz."

Stefan's eyes narrowed. "You had better not be," he said evenly.

Edward did not reply and went back to watching the river Seine; slow and even, it lapped against the Quai in a rhythm that was regular and timeless. "Have you some sort of plan?"

Stefan inched closer to the Englishman and spoke in a softer voice. "I have brought with me Swiss identity papers."

Edward tilted his head slightly. "However did you manage that?" he smiled.

"I didn't," Stefan answered, "my *uncle* did."

"The monk?"

Stefan grinned easily. "Teo," he sighed and shook his head. "Teo is Teo. There is no one like him. I asked no questions and he offered no explanations."

"A monk," Edward said again, somewhat amazed.

"And once, a Prince," Stefan said, this time without rancor. "Sometimes I wonder which of us has the real power."

Edward laughed softly. After several moments, he said quietly, "Franz was your friend."

"He *was*, yes."

"How did you . . ."

"We met at Military School," Stefan interrupted. "And she met him one Christmas when he stayed with us for the holidays. He can be quite charming, when he wants to be."

"Oh," Edward said.

"My best friend," Stefan breathed. "I introduced them. I answered all his questions about her. I encouraged him . . ." He stared at the river. "God forgive me."

"You had no way of knowing," Edward said gently. "To blame yourself is useless."

"You did not find her as I did," he said sharply. "It haunts me still. The sight of her," he said, his voice cracking, "purple bruises, broken bones, caked blood . . ." he swallowed. "She almost died. It is my nightmare, mine, and it will be with me until *I* die."

"When was this?"

"Three years ago," Stefan answered.

Edward grunted. "He whipped her a number of years ago," he said tone-lessly.

"I found her the *second* time he nearly killed her." Stefan looked over to the Englishman and saw the hard expression in his eyes as he stared at the river. He saw a determined look, one he'd seen before, in his own mirrored reflection. So, Stefan thought, he nurtures a hate for Franz, too. A moment later, he told Edward of that night in Vienna when the children had screamed and hidden themselves under the piano, and he learned from Friedrich that the boy did not know if his mother was even alive. He watched Edward take a breath and close his eyes for a second, then that hard angry glare returned as he fixed his eyes on the Seine. "I left instantly," Stefan went on. "In Eisenstadt, I hired a horse and rode the fourteen miles to the Estate. I had to push my way past the butler, but I found her. Franz had taken the baby to his Aunt's house. Julienne was so beaten I couldn't even hold her in my arms." He swallowed, then continued. "I sat up with her for four nights, coaxing her to eat when she couldn't even hold the spoon. I fed her soup. I had the cook make her custards and soft-boiled eggs. And she made me *swear* on my father not to kill that rabid animal, my friend, because she wanted to find a way to escape with the children."

Edward turned his head slightly. "She didn't make me swear," he said calmly.

Stefan saw the chilling look just below the surface of the Englishman's warm blue eyes and felt a tight-lipped smile begin on his own mouth.

They heard a crowd behind them, on the Boulevard St. Michel, and turned to see the spontaneous mass of people on the street, waving their hats, clapping their hands, and saw above the crowd, fixed bayonets. They watched as the crowd parted and the Gardes Mobiles marched the war prisoners toward the Pont St. Michel to their right.

"It never changes," Stefan observed quietly. "Those soldiers are little more than children of seventeen, or twenty years at the most."

"I wonder where the battle was," Edward said.

"Does it matter?" Stefan said, and pushed himself from the stone wall. He walked back up the slight cobblestoned hill of the Boulevard St. Michel, past the men in green-hooded jackets and black caps, the uniform of the newly formed secret police force. They watched the crowds in search of spies.

Egerton was a calm-faced man in his early forties, neatly dressed and ex-tremely proficient in his duties. He had gathered the mail, opened what should be opened, and arranged it all in order of importance. He climbed the stairs of the Berkeley Square house, then rapped gently on the study door. When told to come in, he did so, quietly. He was a dependable secretary with a neat and regular penmanship that made his notes easy to read.

"Excuse me, Your Grace, the mail has arrived," he said in a soft tone of voice.

"Thank you, Egerton," the Duke replied from his desk and dipped his pen in the inkwell. "Place it on the desk, if you would."

"Yes, Your Grace," he said. "I have also taken the liberty of including a newspaper, one that an acquaintance of mine brought to my attention last evening."

The Duke looked up from his report.

"It is the *Morning Post*, Your Grace, yesterday's edition."

"Why?"

"There was an article entitled 'Englishman Ned,' by a correspondent named Tommy Bowles."

"Of what interest is that to me?" the Duke said.

"It is a reported account from within Paris."

"Yes," the Duke sighed, "thank you. I shall read it later."

Egerton bowed and left the room.

The Duke looked at the stack of letters, the delivered reports, and turned first to the *Morning Post*. He read the article and felt a dull ache in his chest at seeing the physical description of this Englishman: lean, tall, dark hair, blue eyes, dimpled grin.

The Duke swallowed hard, then read the article again, as if the second reading would somehow give more information than the first. He read it a third time, and the dull ache persisted, yet, he told himself, there must be thousands of young men who fit the description. But, the "Ned" disturbed him.

Nearly a year, he thought, opening the lower drawer of his desk and removing a small box filled with telegrams and letter-replies. Philippe, Philippe's uncle, the Embassy in Paris, visiting Englishmen to Paris, friends in Paris . . . the same for Lisbon, and any other capitals Edward had expressed interest in visiting. They all told him the same thing: no, Edward was not there—or no, they had not seen him.

People just do not disappear, he thought, unless . . . He pushed the grim thought from his mind and miserably rubbed his lips with nervous fingers.

If only I had gone to his Knightsbridge rooms that night, the Duke thought. If only I had not waited until the morning to speak to him . . . if only he was not so impulsive a boy . . .

Boy, he thought sadly, Edward was not a boy, but it was difficult to think of him as a man. He provoked me to anger, he pushed me to be harsh with him and then, the Duke thought, he deprived me of an opportunity to speak with him and just disappeared from my life. The hurt of his drunken words and my anger had cooled in a matter of hours, but he did not wait, the Duke thought, he did not wait to let me tell him I had changed my mind and that my angry words were as meaningless as his insulting words.

His eyes went to the greyed tin photograph-plate framed on his desk, seeing a younger Edward in full-dress uniform, taken only days before he'd left for India. With each passing year, the Duke thought, I lost just a little more of him, as if he were moving back from me with measured, unbroken steps and I could not bridge the distance between us. Edward held his thoughts and dreams and hopes so tightly to himself and would not share any of them with me. Woolwich seemed to please him for a time, but I have had to guess his reasons, for he never spoke of them to me. My son made himself a stranger, the Duke thought. Oxford did not please him and nothing made him

313

happy . . . even when I offered to buy a commission for him, spite was in his eyes, and his words were cold when I told him the "army" he loved existed only in the mind. I knew his dream was childhood folly, for he never accepted the reality of war. Edward saw only the pomp and the glory, swords flashing in the sunlight as if caught by an artist on a canvas, all so very clean. The army was nothing like that. War is not "clean." India, the Duke sighed to himself. Of all the commissions, he chose a place half a world away. The worry for him, the agony of sending my only boy to war . . . And when it was over, he stayed there. For honor, or pride, or spite, I don't know, but he stayed away from me for eight long years.

What happened to that little boy who'd run to greet me with open arms and a happy smile on his face? What changed that little boy I'd held in my arms, and for whom I'd made a swing with my hands and who laughed and giggled so sweetly when I tossed him in the air and caught him, over and over?

Where are you, he thought, and why have you run away from me?

CHAPTER
22

It was the normality of daily life continuing in an abnormal time that disturbed Stefan the most. After three days of staying with his sister, he began to see how clearly and how completely she'd broken with the past. She lived a totally French life. She thought of herself as French, her children were French now, and Paris was her only home. She had molded herself to this apartment and clung to it as a safe anchor in a confusing violent storm.

He still had not told her about the forged identity papers, now hidden in a drawer she'd given him along with the clothes Edward had managed to buy for him. The time never seemed to be right for that discussion. They were never alone long enough, and though he had a silent ally in Edward, he knew she would resist, very strongly, if the two of them banded together against her. She had to be made to see that leaving was the right thing to do, and she must arrive at that conclusion herself.

His frustration took many forms. He wanted her to leave this place; he was still struggling with her "marriage" to Edward; and lastly, he found it increasingly difficult to sit at table with them and share their rations of food. It was hard for him knowing that the rations were calculated for four, and now fed five people. It galled him to be eating food meant for his niece and nephew. He seriously considered searching out the flourishing black market for food, and wondered in secret how long his money would last and what resources Edward had.

When they sat down to dinner, Stefan could not bring himself to eat their food, and when Julienne tried to insist, he claimed a headache and left the table.

Later, she sat next to him on the sofa and sighed. "Was it that horrible?"

He looked at her. "How can you ask me to eat when you have the ration card and I do not?"

"What an awful thing to say—you're my brother."

"I feel like a thief," he whispered, annoyed. "I am stealing food out of the mouths of children and it sickens me."

"I won't listen to this," she said and got up from the couch.

He grabbed her wrist. "Sit down," he said, and when she did not move, he repeated it in a firmer tone of voice. "I said—sit down."

She did, but gently took his hand from her wrist.

"I cannot, I will not go on like this," Stefan said. "I will not steal food from your children."

"You're not . . ."

"I am," he said, then turned away from her. "I came here to find you, to bring you to safety . . ."

"I am safe," she said quietly.

"Not here, not in this city, and not now."

"This is my home."

"It needn't be."

"It is," she said, eyes beginning to glare.

"Julienne," he said, softening his voice, "listen to me. If you wish to return to Paris after the war, do so."

"Thank you very much, and how kind of you to give me permission."

He felt his jaw tighten. "I am only thinking of you," he said evenly.

"I am not running away, not now, not ever again. You'd better understand that. This is my home and here I stay." She left the couch and walked to the kitchen.

Stefan closed his eyes and smacked the small cushion next to him. He heard a sigh above him, looked up and saw Edward place his hands on the top of the couch.

"Yes, I heard," Edward said.

"You talk with her, if you can," Stefan said.

"Soon," Edward replied.

Stefan got up from the couch and walked to the window. He parted the curtains and looked out to the empty, deserted, dimly lit street below him. "I don't belong here," he said quietly. "I thought she needed me, would welcome my help, as she always had in the past. She is my sister, and I had promised our father I would always care for her."

Edward stood next to him and leaned slightly against the wall. "If you will forgive me, Stefan, you are a man with no patience."

Damn him, Stefan thought, glaring at the Englishman and knowing he had heard words like this before.

"I asked you to give it time, and you didn't. I also told you, that first afternoon, your sister was not the same woman who left Vienna. Since the day they left, she has had to manage and care for herself and the children. That, and the loneliness and fear on the road, changed her. It makes one hunger for stability. She has said, often enough, nothing has ever really belonged to her. It took me quite a long time to understand that, Stefan."

Stefan made no reply.

"Give it time," Edward said quietly.

"We may not have that luxury," Stefan replied.

"Perhaps not, but lack of patience will only add to the problem. Use a little 'diplomacy.' "

"Ahh, yes," Stefan sighed, "my life-long cross: to see too much and too quickly, and to have no one else believe. My father was too good a teacher." He looked at Edward and marveled at the calm expression. A moment later, he gazed at the street again. "You," he commented quietly, "are the most confusing of all, a man of total contradiction. You have no governmental ambition, yet you are more 'diplomatic' than I."

Edward felt a smile beginning. "I like you too," he said, and walked quietly out of the salon.

Two days later, on Wednesday afternoon, Stefan knew he had to try to get word to Rosl that he was safe and had found Julienne. They had arranged a code-name, because Teo had impressed upon him the need for secrecy. He would sign the correspondence "your cousin Joseph." But neither he nor Teo had reckoned with the "pigeon-post."

The queue on the Boulevard St. Germain at the Post Office was a long one. He had told Edward what his plans for the afternoon were, and Edward was to meet him near the Post Office later. Stefan was not used to waiting in queues and felt a growing impatience standing out in the afternoon sunshine, fixed between an older woman behind him who kept humming a song, over and over, and a man in front of him who hadn't washed in days. He tapped his foot on the pavement and tried to close his ears and nose to the annoying situation.

When he finally moved inside, he saw placards were placed all over the walls explaining that the Post Office was not responsible should the messages not be delivered, and each message was limited to twenty words. Government correspondence, they explained, had precedence over private messages.

He waited again, inside the cool building, fidgeting on the line, playing with his hat and, in general, exasperated by everyone and everything.

An officious little man stood behind the counter, a harried little insect of a man with a pinched nose and grey whiskers, jotting down the messages on slips of paper which, with all the other messages from Paris, would be sent to a government photographic establishment, copied onto a sheet, hung on a wall, photographed with a newly developed special lens and unbelievably reduced to a shred of tissue paper that would be placed in a capsule and tied to the pigeon's tail.

Science, Stefan thought, enormous Prussian cannons and pigeon-post photography; what is the world becoming?

"Yes, Monsieur, twenty words, no more," the man said.

Stefan felt his nose wrinkle. "To Madame Rosl Weiskern," he said quietly, and saw the man's eyebrows arch as he stopped writing for a moment. The message was simple, all the family well, hope we may visit soon, your loving cousin, Joseph.

"You are under the limit," the man said.

"It is all I wish to say."

"But you may add words, Monsieur."

Jesus, Stefan prayed inwardly, give me strength. "No, that will do," Stefan replied, aggravated, and paid the exorbitant five-franc fee. He gritted his teeth and strode toward the door with long steps.

"Do not create a disturbance, Monsieur," a voice said quietly as a hand took his arm.

Stefan turned quickly and saw that the man wore the green-hooded jacket and black cap of a secret policeman.

"Step outside, please," the man said firmly with a tight grip on the upper arm.

"Take your hand from me at once," Stefan commanded.

The policeman nodded, and two other policemen stepped forward and circled Stefan.

"Step outside, Monsieur," the second policeman said, "you are under arrest."

"You have no right to . . ." Stefan began, then noticed the bored Gardes Nationals suddenly become interested in this "discussion." He knew he was outnumbered, and the Guardsmen had rifles they were too eager to use. He did not resist and silently prayed that Teo's forgery would stand a very close inspection.

They pushed him into a closed cart and locked the wooden door behind him. As they began to move slowly down the Boulevard St. Germain, he saw Edward walking toward the Post Office. He whistled shrilly, stuck his arm through the slats, waved and called out to Edward.

Edward saw the face pressed against the open side slats and pushed his way to the center of the street, running to catch up with the cart, darting between military wagons and then grabbed the slats with his hands, trying to keep pace with the prisoner cart.

"Do not involve the Embassy," Stefan said to Edward.

"Where are they taking you?"

"I don't know," Stefan said as the cart moved slightly faster.

Edward was losing his grip. "I'll, I'll do something," he said, and had to let go as the cart pulled away. "I'll do what I can," he called out.

He moved from the center of the street and felt a twinge of pain in his chest from the running. The Embassy, he thought, it's closed, they're nearly all closed, he thought, gasping for breath. Good Lord, his identity paper—does he have his identity paper with him?

Edward started down the Boulevard St. Germain, running, walking, loping all the way back to the apartment. He felt his knees and his sides ache as he climbed the stairs, but hauled himself up the three flights without stopping.

Out of breath, he said nothing when he entered the apartment and did not even hear Julienne's questions. He went straight to their bedroom and the bureau drawer used by Stefan. Kneeling down, he opened the drawer and began pulling out the clothes in a frantic search for the identity papers. His hands were shaking when he found them.

"What are you doing?" she asked from the doorway.

He did not reply and kept reading and unfolding the papers.

"Edward?"

He sighed and sat back on his heels. "Oh thank God," he breathed, "he has it with him."

"Has what?" Julienne asked and took an unfolded paper from the floor, seeing her own first name followed by the surname "Dössegger." She felt her stomach tighten. "Where's Stefan?" she asked slowly.

Edward looked up at her.

"Where is my brother?"

Edward leaned on the bureau, then stood up. "He's been arrested. No, don't . . ." he said, taking a deep breath and seeing her eyes go wide and her mouth open. "Let me think, just let me think for a moment . . . for God's sake, stay calm . . ." He tried to take the paper from her hands. "Let go," Edward said quietly, "let me see it."

She felt it drawn from her hands, as if the numbed hands belonged to someone else.

Edward went to the window and studied it in the daylight. Then he took out his own paper and compared the two, line by line, paying special attention to the seal of Switzerland and the ribbon attached to it by the wax. "It looks genuine to me," he said. "Your Uncle Teo is very resourceful." He sat down on the edge of the bed and nervously rubbed his lips. "There must be someone we can trust, someone who knows him and will go to the authorities on his behalf . . ."

Teo, she thought, eyeing the papers on the floor. Teo helped him, as he helped me, with forgeries . . . Stefan, she thought, her mind suddenly sharpening as her eyes began to cloud. He came back to Paris to find me, to see that I was safe, he risked his life for this, he could have been killed on the way, at any time in Paris by anyone. She looked at Edward. "What will they do to him?"

Edward suddenly stood up, walked across the small room and grabbed her by the arm. "Come on," he said, "we must think this out, and quickly, too."

"What will they do to him?" she repeated, staying where she was.

He paused. "I don't know," he said, and saw the saucer eyes grow larger. "They are expelling undesirables, or keeping them in prison. I, I don't think it will go further than that."

"You mean you're not *sure* of that?" she panicked.

He pulled her from the room and as they passed the still-open door to the hallway, he kicked it shut. He sat her down at the dining table, then went to look for paper and a pen. When he found them, he brought them with the inkwell to the table. He noticed her hands were shivering. He touched her shoulder and gave it a slight squeeze. "I need your help and *he* needs *our* help," he said gently. "Both of us must think calmly and clearly."

She looked up at him and managed a nod. "You're right," she said, and then straightened her back.

Edward took the seat opposite her. "In the week he has been here, he had mentioned many names, people he had met during his stay in Paris on the diplomatic mission from your cousin. We'll begin by listing them."

"Why not go directly to Metternich?"

Edward shook his head. "The Embassy is closed," he said. "And Stefan specifically told me not to involve the Embassy. We must forget that, and start listing everyone else."

She folded her hands in front of her, thought a moment, then began to recall the conversations, watching him write down all the names.

He wiped the blood from his cracked lip with the back of his hand.

"Shall we try again?" the policeman prodded.

Stefan made no answer.

"Your name is not Stefan Dössegger. What is your name?"

He cleared his throat and sullenly leaned back into the chair. "You have it before you on my identity paper. Believe or disbelieve, as you wish."

They hovered around him like vultures in the small dank room and their shadows crossed in front of his face. They gave him a back-handed smack again, and his head jerked and hit the wall.

"What is your name," the policeman with the mole on his cheek repeated.

"Dössegger, Stefan. I reside at number eleven, Rosengasse, Zurich."

"You're lying."

"I am a teacher."

"You're a spy."

Stefan gave a hoot of laughter and shook his head, even though it ached. "You see spies under the bedcovers of old ladies."

"Yes, laugh now, but we shall see how much you laugh in the days to come, Prussian."

"I am not Prussian, I am Swiss. And I shall complain to my Embassy about this treatment, and then we shall see . . ."

"Oh, Monsieur," the policeman sneered, "you needn't bother. We shall do it for you."

Stefan had learned a long time ago how to control his facial expressions and let his silence do his bluffing, yet he wondered what would happen to him if they did check with the Swiss authorities and it was then discovered the paper was a forgery.

Edward had spent the following two days waiting patiently on the Rue de Berry, trying to see Ambassador Washburne, but hundreds of other people had the same idea. The confusion was so great on the small street that they could not even form a queue.

The Americans must be at least three hundred strong here, Edward thought, hearing their form of English as they spoke and waited, the accent sounding strange and flat to his ears.

By half-past four of the second day, Friday, October 28th, Edward finally faced a clerk, who then referred him to Ambassador Washburne's secretary, a Colonel Hoffman, on the third floor of the Legation.

Hoffman was a sturdy-looking man in his early forties, and very well versed in handling all the requests made to the Ambassador. Hoffman had seen it all, and heard it all, every story from frightened Prussian servant women begging for help, to the poor workmen denied passage by the French, who feared they would join the Army in their homeland against France, to children without parents, unable to speak for themselves. The Ambassador, in addition to caring for his own countrymen, had become the sentinel of the undesirables; the man who made daily visits to the prisons, and who had already seen to the safe departure of over thirty thousand innocent Prussians. Ambassador Washburne was, undeniably, the most respected and trusted man in Paris, and everyone wanted to plead their cause only to him.

Go to it with a will, Edward thought, and placed his card in Hoffman's hands.

Hoffman seemed slightly impressed, but not overly so, coming from a country that had a different Society. "And how may I help you, Lord Harlaxton?" he finally asked.

"I should like to speak with His Excellency, in private."

Hoffman shook his head. "I am afraid that is impossible, My Lord. His Excellency has been unwell for the past several days, and has fallen behind in his work. But if I may be of service to you . . ."

"With all due respect, Colonel Hoffman, I come on a matter of extreme delicacy, and it must be addressed only to the Ambassador."

Hoffman had heard this countless times before. He sighed, looked at the tall Englishman and said with practiced care, "My Lord, if you are hoping to secure a laissez-passer, I am obliged to inform you that the United States Legation will not issue passports to anyone other than American citizens."

"No, sir," Edward said, "that is not my purpose." He thought a moment, wondering how much to tell Hoffman and decided on a small middle course. "I should be obliged if you might tell His Excellency, this matter concerns a mutual acquaintance."

Hoffman's eyes opened a fraction more. "And the name, My Lord?"

Edward shook his head. "I am not at liberty to speak it." He watched Hoffman think a moment, and saw he was slightly interested.

"Extreme delicacy, you say?"

"Yes," Edward commented, seeing the interest grow.

"And you assure me, you are not seeking an American passport for . . ."

"You have my word on it," Edward interrupted.

Hoffman thought it over. "I am sorry to have asked you twice, but our position must not be compromised on that point. Many many people have tried all manner of deception to obtain a passport, and we have been instructed by our government not to . . ."

"I understand," Edward said politely.

Hoffman sighed, then said, "Do excuse me for a moment. I shall see if His Excellency has time to see you."

He watched Hoffman leave the room, and when he was alone, Edward sighed, thinking the only hurdle remaining was Washburne himself. He rubbed the brim of his hat whilst he waited, then heard a door open, close, and footsteps behind him.

"Yes, he will see you now."

Edward held out his hand to the Colonel. "Thank you," he said. "I am most grateful."

Hoffman shook the hand and smiled graciously. "Follow me, My Lord."

They walked through an anteroom, and after Hoffman knocked at the door, he opened it for the Englishman and then introduced the two men before quietly leaving.

The Ambassador was a pleasant-looking older man with a tired smile. He was pale, owing to his recent illness, and his eyes had an exhausted look about them, but his handshake was firm. And though soft-spoken, his voice was clear and strong.

"How may I help you, Lord Harlaxton?" Washburne said, walking back to his desk and waving the Englishman toward a chair placed before it.

Edward sat down and collected his thoughts. "Your Excellency," he began, "do you recall an Embassy party, sometime in June of this year, where you were introduced to a man from Vienna?"

Washburne wrinkled his eyebrows, then arched them a moment later. "Yes," he said, "and I suppose you have a reason for phrasing your question so mysteriously. Yes, I do recall meeting one very special man. Prince Stefan Weiskern, at the Austrian Legation."

"My reason, Your Excellency, was not to prejudice your recollection in any way." Edward swallowed. "Would you recognize the Prince if you saw him again?"

"Absolutely," Washburne grinned. "He was most pleasant, and I enjoyed our conversation very much." He thought for a moment. "Slight build, about five-feet-nine, square jaw, brown hair, brown eyes, fair complexion."

Edward smiled, then nodded.

"Are you here on behalf of Prince Stefan?"

"Yes, I am," Edward said. "He's been arrested."

Washburne's eyes widened. "On what charge?"

"I would suppose—spying."

"But that's ludicrous," Washburne said. "I realize the times are unusual, but . . ."

"Sir, I myself was arrested not long ago."

"But the Prince, surely they must realize . . ."

"He . . ." Edward said cautiously, "is not traveling under his own name." Edward saw the surprised look replaced by a suspicious one in Washburne's eyes. "Your Excellency, I will take any oath you desire, and I give you my word as a gentleman and a loyal subject to the British Crown, he is not a spy. He came to Paris quietly, and as a private citizen, to search for his sister. He

321

took a different name, and obtained a false passport to prevent any scandal reaching the Court of Vienna and not to embarrass his family."

Washburne's lips set in a line. "You will forgive me, Lord Harlaxton, but it sounds somewhat peculiar."

"I realize that," Edward said.

"The passport is forged?"

"Yes, Your Excellency."

"What nationality?"

"Swiss."

Washburne nervously tapped his desk with the fingers of his right hand. "I, I cannot issue him an American passport."

"I understand that and I am not asking for one."

"What, then, are you asking me to do?"

"Help me," Edward said. "I do not know what to do. I had thought to go to the Assistant Prefect myself, and I am fairly certain he would remember me, but it is doubtful whether he would believe only me. I, I don't even know where they've taken him."

"You want me to identify him to the authorities with the assumed name, is that not so?"

Edward met his eyes. "Yes, Your Excellency."

Washburne sighed and leaned back in his chair, thinking for a long time. "Has the Prince found his sister?"

"Yes, Your Excellency."

Washburne nodded and his expression eased. "Lord Harlaxton, do you restrict this information to me alone?"

"I don't understand," Edward said.

"May I speak of this to one other man?"

"Sir, I trust your judgment. If you need to speak of it, then speak of it. I know you will respect Prince Stefan's wishes, and I also know you will do what is right."

"Thank you," Washburne said. "And as you have not asked, I will tell you. I will speak of it only to my colleague and friend, the Swiss Ambassador, Mr. Kern. What name is the Prince using?"

"Dössegger," Edward sighed, relieved. "Herr Dössegger of Zurich."

Washburne dipped his pen into the inkwell and wrote the name down. "In all probability, they have taken him to Prison de la Roquette. At present, all the others are overcrowded." He looked up and across the desk. "Leave it to me," he said. "I shall do all I can."

Edward stood up and reached across the desk, offering his hand. "I am more grateful than words can express, Your Excellency."

Washburne shook the hand. "One thing further," he said. "One would assume the Prince is desirous of leaving Paris?"

"Yes, Your Excellency."

"There is a quota system now," Washburne said, rising from his chair. "We are in daily communication with the Prussian generals and with Bismarck himself. The lists must be approved by them. On their side of the barricade, nationalities other than Prussian are considered undesirables. The Swiss Ambassador, Mr. Kern, may help in this regard. I shall request that he, personally, oversee the departure of the Prince and his sister." He looked at Lord Harlaxton. "And you, My Lord, shall I include your name as well?"

"Yes, Your Excellency, and two children, also."

"And their surnames?"

"Dössegger."

Washburne smiled. "Well, at least it is consistent," he said. "It is not an easy matter, by any means, but neither is it an impossible one." He walked to the door, but hesitated by the knob. "The legation will be closed tomorrow," he said. "I imagine the 'family Dössegger' will be quite worried."

"Yes", Edward said.

"Then I invite you to come to my home, Lord Harlaxton, in the afternoon and I will tell you what, if anything, has happened, so you may relieve their worry. I live at 75 Avenue de l'Imperatrice. Let us say, sometime after two o'clock."

"Thank you, again, Sir. We are all greatly indebted to you."

On the Rue de Rivoli, Citizen Soldier Dejoux and his comrade Maussion drained the last of their wine and leaned against the cool lamp-post, watching with a growing interest the sight, just a little up the street, of the bobbing hat and then, the tall thin man, weaving in and out of the crowds.

"There is another one," Dejoux said, scratching his cheek and staring.

"The clothes," Maussion agreed. "You may tell by the way they wear the clothes."

"And the hat," Dejoux said. "He is in a great hurry, isn't he?"

"What does he carry under his arm?"

"Newspaper, I think," Dejoux said.

Maussion shrugged. "Maybe. I have heard they carry things in newspapers."

"Yes, I know," Dejoux said, narrowing his eyes to lines. "Come on," he said, and raced across the street.

They didn't have long to wait and with two steps, rifles drawn up to their chests, they barricaded the way.

"Good evening, Monsieur," Dejoux said malevolently. "You seem in a great hurry."

Goddammit, Edward thought, not again. "I am," he said pleasantly, trying to remain calm. "If you would be so kind as to move, I . . ."

Maussion clucked his tongue and shook his head from side to side. "What do you carry inside the newspaper, Monsieur?"

"Nothing," Edward said, opening it. "It is only a newspaper."

"They all say that, don't they," Maussion grinned to Dejoux.

They're drunk, Edward thought, then changed his tone of voice and smiled. "Gentlemen," he said.

Dejoux hooted. "Gentlemen," he repeated to Maussion.

"Yes," Edward grinned, "Gentlemen. I shall save us all a great deal of trouble and embarrassment."

"What embarrassment?" Dejoux demanded.

"Yours mostly," Edward smiled. "How would it look to the Prefect, if you brought me in and you were reprimanded for such a grievous mistake? What would he think of you?" Edward clucked his tongue like them, and shook his head. "You would be embarrassed. He would think less of you. How would he trust you or believe you in future. No, no, it would be awful for you."

Maussion seemed to think about that for a moment.

"It's a trick," Dejoux said.

"No, not at all," Edward said. "I have a way. Why don't you walk with me to a small shop and a Frenchman there will identify me."

Maussion seemed to be wavering. "I say we do."

Dejoux shrugged. "As you wish, and if you are denounced, Monsieur," he smiled, "then we shall see who is embarrassed."

They walked with him to the shop only two blocks away, and stepped inside, hearing the small bell jangle over their heads.

Edward saw the peevish assistant near the counter. He said calmly, "I should like to see Monsieur Simoneau, please."

The assistant, that furtive little man, watched the two soldiers, then scurried to the rear of the shop. A moment later, the shopkeeper came to the front.

"Citizen," Dejoux said, "do you know this man?"

We denounced him, Simoneau thought, and he returned to my shop the very next morning and presented me with his passport and his card. He spoke to me without hatred of my mistake, and bought a second kaleidoscope for his son's birthday. "Yes," Simoneau said. "He is Lord Harlaxton, an Englishman. He is no spy."

Dejoux scratched his neck by the stiff collar of his uniform. "Englishman, I give you some good advice, uhn? Next time, you should not be in so great a hurry. It makes people nervous." He nodded toward the door, and Maussion followed him out.

Simoneau's eyes stared at the glass counter and the display underneath it. He saw an open hand waiting for him, and looked up to the Englishman. He shook the Englishman's hand. "Did your little son like the kaleidoscope?"

"He plays with it every night," Edward smiled. "Thank you for remembering me."

Simoneau smiled.

Washburne felt exhausted and worried whether his recent illness might be recurring again. His head ached and he felt slightly dizzy, but he forced his mind to stay clear as he listened to the dismal report given by Baron de Zuylen de Nyevelt, Minister of Holland at the Papal Nunciature. There was a frustrated hopelessness in the air of the conference room, and the remaining Ambassadors in Paris saw their latest effort thwarted by the Prussians. The Baron relayed a conversation with French President Jules Favre, and told the diplomatic body of the Versailles meeting with Bismarck.

"He declines any responsibility for the sufferings of Paris," the Baron went on. "He lays the fault completely on the shoulders of President Favre, stating that Favre has rejected the proposal of the armistice."

"President Favre has assured me it was Bismarck who rejected the terms," Minister Kern said.

"We travel in circles," Washburne sighed.

"Yes, well," the Baron continued, "Bismarck ended our interview rather ominously by saying, 'he who brings matters to extremities of this kind will have to bear the responsibilities thereof . . .' " He looked at Washburne. "He has said nothing further to you, in any of his communiqués?"

"Just that Paris is doomed to fall, and the German Army would be hard-pressed to supply Paris with food."

"What a horrible thought," the Baron said. "Do you believe the Prussians will commence a bombardment?"

Washburne looked at the Baron. "Yes, I do. The French may reject that possibility, but I do not. I think the only question is 'when,' and not 'if' they will do it. The Prussians have no other choice."

Ambassador Kern agreed. "It is a stalemate."

"Every day, the Prussians bring to their lines more heavy guns," the Baron observed, then looked at the Papal Nuncio. "I have nothing further to add," he said simply, and sat down.

The Nuncio looked at his list and came to the last order of business. "The Prussian historian, Doctor Fontaine, was it?"

"He has been released from prison," Washburne said. "President Favre saw to that himself."

"Good," the Nuncio said. "That is one less complaint on our list from Chancellor Bismarck. Gentlemen, if there is nothing further, we will adjourn."

Each of the Ambassadors began to collect his papers, and chairs scraped on the wooden floor. Washburne leaned to his right and said quietly to the Swiss Ambassador, "A moment of your time, my friend."

Kern graciously nodded.

At half-past seven the following morning, Washburne walked through the gates of Prison de la Roquette and was admitted to the Prefect's gloomy grey office.

Washburne sat in the creaky wooden chair opposite the Prefect and read the list of names. He'd come with his own list, and now inspected the new arrivals at La Roquette. Still so many Prussian and Bavarian names, he thought sadly.

When war had been declared, the Prussian government petitioned him to take care of their nationals stranded in Paris. Bismarck had given a bank-draft to the American Ambassador in excess of fifty thousand dollars to use as the Ambassador saw fit. Washburne immediately deposited the money with the Rothschild Bank on behalf of the Prussian Government for the express use of the Prussian nationals in Paris. The money bought passage for the poor to their homeland, food for the unemployed, and provided temporary shelter for thousands of people until they were permitted to leave Paris.

By eight o'clock, Washburne was visiting the cells at La Roquette, culling from their dank and smelly confinements American citizens, Belgian workers, Prussian sewermen, visiting doctors, teachers, citizens of Alsace, two French Provincial men who had stuttering defects in their speech, and lastly, the Swiss.

He was given permission to enter the solitary wards, and there expressed profound astonishment at seeing his acquaintance, Herr Dössegger of Zurich in so ruined a state.

"This man has been beaten," Washburne said in an official voice to the guard. "I have complained of this before," he said, "and you have been warned of this before." He gave the list from the Swiss Embassy to the guard. "Herr Dössegger's name is listed. I respectfully—and formally—request you release Herr Dössegger to me at once."

"Only the Prefect may do that," the guard spitefully replied.

"Then speak to him, as he has already approved the list you now hold in your hands."

The guard grunted and walked down the narrow passageway.

Stefan stared numbly at the Ambassador.

"This is an outrage," Washburne whispered and helped the Austrian Prince to a small stool with uneven legs in the corner. Washburne saw the blackened left eye, the large purple bruise that had formed on the jaw, the Prince's lip had been split and his clothes were tattered, dirty, and had a rancid odor clinging to them.

Washburne took his handkerchief and dipped it in a basin of water, then wiped the dried blood from the Prince's cheek. "Have they fed you?"

Stefan shook his head. "I . . . I don't remember . . ."

"I shall complain of this—again," Washburne said by way of a promise.

"Who . . ." Stefan swallowed, "who came to you?"

"The Englishman," Washburne said, then put his fingers to his own lips when he heard the footsteps of several persons echoing in the cold stone passageway.

They released him. And leaning against Washburne, Stefan walked slowly to the Ambassador's carriage in the courtyard. With his free hand, he shaded his eyes from the sunlight and saw the blur of the carriage.

Washburne climbed in beside the Prince and shut the door.

"I am indebted to you," Stefan said quietly.

Washburne shook his head. "I do not keep accounts," he said matter-of-factly as the carriage began to move toward the iron gates. "It was my privilege to be of service."

They rode silently for a time. Stefan slumped against the horsehair-filled seat, more tired than hungry.

"I, I know something of your predicament," Washburne began slowly. "And I have spoken with the Swiss Ambassador. I took the liberty of placing all your names on my colleague's list."

"What list?" Stefan asked, turning his head to the right.

"The exit list, for Monday afternoon. We have a quota system now, but my colleague will see to your safe passage out of Paris and then out of France to Switzerland. He knows who you are, I had to tell him, but he has told no one else."

Stefan weakly nodded.

"He assured me, he will see to this personally. He will be waiting for you and your family, and he told me you are not to wait in the queue but to walk to the side of it where he and his aide will be. The aide will accompany you all the way to Switzerland."

Stefan leaned heavily back into the seat and sighed. "This is good of you, Your Excellency. My family will not forget your kindness or that of the Swiss Ambassador. I am most grateful."

Washburne only smiled.

"Where do we go, on Monday afternoon?"

"It is—complicated," Washburne said with a heavy sigh. "Besides being on the exit list, everyone leaving Paris must have, in addition, a pass from my embassy with our seal and my signature. Bismarck demanded this precaution. You are not allowed to bring newspapers, government correspondence or books with you. Bring only the most necessary of personal items—one suitcase per person. You must first go to Porte St. Vincennes. There, the French authorities will inspect your papers, and rather closely, I might add. You will be traveling under military escort. Leaving with you that day will be many Swiss, about twenty Russians, and a half-dozen Bavarians. You will be escorted through the outlying provinces and brought to a point where you will continue alone to the Prussian lines. Then, they will inspect your passes. That is why the aide will travel with you all the way to Switzerland. From there, you will continue, again under military escort, south to Fontainebleau, where you will be permitted to board a train to Dijon, and from there, to Lyons, and finally, to Switzerland."

Stefan nodded as they passed the Place de la Bastille.

"I shall be seeing my colleague, Ambassador Kern, this evening," Washburne continued, then took from his coat pocket a shred of paper and a pencil. "I shall be needing all the names—for the Swiss passes. All, that is, except Lord Harlaxton's. He left his card with me, so I've already sent his name on ahead."

Stefan managed a small smile. "Stefan, Julienne, Friedrich and Gisela."

Washburne wrote them down. "All Dössegger?"

"Yes," Stefan replied.

"It is done. The Ambassador himself will give you your passes along with my pass."

"Where do you take me now?" Stefan asked quietly.

Washburne shrugged. "I thought, to my home, unless you prefer some other place."

"I think I would prefer to go home."

"As you wish. I'll tell my driver to . . ."

"No, no, you needn't bother. I'll get out by the Hôtel de Ville. It isn't far from there."

"Are you quite sure? It is no bother at all to . . ."

"I am sure," Stefan answered. "You've already done a great deal for me."

"But the Englishman is coming to my home this afternoon."

"I shall see him before then."

"Ahh good," Washburne said.

"He may wish to see you anyway, to thank you."

Washburne shook his head. "He's already done that, and I have already accepted." Washburne saw the Hôtel de Ville down the Rue de Rivoli and called up to the driver to stop the carriage there.

When the carriage lumbered to a stop, Stefan turned to Washburne and offered his hand. "God bless you and keep you, Sir. Your country is most fortunate, to have you represent her."

"I hope we meet again," Washburne said.

"We shall," Stefan smiled, "at another time, and in another place."

Stefan had a headache, and the sun still hurt his eyes as he walked slowly up the Boulevard St. Michel, unobtrusively and quietly.

He felt relieved when he walked into the cool lobby of the apartment house, and began the difficult climb of the stairs. It seemed to take forever, and he leaned heavily on the banister for support. A door opened on the floor above him, it closed, he heard footsteps and a moment later saw Edward rounding the landing.

"Good God!" Edward said and dropped his hat, then quickly looped an arm around Stefan's waist and half-carried him up the remaining flight of stairs. "I cannot believe they beat you," he muttered, unstrained by Stefan's weight.

"They . . . did," Stefan said, then stopped when they walked toward the door. "Wait," he wheezed. "I . . . I must walk in, myself."

Edward withdrew his arm and looked closely at the bruises. "How much does it hurt?"

"Not as much as before," Stefan said. He looked into the glittering blue eyes. "I was wrong about you," he said quietly. "I apologize. You behaved better than I."

"Don't be ridiculous," Edward said, brushing the compliment away. "I would have behaved in precisely the same fashion, had it been my sister."

Stefan managed a grin. "Somehow," he said, "I do not think so," and walked unsteadily to the door. "Is she alone?" he asked softly.

"Yes."

"Come inside then, we must talk now." He saw the hesitation, then added, "Please."

Edward sat in the chair as Julienne fretted and brought a basin, a cloth and a bottle of astringent to Stefan and began to clean the bruises.

"It wasn't the hunger, or the dampness, or even the fear," Stefan said bitterly as she held the cloth to his jaw. "It was the humiliation. The second time they came to my cell, they tied my hands behind me. They bound me, like a criminal. There were three of them. They had rotten teeth and disgusting smiles and they took turns hitting me. They called me filthy names, spit at me—at *me*," he said angrily, "and tried to shame me into confessing I was a spy. And when I wouldn't be shamed, they hit me all the more. I've been in fights, I've felt fists on my person before, at the Academy, even in the street, but *this*," he spat, "this was a ritual humiliation and . . ." He stopped speaking and saw Julienne swallow hard. He sighed, thinking, how stupid of me, to go on like this when she *knows* what it is to be humiliated and to be hurt. And now, he thought, trying to give a comforting smile, I have been given but the smallest taste of what she must have lived through for so long a time, humiliated not by strangers, but by a husband. "It doesn't matter," he said aloud. "It's over."

Julienne said nothing and wrung the cloth over the basin. But Stefan saw the hard, pained knowing in her eyes.

Stefan took the cloth from Julienne and dabbed near the corner of his mouth. "Well," he said, feeling tired, "there is much to do between now and Monday."

"Monday?" Julienne asked.

"Yes, Monday afternoon. It's all been arranged by the Swiss Ambassador and Mr. Washburne. Monday," he said, staring at her with unblinking eyes, "we are all leaving."

Her mouth opened.

"Do not argue with me," he warned. "It is done, finished, we are leaving this place and that is final."

"I won't be ordered about like . . ."

"ENOUGH!" Stefan yelled, "you are *still* a part of my family and you will do what I say."

"You are *not* my father!"

"You will do this because it is right and . . ."

Julienne jumped up from the sofa but Edward was out of the chair and blocked her way. "Come back and sit down."

"You've taken his side, haven't you?" she glared.

"That's hardly the point, surely," Edward answered, annoyed that Stefan's exhaustion had prompted so angry a response.

"This," Stefan blazed, "is all wrong. It is enough. You will not live like this any longer."

Edward waved his hand at Stefan to silence him. "Sit down," he said to Julienne.

"Why?" she demanded. "You've *both* decided for me, haven't you? You've just been waiting patiently, haven't you, waiting for your chance to make me leave. Well I will not be ordered to do things—not anymore. You do not wag your finger at me and treat me like a trained dog."

"No one has suggested such a distasteful thing," Edward said. "But we will discuss this, now, all of us."

"What is there to discuss? You've happily taken my brother's side and the two of you think that . . ."

"You have never *once* asked me my opinion, have you?" Edward interrupted.

"You've made it very clear."

"No. It is *you* who have decided what I am thinking, or why I think it, or what I feel is the right thing to do, but you have never actually asked me, have you?"

He had a point and she knew it, much as it displeased her. She gave an angry sigh and looked at him. "Well?" she finally asked.

Edward arched an eyebrow in annoyance. "Are you going to sulk or are you going to listen?"

She felt shamed and her expression relaxed. "I shall listen," she said.

"Good," he commented and waited for her to sit down again, watching as she chose the chair instead of the sofa and folded her hands primly on her lap. He said nothing about her choice, and sat down in his chair facing her. "I am very surprised at you," he began in a quiet tone. "You have been taught so well by your father, to choose life no matter what the sacrifice might be. You once risked your life to save it, to find the peace that had been denied you. That same choice is presented to you now."

"I have already told you I will not run away from my home or my family ever again."

"*This* is your family," Edward said, pointing dead-center to the room.

"I told you I would not leave Cécile and . . ."

"*They* are a different family," Edward answered firmly. "As much as you love them, as much as you care for them, they are a different family and your *first* responsibility is to this family. They have their lives, we have ours, and we make decisions for *our* family, Julienne, not theirs." He paused to let his point settle for a moment. "Our family is no longer safe here. The streets are filled with drunken soldiers, the poor, the hungry, the homeless. And this is only the beginning of it," he said. "I swear to you, I will not sit by, for the sake of an apartment and friends, and watch my children slowly starve."

She looked at him with astonished eyes.

"Yes," he said. "They are hungry now. We must coax them to eat *now*. Do you believe this will change for the better if the Siege continues much longer? The herds of sheep and cattle grow smaller by the day. They've already killed the deer in the zoo for food." He took a breath. "I never told you this. I have seen famine, in India. I have seen with my own eyes what that sort of death looks like. It . . . it was a vision of hell that has been with me ever since, and that I have tried with all my mind to forget. I . . . I could not bear that sight with strangers. Do you think I will allow that to happen to Frédéric and Gisèle? Never. Not as long as I have breath and we have a choice."

She felt ashamed for clinging so tightly to a set of rooms, and knew that she had been blinded by an old familiar weapon—fear; fear of leaving what she knew, what she believed safe, and what had become home.

"This time, and for this journey, you will not be alone. You needn't be afraid," Edward said.

After a moment, she said quietly, "I am not afraid. You are right and I am wrong." She looked at Stefan. "We leave on Monday."

Stefan smiled, then hugged her when she moved next to him on the sofa.

"I'm sorry," she said.

"So am I," he answered.

"When shall you tell Cécile?" Edward asked.

Julienne swallowed. "Now," she answered, then looked at Stefan and then at the cloth in the basin. "In a few minutes."

"I can manage," Stefan said easily. "I'm not a child. Go and be with your friend."

Julienne nodded, then walked with Edward to the door.

Edward stood there for a moment, watching as she walked down the stairs, then quietly shut the apartment door. He turned around and saw Stefan standing up and looking out the window to the street below. "You ought to rest, you know," he said, walking toward the window.

Stefan looked with calm eyes at the tall Englishman. "I was more wrong about you than I have ever been about any man alive," he said. "Julienne was right to call you 'husband,' and right again to have the children call you 'Papa.'"

Edward was caught completely by surprise.

Stefan offered his hand. "I am proud to call you my brother and my friend," he said.

Edward warmly shook the Prince's hand.

"My only regret," Stefan said, "is that my father did not live to meet you. I wish you could have known him. He would have liked you, very much."

"But I have met him," Edward said quietly to Stefan. "I have met him in you and in her."

The boy was nervous when he saw his Uncle's bruises. His eyes kept looking and then darting away from the purple and the yellow and the darkened left eye. He had little appetite for luncheon and would not leave his mother to go outside and play, but followed her from room to room, a tiny protective shadow. He complained of a stomach ache, and strangely, wanted to be held and comforted by his mother.

Gisèle did not want to go outside, either, and spent the afternoon in a corner, afraid to look at her Uncle.

The children did not want to be left alone, and it took great patience to get them undressed and into bed that night.

Several hours later, they heard moans and cries from the children's room and then a small muffled shriek from the boy, still asleep.

Julienne woke him and held him whilst he whimpered. "It was only a dream," she said softly, rubbing the small of his back and feeling the tangle of his arms tighten around her neck. "It's gone now, it is far away and won't come back."

He shook his head against her. "It . . . it was a dark place, and, and I couldn't get out, there was no door, and then, I saw him."

"Who?"

"Uncle Steffie."

"What did he do?"

"Nothing. He . . . he was just there, like today."

She nodded. "Strangers did that to his face, Frédéric. Bad people hurt him. You mustn't be afraid of that anymore. We will never, ever, be afraid of that again. Uncle Stefan is not to blame. He loves you, you know that. He would never hurt you, never."

The boy was shivering, but nodded.

"Lie down again, and I shall fix the covers, just as you like them."

"No," he shook his head, "I, I don't want to go to sleep. I'm afraid of the dark."

"But you need to sleep. It's late."

"No, please, I want to stay with you."

She thought a moment, then said, "You haven't kissed Uncle Steffie all day. He feels very bad about that."

The boy recoiled slightly.

"His face isn't nice to look at, is it?"

"No," Frédéric answered, stealing a look at Gisèle, sound asleep and untroubled by anything.

"It will get better in a few days," Julienne smiled. "He will look the same, once the bruises go away. But he is still the same Uncle Steffie who reads you stories, and plays with you, and looks through the kaleidoscope with you. Do you still love him?"

"Yes."

"Maybe a kiss would help the pain go away. Would you do that?"

He just looked at her.

"When you have a pain, I kiss you. I still love you. It is the same."

Still, he didn't move.

"Come inside, come sit with us for a little while and hold Uncle Steffie's hand. It will make him feel better."

"Will it?"

"Oh yes," Julienne said. "A kiss from you would help him so much." She moved the covers and led him out to the salon as he rubbed his eyes.

Stefan was lying down on the sofa and held a wet compress to his eye. He opened his right eye and saw Frédéric staring down at him. He half-smiled at the boy.

Frédéric looked at the compress.

"Ugly, isn't it?"

"Yes," he said, then looked at his mother with a fearful glance that told more than his words. He, too, remembered.

Stefan took the compress off and held it out to Frédéric. "Be a good boy," he said quietly, "and dip it in the water for me."

Frédéric did as he was told.

"Now, wring it out. Make sure most of the water is squeezed from the cloth. That's right," he said, watching Frédéric. "Will you put it very gently on my eye?"

Frédéric paused, then placed the cloth down.

"Ahhh," Stefan sighed, "that is good. I begin to feel better." He made room on the sofa for Frédéric and let the boy take the cloth, dip it, wring it, and replace it on the eye several times, each time saying he felt better, and each time Frédéric grew less and less afraid of the ugliness and the uglier memories.

Stefan groaned slightly when the child poked a most tender spot. Frédéric kissed the bruise and announced it would be better now.

"Oh," Stefan smiled and touched the spot. "I do believe you're right. Yes, it is slightly better."

Frédéric eyed him. "It doesn't happen that fast," he said. "You're only pretending."

Stefan laughed quietly. "I was, yes. And you should go to bed now, shouldn't you?"

The boy nodded.

"Come kiss me goodnight then, and tomorrow, Doctor Frédéric, you must promise me to tell me if I look better."

"Yes, I promise," Frédéric said, hugging his Uncle. After a kiss, he scampered off to bed alone.

Sunday was a bittersweet day. After they had packed only the most necessary of possessions, they walked the boulevards of their beloved city, now changed into a military camp. Julienne silently said goodbye to the city that had become home.

Paris, she thought, my Paris. You are elegant and beautiful, timeless and constant, the heart of France. You are the dream I clung to in my most desperate hour. You gave me a home, friends, and I, too, found life here. My Paris, she thought, you are part of me, and will be with me forever . . .

That night in Edward's arms after quiet loving, she thought of the dresses still in the wardrobe, the dresses he'd given her that had to stay behind, for they had no room in the small cases they would be permitted to carry with them. She kissed his chest, and gave a constricted sad sigh.

"What is it?" he whispered, holding her closely. "Tell me what's wrong."

She shook her head. "Nothing," she said softly.

"Rubbish."

"You'll think me foolish."

"Tell me," he said.

She shrugged beneath him. "So many things must stay here."

He thought a moment. "It's like the last time, isn't it? You left so much behind, didn't you, you had to, of course."

Julienne slowly nodded.

He smiled in the dark and rubbed his mouth with hers. "Old things were replaced by new things," he said, "and now these old things will be replaced by newer things—things you shall never leave behind or part with again."

"I know that," she said gently. "It just makes me sad to leave behind the first things you gave me."

"I'm the first thing I gave you," he said, butting his cheek softly against hers. "Silly . . . to be sad over dresses, beautiful dresses, but only cloth."

"It isn't the same for you, is it? You left a life behind you without ever looking back, didn't you?"

He chuckled. "Oh this is hardly the time to bring that to mind, my love."

"And what a clever way not to answer a question," she said, bringing her hands to his face. She felt him nod.

"And I shan't answer it, either," he said rather glibly.

"Someday," Julienne said.

"You never give it up, do you?"

"Not 'it,' " she corrected quietly, "you. I shall never give you up for lost."

He shifted his weight and moved to his side. "I'm not lost," he said softly, "not anymore."

It was raining. And the solemn walk down the Boulevard St. Michel made the grey buildings and dark green ironfronts to the newer stores more oppressive than ever. They hardly spoke, but Julienne walked with Cécile's arm in hers and felt the warmth of the woman's hand in her own.

When they crossed the streets, Armand picked Gisèle up and then set her down and took her hand as they moved closer to the Seine. Though he knew they must do what they must do, he felt a weighty sadness in his heart at saying goodbye to them, all of them, but especially the little ones, his "little fleas."

They made their way over the bridge, and then, the Île St. Louis, and saw the crowd massing in front of the cream-colored Hôtel de Ville.

"We must go this way," Armand said, and motioned toward the Quai de la Grève. "It's better. There are too many people there."

"Something awful must have happened," Cécile said, staring at the angry crowd, the people at its edges raising their fists and baring their teeth in rage.

The crowd began to chant. "Long Live the Commune! Long Live the Commune!"

"My God," Armand muttered, "the Reds are overthrowing the government . . ."

The mob began to grow, as passersby molded themselves to the fringes and added their support.

"Come along," Armand said, "this way."

They could still hear the crowd as they turned left on Place Lobau, at the rear of the Hôtel de Ville. People were running down the street, running toward the Hôtel de Ville.

A man bumped into Cécile and excused himself.

"What has happened?" Cécile asked the stranger.

"Do you not know?" he shrieked. "Bazaine has surrendered. The city of Metz has fallen." He saw the blank look in her eyes. "Madame, Madame," he said, frenzied, "the Prussians have our arsenal. The Prussian Army, all the troops fighting at Metz are now free to attack Paris! We stand alone. We are betrayed by the government, we are betrayed! Only the Commune will save us now . " He left her standing there and joined the mob at the mouth of the street.

Armand stiffened his back. "What does it matter who is in charge, they are all the same—pigs and cowards. Only the faces change."

"Armand," Cécile said and nodded toward the children.

"Let them hear," he said loudly. "They should know how to recognize a pig when they see one . . ." He took Gisèle's hand and pulled her down the street and only slowed his pace when she complained he was walking too fast.

At the mouth of Rue Lobau where it met the Rue de Rivoli, the Hadean gates opened wide. Gardes Nationals were running with fixed bayonets toward the Hôtel de Ville. The crowds thickened, people were uncontrolled and ran madly in the streets, bumping and shoving each other and anyone in their way, as they shouted words lost in the soaking confusion. Everywhere, frightened people ran and splattered mud from the rain-drenched clay that had collected in the streets. Horses and carts were being driven in the midst of the crowds and the scent of panic hung real and evil-smelling as the animals began to rear up and bolt in the contagious anxiety.

334

Garde Mobile troops, troops of Gardes Nationals, a veritable avalanche of avenging furies, separated them from each other.

Frédéric looked up as the man with the criss-cross white belts on his chest ran between him and his uncle and parted their two hands. The crowds buffeted him, pushed him and shoved him and turned him around many times in a sickening whirlwind of the blindman's game in a sea of terrified people. He was drawn away from the pavement, away from his mother and his family, out toward the middle of the street. They were all so big, so tall, so frightened and running so fast, he didn't know what to do, and was so confused he stood where he was and began to scream for his mother and his Papa.

Julienne had seen Stefan searching the crowd. She had seen him begin to push people out of the way and heard him calling out to Frédéric.

As the crowd thinned and turned left down Rue Lobau, Edward heard the frightened voice and saw him, muddied, dazed and confused, rooted to the spot in the middle of the street looking toward the sidewalk, and in the way of a charging cart.

Instantly, Edward dropped his bag and pushed his way to the street as the cart-driver began pulling hard on the reins. Behind him, Edward heard the mother's voice, loud and shrill and with all the strength she possessed, calling out the name she'd given the boy: "FRIEDRICH!"

Edward reached, he stretched out his arms and reached for his son as the cart-driver stopped the horse five feet away from the panic-stricken child, while four Gardes Nationals whirled around.

Edward's hands grabbed Frédéric's shoulders, but he let go when he felt his own neck suddenly burned and bleeding on the left side, seared by the bullet. One second later, he screamed from the bone-splitting agony, the blinding white light of unimaginable pain as his left leg gave way beneath him, and his body jerked convulsively, tumbling down.

He grabbed for his son as the black tunnel began to close out the sounds and the air, not hearing Armand's screaming voice above him, "He's English, he is an Englishman!"

The crowds had shouted and yelled when the Guardsmen had fired, they had parted and rushed from the street and now, the Guardsmen could only look at the man in the mud, and the woman pushing her way to him, shoving the curious people out of her path as they all stood and watched as the man's blood mixed with the mud and the clay and the rain.

But I heard a German name, one of the Guardsmen thought. He was German, I heard the name shrieked by a French woman. I know I heard it.

Shivering, Julienne dropped to her knees and hauled Edward onto her lap, holding him in her arms as the blood from his neck trickled out from the burned skin where the bullet had grazed him.

Frédéric was white and closed his eyes against his mother as he wailed, afraid to look, yet still calling "Papa, Papa . . ." in pitiful moans.

Stefan ran out to them and held his handkerchief to the wound on the neck, but when he saw the knee and vainly tried to stem the flow of blood with the small soaked linen cloth, he watched with horrified eyes as it turned bright red immediately.

"You COWARDS!" Armand raged at the Guardsmen. "Your mothers were scum and you know it, you filthy murdering pigs! He is English! ENGLISH!"

The confusion began to grow with the shame, and the crowd began to slink back and disperse from the sight.

"Go," Armand shrieked, "that's right, go . . ." He stood guard until the soldiers melted with the crowd and, anonymous once more, left.

"Armand," Stefan called out.

The proud Frenchman turned around.

"Tell Cécile to take the boy and Gisèle back to the apartment; to manage as best she can with the bags. If she cannot, leave them. Hurry . . . he's . . ." Stefan stopped speaking.

Julienne saw the end of the phrase in her brother's eyes. He's dying, she thought.

Armand had to pull Frédéric away from Julienne; he had to ignore the weak kicking and the plaintive screaming of the child for Papa, for Mama, and not watch the outstretched arms flailing at the air, or the tears that blended with the rain. Cécile held both children to her skirt. A shopkeeper, a witness to this despicable mistake, offered to help her with the bags. And with trembling lips, she accepted.

"Madame," a voice above Julienne said.

She looked up and saw the soaked cart-driver.

"Let me help you," he said. "We'll put him in my cart."

"Julienne," Stefan said, "where is the nearest hospital? Look at me—where?"

She tried to think, but saw only the closed eyes, the dark hair wet and matted by the rain, and the blood from the neck wound disappearing into the stained cravat. Stefan's hands grabbed her shoulders and she felt him shake her, hard and quick. "Boulevard St. Germain," she mumbled. "The Sorbonne . . . Ecole de Médecine."

Stefan looked at the cart driver. "That is the nearest one?"

"Yes, Monsieur. It is only a school . . ."

"It must do," Stefan said, and tried to take Edward from her.

"Let him alone—don't touch him," she yelled.

Stefan smacked her hand away and grabbed Edward under the shoulders. "Please," he said to the cart-driver, "help me to pick him up."

They held him and lifted him to the cart and laid him on top of the tarpaulin covering bolts of material.

"Madame," the driver soothed, "ride with him." He then looked at Stefan and Armand, and shook his head. "It will be too much for the horse to bear."

"Then we'll follow alongside," Stefan said, and tried to keep pace with the cart as it moved and jerked through the streets back toward the Left Bank.

Julienne held him tightly and saw the eyes open, but dazed. "Edward," she said. "Edward?"

He was breathing through his mouth, short quick gasps as his head was jostled from side to side. The cart wheel thudded on a large cobblestone, and after giving an agonized moan, he passed out again.

God, don't let him die, she prayed, staring at him with eyes stretched open and wide, touching him, trying to keep him warm, and seeing her skirt near the knee red and wet with his blood.

The cart slowed and stopped at the doors to the Ecole de Médecine, its white columns slicked by rain and the grey steps slippery and glistening. Armand ran up the steps, grabbed a robed student near the doors and gestured wildly toward the cart. The student followed him back to the cart and helped them carry the man to the Clinic around the corner on the Rue Dubois.

The small waiting-room was warm and filled with people. They pushed their way through the crowd of soldiers, children, men and women, and parted the wooden doors with their backs as they blindly followed the student. They carried Edward down greyed halls with flickering gas-lights, halls that smelled and had wounded soldiers sitting and sleeping on the floor. The passageways were narrow, and dying men lay unattended on litters; wounded soldiers in stained uniforms moaned and cried. The young student began to feel the dead weight of the man in his arms, and he struggled to keep the flopping arms from smacking into the walls. He looked for a familiar face and, at the doors to the surgery, saw one of his professors.

"Doctor Vadon, Doctor Vadon," he called, seeing the older physician turn and come quickly to him.

One look at the knee and Doctor Vadon helped shoulder the weight of the unconscious man as they took him into the operating theater.

Julienne tried to follow, but Vadon stopped her. "No, Madame, stay where you are . . ." and then sent everyone out of the surgical theater to wait in the halls.

They set him on an ordinary wooden table, stripped him, covered him partly with a sheet and saw the full extent of the gaping wound in the leg, and a second bullet wound near the waist.

"Try to stop the hemorrhaging," Vadon ordered, as he tied an apron about himself, then rinsed his hands in phenol, the antiseptic recommended by Lister and currently under experimentation at the Ecole de Médecine.

The graduated stalls were filling up again with students who leaned on the barriers and began to open their notebooks.

Vadon looked at his colleagues. "How much is left in the bottle?"

Doctor Porlier, a stocky man with brown eyes, held the Mills Chloroform bottle up. He shook his head. "Perhaps enough, Vadon; perhaps for him and one other patient. This is the last of it. The supplies all over Paris are nearly gone."

"God help us," Vadon mumbled.

Porlier expertly folded a piece of lint cut to a square shape and of double thickness. He held it just above the man's nose and began to shake the chloroform ether, once every thirty seconds, and then, three shakes every thirty seconds from the Mills bottle.

"Notice, Gentlemen," Vadon said in his clear professorial voice, "Doctor Porlier again demonstrates the St. Bartholomew's method of anesthesia . . ."

Edward's eyes fluttered open as the strange smell raced quickly through his nose and down to his lungs, a strange hypnotic mixture of scents, sweet-smelling, heavy, something metallic and, yet, like a perfume that oddly had a sharp underscent to it . . .

"As we have explained," Vadon went on, "the liquid anesthetic is harmful to the skin and mucous membranes, but not the vapor. Hence, one must be very cautious indeed whilst shaking the Mills bottle, else you burn the patient and yourself."

I'm cold, Edward thought blandly, drifting, eyes blurring, people . . . all the people watching from above, who are they, he thought, hearing a man's voice drown in confusion at the far end of a tunnel that stretched forever . . . The smell was like a hand that covered his face, his eyes, his mouth and reached deep inside of him to muffle sounds and sights, and it slowed time to a dulling, creeping, numbing halt. He closed his eyes.

"We have two bullet wounds; a third, on the neck, was merely a grazing. But the leg is a compound fracture," Vadon said, "and the hemorrhaging is barely contained." He inspected further and said, "The blood near the bone is dark and contains fat droplets from the marrow." He used the metal probe, strained and bent closer. "Muscles lacerated, massive tissue destruction . . . the tendon is severed, but the joint, I believe, is intact. The tibia, below the joint, is shattered, and splinters are piercing the surrounding tissues, which means a disarticulation of the knee, and amputation . . ."

He heard a murmur from a group of students to his right and looked up. "Ahh, Doctor Swinburne, I thought you had already gone . . ." Vadon smiled.

The American shook his head and perched over the wooden barrier. "One of your young fellows came after me when this patient was brought in."

"Would you like to examine the wound?"

"Yes, thank you," Swinburne replied, and left the row of students. A moment later, the Chief Surgeon of the American Ambulance-Hospital entered the theater. Swinburne was of average height, had pale clear skin and a calm face. His hands, however, were remarkable. The square strong palms were off-set by long fingers, deceptively delicate-looking, but strong and steady. He had saved countless lives, first in the American Civil War and now here, in Paris, tending the wounded consigned to his hospital. All morning long he had assisted in operations and demonstrated methods to the students. Though tired, he always found new energy somewhere within himself when he approached the table and rinsed his hands and the probe in phenol. The energy always returned, as it did now when he parted the tattered skin on the leg.

They heard moans and cries from the men in the hallways, from the waiting room crammed with the wounded and the sick, echoing sounds that had little reality in the dim grey halls as attendants and volunteer nurses stepped over the wounded and the dying on the floors. It was a grim sight, and the smell of blood, urine, and the unwashed men nauseated them.

Stefan tried to convince his sister to wait outside. The fresh air might help her and calm her. She had refused and leaned against the wall, closing her eyes and seeing Edward's face in her mind, smiling, laughing, speaking . . .

She was unaware of the dried blood caked on her hands, on her skirt. She felt cold and damp but refused to move. Why am I still breathing, she thought in a daze. All these people in the halls, sitting in their own worlds, don't they know . . . is it an hour, less, more . . .

She heard the doors of the surgery open. She opened her eyes and felt her body stiffen as a middle-aged man with greying temples walked towards them, drying his hands on a small towel.

"Excuse me," he began, "are you the family of . . ."

"Yes," Julienne said, stepping closer.

"My name is Swinburne, Doctor John Swinburne of the American hospital and . . ."

"Is he alive?" Julienne asked.

"Just," Swinburne commented. He eyed the anxious woman. "Your husband, Madame?"

She nodded.

"Madame, let me give you some good advice," he began quietly. "My French colleagues and I differ on this point, but this is my second war and I have had much experience with this sort of wound."

Stefan felt his stomach turn violently, sensing what had been done.

This had never been easy for Swinburne. And years of experience did not help him in the least when he had to speak to patients or their families. He was a surgeon, and felt at home in the operating theater or lecturing to students or colleagues. As he looked at the young woman with the large brown eyes, he just went ahead with it, saying as gently as he could, "I recommend you to expect the worst." He paused, then said, "The bullet shattered part of his knee and the bone of his leg. We separated the knee joint, saving what we could, and had to amputate the left leg." He noticed she seemed to will herself to listen and be strong, then after looking at the two men, said directly to her, "I'm sorry. He's dying."

Stefan, holding Julienne firmly with his arm around her waist, said to the doctor, "Is there nothing we can do . . ."

Swinburne sighed. "I will not lie to you. It is very bad. But, I have seen worse, and indeed, some of those men have recovered, yet, it was under better circumstances. All you can do is keep the wound clean, change the bandages several times a day, and one other thing. This is where my French colleagues and I differ. The wound needs—must have—fresh air. Do not keep him in a closed stifling room. I know my colleagues have a horror of drafts, Madame, Gentlemen, but please believe me when I tell you a closed room will definitely kill him. Keep him warm, yes, but keep the wound in the open air."

The doors to the surgery opened and Doctor Vadon stepped out.

"What is his name, by the way?" Swinburne asked.

"Edward Atherton-Moore," Julienne answered.

"English?"

"Yes," she managed.

"And how old is he?"

"Thirty-four years old."

Swinburne thought a moment. "He seemed fairly strong . . . perhaps it will make a difference."

Vadon approached them. "Doctor Swinburne has told you?"

Stefan nodded.

"Monsieur," Vadon said in a weary voice from a man who had seen too much, "take him home. We can do nothing more for him here. We have no beds, little medicine, and diseases from the war-front are everywhere. Take him home. If he dies, he will die in his own bed and not lying forgotten in a passageway here." Vadon paused and looked at the chalky-skinned woman watching him along with her two companions. It is always the same, he thought, a stupor surrounds them like a vapor, shock. It will wear off soon enough. "I . . . I am very sorry," he said. "I wish I could have told you something else."

"Are we to just change the bandage and watch him die? Is there nothing more we can do for him?" Armand asked.

"Monsieur . . . ?" Vadon said, raising the inflection.

"Mabilleau," Armand answered.

"Monsieur Mabilleau," Vadon said with a shrug to his shoulders, "would you prefer me to lie to you? There is no medicine. If there was no war, and if he were here and we were caring for him, we would give him morphia. But there is no morphia. Not here and," he turned to Swinburne, "and not at your hospital, correct?"

Swinburne shook his head. "We finished our supply two days ago."

"What can I tell you, Monsieur Mabilleau?" Vadon continued. "The young man will be in terrible, terrible agony, and it will not be an easy thing to watch . . ." He suddenly stopped and raised his eyebrows with a thought. "However," he breathed, "if not morphia—Monsieur, see if you may find, somewhere, Laudanum. Those supplies are nearly gone as well, and I tell you, quite unofficially, you may have to search the black market for it. If you cannot find Laudanum, try to buy absinthe, and if you cannot find that, and he lives through the night and tomorrow morning, get him drunk. And keep him drunk until he feels nothing and passes out in a dead sleep."

"Good idea, Vadon, very good," Swinburne said, noticing the eyes of the family had suddenly sharpened. "Should he live, you must do several things. Madame Atherton-Moore, none of them are pleasant."

Julienne inhaled deeply, then stepped away from Stefan's arms and stood straight, staring at the doctor. "I will do it, whatever you ask of me, I will do it."

Swinburne nodded, then made a fist with his left hand and pointed to the "ball." "This is what remains of the knee joint. We have made a double flap of skin over the joint. It must be washed and the scab that will form—and the incisions—must be kept soft. A hard crust should not form, Madame, and do not let it form. You . . ." he said gently, "you must knead the skin, like dough, and it must be done several times a day. Do it when he has passed out. The kneading causes a horrible pain, beyond words."

"And the stump," Vadon said, "keep the stump on several soft pillows. This, Madame and Gentlemen, is to prevent the muscles and the veins and the tissues from drawing back and . . ." He saw the blank looks. "It prevents them from shrinking," he said with an embarrassed smile, remembering they

340

were not medical students listening to a lecture. "The shrinking is very painful, also."

"If you see pus, or lumps under the skin," Swinburne went on, "or lumps under the stitches, or smell a foul odor . . ."

"Gangrene," Stefan said.

Swinburne and Vadon both nodded. "Then he will die," Swinburne said, "then there is no hope at all."

Vadon studied the young woman's dry, determined eyes. "Madame, there is one other matter. It may seem bizarre to you, to all of you, and you may think that he has lost his mind." Vadon shook his head for emphasis. "I assure you he will be quite sane, but it is common, and happens to patients who have had this sort of surgery. He will complain of a pain, a pain in the leg that is no longer there." Vadon shrugged. "It may take the form of a burning pain, or a pulling sort of pain, sometimes an itch, sometimes a throbbing pain. In the old days, they used to call it a 'sensory ghost.' But we have given it a new name. We call it a 'phantom.' And, oddly, we have noticed—as you must have seen, too, Swinburne—the patient seems to experience moods of mourning."

Swinburne nodded vigorously. "Yes, exactly."

"Madame, you must know what it is to mourn a loved one, yes?"

Julienne slowly nodded.

"It is, in a way, similar. Patients, sometimes, become angry, or they cry, or they become morose, as some people do in mourning. I have seen soldiers, grown men, weep and wish for death itself. When they give up, they die. It is very strange. Others, the anger helps them. Still, he must want to live. Some men, and women too, do not find that desire within themselves."

"I understand," Julienne said clearly.

"How far must you go to reach your home, Monsieur Mabilleau?" Vadon asked.

Armand sighed. "Not too far, Doctor. We live a little ways from here. Just off the Boulevard St. Michel."

"Good," Vadon said. "We will lend you a litter in which to carry him. Please return it to me. We are in great need of them, Monsieur."

"Yes, of course," Armand answered.

"I only wish I could do more," Vadon said.

Julienne watched as Vadon disappeared into the operating theater.

"Remember," Swinburne said to the young Madame Atherton-Moore, "fresh air, clean bandages for both wounds, soft pillows, knead the stump, and feed him whatever food you may find—good food, if such a thing still exists in Paris. And keep him drunk."

"For how long?" Julienne asked.

Swinburne shrugged. "At least a week, perhaps two, or until he stops screaming."

Oddly, as she and Stefan held the two front bars of the litter and Armand supported the back-end, she saw clearly, thought clearly, and felt the familiar strong angry will to survive.

They walked quickly through the rainy streets, and though the litter was heavy, Julienne did not stumble and absolutely ignored the strained pulling in her right arm as it ached from the weight.

Her apartment was stuffy when they opened the door.

"No," she said to Stefan as he began to walk toward her bedroom. "Not there. The children's room. The window is closer to the bed there."

"But the drafts . . ." Armand said, amazed.

"I will do what he said," Julienne answered. "I do not understand it, but I will do it. I will do *everything* he said."

They carried him to Frédéric's bed, put the litter on the floor and lifted him from the canvas to the mattress.

Julienne walked between the beds, parted the curtains with one violent pull, and without hesitation, opened the window, watching as the cool brisk breeze billowed the curtains and filled the room with fresh air.

Her hands were shaking, but her mouth was set in a line and her eyes were narrowed. "We must change his clothes," she said to Stefan.

"Do you have brandy?" Armand asked.

"Some, at least there was some left."

"I'll see to it," Armand said. "Use the brandy until I see what may be done about the other things Doctor Vadon suggested."

"Thank you," she said in a tight voice.

"Tut," Armand said, and briefly hugged her before he left the room, and then, the apartment.

She looked at Edward now, grey-skinned, breathing through his mouth.

Stefan walked over to her, placed his hands on her shoulders and led her out of the room. "We will wash our hands first," he said.

She looked at him, not understanding, then turned her palms over and saw the dried blood. Her lips trembled, but after several angry breaths, she steadied herself and followed him to the kitchen. She held her palms under the spout as he pumped the cold water into the sink. Her hands shook as she washed his blood from her fingers and her palms.

"I'll change his clothes," Stefan said quietly. "I've . . . I've already seen that sort of wound."

Julienne's shoulders sagged and she felt the tears brimming in her eyes. "I should have listened to you . . ." she said, shaking her head from side to side. "God forgive me, I should have listened to you. None of this would have happened if we had left ten days ago . . ."

He drew her close and kissed the top of her head. "You don't know that. No one knows the future, despite Napoleon and his stars . . . Don't do this to yourself. There is no blame, none. The soldiers did this to him, not you, and not the delay. It is done. Now, we must think only of him and the work we were told to do to save him."

Julienne held him tightly around his waist. "I need you, Stefan. I don't think I can do this alone."

"Hah," he said quietly and shook his head. "Julienne, my dear, if you were alone, you would do it alone. We were raised that way."

She looked up to his eyes.

"Papa made us strong," Stefan said proudly, "and don't you ever forget that." She smiled.

Edward had been changed and now wore a clean nightshirt. They put many blankets on top of him, but the bandaged stump was resting on pillows and exposed completely to the cool air in the room. The bandages were already stained a dark red.

Stefan was sleeping on the sofa and the children were still downstairs with Cécile.

Julienne poured herself a glass of brandy, drank a third of it, then replaced the glass on the table next to the bed. She sat down near him, looked at him, then wrapped her hands around the shoulders of the nightshirt, twisting it between her fingers and lifted him slightly up from the pillows. She bent to his ear. "Listen to me, Edward," she whispered evenly, "listen well. You swore to me you would never desert me. You swore to me I would never be alone. I swear before Almighty God, I will force you to keep that promise. I will not let you run away from me," she said, seeing his head hang limply back, the hair, damp from perspiration, falling in wisps and matted clumps. She kissed him, then placed him gently back upon the pillows, smoothing his hair and then the wrinkled shoulders of the nightshirt. "You will have what you need to live," she said, "I swear it, for as long as I have breath. I will never give you up for lost."

She got up from the bed and took a seat on the chair she'd brought in from the dining room. With the light of the small oil-lamp, she picked up the old petticoat from the floor.

Without hesitation, she took her scissors and ripped open the centers of every embroidered flower.

CHAPTER

23

Several days later, Doctor John Swinburne was again holding a medical seminar in the large tent of the American Ambulance-Hospital near the Avenue de l'Imperatrice. The visiting doctors of French, English, and Swiss nationalities were quite impressed by the clean surroundings, and though the tents housed countless wounded soldiers all bedded in lines, they seemed in good spirits despite their wounds and amputated limbs.

He saw the horrified looks of the French doctors at the rolled-up canvas sides and the drafts that raced unhindered through the tents.

"We heat the ground," Swinburne explained, and showed the doctors the many small round iron stoves and coal fires in holes in the ground. But he knew they would not be convinced.

He allowed the surgeons to examine his patients, question them, and at the end of the afternoon explained that the modern equipment had been purchased from the Union Army by an American dentist-friend of the Empress Eugénie.

"It was rather a good purchase, wasn't it," an Englishman commented in rounded public-school tones, pausing at the tent's entrance.

Swinburne's ears delighted in the sound. "Yes," he said. "Why he bought the equipment, I've no idea, but thank God he did. You are . . ."

"Herbert," the gentleman with the whiskers said, "Doctor Alan Herbert, of the English Ambulance-Hospital, Doctor Swinburne."

"Delighted to meet you," Swinburne said, and shook the man's hand.

When the others had gone, Herbert commented further, saying, "The fresh air and the stoves in the ground are really quite a remarkable concept, Doctor."

"Yes, well, have you seen the conditions at the Grand Hotel?"

Herbert solemnly nodded. "It's quite like Dante's seven levels of hell, I think."

"Overcrowded, poor ventilation, infections rampant," Swinburne added.

"Have you a death-tent?"

"Yes," Swinburne said, "but it is, naturally, quite a distance away from our open-air wards."

Herbert nodded. "So many soldiers have been consigned to our hospital. We've been treating them, as well as my own countrymen who arrive for a variety of reasons. The same as you do here, I imagine, for your American countrymen."

Swinburne tilted his head. "I operated on an Englishman, not long ago."

"Here?" Herbert asked.

"No, at the Ecole de Médecine. I was assisting and demonstrating that day, Monday, I believe."

"What was the nature of the operation?"

"Bullet removal from the waist, disarticulation of the left knee, amputation of the left leg."

"How very sad," Herbert commented.

"He was a young man, thirty-four years old, quite handsome, too. Atherton-Moore was his name, I believe."

Herbert's eyes shot open. "Are you quite sure of that?"

"Yes, Edward Atherton-Moore, that was his name. Why?"

Herbert's brows knit into a frown. "No special reason. You say 'was.' Then the young man . . ."

"He'd already lost a great deal of blood prior to our surgery," Swinburne said quietly, "and owing to the expense of food these days, the people with him looked rather needy, if you take my meaning." He shook his head. "No, my feeling is that the young man has already died."

Herbert shook his head, then looked at the men in the tent. "What a waste," he said.

That night, Alan Herbert wrote to his elder brother, the Earl of Carnarvon, Patron of the British Charitable Fund which was helping to support the Britons in Paris. Herbert described, as he usually did, what he had seen that day, what had happened at the hospital, and then wrote about Doctor Swinburne and the surgery performed on the young man at the Ecole de Médecine.

"I trust you will inform the Duke of Middlesex of this sad business, and add my most sincere regrets."

He signed his letter, folded it, slipped it into the envelope and addressed it to his brother's London residence.

"Well?" Julienne asked nervously as Armand took off his coat.

He nodded wearily and handed a slender bottle to her, a bottle filled three-quarters full with a red liquid, sloshing slow and thick up the sides to the stopper. "It was," he breathed, "so very expensive." He sighed. "Four hundred francs."

Julienne shrugged. "No matter," she said, thinking it had cost four diamonds. "Can we buy more, should we need it?"

Armand shook his head. "The uh, 'gentleman,' told me this is the last of it, anywhere, at least in his opinion."

"How much do we give him?"

"I'm told we mix it with brandy. The taste is very strong. The 'gentleman' seemed rather proud that it is a very pure blend, whatever that means."

"Perhaps Stefan knows how much," Julienne mumbled and walked to the children's room.

She watched Edward sleep, pleased that they had managed to force an adequate amount of brandy down his throat. He moaned, a small haunting sound that lingered in her mind, and she wondered if it was from pain, or the drink, or because of a dream, if he dreamed. She'd held him in her arms most of that first night after she'd removed the diamonds from the petticoat. It was her family's way, she knew, holding him as he shivered, moaned, wiping the sweat from his forehead, praying and waiting for him to die or to live.

The moans were bearable, she thought, but the screams—she shuddered. What did it matter what the Laudanum cost, she thought, knowing she would have given all the diamonds to buy it and help him. She considered selling the remaining twelve diamonds now. The jeweler had been firm—one hundred francs each. He had apologized, but said she must blame it on the times. They were perfect stones, worth small fortunes, but, he had said, everyone was selling their jewels.

She looked at Edward. His face was drawn and the skin had a greyish cast to it. His cheeks and eyes seemed to have become hollow overnight. "Stefan," she said softly, and held up the bottle of Laudanum. "Do you know how much to give him?"

Stefan looked up and nodded.

"When?"

"When the brandy wears off," he answered quietly.

Edward slept for hours, but by two that afternoon, they heard the special drawn-out moan followed immediately by the full-throated high-pitched scream.

They ran into the room and Stefan grabbed Edward from behind. He had prepared the large glass of brandy and Laudanum a half-hour earlier, so it would be ready and they would not cause him needless agony.

Julienne knelt on the bed and with her left arm, tried to keep Edward's head still. "Edward," she said loudly, "Edward, don't fight us, please, for God's sake, drink it . . ." She tried to pour the drink into his mouth, watching as he screamed and sputtered and spit it out, jerking his head away as the brandy and Laudanum ran down his chin.

"Drink it," she said and forced it into his mouth.

He jerked his head away again, and tried to free his arms from Stefan's grip. "No," he coughed, fighting them, recognizing the taste. "NO, take it away, I don't want it, no, oh God in heaven my leg . . . my leg's on fire, for the love of God somebody help me," he screamed.

"Stefan, lean him back a little more," Julienne said loudly above the scream, holding the glass near Edward's lips.

Stefan, sitting behind a propped-up Edward, did as she asked.

She forced his mouth open and made him drink the Laudanum, ignoring the coughing and spitting and sputtering.

"NO," he shrieked, trying to spit it out again. "NO, GODDAMMIT, I don't want it, I . . . I'm afraid of this . . ."

"Um-ma-num? Um-ma-num," Julienne cooed into his ear, pained at his wild-eyed stare. "It's good for you, drink it, drink it . . ." She watched his fluttering eyelids and kept repeating the phrase "um-ma-num," as the dazed hot eyes seemed to calm at the sound.

"It . . . they . . . come back . . . no . . ."

He was sweating and shivering at the same time but he stopped resisting. There was a slight stream of the red liquid trickling down from the corner of his lips, but he finished the mixture as a child drinks milk. She wiped his cheek and his chin, then caressed the side of his face with her shaking hand.

He groaned.

Stefan held him and waited as the drug slowly began to take effect.

"They, they come back with it . . ."

"Who?" Stefan asked.

"They . . . Oh God, my leg. It hurts, it burns, do something, do . . ." His head began to flop slightly, his lips moved, but he made no sounds. His eyes opened, staring at nothing.

Stefan released his grip and set Edward back upon the pillows. "What was that you said?" he asked Julienne.

She shook her head. "Something from childhood, something his governess used to say to make him eat."

The taste lingered in Edward's mouth and burned all the way to his stomach and began to radiate out to every part of him. He felt dizzy and watched with open eyes as the room began to move and the fading sunlight grew brighter and sharper to a white solar heat.

He watched, fascinated, as Julienne began to melt away, and saw a face, walking from the wall, growing out of the papered stripes and hovering above him. "John?" he said. "John?" he repeated, feeling his jaw slacken, heavy with a weight, and lost all feeling in his body as he seemed to float, lighter than a feather in a wind.

Julienne sat down in the chair at the side of the bed and brought her nose to the bandaged stump and smelled it. "Nothing," she said to Stefan, relieved.

"That is encouraging," Stefan said, rolling up the sleeves of his shirt. Julienne changed the dressing on Edward's waist, then Stefan helped her remove the bandages on the stump.

It was an ugly, hideous sight, flaps of skin sewn over the remaining part of the knee, and though she swallowed hard every time she saw it, it did not stop her from touching him. She placed her hand lightly on the stump and watched Edward for a moment. He did not react. She pushed the stump slightly, and he did not even know it. Looking up at Stefan, she sighed, then nodded.

Stefan walked to the other side of the bed, listening to the steady stream of rambling English phrases. He knew some of the words, but they made little sense under the drug's powerful influence. "He is talkative today," Stefan commented, and began to knead the stump.

<hr>

He saw the cave, and in a drowning mist, the statue moved. The three faces moved all at once. Shiva. Destroyer. Giver of death. The voice came from somewhere else. Famine. Famine in the Northeast Province of Madras.

Sherringham's face appeared, then grew a body, but he was a transparent phantom, not a man. "It is strictly volunteer, Neddy. I must go. They've been starving for nearly a year and we've only just heard of it now."

The trees behind him burned brown and shriveled to scrub, and the lawns washed to the brown dust of the road.

"Tupakulanu bhujamula-pai pattandi . . ." The Indian troop commander, Subedar Mohan Dubashi, called out, his skin forming from the dust and the blue turban swirling from the sky as the troops shouldered their arms, beginning to march again.

"Damn this place," Sherringham said. His eyes were large and the heat wrinkles in the corners were caked with dust. "Ten months before we knew. Ten months of suffering before anyone knew . . . it's so big a country no one knows anything until it's too damn late."

"Easy now," Edward said, suddenly appearing next to him.

"That old man, Ganesh Chaterjee, I hope he's still alive . . . he's probably rotting somewhere, in that Godforsaken province, separated from the rest of the world with no roads to reach it, no inland water-routes to service it . . . what skill that Indian man has, what talent, to make such beautiful musical instruments, I must try to help him, I must . . ."

But the words were fading in the heat haze and the damp. The column of volunteer Indian and British from Madras escorted the convoy of food supplies that stretched for miles ahead and behind them. The inland climb grew steeper and more congested by the growth of the trees and vegetation, isolating them further from the world.

In the burning vapor of oasis dreams, it was the smell that told them they were near. Three months of dust, and damp musky smells from smothering forests abruptly changed as the sky went black with heavy smoke in the sun's full heat at midday. Funeral pyres of bodies stacked like sacrificial logs against pestilence.

The devils were loosed by the Laudanum, and faces long buried yet forever imprinted on his mind, cracked free. The village . . . flies in thick black masses made a wall over the huts . . . the smell was of the last to die, corrupting where they had fallen in the streets. Liniment-soaked linen was tied over his nose and mouth, but the stench filtered through. They dug shallow trenches for mass graves. Half-dead women sat in the shade of their huts holding skeletal babies in their arms, babies who no longer had the strength to suckle empty breasts . . .

Edward knelt and gave his water canteen to a woman, watching as she pushed it away from her own mouth and held it for her child. The woman's tiny hand poured the water, but it made a pool and dribbled out of the child's open mouth, toothless because of starvation.

Her large, staring, melting eyes grew to white, and in the white, black silhouettes with large wings riding the heat currents in a lazy patient pattern, circling, circling, lower, lower, vultures . . .

∽

Stefan ran to the bedroom when he heard the first scream, and in the lamplight near the bed, saw Edward's arms beating at the air above him.

"Should we give him more?" Julienne asked, wiping the pouring sweat from Edward's face. His body was soaked and the nightshirt had become a drenched second-skin.

"No," Stefan answered, seeing the still-dazed eyes with the large black pupils staring at a point on the ceiling. "Edward," he shouted, "Edward . . ."

There was no answer. He wept, moaned, and continued to babble uncontrollably in English.

His swinging fists grew more frantic and panic-stricken. He was so terrified, he tried to get up from the bed. Stefan had to straddle him to keep him still. Then, slowly, whatever the torment was, it passed. Exhausted, gasping, he grew quiet again.

∽

The moneylender. A broken-toothed smile floated from the corner of his hut. "I did not hear any word from you, Lāt Sahib. You were away, far away, and I thought you had died. I reported my troubles to your Colonel, Lāt Sahib. Your debt to me was very large."

The rain made grey walls of light across the compound, but the people were made of dust, gone and blown away in the fragment of a moment . . .

"It wasn't my fault," Sherringham said. "You believe that, don't you? I borrowed from the moneylender and the others only to help the men. They needed . . ."

"You silly puppy," Edward slurred as he fell against the base of a tree in the forest. "I know that. You haven't a dishonest bone in you. I know the truth."

"Why'd you do that? Why did you resign as well?"

"Because you're my friend, that's why . . ."

Sherringham pulled him up and draped him across his lap. "You throw away the only dream you've ever had—for me?"

" 'Tisn't a dream any longer," he shook his head. "It's a nightmare."

Sherringham held out his linen handkerchief to the rain, and when it was wet, began to wipe the mud from Edward's face, tracing the handkerchief over the high cheekbones, around the mouth and the jawline, gently, kindly. Then, supporting the wide shoulders with his left arm, drew Edward closer and kissed the slightly parted lips in a tender embrace. "I've always loved you," he said, the voice faraway. "Forgive me, this," he said. "I had to speak it, just once. I'm tired, Neddy. I'm tired of being different, of never belonging. It . . . it doesn't matter anymore. Nothing does. I know you'll forgive me. You're the only one who ever could . . ."

He turned the face toward the crook of his arm to protect him from the invisible rain.

∾

Julienne heard him stir and slipped out from under the covers of Gisèle's bed as slowly as possible so the child would not wake.

The scandal followed him, Edward thought numbly, as a shadow crossed in front of the oil-lamp next to him. It followed him to London, Edward thought, and his father; consorting with Indians, a supposedly "ignored" debt to a moneylender—against regulations to borrow from Indian moneylenders— and he borrowed from other officers—such "bad form." It didn't matter that we *replaced* the money by selling our commissions, no, it made no difference. In London, John gave up a little bit more every day. He knew it was just a question of time. He was looking for a moment in which to die. I suppose I've always known, yet never allowed myself to know that particular truth. Edward felt a weight next to him on his right in the small bed, as cool dry hands wiped his face and cradled his head. He felt trapped within a drowning body, and fought the drooping eyelids, listening to the rhythmic heartbeat in between soft breasts. I couldn't help him, Edward thought. I didn't know how to help him. John, he thought, I'm sorry . . . I, too, am very tired . . .

"Sleep, Edward," Julienne whispered. "It's best. It will help you to live."

"What for," he answered, and closed his eyes.

For two weeks, they fed Edward whilst he was drunk. They made him soup, and ground the meat down to the smallest of slivers. Cécile had found a pottery feeder in one of the wicker baskets in the cellar, a large cup with a handle and spout that she had used for her children when they were small. It worked very well and Edward was little more than a child anyway when he was drunk.

When the Laudanum was gone, they went back to large doses of brandy. He had stopped screaming though still had a great deal of pain. Julienne knew he would be in pain for quite some time. It is natural, Julienne thought, but what settled in place of the screams was worse.

349

He barely spoke, and spent most of his partly drunk hours just staring at the wall. He had never once looked toward his left knee and seemed to avoid it at all cost. They bathed him daily, shaved him, changed his position in the bed, powdered his back first with cornstarch and when that was gone, rice face powder to keep him dry and to prevent bedsores. He never resisted, and he never helped.

He had become a shell, as lifeless and pliable as one of Gisèle's rag-dolls. When Frédéric returned from school each day, he went to Edward's bed, held him, and stayed next to him as long as he could. Edward stroked the blond hair for hours, not speaking, never looking anywhere but at the wall, just touching the boy. It was the same with Gisèle each morning.

It grew worse by the end of November. He woke in the nights, startled and frightened, yet would not speak. Now, not even the children could comfort him.

Cécile had remembered a drink her grandmother used to make when the children were ill. A large cup of milk, with a raw egg mixed in, a touch of sugar and this was laced with brandy. It was very good, she had said, and most nutritious.

The ingredients were expensive and rare, but they were searching the black market for food and supplementing their rations by buying additional meat, or chickens, or goat's milk from the poor farmers who had come from the provinces and were now forced to sell their products for a high price on the streets in order to survive.

One sleety wet day at the end of November, Julienne brought him the mixture. "Here," she smiled, "drink this. It's good for you."

He shook his head and looked away.

She sat down next to him. "Edward, we made this especially for you. The least you can do is drink it."

He did not answer.

She brought it to his lips, but he jerked his head away and did not even bother to wipe the trickle from his chin.

Julienne looked at the large cup for a moment, then smacked it down on the wooden table near the oil-lamp, spilling some of the precious liquid on the tabletop. "Shame on you," she said. "Armand and I spent most of the morning, in the sleet, trying to find anyone selling milk and eggs. We were cold, and tired, and wet, but we did it for you, Edward. You make me feel like some sort of poisoner."

"Give it to the children," he said quietly.

"It isn't for them, it's for you," she snapped.

He shook his head and pursed his lips for spite.

"You don't want it? Then I've other plans for it," she said and quickly got up from the bed, knelt down and pulled out the chamber pot. "If you don't want it, we'll throw it away, we'll *waste* it . . ." and she grabbed the cup to pour its contents into the chamber pot.

His eyes widened. "NO, don't do that, don't waste it, don't," he said and reached for her wrist.

"Then drink it," she answered firmly, watching his eyes fill.

"How can you do this to me?"

"Because I love you," she answered, her voice straining, "and I will *not* help you to die." She put the chamber pot down and stood there, holding the cup out to him. When he didn't reach for it, she said, "I'm warning you, for the last time, take it, or I'll throw it away."

He took the cup, held it for a long moment, then narrowed his eyes in a mean stare as he drank the warm milk.

"Thank you," Julienne answered, seeing him gag, and pulled the empty cup from his hands.

"Why don't you leave me alone and stop bothering me with all this nonsense," he snapped.

"Nonsense," she countered, her voice getting louder, "I'm sick to death of you. You tell Frédéric this is nonsense. You lie to him that you're getting better, you wipe his eyes when he has nightmares about seeing you shot and cries every morning because he is afraid you won't be alive when he comes home from school. You shameful, selfish man," she yelled, and slammed the bedroom door on her way out, storming past an open-mouthed Stefan in the salon and again slammed the door out of the apartment.

She bounded down the stairs to the second floor and met Armand coming out of his apartment.

". . . then complain to them and not to me," he said in a loud voice. He bumped into Julienne. "You talk to her, I cannot," he said, and left her standing there as he took his rag and bottle of oil and went to calm his nerves by polishing the banister.

All the world is irritable today, Julienne thought and found Cécile crying in the kitchen.

"What are you doing here, you leave him all alone?" she said, wiping her eyes.

"It will do him good," Julienne said in a starchy voice. "He makes me so angry I could scream. I'm sick of begging him to eat, arguing with people on the streets, waiting on queues, the weather, the world, everything ought to be swallowed into the earth to give me a moment of peace and quiet." She saw the large bowl filled with cloudy water and a piece of meat soaking in it. "Why are you crying and what is that?"

"That is the reason," Cécile whimpered.

"What is it?"

"A very good question," she said, staring at the meat. "It is the government's latest idea," she sneered, poking the meat with a fork. "Salted meat. Well, they've done such a splendid job of salting it, I cannot remove the salt. I have tried since last night, soaking it, again and again and again, and it is *still* grey with salt. Look at the hateful thing!"

"What kind of meat is it?"

Cécile looked at her. "I haven't the slightest idea," she answered. "Would you like a little wine?"

"Yes, thank you," Julienne said, shaking her head at the sight of the discolored meat. She followed Cécile into the salon and then slumped into a chair. "God help us all," she sighed, "it is impossible." She took the wine glass from Cécile, clinked her glass against Cécile's glass, then took a long sip.

Cécile sat down. "We cannot go on like this," she said quietly. "Armand is right. They are all swine. Armistice, no armistice, back and forth like a swing, and all night we hear the cannons thudding from the provinces. Armand says they have reduced the coal rations—again."

Julienne felt her blood boil, and shook her head. "What will you do for tonight, Cécile?"

She shrugged.

"Why don't we combine what we have," Julienne said. "I still have a little of the chicken from yesterday, and potatoes . . ."

"I have some rice and a few carrots," Cécile said, "and a tin of beef—they *say* it is beef, but I wouldn't believe them now if they swore before Almighty God that it was beef."

"At the very least," Julienne continued, "it will be filling. And that is something to consider."

"Are you sure of this, though? Is there enough for all of us, for the children?"

Julienne shrugged. "We worked together to buy meat and vegetables before. What difference is there in cooking together now, and making a large stew of something to feed all of us?"

Cécile studied her wine glass, then sighed. "I must think about this," she said. "It is generous of . . ."

"Tut," Julienne interrupted. "We are a family. You said that to me and I believed you. Then, we must *be* a family, and work together for the family's survival."

Cécile smiled. "I shall speak with Armand."

Edward looked around the children's small room, the angry words still hurting and lingering, hurting more than the pulling and itching pain from his leg. Leg, he thought miserably, what leg, and began to cry, seeing the dolls he'd bought for Gsèle, arranged neatly on the small bureau. And Frédéric's kaleidoscope, in the leather box, open with the top leaning against the wall. He wept, frustrated and guilty, tired and in pain. Drinking milk when they had none, he thought, eating food I have not helped to buy. Goddamned useless, he thought. His hands shook and he felt cold. Drawing the blankets up to his chin, he shivered under them and looked now at the bandaged stump resting on the pillows. A cripple, he thought, closing his eyes and wanting so very much to die.

"Does it hurt?" Gisèle asked from the doorway, her lips trembling.

He looked, then nodded, watching as she walked timidly into the room, gave a quick glance to the stump, then looked at him with sad eyes as big fat tears rolled down her pale and thinning cheeks.

She kissed her doll's forehead, then said, "Here, you may hold Marie."

His throat pulled when he tried to smile, but he tried. Then, he brushed his cheeks dry with the flat of his hand. "I'd, I'd much prefer to hold you," he said, and let her crawl under the blankets with him after she had taken off her shoes.

She cuddled and curled into his side, then lifted her head above the blankets and made a face at the stump.

"Horrible, isn't it?" Edward said, staring at the opposite wall.

She propped herself up on his chest and looked him in the eyes. "Will it grow back someday?"

Innocence, he thought, then slowly shook his head.

"Gone?"

He gave a nod.

"Will it always hurt so much?"

He managed a small shrug. "Let's not talk about it," he said and kissed her chin.

"Will you tell me a story?"

"I, I can't think of one just now."

"Why not?"

"Gisèle, please," he said quietly, "you ask far too many questions."

"Do you want to sleep?"

"Yes."

"Then I will tell you a story, Papa," she said, and held him with her small arms around his neck and partway across his chest, weaving some fantastic childhood tale of knights and horses and magical kingdoms with no thundering in the distance.

Edward listened to her voice and somehow, in the darkness of his closed eyes, felt smaller than she, feeling safe and comforted in the grip of the tiny hands that were warm and sweet and gentle.

Later, Julienne found them, and it gave her an idea. That evening, when she prepared the warm milk drink again, she sent it in with Gisèle.

The child carried it in with great care, and then sat down on the edge of the bed. "Mama said," she smiled, "that I must give this to you and stay here to make sure you drink it all. It's good for you and will make you feel better."

Edward's eyes narrowed and began to blaze. "Put it down, right here on the table, and ask your mother to come to me, but you wait in the salon."

She did as she was told and disappeared.

Goddamn that woman, Edward thought in a fury.

Gisèle returned a moment later. "Mama says she won't come in until I bring her the empty cup."

He stared at the child, grabbed the cup, swallowed all of the drink, gagged, and gave it to Gisèle's waiting hand. She scampered out, happy and delighted.

Edward propped himself up on his elbows, feeling the sudden pain in his leg but too angry to care. The smug look in Julienne's eyes enraged him. "Never do that to me again," he breathed. "You cruel, hateful woman. That was contemptible, do you hear, absolutely contemptible. I shall hate you for that for the rest of my life."

"Good," she answered. "Nurture that hate, for a very long life."

"You think you've won, don't you, of course you think that. You think you'll shame me into drinking that, that *thing*," he spit out with narrowed eyes. "You haven't won, Madame," he sneered, "I shan't drink it ever again."

'Then *you* will tell Gisèle why you want to die."

"I hate you," he whispered, flopping back on the pillows.

Julienne closed the door and stepped closer to the bed, looking down at him with hurt eyes, seeing his own pained expression and his angry eyes staring hotly at the wall. She sat down next to him.

"Don't touch me," he snapped, pushing her arms away. When she put them back, he smacked them away harder, but she grabbed the sides of his face and made him look at her, feeling the vise-like grip of his hands on her shoulders trying to push her away.

"Why do you hate me?" she asked quietly.

His eyes filled. "What do you *want* of me?" he cried. "Do you think me deaf? Goddamn you, even when you get me drunk I hear them. I hear them at table . . . what is it? I don't like it, I won't eat it. I'm not blind, either, Julienne. Look at you, for God's sake," he grabbed her face and pinched her cheeks together with his right hand. "Your face, Gisèle's, Frédéric's, Stefan's, all of you, thinner, all your eyes so big and staring . . ." He let go and then loosened his hold on her shoulders. "Give it up," he said. "I should have died long ago," he added, tears spilling down his thin, ashen cheeks.

She shook her head at him and wiped her own eyes. "I, I never realized before, just how selfish you truly are."

"How selfish *I* am?"

"Yes, you."

"I told you once I'd seen famine," he swallowed. "All their eyes have come back to haunt me. I see them, every night, all those children, thousands and thousands of people . . . we, we tried to help them, we tried to bring food to them, but by the time we'd arrived one quarter of the province had died of starvation . . . My God," he wept, "how can you do this to me, none of us could eat a thing when we were there, none of us. I couldn't put food in my mouth whilst strangers died in front of my eyes and you expect me to steal food from the mouths of my children, Goddamn you," he breathed, "Let me die . . ."

"How kind of you, Edward, to choose to die, and leave your wife and two children to face hardships all alone. How noble you are, to desert us when we need you the most."

"Stop it," he said. "It isn't like that at all." He took a breath. "I'm, I'm a burden, a useless mouth, useless," his lips trembled. "Nothing more than a helpless child."

"Why, because they cut off part of your leg to save your life?"

"YES," he shrieked, and felt a convulsive shiver close his throat. He stared for a long time at the wall. "You don't understand, it didn't happen to you. You can't feel the bullet shattering the bone all over again, day after day, and you aren't frightened by the dreams . . ."

She moved closer to him, wrapped her arms around him and drew him to her. "What dreams?"

"I, I dream about it," he said, eyes wide, shoulders shaking. "I dream, I dream about dancing, I dream about running, but the leg grows shorter and

354

shorter, and everyone is watching—Philippe, John, my brother, everyone, even you, people all around me watch it grow shorter and shorter, then I start to fall, and no one helps me to stand up . . .”

“Why did you never speak of this before?” she asked quietly, gently rocking him back and forth.

He shook his head. “It seemed too silly. I’m not a child. My nightmares belong to me, and they are so unimportant when my children cry and carry on at table because they are hungry and won’t eat the food you give them.”

She caressed the back of his neck. “I’ve had my nightmares, too, Edward.”

He looked up at her and brushed her cheek with his hand. “That life is gone. He will never hurt you again, Julienne.”

“I don’t dream about Franz,” she said. “I dream about you.”

“I don’t understand.”

She looked into his eyes. “I crawl into Gisèle’s bed and watch you breathe. For the first few nights, I sat by your bed forcing myself to stay awake because I thought, if I closed my eyes for just a moment, you wouldn’t be alive when I opened them. I was so frightened, I kept poking you, to make sure you were breathing, because the light kept playing tricks on my eyes. Half the time I wasn’t sure, so I listened to your heart beating, and tried to hear only your heart instead of my own. They told me you would die. They told me that, to expect the worst, and everything they told us to do for you always had the phrase ‘should he live . . .’ My nightmares are different now. It is a deadly emptiness, and I wander in a terrible place, lost, without you. You’re not the only one of us who has bad dreams . . .”

“I didn’t know,” he said quietly.

“No one does,” she replied. “It is my private cross.”

He tried to sit up, but felt a wave of dizziness and had to lie down again. “It is hopeless,” he whispered.

“Only if you let it become so,” she said. “This is the burden,” she said, giving a tired wave to the air, “not you. Trying to manage alone, think and plan alone, trying to be everything to everyone, *that* is the burden, Edward. I could manage before you came into our lives, because I had to, but not now. We need you, but you won’t believe this, will you? Only you can ease the burden, but you don’t want to help, do you?”

“How can I when I’m not even able to sit up?”

Julienne shook her head. “I don’t know, but I’m tired of fighting all the world for every single breath and every miserable scrap of food we’re able to find.” She unwound his arms from her and left the room quietly.

She went for a walk to calm herself and to escape the heavy pall for just a little while. The rainy sleet had stopped, and though it was cold, the crisp air had a reviving effect upon her. She walked in the twilight toward the Jardin du Luxembourg, her favorite place, and saw in her mind that winter’s day, and a shadowy picture of Gisèle being lifted by a tall, smiling Englishman, determined to carry on a conversation.

The flocks had long since disappeared, and it was a silent testament to passing time and growing hunger within the barricaded city. Many of the magnificent trees still held some of their autumn leaves, brightly colored patches in daylight that moved with the wind but now, dark and gloomy splotches against a pewter-grey sky.

It began to rain again, a cold winter's rain, and Julienne went home in the dark to help Cécile with what little energy she still possessed. They combined what they had into some sort of stew, and covered the whole thing with wine.

When it came to warming the milk for Edward, she did it, and wordlessly placed it next to him on the table in the room.

"Just a moment," he said, and then drained the cup. He held it out to her and when she grasped it, caressed her fingers with his own. "Next time, a little less brandy, please. I'm tired of being drunk."

Later that night, Julienne and Stefan counted the money again. He had come to Paris well-provided, he told her, but the majority of that money had been confiscated at the hotel. He only had two hundred francs left.

Edward's resources were better. The last of the money given by Philippe totaled eleven hundred francs. The carriages were useless and were abandoned at the stables. The horses, including the pony, had been commandeered by the government. Vouchers were given and promises made that they would be replaced at the end of the war. Julienne had the black thought that they'd been slaughtered and eaten in order to help fill the Government's quota of five hundred horses per day.

Stefan had advised her to sell the remaining nine diamonds at whatever price she could get. The price at the beginning of November had been a pitiful one hundred francs per stone. That had dropped quickly to fifty francs, and it was at that price she sold them, adding only 450 francs to their total of 1,750 francs. The pearls were held in reserve.

"It isn't very much, is it?" Stefan observed quietly.

"Not when eggs are twenty-four francs a dozen, when and if we can find them."

He tapped the pencil on the paper. "What do we spend each week for food?"

"It varies, Stefan," she shrugged. "Prices change every day. Let us say, twenty-five francs for a chicken, fifteen francs for a bushel of potatoes, four francs per cabbage . . . I cannot give you definite amounts for each week because it varies both in price and in what we find."

"And bread and wine," he said. "We'll approximate. We'll say sixty francs per week . . ." He worked it out and said, "It should last us twenty-eight weeks, or roughly seven months. God, what a grim thought, living like this seven months from now . . ."

"You're forgetting the coal, and the cost of lamp oil, and candles, and what if the prices rise again, which I am sure they will, and the rent, or if by some miracle we find butter and cheese. The last price for cheese was twenty-five francs a pound, Stefan."

"This conversation has made me delirious with joy," he quipped, then said more seriously, "You have many valid points. At the very least, it's a start. We have a fixed amount with no other resources available to us. Pity about the diamonds. Ordinarily, they would have lasted you for years."

"That was the general idea," she smiled, then shrugged. "We must do what we must do . . ."

A grey rain pelted the stained-glass windows of the House of Lords at the end of November. The Duke of Middlesex and his peers listened quietly to the latest report of the war raging in France. So many long months ago, at the onset, the Government had been decidedly pro-Prussian, distrusting Louis Napoleon's motives and believing the declaration of war had itself been made on a trifling issue while so many governments were trying to defuse the situation.

That was lost in memory now, as journalists reported the daily tragedies in Paris: Tommy Bowles gave his version; a gentleman known only as the "Oxford Graduate" wrote what he saw; and a third man, Henry Labouchère, called himself the "Besieged Resident," because at one time he had been extremely unpopular with the Queen and he did not want his name to prejudice his reports. These three gentlemen, along with the Earl of Carnarvon and his younger brother, Doctor Alan Herbert, began to make the Government wonder about the confusing situation.

Had Bismarck, indeed, refused the offer of armistice? For what reason? Or had the French refused his offer? No one knew. The Duke thought them both reprehensible in light of the daily wagons with white flags being drawn through the streets of Paris collecting the bodies of citizen and soldier alike. Tommy Bowles often wrote of the daily funeral processions to the cemeteries, describing the terrible sight of men carrying the coffins of children on their shoulders.

The Duke shook his head and listened to the grim happenings in Paris. The death rate had risen sharply over the last two months. One expects that in a war, he thought, the men who die from their wounds, men killed outright in battle. But it was the remaining categories that disturbed him. Smallpox was reaching epidemic proportions, and more diseases of war would follow. It was the last category that made everyone pause, the one simply called "other," the polite euphemism for starvation. The French refused to recognize this, and denied to the world and themselves the hardship of the winter, the dwindling food supplies, and the resulting deaths. It was a despairing stalemate: no large amounts of relief could pass through the Prussian lines, and the gates of Paris were closed to the outside world. And one or both of the forces had refused an armistice.

An attendant opened the door and gave a note to the peer nearest him. It was passed along and finally given to the Duke of Middlesex.

"I must speak with you now," he read, "am waiting in the lobby, Shaftesbury."

The Duke wondered what his old friend had to say, and waited until the

Peer had finished speaking, then unobtrusively got up, walked toward the doors, turned and bowed to the Lord Chamberlain on the Woolsack, then went out beyond the bar into the Peers' Lobby.

He saw Shaftesbury, slightly wet from the rain. "Ashley?" the Duke said softly, "is something wrong?"

Shaftesbury took a breath, "Do me one kindness," he said. "Ask no questions and just let me take you home."

The eyes, the tone of voice, the drawn angular face made the Duke uneasy. "What's happened?"

"Richard, I beg you, this isn't the place."

"Tell me what's happened," the Duke insisted, his breathing beginning to quicken.

Shaftesbury looked around the deserted lobby. He knew he had no choice now. "Edward . . . " he said quietly, "Edward is believed dead." He saw the color drain from the Duke's face and helped his friend to the chair against the wall.

"How . . ." the Duke whispered hoarsely.

"He . . . he was shot in Paris."

The Duke's wide shoulders sagged and he collapsed in the chair, not even feeling his head bump against the wall behind him. Why is there no air, he thought vaguely, feeling his heart pounding in an unnatural rhythm. There is no air . . . "Paris?" he managed, watching Shaftesbury bend to him. "What did they do to my son?"

"Let me take you . . ."

"What did they do to him?" he repeated, as he rubbed his left forearm, feeling the pain now.

"Richard, please . . ."

The Duke shook his head as streams of perspiration dripped from his temples.

Good Lord, his skin is grey, Shaftesbury thought, then said to the stubborn man, "Carnarvon had a letter yesterday from his brother. He would have come to you himself, but he is ill, and asked me to help. I have the letter with me."

The Duke held out a shaking right hand, waiting until the folded letter was given him.

"It's the last page," Shaftesbury said.

The Duke read the words, then read them again. "My dear God, what did they do to my son . . ." He struggled to stand up, trying to breathe, soaked from the sweat glossing his whole body. There is no air, he thought, I can't breathe, I can't . . . He staggered from the Lobby, leaning against the walls and walked unsteadily toward the Law Lords' Corridor, trying to reach the staircase which would bring him to the river terrace one floor below. No air, I can't breathe, my son, he thought in a haze, my beautiful boy, my Edward, what have they done to you . . .

He thought he heard an agonized cry, and then no sound at all as the carpet in the hall bruised his cheek and he felt nothing except the radiating pain from his chest.

CHAPTER
24

The Prussians were advancing. In the dark streets, blackened without the lights of the gas-lamps, they heard the distant cannon-fire.

They were numbed by the routine of finding food, waiting on long queues and huddling against the bitter cold of December, the coldest December anyone could remember. Shock replaced the lethargy. On Sunday, December 11th, there was no bread.

After an hour's search, Julienne gave up. Well, she thought, at least we have a few pieces left from yesterday and they will be saved for the children to eat tomorrow morning. She returned to the apartment after having spent all morning trying to find oil for the lamps and pushing her way through crowds of women buying cabbages on the Boulevard St. Germain.

She found Stefan reading a newspaper to Edward.

"You're sitting up," she smiled to Edward from the doorway.

"Somewhat," he corrected with a grin.

"For how . . ."

"Nearly ten minutes," Stefan said proudly.

"And uncomfortably, too," Edward sighed. "I'm still dizzy, and nauseous."

"You must expect that, you know," Stefan reminded him. "You've been on your back for a long time. It will pass." He stood up and walked to the bed. "It is enough for today," he said, and eased Edward to his back once more.

"We will try again . . . later," Edward said.

"Maybe," Stefan replied.

Edward shook his head. "The longer I sit, the less dizzy I shall become, you said so yourself."

"Let's not do too much in one day," Stefan cautioned.

Edward did not answer, but looked at Julienne and asked, "How was it today?"

She shook her head. "No bread at all, hardly any lamp oil, no candles, a box of small carrots at the despicable price of two francs eighty centimes, three cabbages that I had to fight for," she paused. "Where are the children?"

"Out with Armand, why?" Edward asked.

"It's better if you don't know."

Edward propped himself up on his elbows and waited a moment until his head cleared. "What do you have in that basket?"

"A zoo animal?" Stefan asked with a steady voice and stare.

She shook her head. "It's . . . it's a dog," she shivered. "Jevelot's was empty by the time it was my turn . . . I . . . I had to buy it from a man on . . . on a little street."

Edward leaned back on the pillow and thought for a moment. He looked her straight in the eyes. "It isn't a dog. Call it anything you wish, and we'll lie with you."

"They'll never eat it," Julienne said.

Edward looked at Stefan. "If you must tie me to the chair, do it, and I swear, I shan't complain."

"You'll be dizzy," Stefan said.

"Bother that," Edward answered firmly. "I will do it, with—or without—your help."

"You probably would," Stefan commented. "The sofa might be better. If you pass out at table, that might frighten the children more, you know."

"The sofa it is," Edward answered, then looked at Julienne. "I imagine you and Cécile will disguise it as best you can."

She sighed. "They have become very suspicious of any heavily spiced meat . . . "

The dizziness had not passed, and though Edward's stomach turned slightly from sitting up, he steadied himself on the sofa and dipped his spoon into the soup-bowl set before him on the nightstand. He was balanced by pillows, and the left knee rested on top of the bedpillows, uncovered by the blanket draped across his lap.

"I don't like it," Gisèle said, sniffing at the soup-bowl.

"But of course you do," Julienne smiled. "You like lamb."

Edward watched her squirm around in her chair. "Gisèle," he called, "come sit with me and bring your bowl. We'll eat together."

Armand glanced quickly at Cécile, and then continued eating, smiling and pretending a grunt of approval, then drank his wine.

Julienne helped the child carry her dish t Edward's table.

She looked at Edward's bowl. "You . . . you haven't eaten it," the child pouted.

He sighed. "It is difficult for me to sit up for so long," he said calmly. "I'm just taking a rest, Gisèle."

Frédéric was only pushing the meat around the bowl, eating the beans and the reddish tomato stock.

"Pick up your spoon," Edward said, "and we'll eat it together."

She shook her head.

"It's . . . it's not a proper cassoulet," Cécile said nervously. "A proper cassoulet should have two layers of bread crumbs and . . ." she stopped trying to fill the silence.

Edward chewed thoughtfully. "It's very good," he said, "though I think it was an old lamb, a very old lamb," he said, seeing her smile just a touch. "You'll see for yourself how old and craggy a lamb it was . . ." Using his spoon, he dipped it into her bowl and brought it to her lips. "Taste the old craggy lamb, just for me."

She drew her head back from the spoon. "It . . . it has black things in it."

"Pepper," Edward explained.

"I don't like pepper."

"You did yesterday," he answered patiently, then said, "What about beans? You like beans, don't you, of course you do, everyone likes beans and I've seen you eat them thousands of times."

"Does it have black things on it?"

He inspected the spoon rather carefully for her benefit. "No. Not one black thing on it."

She inched closer, opened her mouth a fraction, then closed it immediately and wrinkled her nose. "It smells bad."

Edward brought it to his own nose and gave an exaggerated sniff. "It certainly does not smell bad. It smells just like lamb ought to smell."

She opened her mouth, took three beans off the spoon, tried to swallow and gagged a moment later. "No," she insisted, eyes beginning to well up, "it'll make me sick, I don't want to be sick . . ."

"Gisèle . . ."

"NO," she wailed.

He sighed and put the spoon down in his bowl, exhausted by the effort. "I shan't force you, then. Come here," he said and waved her closer, watching her step around the small table and cuddle next to him on the sofa. He wiped her eyes with his napkin, thinking for a time as he caressed the child. "Be a good girl, won't you, and bring me my wine."

She stood up and with two hands, picked up the wine glass, then gave it to him.

He took a drink, then winked secretly at her. "Would you like a little of my wine?" he grinned.

She gave a pouty nod.

He held the glass to her lips. "Just a little," he said, watching as she obeyed. He took a sip. "Have another," he said, "a good drink this time," watching her drink more of the red wine. He took the glass back and held her against his right side. "It is good, isn't it?" he asked softly, and felt her nod. "It makes one feel warm, doesn't it?" and felt her nod again.

He waited. She was small and thin and was used only to wine diluted by water. It would not take long for her to feel calm, perhaps sleepy. He unwound his arm from her, took the spoon and tried again, but she hid herself deeply against his side. Edward gave it up, wiped her eyes, then kissed her forehead. "You'll feel much better if you go to bed and lie down. Will you do that?"

She nodded.

"Try to sleep," he said quietly, then kissed her again before she left the salon. He looked at Julienne, and shook his head.

Frédéric had fared only slightly better. He'd eaten everything but the meat, having tasted two pieces of it and hated it. He, too, was given a moderate amount of undiluted wine to fill his stomach, warm him slightly, and help him to sleep.

Edward could bear the dizziness and the pain no longer. When he'd nearly finished his supper, he put the spoon down with a shaking hand and called out to Stefan for help. The two men carried him to his bed, and then Julienne and Cécile carefully adjusted his pillows and blankets. The room was cold, and they now had to shut the window against this most bitter winter.

"A noble effort," Julienne whispered to him.

"But a failed one, nonetheless. I'm sorry."

Julienne shook her head, then looked at Gisèle, who had fallen asleep on the other bed, still in her clothes. "I shan't wake her," Julienne said softly. "She's warmer this way."

The newspapers the following morning were filled with government denials of bread shortages and scoffings at the rumors of bread rationing. Sunday's misfortune, they claimed, was bad planning, nothing more. There was enough white flour in the city to keep Paris in bread for several months. When the white flour was gone, brown bread would be sold by the boulangeries.

Edward tossed the paper down. "Rubbish," he sneered at *Le Figaro*. With Stefan's help, he sat up again, hoping for twenty minutes this time before the dizziness and the pain became unbearable.

As the days wore on, the coaxings at table increased, and the tears and the gagging seemed interminable battles in themselves. In desperation, Julienne held Gisèle on her lap, cuddling her and feeding her like an infant and finally forcing the spoonfuls into the mouth, only to have the child vomit later.

It was an awful sight, watching Gisèle nibble a biteful here and there, but refusing to eat anything disguised with onions, sauces, and finally, any meat whatsoever.

But she liked eggs.

Julienne and Cécile, and then even Armand began searching for them, and they considered it a major triumph on the 19th of December when Julienne found a dozen eggs and paid the price without blinking an eye.

What does the cost matter, Julienne thought, pleased to see Gisèle scraping the sides of the soft-boiled egg. No one may put a price on this, to see my child eat without tears. She pushed her own egg-cup, untouched, to Gisèle. "I'm not hungry. You eat this," she said, her eyes filling as the thin child tapped with her spoon and broke the shell.

They heard the sound of the bugles at two o'clock in the morning on December 21st. The Army was mobilizing. At dawn, the forts that ringed Paris and protected the city opened fire on the Prussian Army.

The thudding kept up for most of the day and frightened Gisèle to pitiful screams. She clung to her mother's skirts, begging her not to go outside. The child calmed slightly when hidden under the blankets of Edward's bed.

Weary, Julienne carried the laundry basket down the Boulevard St. Michel. When she turned the corner off the main boulevard, she saw the old laundress, gazing up at the blue sign and shuttered windows. "Good morning, Madame Bédard," Julienne said.

The old woman barely nodded. "You have carried the laundry for nothing, Madame Atherton-Moore. I have only come here to say goodbye to my shop— the shop of my mother and my grandmother, my little corner of France."

"But why," Julienne began.

The old laundress lifted her chin. "Why," she repeated tonelessly. "There is no fat to make soap, so we cannot buy soap. And there is no fuel to heat the water or the irons." She looked at her shop, at the door, at the windows and saw that an inherited lifetime had been taken from her. "I have lived so long to see this happen," she said in a small voice. Then, she managed a proud smile. "Good luck to you, and the little ones," she said.

Julienne impulsively kissed both cheeks of the old laundress' wrinkled face. "And to you, Madame."

"Damn them," the old woman whispered with trembling lips. "They are damned for what they do . . ." She straightened her shoulders, walked down the street and turned the corner without ever looking back.

They began hoarding the soap they still possessed, and tried to find whatever little bars of it they could on the streets and in the alleyways of the fifth arrondissement.

In desperation, Julienne tried the Right Bank.

The jewelry shop on the Rue de Rivoli caught her eyes. She walked a little closer to it and stared at the elegantly feathered carcasses of three ducks spread on a black velvet cloth, eggs held in gold cups in a half-circle around them and the hand-lettered sign saying "Roast Goose—125 Francs."

She saw her reflection. I look ten years older, she thought, then closed her eyes. Papa, she thought, walking away from the jeweler's and sloshing through a deep puddle of slush that nearly covered her shoes, I'm tired all the time . . . my arms hurt when I carry the basket, and climbing the stairs takes so much effort I have to stop and catch my breath every single day . . .

Christmas, she thought, remembering a Vienna childhood with Roast Goose, many vegetables, sweets for dessert, hot coffee with thick dollops of cream, and the silver punch bowl with wine and apples on Christmas Eve and the brandied sugar lit by a taper that sent burning sweet droplets to the Wassail Bowl below it. And my father, smiling, singing, toasting the family and giving extra portions to his children, she thought sadly.

She crossed the Seine by Pont St. Michel and paused mid-way over the bridge, looking at the white ice and at the people living and dying on the Quai in their open-air homes. We were taught that hell was a crucible-fire without end, she thought, an ever-lasting heat that would burn but not devour us. No, she thought. Hell is cold and filled with hunger.

She managed to get home, tired, and out-of-breath from climbing the stairs. She threw her cloak onto the sofa and felt silly after doing it for it made her feel no better. She undid her wet shoes and curled her feet onto the sofa, digging them into the cushions to warm them and ease the tingling. Then, looking around the apartment and seeing the small stack of wood they conserved for the evening, she burst into tears.

"What's wrong?" Stefan asked.

She pushed him away. "Nothing," she snapped, still crying. "Leave me alone. I want to cry, I deserve to cry, and why shouldn't I? I hate everything, everyone, I'm tired, cold, my head is pounding and, at the same time, feels as if it is being squeezed together. All I want to do is scream, leave me alone."

He sat down next to her on the edge of the small sofa and waved a linen handkerchief in front of her nose. She grabbed it, blew her nose and wiped her eyes. "Better?" he asked.

"No."

He warmed her hands with his own, then left the sofa and poured her a small brandy. She took it without comment.

The depression did not ease as the day wore on, and later, after a second brandy, she still felt no better. The brandy seemed to heighten the sadness and she moped through dinner, barely eating and never speaking.

By half-past nine, everyone was in bed. And why not, she thought miserably, cuddling next to Gisèle. The streets are dark, the fire in the grate is out, we have no candles . . .

"Julienne?"

She turned her head in the dark. "I thought you were asleep."

"No," Edward whispered. "Come to bed."

"How," she asked sadly.

He tapped the right side of his bed. "Here. Mind the leg, though," he said, and swallowed a groan as he moved over toward the left.

After a moment, she crawled out, covered Gisèle, and walked to his right side, moving as gently as possible into his bed and wincing in pain for him as he gasped when the stump was jostled slightly by the weight of another person on the small mattress. "Are you all right?" she asked, stretching out beside him, holding him and beginning to feel warm for the first time that day.

"Are you?"

"What a question," she said.

He rubbed the small of her back and kissed her lightly on the forehead. "This mood of yours will pass."

"I certainly hope so."

"Hoping isn't enough, you must help it pass."

Julienne sighed. "Sometimes, I fear I am going mad."

"No," he answered. "You aren't."

"Hah," she said sarcastically, "if I tell you what I wanted to do this morning, you will think me unquestionably a madwoman."

"I'm listening."

She told him about the ducks and the Roast Goose, and the terrible sadness that overwhelmed her in a gigantic wave as she walked home, remembering past Christmases, and thought of this Christmas as a day of tears and their children hungry. "Edward, I swear if I had the money with me, I would have walked into his shop and bought the food, and felt no remorse in doing it."

"Then do it."

"How can I," she said, tears springing to her eyes. "The money is disappearing as fast as the food. It would be reckless, silly and selfish—to spend money just to make me feel better."

"It would make us all feel better. Do it."

"I can't," she said, and felt his hands on her chin.

"What difference can it make now?" He wiped her eyes with his thumbs, then said lightly, "I shouldn't buy the goose if I were you."

"Why?"

"It would be too vulgar," he chuckled.

She laughed slightly and it eased a pain inside, feeling a most intimate comfort from just being in his arms. "It's a hateful world, isn't it?"

He turned slightly in the bed. "Once, I would have agreed with you, but not now. Oh, sometimes, nature is vicious. The Indians had a saying— 'Whatever the gods wish, so it shall be . . .' but theirs was an acceptance of natural disasters. Hateful? No. The world isn't hateful. People may be hateful to one another, but the world isn't to blame. There is a difference, you know." He smiled in the dark. "My father would have been pleased to hear that observation from me."

"Why?"

"He used to say that. He used to say it was far too easy to blame the 'world' for the problems men have caused themselves. What was it now . . ." he said, thinking, "yes, I remember. He called it a 'flexibility of mind,' the ability to loosen the rigid constraints, to see a problem for what it was, and thereby the root of the problem. That, in turn, would show a way to solve it. He used to say a lot of things I never understood—or rather, things I didn't wish to understand."

There is no hate in his voice, she thought, amazed. "What brought this to mind?"

"The oddest thing happened this afternoon," he said calmly. "I can't explain it, I don't know why, but Gisèle was holding her doll and in my mind, I saw him. I think it is my first memory of him. Haven't thought of it for God knows how many years."

"What was it?" she asked, propping herself up on one elbow.

"Well, he's a very tall man, with great long legs and . . . I have it, it must have been the *way* she was holding the doll."

"What was it?" Julienne prodded, enthused for the first time in a long while.

"He used to hold me when I was very small. And make a sort of swing for me with his hands as the seat. And, I'd hold onto his arms and he'd swing me, back and forth, and then, toss me in the air and catch me. I could see it in my mind. Isn't that odd, to think of such a silly thing now?"

"I think it's wonderful." She traced her finger over his lips. "You're smiling," she said.

"I suppose I am," he grinned. "It gave me pleasure for just a moment. I imagine it was because everything was so good then, and I was so—innocent."

She noticed the change in his voice. "What does he look like?" she asked, hoping to keep Edward in a pleased, calm frame of mind.

365

"I'm told I resemble him, but I don't agree."

No, you wouldn't, she thought, wondering if he spoke the truth.

"He's tall, broad shoulders, a squarish sort of jaw. Not slender, but very solid in a muscular sort of way. At least, he was when he was younger."

"Dimples?"

"Yes, and dark hair, well, it's greying now."

"Blue eyes?"

"Yes."

She shook her head at him, hearing the physical description of both father and son. "Do you have a photograph-plate of him?"

"No."

She thought a moment. "Does he have one of you?"

"Yes, several in fact. When my dress uniform was finished, he had a photographer take pictures of me. I'd quite forgotten that. I thought it was all a great bother, but he was very insistent, and . . ."

"And what?"

"Nothing."

"That's not true. What were you going to say?"

He paused, then said, "It never occurred to me, then, that he wouldn't see me for years. I wanted to leave as fast as I could and live my dream of being in the Army. I never thought of him, not once. I . . . I don't know what to think anymore . . ."

She lay down and smiled. And I thought this day was lost . . .

"Are you quite sure you want to do this?" Julienne asked Cécile the following morning in front of the jeweler's shop.

She nodded, and sold her mother's brooch for thirty francs; Julienne sold Philippe's pearls for forty francs, and added that to the one hundred francs they had brought with them.

They bought a duck for forty-five francs and were pleased to discover the jeweler was selling butter for thirty-five francs a pound, so they bought a pound.

The thin jeweler with the grey frock-coat wrapped the butter in paper, saying, "If you are at all interested, I have chocolate bon-bons."

Julienne's eyes sparkled as her mouth watered slightly, knowing how much Gisèle and Frédéric loved bon-bons, even more than she did. "How much?" she asked.

"They are very expensive, Madame," he replied. "I sell them only by the pound."

"How much?" Cécile asked defiantly.

"One hundred francs."

Julienne did a fast calculation, and then undid the clasp of the gold chain holding the cross around her neck. "Will this do, Monsieur?"

"It will cost one hundred and . . ."

"Yes, I know. One hundred and eighty francs. We have one hundred and seventy francs, Monsieur."

He looked at the cross, touched it and found that it was still warm from her. "Gold, Madame," he began, "is worth very little these days. I, I am not a thief. In better times, the pearls and the brooch would have been worth much much more." He gave her back the cross. "I will not accept this. Not for the price of a bon-bon. Think of me with kindness at your Christmas dinner." He wrapped the bon-bons in a paper cone and placed them in the basket resting on the glass counter.

"Thank you," Julienne said.

He nodded, and lowered his eyes as they left the shop.

They walked back and crossed the Seine near Notre Dame and there, saw the sign posted on the great doors: "Owing to the scarcity of fuel, there will be no Midnight Mass on Christmas Eve."

"Even the Church has no candles," Cécile commented with a shake of her head. "Disgraceful."

Walking quietly up the Boulevard St. Michel, Cécile saw the make-shift counters and booths and shabby-looking vendors selling hand-crafted toys for children. "When I was young," she said quietly, "Christmas was so beautiful a time for us. When my children were young, Armand and I had such fun. We went to Mass on Christmas Eve, and came back to Le Reveillon—our special dinner of oysters and Roast Goose, salads, a special yule log cake and fruits and bon-bons . . . We sang, and the children placed their shoes by the fireplace, waiting for Père Noël. Armand," she sighed, "Armand could barely wait for them to go to bed. When they did, we laughed, and giggled and put little candies and fruits on the tree branches, next to the stars and little gifts. They were such happy times. It is all so different now."

Julienne nodded in a melancholy way. "My uncle used to dress up as St. Nicholas. We knew it was he, but we played the lovely pretend game. He would come to us on December 6th, St. Nicholas' Day. And someone else would dress up as the Devil. We had to tell 'St. Nicholas' if we had been good or bad, and if we were good he'd chase the Devil away and give us bon-bons and fruit. Then, on Christmas Eve, the monks would go from house to house, showing the Christ Child in the manger, and everyone would sing and join the torch-light procession to the Mass." She then told Cécile about the Wassail Bowl, and the family dinners on Christmas Eve and Christmas Day, and that they, too, had Roast Goose and special jellies and sweets. "We torment ourselves for nothing," Julienne sighed, "when we should be grateful for the duck."

"Yes," Cécile answered, following up the stairs of the apartment house. "You're quite right." She opened the door and they felt the chill from the unheated rooms. "Where is everyone?"

"In the cellar," Edward called from his bed.

"Ooh-lah, they leave him all alone," she complained to Julienne.

"I'm fine," Edward answered. "Did you buy it?"

"Yes," Julienne answered and walked to the door of his room.

"Wonderful," he smiled.

Armand and Stefan took turns sawing the doors which Armand had removed from the cellar and his apartment rooms. Both men were sweating, but it felt good to be able to do something to help.

367

"I still think," Stefan breathed heavily, "that we should have gleaned some of the wood from the trees being felled . . ." He stopped and wiped his brow. ". . . felled, on the boulevards."

Armand clucked his tongue. "It will not burn—it is green wood and will only smoke," he said. "There is a terrible surprise waiting for those people. We will do much better this way: the doors, the chairs, bits of fences, old wood, Stefan. Dead wood. This will burn."

"Yes, but for how long?" Stefan asked, wearily handing the saw to Armand, and then flexing his hands, smarting and aching from the effort.

Armand shrugged. "How long?" he repeated. "It will last long enough to keep us warm for a few days until the wood merchants open their doors, the swine." He began to saw the door again, long strokes with powerful arms.

"And if they don't?" Stefan asked. "What then?"

"I have already thought of that," Armand said by way of an answer, then went back to concentrating on sawing the heavy door from his bedroom into foot-wide strips.

After Mass, as snow fell again on Paris, the smell filtered and drifted through the apartment in a slow, teasing, mouth-watering glory. Although they all had grown thinner, they dressed in their finest clothes. Julienne's dress seemed much too large now, so she tied a sash about the waist to girdle the material.

They had cut most of the left leg from a pair of Edward's trousers and he, too, sat at table for this dinner. He willed himself to ignore the discomfort. Julienne had tried to encourage him to sit on the sofa, but he was determined and had made up his mind to sit with the family and would not be swayed.

No one could speak. Real butter, a tasty duck, some glazed vegetables, wine . . . they savored each and every mouthful trying to make the tastes linger and last, but like all good things, it was finished much too soon.

The bon-bons were marvelous, and Cécile indelicately licked her thumb where some of the chocolate had melted. She blushed. "I do apologize," she smiled, "but I don't care."

"My love," Armand chuckled, "we have all licked our fingers."

"Then I do not apologize," she smiled.

Frédéric had been given a book by Père Noël, and Gisèle found a small hand-carved doll with painted features and black horsehair glued to the head. The little dress had been made from a piece of Julienne's petticoat.

Edward had been sitting for nearly an hour, but the pain began to throb and was not dulled by the wine. Armand and Stefan carried him back to bed and helped him to lie down.

Armand hesitated by the door, then decided to stay and shut the bedroom door. "I . . . I have been wanting to speak with you for some time," he began, "but I did not know if it would be an intrusion."

Edward looked at him. "Say anything you wish," he said simply. "There is nothing secret or unapproachable between us, Armand, not anymore," he smiled.

Armand nodded thoughtfully, then dragged a chair to the left side of the bed. He sat down near the bandaged stump. "It is about this," he said, and jutted his chin toward the stump.

"It hurts," Edward said. "All the time."

"What will you do about it?" Armand asked in a delicate way.

"Nothing," Edward shrugged. "Gisèle still believes it will grow back," he smiled, but it was a hollow grin.

"It can," Armand replied gently, eyeing Edward, "in a manner of speaking."

Edward frowned at him. "What do you mean—a peg?" He sighed nervously, then quickly shook his head. "No. Never."

Armand's eyes remained in a stare. "Tell me something. How much do you want to walk?"

"What a question. I'll never be able to walk."

"So you want to spend the rest of your life on your back and have people carry you until you are old and feeble-minded?"

"No, of course not."

"Well?"

Edward shook his head. "I don't want to think about that. It's, it's too horrible."

"What is horrible about standing up, walking, going where you want, when you want?" Armand asked. "What does it matter how or by what means, except that you are able to do it?" The expression had changed, and Armand could see that Edward was thinking it over, eyeing the stump, looking away, wondering. "I have given this much thought," Armand continued. "I have seen soldiers on the streets, the wounded, and men with pegs, walking. If they may do it, why not you?"

Edward glanced at the stump. "The pain . . ."

"I see no pain on their faces," Armand said. "It must go away, eventually."

Edward sighed.

"Look, I will show you," he said, and pulled a slip of paper from his pocket. "I am not an artist so pay little attention to my poor drawing. You see, at the top, rounded like a deep bowl, but more narrow at the bottom. In here, we will put a cushion, something soft, with lambswool or goosedown from a pillow. Soft and pliable. When I see those others on the street, do you know what I notice?"

Edward shook his head.

"It is the crutch they use. Only one crutch and it makes them walk in a strange way. It isn't balanced. I learned as a carpenter, that all things must balance. I don't like the way they walk, so I thought of something else. Two walking-sticks, you see, look," he said, tapping the paper with his fingers. "You are young, strong, and tall. Perhaps the crutch does not look so peculiar on a smaller man, but on you . . ." he shook his head. "It would look strange, uneven. However," he smiled, "two sticks, with very large flat thick handles to fit your hands exactly, ah, they would hold you."

Edward studied the paper with the thin pencil lines, trying to imagine it. "Where would you buy such things?"

369

"Buy?" Armand shook his head. "I will make them. And I will make them to fit you." He took the paper from Edward's hands. "But only if you are interested and will really try. Otherwise, we burn the wood like all the rest, in the stove."

"How will it stay on?" Edward swallowed.

"I have thought of that, too," Armand smiled. "The bowl, you remember, snug, tight like a leather riding glove to fit the size of the . . ." he waved toward the knee.

"The stump," Edward said.

"Yes. And, and perhaps straps, in loops, to tie about your thigh or your waist. I don't know that, yet. I have never made anything like this before. It is a challenge. I think, and then I invent as I go along."

"It might work," Edward said.

"Ahhh," Armand chuckled, "so you are interested and wish to try, uhn?"

Edward nodded. "You'll need some strong wood."

"I have it already," Armand answered.

Edward studied the expression on Armand's face, the calm resolve in the eyes that had already made a decision. "Where will it come from?"

Armand shrugged. "The last supply."

Edward paused, then said what he suspected from the first. "The banister."

Armand nodded.

"It isn't fair," Edward said quietly.

"How much of life is fair?" Armand answered, and when the sad blue eyes looked at him, he smiled easily. "If it helps you to walk, I shall be satisfied. I will always have in my memory, the pleasure of those days with my son in making our banister. But now, I will have a second pleasure, too. It will be good to know that a small part of that banister was not burned for fuel, and was given to the living. It gives me hope to know it will last beyond these terrible days."

On the 28th of December, they read that the Prussians were shelling the Avron Plateau just east of Paris. The shells were reducing the village to rubble. It was abandoned by the French on the 29th, the day the two young elephants, Castor and Pollux, were slaughtered in the zoo and were sold for forty francs a pound.

The first week of the New Year, 1871, was quiet and cold. Then, on a placid grey morning at ten past eight, Thursday, January fifth, came the howl.

It pierced the air in a scream all its own whilst Julienne was standing, half-asleep on the queue at Jevelot's.

The queue scattered and everyone flattened themselves against the building as the first Prussian shell exploded a few blocks away.

Gisèle ran from room to room shrieking and wild-eyed, the nightdress clinging about her ankles as she tried to find a safe place to hide. She had heard the cannon-fire, far away, for nearly two months, but now the whistling and the howling were on top of them, the explosions on the streets near them. She collided with her Uncle, then pushed away from him and ran to Edward's bed screaming into his arms.

"I'm going out," Stefan said, half-dressed, from the doorway.

"Don't worry about me," Edward said quickly, "Frédéric and . . ."

"He can't have got far," Stefan answered and left to finish dressing.

The boy dropped his books on the street and ran back to the apartment house, shivering and shaking all the way up the stairs. He did not even stop to shut the door to the salon and ran straight to Edward. "Mama," he breathed anxiously, "where's Mama . . ." He flattened himself against the window searching the street.

"Get away from there!" Edward yelled and tried to reach the boy with his arm. "STEFAN!" he shouted, and tried again to grab Frédéric.

Stefan hauled the boy, kicking and screaming, away from the window and set him down on the floor on the other side of Edward's bed as an explosion rocked the building itself. "Stay there," he said to Frédéric, then pulled a woolen blanket from the other bed and covered the three of them to protect them from the window should it shatter. "I'm leaving now," he said, and a moment later Edward heard the hallway door slam shut.

Black smoke mixed with grey smoke and the dust of crumbling buildings as the whine of shells continued overhead. Stefan saw Army Corpsmen running in all directions, in and out of the dust clouds settling on the streets as they searched for the injured. People crowded in doorways and watched the shells flying and diving in the air.

He saw the size of the enormous shells and had the fleeting thought that the Krupp Foundry had improved on the guns used against the Austrian Army nearly four and half years ago.

Three blocks away, Stefan heard a deafening explosion, and a few moments later, saw that a bistro had been leveled. The sides of the building had collapsed into the street. Black smoke poured from the blown-out windows and flying glass slivers had cut the faces, hands and eyes of people in that street.

He found Julienne near the doorway of Jevelot's. The queue was moving quickly, but the women and the men stood patiently, defiantly, and waited their turn with a calm born of spite.

"Frédéric . . ." she asked quickly.

"Home," he nodded.

"Good," she sighed and shivered when a shell exploded near by.

"The swine," a man on the line said, wiping dust from his face. "The filthy swine. We *knew* they would do this, uhn?" he said to the queue in general, and heard murmurings of agreement. "All this time," he went on loudly, "all these many months, we knew they would do this . . . Prussian swine. They corner us, starve us, and now they try to blow us apart, well they do not frighten *me*!" he spat.

"Nor me!" the queue echoed.

"Yes," the man continued, "we will show them, citizens. We will show them how strong we are. We are the heart of France and we will never give up!"

Julienne stepped inside Jevelot's as the crowd outside loudly agreed with the angry man.

After buying the small ration of meat, they walked home under the daylight canopy of smoke from fires that were burning themselves out but did not muffle the sound of the shells still whining overhead. The moment she stepped into the salon, Frédéric bolted from the bedroom and stumbled into her arms.

"I was more worried about you," she soothed.

"Don't go outside," he wept, "never, never, never again . . ."

She held him and wiped his eyes. "It's all right now," she said quietly, but he gripped her tightly and would not let go.

Stefan poured himself half a glass of wine and finished it in two swallows, then looked in on Edward. Gisèle was still hidden under the covers and Cécile was now sitting in the corner of the room, leaning her head against the wall.

"Where's Armand?" he asked.

She turned and looked at him with tired eyes. "The old fool," she said. "When the shell hit the roof, he went up to see . . . He is on the roof. He will not come inside."

"I'll get him," Stefan said.

"He won't listen to you," Cécile called out after him. "He won't listen to anybody, the silly old fool . . ."

Stefan climbed the stairs and felt very tired and drained. Opening the door to the roof, he saw the shell had hit on the extreme right side. Half the apartment underneath it was gone, as well as a section of the roof and side wall. Then he saw Armand, staring at the sky with a hate in his eyes Stefan had never seen before.

"German swine," he yelled, "the blood is on your hands, you murderers . . ."

Stefan walked closer to Armand and saw the view with unbelievable clarity—red flames consuming buildings in streets far away; the black shells streaking in a wide pattern in the grey sky. He watched the shells for a moment and saw they were being aimed at the Pantheon, only three blocks away, a high target for the Krupp cannons and visible above the rooftops of the Latin Quarter. "Was anyone hurt?" he asked Armand.

"No," Armand clucked his tongue.

"Is the building safe?"

"Until it falls over, it is safe."

"Come inside now," Stefan said.

"NO," Armand snapped. "They think this little display will frighten me, uhn?" He spit to the side. "That is what I think of them, the bastards, the pigs. LOOK! Look what they did to my building. Look what they do to my Paris," he yelled, jutting his chin toward the city. "They killed my son and now they hope to destroy my home. Nameless, faceless pigs who kill from far away," he shouted. "You will have to kill me and everyone like me, and even then, you will never never win. Paris will *never* be yours!"

CHAPTER
25

From the salon window, Julienne and Cécile watched the steady exodus of people stepping carefully about the rubble strewn in the streets. The people walked to Rue Gay Lussac, and from there, to the rubble on the Boulevard St. Michel. It was a mid-morning ritual now. The Prussians usually bombarded them at night, and in the morning, those without homes left, carrying on their backs what little they had salvaged and tried to find shelter on the Right Bank.

By the third day of the cannonade, the hundred-pound shells had leveled Jevelot's and it had burned to the ground. The Sorbonne, many homes and businesses on Boulevard St. Michel and Rue St. Jacques, the Jardin du Luxembourg and even Montparnasse Cemetery had all sustained heavy damage as the Prussians continued to aim their shells at the high dome of the Pantheon and spread them in a wide pattern over the Left Bank.

At the end of the first week, two apartment houses across the street had been repeatedly hit by shells. While the children stayed with Edward, the rest of them and all the lodgers joined the queue and passed countless leather buckets filled with water to stop the fires, but to no avail. They watched helplessly in the middle of the night as the buildings burned hideously and caved in, leaving forty or more people homeless and destitute, and several dead from the explosions, the shell fragments, and the fires.

In the dusty sunlight, Julienne watched as someone came out of the doorway directly across the street. The old one—man, woman, she could not tell—was bent, and had grey straw-like hair partially hidden by a woolen hat. A piece of rope was used as a belt around the waist of the frock-coat, and from the window, Julienne saw the old one remove the woolen hat. Ahh, a woman, Julienne thought, seeing the braid and noticing the tattered fragments of a skirt which was too short and showed her ankles. Still, a man's coat, and a man's shoes were all she had to keep her warm.

"God in heaven," Edward gasped, gripping the sides of the bed.

Julienne turned her head to the now doorless bedroom, but did not move.

"Too tight?" Armand asked.

The tension in Edward's arms eased and he flopped backwards onto the pillows. "It hurts," he breathed quickly. "Oh my God, it hurts . . ."

"Well, do not try to move it."

"I'm not moving it," Edward argued, staring at the wooden cup with the peg resting on the pile of pillows.

"I must see if it fits correctly around the sides. I have to touch it," Armand said, raising his eyebrows and causing the wrinkles in his forehead to deepen. He leaned slightly over the bed. "Ready?"

Julienne looked at Cécile as they listened to the conversation only a few steps away. She wanted to go to Edward, but thought it best to leave him his privacy just now. She motioned to Cécile and they moved to the furthest end of the salon and sat down in the chairs near the empty fireplace.

Armand poked his finger in between the wood and the thigh, hearing the sharp intake of breath. "Snug. Yes, good and snug. It should hold nicely."

Edward wiped the gloss of perspiration from his forehead.

"How does it feel? Inside, I mean. Do you feel the bottom? Is it smooth? Are there any rough spots that bother you?"

Wearily, Edward waved a hand at Armand. "One . . . question at a . . . a time," he said, gulping the air. The hot pain stopped pulsing and after a moment he could speak. "I cannot feel the bottom, no."

"Is it smooth?"

Edward nodded.

"No rough spots?"

He shook his head.

Armand smiled and jauntily placed his hands on his waist. "Not bad, uhn? Not bad for my own invention, uhn? Look at that wood. Magnificent, that's what it is, magnificent. It will last longer than you."

"What a comforting thought," Edward quipped. "Is the padding inside it?"

"No, no," Armand answered instantly. "I had to see first how much room you have inside. Now I measure. Then, I'm sorry, but I have to take it off again . . ." He looked at Edward's suddenly wide-open eyes.

Edward steadied himself by clenching his jaw. "Go ahead."

Armand shook his forefinger in the air. "I said I have to measure first. You upset yourself for nothing." He placed a string around the thigh at the top of the cup. "*Now* we take it off," he said and gently eased the cup from the stump. He compared the two and saw that there was a space of about two inches at the rounded bottom. He grunted. "Not too terrible," he said and looked at Edward.

"No, not too terrible," Edward wheezed sarcastically, amazed at the searing, burning pain.

"Cécile," Armand called. "Two and one-half inches."

She appeared at the doorway, grinning. "What did I tell you?"

Armand shrugged. "So you were right. But I had to be sure. Nice and soft now, very smooth, and no wrinkles in the fabric."

"Yes, Monsieur," she smiled.

"What are you waiting for," he said, "go, go . . ."

She arched an eyebrow and muttered all the way back to the chair in the salon. "Impossible, he is impossible, go, go," she mimicked, then sat down across from Julienne. "Monsieur says no wrinkles."

Julienne tightened her lips to hold back the laugh.

"Monsieur says nice and soft," she grinned meanly at Julienne. "He thinks we're idiots," she added and picked up the small silk pad. "Do you see any wrinkles?"

Julienne shook her head.

"Have we put the seams on the sides so it will be nice and smooth?"

Julienne started to laugh.

Cécile pinched the pillow in between her fingers. "Haven't we stuffed it with muslin and the down from a pillow?" She closed the last seam on the pad. "The Inventor," she sighed, snipping the thread with her scissors.

As Cécile was walking across the salon, the door opened from the hallway and Gisèle raced in. Cécile blocked her way to Edward's room. "Tut, tut," she clucked, "Papa is busy just now. Leave him alone."

The child shivered and ran to Julienne, scrambling into her lap.

Stefan closed the door behind him and placed the basket down on the dining table.

"Any difficulty?" Julienne asked.

"No," he replied. "No shortage of wine. Just a long wait."

She caressed Gisèle, then raised her eyebrows in a question to her brother.

Stefan shook his head. "No better today," he replied softly.

"Gisèle," Julienne said, "go put your coat in Uncle Stefan's room and wait for me there."

After several quick breaths, she did as she was told.

"What happened?" Julienne asked quietly when the child had gone.

"The same," Stefan answered. "She clings, she cries, she says I'm hungry, I'm thirsty, I want to go home, I don't like it here . . . she's terrified of everything now—people, the rubble in the streets, waiting on the queue. She looks at the sky all the time." He sighed. "This will not do, Julienne. She grows worse every day. It hurts me to take her outside and see her so frightened."

"If she does not go outside, that is worse still," Julienne said. "She hides too much. She must see that people continue to live despite the hardships we suffer. Papa always made us speak about whatever frightened us, to chase the phantoms away."

"Yes, well, the trouble is, she isn't speaking about it, or anything else, for that matter."

"Yes, I know," Julienne said, trying to decide what to do.

Armand studied the pad carefully, then gave an appreciative smile to Cécile. "Very good," he said, "yes, very good. It will do."

Cécile's nostrils flared. "Wrinkles?"

"No wrinkles," Armand smiled.

"Smooth?"

"Quite smooth," Armand answered, raising an eyebrow in annoyance.

Cécile winked to Edward before she left the room.

Armand pinched the padding. "Impossible woman," he muttered, but half-smiled in spite of himself. He made a fist and pressed the pillow against the sharp ridges of his knuckles. He nodded, pleased, then put the pillow inside the cup of the peg. "We will try it again, yes?"

"Yes," Edward answered, stiffening his arms to absorb some of the pain, gasping with the initial white-hot throbbing, then breathing easier as it subsided in slow warm waves. "I . . . I can feel the padding," he said, tilting his head slightly, having to think and concentrate about the sensation at the end and on the sides of the stump.

"Is it unpleasant?"

"No," he said, surprised. "No, it isn't. Help me up."

"I will not," Armand replied quickly, then waved the flat of his hand at Edward, pushing him back by pushing the air back. "You stay where you are. Let yourself become used to it. If you are impatient . . ." he said, and shook his head as a way of finishing his thought.

"But I want to try," Edward insisted.

"At another time, not today. Just keep it on for a little while. Perhaps later, we will put it on again and leave it for a little while longer."

Armand was firm, and Edward knew he could not do it alone. "You're right, of course," he said, then shrugged his shoulders. "I am damned tired of sitting and lying down all day."

"You only sit for an hour at a time," Armand caustically reminded him.

Edward looked at the peg, then slipped his right leg out from under the covers and compared the two distances. "Well," he said, "today I shall sit with the thing on for an hour, at least an hour." He hauled himself up, leaning back against the wall of pillows behind him, clenching his jaw tightly against the sudden pain.

"You see," Armand said, arching a victorious eyebrow. "It hurts, doesn't it?"

"I don't care," Edward breathed.

"But it hurts. Admit it."

"What if it does?"

"Edward, you must grow used to it," Armand said. "In time, it will be part of you, and not something strange and heavy at the end of your body."

"Then we'll hurry it along, won't we, of course we will," Edward answered, determined to sit despite the radiating pain.

"You are a very stubborn man," Armand said.

Edward folded his arms across his chest. "Quite," he replied. "I will do this, I will stand, and I will not spend the rest of my life looking up to people whilst they look down upon me," and he gave a quick, final nod to his head and sat in spite of the pain.

Armand enjoyed the fire in the eyes. "Would you like some wine?"

"Yes, please," Edward said, then smiled. "Do forgive me. I was taught to say 'thank you.' You've done well, my friend. With every step I take, I shall remember you for the rest of my life."

"A long life," Armand said.

"Definitely," Edward replied.

Luncheon was nearly ready. They had a brown bread now with an unpleasant texture and taste. The soup was thin, and Armand, sitting quietly, make a quick estimate as to the amount in the tureen. He saw there would not be enough. He tapped his fingers on the table, then gently turned over his bowl. "No," he said, "none for me, thank you. I wish to begin work on the walking sticks. Share my portion between you." He poured himself wine, then left the table and the apartment.

Cécile smiled at his overturned soup-bowl and his quiet sacrifice.

With Jevelot's gone, they had to find another butcher, and the new man, Davadant, on Rue d'Uln, usually gave preferential service to his regular customers. He was a squat little man with an attitude of rude indifference to strangers. Julienne discovered soon enough he had disliked his competitor, Jevelot. Twice a week, she and Cécile had to suffer his comments about strangers in his shop, and strangers buying up his allotment of meat. The rations had been cut again, this time to a mere four ounces per person.

There was still coffee to be found, and that continued to be breakfast. Luncheon was a thin soup of whatever vegetable they could find with a few teaspoonfuls of dried beans added to the stock every other day, and dinner was the shreds of meat in a stew with potatoes. It never varied and they began to institute their own rationing within the family. Cécile, Armand, Julienne and Stefan took turns giving up their portions for dinner, and the one going without would take a glass of wine and wait downstairs in Armand's cold, dark apartment, an apartment without doors to the rooms and beginning to be stripped of all wooden furniture that they burned for fuel.

By the sixteenth of January, snow was still falling lightly and at night, the shells kept them from sleep. Frédéric had stiffened his back to the terrible sounds, and like other schoolchildren in Paris, was instructed by his teacher to be brave, to think only of France.

"The enemy," Brother Thomas stated, "has turned his cannons on the innocents in order to defeat us. They aim at the hospitals, yes, the hospitals, where the sick and the dying cannot escape. Is that brave?"

"No," the children answered in unison.

"Is that honorable?"

"No," they replied again.

"We must pray for our soldiers, our brave soldiers. This is our lesson today, my children, the lesson of strength, the lesson of our will . . ."

On Saturday morning, January 21st, Gisèle sat in a corner with her back to the room and played with her smallest dolls, the ones no bigger than her fingers. She put them down in pretend chairs, poured them make-believe milk, gave them make-believe cakes, and carried on a conversation with them in the barest of whispers about green ponds and lovely houses and quiet. She saw the hem of her mother's cloak appear to her left, then felt the hands smoothing her hair.

"Gisèle?"

She looked up with large round eyes.

"Come with me. I am going out for a walk."

She shook her head.

Julienne bent down, then knelt on one knee. "Why not?" she asked.

"I don't want to," Gisèle answered.

"But why? It's warm outside, much warmer than it is in here, and it isn't snowing or raining. It's just a bit foggy. It's nice to walk in the fog, it feels so mysterious. Why won't you come with me?"

"Because."

"That isn't an answer," Julienne replied softly. "Tell me why."

Gisèle turned away and pressed her lips to a straight line.

"Won't you tell me what frightens you, so I can try to make it go away?"

"You can't," Gisèle pouted and caressed the head of the wooden doll.

"Is it the people?"

She shook her head.

"What, then?"

"It's . . ." Gisèle began, then stopped.

"Tell me," Julienne coaxed.

"Ugly."

"What is ugly?"

"Ev . . . ev . . . everything," Gisèle sputtered.

Julienne held her for a moment, thinking and trying to imagine the secret language of children. She spoke with her dolls about beautiful trees, and for quite a long time, relived in the corners of the salon, the time spent at Philippe's country house, and the gardens and the sweet smells of lawns and flowers and playing there. "Are the buildings ugly?"

Gisèle closed her eyes against her mother's breast, nodding.

"And the pavements and the streets?"

Again, several nods.

"Ahh," Julienne sighed, caressing the child's face. It is the Prussian shells, and what they have done to her very small world—burned-out buildings, rubble in the streets, everywhere confusion and disorder. She smiled and lifted Gisèle's chin. "It won't be like this forever," she said gently. "It is only for now. When we are able, we shall go away to a nice place."

"Like the place in the country?"

"Yes, and just as beautiful."

"Where is it?"

Julienne shrugged. "I don't know, perhaps Switzerland, or England."

"England?"

"Yes, Papa's family is in England."

"Will Uncle Steffie come too?"

Julienne shook her head. "He must go back to Vienna, to Tante Rosl and your cousins.

"Why?"

"Because he lives there."

"Where, where will we live?" she asked, eyes filling.

Julienne brushed a tear from the thin cheek. "Somewhere very beautiful, I promise."

"Does England have trees?"

"Yes," Julienne smiled.

"And, and a house?"

"Yes."

"What does the house look like?"

"I don't know," Julienne replied easily. "I've never been there. You must ask Papa about that." She watched Gisèle thinking it over and it seemed to calm her and please her. Julienne felt her chest tighten seeing the shadow Gisèle had become, knowing the child had reduced her world to the apartment and the hallway's convenience. She was even frightened to go downstairs to Cécile's apartment and had not been outside for over a week. She was pale and drawn, thinner than ever and her normally large eyes were now enormous saucers set above the sharply defined cheekbones. She looked old. "I am going for a little walk," Julienne said. "You know the place, Jardin du Luxembourg, the pool by the big house?"

Gisèle nodded.

"The very place where we met Papa so many many months ago?"

She smiled.

"Please come with me. We'll walk around the small pool, just for a little time, and if we talk about how it used to look, and how beautiful it was, perhaps it won't be so bad after all. And the fog will hide a great many things."

"You'll, you'll hold my hand?" Gisèle asked.

"Very very tightly," Julienne answered.

"And, and you won't let go?"

She sees everything and remembers everything, Julienne thought and kissed the small forehead, hoping to chase from the child's mind the memory of that October day's madness. "No. I won't let go of you. Will you come with me?"

"Yes," Gisèle said.

"Oh my good girl," Julienne beamed and cupped the hollow cheeks in her hands and gave several quick kisses all over the small face.

Gisèle found her coat and Julienne did the buttons, then wrapped a scarf about the tiny head and neck. After Gisèle put on her gloves, they went out of the apartment, and into the street.

The momentary courage seemed to wane with every block and every pile of rubble they had to step over or around. The sights of the burned-out buildings showing through the swirls of grey fog made the child nervous. She clung tightly to her mother's hand and skirts as they walked.

There was a substantial change in the Jardin du Luxembourg. Many trees had been cut down, and in the foggy distance, they could see several large gaping holes in the ground where children in rags now played games of war and explorers. The lawns by the Palais were brown. Gisèle winced at the ugliness and turned her face away with a shudder.

Yet, there was one moment of beauty.

In a bare tree by the stone steps, a bird perched in the higher branches and

379

sang its song. It hopped down the branches, one by one, pausing to sing a few notes, and then finally settled on the ground by the base of the tree.

Gisèle inched closer to the stone barrier and peeked over. "Look," she breathed quietly, "isn't it beautiful?"

Julienne stood behind Gisèle and watched the bird. It listened to the ground, then hopped to a clogged cluster of brown decaying leaves at the base of the tree. Using its beak, it sifted and separated the leaves, flinging bits of them to the sides in a patient search for food.

"What is it?" Gisèle asked.

Julienne knew the bird. It was a year-round resident of Paris. The black head, the white feathers in an oblong pattern on the sides of the head just under the eyes, the pale yellow breast, light brown wings and the three-note song that it varied at will was sad and delicate and haunting. "It is a Mésange Charbonnière," she said, "and the song that it sings?"

"Yes?"

"He sings it to make the winter go away. They always do that. They always sing more as the days grow longer and the spring is very near."

The bird found something, and flew to a branch near the foggy top of the tree. They heard the song a moment later, a most beautiful sound on a quiet Saturday morning.

They walked around the pool and noticed several people just sitting on iron benches watching the grey water or gazing out in memory at the mists, thinking of a time before hunger and cold and war. They circled the pool near the Palais, and then headed towards the steps.

Passing the benches and the people sitting on them, a man from behind called out, "Good morning, Madame Atherton-Moore."

Julienne turned around and saw Monsieur Jevelot. She stopped walking by a bench with a man sitting on it and waited for Jevelot to come closer. "Monsieur Jevelot," she said, "how nice to see you."

"And you, Madame. It is a sorry business, isn't it?"

"Oh yes, the Army. I heard about that this morning." She shook her head. "Pity."

"In retreat, coming back to Paris. Another failure we must lay at the feet of General Trochu. The man is no good. I have said so from the first, he is no good. Where do you buy your meat now?"

She felt uneasy about the words, but said them anyway. "I am sorry to say, at Davadant's."

His eyes blazed. "Madame," he complained, "Madame, this is awful. He is a swine. No, no you must not go to him."

"But what choice do I have?"

"I work now with a friend of mine. He has kindly placed me in his employ. Monsieur Moiselet, on Rue du Cardinal, do you know it?"

"I know where the street is, but not his shop."

Jevelot shook his head many times. "You must forget that swine Davadant. He is a cheat and a liar. Come to me, Madame. You and my old friend, Madame Mabilleau, you come to me. She is well, I trust?"

"Yes," Julienne answered.

Gisèle ignored the conversation going on behind her, and still clutching her mother's skirt, was more interested in the man sitting on the edge of the bench. He turned and smiled at her. He was a soldier with a uniform that had brown stains on it, and an empty left sleeve tucked into the belt.

He noticed she seemed a bit frightened of his missing arm, and he smiled again, gently, a lovely smile on a sad and thin face. "Does it scare you, little one?"

She shyly looked away, then turned back to him saying, "My Papa has one leg."

"Oh," he said, pleased at the sound of a child's voice. "And was he a soldier like me?"

She nodded, remembering Papa had said he'd been in the Army.

"Ahh," the soldier sighed. He swallowed, feeling his mouth go dry. With his right hand, he placed a metal flask between his knees and pulled out the stopper. He took a long swallow of the cold water and sighed, then noticed the child had been watching him, licking her lips. "Are you thirsty, little one?"

She nodded.

"Would you like a drink of cold water."

She nodded again.

He held out the flask to her with a smile. "Take," he said. "I share with you. For your Papa," he added. "Take as much as you want," he said, waiting while she let go of her mother's hand and grasped the flask with both hands and took a long drink, and then, a longer second drink which finally slaked her thirst. She gave him back the flask. "Thank you, little one," he said and put the stopper back into the flask. She stepped back from him and took her mother's skirt in her left hand. Like all the rest, he thought, all the children of Paris look like this one, he thought, and they never seem to smile anymore. He offered his hand to her.

She studied it for a moment, then cautiously put out her own little hand.

With a tired elegance, he leaned, and kissed her small gloved fingers. "My little one," he said, "someday you will smile again. Someday you will play here again, when happy people walk here and listen to the band music and buy sweets for their children, and when the trees are filled with the songs of birds. Someday," he said, and let go of her hand. "They have taken so much away from you, but someday, you will have it back again. Remember, I have made you this promise."

Shyly, she hid behind her mother's skirt.

"I wish you well, Madame," Jevelot was saying.

"And you Monsieur," Julienne responded, having promised to buy meat at his new location. She watched as he left, and wondered how long his shop would be open for business. She tugged lightly on Gisèle's hand and began the long walk home.

Later, the child sat next to Edward on the small bed and peered down at him as he rested on the pillows. After six questions about England, he stared back at her. "Why this sudden interest?" he asked.

"Mama said we might go there, when we leave here."

"Oh she did, did she?" Edward said, raising himself up on his elbows. "And why would she say a thing like that?"

"Because we're going to leave here," Gisèle answered, startled by his question. "We will move to a beautiful place."

He paused, then called out in a loud voice, "Julienne," and waited, tapping the edge of the bed with the flat of his hand.

She came to the doorway, drying her hands. "Yes?"

His smile was menacing. "Are we planning to move?"

She knit her eyebrows. "What?"

"Gisèle tells me we may move to England," he said in an even tone of voice.

She thought a moment. "Oh," she sighed, then stepped closer. "Gisèle," she said, handing her the dish towel, "be a good girl and put this in the kitchen for me, will you?"

The child took the towel and left the room.

"Before you start blustering like some angered bull, let me tell you why."

He stared at her with narrowed eyes.

"She was afraid to go outside because it is so ugly. I told her, after the war, as soon as we're able, we would go to a place that was not ugly. I said Switzerland, or perhaps England. She was curious about England and I told her to ask you, as I've never been there. She seemed calmer, thinking about a place that had trees and a house. That's all."

"Oh," he said, feeling very silly. "And I don't bluster," he added.

Julienne only smiled. "Talk to her about your home. What harm can it do?"

"None, I suppose," he answered, then looked up at her. "She was calmer, in thinking about a home and trees?"

"Yes," Julienne said, then nodded toward the window. "It must be very confusing and upsetting for her to see the streets and the houses as they are now—blown apart, uprooted. She doesn't understand, and I often wonder if anyone understands . . . She likes beautiful things, always has. She's very sensitive that way."

He nodded, then slowly inched his way to a sitting position. "No, I will do it myself," he said, seeing that she had stepped closer to help him. "There," he sighed, "you see? I did it."

"Good for you," she grinned and kissed his forehead.

"Is that the reward you give for so great an effort?"

She sat down next to him and kissed his partially open mouth, then held him tightly for a moment.

He played with her hair, saying with a sigh, "What wouldn't I give for a room with a door, a night without Prussian shells exploding and a slightly larger bed . . ."

She laughed slightly and ran her fingers through the rumpled hair near his temples. "I do love you," she said. "And I hope for those things as much as you."

"Do you really?" he asked quietly.

"Yes of course," she said, surprised at his question.

"Wretched, bony, half-man skeleton—or rather, 'angered bull' that I am . . ."

Exasperated, she shook her head and traced her finger over his lips.

He liked her answer, then looked up and said, "Come in, Gisèle," seeing her waiting in the doorway. Edward held Julienne's hand as she stood up, then gave a quick kiss to her palm before opening his arms to Gisèle. She crawled up onto the bed and he wrapped his right arm around her. "You want to hear about England, do you?" He took both her hands in his own and spoke quietly. "You have a grandfather. And a grandmother, too."

"Where do they live?"

"In two places, for we have two houses. One house is in London—that's a big city—and the other is in the country, a very, very large country house. It has a name. Chadwell."

"Is it like the house we went to once?"

He smiled. "Larger."

Her eyes brightened. "Really?"

"Really. A very, very large house, and my father's property stretches for miles and miles and miles. There's a stream with all kinds of fish, and a lake, and meadows with huge trees that are over two hundred years old, and a forest. I have a sister, and she has married by now, so you have an Aunt Margery and an Uncle William. And perhaps, a little cousin, too."

"And my grandfather's name?"

"Richard Atherton-Moore, Duke of Middlesex."

"And my grandmother?"

"Elizabeth Atherton-Moore, Duchess of Middlesex."

"And the house, the one in the country, the one with the name, what does it look like?"

"If you fetch me a pencil and a piece of paper, I will draw a picture for you."

He entertained her for nearly two hours, drawing pictures of the magnificent house, simple maps of the land to try to give her an idea of what surrounded the house and how large the estate was. He gave word pictures in stories of his youth, of playing in the gardens with their mock Roman ruins, and imitation Greek temples, and described how cool they were in the summers. His words were so vivid she could taste the tarty sweetness of the lemonade, and smell the blossoms of the trees in the orangery.

He spoke without rancor, without hate, and culled from his memory every pleasant thought unsullied by later troubles. Her eyes seemed so hungry for peaceful nights with large white stars in the sky, and softly blackened silhouettes of trees rustled by a gentle wind. In her mind, she saw open meadowlands in daylight, warmed by the sun and shaded in various gradations of green. She could smell the fragrant roses in garden walks, and the lilac trees with bees darting around the heavy and sweet blossoms dampened by dew.

Frédéric, too, listened to every word of the descriptions of this land so far away, and by dinnertime, they took their places at table, calmed and relieved, Edward thought, to be reminded that not all the world looked as battered as Paris looked now.

It was Stefan's turn this night. He filled his wine glass, took Armand's apartment key and left them for an hour.

Gisèle wrinkled her nose at the stew and only ate a small portion of it, relying mostly on shreds of the black bread for food. She was sent to bed early with a large glass of wine and by nine o'clock as Julienne was just settling in bed next to her, she sat upright with a groan.

"What's wrong?" Julienne asked.

"I, I, I don't feel well," she said and jumped out of the bed.

Julienne followed her quickly and saw the mad scrambling at the hallway door. "Gisèle, Gisèle, what's wrong . . ."

"Hurry, hurry," she cried, and doubled over slightly with a cramp.

Julienne helped her down the hall to the convenience, then returned to the apartment to find a fresh nightdress for her. Perhaps a cold in the stomach, she thought, after the massive diarrhea attack and bout of vomiting. She cleaned Gisèle, and disposed of the soiled nightdress, then brought her to the kitchen, pumped water on a towel and wiped the child's face clean.

For the first time since the bombardment had begun, Gisèle was unconcerned by it. When the shelling started promptly at ten o'clock, Gisèle had already gone to the convenience several times, complaining of cramps in her stomach.

Julienne sat up with her for most of the night and had moved her to the sofa in the salon, bundling her in the covers from the bed. There seemed to be no end to the visits to the convenience, she thought, and though the child's bowels had calmed, how was it possible so small a child could have so much *liquid* to pass?

When the bombardment ended at four in the morning, Gisèle had dropped off to sleep after several dry heavings and several glasses of water.

By half-past four she was back in the convenience, relieving herself of the water.

All day Sunday, the child could not find a comfortable position on the sofa. She tossed and turned, groaned and whimpered, slept a little now and then and continually went to the convenience. Even Frédéric, who hovered about her like a mother-hen, adjusting the pillows and the blankets, reading to her, fetching her dolls and then bringing her others when she tired of the first group, worried about her and tried his best to make her smile.

"Has she eaten anything?" Edward asked when Julienne brought him his dinner in the bedroom.

"No, she wants nothing. Only water. She is terribly thirsty all the time."

"Fever?"

She shook her head. "No, that's the strange part. None at all. She's quite cool, but complains now of pain in her arms and legs."

"What sort of pain?" Edward asked, swallowing a shred of meat and grimacing at the taste of it.

"I don't know," Julienne said. "She can't seem to describe it to me. She just says her arms hurt, her legs hurt."

"No pulling pain, or burning pain, or throbbing pain, nothing like that?"

Julienne shrugged helplessly. "She doesn't know how to tell me about it."

He thought a moment. "Maybe influenza?"

"But she'd have a high fever with influenza."

384

He thought again. "What is she doing now?"

"Sleeping."

"It's probably best," Edward said and scraped the bowl clean with his spoon. "Here, he said, "and thank you."

"Well, that didn't take long, did it?" she sighed and took the bowl away from him.

He looked out to the salon again. "She really ought to eat something."

"Edward, I've tried. I can't force her to eat."

Absently, he nodded, still watching the back of the sofa as if it might tell him something.

She was quiet for several hours, and woke when startled by the evening's bombardment. She sat up, looked around the salon, and began walking toward the open doorway of Stefan's room, bumping into the side of the bed.

"What is it?" Stefan asked, instantly awake.

"I . . . I," Gisèle began, looking around the dark room.

Stefan flung the covers back, which woke Frédéric. "What is it, Gisèle, what do you want?" Stefan asked, sitting up. "Are you hungry?"

"I, I, can't find it."

"Find what?"

"The, the convenience."

He took a match from the bedstand, lit it, and held the small flame near her face. "Look at me," he said, and saw her hesitation, the dazed look in her eyes that darted around the room yet did not seem to focus on any one thing. Her expression was confused and bewildered. He touched her forehead but found it cool. "Gisèle, what's my name?"

She looked at him. "Uncle Stefan."

He nodded. "And where do you want to go?"

"To, to the hallway."

The match burned down and he blew it out, placing the smoking stubble at the base of the oil-lamp. He got up and led her to the salon and walked with her to the hallway's convenience. He waited outside wondering why she'd become confused. Perhaps a dream, he thought. It happens. One wakes, and doesn't know the room, still confused by the dream. She has no fever, he thought, so it is not delirium from a fever. Still, it bothered him. And her eyes had seemed a bit sunken, but he thought it might be from the distorting matchlight.

She grew worse, all the day long, and early in the evening collapsed in the hallway on the way back from the convenience. Julienne carried her to the apartment and brought her close to the small fire burning in the grate. She was ice-cold, shivering, her teeth were chattering uncontrollably. Her eyes seemed to have sunken back into the small face in a matter of hours, but the skin was the most disturbing of all—it had a grey cast to it, and was horribly loose.

They took the blankets from Stefan's bed and wrapped Gisèle in the additional covers, but her teeth still chattered. They tried to warm her by boiling water and then putting it in a closed bottle, holding it against her, but it made no difference. Her arms and legs still shook.

385

Julienne held the blanket-wrapped child in her arms that night near the small fire. "We ought to take her to a doctor," she said, looking up from the floor at Cécile.

Cécile looked out the window. "It's raining," she said. "It might make her worse."

"But what are we to do?" Julienne said, trying to control her voice.

"I don't know," Cécile answered, walking past Frédéric, who stood in the doorway to Edward's room.

Julienne drew Gisèle closer to her, and caressed the face resting in the crook of her arm. When she bent down to kiss Gisèle, she smelled the odor from the child's open mouth, a sweet smell, as if she'd just eaten fruit. Julienne smelled it again and then a third time, wondering what could have caused that.

Stefan held Gisèle for a time, watching Julienne pace the room and shudder from worry, biting her thumbnail, watching the window splattered by rain. Which is worse, Julienne thought, to do nothing or to risk going out with her now in the rain . . .

"Julienne?"

She whirled around, seeing Stefan suddenly touching Gisèle's face. She ran to the fireplace and dropped to her knees.

"Touch her," he said.

She did, tracing her hands all over Gisèle's face. The grey skin was very very cold, and now, clammy as well. "Gisèle?" Julienne called.

The child made no response.

"GISELE," she said louder, and when there was no answer, she grabbed the thin shoulders and shook the limp child. She looked at Stefan with filled eyes.

"No, she's still breathing," he said, listening to her.

"Damn the rain," Julienne said, beginning to cry. "She needs a doctor now."

"We're wasting time here," Stefan said, standing up. He tossed Julienne her cloak and put on his own coat. Then they bundled Gisèle to protect her from the rain.

"We're leaving," Stefan said to Edward. "I don't know when we'll be back."

Edward nodded, suddenly numb.

Armand heard noise from the stairwell, and when he saw them with the bundle, went back and grabbed his coat. "You go to the hospital?"

"Yes," Stefan said.

"I am coming with you," he said, and left Cécile standing in the doorway. "Which one?"

"The Sorbonne . . ." Julienne said with a question in her voice.

"No," Armand said. "There is a children's hospital not far from here, on Rue d'Enfer. Why not bring her there, where they care for children all the time?"

"All right," Stefan huffed, his arms aching from holding the child. He wondered why. She wasn't heavy, still, he had to shift her weight in his arms.

In the lobby, Armand held the door open for him.

"Let me," Armand said, "we will take turns," and took Gisèle as they walked quickly in the rain.

Half an hour later, Armand held the door open to the Children's Hospital. They walked into the darkened lobby of the building, lit only by a few candles. In the dim light, Julienne saw many people, mothers and their children, waiting. Some children were crying, others were sleeping against their mothers or lying on the floor.

She walked with Stefan to the desk which blocked the entrance to a narrow corridor. A woman with a large red cross on her chest looked up at them.

"Madame," Julienne said, wiping her eyes, "my child needs a doctor."

The woman brought the candle close to the face bundled in blankets. She saw the greyish skin and the wrinkles. She'd seen this before. "One moment, Madame, I shall find a doctor for you." She left, and walked down the corridor behind the desk.

Long moments passed. Julienne stood close by, pacing and trying to see down the hallway. She saw the volunteer sister. A man followed her, a man in his fifties with white temples and wearing a dark coat, of what color, she could not tell in the dim light.

He stood behind the desk on the small platform nearest the candle. He had ·a tired face, but a kindly smile. "I am Doctor Lacelle," he said quietly. "Bring the child to the light."

Stefan stepped closer as the doctor gave the candle to the sister to hold.

Doctor Lacelle parted the blankets, touched the skin with the back of his hand, then brought his nose to the mouth and sniffed the breath quickly. He held his hand near her nose, feeling the shallow rapid breaths. His face betrayed nothing as he turned to the anxious mother, saying, "Has she eaten?"

"No, not for nearly two days," Julienne rasped.

"Loose bowels?"

"Yes, once, on Saturday, but not since then."

"She has insatiable thirst, and passes a great deal of water?"

"Yes," Julienne answered, feeling her throat tighten all the more.

"How long has she been unconscious?"

"A little over half an hour," Stefan replied, "and we brought her here immediately."

"She . . ." Julienne began, "she has complained of pain in her arms and legs."

Armand watched quietly for a moment, then looked away from Gisèle's face.

Doctor Lacelle nodded. "Give the child to me," he said. "You, Madame, wait here. Monsieur, will you come with me, please."

"Yes of course," Stefan answered.

"Sister Anne," the Doctor said, "take the blankets. You know what to do with them."

"Yes, Doctor Lacelle," she answered, and helped to unbundle the child.

"Where are you going?" Julienne asked frantically and felt the flat of Stefan's hands on her shoulders.

"Do as he says," Stefan said quietly. "Wait here."

387

"But . . ."

He nodded to Armand. "Do as he says," he repeated to Julienne in a soft but firm voice, then followed the doctor down the hallway.

She leaned heavily against Armand and felt her hands turn cold as she began to shiver. "Where are they going, what are they going to do to her . . ."

"Shh," Armand whispered, holding the shoulders tightly. "They know what to do. It is no mystery to them."

Stefan followed the Doctor to a set of double wood-and-glass doors at the far end of the hallway. They stepped inside the ward and he saw rows and rows of children in small iron beds and cribs, all bundled up, all shivering, some moaning in their sleep and others, like Gisèle, unconscious and quiet. The terrible sight made him pause at the doorway and he watched as Doctor Lacelle placed Gisèle in an empty iron bed at the head of the fourth row.

"You are the father?" Doctor Lacelle asked.

"No," Stefan replied. "The Uncle."

"Her name?"

"Atherton-Moore," Stefan answered, "Gisèle Atherton-Moore."

Doctor Lacelle wrote it down in a book and placed the number of her bed next to her name. He sighed. "I rarely go home now," he said quietly. "These are awful times, Monsieur." He put his arm around the man's shoulder and eased him away from the beds. "Monsieur," he began softly, "you saw me smell her breath?"

"Yes," Stefan answered.

"It was sweet, a very sweet odor," he said. "There is no easy way to tell you, so I will just tell you the truth. Sweet breath, the skin as it is—loose and grey and with a clammy touch—and all the other questions I asked, they are symptoms of cholera. Your niece is already in shock, and may possibly slip into coma. I do not believe she will live through the night, Monsieur."

Stefan's mouth opened, and he felt a dizzy wave, but stood where he was, staring at her, so still in the bed, so quiet. Gisèle, he thought, his eyes filling.

"The mother is your sister?"

He nodded.

"Monsieur, there is no point in her waiting here as so many others are doing. We will do all we can to help the child, but she is weak and there is no medicine we can give her. I placed her here because this is the cholera ward. We isolate them from the rest of the children. There is, perhaps, the chance she may come out of the shock. I have seen this happen, but in all truth, it happened in better times, with heavier children. I . . . if it were me, Monsieur, I would not place too much hope in that. Take your sister home, and I recommend you give her a great deal of brandy to steady her nerves. You decide what to tell her. Come back in the morning. We, we may have news for you then."

Stefan stepped closer to the bed. Bending down, he touched her hair and saw his own tears spill and run down her grey wrinkled cheeks. "Should . . . should we have brought her to you sooner?" he managed, somehow, still touching her.

"No, Monsieur. It makes little difference with cholera. Some survive, most do not. We know not why. It, it is a strange disease."

"How could . . ." Stefan began, then shook his head, trying to breathe.

"We don't really know. Some believe it is from water, others believe from food." Doctor Lacelle looked with sad and weary eyes at the long lines of filled beds. "There is no end tó them," he said quietly. "They come, and they come, and they still come, all wrapped in blankets which we burn, all shivering, all grey and wrinkled like old people in the arms of their mothers. It is . . . epidemic, they come with this, and typhus, and pneumonia, and smallpox." He gently eased the Uncle away from the bed, walking with him all the way to the doors. "Go home," he said softly. "There is nothing to be done here."

Stefan took several deep breaths, wiped his eyes and steadied himself as best he could. He turned to look at her just one more time, then walked quickly down the hallway. He paused before the entrance to the main lobby and leaned against the wall, thinking she must be told at home, where we may care for her quickly, and efficiently, and give her brandy after brandy to numb her to sleep. That is the only way, he decided, knowing Doctor Lacelle was right about this. Yes, but how, he thought, and realized anger might make her leave. He might make her angry at himself, and force her, with Armand's help, into leaving. Stefan straightened his shoulders, then strode out, doing what he had to do, ignoring his sister's frantic questions.

"Not here," he replied curtly, grabbing her firmly about the waist and trying to lead her to the door.

Armand blinked at the sharp tone of the voice.

"I won't leave, let go of me," Julienne said, beginning to raise her voice.

"Control yourself," he glared, narrowing his eyes. "Do it, right now." He glanced at Armand, as a Colonel to a soldier.

"Tell me what's wrong with her," Julienne pleaded.

"With all these people about?" he said offensively in a strained whisper. "Are you mad? How much attention do you want to bring to us?"

Armand was beginning to feel uneasy, and clearly saw in Stefan's eyes that they had to leave. "Do as he says," he whispered to Julienne.

"Behave yourself," Stefan said and jerked her through the doors, half-pulling, half-dragging her down the street away from the hospital at a furious pace.

He clenched his jaw and answered no questions from her, and could see her eyes glowering at him with every block they crossed, leaving the hospital further and further behind.

"Tell me," she snapped and smacked his arm away from her.

He grabbed her cloak and twisted it in his fist. "Stop it," he snarled. "I shall tell you when we're home and not before. Hit me once more, and I shall slap you, do you hear? It will kill me, but Goddammit, I shall do it! Remember who and what you are and behave yourself. You shameful woman, acting like a common spoiled brat in the streets . . ." He pulled her cloak and made her walk faster and faster, and had to turn his face away from her so she would not see the tears in his eyes.

When they entered the apartment house, Stefan directed them to Armand's flat and they went inside. Brandy, Stefan mouthed to Armand, and nodded discreetly toward Julienne. He motioned for a large glass.

Julienne stared with blazing eyes at Stefan. "Tell me now," she demanded.

He took off her cloak and tried to hold her but she stepped away from him.

"Don't you touch me," she snapped, "you just tell me what's wrong with her."

He stepped closer to her. "Sit down," he said quietly.

She started to cry. "It's something awful, isn't it? It's something horrible, tell me, tell me the truth . . ."

He looked at her, then said, "She has cholera. She's dying."

She couldn't scream. She wanted desperately to scream but suddenly had no voice. Why was he blocking the door, she thought, trying to push past him. Why . . . why . . . "Get out of my way, let me go, let me go . . ." she shrieked, beating his shoulders with her fists, but he would not move and closed his arms around her and when the pelting grew weaker, she collapsed against him. He held her and cried with her for a long time, then helped her to sit down.

The nightly shelling had begun but she didn't hear it. They began to ply her with brandy but it had no taste in her mouth. "My child . . ." she wept in between swallows. "My Gisèle, my Gisèle . . ."

Cécile held her on the sofa as Stefan sagged in the chair facing them. He hung his head and rested his arms on his knees, wiping his eyes and suddenly feeling very, very cold.

"Could . . . might we have done something?" Cécile asked, breathing quickly and hard and holding Julienne's face to her breast.

Stefan shook his head as he stared at the floor. "I asked," he said, his voice in a hoarse whisper. "The Doctor told me there was nothing we could have done."

"Armand," Cécile said and nodded toward the large glass. "Another."

He filled it for Julienne a fourth time and Cécile made her drink it all, waiting for the weeping to subside every few minutes, waiting for the string of nauseating gags to stop, and always the brandy glass was at the lips, ready to be drained. Julienne struggled, she fought them, she cried, but they held her down and made her drink until she grew dizzy and tired and looked at them with stunned frightened eyes.

Stefan knelt down next to her as she lay on the sofa watching as her dilated eyes fluttered.

"I . . . I . . . I have to be . . . with my baby, she's all alone," Julienne mumbled, trying to sit up, but he held her shoulders down. She was too exhausted and too drunk to fight him. "Gisela," she whispered. "My Gisela's all alone . . ." and she started to cry tears of exhaustion and pain.

"She's not alone," Stefan said quietly. "Papa's with her." He knelt near her for a long time, holding her hands and letting her drift into a stupored sleep, fitful at first, then drugged to quiet.

In the morning, he left her sleeping on the sofa and went alone to the hospital.

The change from dark to light woke her. Her head throbbed at the temples and felt heavy, as if stuffed with cotton. She tried to lift her head from the pillow and had to wait a moment until her vision cleared. Her mouth was dry and she licked her lips. His coat was gone and the chair was empty. She heard the heavy breathing of sleep from the bedroom without a door.

How could he, she thought, finally sitting up and feeling queasy. She used Cécile's hook and buttoned her shoes, then walked slowly to the chair with her cloak draped over the back of it. How could he go without me, she thought, and quietly left the apartment.

There was a thick fog in the streets, and it made her nervous. She still felt drugged and slowed by the brandy, and walked as best she could in some half-state between sleeping and awake, in a grey cloudy fog that hid the buildings and made all look unreal.

She stopped at a corner and leaned against the cold lamp-post. How long has he been gone, what time is it, where is everyone, she thought, and wondered if this were only a dream.

She saw him walking through the fog like a phantom in the night. He came closer. His walk, and then his face, his eyes and then his tears told her everything.

"They . . they haven't any wood for coffins," Stefan said, trying to breathe "They . . . have to use tarpaulin, like a burial at sea . . ."

Edward wept, closing his eyes.

Stefan swallowed. "She is to be buried right away. They're afraid of the disease spreading even more. Lacelle, the Doctor, told me it is rampant all over Paris. They can't give her back to us at all. Nine children died last night, and all of them are being taken straight away to Montparnasse Cemetery. We . . . can't even have a funeral Mass," he said, tears streaming from his eyes. He gulped at the air. "Some sort of graveside service, that's all. The Mass itself will be at another time—but without her . . . The Public Health people are terrified. Cholera and typhus are spreading." He shook his head and rested his arms on his knees, shifting slightly on the edge of Edward's bed. "He apologized, of course, but said they must think of the living. I . . . I haven't told Julienne any of this yet."

"Can't we make a coffin for her?" Edward whispered. "Armand could do it, why can't we make a coffin for her?"

"There isn't time," Stefan said. "We only have an hour before we go to the cemetery."

"Will you be able to see her before . . ."

"They . . . God," he said, and broke down with a sob, "they've already put her in the tarpaulin . . . they burned her clothes last night, and the blankets were burned before we even left the hospital . . . no coffin, no funeral Mass, no marker, just a name and a location in their damned registry book . . . this . . . my sister can't . . . it will kill her . . ."

"Where is Julienne now?"

"With Cécile."

Edward wiped his eyes and set his jaw. "She must know this," he said. "She mustn't see all that at the graveside, it's, it's too horrible."

Stefan sighed and agreed.

"I'll tell her," Edward said. He thought a moment, then took a breath and stretched, reaching to the side of the bed and felt for the wood of the peg on the floor. He picked it up, slowly eased himself further into a sitting position, paused, then pulled the peg onto the stump as he wheezed with the pain. "Help me up," he breathed, turning his body toward the left.

Stefan thought it madness, but walked to the other side of the bed knowing precisely what would happen, but also knowing Edward was stubborn and had to discover it for himself.

Bracing his arms against Stefan's, Edward tried to stand, feeling the unbelievable ricocheting pain, the quick loss of blood draining away from his cheeks and a thudding in his ears. He fell backwards on the bed on his side, and when his breathing was normal again, he slammed an angry fist onto the mattress.

Stefan took the peg off and helped him to sit up, adjusting the pillows behind him and under the stump.

"Goddamned useless," Edward snapped, giving a pull to the blankets. He looked at Stefan, then forced himself to be calm. "If she is able," he finally said, "ask her to come to me. If not," he sighed, "you must tell her."

"All right," Stefan said, and left the room.

Alone, Edward felt a cold emptiness circle him as he looked at the bureau and saw her dolls with their painted smiles, all neatly aligned in a dumb mockery, as if they were waiting for her to walk in at any moment and cuddle them. Was it only a year, he thought sadly, eyes beginning to burn with tears. One little year, searching for a woman named Jeanne Barbier and seeing her, and the little scamp that looked so like her mother . . . He closed his eyes and leaned his head back, staring at the ceiling to avoid the sight of her dolls. It did no good. His hand touched the center of his chest, where she had placed her head only three days before, asking questions about England, hugging him and smiling an innocent lovely smile. It is a living death, he thought, vainly trying to deafen his ears to the memory of her voice and childish giggle, blinding his mind to the sight of her smile and her large, open eyes. Gisèle, he thought, my little Gisèle, my child . . .

He heard the door open, then close. Slow footsteps walked closer and he saw her pasty skin and sunken eyes that were red-rimmed and still crying. He held her, shouldering the grief as best he could and gripping her tightly as if to deaden the pain. He waited until she had calmed slightly, then wiped her eyes and let her rest for a moment, hiding her face in his neck whilst he caressed her back with firm, gentle circles. "I feel so useless," he said quietly to her ear. "I wish I could go with you, I wish I could walk with you, help you . . ."

She shook her head. "It doesn't matter anymore."

"No," he said, his voice cracking, "I suppose it doesn't." He paused, swallowed, and cleared his throat. "I want you to remember something this morning. I want you to think of this and remember what I say to you."

Julienne looked up, then straightened to a sitting position on the bed. "What?" she asked, confused.

He thought a moment, then said, "We, all of us, all that live are very like cocoons, aren't we? This," he said, pinching his own ribs, "this is but a shell, isn't it? When we die, this shell is all that remains, and it is useless, isn't it? It is meant to be so. But we live on, in God's peace, don't we?"

"Yes," she said, "I know that. Why are you . . ."

"Remember," he said gently, placing his hands around her face. "A ceremony is simply that, be it in church or at the graveside. Gisèle . . ." he had to take a quick breath, "Gisèle is beyond pain, beyond hunger or cold and nothing we do will change that or disturb her peace with Christ."

"I know that," Julienne said again, eyes opening wide. "What are you trying to tell me?"

"That what we do—or what we do not do—doesn't matter."

She continued to stare at him, waiting, panting in quick little breaths.

"What they will not do, was not decided by caprice, or to shock you, or hurt you or any of the other families who suffer what we suffer now. It is of necessity, for the living and to protect the living."

"My God," she said, beginning to cry, "what are they going to do to my child . . ." she shuddered.

"Nothing," he said, drawing her close and holding her with his arms again. "They can do nothing to her—not anymore. It is unfair, it is horrible, but there is no wood and there will be no coffin."

"They're going to put her in the ground just like that?" Julienne shrieked.

"No, no," he said quickly, "she will be buried in a tarpaulin, like a burial at sea." He waited until she stopped crying again. "Listen to me now. All through time, sailors have been buried that way with great respect and greater dignity. Remember that. And remember Gisèle's soul is already safe in God's loving hands."

It was but a short walk from the hospital to Montparnasse Cemetery. The cortege comprised nine families who had lost their children to cholera in the night. They walked slowly, dazed by the grey fog in the air, and in their minds. They followed the hand-drawn black wagon as a priest led the solemn procession past the lines of white crosses and monuments, to the line of small open graves. The air was heavy with the scent of freshly dug earth.

Despite his tender words, despite his kind warning, the shock of seeing the off-white tarpaulin with her name written across it, so small a tarpaulin, so small a bundle being given to a man and then laid in the earth, nearly buckled Julienne's knees. Nine children were passed from the cart. Nine families wept and moaned and held one another, supporting each other to somehow bear this terrible sight.

The priest sprinkled consecrated water over the bodies and the graves. As they began to pray, a howl from the grey foggy sky shattered the stillness of the morning with its explosion.

"Our daughter Gisèle . . ." the priest intoned.

Julienne shook her head. "Gisela," she whispered, unable to see clearly through tear-filled eyes. Stefan gripped her tighter.

The howls continued, the ugly noises of explosions grew closer until one of the shells fell in the cemetery not far away from them, the blast spraying them with dirt and giving up the dead in a too-soon resurrection, disturbing the bones as they now lay in open graves.

Julienne shivered at the paralyzing sight. No more, she thought, no more. The howls continued from the sky and she felt as if pieces of herself were flying off in all directions, scattering to the winds and leaving only the outline of a grief-stricken woman. She couldn't help herself anymore, she couldn't stop herself and began to scream "GODDAMN YOU all to hell and its everlasting torments! No more, no more, stop it, stop it!" In a madness, she grabbed Frédéric and began to shake him violently. "You're French, do you hear, French, French, only French . . ."

Stefan pulled her hands from the boy. She slapped her brother and broke free from him.

Breathing frantically, she stooped in one instant, gripped a fistful of the cold earth and tossed it into Gisèle's grave. "It's done," she screamed, "done . . . there's nothing left!" and she staggered blindly away from the edge, deaf to Frédéric's sobbing, not caring about anyone, anything, not even the shells exploding all around them. Like a wounded, cornered animal still lashing out with one last breath of self-protection, she turned and ran from the cemetery.

"Let her go," Armand said to Stefan, holding him back. "Let her scream all she wants to."

Cécile took the boy from Stefan and held him as he hid in the folds of her skirt. "Armand is right," she said firmly, "let her have this kindness. Let her go."

Edward smoothed the folded edge of the blanket, then wiped his eyes after a heavy sigh. To be starved all of my life, and then finally to live and grow in love with a wife and children, only to discover the evanescent sands upon which we build our lives . . . Three days and she is gone, he thought. Three days—minutes really, in a life's time.

Minutes.

He thought instantly of his brother. Minutes. Twenty-four years ago and the pain is still fresh, still unspeakable. Nothing has changed, he thought, trapped in the twinned grief of the past and the present. The living still watch helplessly, lost in their own small worlds of a swirling, drowning agony in the mind, that clouds all the remaining world and renders it unreal. Lost, yes, lost as— He opened his eyes, staring at the wall in front of him, remembering the shocked expression on the face, in the eyes, his father's eyes mirroring the grief as they tried to take Michael from his father's arms, the final act of loss. He was lost then, Edward thought. He saw in his mind a father unable to eat, a man wandering the hallways, vainly touching portraits as if they were warm skin, instead of oil-based paint from an artist's palette.

I know, he thought, aching deep inside. I know what it is now, he thought.

blinking his eyes, not knowing where to look in the room, a room burgeoning with memories and sights of her. I know what he suffered, Edward thought. He watched his son die, my God, the nightmare of that sight, coupled with the loss. And I hid in a corner, he thought, looking at the corner of the bedroom, seeing in his mind, himself, crouched and hidden so long ago, a frightened living son momentarily forgotten, a little boy calling out to his father, half-spoken words never heard over the parent's tears.

Frédéric. The name came to his mind, jarring him.

He hadn't thought of Frédéric since—when? Today? No, he thought, yesterday? Did I speak with him yesterday, last night, when, *when?*

The boy had been forgotten in the hurry and the pain and the tears, lost in the confusion, lost . . . as I was lost, Edward thought, feeling the buried guilty tears come to his eyes.

It is normal, isn't it, so Goddamned normal to succumb and forget, to be consumed by the shock, not to know what to do, where to look, what to say, to think of no one except the agony that hovers all around, and stings with every . . . He turned his face into the pillow and wept. To hate him all these years for forgetting me, when I've done it too . . . He has reason to hate me, but I've none for hating him . . . I cannot blame him, I cannot, he was stricken, he was numb, his son, of his body, his son of fifteen years and I am the same *now* when she wasn't even mine . . .

He felt the ache in his heart from the crushing shame. John was right, he thought. My father tried to talk with me, but I never, never spoke to him. Julienne was right. He stood by me when no one else would, he granted me everything I wanted and I punished him, hated him for all of my life since that day when the shame was all mine; I blamed him when the blame was all mine . . .

He saw the wreckage of those years in his mind's eye, his sullen arrogance and the punishment of his absence. God, God forgive me, he cried, what *have* I done to my father . . .

The sound of the shovels echoed in their minds as they walked from the cemetery and blended with the people on the avenues who taunted the shelling. People continued with their lives and no one noticed their grief. The air was too crisp, noises too loud, and any fading color on anyone's clothing, any color other than black, seemed out of place and so disrespectful to a child's little life.

They climbed the stairs to the landing and were grateful for the quiet in Armand's salon, and wine, instead of food, warmed their stomachs.

Frédéric had watched them from the hallway and had stayed behind on the landing, first sitting on the stairs, looking and picking at the sawn stubs where the banister used to be, then felt cold and didn't know where to go. With them, he shrugged, then shook his head. They're so quiet and the shells are so loud. He glanced up to the third landing and meekly climbed the stairs.

But it was empty here, too, and he looked around the salon, half-expecting his mother to be there. Why is every place so cold, he thought, shivering by the door, then slowly walked to the window to watch for his mother.

395

"Frédéric?" Edward called.

He turned his head and paused by the door.

"I've been waiting for you."

The boy's shoulders sagged and he tumbled onto the bed, pressing and hiding himself in the arms and against the chest. The warm arms held him and smoothed his hair and smothered out the sound of the shelling. The big warm arms made a safe world around him and let him cry.

The rage in the sky and in the fires of burning buildings went unmatched by the rage in her heart. She walked and ran, then walked and finally crumbled against a building on a street she didn't know, and wept until the tears were wrung from every part of her. A grey woman, against a grey building, with grey-sooted snow near the shoes and the cloak, was a common sight and no one noticed her as the world around her lost the last fibers of its humanity.

She sat there, shivering and numb, until the night sky was thick with a cold fog and filled with the sounds of howls as the shelling continued, uninterrupted, as always.

There is no end to it, Julienne thought, dazed and struggling to stand. Homeless people, the old, the abandoned, clutch at the rags they call clothes, mismatched things taken from the garbage or stolen from one another.

They kill us piece by piece, Julienne thought, lost in a slow and morbid dream. I cannot bear it anymore, all of this, this ugliness . . . I'm empty inside and ache all the time and now, my child, too. My child, my Gisela . . . Kill me now and have done with the torture of life . . . I am as good as dead anyway . . .

There was a certain calm in hearing the Seine lap against the stone bridge. Even the fires' smoke carried by the wind had a certain seductive perfume to it, like trailing fingers pointing a way. The slight fog and the mist from the river hid the sights of ugliness and made a soft gossamer wall against the world that was dying around her.

Leaning against the bridge, she removed her gloves and touched the lifeless stone with her hands, desperate to feel something, anything, even the bitter cold of stone. I want, she thought sadly, I want everything to stop. I don't want to hurt anymore.

She stared at the water for a long time. Will it give me rest, she thought, or is it a slow death, an eternity of cold slipping through my nostrils and mouth, and stilling my voice before it takes my life?

God help me, she thought, I cannot feel anything, every part of me is dead—it scares me. She rubbed her hands together. If I had not run away, they would still be alive, I would be dead, but they would still be alive, so they have died in my place, and it is a punishment, then . . .

She paused with a shiver. Punishment? The word was peculiar and touched a memory with a warm burst within her mind. Who said that, when I was a child . . . she tried to think through the thick veils covering her mind. I, I was crying, she thought, eyes darting from her hands to the gloves in front of her lying on the stones. Yes, I remember, I was small, and I was crying for something, what? My mother? Was it when my mother died . . . Yes, I remember now—standing in the doorway crying for her, after she had died, long after they buried her. I stood in the doorway to the room and cried. One of the housemaids stood behind me, and she said "come away from there. It's wrong to cry over God's will, His punishment." A stupid woman, such careless words that hurt and frightened me so deeply.

Papa was furious, she thought, her back stiffening slightly. He dismissed the maid instantly that very day. He took me in his arms and dried my tears, then said I mustn't believe such silly words. He said the sevant had told me a terrible lie. He said, try to understand as best you can, but remember what I tell you—death is not a punishment. We will all die, we must all die, someday. It is natural, as natural as a flower picked from a garden that lives a week or so in a vase, then wilts and dies. There is nothing to fear in that. It is God's will, and the way He has made the world. Then, he smoothed my hair and said, I wish you were older, I wish you might understand that life is a gift, God's gift, for however long He chooses us to have that gift. Remember, my child, my Julienne, keep these words with you always—God has said, "Let your hearts be broken, not your garments torn, and return to the Lord your God. For gracious and merciful is He, slow to anger, rich in kindness, and relenting in punishment." *Relenting* in punishment, Julienne. It means God forgives. Punishment, he said, then shook his head, we hurt and punish and humiliate and shame each other. That is all our doing.

She felt her throat tighten. From the Bible, she thought, one of the prophets . . . Joel, I think.

I miss Mama, I said. He looked at me with sad eyes. I miss her too, he said, and your little brother. We must go on, we must live. I love you so much, my child, and you need me now, don't you? I am here.

A hot tear stung the deadened cheek and left a burning trail as it fell downwards to the jawline. My child, she thought . . . my Frédéric. I have been as silly and stupid and as thoughtless as the housemaid. I frightened him, and deserted him when he needed me most.

She took her gloves and stepped back from the bridge.

The sound of the door opening and closing roused Edward from a light sleep and in the oil-lamp's light, he saw the large brown eyes still beautiful even in their agony. She undid her cloak and let it drop to the floor.

"I wondered when you'd come back."

Julienne turned at his voice and saw that the sofa had been moved to face the door. A small table was within Edward's reach and on it were two glasses, a bottle of wine, the lamp and a dinner plate. "Where's Frédéric?"

"Downstairs, probably asleep by now. He stayed with me all afternoon and we had a long talk. Stefan is with him. You and I are quite alone."

She felt a small relief knowing Edward had comforted the boy and had not deserted or forgotten him. "Have you been sitting all this time?"

"Yes. First time in my life I'd fallen asleep sitting up—sober, mind you, drunk doesn't count."

She sighed and took a few steps closer to him, wincing at the sight of the strange shadows playing on his face, accenting the high bony cheeks and sharp jawline, the terrible thinness from hunger. She slowly brushed his hair from his forehead and then saw the dinner plate still had food on it. "Your supper's gone cold," she said.

"No, yours. I saved it for you."

She shook her head. "I'm not hungry."

He took her hand and she was surprised at the grip, the moment of strength gently drawing her down to him to a sitting position on the sofa, and then, making her lean across his lap.

"Your leg . . ."

"It doesn't matter," he said and supported her back with his left arm. With a trembling hand, he tried to pick up the fork, but couldn't hold it. He used his fingers instead, bringing the first small piece of meat to her mouth. "Open your mouth," he said, then put it inside.

She chewed and made a face. "It's horrible."

"I'll wager it is," he answered.

"Don't you know?"

He shook his head.

She looked at him, and then at the dinner plate. "This is your portion, isn't it?"

"Yes."

"Edward, no, I don't want it, you need . . ."

"Shhh," he said. "Everyone has gone without to coddle me. There'll be no more of that, do you hear? It's my turn now." He reached for the second of the three pieces, but she'd clamped her mouth shut. He looked at her for a moment, then said, "I'll push it past your teeth, I will, you know I will . . . for God's sake, don't deny me this, don't do this to me, I love you too much . . ."

She could see the truth in his eyes and opened her mouth as her own eyes filled. She chewed, then swallowed it with difficulty. "What is it?"

"It's grey," he said, giving her the glass of wine.

She drank half of it, then gave the glass back to him.

He held the last small piece of meat, and this time she did not resist. Leaning against him, she felt the clear outline of all his ribs, and traced her hand over the bony shoulders, hearing the rapid beating of his heart and the shallowness of his breath.

She tasted a warm salty taste in her mouth, and touched her gums with a finger, seeing the slight redness trickle slowly down to the knuckle. "My gums are bleeding," she said quietly.

"Mine have done that, too."

"You never said."

He shrugged. "What would be the point . . ."

"Headaches, too?"

"Constantly."

"All I seem to want to do is sleep."

He nodded.

"You've seen this before, haven't you?"

He looked at her but did not speak.

She paused, touched the thin, handsome face, then said slowly, "Are we . . . are we dying?"

"No, Madame," he smiled defiantly, "not yet."

CHAPTER
26

Standing on the Boulevard St. Michel, Armand read the newspaper article which made the rumors true. The swine, he thought, the rotten miserable swine, they ought to be lined up against a wall and shot, every last one of them. He crumpled the newspaper in his hands as his eyes stung and burned bitterly with new tears.

Moral energy, moral courage the Government says, he thought as the fury built inside. I'll give them moral courage, those thieving swine . . . and they have the nerve to call it a "convention?" He spit, then strode with long painful steps back toward his house. Convention, uhn? Why don't they call it what it is—surrender.

He looked at his house, and though it could not be seen from the front, he knew in his mind what the shell blast had done to the rear of the building. Walking inside, he saw the stairs, bare of warmth, bare of his banister, stripped clean by necessity to survive the terrible months of cold and dark. He stood there, staring at the emptiness and could only think "Why?" as he wept for his son, his country, and the shame.

"It says there will be food from the provinces," Julienne said, wiping her eyes and trying to read the newspaper Stefan had brought.

Cécile grunted.

Placing the newspaper down on the table, Julienne sighed. "It is over . . . and we're alive."

"Just."

"Where is Armand?"

"Downstairs."

Julienne saw the curious mixture of sadness and anger in Cécile's eyes. "What is he doing?"

"Leave him alone," Cécile said. "He has his own way, Julienne."

From the shavings of the banister used for the walking sticks and the peg, and the little pieces of wood that had been saved, Armand had built a fire.

He carelessly wiped his tears as he set the two wicker baskets down on the floor in front of the small fire. What have they done to all of us, he thought sadly, to the parents of the children who fought and died for nothing . . .

He took the clean baby clothes that Cécile had made so long ago, kissed them goodbye and gently fed them to the fire. The schoolbooks followed the clothes, then the toys he had made. He watched with dead eyes as a lifetime was reduced to ashes and smoke, and a few glowing embers escaped up the flue to the cold Paris daylight.

Holding the letters to himself, he could not burn all of them, just a few, three, three written by Denis' hand, three to represent him. My son, he wept, my beautiful son, they did not even bring you home to me . . .

Taking the last two good-sized pieces of wood, he began to carve dovetail joints.

There was a noise below the bedroom window that faced the courtyard and the small garden. It was a foreign sound and it woke Stefan from a light early afternoon sleep.

A shovel bit angrily into the soil near the rose bushes. Again and again, Armand dug, deeper, wider, deeper in the frozen soil, then, he stopped.

Stefan watched Armand tip the coal scuttle over the hole and reverently spill the ashes, slowly, losing none of them. Then, he began to cover the hole with the earth.

"Is it finished?"

Stefan turned to the doorway and saw Cécile, tightly holding herself and leaning against the wall. He didn't understand and looked out the window again. When Armand smacked a small wooden cross into the ground at the head of the mound, Stefan's eyes filled. "Yes," he whispered, as Armand sat down and caressed the earth, "it is finished."

Two long dismal months of winter spent on my back, obeying them, suffering their repellent advice and seeing the sleet and snow from my bedroom window, he thought. Watching the Dover Cliffs jagged and white against the blue cloudless sky, he sighed as they receded, then disappeared from view. So it is over, he mused, walking slowly on the deck and holding the railing for support. The last shot fired just before half-past eleven, one week ago, on Thursday night, January 26th. Surrender.

He touched the doorknob of the inner cabin, then let go of it, deciding to stay outside in the reviving air as the spray from the Channel soared over the bow and mixed with the steam from the port funnel. His tired blue eyes drifted to the flag of the P. and O.'s steamer *Fleet*, the four triangles of indigo, red, yellow and white, flying and flapping, a snapping sound barely heard against the choppy water. Then, he saw the larger flag at the top, flying on the steamship *Victoria*, the British Flag.

Soon, he told himself, it is not a long journey. One hour and a half, and we land at Calais and from there, on to Paris. I have waited a long time for this, and tomorrow they will let us enter the city.

400

He saw in his mind the food supplies traveling with them, the Lord Mayor's Relief Fund, donated by the English people for their countrymen and the starving of Paris.

Watching the whitecaps on the Channel, he felt an ache in his chest. He swallowed, then took a deep breath. Gently, old fellow, he told himself, breathe gently and easily. Ahh, I've lain in bed too long and done precisely what those charlatans ordered—rest, and more rest, that beastly infusion they made me drink, no strain, sleep and then more sleep until I hated the bed and the pillows and the fuss. How pale they turned when I had my bags packed for this journey. Too much of a strain, they said. Rubbish, I told them, firm as a rock. He sighed. I must know, he thought. I will keep the oath I made to myself: when the barricades are opened, I shall be there.

"Your Grace?"

He turned his head and saw a Steward, waiting respectfully a few yards away. "Yes?"

"It's turning colder. Won't you come inside and let me get you something warm to drink?"

He shook his head. "Thank you, no."

The Steward nodded, and left the Duke of Middlesex leaning on the railing and watching the Channel with brooding eyes.

Soldiers tossed bread to the crowds. Bony fingers scrambled for the loaves in the air. Julienne gathered up her tattered skirt as other women did, and held all the food there, all the food being given by the soldiers. Bread, and it looked like bread, real beef, garlic cloves, potatoes, cabbages, bacon, beans, leeks, eggs, butter, chickens, rabbits, *food*—from the Prussians, from the provinces, no one knew and no one cared. She pushed and grabbed and wept, edging her way closer, closer to the wooden tables set up near the Orleans barricades, and filled her skirt in the mad, hungry confusion of starving people. She took as much as they would allow her to take, and a weeping soldier gave her one more loaf of bread before she left the tables and began the long walk home, down Avenue d'Orleans, which turned into Rue d'Enfer.

She knew she was approaching it, and she knew she had to walk by it. Turning her head away, she forced herself to stare either down or to the right, not to the left, not towards Montparnasse Cemetery. She clutched the food closer to herself, though her arms ached, and her knees felt weak, and the headache had not gone away and her gums still bled. She held it tighter and tighter, thinking of the food, the life-saving food, and cried weak tears knowing it had come too late for Gisèle. She slowed the agonized pace only when she was five blocks past the cemetery.

The stairs to the apartment were like a mountain, and she barely had the strength to climb them, panting and aching, dry-mouthed and in pain, yet frantic to cook the food and eat, truly eat . . .

She walked through the salon and only let go of the skirt when the bundle rested safely, gently, on the table so nothing would break or be bruised or dirtied.

She and Cécile did not speak as they prepared the make-shift Garbure, cutting and paring, with anxious hands, all the vegetables they had not seen for months, using chickens in place of the wings and fat from a goose.

"It doesn't matter," Cécile said, heating the bacon and then pouring boiling water over it. "It will be wonderful, it doesn't matter at all that we use other things. It will be a Garbure to us."

Julienne put another cut slat of wood into the oven fire, then urged it along with still more pieces of Stefan's headboard.

"When will we find coal," Cécile said, tapping a nervous foot.

Julienne shrugged and watched the large pot.

"It has a long way to go," Cécile said, and took Julienne's arm, leading her away from the kitchen. "We ought to do something to keep busy."

"Could we, should we, perhaps, a little bread and jam?" Julienne sighed, hoping.

"Yes, why not," Cécile said. They went back to the kitchen and prepared the slices.

Julienne gave the first piece to Frédéric. "My good boy," she said, and kissed his forehead. Then Stefan was given his, and he savored every bite.

Armand was in the cellar working on the walking sticks and Cécile brought him his slice. Julienne took hers and Edward's into the bedroom.

He was sitting up in bed, using a book as a desk, and was writing with a pencil on sheets of paper torn from one of Frédéric's exercise books.

"Here," she said, and waved the bread under his nose.

He put the pencil down, and leaning back against the pillows, enjoyed the sheer pleasure of untainted food. "Marvelous," he sighed when finished. "Dear Lord, I never realized how good it could taste." He felt a pull in his stomach. "Ow," he said, and rubbed the center of his stomach. "Hurts a bit."

Julienne nodded. "Feels heavy, doesn't it?"

"Are we to be sick yet again, and this time because of real food?"

She shrugged.

"Well," he sighed, "I suppose real food—and plenty of it—will be a bit strange in our stomachs, after the things we've eaten."

Julienne looked at the pages neatly stacked at his side. "What is that?"

He paused, then said, "A letter."

"You write it in English."

"It *is* my language—my first language—you know."

She gave him the pencil.

"It's a . . . a letter to my father," he said quickly, then looked away from her and stared at the bureau's empty space where the dolls had been a scant ten days ago. "I've much to explain to him," he sighed.

She touched his thin hand, feeling the ridges of the tendons and the veins in an intricate pattern on the top as he gripped the pencil. "Why not just tell him?"

"What do you mean—to his face?" Edward shook his head. "No. I couldn't."

"But he's . . ."

"No," he repeated. "I forfeited that right long ago."

Julienne saw the telling look in his eyes. "It is good that you write him. At least it is something."

Edward touched her hand with his thumb. "Try to understand," he said. "I've shamed him, embarrassed him, hated him, and I was wrong to do so. I no longer have the right to be called his son. His tenant farmers behaved better than I . . ." He cleared his throat, which eased the taut pulling. "It's a long-overdue apology. It cannot undo what I have done but . . ."

"Why do you say that?"

"The punishment suits the crime," he said.

"You are so unforgiving with yourself."

"I know what I have done," he said quietly. "Leave this to me, Julienne. Please. Let me do what I know is best in this."

"You've changed a great deal," she said.

"Too late, I'm afraid."

She shook her head. "No change comes too late, Edward. Perhaps someday you will see that yourself, and learn to forgive yourself."

"Someday," he said, "I hope only to learn how to *live* with myself. And that's the difference between us."

As they said Grace, Armand stared at the filled bowl in front of him. His jaw was tight and the veins danced at his temples. "It's their food, isn't it?" he whispered, eyes narrowing at Cécile. "Answer me, it's from the Prussians, isn't it?"

Cécile returned the stare. "Don't be absurd. Food has no nationality."

"French soldiers gave it to me," Julienne said.

"The Army has been as hungry as we have. I don't believe you. And I will not eat their food," Armand pronounced and started to rise from the table.

Stefan planted his hand on the thin shoulder. "Sit down. None of us will eat unless you eat with us."

Armand was about to argue, but he saw the hungry eyes of the boy watching the soup-bowl. "You ask too much," Armand said, tears beginning at his eyes. "You, the Government, everyone asks too much of me. I will not stay inside when they come to march in Paris. I will buy a rifle and wait for them outside, and when I see one of their helmets . . ."

"You'll do no such thing," Stefan said quietly. "It's over. Silence is the only reply now." He picked up Armand's spoon and held it out to him. "How much *longer* must we be hungry?"

Armand wiped his eyes. "I will eat for those who died so we might live. I will live. And I swear to Almighty God, I will *never* forget what they have done to us."

Still, real food in small stomachs, used to a pittance and self-imposed rationings, made them queasy and gave them horrible pain for two days until they grew used to it. Armand ate, and suffered the pain, and insisted all the time that they had been poisoned by the Prussians.

"Look at them," Doctor Alan Herbert said to the Duke, indicating the long queue stretching around the distribution center for the English Lord Mayor's

Relief Fund, temporarily housed in a store on the Rue Pont Neuf. "So many cases of scurvy," he said. "I have heard that the Americans have also given a shipload of food."

"Have you been able to speak with Doctor Swinburne?" the Duke asked.

Herbert shook his head. "He has not replied to my message yet. They are as busy as we are now."

"What was the Doctor's name, at the Sorbonne, do you know?"

"No, Your Grace. Doctor Swinburne never told me. I wish I could be of more help to you."

"Thank you," the Duke replied, shaking Doctor Herbert's hand. He left the distribution center. What to do now, he thought. No records of him at the Embassy . . . perhaps, just go to the Sorbonne myself, and hope for the best . . .

Walking by the Seine to the Quai des Grands Augustins, he had the plaguing thought of the records kept at cemeteries, but dismissed it and decided again, for the fourth time that day, that the cemeteries would be last.

He was a stubborn man and would not believe Edward was dead until he saw the name plainly on a gravestone, or on a record sheet, or heard the words from someone who had witnessed his death.

He looked at the shelled buildings, the remains of homes and businesses, the burned rubble and partly standing buildings that had once been the center of people's lives. The further he walked on the Left Bank and the closer he got to the Sorbonne, the more rubble he saw. The Sorbonne itself bore the scars of war, and the blown-out windows made their own testament of a bleak winter's mutilation.

He asked the students where someone would have been brought for medical attention, and they showed him to the clinic. There, in the jammed waiting room, he asked the volunteer sister which doctor might have helped in an emergency operation on an Englishman. She looked at him with blank eyes, not knowing who might have performed it, and he could not tell her precisely when the surgery took place. She said she would ask the doctors. He was told to wait, and found a spot near the door where he could stand and breathe fresh air.

As the waiting room began to thin and clear, he wondered how many hours it had been. People came and went, others disappeared into hallways, and still many more were carried out on litters.

"Monsieur?"

He turned his head and saw a man. "Yes?"

"My name is Vadon, Doctor Vadon. What is it you wish to know?"

"Are you poisoned today?" Cécile sniggered, chiding Armand as she had done for five consecutive days.

He glared at her. "Isn't it enough that I eat the hateful food? Why do you pester me with your nasty remarks and make fun of me?"

She took the broom from his hands. "Because you are a foolish man and you frightened the boy for nothing."

Armand held the dustpan for the broom. "I was upset. What do you want from me, you silly old woman?"

"Ahh, I am old now, am I?"

"You were born old," Armand snapped. "I have lived my whole life with an old woman."

"It is you who have *become* old, and sour, and I think mean as well. The newpapers claim it is 'Siege Fever,' and I think with you, you are too far gone to be saved." She tossed the broom to the floor. "Do it yourself," she said, and walked back up the stairs from the lobby.

"I will," he shouted. "I don't have Siege Fever, and I don't need you to help me, to do anything at all for . . ." He heard the door slam. "*I* am not sour. *She* is sour. She has always been sour. She was born sour. Her miserable mother must have eaten nothing but rotten, sour, miserable . . ." He noticed the tall man, elegantly dressed, waiting in the doorway and looking cautiously inside. "Yes," he snapped, totally aggravated, "and what do you want?"

"I am looking for Monsieur Mabilleau," the man said in flawless French.

A foreigner, Armand grunted to himself. "I am Mabilleau," he said, brushing his dusty hands on the legs of his trousers. "And who are you?" he asked petulantly, angry at the world.

"I am Edward's father."

Armand's eyes sharpened. He stepped closer, seeing the face, the eyes. "Yes," he said. "I see the resemblance."

Richard Atherton-Moore took a breath. "Is my son alive?"

"But of course," Armand smiled, seeing the large blue eyes close for a moment and relief ease the taut lips.

"Where is he, I've been trying to find him for . . ."

"Upstairs," Armand said, then stepped in front of the anxious father, who had moved quickly to the stairs. "One moment, Monsieur," he said gently. "There is something you ought to know."

The Duke nodded. "I know of the surgery."

"Ahh," Armand said. "Then you must not be surprised when you see him. You see me? You see my face, how thin I am?"

"Yes," Richard answered.

"He is no different, Monsieur. We have been hungry for a long, long time. He is very thin, and weak, but he is alive. We saw to that."

The Duke looked full into Mabilleau's eyes. "I am indebted to you, Monsieur. I do not know how you came to know my son or to care for him, and later, you must tell me everything, but take me to him now, please."

"Yes of course," Armand said. "He lives on the third floor," and he led the father upstairs, noticing the strain on the face and the pale color in the cheeks. He wondered if the father was ill, but he knew that determination does magnificent things, as it had done with Edward. How did he find us, Armand wondered, and told himself he would ask later. He knocked on the door and waited, holding the father back slightly with the flat of his hand.

Stefan opened the door.

"You have a visitor," Armand said, and tilting a nod toward the man, said,

"I introduce you to Edward's father. Monsieur," he said, "Stefan . . ." He looked at Stefan and suddenly wrinkled his brow. "Isn't that strange," he said. "I never knew your last name."

"Weiskern," Stefan answered, holding out his hand.

The Duke's eyes opened a fraction.

"Come inside, Your Grace," Stefan said, then looked at Armand.

"No, no," Armand said, "I would intrude. I will come back later," he said, and went to the stairs.

Stefan closed the door quietly.

"Weiskern," the Duke said. "Prince Stefan Weiskern?"

"Yes."

The Duke looked at the salon, and then at the Prince. "I'm sorry, I don't understand any . . ."

"There is time for that," Stefan replied. "Has Armand told you . . ."

"Oh, you mean Monsieur Mabilleau," the Duke said. "Yes, he has, and I am aware of what to expect." He looked at the salon again, at the poverty, at the small boy with the large round eyes watching him from the chair. He heard footsteps in the kitchen and a young woman came out. He looked at the Prince. "Where is my son?"

"Sleeping," Stefan replied, then introduced Julienne to the Duke. He saw the pleasure in her eyes, and wondered why she had such a satisfied look about her, as if she'd known a private truth and it was now confirmed. He thought it best to leave father and son alone, and with Julienne and Frédéric, left the apartment. They would wait downstairs with Armand and Cécile. There is time to answer his questions, Stefan thought.

The Duke walked slowly to the doorless bedroom and stood there for a long moment watching Edward sleep. He wiped his relieved eyes, and simply enjoyed the placid sight after so many months of nightmares. He took off his coat and gloves and walked into the bedroom.

The tousled dark hair, the closed eyes and steady breathing, he sleeps as he has always slept, Richard thought, rumpled sheets and one arm out and the hand laced within the sheet, holding it tightly with his fingers.

He swallowed, then walked to the other side of the bed and looked down at the stump resting on pillows and half-covered with the thin blanket. He lifted the covers and felt a pull in his chest. What kind of suffering have you endured, he thought, shaking his head slightly, seeing his son ravaged by hunger, and a once-strong body violated by a bullet that claimed his leg and nearly his life.

The Duke of Somerset's boy, he thought, almost six years ago. He died from an amputation; most do, but you haven't. God has spared me that unspeakable loss. What have these people done to keep you alive?

He felt a bit weak and sat down on the edge of the bed. Gently, he brushed the hair back from Edward's forehead and caressed the right cheek. You are so thin, so horribly thin, he thought.

Edward stirred and leaned slightly into the palm. It felt smooth and warm— and large. He opened his eyes, and when they cleared, he saw a cuff, a man's cuff. He slowly turned his head and saw his father. His eyes shot open and he looked around the room quickly and discovered he wasn't dreaming. "How . . ." he said, turning his face away from the palm, then struggled to sit up.

"Let me help you," Richard said.

"No, no I can manage," Edward said, the English sounding peculiar to his ears. He was breathing hard and quick through a partially open mouth. "I, I don't know what to say to you," he said, staring with wide eyes at his father sitting on the edge of the bed not two feet away. "I, I never expected this, never."

Richard stared at him in disbelief, seeing the stunned and furtive look in the blue eyes, and the way they avoided his own.

"I," Edward said, more unnerved by the silence than anything else, "I, I was writing you," he said, glancing first at the empty bureau-top behind his father, and then uncomfortably at the empty corner. "I was writing you to explain everything. I'd nearly finished it."

"Explain what? About the leg?"

Edward shook his head. "It's all in the letter," he said quickly, reaching to the small table. "It's all been explained, in my letter . . ." He pushed the small stack of papers at his father's hand.

Richard looked at the top page but did not read it, and gently put the letter aside.

"Don't you wish to read it?" Edward asked, sounding like a small boy.

"I am here," he said simply, "I am sitting here, and not thousands of miles away. Has it not occurred to you I would rather hear your voice than read your handwriting, Edward."

"If I could speak the words, I'd not have written the letter," he said, leaning his head back and staring at the ceiling. He glanced at his father. "Philippe is dead, you know."

"No," Richard sighed, "I didn't know. How very sad. In the war?"

"Yes," Edward answered. "In battle. I, I read his name in the newspaper."

"You have suffered much, haven't you, and in so short a time."

"Hunh?" Edward said, and stopped looking at the ceiling and looked now at his father. "Whatever made you say that?"

"It's true, isn't it?" Richard said. "Two close friends, within a year, a terrible injury to yourself . . . I have heard, it is most painful. Is it, still?"

Edward swallowed, amazed. "Doesn't hurt quite so much anymore. Mostly a dull ache. Except when the peg is on . . ." He saw his father wince slightly, but then steady his expression. "I, I stand a bit now. Just for a minute or two. That is quite painful, but I try to stand a little more each day. It is still so strange, in the mornings, if my mind wanders, the memory of it comes back, as if to surprise me. I still feel the spot where the bullet shattered the bone. I still feel it, even though there's nothing there."

The Duke closed his eyes for a moment.

Edward saw the pained expression on his father's face, then smoothed the edge of the blanket with the flat of his hand. "Is my mother well?"

"Yes," his father managed.

"And my sister?"

"Wed. Happy and content."

Edward nodded absently, and looked at his father again, noticing now the pale color, the wrinkles that had deepened with time, and perhaps, worry, and saw so much more grey in the hair. He's aged, Edward thought, and suddenly realized it must have been more than aging. "You don't look well," he said quietly.

"I . . ." Richard began, then said, "it doesn't matter."

There was a long silence and Edward found it difficult to withstand. "You've been ill, haven't you?" then added, "You work much too hard, you know."

The Duke weakly smiled. "Not any longer. I haven't been to the Lords for months now."

Edward felt a chill crawl up his back. "Why?"

Richard met the stare. "Blame the doctors, the silly old hens." He saw the worry in the blue eyes. "It's nothing. Don't think on it. A little pain, a lot of rest, nothing more." He paused, then said, "Not when one thinks of this," and nodded slightly towards the leg.

He's had a heart attack, Edward thought, feeling a heaviness settle on him. Always knew he might, then he looked away. "How did you find me?" he asked, mostly to fill the aching silence.

"Why did you leave so quickly?" Richard asked, feeling a strain in his voice. "Why did you up and leave without waiting for me? I went to your rooms that next morning to tell you you needn't go, you needn't leave, but you'd already gone, hadn't you?"

"I," Edward began, "I was angry, and filled with spite. You'd changed your mind?"

"Yes of course I had," the Duke said quickly, knitting his eyebrows in a frown. "I, too, was angry, but it passed, and so soon afterwards, but you," he said, "so impulsive, so eager to disappear and never once look back. In all your life you have never once stopped, and paused, and reflected on a situation."

Edward hung his head slightly, knowing it was the truth, shamed by the truthful words and knowing it had been the way he'd lived all his life, before her, before seeing that the world did not end at his fingertips and there was a larger view of things outside himself.

"How did I find you?" Richard continued. "Well, it wasn't easy, Edward. From the day you left, I began writing letters, and sending telegrams to everyone I knew, and without exception, they told me they hadn't seen you. Even Philippe," he said, raising an eyebrow.

"Yes, I knew of that letter," Edward confessed.

"Quite," his father nodded. "At the end of November I read you'd been shot, and about your leg, and that as I was reading this, this hateful note, you most probably had already died. That," he said in a sigh, "that was the hardest of all."

"What note? Who told you?"

"Carnarvon. His brother, Doctor Alan Herbert, learned of you from an American Doctor named Swinburne. He assisted in your surgery." He saw the blank look. "No, you couldn't have known. I've been here for nearly a week, searching for you. First at the Embassy, then to see Herbert. Tried to see the American, but could not. Then I tried the Sorbonne myself and learned your friend's name, Mabilleau. The Doctor didn't remember where he lived, just the name and that it wasn't far from the Sorbonne. I've been knocking on doors and asking all sorts of people about this man Mabilleau for four days," he said. "Always, at night, in a corner of my mind was that last choice, that awful specter following me—reading the registry lists of the cemeteries." He took a breath. "I, I was prepared to do that, I was, because otherwise I would not believe it. Happily, thank the Good Lord, I did not have to."

Even now, Edward thought miserably, I am the cause of grief for him. He felt his lips trembling and his eyes burning as they filled. He tried to stop it, to compose himself, but it was a failed effort as he thought of his father walking the streets, asking people about Armand, being told God knows what, yet continuing, in despair, and a nightly torment of seeing a name on a gravestone. "Why . . ." he whispered, "why did you *do* all that when you're unwell, after all that's happened, when . . ."

"Because you are my son and I love you."

Edward felt himself aching inside. "How can you say that to me after all I've done   ."

"The past doesn't matter at all," his father said.

"No, no," Edward shook his head, feeling frantic, hearing the words escape his lips. "It should have been me, *me*, and you would never have had all that suffering, all that anguish . . ."

Richard took Edward's hand in his own. "I don't understand, what are you talking about?"

Edward felt the warm caress, and instead of calming him, it made him more upset. He couldn't look at his father, yet he could not pull his hand away. He felt unbearably dirty. "I've always known it should have been me. I . . . I know how much you loved him, and how much promise he had. Sometimes, I was so jealous. I loved him, and God forgive me, I hated him at times, too."

"Hated whom?"

"I should have died in his place," Edward said, his jaw slackening, a tremble shooting through the thin shoulders.

"Whose place, what are you talking . . ."

"Mi . . . Mi . . . Michael's," Edward stammered, and felt the hand loosen about his own and slightly withdraw as the great shoulders slumped and his father stared at the floor.

"It was my fault," Edward said, closing his eyes, ashamed to look anywhere, hiding in the false darkness of wet eyes. "I made him laugh, and, and he choked, and it, it was all my fault."

"No," his father said slowly.

"YES," Edward said, biting the word out, feeling the ghastly shudder inside of him as he stared at his father. "I saw what I . . ."

"You saw nothing," Richard said, facing his son, seeing the guilty, tormented eyes of his boy. "*I* saw—*I* saw him eating too fast. He *always* ate too fast. It was a habit from childhood he never, never broke. I saw *all* of it, Edward," he said, his voice straining. He took a breath and continued. "You leaned to him. You whispered something to him. He laughed. *Then* he put the fork into his mouth and barely chewed the blasted fish before he swallowed. Only then, did he choke." He saw the color draining from Edward's face. He reached quickly and placed his hands around the thin cheeks, wiping the tears with his thumbs. "You had nothing to do with it, you were not to blame." He drew his son closer, wrapped his long arms around the thin back, touching the sharp outlines of the shoulder blades and the spine, and felt his own eyes stinging and wet. "What sort of hell have you fashioned for yourself all these years," he said slowly, "blaming and punishing yourself for something you did not do . . ."

Edward leaned into his father. He hesitated, then touched his father's side, then placed a timid hand on the back. He waited, still guiltily expecting a rebuff, and when none came, pressed the hand on his father's back. Then he brought his other arm around his father. He felt warm and safe, as adult eyes cried a little boy's tears.

"What am I to do with you," Richard managed, not meaning it as a question, but more a statement, seeing clearly this guilt borne for so many wasted years.

"I . . . I should abandon me, if I were you," Edward whispered.

Richard firmly held his son. "No," he sighed, "I have never done so and I shan't begin now, when you have finally come home to me." He felt the grip tighten across his back. He felt the stubbled cheek brush his smooth skin, then closed his eyes, content when, for the first time in twenty-four long and empty years, he felt a son's kiss.

Julienne lingered in the hallway by the stairs, listening for any sound, any door opening or feet shuffling upstairs. How maddening, she thought, I wish I knew what he was doing up there for two hours, I wish I could read English and could have known what he'd put in that letter . . .

"What *are* you doing?"

Startled, she turned to the accusing voice and saw Stefan closing the door behind him. "Come away from there," he said. "This is shameful, listening like that. What is next, peering through keyholes?"

She grinned. "I considered that." She saw his expression harden. "It was only a joke, Stefan, you needn't look so disapproving. His father is a handsome man, isn't he? Edward insisted he looked nothing like his father."

"He must be blind. The resemblance is extraordinary."

"I wonder how he found us."

"I wonder what he'll think of us, and this 'unusual' situation," Stefan said. Her grin faded.

"You hadn't thought of that, had you?"

"No," she answered. "Not once. It won't make any difference."

"Really?" he said rather pointedly. "I recommend you think again." He took her by the hand. "But, my dear sister, not in the hallway. The days of being common are over."

"What is that supposed to mean?"

"It means," he said, eyes glancing around the hallway, "that *this* is over. The war is over, and the charade is over. You must, and will, turn your eyes toward a lasting future for you and Frédéric. And it is not to be found in some little apartment in a ravaged city, giving you a life you were not born to, and most certainly do not deserve."

"Edward won't leave me," she said.

"I never suggested he would."

"And I won't leave him."

"I never suggested you should."

"Then what are you suggesting?"

Stefan's eyes brightened, but he only smiled and did not answer with words.

Julienne saw the veiled menace in his eyes. "Stefan . . ."

"No," he said with a finality in his voice. "We shall speak when we have a moment of privacy—and not before." He opened the door to the salon, to a waiting Armand and Cécile and Frédéric, effectively ending this conversation and behaving once more as head of his family and very much a Prince.

As the Duke crossed the Seine, he paused for a moment, absently watching a child with large vacant eyes walk in the opposite direction. He turned away and stared at the Seine, his mind reaching back to that June evening. I lost two sons that night, he thought sadly, and in my grief I believed that only one had died. He sighed. What to do about this, he thought, mulling over the long and complicated story Edward had told him about his life, and the people who had become his life.

He left the bridge and made his way through the crowds of people, all angry, all speaking of banding together to continue the revolution and a war already lost.

Edward said he thought her a widow, and only later knew the truth. Can one call what she has fled a marriage? I think not, he decided. They have survived unthinkable hardships together, and are bound by both love and grief. Tragedy, as I have seen in my own life, will either separate two people, or draw them closer together.

Well, he thought, walking into his hotel, I have never flinched from any argument and the words "unsolvable problem" have never had meaning to me. Every situation has a solution, and my mind is not bankrupt of imagination yet. He smiled to himself. My friends described Edward as willful and stubborn. They have forgotten he inherited that from me.

Julienne hid her face into Edward's neck, then sighed and edged nearer to him.

"Careful," he said lightly, "I shall fall off if you move any closer. This bed wasn't fashioned for two."

"I cannot sleep in the other bed," she said quietly. "Sorry."

He wound his arm around her, caressing the small of her back. "It was only a joke." He kissed her hair, saying, "You are so serious tonight. I would have thought you'd be so pleased, about my father, I mean. You're not even enjoying the fact that you were right."

"It isn't that," she answered. "My brother is behaving strangely again."

"How so?"

411

"He said, 'this charade is over,' and I must think of the future now."

"He's right."

Julienne propped herself up on her left elbow. "Not you, too? You agree with him that everything has changed?"

Edward turned his head on the pillow. "Planning to leave me, my love?"

"Never," Julienne answered, laying her head across his chest.

"And I won't leave you, so tell me, if you please, precisely what has changed?"

"Nothing."

"Exactly so."

She sighed. "Stefan says I am living a life undeserved."

"I agree."

"How . . ."

"Oh, come now," Edward said, winding his fingers through her hair, "you *know* I have never wholly approved of this. Yes, I agree that the time has come for a calmer life where you do not do the work of servants."

"I don't think I wish to discuss this just now," Julienne said.

"You're a fine one to talk," he said quietly. "When it suits you, you accuse me of avoiding things, but you, too, have a fondness for 'not discussing' unpleasant things. You needn't run from this, you know. We shall face it as we have faced everything else—together, with our strength combined."

She thought a moment, then said, "Your father wasn't pleased, was he?"

"Was your brother at the start?"

"No."

"Well how can you expect him to be pleased, when he hasn't had the time to understand? Be fair, Julienne." When she said nothing, he poked her. "Aren't you forgetting one little point? Whether or not he approves doesn't matter a trice. Nothing will change." He sighed, then said softly, "My father is not an ungenerous man and he will not leave us destitute. He knows what we have survived. I told him everything, especially what you and the others sacrificed for me."

"It wasn't . . ."

"It *was* a sacrifice," he said, firmly interrupting her. "It was a great sacrifice and one made out of love. We shall have a suitable income, of that you may be certain. Wherever we go, we shall live well."

"We've been mostly happy here," she began. "Shall we live here?"

He held her, and said very gently, "It's finished here. Can't you sense it? The Paris we knew has gone. We must let it rest, and begin again."

In a borrowed carriage drawn by newly purchased horses from the provinces, Richard returned to the apartment the following day and felt like Father Christmas bringing packages and food. It seemed very quiet, and as Prince Stefan helped him carry the packages to the sofa, he asked where everyone was at this hour.

"My sister is with Cécile downstairs. Frédéric is in school. Armand is sulking somewhere on his own. He's been doing quite a lot of that lately."

Richard nodded and was about to walk into the bedroom to see Edward, but the Austrian Prince stood in his way.

"We have a small surprise for you. I told Edward it was too soon, but he is rather determined. He can be very stubborn."

"True enough," Richard chuckled.

"Turn your back, just for a moment."

Richard did so, hearing shuffling behind him, then a heavy sigh. He then heard the scrape of wood upon wood, and turned around to see Edward, shaved, dressed, and standing with the help of two walking-sticks gripped in his white-knuckled hands. The arms were bowed at the elbows and his shoulders were hunched, unused to supporting the weight of his body. His head was slightly bent down, and his eyes darted from the floor to his father. Even though he seemed uncertain, the smile was as warm as it was fast. He was in pain, and was visibly ignoring it. Richard stepped closer.

"No, Sir, wait there," Edward said, jutting his chin. "Let me come to you."

Richard waited, and as he watched, he had the strange feeling of reliving a moment that had disappeared with time and growth and was preserved only in memory. He opened his arms as Edward again took his first steps to his father. The Duke let his son lean against him, and felt the shivering in the arms from the strain.

"Three," Edward wheezed, breathing fast and hard. "Can you imagine, three steps . . ."

Richard patted Edward's back. "You ought to sit down now," he smiled. "It's a marvelous beginning. You've made me very happy and I am so very proud of you. Where do you wish to sit?"

Edward nodded to the chair at the table. "There," he said.

Stefan took both walking-sticks, and he and the Duke wrapped their arms around Edward's waist and half-carried him to the chair. He sat down heavily, wiping the sweat-beads from his brow and upper lip.

Richard took the chair nearest him and brought it even closer. "I should like you to see a doctor, and have the knee examined."

"Yes, I will," Edward answered, then opened his eyes. "Oh the stairs." He looked at his father. "I can't imagine how I will manage those. Three flights of them . . ."

"We might carry you," Stefan offered.

"Yes," the Duke agreed, "we could make a seat for you with our arms and hands and . . ." He paused, then smiled to himself.

"I remember that," Edward said, watching his father.

"Do you?"

"You made a swing for me with your hands as the seat, and then you tossed me in the air. I remember." He saw his father smile. "I was a bit lighter then." He thought a moment. "Suppose I were to sit down on a step, then, using my hands and arms, lift myself and ease myself down to the next step. I could do it. I've still got the good right leg to help in this, when I lift myself up. I haven't the strength nor the balance to stand on a step now, and with no banisters for support, it would be courting disaster to try to manage them otherwise. It's worth a try, don't you think? If I cannot do it, I shall have to be carried, but I should like very much to try it myself, first."

"Why not?" Richard said as a way of agreeing.

413

"It's settled then," Edward said.

"Well, one issue is settled, isn't it?" Richard said.

Edward nodded thoughtfully. "Have you considered the other matter, Sir?"

"I have thought of nothing else," the Duke replied.

"Whoever you are, go away and leave me to myself," Armand growled to the footsteps on the stairs.

Julienne continued downstairs to the cellar anyway.

"I said, go away," Armand said, and scowled at her when she first appeared.

"I do not deserve that," Julienne said, lifting her chin to defy the scowl.

"Perhaps not," Armand relented, sitting in the corner on top of wicker baskets.

She shook her head at him.

"The old woman sent you, didn't she?"

"What old woman?"

"The old sour one I am married to, she sent you here, didn't she?"

"If you mean Cécile, yes."

He grunted, defiantly, whilst his right leg swung carelessly over the side of the large basket. "Leave me to my misery, Julienne. There is nothing for you to do here."

"I think it is more than misery, Armand," she said. "I think the misery has crossed into another feeling. Hate."

He nodded.

"Why?" she sighed.

"Why," he repeated in a colorless tone, then felt his jaw tighten. "You have the courage to ask me why?" He looked at her standing there, waiting, thin and tough and hardened by life. "Half my home is destroyed, my country vanquished, my sons are dead, and my life, if one may call it so, stretches out before me—empty: empty years to finish an empty life, nothing but emptiness waits for me and you stand there and ask me why I hate . . ."

"You speak as if you have nothing, and no one, and it isn't true. A loving wife is a good friend, Armand. And she has been your partner through the most terrible times in memory."

He vaguely nodded.

"Where is your emptiness then?" Julienne asked, stepping closer.

"You would not understand," he said quietly.

"Why not?"

He looked up with softer, sadder eyes. "Because you are young, my dear Julienne, and I, I am not." He looked away. "The years left to Cécile and me, will be empty ones. I have been robbed of my sons, my children. When I die, she will be alone, and if she dies before me, I shall be alone. You cannot understand that, because your situation is unlike mine."

"But in the beginning, when I first came here I was alone."

He shook his head. "You had your children," he said quietly, "and both of mine are in their graves."

She walked over to him and took his hands. "We are like a family now," she said. "You will never be alone. Come with us."

He shook his head again. "That is kind of you, but you have a path you must follow. You and the others will live your lives in some other place, yes?"

"Yes," she said. "Edward wishes it."

"So it must be," he said. "This is my home, just as you must find a place to call your home." He paused, then sighed. "I thought it would be so different. I thought, so many years ago, looking at my two sons, it will be a good life. I remember thinking, Claude will grow strong and tall, and Denis, what a fine boy he is, what a loving son I have. They will marry, and have many children, and when we are old, the house will still be filled with the sound of children calling out Grandpapa, Grandmama . . ." He swallowed. "It was not to be," he said simply, then squeezed her hands and withdrew his own from hers. "There was no time to think of such things before. I shall have the rest of my miserable life to think of nothing else. Please leave me alone. I . . . I don't want to talk anymore . . ."

"Once, Julienne believed her only course was to run away," Stefan said thoughtfully at the table. "I never agreed with that. She denied me any say in the matter and did not seek the help of . . ."

"Be fair," Edward interrupted. "She was terrified, and with good reason. She fully believed he would kill not only you, but the rest of your family as well."

Stefan shook his head. "That idea—and her choice—defy rational belief."

"And we are not speaking of a rational man," Edward countered. "The situation, and the man, are most irrational. To understand why she did what she did, you must appreciate how isolated she was, how confused she had become, and at the base of it all, how terrified she was of him. Stefan, consider what it is to be inundated by criticism, to be reminded one has failed as a wife, mother, and a woman, to be in constant fear of one's life and for the lives of one's children and beloved family, day after day after day for years. All of this heightened her desperation. Given the circumstances, it is amazing she could think at all!"

Richard agreed. "Earlier, you mentioned the Esterhazy scandal."

"Yes," Stefan nodded.

"What was the outcome?"

"Well," Stefan began, "the situation is slightly different. The Count— known to most of us as 'Mysterious Móricz'—has always been 'peculiar.' He had moments of genius, and longer periods of exceedingly strange behavior. He was our Ambassador to Rome for only five months because he sent no dispatches, answered no questions, attended no meetings, and regarded himself above inquiry of any sort. Later, his abuse of his wife was an embarrassment to my cousin who trusted him. No amount of talk could stop the beatings. At any rate, one act put an end to it. He set his castle on fire and was committed to a lunatic asylum." He sighed. "The public was outraged over Esterhazy's actions. So was my cousin. But I tell you this—as far as Franz is concerned, he does not have to set *his* house on fire to catch my cousin's attention. One look at Julienne, and Franz will be banished or imprisoned. My sister may insist all she likes that Franz will not obey, but that is nonsense. He has no choice in the matter. My family *is* Austria, and her husband Franz is a subject to that power."

The Duke thought a moment, then said, "In England, cruelty is a sufficient—and acceptable—reason for a woman to sue for divorce." When the Prince made no reply, he continued very gently, saying, "I realize it is different in your country."

Stefan nodded. "Still, there is a way. I will put the situation before my cousin. Franz will be imprisoned or banished, and he will obey. Then, I will go to Rome and speak to the Pope myself."

"Do you expect her to go back to Vienna for this?" Edward asked.

"She will—because she must," Stefan answered.

"She won't do it."

"She has no choice," Stefan glared, growing annoyed. "I cannot, in good conscience, allow her to continue living like this. My family's power and influence will be used to one end—to aid my sister. I want my cousin to see what Franz did to her."

"And what of the scandal?" Edward asked.

"There will be no scandal in Vienna," Stefan said evenly. "It will be handled with great discretion, and with little or no interference from Franz."

"How can you be so sure of that?" Edward asked.

Stefan slowly smiled. "You leave that to me."

There was something chilling in Stefan's warm and easy smile. Edward looked away as Stefan refilled their wine glasses.

"We are all agreed, then," Stefan said. "She returns to Vienna and my family will take charge of this matter. After that, you will live in England, as your father suggested earlier, Edward." He took his glass and touched it to the others. "To—a speedy journey, from one life to another," he quipped.

Edward looked at Stefan and noticed that behind the calm expression, his eyes held flint-like sparks.

The doorknob turned and Julienne stepped into the room, still brooding to herself about Armand. Walking closer to the table, she saw three sets of determined eyes watching her.

CHAPTER
27

She liked Edward's father. Frédéric warmed to the Duke very quickly and it pleased Julienne to see this. She spent many hours talking to the Duke, learning a little of him, his background, his work and enjoyed the respite from pressure regarding her return to Vienna. He never once mentioned it and she knew it was not his place to do so.

Still, it was difficult to fight a conspiracy. Over the next few days, there seemed to be no corner where she might find peace. She mistrusted Stefan's reasons. He had, she knew, a deep hate for Franz, a hate he had nurtured for several years. He felt betrayed by his friend, and perhaps, she thought, guilty that he somehow betrayed me by not knowing of this, by not protecting me from Franz and the violence.

Edward's reasons, she thought, ran a parallel course with Stefan's: hate; hate for a man he's never met, hate for what he has learned, hate for what he has seen with his own eyes, in me, on my body and in Frédéric.

Even Cécile and Armand joined the ranks against her. This was a surprise. There was a vindictive undercurrent in them as well. Sever him from your life, they said. It is not worth the trouble thinking and fretting over him. Do it quickly and walk away from him forever. You'll be free of him, they said. He is worth less than a flea. Swat him and be done with it.

Everywhere she turned, there was a firm resolve against her, and in desperation, she looked to Edward's father. She felt he would give, as he was trained to give, an opinion based upon fact and not one colored by emotion.

She met him away from the apartment, away from the nagging voices and knit eyebrows and obstinate eyes. She walked with him in the remains of the Jardin du Luxembourg, the devastation and bleakness perfectly suiting her mood. "I am afraid," she said quietly, keeping pace with the Duke.

"I know that," Richard answered.

"Then why do you agree with them? Why do you want me to return to the place that has been nothing but agony for me? Everyone has their arguments and all I have to speak for me are the words of my Uncle and the memories of what I have survived."

Richard thought a moment, then stopped by one of the cast-iron benches near the pool and sat down with her. "You are joining issues in your mind. First, we must separate them."

She waited, willing to listen.

"A place is not an agony, the man has caused you the agony."

"Yes," she said, not wishing to argue over the small semantic point.

"Secondly, your Uncle's words were given you when you were alone. He sought your safety and knew if you returned alone, if you had failed to reach France and returned to Vienna, frightened to go on, unable to keep to your resolve—or, were brought back to Vienna—the misery would probably be worse, and the punishment more severe."

Yes, she thought, he did have a point.

"Lastly, why do I agree with them?"

She nodded, and let him take her hand.

"My dear daughter," Richard said, "if I may presume to call you so?"

She smiled and squeezed his hand in assent.

"I urge this because it is the right thing to do," he said calmly. "You must think of your son's future, and questions that may arise later. But mostly, Julienne, you must realize that living a life in hiding is not living at all. It is a perpetual charade and there is something mean in that. It isn't that you live a life unsuited to your position or your birth. I do not speak about doing your own work within the house—you are most brave and did what was necessary to survive. I speak of a denial of yourself. You have an absolute right to be you, to call yourself by your own name. It is one thing to make that choice, however willingly, when none other presents itself. But you have another choice now—to end that marriage and begin life again, this time in freedom and not in shame. That is what you would deny yourself by continuing this charade. You betray yourself, and that is wrong."

She knew he was right. Still, she was afraid of Franz and told him so.

"But why live a half-life, when you are presented with a choice of a full one?" He paused, suddenly fascinated by the expression that softened her eyes and the small smile easing her lips. The lovely face calmed.

"In other words," she said quietly, "choose life. That is what you mean, isn't it, by choosing a full life instead of a half-life?"

He was puzzled by the phrase, but nodded. "Yes, I would choose life, always."

She warmed to the sound of a father's words bridging time in another man. Despite the gnawing fear, she said quietly, "Then I will."

The days came and went with an alarming speed, and all arrangements rested in the capable hands of the Duke. Edward, more stubborn than ever, managed the stairs by sitting on the steps and lowering himself, one at a time. At each landing, Armand and Stefan picked him up and helped him to the next set of stairs. Edward felt more satisfied by overcoming this obstacle than by Doctor Vadon's astonished pleasure at seeing him alive. The Doctor examined and poked, squeezed and touched, saw that the stump had healed and then removed the stitches. He nodded approvingly at the hand-made peg with the straps and commented that it had been fashioned by a talented craftsman.

Tailors were brought in and new traveling clothes ordered. A dressmaker came, and Julienne chose material for her traveling outfit. Suitcases were purchased, and empty crates were delivered. Julienne packed what clothing remained, the books, and a few personal items she'd purchased for the apartment, which filled only one of the crates. She kept two of Gisèle's dolls and one little dress, unable to part with them, but the rest would better serve a living child in need. She brought them to an orphan asylum and did not have to explain the gift.

Armand watched the tradesmen come and go and spoke very little to anyone. Each day, he felt the ache within him growing, but it was not his place nor his right to speak it aloud. He seemed lost within himself and clung mostly to Frédéric. With the boy, he seemed to be a boy in telling youthful stories filled with dreams, but the narrative was noticeably without hope.

On Friday afternoon, they heard the door to the courtyard open behind them. Frédéric turned and smiled. "Grandpapa," he said.

The Duke saw Armand's pained expression, and watched as he let go of Frédéric.

"Your mother wishes to speak with you," Richard said. "Go along now, upstairs with you. I wish to speak with Monsieur Mabilleau."

He closed the door after Frédéric and sat next to Armand on the stone ledge surrounding the bare-branched tree. "It will be a lovely garden in the spring," Richard said.

Armand grunted. "You are a lucky man," he said. "Your life is untouched by this tragedy."

"No. My son was hurt. His pain is my pain. But I take your meaning. I, too, have buried children."

Armand nodded, then sighed as he looked up at the gaping hole in the side of the building near the roof. "Look at it," he said, mostly to himself. "A shell of a building, a shell of a life . . . and a shell of a grave," he said, his voice straining slightly as he gazed on the small wooden cross, marking the spot near the rose bushes, bare and filled with thorns.

"Will you stay here?"

"Yes," Armand replied. "It is my home."

"Shall you repair the side and the roof and the banister?"

"I must. It is not safe." Armand shrugged. "When I am able to buy bricks and wood, I shall. Some of my tenants have no money now. I cannot turn them out. They have been with me a long time, through good and bad. I let them live on credit for a time, until we pick up the pieces of our lives, and are able to make a living again, such as it is." He sighed again. "I came here with such dreams. My wife and I, we built our lives together. In the things I made, I was able to write my name. The banister had my name. The building had my name. My sons had my name. Now, all is gone."

"Those are the feelings of an orphan, Monsieur Mabilleau."

"Yes, well, I feel orphaned—we must blame the war for that."

"Then you are not alone," Richard said.

Armand shook his head. "Monsieur, I am more alone than you know."

"I meant that many share your situation."

Armand looked at him with puzzled eyes. "You mean it has killed something in all of us?"

"That, and the other meaning. The streets and hospitals are filled with orphaned children."

"What do you suggest, that I . . ." Armand shook his head. "No. It is impossible. They are other people's children, not mine. Mine are dead."

"Frédéric is someone else's child," Richard said carefully, "or had you forgotten that?"

Armand turned away from Edward's father. In the daily struggle to survive over so many long and terrible months, when they thought only of the hardships and death and despair, he had grown so used to hearing Frédéric say "Papa," he had forgotten the boy had been fathered by someone else.

"Frédéric loves my son, needs my son, and has become a son to my son."

"That is different," Armand said.

"Why?"

"Because your son has never had sons of his own."

"A child is just a child. You know that yourself. You've raised two sons, and helped greatly in the raising of Frédéric and Gisèle. Were they all so very different? Did they require different things, or play different games or sing different songs?"

"No," Armand had to admit, however, grudgingly. "Is that why you came to me? Has someone suggested this little talk?"

Richard smiled. "A word or two was whispered in my ear, yes."

"Cécile," Armand said flatly.

"No."

"Then it could only be Julienne, who was sent by Cécile in the first place, so it is *still* Cécile who sent you," Armand announced.

"I came for another reason as well," Richard said. He reached into his breast pocket and saw Armand shaking his head.

"No," Armand said, "I accept no charity, Monsieur."

"It isn't charity," Richard said. "It is a gift."

"No, thank you, but no."

Richard considered Mabilleau's answer, and not wishing to offend a man holding onto the last shreds of his pride, said in a diplomatic way, "What you did for my son, was that charity?"

"Of course not," Armand said.

"Your help and concern and friendship gave my son his life. You know that. What I do now, is return that gift of life to you. It is yours, to accept or reject as you see fit. I have placed a sum in the Rothschild Bank on Rue Laffitte in your name. Claim it, and use it, and let it help you make the repairs that need to be made." He stood up, then said with a smile, "You know, so many homes have been destroyed by this war. In rebuilding, the work lies not only in the bricks and the mortar, but with people. A country's future rests on the shoulders of its children, Monsieur Mabilleau. There are too many children in need, deeply scarred by loss. They are not just other people's children. They are the children of France. If you open your eyes and see them, Armand, you will open your heart." He left the Frenchman nodding thoughtfully, and walked alone to the door of the building.

Julienne had never liked goodbyes, and Sunday was a day filled with little else. She wept with Cécile, whose own eyes were wet with sorrow. The last time they had planned to leave, the pain was not as it was now. This, Julienne knew, was permanent. They would visit, they would write, but it would never be the same again. In saying goodbye to Cécile, she was losing a part of her life, for in the one woman was friend and mother, and no words could say what her tears said.

Holding Frédéric for a long time that evening, Julienne sat with him on the sofa, smoothing and adjusting the silky blond hair with her fingers whilst he sat as close as he could to her. Leaving him, her only child, even for just a short time made her anxious and worried, yet she knew his safety was the most important thing in all the world. Bringing him to Vienna just to have him with her, would place him in needless jeopardy. He had suffered too much in too short a life, and she swore to herself there would be no more of it. It was best for him to go to England, and she told him so, and was touched deeply by his questions of would she be all right, would she be safe, and she had to promise many many times that she would be.

He hadn't really forgotten, she'd learned. He was still terrified of Franz, as she was. She lied to him. She said they were going to Vienna for business reasons. Uncle Stefan needed her help, it was too complicated and not really important for him to understand, and she would be in England in less than a month. He seemed to believe her, but still held her tightly as if his small and frail little body might be an armor against the world and against what still waited in Vienna.

"You needn't worry or be frightened," Julienne said. "But you must promise me something."

He looked up at her.

"You must promise me to be the very good boy that you are, when you go along with your Grandfather to England. You must do as he says, and not cause him to fret over you."

"I promise," the boy smiled. "I love him."

"So do I," Julienne said. "It will be a good life, Frédéric. You shall see."

"Shall I go riding?"

"Yes, I imagine you will."

"But not with Papa anymore," he said wistfully.

"Well," she sighed, "you will ride a horse, and perhaps we shall ride alongside you in a small carriage. That's nearly as good, isn't it?"

He nodded. "Grandpapa said I will have Papa's old room which he had when he was a boy; and, and I shall have a tutor in the schoolroom at the house, the one with the name . . ."

"Chadwell."

"Yes. And I shall learn to speak English."

"I must learn it too," Julienne said. "We will learn it together, then."

"Will it be difficult?" he asked, wrinkling his nose.

She tapped his nose. "Probably, but you are such a clever boy, and we shall practice together. Papa will be there to teach you as well. You know he is a very good teacher."

Frédéric nodded. "Shall I have a new name?"

Her eyes opened slightly. "What a strange question, why do you ask?"

"You gave me a new name when we came here," he said, "a French name. Shall I have an English name now?"

"I suppose so," she smiled.

"What will it be?"

"Very like your name. Frederick. It's almost the same."

He sighed, confused by it all.

"It's time for you to go to bed," Julienne said. "You need to rest. Tomorrow will be a very busy day and we've both a long way to travel."

He hugged her tightly. "I love you, Mama," he said.

She returned his hug. "And I love you, and I will miss you every day."

He kissed her, then scrambled off the sofa and went to bed.

•   •   •

The Gare du Nord was filled with people carrying packages and suitcases, mixing freely with the beggars who shook their cloth caps and called out in small voices for a sou. The black steam engine was huffing as it built up its power, and the passengers were stepping aboard to their compartments, whilst others had opened their windows and were leaning out, speaking a last few words to their friends and families.

Edward moved slowly and was a bit nervous in the crowds. He was sweating from the strain of walking, and had to stop every so often, and lean against a stone pillar to ease the throbbing ache in the stump. The only thing that really worried him was the metal steps on the train itself. When they reached the train car, he stared at the steps, then looked at Stefan. "I'll never manage it," he said quietly, frustrated and embarrassed.

"Of course you will," Stefan answered. "Use the railing on the left side."

"And on the right?"

"I'll be the railing, one step above you." He hopped up on the first step, turned around and braced himself against the side of the train while he held out his right arm. "Come on," he said. "You're not going to fall. I won't let you fall, you can do it."

Edward inhaled deeply, inched closer to the step, then gave the walking-stick from his left hand to his father and grabbed the railing, holding it tightly. He saw Stefan's waiting arm just out of reach on his right, and with Julienne's help, gave up the other walking-stick and held firmly to Stefan's upper arm. After a moment, he felt reasonably secure, but that first step seemed high.

Stefan half-held and half-pulled as Edward stepped up.

"I will have to practice this," Edward wheezed. "I feel so clumsy."

"You're doing very well," Stefan said. "Two more now."

He took them one at a time, having to rest each time on each step, but with Stefan's help, he did it. His hands were aching and shivering from the effort, his breathing was shallow and the sweat-beads trailed down from his temples, yet, he felt a solid pride in the accomplishment. Stefan returned the walking-sticks to him, and he moved slowly and unassisted into the private compartment.

The Duke and Frédéric climbed up after Edward.

Julienne waited a moment longer on the platform with Armand. She missed Cécile already, but respected the older woman's wish not to come to the station. Cécile had said that watching the train leave would be too much for her to bear. It was better to say goodbye at home, and cry alone.

"I don't know what to say to you," Julienne began, seeing the soft yet sad smile on his face and in his eyes. The wrinkles had deepened and made him look much older. She remembered that first day, when he seemed to be an overgrown boy in a man's body, that friendly, toothy grin, his sparkling eyes, a helpful gentle man to frightened strangers.

"Say nothing then, you needn't speak words to me," Armand replied.

She nodded, then kissed his cheek and hugged him tightly for a moment, the first friend, a most special man who had given so much and lost even more. "You are part of my life, Armand, and will always be so. I love you. Be well."

The craggy-faced Frenchman kissed her forehead, then stepped back. "See . . . see that he takes care of my wood."

Julienne smiled. "I will. Won't you come up and say goodbye?"

He shook his head. "I've already done so. Go and kiss your son, quickly now, they are nearly ready to leave." He thrust his chin in a jaunty manner at the advancing trainman, closing the compartment doors.

Julienne nodded, and slowly climbed the steps.

Inside the compartment, she saw Edward holding his father, and heard him say "thank you," before giving a kiss to his father's cheek. The Duke had smiled, then helped Edward to sit down.

Edward opened his arms to Frédéric, held him for a long moment and said, "Be good, and we shall see you very soon."

After several kisses, Julienne fussed with Frédéric's hair for the hundredth time, then stood by the window of the compartment after they had left and watched her son as he walked with the Duke toward the doors of the station. A carriage was waiting for them there, and they were to go to a different railway station. The train would take them to the Channel steamer, and then, the boat would take them to Dover, safe in England.

She opened the window and leaned slightly out. The train began to move. She wanted to see Frédéric one more time, but didn't. Instead, she saw Armand, lingering at the pillar near the station doors, first watching, then stepping closer to a beggar-boy with a torn cloth cap in his hands. The dark-haired child barely came to Armand's waist and had to lift his chin high to speak to the tall Frenchman. She wondered what they were saying and tried to watch as the train moved slowly down the track, but a blast of steam clouded the view. The last sight she had of Armand, was of the tall man bending down closer to the boy's level, as he had done so often with Frédéric.

CHAPTER
28

It was a long and difficult journey. The countryside of France, ravaged by the war, gave way to the placid beauty of the German lands. The more miles they traveled, the more naked and taut Julienne's nerves became. The beauty of the countryside heightened the past ugliness and gave her no peace, because here was the proof that life had gone on, whilst hunger and cold and death had stung their lives and changed them forever.

The German names of the towns were familiar now, and the three-day journey was drawing to a close.

Teo had said never look back and never come back, yet she was back, looking out the window of the train in the early-morning light and seeing the station just ahead, with a grey mist clouding the window. She reached up to her hat and slowly drew down the veil. It made her pause. How many times did I hide my face, she thought, how many times did I feel like a dead woman, shrouded, to hide what he had done? This is wrong, she thought weakly, so very wrong. We should not have come back.

The train stopped and her heart began to pound harder and harder as she stepped from the compartment behind Edward and Stefan, almost expecting Franz to be there, leaning against a stone column, his animal-like eyes narrowed and accusing.

He wasn't there. She looked and searched the crowd of people at the station and he wasn't there. She sighed, relieved, but knew the relief would not last.

Stefan hired a closed carriage and had the porters see to their baggage. He walked alongside Edward, and noticed every step Julienne took was a hesitation, and when they were inside the carriage, she did not even lift the veil.

"You needn't hide behind that now," Stefan said lightly. "No one can see you."

She did not answer and smoothed the gloves on her hands, barely watching the street. "You . . . you should have sent a telegram to Rosl," she managed, some ten minutes later. "You really should have, Stefan. What if . . . what if someone is . . ."

"I doubt very much Franz is visiting my wife," he frowned. "She and the children are quite alone at the house. I am sure of that."

"But . . ."

"Stop it," he interrupted. "You are frightening yourself for nothing. He isn't here. He isn't even in Vienna, Julienne. Without you and the children . . ." he stopped, then corrected himself, "without you and Frédéric, there are too many questions he would have to answer. If he is anywhere, he is hiding in Eisenstadt. Don't you realize that? Don't you know he could not dare to show his face in Vienna without you? He's been hiding for as long as you've been gone, don't you know that?"

She looked up from her hands. "No," she said.

"Well he has. How many times could he lie the same lie before people began to wonder about it?"

"I . . . I never thought of that," Julienne said.

"Well start thinking of it. He's just a man, as mortal and fallible as the rest of us. There's nothing supernatural about him, my dear sister, as you will soon see." He looked out the small carriage window and smiled. "We're here," he said, pleased and calmed by the sight of his home.

Their voices carried in the courtyard. Stefan's voice could be heard inside the house and, as he helped Edward down from the carriage, the front door flew open and a beautiful, healthy-looking blond-haired woman raced out. She ran to Stefan and closed him in her arms.

"Rosl?" Edward whispered to Julienne.

"Yes."

"She's lovely," he said, admiring the woman in the lilac-colored velvet dress.

Julienne lifted the veil and placed it on top of her hat. "She's very kind, as well."

Rosl wiped her eyes, kissed Stefan again, then walked over to Julienne. She hugged her sister-in-law and said in a tight whisper, "Why have you come back? It's too dangerous . . ."

"Tell my brother that," Julienne answered.

Rosl nodded. "I understand now," she said softly.

Stefan took her arm and introduced her to Edward. "I will explain everything to you later, tonight," he said to Rosl in German.

Rosl smiled, but the way Edward looked at Julienne, and the way she looked at the Englishman, explained most of it.

They brought Edward to the drawing room, and there he would rest for a time, while Stefan was upstairs with his sons.

"This house is warm and comfortable," Edward said, sitting near the blazing fire.

"It has always been so," Julienne answered, touching the mantelpiece.

"Then why are you so nervous?"

"You must not expect anything else from me," she answered. "I'm frightened. I cannot help it, and no matter what you, or Stefan, or anyone else tells me, it will not go away just because you wish it to. I don't want to face my cousin with this. And Franz . . ." she said, shaking her head from side to side.

"He's just a man," Edward reminded her.

"Yes, just," she said sarcastically, then stopped speaking when the door opened and a servant brought in hot coffee and sweet rolls and cheese on a large platter.

Edward loved the house; and more, he loved seeing it through Julienne's eyes, a story in every corner, a memory in every room. It was part of her, and in that, it became part of him. He wished he could speak with Stefan's children, but they spoke too fast for his slight knowledge of German, and the vocabulary and Austrian pronunciation were different from his German lessons and studies long ago and mostly forgotten. Rosl spoke French, and Edward knew they spoke it for his benefit.

The food and the company, the elegance of this small palace and the family unaffected by war seemed odd at the beginning of the day. A few weeks ago we were starving, cold, and in bitter despair, Edward thought, and now, after a three-day train-ride, it seems a nightmare dreamed by someone else. The mind has strange powers, he mused.

The servants had been told to take Julienne and Edward's clothes to her room. There was a sweetness to the room he found particularly enchanting. It was a young girl's room in shades of green and white with flowered silk wallpaper and large windows. A peaceful expression had come to her eyes when she had said, "This is my room." He took notice of that. She had not said, "This was my room." She knew it still belonged to her, as she would always belong in the house that had become her brother's home.

Sitting on the edge of the four-poster bed, Edward watched her comb her hair, then blew out the oil lamp on his side of the bed when she was settled under the covers. It felt strange, and he smiled. "The bed seems so large, doesn't it?" he joked.

She turned her head slightly on the pillow. "Didn't you once wish for a larger bed and a room with a door?"

"Yes," he said, "and now I'm rather sorry I did. You seem miles away." He felt her move on the mattress.

"Better?"

"Closer," Edward said, waiting as she moved again. "Closer still," he said, turning on his right side and feeling her shoulder press against him. "Oh much closer than that," he said, cradling her beneath himself and kissing her deeply as lover and husband, with his whole self, and his whole heart.

Seven long months without a wife's tenderness and love, without hearing her voice or sharing her life and thoughts, evaporated in their bed. Stefan loved her, and held her, and wept with her when he told Rosl all that had happened and all they had suffered.

She knew him so well and was not surprised when there was a change in his voice in speaking of the Englishman. She heard in his voice that initial anger when he met Edward. As Stefan spoke, Rosl saw the change in his attitude: anger to acceptance; acceptance to respect; and finally, friendship for a stranger became love for a brother.

"Edward was a true father to them both, as he is now with Frédéric. I shall never forget the look in his eyes when I told him Gisela died. I think he had a very special love for her, and I believe a part of him died with her. I could see it. I could tell by the way he cried."

"He seems so very kind," Rosl said, combing her fingers through Stefan's hair.

"He is, and strong. Make no mistake on that."

"Strong? Do you mean stubborn?"

"He is that, yes."

"Well, so are you."

Stefan laughed softly. "There is another kind of strength: strength in one's chosen course. Sometimes, a situation requires strength of will, and often, returns that strength, many times over. Frédéric must have been an awesome burden at first, yet, he never gave the boy up for lost, and he did not give up on my sister. What strength and courage he has, to sift through the chaos of their lives and help them piece it together again. Remarkable. I could not be a hypocrite in my own home by giving them separate bedrooms. You understand that now, don't you?"

"Yes," Rosl said. "I never doubted your reasons, Stefan. I knew you would tell me why, once we had time to speak privately."

He kissed her bare shoulders. "I knew you and the children were safe. That alone helped me to bear our hardships."

"I seemed to be living our war with Prussia all over again—not knowing what had happened to you, not hearing any word at all for . . ."

"If I could have written, I would have done so," he said.

"I know, but it was little comfort to me at night."

"I understand," he said. He rubbed his cheek against hers. "Isn't it odd? I worked so hard to prevent a war, and in the end, I suffered its deepest agonies, and in a country not even my own . . ."

"It's over now," Rosl said. "You must let the past stay where it belongs."

"I want to," Stefan replied, "but there is only one thing left undone."

"When will you speak with Franz?"

"If it were only myself, I would go tomorrow."

So typical of him, Rosl thought, at times, so impatient.

"However," Stefan continued, "I cannot subject Edward to another train journey so soon. It is uncomfortable for him and he is still suffering some degree of pain."

"When you do go, go by carriage instead of by train. The journey may take a little longer, but it will be more comfortable for him."

He thought for a moment. A carriage, yes. He'd planned on hiring a carriage at the stable near the station in Eisenstadt. Three hours or so by carriage from Vienna . . . a light carriage, and a strong team. And I'll drive it myself, he thought. No witnesses. He kissed Rosl deeply. "Splendid idea," he breathed in her ear. "Edward, Julienne and I will go tomorrow—by carriage."

"I am not to go with you?"

"No," he said calmly. "I don't want to involve you in this. I want you to stay here."

"But why?"

"I'll tell you that tomorrow night," he answered, then jabbed his pillow with his elbow.

"NO," Julienne said. "Absolutely not. It isn't the right time. We're all much too tired and . . ."

"There is no 'right' time," Stefan argued, his eyes flaring slightly. "The sooner we finish this the better."

"You don't know him as I do."

"Oh yes I do," Stefan shot back. "I know him, I know him very well."

"Do you?" Julienne said with a defiant nod of her head. "Did you know that he was capable of such anger, and did you know that he would do what he did to me?"

Stefan flushed. "I know him," he insisted after a moment.

"Not as I do," she said, staring at her brother. "We are too tired, too weak to . . ."

"WEAK?" Stefan said, rising from the dining table. "Not in the least. On that you are quite wrong, Julienne."

"A few good meals have not given us back our health or our strength, Stefan. Be reasonable. You are not seeing this situation with . . ."

"I want it to end," Stefan said, standing at the head of the table. "And end it shall. Now."

"Papa always said, when you are tired you do not think clearly. What harm will a few days, or a few weeks of calm rest do? I don't agree with you and I will not go today."

Stefan felt his eyes narrow. "Fine," he said with a menacing smile. "Then I shall go alone. Do you want *me* to tell him in *my* words? I'm happy to do it, Julienne, and by God, it will be a pleasure to go there alone."

"NO," she said quickly, realizing that would be worse and Stefan's temper would be completely unchecked.

Stefan smiled. A very easy maneuver, he thought. "Get your coat then," he said and glanced at Rosl. "We'll be home for dinner." He left the dining room with long strides.

Rosl sighed.

"Now do you understand why I've come back?" Julienne said to her sister-in-law.

"He's been angry for a long time," she said simply, noticing the hard expression in Edward's eyes. Rosl watched as Julienne looked to him for support, but those eyes told her none would be found there.

"You, too?" Julienne asked Edward.

"Yes," he replied. "We came here for one reason. Why prolong it? I want us to be able to go on with our lives."

"You don't understand," Julienne said, "you don't know him or what he's capable of . . ."

"I don't want to hear that," Edward interrupted, then stared at her. "He's just a man, nothing more. You are not that frightened shadow he made you become, and I do wish you would stop behaving like that."

"Edward, please don't come with us. Please stay here. There's no reason for . . ."

"There is every reason," he answered. "*I* want to see him. *I* want to put a face to that ghost and end my own nightmares."

She felt caught and trapped and did not know which was worse—to stay behind, or to go with them. Seeing Stefan in the hall with his heavy coat already buttoned told her she must go with them. Stefan would not speak to Franz in the right tone of voice; Stefan would not know how to phrase things to Franz; and Stefan might not be delicate in telling a father that two of his children had died. No, she thought. He must hear that from me. But how . . . Stefan was tapping his foot. She put on her coat.

Sitting next to Edward in the carriage, she wondered why Stefan was driving the light black coupe. It was too familiar and unnerving. She heard Edward sigh and felt him shift his position. "Are you uncomfortable?" Julienne asked in a soft voice.

"Yes, a little."

"You should have stayed with Rosl."

"No, and please do not mention that again."

She leaned her head against the side of the carriage. I don't understand any of this, she thought. Edward is tired and in pain, he isn't used to walking and is not able to walk far; I am still tired and weakened from all those months and Stefan *must* be the same. *Why* is he so determined to do this now? And why, in God's name, go to Eisenstadt? She shook her head. He should have sent a telegram to Franz and made Franz come to Vienna. We could have told Franz what we had to tell him, then sent him away. It would have been so much more reasonable, and so much safer.

As the hours passed, memories and sounds faded by time, came back with a sharpened clarity—the sound of scissors next to her ear woke her from sleep. She did not move and felt him sprinkle the hair in delicate wisps all around her, like rose petals on a funeral bier, and all the time, he wept as he did it. She remembered the sound of an axe, splintering her locked bedroom door . . .

She stared at Edward for a moment, then looked away. What does he know of a short temper, she thought. Edward has great patience and he cannot conceive of a man with no patience. It does not take very much to spark the fuse in Franz's mind, not when it concerns his pride or his unreasoning jealousy . . .

She gave it up and tried to remember only the Duke's words and his reasons for this journey. She felt a moment's comfort in a father's advice and held it in her mind as long as she could, instead of crossing off the miles bringing them closer to Eisenstadt.

I never wanted to see Franz again, she thought, or hear the sound of his voice and the lies he would scream at me. Stefan left me no choice. I suppose that is only partly true. Life leaves me no choice. Edward's father is right. Why should I be content with half a life, when a full one awaits me? We'll speak our words and leave. I shall finally shake the dust of that place from my shoes . . .

A few more miles, Stefan thought single-mindedly. He scowled at the road ahead of them. He felt the weight of the loaded pistol press inside the waist of his trousers. Exile and divorce, uhn? He nodded to himself. I shall divorce Franz from this life. She has cried enough tears for ten lifetimes because of him. Today he pays in full for every scar on her back, for every slap he's ever given her and for every bone he's ever broken. I will return all of that to him—tenfold. Humiliate my sister? He will know what it is to be humiliated, and hit, and shamed by someone with more strength than a woman, by someone able to fight back. He will know all of this before I kill him and send him straight to hell where he belongs. I swear it, by God, because it is what I should have done three years ago when I first learned of this madness— despite the oath she begged of me.

Stefan pulled the reins slightly to the right, guiding the team of horses through the open iron gate.

Julienne felt a morbid chill the moment she saw the house.

Edward noticed the change in her expression. "Julienne, I survived the ghosts of my past. I faced them full with your help. You know you have my . . ."

"I know," she said quickly, then smiled softly. "I know."

He took her hand and squeezed it. "Then also know that this time, the three of us face the past together."

"I know that too," she said. "It is just a . . . a shock, to see it again."

"Madame," he said with a smile, turning the word for her into a gentle joke, "look well, for you shall never see this place again."

"Thank God for that," she said.

With Stefan's help, Edward got out of the carriage. Julienne hesitated for a moment, then she stepped out.

Stefan saw the concerned look on her face and tenderly touched her cheek with his gloved hand. "He'll never hurt you again. I swear it. Today it is finished. I . . . I owe you this."

"Stefan, you don't owe . . ."

"No. He was my friend, and it is my shame," Stefan said simply, then helped Edward to walk up the steps, and then, to the large double doors. He pulled the bell three times.

Julienne felt an ache when she saw Kollmer's widened eyes.

"You mustn't," Kollmer began, "you . . ."

"Is he here?" Stefan asked.

Kollmer did not reply and did not take his eyes from the woman he'd tried so hard to save.

"He is here, isn't he?" Stefan asked, and pushed the butler aside.

Kollmer stared with glassy eyes at her. "Please, I beg you, get back in the carriage and leave now before he knows you are here. He . . . he is greatly changed, Your Grace. He is despondent, he drinks in the afternoons, he tried to kill . . ."

"Kollmer," Stefan demanded, "announce me to my brother-in-law."

Julienne met Kollmer's eyes as Stefan walked back outside and took her by the arm, leading her into the house.

"Kollmer, tell him I am waiting in the drawing room," Stefan said.

The butler did not move, still watching her and pleading with his eyes.

"DO IT," Stefan commanded.

Kollmer only moved when she gave him a small nod.

Stefan parted the doors to the drawing room and stepped inside, closing them after Julienne and Edward. He took his coat off and tossed it over the back of a chair.

Edward had only given a quick glance to the vestibule and the large domed ceiling three floors above him. In the drawing room, he stood on the right next to a rosewood table. He listened to the quiet ticking of the large clock resting there. The table stood between two large windows with curtains partially drawn back. It is an attractive room, Edward thought, and has been decorated with taste, but it belongs to a tasteless man. He tried to imagine Julienne in this room, but it was so at odds with her. She had said she never felt this house to be hers, and he could see now that she was right. There was a cold dead perfection to the room, very like a museum, he thought: one admires the room, speaks in a whisper, and moves on.

The only object in the room that held his attention was the portrait of Julienne over the mantelpiece. It was an early portrait of a young and happy wife, dressed in a light blue silk day dress, with white lace cuffs and collar. Her beautiful hands held a white parasol, open behind her right shoulder. The artist had caught an enchanting smile, a summer's smile. What innocence, Edward thought, staring sadly at the portrait's lovely eyes.

The sound of boots clicking on the marble stairs, as they had done so many times in reality and in nightmares, closed her eyes for a moment. God help me, she prayed, watching quietly as Franz walked through the doors, closed them, and then turned his eyes to Stefan.

He has changed, she thought, and when she saw his eyes, knew instantly Kollmer had been right. Too many years of seeing those eyes, of having her life depend on every nuance of expression in his eyes, his voice, his stance, had taught her well. She knew he had been drinking.

"Stefan, I never expected . . ." Franz said at the door, then stopped speaking when he saw her. Shock held him motionless. He blinked as if she might be a vision or a phantom in his mind brought to life by several brandies. She's come home, he thought, and tried to speak her name as he stepped closer to her, wanting only to take her in his arms, but she stepped back from him.

"Franz," Julienne said quietly in a self-trained placating voice, "speak to me in French, please, only in French."

Stefan's jaw clenched, hearing the tone of her voice, seeing the timid smile on her face, all for a worthless animal.

"French?" Franz said, with a slightly thickened tongue and tried to see her clearly through his tear-filled eyes. "Of course, Julienne," he said. He wiped his eyes and saw now how thin she was, how wan her complexion. Her eyes were so large and the bones in her cheeks seemed more sharply defined than he had remembered, or saw in the photograph-plates he treasured and examined in a daily ritual of longing and pain. "You, you don't look well," he said plaintively, then sighed. "No matter. You're home, you've really come home to me and, and everything will be wonderful, I swear it, you'll see. You've really come home . . ."

"Only for today," Stefan said acidly.

Franz felt confused. Standing mid-way between Stefan and Julienne, he'd quite forgotten Stefan was there. His eyes had been only for her, filling the emptiness he'd suffered for such a long time with the sight of her. "Huhn?" he said, turning around, walking closer to Stefan, puzzled by the arrogant blaze in the eyes.

So this is Franz, Edward thought. He's just a man, not the rabid animal she'd painted in her mind. He must be about six feet, Edward thought, average weight, yet, standing next to Stefan, he looks so much larger, so much heavier. Edward mentally scolded himself for being silly and realized it was because

431

Stefan had lost weight, as they all had during the war. Edward shook his head. And I expected some sort of giant, he thought, with gnarled knuckles or something equally as hideous. How totally absurd.

"What are you talking about?" Franz said to Stefan. "You've found her and brought her home to me and that's . . ."

"You'd like to believe that, wouldn't you?" Stefan said in a clipped tone of voice. "You'd like to believe that I found her *for* you and brought her *to* you. You'd like to think we are still friends," Stefan said sarcastically.

Franz arched an eyebrow and his shoulders hunched slightly.

Julienne noticed.

"I trusted you," Stefan continued, raising his voice and stepping closer to Franz. "I brought you to my family, I shared my family with you. I encouraged your attentions to my sister. I even stood up to my father in the very beginning and explained away your family's disgraceful behavior. I've lied for you to my cousin, I've made excuses for you to everyone, and this is how you repay me, you Judas . . ." He backhanded a smack to Franz's face.

Franz felt his stomach tightening as he touched his cheek with a shaking hand. He stepped back from Stefan, maintaining a distance between them. He began to feel edgy, cornered. He looked at Julienne, and now saw the tall man standing near her, the one-legged man holding on to two walking-sticks. "Who is this?" he asked her a little sharply.

"A friend," Julienne replied quickly, trying to remain calm.

"A very good friend," Stefan added.

She saw Franz's jaw clench as the veins near the temples began to pulsate. His eyes narrowed. She saw the anger beginning in the way he held his head, his hands. It was the way he looked when he felt himself trapped.

"What Goddamned nerve you have," he said.

Julienne shuddered. He's never done anything in front of people, she told herself. He was always afraid people would know . . .

Stefan stepped closer to Franz, who still maintained that distance by stepping back.

"A good friend, is he?" Franz said with a razored edge to his voice.

"You always were perceptive," Stefan taunted.

Mother of God, Julienne thought, his eyes, his eyes . . . Stefan is deliberately provoking him.

"I *knew* you'd do this one day," Franz glared at her. "How many times did I . . ."

"Stefan," Julienne said, her skin alive with cold prickles, "not now. Let's go home."

"You are here," Franz breathed quite suddenly, "and here by God you stay!"

Stefan hit Franz a second time, and stepped closer to the startled man. "You do not speak to my sister like that," he yelled. "You will show proper respect to my family, Goddammit, *my* family," he repeated with a malevolent emphasis. "Did you think I did not know? Did you imagine I would never find out what went on in this house and what you did to my sister?"

Franz stood still as his lips tightened.

It's coming, Julienne thought nervously, I can see it . . . and suddenly remembered Franz *had* fought in front of other people. Her eyes widened. Stefan told me, she thought, I remember now . . . They had been drinking. It was in the street, three people were against Stefan and Franz. Stefan was too drunk. Franz did most of the fighting. He did it, I remember. "Edward, say something, make Stefan stop."

"No," Edward answered.

"Edward, is it?" Franz said, turning his head. "Is that his name?" He took a step closer.

Oh my God, she trembled, his hand. He's tapping his hand against his thigh.

"I know all of it," Stefan ranted, "and I will see to it that *everyone* knows what you are. You *know* I have the influence, and I will use all of it now. Upon my soul, I swear I will ruin you."

Franz was breathing shallowly, quickly.

Julienne could see he was no longer listening to Stefan and had not once moved his eyes from her.

"Everyone will know," Stefan spit. "Especially my cousin."

"Stefan, enough," Julienne said firmly, but her words went unheeded as she watched her brother begin pushing Franz, who still had not moved his eyes from her.

"You not only brutalized your wife, but your children as well," Stefan continued, punctuating his words with irritating little shoves. "They fled from you, hated you, and my sister had to suffer the deaths of two . . ."

"STEFAN!" Julienne shrieked and instantly covered her mouth with her hands.

Franz's eyes went from her to Edward, then back again. "What have you and the cripple done to my children?" he hissed.

"Nothing, Franz, nothing," Julienne answered.

He took a step closer. "You and your crippled lover, what have you done to my children?" he repeated, feeling Stefan's palm press against his chest.

"Stay where you are," Stefan warned.

Franz brushed the hand away.

"You ran off with him, didn't you?" Franz said, baring his teeth. He brushed the arm away again, more quickly now, with more strength. "I knew you couldn't do it alone," he snapped. "You hadn't the brains to do anything alone, Goddamn you, and you've come back to ridicule me with this, to torture me, haven't you?"

"No," she said.

Edward felt his jaw slacken with the horrible surprise. What in God's name is happening to that man?

"How could you . . ." Franz glared.

"It's not what you think," Julienne said.

"Don't you tell me what to think, you whoring bitch," he yelled.

Stefan punched the filthy mouth and unexpectedly, instantly, a fist was returned to his own face.

Edward heard the scream next to him and then saw Julienne run toward Franz and try to pull him away from her brother.

"Stop it, stop it," Julienne screamed.

In the rage, Franz hit her quickly, hard, and the force knocked her backwards out of the way, as he went back to Stefan.

Edward tried to step closer to Julienne.

Stefan felt the power full in his chest from the closed fists, another, a third, a fourth, as the punishing blows continued without end. He couldn't breathe and the knuckles hit his jaw again and again. His head was swimming from the beating, he felt his knees hit the floor and then, two hands, at the collar, twisting it, dragging and hauling him up as curses spewed out with limitless ferocity. The last thing he saw was the sight of the wall looming before his eyes and then, the awful sound of his nose breaking against the wall while somebody screamed.

Julienne staggered up from the floor, tasting the warm salty blood in her mouth and watching helplessly as Franz repeatedly slammed her brother against the wall. He let go. A trail of blood stained the wallpaper and pointed to the man on the floor.

Franz turned around. "I warned you," he babbled in German. "I *told* you I would kill him and now you've made me do it, you bitch, you whoring bitch . . ."

Edward tried to place himself in front of Julienne. She kept moving away from the rabid animal with the flushed face and the lips drawn back over bared teeth.

"I'll kill you for this," Franz swore, staring at Julienne. "It's your fault Stefan is dead. You always make me do these things . . . You *killed* two of my children, didn't you," he said, stepping closer. "You and your crippled lover stole my children and murdered two of them. Is that what you came home to tell me? Did you think I wouldn't mind, you whore . . ."

Edward didn't know the words being yelled at her, he didn't have to know the words. He saw what they were doing to her—her face had lost all its color, she was wide-eyed, haunted, and kept stepping away. Edward moved again and tried to place himself in front of her.

"It's cripples now, is it? Half-men you find in the street? Anyone will do for you, isn't that right? Soldiers, gardeners, my friends, strangers, stable-boys, cripples, anyone at all . . ."

"Stop it," she screamed, "stop it, it's not true, it was never true, never . . ."

Franz simply pushed Edward out of the way and heard the walking-sticks clatter to the floor. Edward held onto the table to steady his balance.

"He's last," Franz promised, then kept walking closer at a deliberate pace.

He crossed in front of the window, the window with the hard bright light as in the dream. Her ears were numbed by the filthy words he was yelling at her. He's killed Stefan, she thought, and he's going to kill us all . . . She began screaming for help, backing away from him as he shortened the distance between them. She suddenly stopped screaming when she felt the mantelpiece at the back of her head. It startled her and she inched along it to the right.

Edward saw her bare hands fluttering and feeling behind her, for the way, for a weapon, as the verbal assault continued unabated.

Julienne felt the metal, something cold and heavy by her right hand. She wound her fingers around it, never taking her eyes from Franz.

"You belong dead in the gutter. I'll kill you for what you made me do, Goddamn you," he spit at her.

Edward grabbed for the clock, then hurled it before he fell.

She saw Franz turn his head sharply to the left, away from her towards the sound. Stop it, she thought, for God's sake, stop it . . .

He glanced at the shattered clock on the floor.

Lifting the metal rod, she gripped it now with two hands and hit him hard on the back of the head.

His back arched, he raised his hand slightly in the blinding white pain and staggered as he turned around. Julienne? My Julienne, he thought, his eyes wide with a stunned surprise.

Stop, stop, stop, she thought, hitting him again, and again, and again, her eyes darkened to everything except the man on the floor. Stop, stop, stop . . .

Edward's left hand reached and gripped the armrest of the settee while the right hand held onto the table leg. He felt droplets. Warm red droplets rained down on him as he tried to pull himself up, hearing the thudding sound. He pulled and pushed himself to a standing position and saw her. "JULIENNE!" Edward yelled.

She didn't hear him, didn't see him. Her arms kept rising and falling; the heavy brass fireplace brush with the thick boar bristles mounted on a circular base was sopping wet as it sprayed her face and clothes, the walls and the ceiling, as long trails of blood criss-crossed in strange patterns on the portrait behind her.

Edward saw the bloodied heap on the floor, and then heard footsteps and voices in the hallway. He took two steps, then slumped against the mantelpiece, using it for balance. He dragged himself closer to her, one step closer, then pulled the long, heavy metal brush from her hands.

Her arms kept moving, up and down, up and down, though she held nothing and stared at nothing and continued to mouth "stop, stop, stop," with no sound coming from her lips.

They must never know, Edward thought quickly. He looked at Julienne, covered with blood, and pushed her out of the way, not seeing or caring that she had fallen down. He held the wet bloodied weapon in his own hands. God forgive me, he thought, waiting until he heard the door open, then willingly took her place and would take all the blame, and powerfully hit the dead man twice before he lost his balance and collapsed to the floor.

Kollmer stood there, saw the blood on the walls, then quickly shut the door.

Edward looked at his own shaking hands, stained with blood. He saw the butler's legs, then looked up saw the pistol in Kollmer's hands, watching as the man put the pistol on the mantelpiece.

Kollmer took out a handkerchief and went to the space next to the fireplace, to the shivering woman staring at nothing and leaning with her head against the wall. He knelt down and wiped the blood droplets from her face, from her bare hands as best he could, took off his own jacket and placed it around her shoulders. He heard a groan behind him.

Pivoting, Kollmer placed a knee on the soiled carpet and saw the bloodied beaten face, and this time, it was not hers.

Stefan tried to lift his head, then fainted.

Kollmer went to the Archduke, loosened his collar and looked at the bruises.

"Kollmer?" Edward said in between deep breaths and in a faltering German. "Do you speak French?"

"Yes, Sir."

Edward was still breathing hard, and pushed himself to a sitting position. He held the bloodied metal fireplace brush in his right hand. "I did it," he lied.

Kollmer stood up, stared at the stranger, then let his eyes sadly find her, sitting on the floor and hiding in a corner, so cold, so frightened, and the brown traveling dress and mantle-coat so soiled with another's blood. He shook his head.

"I killed him," Edward repeated.

"No, Sir," Kollmer answered, still watching her. "You did not."

"I needn't explain to you," Edward said in an authoritative voice, "only to the courts."

"You needn't explain to them, either," Kollmer replied in a servant's voice.

Edward's eyes opened in a stare.

"You misunderstood me, Sir," Kollmer softly continued, still watching her with protective eyes as he had always done. "My employer had an accident. No one killed him." He looked now at the stranger. "No one."

Edward shook his head. "You don't understand," he said, "this will not go unnoticed, there will be questions and . . ."

"With all respect, Sir, you do not understand."

"He has family, they will demand . . ."

"No," Kollmer shook his head. "His only Aunt died last July. His mother still lives, but in Hungary now, and will never return to this house and her nightmares of it."

"But his friends, his associates in the Government . . ."

Once again, Kollmer shook his head. "He tried to kill himself last year. He should have died then." Kollmer paused, then continued quietly, "My employer was a drunkard. Everyone knows that. My employer frequently rode his horses whilst he was drunk. He was cruel to them, did you know that? Everyone knows that. One of them trampled him in the stables. One of them could stand the maltreatment no more. The funeral arrangements will, of necessity, be made quickly." He stared with filled eyes at the shell of a woman in the corner. "All who worked in this house knew the truth of what he did to her. We could do nothing to help her. We could only try to save her later and ease the pain later. We . . . we are servants and had to keep silent." He looked at the stranger. "This time, I will keep silent and not be shamed by it." He stepped closer to the gentleman and said, "Let me help you up, Sir."

Edward crooked his arm through Kollmer's and allowed the butler to lift him, then leaned heavily against him as he hobbled to a chair and was eased to the seat. Kollmer stepped gingerly around the body to the other side of the sofa and picked up the walking-sticks. He handed them to the gentleman.

"Why are you doing this?" Edward asked.

Kollmer gently smiled. Why, he thought, because she was always kind to me and all the staff; because she was generous to us and thought of us as people, not things; she worried for us, protected us when she could and saw to our welfare; because I saved her life more than once, and helped her to escape, for we were all bound together in this sickness, this silence; because she needed me, being friendless and alone, and unprotected. We protected each other, as best we could. Why, he thought, because I am not a stupid man and I know what he was, and what he did to her because I am the one who cared for her later. He swallowed, then said aloud, "Why, Sir? Because I love her, I always have. I am a good servant, Sir, and it is a servant's loyal love I feel. I am *her* servant, not his, though he was my employer and I served in this house in his father's time. I was, and always will be, her servant."

Edward nodded.

"You must leave this to me," Kollmer said quietly. "He . . ." nodding in the direction of the dead man, "he was just like his father. I was here for that reign of terror, too," allowing for the first and only time a touch of bitterness to show through the servant's respectful tone of voice. "But she suffered more than his mother ever did. You must trust me and leave this place now."

Edward looked at the walls, the portrait, but did not look down at the dead man or the blood-soaked carpet. "It . . ." he swallowed, "it is an awful mess."

Kollmer looked to her in the corner and said quietly, "I have cleaned . . . far worse."

Kollmer helped him to the carriage outside. In the cold air, Edward asked, "Why did you stay, after she'd gone?"

Kollmer shrugged slightly. "I set a time for myself. I said three years, from the day she left, just to be certain she did not come back—or that he did not bring her back. There are very few of us still here. Most left after she escaped. When I was certain, I, too, would leave." He paused, then asked, "Forgive me, Sir, but are you able to drive the carriage?"

"I shall have to manage, as we have no other choice," Edward answered, then shook his head to silence the servant. "Let us not involve anyone else. If you can help me up to the seat, I will manage the rest."

With tremendous difficulty, and a great effort on both their parts, Kollmer lifted and pushed Edward up to the driver's seat. They both knew Stefan would be unable to drive the team. His eyes were beginning to blacken, he was breathing through his mouth in shallow gasps, the nose was swollen and twisted and bled, off and on, as did the split lip. From experience, Kollmer knew he'd probably suffered a vicious beating elsewhere on his body. He would not be able to endure several hours driving a carriage and would endanger all three people.

Kollmer took charge. He brought a blanket to the stranger, wrapped it around the man, then gave him a bottle of brandy to help him stay warm on the long journey back to Vienna. He then guided Stefan out and helped settle him inside the carriage. Then he half-carried her out, and wrapped her in a blanket alongside her brother. She was deathly cold, dazed, and appeared to hear nothing, and see nothing.

He made sure all the oil-lamps mounted on the carriage had enough fuel for the journey, gave the stranger a supply of matches, and even had the presence of mind to draw a simple map to Vienna, and once there, to the Archduke's home. When he finished all his duties, Kollmer looked up at the tall man holding the double-set of reins. "Sir, please tell her I still have them," he said, and took from his breast-pocket the wooden rosary beads.

Edward shook his head. "When your bags are packed and this hateful place shuttered, bring them to her yourself. Come to the Duke of Middlesex' house, Number 9, Berkeley Square, London. I am his son, Marquess Harlaxton. Send word to me if you need the fare. We shall meet again," Edward said, then looked at the horses. Shoulder to the wheel, he thought, and in the cold grey light of late afternoon, smacked the leather on the rumps of the horses.

There was a crypt-like cold in the carriage. In a stunned quiet she watched the countryside come and go with no feeling in any part of her body, grateful for the sunset and the darkness that followed it. Was it hours that had gone by, or minutes, she wondered, feeling like a stranger to herself, not aware, not caring, floating in a daze of silhouetted trees that moved but made no sound. Someone touched her hand, her bare cold hand with the filmy dryness caked on the fingers and the palm. She pulled her hand away and huddled closer to the corner to be more alone, closing her eyes, unable to cry.

She slept, or thought she did, and didn't know the difference as she listened to the rhythm of the carriage wheels, turning and turning, watching the darkness and drowning in its emptiness. Faint lights in the distance grew larger, diamonds in the night sparkled closer, the gas-lights of Vienna's streets appeared. Bumpy cobblestones told her it was real and not a dream, for she no longer trusted her eyes.

When she saw the doors of her father's home, she believed her eyes and opened the door while the carriage was still moving. She stepped out, stumbled, then picked herself up and ran, half-dead from exhaustion and totally spent by the fear.

Mid-way up the stairs, she heard the drawing-room door open but did not stop to see who it was. She ran from the sound and staggered to the bathing room at the end of the hall on the second floor. The tiles were cold, colder than her skin. The room was cold and dark and quiet. No noise at all, she thought, breathing very hard. No screams, no noise. I want to be still, I want to be quiet. She leaned against the cold wall for a long time in the dark, then felt terribly dirty. She felt for the matches, struck one, then turned on the gas-light, hearing the puff just before the flickering light lit the small blue-and-white room. She blew the match out and dropped it to the floor. Her hands. She stared at the dark dried blood on her hands.

Quickly, madly, she poured water from the pitcher into the white porcelain basin. The water turned red and she kept staring at her shaking, red-stained hands.

Her knees gave way and she leaned against the wall as she began to cry. God . . . I . . . only meant to stop him, just to stop him, not to kill him . . .

"I'll stay in the drawing room tonight," Edward sighed. "Have someone make up the fire and bring me a blanket. I . . . I can't move anymore."

Rosl nodded as two servants carried Stefan upstairs. "I'll send for the doctor, and then, I'll sit with Julienne for a time."

Edward shook his head. "Leave her alone tonight. Stay with Stefan, but leave her time to herself just now." He knew, sometimes, Julienne had to sort things out alone. He moved very slowly into the drawing room, aching and hurting in every part of his body.

It was a death-like sleep, deep and warm and hidden from prying eyes under the covers in a dark and silent room. When grey light edged through the parted curtains, she woke and sat upright in the bed. It was a night without nightmares and she knew why. She'd lived the nightmare during the day and there was nothing left to torment her in the blackness of the night.

The bloodied clothes were in a pile in the corner and she barely looked at them whilst she dressed methodically, as if still trapped in a dream.

The hallways were not frightening here, and she walked down them, and then the stairs, and went out the front door.

The Paris cloak kept her warm. The cloak she'd lived in, cried in, suffered in and survived in made a woolen barrier against the mind. Julienne walked slowly on the streets, listening to the rattle of the carts of vegetable men, dairy men, coalmen, as life went on, as it always did, unconcerned.

I never meant to kill him, she thought quietly, I only meant to stop him. I was afraid to stop myself, lest he get up and just keep coming and coming, and beat me once more. She looked up at the bare-branched trees and heard the faint songs of hardy morning birds. He thought he'd killed Stefan, she remembered. He would have killed Edward. And *this* time, he would have killed me.

She looked at her ungloved hand, expecting to see stains on the palm. I ran to my room like a frightened child, and I suppose for a short time, I was.

She continued walking the streets, only listening in part to the distant bells of church steeples singing their own morning songs. She stopped walking when she'd crossed the small cobblestoned courtyard and pulled on the bell of the great wooden door. She lowered her eyes, listening and waiting, an eternity of minutes passed before it creaked slightly, and opened slowly.

"Good brother," Julienne said in a soft haunted voice, "I . . . I must speak with my Uncle."

"Come inside," the monk replied softly. "I will find him for you."

Edward had calmed Rosl's fear in not finding Julienne in her room, and sent her back to Stefan, to wait with him for the doctor's second visit. They had been told the previous night that with time, Stefan would heal.

Alone in the drawing room, Edward watched the newly made fire in the grate. Julienne is frightened, possibly ashamed, he thought, and she has gone to Teo as she did once before—for help and guidance. He will find a different woman now, Edward thought. The last time, she crept to him and cried to him and was bewildered and abandoned by all around her. That woman was created by Franz and fashioned from his sickness.

At half-past the hour, he heard the front door open and close. He knew the sound of her footsteps. "Julienne," he called, and saw her pause at the door. He studied her face and saw in her eyes the remnant of the storm that had passed.

He stretched out his arm and opened his hand to her. She walked to him and put her hand in his without hesitation.

"Feeling lost?" he asked.

"I'm not lost anymore," she smiled.

AUTHOR'S NOTE

I have always loved history. It defines who and what we are, and provides a guide not only for the "now" of our lives, but for our future as well. Because of my desire to conform to historical facts, this historical novel required seven and a half years of work.

In researching this book, I was fortunate to be able to spend time in London and Paris, reliving the events in imagination and haunting numerous antiquarian bookstores for maps, photographs and memoirs. I give special thanks to my French family for their untiring efforts in taking me around Paris to actual sights described in this book and for reading to me their translations of original French works of the period. Very special thanks and appreciation goes to my British friends: Grace Pine, for literary criticism and editing suggestions, and L. G. Pine, for literary criticism and genealogical research.

My thanks, also, goes to those dedicated, respected and eminent historians whose works provided insight into that period of history: Theo Aronson, Eugene Bagger, Robert Baldick, S. C. Burchell, David Duff, Alistair Horne, Michael Howard, Melvin Kranzberg, Robert Howard Lord, Lawrence D. Steefel, and Louis L. Snyder. If I have inadvertently omitted anyone, it certainly is not intended to reflect adversely upon their capabilities and standing in the academic community.

Additionally, of particular note, are the memoirs of those who lived the events: Otto, Prince Von Bismarck; Dr. Moritz Busch; Dr. Thomas W. Evans; Comte Fleury's memoirs of the Empress Eugénie; Emperor Frederick III; Edmond de Goncourt; Emille Ollivier; and E. B. Washburne.

Listed separately in the acknowledgments are those individuals I interviewed, who willingly shared their knowledge and expertise.

Vive la France and God Save the Queen.

LINDA J. LaROSA

New York, March, 1984

ACKNOWLEDGMENTS

The author is grateful for the help, cooperation and encouragement of the following people and institutions.

In England: H. S. Cobb, Clerk of the Records, House of Lords; Ralph Hart, formerly of the Photo and Map Library, Greater London Council; Helen Hayward, A. D. Peters and Co. Ltd.; Dr. T. A. Heathcote, Curator, R.M.A.S. Collection, Royal Military Academy, Sandhurst; Bridget D. Malcolm, Archives Advisor and Researcher for Victorian Military History and the Royal Military Academy, Woolwich (1850–1870); K. S. Morgan, Editor, Hansard Report, House of Commons; Newspaper Library, British Museum; Readers' Service, National Army Museum; Readers' Service, National Maritime Museum; Nick Saloman, formerly of the Photo and Map Library, Greater London Council; H. O. Wilson, A.L.A., Librarian, Greater London History Library, Greater London Council. *In New York:* Rica Monique Asaban, for translation assistance; Amelia Benson, for translation assistance and criticism; Patricia Boyce, K-6 teacher; Trudy Citron, for material pertaining to Vienna; Siegfried M. Clemens, Technical Information Specialist, National Institute of Mental Health; M. Freddolino, Registered Dietician, Veterans' Administration; Walter and Elsie Friedle, for material pertaining to Vienna; Carolyn Hecht, R.N.; Ralph R. Hochberg, Esq.; Dr. and Mrs. Bernard M. Jaffe, for their help with the New York University Library; Nandita Kapila, of Bombay, India; Harold Koda, Design Lab, Fashion Institute of Technology; Suzanne Konowitz, Information and Public Relations, Artistic Division, Cultural Services of the French Embassy; Michele LaRosa; Miriam LaRosa, for assistance in typing and correcting the manuscript; Robin Massee, Head of Information and Public Relations, Cultural Services of the French Embassy; Patricia Petretti, preschool teacher; Naomi Sanderson; Joan Sanger, of G. P. Putnam's Sons; Neil M. Solomon, Ph.D., Family Therapy; Dr. Barbara Stoerck, Austrian Institute; Bernard Tawfic, M.D., Fellow of American Academy of Otolaryngology, Head and Neck Surgery; Friederike Zeitlhofer, Librarian, Austrian Institute Library. And *in Paris*, those extraordinary guides Leslie Dahlgren, Kim Massee, and Ninette and Jo Zagury.

And most especially,
Don Congdon
whose help and encouragement are beyond measure.